KISMET TASK FORCE

THE BLOODLINE REVELATIONS

ΑΩ

MISSION: TWO

KISMET TASK FORCE

Ryan J Alls

Printed in the United States of America

First Printing, 2015

Alls, Ryan J

Kismet Task Force/by Ryan J Alls

Summary: A young man joins a squad in hopes of finding a way to free his now enslaved home from the hands of an unknown adversary.

ISBN-13: 978-0-9893454-3-9

HUNTED

The night held its breath, as if in fear of the fatal consequences that would follow if anything stirred within its depths. While the breeze had ceased and nature's kin remained absent, Jude took in the saliva that fell from Jed's fangs. The sight screamed hunger while filling Jude with the same thirst that stared back at him. As Jude continued to try and hold his ground, he felt Jed easily overpowering him, and soon felt the *crunch* within his hands. A cloud of black smoke erupted at the watering hole's shore, as a black raven took flight, departing from the chaos that once imprisoned it.

The night began to breathe and soon Jude felt the comforting breeze blow across his feathers, while he evaded the large trees that rose up ahead of him. He found a precariously but covertly placed tree hiding behind a group of larger trees. After landing on a sturdy branch, he surveyed the area. There were no signs of movement, which meant that there was plenty of movement.

"You know little brother, I always knew you were intelligent. However, I have to confess that you are too smart for your own good," said Jed. His voice sounded calm and both close and far away.

The breeze began to blow and the branches of the countless number of trees began to sway, thus concealing any movement beneath.

For the first time, I do not know what to do. If he finds me, he will kill me. If I find him, I cannot bring myself to kill him, even if I was lucky enough to land a fatal blow. He is my brother, and he wants my life.

"You know, it was so tiring and repetitive to follow you around these past few years, to make sure that Mathias—excuse me, dad, did not try and contact you. You would think a creature, that had all the time in the world, would be immune to the claws and wounds of boredom and repetitiveness," said Jed. His voice sounded directly beneath the tree that Jude sat perched on.

Jude looked down to find himself staring into the translucent eyes that glared back at him.

"Shall I come up, or will you be a good little brother and come down?" asked Jed.

Jude's normal form felt both natural and vulnerable when he felt his legs dangling from the branch he sat on.

"Now there's a good boy," said Jed.

Keeping his hands covertly at his sides but behind his back, Jude lightly loosened the vial in the last slot of his belt. His stomach sank when he dropped down from his once safe haven. When his feet hit the ground, he expected an ambush, but only saw the slow movement of the eyes of his predator.

"I still do not understand why you attacked me. All I want is to see dad. Why is that so terrible?"

Jed glared back, forfeiting any movement, or signs of life. "If you plan on using that vial in your left hand, I suggest you use it before—."

A flash of movement forced Jude to quickly inject the vial. The sky twisted and turned in his vision until his body collided with a rough and unyielding object. His head jerked up and caught the fast but identifiable movement of Jed, running straight for him. Jude felt the effects of his Faliche vial surface just in time for him to return to his feet and evade Jed's charge. He darted behind Jed, grabbing him behind the neck. A second later, Jed was behind him picking him up off of the ground. Jude's body fell a short distance before collapsing into Jed's knee, causing his back to go into spasms. He injected himself, and soon found himself towering over Jed as his arachnid form prepared to strike.

"Refusing to play fair huh little brother? I can play that game—I can play that game very well," said Jed. He was gone. The silence of the night soon returned, but the hairs on Jude's eight legs sensed vibrations close-by.

Jude barreled towards the surrounding trees, spinning web around them all, until he found himself perched a few feet above the ground on a tightly secured net of webbing. He waited.

"You know little brother, there are a few things I did not tell you about us vampires," said Jed. His voice seemed to echo from every direction causing Jude to look around frantically. "After we are bitten, and our souls are immediately dragged to Anim's realm of flames and darkness, we are rewarded with an ability reflecting the realm of suffering we will spend the rest of our lives in. Mine happens to be deception."

A fuzzy ripple appeared and then vanished between two trees in the span of a second. Jude's eyes quickly closed and opened, in an attempt to confirm whether or not he had seen what he thought he saw.

"This is why whenever you see a vampire—run!"

The webbing snapped and the ground shook, as Jude's enormous legs came in contact with the floor beneath him. The ripple appeared a couple of feet ahead of him, and then cold pain sliced the side of his body. He felt his pincers open up for a scream, but all that came out was a foreign screech of pain. His body forced himself into his normal form. Blood ran from his shoulder and stomach while his hand attempted to apply pressure, and soon the sky turned quickly and then ended with the unforgiving forest floor. A sinister laugh echoed all around Jude. His body failed to respond to anything but the pain that caused his body to tremble. Forcing himself to his feet, he closed his eyes.

I cannot see him, or even react in time. I need to calm down.

He meditated on his surroundings. He tried to open his eyes, but his brain refused the request. His breathing slowed and his heart began to beat regularly. His eyes opened automatically, showing a ripple coming straight for him. His eyes began to burn as a sensation trickled down the back of his brain. The ripple disappeared and Jed took its place. Jude's body hurled around and crashed into what felt like a tree. He cried out in pain as he felt his teeth pierce his tongue. The chilling laugh returned.

What is that? It was almost like I could decipher his camouflage.

Returning to his feet, he slowly turned in place, taking in every angle around him. He let the sensation in his head spread, and soon the trees and everything he saw, was covered with a white tint. He quickly counted two hundred and seventy-three pieces of bark on a neighboring tree. He stood dead center of nine large oak trees. Everything was white and appeared to be too clear for his brain to process. A ripple transformed into Jed, as he charged in for another attack. Jude injected himself with the rest of his Faliche vial and challenged the charge. A flicker of alarm teased the corner of Jed's eye before Jude felt his brother's neck in his grasp. A snarl jumped from Jed's throat and was soon replaced with the crashing of a tree, as Jed's body crashed into it. The white tint in Jude's vision began to flicker on and off until he saw normally once again. Jed was gone.

"I have to say, my optical tactics didn't develop until I attained at least twenty-two years of human age. I always knew you were the favorite," said Jed. His voice assaulted Jude from every angle.

Optical Tactics? Of course!

Jude had read about the ability in a book that he had checked out from the library. The description of it was complex and unappealing, causing Jude to foolishly skim over the chapter. He closed his eyes and began to meditate. After a few seconds his eyes opened and his lips parted.

"Optical tactics!" A rush of white tint filled his vision causing a smile to force itself to his lips. "Foolish!" yelled Jude. He immediately turned around, catching Jed's wrist, hurling him at a nearby tree. The tree uprooted and fell over as Jed's body crushed the base that supported it.

Jed's body showed no signs of movement. Jude expected his brother to be on his feet and retreating to camouflage where he would prepare for another onslaught. The only movement was the leaves that cascaded down in an endless cycle from the tree that once inhabited the area. Pain shook Jude's heart.

Two figures sat at the shore of a watering hole's edge. The moon seemed to watch over them, as the motionless water reflected the bond between them.

"Jed."

"Yes little brother?"

"You are not alone anymore. You have me; and I promise you, no one will ever harm you again."

Jed cracked a full smile.

Jude shook his head violently in an attempt to shake off the image. He approached Jed's lifeless body with grief in his heart and red flags in his mind. As the tips of his toes touched the heels of Jed's boot, Jude felt his eyes water.

I'm sorry—I really am. I did not mean to hurt you, only protect you.

Jude reached down and soon his throat gasped for air beneath the crushing grip of Jed's grip. Jude's feet left the ground and soon he found himself staring down into Jed's smiling achromatic eyes. A smirk touched his lips while his fangs extended. He hissed.

"Why..."

"This you brought on yourself little brother. I tried to warn you—warn you to stay away. But no, you had to keep on pushing, keep on asking questions. Since I cannot trust you to not go snooping around for our fallen father," started Jed as he cracked his neck. His tongue began to bleed as it ran across the tip of one of his fangs.

Jude kicked in an attempt to break free. His hands refused to budge from the hands that ceased his breath. Lightheadedness soon followed along with heavy eyelids.

"Oh yes—yes! I have yearned and thirsted for your blood for quite some time now; and if I cannot trust you to obey me, then I will just have to control you," said Jed as his lips parted. A hiss slithered from his mouth and his fangs striked.

"Blood trauma!" yelled a voice.

Jude's vision ceased the urge to cave in when his body hit the floor. His violent coughs hammered at his chest and allied itself with the pain that already pulsed from his neck. When his vision began to clear, he rose to his knees and set eyes on a pair of colorless eyes, staring motionlessly back at him.

"I said, yes you said—kill them all—all of them, even the children," said the voice.

Jude looked up to see Pang on one knee. His chest rose and fell rapidly while his gasps for air filled Jude's ears.

"Pa—," started Jude before he began to cough again. "Pang, how did you find me?"

Pang's body fell to the floor. Jude forced himself to his feet and limped over to his comrade. Bending down, he rolled Pang on his back.

"What did you do?" Is Jed—is he—dead?"

"Why do you deprive me of what is mine—it's mine! Mine you hear me!" yelled Pang in no apparent direction.

Jude became alarmed by Pang's behavior. The pitch in his voice rose and fell, and the sweat that poured from his body began to drench his shirt. Jude helped Pang to his feet, and just when he thought that Pang was regaining his footing, his body attempted to collapse. Throwing Pang's arm over his shoulder, Jude helped his friend back to his feet.

"I drained his body of all of its blood. His body thinks that it starved, and in turn rendered him unconscious. It won't be long before he is a threat, we should—we should..."

"We should go," said Jude finding the words that Pang could not. "Will you be okay?"

The orange and red in Pang's eyes separated and began to circle one another. Jude became both mesmerized and terrified by the sight.

"Only their blood will end the madness. Take them—take their lives. Take their souls!" yelled Pang as he erupted into laughter.

Jude injected himself with a vial, and as soon as his raven form took control, he amplified its size and took to the sky with Pang dangling from the grip of his claws.

"They will all come to know true power," mumbled Pang. His eyes stayed closed and his head wobbled in place, while the wind blew fresh air throughout his slate black hair.

Jude felt a brief moment of freedom when the night air kissed his feathers and hugged his wings. A screech echoed throughout the night filling the silence with an aura of sorrow and triumph.

CONFLICTED

"Agents are taken care of," said Sia. She gave Eli a quick kiss on the cheek before returning her glare to her father.

"You insist on infuriating me don't you—you insufferable brat!" said Mr. Wyatt.

The sound of the waterfall was all that filled the air. Eli looked to Sia assuming a response would soon leave her lips. However, all he saw was determination and rage in the recess of her eyes.

"I will give you one last chance—come with me or die!" scowled Mr. Wyatt.

Eli felt a hand grab his. He looked down to see his hand interlaced with Sia's. He looked up at her face and was surprised that her gaze still stayed glued to her father.

"All of my life I made myself believe that all of the physical and emotional abuse you put me through was because I deserved it. You manipulated me into believing that I was a bad child and deserved the afflictions fueled by your rage. I used to lie to everyone, including those who cared for me, about the pain and scars you inflicted—all because I was ashamed. Luckily I met someone amazing that reminded me of how special I am and how Mik and I deserve to be happy," said Sia.

"Enough of your disrespect!" yelled Mr. Wyatt. His hands raised and soon Eli found himself captured in the same memorable cold pain from that unforgettable night. His feet rose from the ground and his body began to spasm, he looked over and saw Sia in the same state as him.

A roar sounded from below and soon Eli saw Spiffy take charge. The canine leaped at Mr. Wyatt with its fangs drawn. A soft cry echoed throughout the meadow rising from the ground and shrouding the trees. Spiffy's body tumbled across the meadow until a large tree abruptly stopped his movement.

"No!" screamed Sia at the cruelty.

Pink petals cascaded down over Spiffy's body, covering him with a soft blanket. Eli felt his eyes burn and water just when he anticipated the tear that fell from his eye.

"Target acquired!" boomed a voice.

A cloud of white smoke shrouded everything.

"What kind of tomfoolery is this!" yelled Mr. Wyatt between coughs.

"Kai engage!" ordered a woman.

Eli felt himself land on top of a body. Assuming it was Sia's, he dragged her out of the smoke. Sia coughed rapidly as they exited the blinding smoke. Commotion and explosions radiated from the smoke causing the ground to tremble beneath their feet.

"Daddy!" screamed Sia. She started to run towards the chaos but Eli grabbed her. "Eli let me go! That is my father in there!"

"You can't go in there," started Eli as he struggled to apprehend her. "You'll die!"

An Operative leaped from the smoke and landed in front of them. Eli instantly recognized the black combat gear, hood and scarf that concealed the Operative's identity.

"Return to your base, effective immediately!" said a woman's voice.

"No! I won't let you hurt him!" screamed Sia.

"Second request, return to your base. This is your last warning," said the Operative.

Something told Eli not to leave Mr. Wyatt. Even though Sia's father had just been his enemy a few minutes ago, there was something about the Occult Operatives that terrified Eli.

Grabbing hold of Sia's waist, Eli hauled her towards the Forgotten Forest.

"No! Eli let me go! screamed Sia. Her arms and legs flailed in all directions, as she struggled to break free from his grasp. "Let go of me! Someone help!"

He picked her up and threw her over his shoulder. The jabs in his stomach and back from her hands and feet caused him to recoil, but he knew that the pain paled in comparison to the consequences that would follow if they disobeyed the Occult Operatives. As they exited, Eli took one last look over his shoulder and noticed the lifeless bodies, deep trenches and demolished trees that lay scattered around him. Where he was felt alien and melancholy and soon his body felt the same.

UNCERTAINTY

The sound of crickets chirping and neighboring owls masked the mud and water that swallowed their feet—while Eli and Sia trudged through the flooded and perilous terrain of the marshlands. The silence was unnerving and eerie. The sound of boots squishing the wet soil below began to drive Eli insane when the lone shack made its appearance known. He turned back towards Sia, whose hands still hugged her body tightly.

"Hey—we are here," said Eli extending a hand to her. His hand remained motionless while she continued passed it, as if unaware of its presence.

How long is she going to stay mad at me? I was only following orders and doing what I thought was right.

She knocked on the door once—twice, and then coughed. The door immediately opened. Agent Val stood in the doorway with a bow ready to fire. Eli leaped in front of Sia spreading his arms.

"Whoa! Wait—it's us!"

Val stared back unaffected a few seconds before lowering his bow and nodding his head for them to come in. The temperature inside the cabin was warmer than the marshlands around it. A handful of candles cast a dancing flare of lights and shadows. Two familiar figures occupied one of the small couches that surrounded a lone table.

"Has the Lieutenant or General returned yet?" asked Sia.

"No—not yet," said Val closing the door.

Eli followed Sia to one of the couches that sat next to the couch which Jude and Pang occupied. Jude instantly rose to his feet when Sia was in close proximity. Worry and shock ravaged his face.

"Your face! Are you okay?" asked Jude.

"Yes Jude—I am fine. I will be fine," said Sia.

Jude threw his arms around Sia and soon muffled sobs came from her lips. He extended his hand towards a spot on one of the couches, and soon she took her seat. Eli felt both conflicted and annoyed when Jude left for the kitchen and came back with four cups and a kettle. He poured Pang a cup of tea—who ignored it and closed his eyes—and then held a cup in front of Sia. She took the cup between her hands and released a breath, which seemed to have been begging for release.

"What happened—tell me, please," said Jude.

Eli took a seat next to Sia as she went into extreme detail about their battle in the meadow. Jude's eyes never left her gaze and his blinking was abnormally minimal. Pang's closed eyes showed movement, but never exposed the livelihood they were hiding. When Sia was finished with her story, silence took a seat amidst them all.

"I am glad that you both are okay," said Jude.

"Thank you Jude—really," said Sia.

Eli felt himself clear his throat, and became confused as to the reason behind it. Sia's and Jude's gaze simultaneously turned towards him.

"So—how did you guys fair?" asked Eli.

Eli felt his brows curl in response to the complex expression that came and went from Jude's face.

"Fine," said Jude.

Silence moved in closer to listen, causing the rustling grass outside to sound more prevalent.

"Pang are you okay?" asked Sia.

For the first time since the conversation had begun, Pang's eyes opened. His eyes were heavy but hostile. Eli felt himself grimacing in response to Pang rising up from his slouch. "Die, all of them." The dark-haired boy seemed to be struggling in the spot where he sat, while his lips seemed to imprison one another in a repetitive cycle.

"I am—good—I am okay. Much appreciated for asking. I am content to see that you are still among the living as well," said Pang.

"How long has it been since the sun has set?" asked Sia.

"About two hours," answered Jude.

"Then I guess all we can do is wait," she said.

After a few awkward and idle minutes, Sia slowly rose from her seat, and walked towards the backroom. When she was nearly out of sight, her gaze fell upon him. Eli felt himself clear his throat. Jude was reading an unidentifiable book while Pang's chest rose and fell in what appeared to be a pleasant slumber.

Eli rose from his seat and headed towards the backroom. The last door at the end of the hallway creaked open. The room was bare and the air was stale. He walked passed the center of the room when the door closed behind him, causing his footsteps to come to an abrupt halt. He turned around to find pools of amethyst dubiety, ever present in their core.

"You scared me."

"I apologize," said Sia as she drew closer. "That was not my intention."

Her eyes moved slightly from side-to-side as if studying his.

"I must apologize for the coldness I have inflicted tonight. I was not being fair," she said.

He took a few comforting breaths while his hands found hers. Her blue combat tunic was torn and stained with blood and dirt. Dry blood clung to the side of her neck. His eyes came to hers just as his hand began to remove the dry blood from her.

"It's okay. I understand."

"Why is it that even amidst all this pandemonium and pain, this moment has never felt so perfect," she said.

"We both know the cause of this perfect moment," he said as his lips touched the back of her hand.

A small laugh and tiny smile teased at her lips as her eyes fell to the floor and then back up to his face.

"Eli I—," started Sia before her voice halted at the sound of an opening door.

"General Briars, Lieutenant Conall—they must be back!" said Sia as she swung open the door and exited.

Eli followed Sia back to the main room where he found it livelier than before. Lieutenant Titus stood by the door speaking with Agents Laia and Val, who both nodded and exited. Jude and Pang had taken a seat at the roundtable that embodied most of the room.

"Great, you are all here," said Conall as his eyes stopped when they came to Sia. "If you will all take a seat, I have a rather disturbing update."

◆◆◆

Jude realized his long list of questions, which he had accumulated for Conall, grew longer as more time passed. Everyone's eyes seemed to bore into the Lieutenant's face as he took his seat.

"First things first," started Conall as he clasped his hands in front of him. "The General will not be joining us. As we have expected, Kismet has fallen."

A cup crashed against the table which held a variety of parchment and cups. Jude's head shot towards Sia and found her soaking up a spill with a blank piece of parchment.

"Excuse me, I apologize—I was just caught-off-guard," said Sia. Conall stared at Sia for a few seconds before continuing.

"The Necrosis and Necroborns were all a ploy to weaken the city's defenses. The enemy appeared to have entered through the Western Gate of the city. The Western Hold and Market District are littered with the lifeless corpses of our people."

"What about the children? Did you see any children—Lieutenant?" asked Sia frantically.

"No—I am afraid I did not," said Conall as his head tilted down for a few moments before rising. "Anya has chosen to stay behind, to uncover anything we may have missed and to be our informant within Kismet's borders."

It took Jude a few moments to process everything. He was unaware that he had not really spoken since Conall had begun. However, one question stabbed at his mind, begging to be answered.

"What of Lord Bishop—is he okay?"

The melancholy cloak of inevitable despair and anxiety, descended upon the table.

"Lord Bishop has fallen," said Conall.

"No!" yelled Eli slamming his fist on the table.

Jude was confused by Eli's outburst. He never knew that Eli cared so much for Bishop. Of course he was the Lord of Kismet, and held a special place in the hearts of all of Kismet's people; however a more intimate feeling of sorrow seemed to overwhelm Eli in a way that was both shocking and revealing.

"Who is the enemy? What is their purpose? When do we kill them?" asked Pang.

Conall stared motionlessly back at Pang, as if cycling through a long list of applicable responses.

"Before I can disclose any further information, other duties must be adhered to."

"Other duties? Are you serious? Our city has just—."

The table vibrated with a *bam* that sent empty cups tumbling over.

"Brassie! One more outburst of disrespect and I will personally hand you over to the enemy myself," said Conall.

Jude looked over to Eli to see a both shocked but hostile expression present on his face. Jude wished his legs were longer so he could kick Eli from under the table.

What is wrong with him? He complains about not passing the Trials and not being enlisted on the squad. Then everyone puts their neck out for him to give him a chance, and he just spits on this unearned opportunity every chance he gets. Disgraceful!

"Try me!" said Conall in response to the silence.

"We apologize Lieutenant. Please—if you will—continue," said Sia.

"I am offering you a chance to become more than an Agent. I offer you a chance at becoming stronger, and have an opportunity to save Kismet. I understand that this may not be for everyone, so anyone without a backbone or loyalty to Kismet can feel free to leave—effective immediately," said Conall.

Jude found himself extremely anxious, and could not stop himself from fidgeting in his chair.

"I am asking for volunteers for a covert squad that would leave for Kismet as early as tomorrow. Due to safety and confidentiality, I cannot elaborate on what the mission will be, but what I can say is that it will impact Kismet and every land in existence. Any who decline this invitation shall leave now, and never return. Those of you who accept what I am offering, speak up," said Conall.

Jude thought about all of the pain that his mother and brother had put him through. All of the lies they weaved around his youth. There was so much unfinished business with both of them. He knew he was angry now, but the fact that his home and family may still be able to be saved, gave him enough incentive to know what to do.

"Lieutenant, Agent Jude Bray accepts your offer," said Jude rising from his seat.

"Lieutenant I accept as well—Agent Sia Wyatt," said Sia as she came to her feet. "I need to find my brother, and I do not know if I can do it alone."

"That goes the same for me Lieutenant, my dad is still back there," said Eli.

Jude was surprised when he did not hear the last voice that he had expected would immediately rise. Pang sat scowling examining the room while mumbling to himself. Jude had been worried about Pang, ever since he had rendezvoused with him in the forest. He seemed—off.

"Lieutenant will we be paid for our services?" asked Pang.

"You will be taken care of. Matter of fact, I have your payments with me for the Necrosis mission. Anya will continue to provide as much funding as she can, but we do ask for you to be patient. As far as we know, she is the only Agent left of our people—her and one other," said Conall.

Pang's eyes met Jude's. They harshly stared back for a short moment before returning to Conall. "Let's kill someone!"

A wave of relief washed over Jude. He could not picture going on any missions with just Eli and Sia. While he valued his new-budding friendship with Sia and had no harsh feelings towards her, he felt like he and Sia would not be able to carry an entire squad alone. At least now he would have both some help and a friend.

"Okay. The rest is not for my lips to disclose for I do not have all of the necessary knowledge to fully brief you. That is why I have invited him here tonight," said Conall.

"Him Lieutenant?" asked Sia."

Conall rose from his seat and approached the front door. He opened the door and exited, closing the door behind him. In his short absence, Jude found himself mirroring the same curious and anxious expressions that displayed all around him. After a few minutes the door opened, unveiling a robed and hooded figured, who froze at their presence.

TRUE COLORS

Jude was unaware that a grandfather clock had surreptitiously made its nest of time and secrets somewhere within the cabin. As the four of them sat anxiously in the silence with Conall and the hooded figure, the clock's pendulum sent Jude's mind on a personal mission to discover its location.

"I have had more time to prepare for what I am about to tell you—but still even I am having trouble coming to grips with what has transpired," said the stranger. His voice was raspy and the laugh he released was low.

"Professor?" asked Sia with a flicker of enlightenment in her voice.

The navy hood fell and was replaced by crumpled long white hair. His wrinkles were just as prevalent as the worry and shame on his face. His head slowly tilted up, until his eyes barely met Sia's.

"It is good to see you my young friend."

Sia's chair rocked in place as she crossed the room and flung her arms around Vance. He embraced her arms for a few seconds before nodding towards her seat. Sia's eyes stayed glued to Vance once she returned to her chair—a newly-displayed confidence and determination present on her face.

"Since all of you still remain here tonight, this means that you have decided to accept what Lieutenant Titus has presented to you. That will be the most honorable and most regretted decision of each of your young lives. However, it is a necessity that would have proven fatal for many, if you all had chosen otherwise. Before we get on the discussion of Kismet, there is much that you need to know about this world, and the past it hides in its shadows," said Vance turning to Conall. "Lieutenant, do we happen to—."

"On it," said Conall leaving his seat and exiting to the kitchen. After a few minutes he returned with a platter containing six steaming cups and a kettle. He set them down in the middle of the table before taking his seat. Everyone, excluding Conall and Vance, took a cup before returning their attention to the Professor.

"Long ago after the War of the Heavens, the gods met in seclusion with a handful of preordained individuals. These individuals would prove to become instrumental in the creation of what you see today. The gods, now referring to themselves as the Three Brothers due to their shame of defeat, had made a decision to create a seal that would imprison Anim beneath the Earth's surface. This seal would embody the very life force of the Three Brothers. Their ancient slumber beneath the Earth's surface would power the seal that would be Anim's prison. Knowing how inquisitive the human mind would be, the Three Brothers feared that through time and whispers, their sacred resting places would be unveiled."

A knock sounded at the door making the entire table jump with surprise. Vance and Conall locked eyes briefly before Conall stood slowly from the table.

"Ensconce," whispered Vance.

Conall's hand lightly gripped the knob on the door before he took one final look over his shoulder towards Jude. The door opened, and soon Val and Laia stepped through.

"Lieutenant!" said Val and Laia in unison.

"Val, Laia—have we made contact?" asked Conall.

"Affirmative Lieutenant!" said Val.

"E.T.A?"

"Two hours, they discovered something on their last mission," said Val.

"Copy that. Survey the area and report back when they have arrived."

"Yes sir!"

Laia exited, and just as Val was nearly out of vision, he stopped and turned around.

"Pardon my intrusion sir, but it is not healthy to be sitting alone in the dark. You should get some fresh air when you get the chance," said Val.

"Thanks soldier—I will," said Conall. Val quickly exited and soon the door closed behind him.

Conall retook his seat and clasped his hands. He nodded to Vance and then returned his gaze to Jude. Jude's stomach began to do more flips than he could count. There was something about Conall's gaze that disassembled his confidence and made him feel like he had failed in some unknown task.

"You may continue Professor. We will not be disturbed again until we have accomplished what we need to accomplish," said Conall. Vance nodded in response.

"While both the seal and the Three Brothers' resting places are secured with unimaginable power, if even one of the Three Brothers is released from his slumber—or worse—the seal will be weakened, and Anim may have the power to escape. So before retreating to their hallowed places of slumber, the Three Brothers bestowed a portion of their power onto the preordained individuals. These individuals came to be known as The Guardians. They possessed prodigious power and went on to pass down fractions of their power throughout the generations. Each Guardian bringing their own signature blessing to each of their people, helped to spread the Three Brothers magic through generations of inherited bloodlines across the lands."

Vance's gaze went to Conall, who held his gaze for a few moments before turning away. Jude's mind instantly tried to decipher the unspoken meaning of their gaze, but was quickly interrupted as Conall rose from his seat.

"If all of you are who you claim you are, then I apologize for this next part," started Conall as he clasped his arms behind his back and began to circle the table. The sight made Jude's heart race and fueled the anxiety that now crawled through every nerve of his body. "Because of the gravity of the situation, and the minimal amount of trust we have at our disposal, my actions are justified."

Jude noticed the candle on the table began to blur until it multiplied. Dozens of lit candles now infested the table at every side. Jude's stomach became nauseous, his mind became cloudy, and the presence of his blood energy began to fade when his eyes set on the cup he once held.

"You've poisoned us!" yelled Jude as he fell from his seat.

"Jude! screamed Sia. Her scream was followed by an abrupt *thud* and soon another followed.

"Blood—," started Pang, before Jude heard another *thud*, and he knew that his friend had met the same fate as the rest of them.

Eli was unaware of how he had returned to his chair. The flame of the single-lit candle in the center of the table seemed to dance slowly and lightly to the drum of his heart. His throat was dry and his mouth tasted of unknown chemicals and grass. As his eyes flickered around the table, he found Jude and Pang looking as disheveled as he imagined he did. A cough jumped next to him causing him to look over until his eyes fell on Sia. His hand felt warm, and when he looked down at it, he noticed that his hand was interlaced with hers.

"Now that you are all awake and calm, we can begin," started Conall. He was standing between Jude and Pang, and after a few seconds, returned to his seat. "In your cups I added a substance known as antiom. It is used by a few of our Operatives when interrogating enemies. While it was outlawed by Lord Bishop some time ago, a few of us still carry a healthy supply of it."

"But we are not the enemy! You dishonor us with your treachery!" yelled Pang.

"Enough!" The silence leaped to Conall's side as soon as his words faded. Even Vance seemed to fight back the urge to move even the slightest. "Antiom is not a poison, but a brain altering substance. Since we never had the time to truly check into all of your 'innocent' pasts, we cannot be sure that none of you are in fact—Rogues," said Conall.

Rogues? What the heck is a Rogue?

The word was new to Eli, and the lack of knowledge he had on it started to irritate him. Whatever a 'Rogue' was, he was positive that he was not one.

"I am not a spy. My family has lived in Kismet their entire life. Jed Bray is my—is my—he is a part of my family and a well-respected and honorable Operative," said Jude.

Eli noticed a bit of hostility in Jude's eyes. For the first time since Eli had known Jude—which was his entire life—Jude appeared caught-off-guard, violent and unpredictable.

"All of that is irrelevant," started Conall. He rose from his seat and approached Jude.

The tension in the air was palpable. Anger warmed the air and clouded the senses. Vance offered no explanation, guidance or comfort when Conall assumed his position behind Jude's seat, absent from the green-eyed boy's view.

"Antiom apprehends the subconscious, and forces the person to reveal anything he or she has lied about, is purposefully keeping a secret, or anything they have deceived others about—even once. While this may seem intrusive, it is necessary, so let us begin," said Conall. He placed two fingers in the middle of Jude's forehead, and tapped twice.

Eli felt himself recoil in his chair at Jude's eyes. Sia gasped next to him and soon tightened her grip on their still interlaced hands. Both Jude's eyes turned completely black, relinquishing every particle of Jude's identity that Eli had come to know over the years. Jude's eyes were evil, cruel and frightening.

"Of course I ate my vegetables mommy," said Jude. His voice was young and strange.

He sounds like Mik!

"Do not tell them about your encounter with your brother last night and how he attacked you," said Jude. His voice was deep and vast before returning to the young voice he once had. "It's okay mommy, I know I am strong enough to protect you."

Jude's eyes cleared and soon the green eyes, which Eli had come to know so well, returned. Jude's eyes turned slowly from Pang, to Sia and then to Eli.

"You are all staring—which means—which means you know about Jed," said Jude. His eyes tilted down before meeting Pang's.

"That is all?" asked Conall.

"What?" replied Jude.

"Nothing," said Conall as he passed Pang and stood behind Sia. Her eyes met Eli's, and soon a small smile came and went. Conall tapped her forehead twice with two fingers. The sinister and nefarious eyes that had once inhabited Jude extinguished the purple essence that always swam in Eli's thoughts.

"Do not worry Mik, mom is coming back," said Sia. Her voice sounded slightly younger than normal. "Stop it! Stop hurting him! I was the one that put the milk on the bottom shelf—not him! Punish me!"

Eli felt her hand detach from his, leaving him feeling anxious and terrified that his turn would be next.

I never got the chance to tell Sia that I was discharged. She is going to find out.

"My stupid cat scratched me and left the ugliest mark," said Sia. Her voice appeared normal, closer to the lightness and sharpness that he loved about her.

Eli giggled slightly at Sia's lie about her cat. Even though they had already talked about it, and he knew it was not true, the hindsight proved amusing to him.

"I do not wear heavy makeup. It must be the stupid trees and plants around here," her voice was heavy with worry and hostility. "They cannot know about my father and his cruelty," said Sia in a heavy and vast tone, before returning to its normal state. "I don't know how I got it. It must have been when I fell down the stairs at home. I do too have stairs at home, you just haven't seen them Markus!"

Eli began to feel embarrassed and did not know why. He found himself shading his face with one of his hands, while his breathing grew more rapid. He snuck glances up at Conall, Vance and Pang a few times, before returning his gaze to the cup in front of him and pushing it away.

Get this crap away from me!

"Go ahead and break up with me, I really could *not* care less!" said Sia.

The sound of Pang rocking back-and-forth in his chair was the only noise in the room for a few minutes. Eli began to hear deep breaths beside him, and wondered if the "not poison" that Conall had snuck into their cups, had finally wore off for her. Eli reached down and grabbed her hand. It was hot and sweaty but quickly clung to his when he grabbed it. He looked at her face and reveled in the comfort of her eyes. They contained sorrow causing Eli's brows to curl.

"Eli," she whispered with her head tilted down at their clasped hands which hung underneath the table. "Do they know? Do they know about my father?"

Her eyes slowly rose to his, and her lips trembled. He saw a tear forming in her eye, and quickly thought of whatever he could say to keep it from falling.

"Hey, stop being spiffy. We have been through worse," he whispered.

It was not the original use for the word, but it was all he could think of. An abrupt laugh left Sia's lips causing the tear to break free and cascade down the side of her face. The sight pained him until he saw the small smile that clung to her lips.

"Two down—two to go," said Conall taking a firm stance behind Pang. The sight immediately drew Eli's attention causing him to smile. He had always thought that Pang could not be trusted and had some kind of hidden agenda. He began to laugh hysterically.

Pang and Conall instantly stared at him. Eli looked over to Jude and Vance and noticed the same expression. He turned his gaze to Sia, and was embarrassed when he saw her lightly shake her head a few times. The smile was gone and her brows were curled. He looked away from her prying eyes which seemed to read his every thought. "Sorry."

Conall's fingers lightly tapped Pang's forehead, and soon the madness, which would soon be a part of Eli, appeared in Pang's eyes.

It actually looks natural on him—of course.

"I will go easy on you," said Pang as his eyes began to squint in a manner that intimidated Eli. "Don't worry, I am not going to kill you—I promise."

Eli's eyes were drawn to Pang's hands that seemed to clench the table. During Sia and Jude's turn, their bodies were still, except for their lips.

"Don't worry about me Issac, I will be fine."

I bet Issac is his spying comrade.

As Pang leaped to his feet, the table flipped over, flying over Vance's head, and colliding with an adjacent wall. Everyone in the room seemed to jump to their feet, except for Jude and Vance. "Fight me! Don't worry—I am weaker than I look." Fresh blood fell from Pang's lips after his teeth pierced the flesh. "Give me your other leg! It is *mine* now!"

Eli found himself hovering above the floor, along with Sia, Jude and Conall. Eli tried to move his legs, but his body refused to respond. It was blood magic. He felt scared, helpless and vulnerable. He felt as if he was in a nightmare—a nightmare that he would never wake from.

"Do not tell him that his friend will die," started Pang. His voice was foreign and seemed to echo with every word. "Do not tell him about the pain that he will endure!"

Pang slowly sat in his seat, resting his hands on his lap. "If you leave now—at this very second—I promise I will not kill you."

Eli felt himself slam back down into his seat, nearly toppling over. He had not realized that he had been holding his breath. He looked around and noticed that Jude, Conall, and Sia were back in their seats as well. Vance appeared to have been unaffected by the entire scene.

"What is the tear for Brassie—your too good for you girlfriend dump you already?" said Pang. Eli's head whipped to Pang only to find that the blackness was gone and the familiar glow of his red orange eyes had returned.

"That must have been some crazy drug because I could have sworn there was a table here a few seconds ago. Whatever," said Pang.

"Bray—a hand please," said Conall getting up from his seat and walking towards the turned over table. Jude helped Conall return the table to its original position. No other noises were audible.

"Pang is it?" started Vance. "Where might you be from my boy?"

"Boy? Just so things do not get twisted and remain clear, I am not a boy. I am twenty-four, and I do not know if it is different in the Land of Kismet, but last time I checked, twenty-four did not earn you the rank of 'boy."

"My apologies, I did not mean you any disrespect," said Vance.

So he hates being called boy.

Eli felt himself smile as the giddiness swelled within him.

"I mean, isn't the Lieutenant the same age as me? You don't call him boy. So I would appreciate the same respect," said Pang.

"I do not believe that Professor Vance meant any disrespect Pang," said Jude quickly interjecting.

Pang's anger seemed to subside and his shoulders seemed lower.

Oh how cute. The best friends coming to each other's rescue.

"Apologies then, I clearly had mistaken your intent then," said Pang.

You both make me sick.

Eli realized that Jude's eyes had been fixated on him. The greenery seemed to pry into Eli's every thought, causing him to recoil at the sight. Looking away, he stared at a picture that hung on a nearby wall for a few seconds. When his eyes returned to Jude, he noticed that he was still staring.

"What are you looking at?" asked Eli.

Jude seemed taken aback. He looked from Pang to Vance as if unaware of who Eli was talking to.

"Yeah I'm talking to you Jude. You've been staring at me for the past few minutes. What's your problem?"

Jude's eyes glared and his breathing appeared to quicken. His chest rose and fell quickly and his nostrils flared up. He mumbled something under his breath before responding.

"You're so lucky Rune just found me some patience because you don't want to know what I was originally going to say to that ignorant comment. I was not looking at you, I was looking at the mirror behind you. It appears that Laia and Val are arguing about something serious, and I was making sure that we were not ambushed since no one is watching the perimeter right now."

"They are what?" said Conall as he leaped from his seat.

Eli turned around and noticed a mirror that showed the reflection of the opposite window. Val had his hands up and appeared to be yelling at the top of his lungs. Conall crossed the room with haste, opened the door, and closed it behind him as he left. Everyone in the room, except for Vance and Jude, stared at the commotion outside of the window. Soon Val and Laia ran off in different directions, and Conall reentered the cabin.

"I apologize. Val and Laia got—distracted. We can continue," said Conall. He crossed the room until he was behind Eli.

Eli felt his nerves get the better of him. He was concentrating on calming down until his eyes met Jude's, who was sitting right across from him. They were set aflame with a rage and hostility that made Eli's adrenaline pump furiously. He began to feel like he was in the middle of combat, and needed to summon a weapon immediately.

So what. I thought you were staring at me and was mistaken. Are you going to be mad at me over that now too?

Blackness spilled across Eli's vision as if a thick black liquid had been spilled at the center of his eye. His breathing felt faint, but he did not feel any need to accelerate it. A heaviness descended within his head, and soon he felt his heart begin to race.

THE LIFE OF A
GUARDIAN

Jude's blood actually felt like it was boiling for the first time in his life. He finally knew what the sensation of grinding one's teeth was, and really felt like he needed some fresh air.

"If you will all excuse me for a few minutes please," said Sia. She politely rose from the table, and just as she passed Eli, jerked her hand away. "Don't touch me!"

The tension was unbearable, but not as overwhelming as the rage that dominated Jude. Eli's confession had proven to be a lot more revealing than Jude had anticipated—and clearly more than Sia had anticipated as well. There were so many situations that Eli had lied and deceived, that Jude found it difficult to add them to his list that he had planned to lock away for future reference. A voice in the back of Jude's head, made him wonder if he had confessed about his attempt on Eli's life; and then worry moved in alongside his rage.

Jude took a look around the table at each of the faces, and noticed that there were no signs of aggression or distaste directed towards him.

If I would have acted on it, whether I was successful or not, I would be apprehended and...

A door slammed in the back of the cabin. Running water sounded for a few seconds before the water stopped.

"My, I have never seen her that angry before. She is usually so calm and collected during my lectures," said Vance taking in a few deep breaths. Let's just give her a couple of minutes shall we?"

"No matter how she is feeling, we are running out of time. Someone needs to go get her so we can finish," said Conall.

"I will go!" said Eli jumping up from his chair. He quickly exited down the hallway and out of view.

A door opened in the back of the cabin. Unidentifiable conversation and muffled sobs sounded down the hallway.

"I said leave me alone!" screamed Sia. Her voice carried both volume and finality. A small struggle erupted causing everyone at the table to change their posture. "You deceitful bastard!"

"Alright that's it," said Conall getting up from his seat. He exited down the hallway with his heavy footsteps shaking the paintings on the walls.

"What are you talking about? We were fine before you came!" yelled Eli. A loud *thud* made Jude leap to his feet.

"I will be right back," said Jude.

Off-centered paintings and loud voices greeted Jude when he turned down the hallway. A body laid on the ground propped up on one elbow, while two people stood in a backroom.

"Eli just get out of here!" yelled Sia.

Eli leaped up from the floor and stormed down the hallway mumbling to himself. He stormed passed Jude as if unaware of his presence, and soon Jude heard a chair scrape across the floor. Jude walked to the backroom and found Conall saying something to Sia. Her lips were quivering, her eyes were pink, and her face was fresh with an infinite waterfall of tears that moistened her skin. His voice was low and soft, which confused Jude.

"Hey," started Jude. Conall and Sia's eyes looked up and stared at him. "If there is anything I can do, let me know."

"No I am fine Jude—I will be fine," said Sia.

"Okay."

"We should be back in the next minute," said Conall.

"Copy that Lieutenant," said Jude turning for the hallway.

"Hey Jude," said Sia quickly. Jude turned around to see her wiping her eyes. "Thank you."

Jude smiled before quickly exiting into the hallway. He noticed a few paintings that reminded him of one he had seen in Pang's house. Taking his seat at the table drew a lot of attention.

"I have been in many fights in the past, so I am a master at breaking them up," started Pang as he crossed his arms. Jude said nothing in response. "I am just saying, if you need someone to play mediator, I am your guy."

Jude looked to Eli and noticed that his eyes were digging into Pang. A black bruise was already beginning to darken his right eye. Just when Jude was about to turn to Vance, Eli's eyes shot to him.

"So—you just stood there and let him punch me. Some friend you are," said Eli. He spit into the cup in front of him and turned his gaze towards the front door.

Jude ignored the comment and turned his attention to Vance. He felt embarrassed about how his "comrades" were acting, and hoped that Vance would not see it as a reflection of Jude as well.

"Conall said he just needs a minute."

"Very well—thank you," said Vance.

A few seconds later, Conall and Sia calmly entered the room. The evidence of a private conversation was present on their faces. Conall pulled Sia's chair out and waited for her to sit. She quickly sat down thanking him once he returned to his seat.

"I owe everyone an apology, it really is not like me to lose my composure like that. Please forgive me," she said.

"No apology needed," started Vance. A warm smile spread across his face. "We are all human after all."

"Back to more important matters," said Conall. He clasped his hands in front of him before he began. "Now that we know that none of you are Rogues, at least as of now, I believe we can trust you with what you need to know. What Vance and I are about to tell you, cannot leave this room. Vance will you continue please."

"Of course Lieutenant. Now even though their magic was absolute, and they had created The Guardians as added security, the Three Brothers also created Protectors. When it comes to the Protectors, things become a tad bit complicated since Protectors are Guardians as well. The Protectors were tasked with the immediate protection of their god first, and the other gods second. This is because only that god's Protector can release them from their ancient slumber if the world is in dire need—or so it is foretold."

Vance pointed to something. Jude looked over and noticed that Sia had her hand up.

"But Professor, does that mean that all Guardians can sense other Guardians and Protectors close-by?"

"No my friend. You see, the Three Brothers feared that if even one Guardian was corrupted by sin, they would be able to hunt other Guardians, and eliminate them. So when the Guardians were created, they were created to not sense other Guardians, but only sense when the Order and their cause was in danger. Protectors on the other hand, are capable of sensing other Protectors—for that is one of their purposes," said Vance.

Since Vance was answering questions, Jude felt like it was an appropriate time to ask one of his own, so he raised his hand.

"Yes Jude."

"Since Guardians are human, when they received their powers, did they acquire immortality? Because if not, then the Three Brothers would have to choose a new Guardian, every time one died."

"Ah very good question. Yes, they did acquire immortality as a result of their amazing power."

"So, they live forever—like the race of Vampires do," said Jude.

"No, I am afraid not. You see, even with their amazing powers, Guardians are still human. Their immortality is different from the Vampire. While Vampires are nearly invulnerable to all kinds of physical damage, Guardians are not. When a Guardian dies he does not sleep or go to heaven or hell, he is eternally bonded to The Order. He wakes up in a different dimension of time as himself. That time period is in the future, sometimes long after the people of his current world have passed—as to divert any suspicion. He is eternally bound to the sacred reincarnation, until there exists no threat to the gods. When all threats have been destroyed, it is only then that all guardians can take their place in heaven among the gods after their next death."

"I apologize. I hope this is my last question. How do you know all of this if you yourself are not a Guardian?"

Vance's eyes met Conall's. "I know this because a Guardian gave me his ability of insight. You see, sometimes it is a difficult responsibility as a Guardian to utilize all of their talents fully. So a Guardian is able to give one of their abilities to another, at the cost of losing it until their next rebirth."

"Even their immortality?" asked Sia.

"Yes my friend, even their immortality." Vance stopped as if giving everyone a chance to absorb his words. Silence did not last long, before Jude deciphered Vance's meaning.

"Bishop was a Guardian..."

"Yes, he was a Guardian—and a Protector of Rune," said Vance.

"So whoever assassinated Bishop, did they know his true identity?" asked Pang.

"Perhaps," said Vance. His small smile fought for expansion, as the professor's eyes washed across everyone.

"Professor," started Sia. Her mind appeared to be cycling through her thoughts. "You know who Bishop's assassin is—don't you?"

"Yes my dear, I do." Vance's head tilted down for a few seconds, before rising to meet her gaze. "It was Lord Egon and our Emissary—Fox."

"What?" said Eli. It was the first time he had spoken since his altercation with Sia. "Fox?"

"Yes, I am afraid so," said Vance.

"Another snake," mumbled Jude. He had not intended to think aloud, and became nervous when he saw everyone's stare turn to him for a few minutes, before returning to Vance.

"But he has been on The Council for years Professor. Why would he betray us?" asked Sia.

"I do not know. But Bishop trusted him dearly," said Vance dropping his head.

The look of betrayal, shock and sorrow was present on everyone's face, when Jude raised his head. He looked around at everyone's face starting with Pang and ending with Vance. When Vance's eye's finally met his, Jude decided that he would be the one to ask what was subtly being asked of him and his comrades.

"When do we take him down?

DIFFERENT PEOPLE

The night air was brisk and sour, when Jude exited the cabin. The marshlands appeared to be both sleep and awake, causing Jude's mind to wonder off before getting lost in the countless thoughts that surrounded him. Vance and Conall had decided that further discussion of what lay ahead would be more productive if they waited for a small group that would aid them in their mission. The information comforted Jude. Even though he was somewhat confident in his abilities, he knew that he was far from ready to be able to take on such a high profile mission without some guidance. The thought of other more experienced Agents aiding them in their mission, brought on a much-needed calm.

Jude thought about one of the things that Eli had confessed, about how he had purposefully not told Jude about the Trials, because he wanted an advantage over Jude, just in case they were selected for the same round.

I don't know why I am mad about that. I mean, I should be applauding his initiative to think ahead, and to see me as that much of a threat. I did not even anticipate facing him in battle, let alone prepare.

However, the thought that his best friend was willing to go to such lengths to put Jude at a disadvantage—as well as continue to lie to him—fueled the rage even more. Another one of Eli's confessions surfaced, of how when they were kids they played in Marius' weapons room without permission. It was Eli's idea, and even though Jude resisted in fear that they would get caught, he followed Eli anyways. It wasn't long before Marius, who seemed to not be angry at all, caught them. However, after a few minutes, Jude learned that Eli had blamed it all on Jude, saying that he had forced Eli to go down there, against Eli's wishes. It made Jude nauseas. He had always looked at Marius as a sort of replacement dad in his father's absence. He always tried to make Marius proud, as well as Aileen, and never wanted to do anything to disappoint them.

Countless lies and deception from Eli's confession ambushed Jude from every angle. His head began to hurt and he could never find the right angle to crack his neck.

Two brown frogs leaped one behind the other, across a small pond that sat between two soggy patches of land. The first frog leaped into the pond, paused briefly, then leaped onto the moist soil on the other side of it—then paused. The second frog followed, leaping into the pond only to pause momentarily. Just as the second frog was about to leave the pond, a larger object emerged from the pond, imprisoning the frog in its sharp jaws, and dragging him down to the cold, wet and unknown depths beneath him. Many ripples continued to travel towards the edges of the pond for a few seconds, until all was still and quiet once more. The marshland air was filled with the lone croak of a brown frog. The frog hopped contently into the marshland's lush sweating trees and slippery surface, void of any worries or troubles.

"Use some company?"

Jude turned around and found Sia staring back at him. She wore a pair of black leather combat pants with a matching tunic. A long pure-white scarf, fell from her small pale neck.

"Oh hey."

"I can go—if you prefer to be alone," she said.

"No I apologize—it's just—I have a lot on my mind. I probably could use the company."

The mud squished beneath Sia's feet when she took a stance next to him. The brisk air seemed to calm in response to her presence, allowing Jude to finally begin to breathe normally.

"If a field mouse leads another blindly into the nest of a snake pit, who is to blame—the leader or the follower?"

"Both," she said.

Jude slowly turned his gaze towards her. Her hypnotic gaze seemed to trap the marshlands into an overpowering trance. Both pain and strength were present in her piercing amethyst eyes.

"The follower is guilty for being blindly led. If one is blind to who they follow, don't they deserve the manipulation—since they show no mind of their own? Don't they deserve the snake pit?"

"And the leader?" asked Jude.

"Is a predator, and leads those who are easy prey. They will remain predators until they blindly become prey—and in turn will meet their justified end."

The sound of trees blowing in the wind crept up from behind them. The world seemed to conceal more than Jude could anticipate, causing him to surrender to whatever the gods had in store for him.

"Thank you," said Sia.

"For what?"

"For going to Vance after my match and asking him to check-up on me. Thank you for saving me, I had no idea that you were the one responsible for me standing here today. Eli originally told me it was him. He took credit for bringing Vance to my bedside. Because of you my little brother still has a family that cares for him."

"I cannot take credit for you being alive today. Vance was the one that saved you, his abilities are why you are standing here today—not me," said Jude.

"Yes, but if you had not talked to him, I would not be here today. The three brothers work in almost perplexing ways. I believe they saved me through you—and Vance."

Jude recoiled at the tight embrace that assaulted him. Sia's arms held him in place, casting the sent of honey and spices. He hugged her back, grateful for her appreciation. After a few seconds, they detached, and their gaze set on the dark night air.

"He cares about you."

"If he cared about me, he would not have lied to me," she said.

"I refuse to neither defend him nor make any excuses. I have known him all of my life. We grew up together and he is like a second brother to me. I thought I knew everything about him and who he was—well I was wrong. However, what I do know is that he cares about you. He turned his back on me and everyone else when he first met you. You were the only thing that was important, and he would have sacrificed anything to have you feel the same—even at the loss of our friendship of so many years."

"Jude I am sorry, I had no—," she began.

"Do not apologize. I do not blame you. Him and I have just grown into different people. There is no one to blame for that. I just blame myself for not being wise enough to see it."

"I must apologize," she said.

Jude looked at her and found her head tilted down at the impressionable gray soil beneath them.

"I apologize because I feel comforted that I am not the only one that he hurt. I am selfish."

"It's fine. I completely understand," said Jude.

"I am going to talk to the Lieutenant, I refuse to allow you to be dishonorably discharged because of Eli—it is unjust."

Jude felt himself smile. It was nice to have someone amidst this chaos, actually care about what happened to him. "Thank you Sia, but I don't think that anything can change the General's mind. I think that the Lieutenant only includes Eli and I in these discussions, because he does not want to bring shame and embarrassment in front of you guys."

"That isn't true. Do you think they would disclose so many of Kismet's secrets, as well as the secrets of the Three Brothers, if you were intended to remain dishonorably discharged?"

"You have a point. I just like to prepare myself—you know—be one step ahead of what could happen," said Jude.

A lone brown frog hopped towards them before halting a few feet away. The vial pinned the frog instantly and silently, as soon as Jude threw it. The frog's eyes turned crimson, before its body flattened with the ominous signs of relinquished life.

"Why did you do that!" yelled Sia.

"He was a predator—a predator who met his justified end."

THE OCCULT OPERATIVES

Eli found himself struggling to resist the urge to punch Pang. The slow time that passed by appeared to take its toll on not only Jude and Sia, but Pang as well. Jude had left the cabin a few minutes after Conall had informed everyone that they were expecting other Agents. Sia followed him a few minutes later. They had been gone for over fifteen minutes, which gave Eli much pause. Vance and Conall had disappeared to the back room, but the sound of loud and unidentifiable conversation was still audible through the walls. This left Eli alone with Pang, who was finding it difficult to bide his time.

"I always knew you were a snake," said Pang.

"Is that so?"

"That filthy, matted, poor excuse for hair looks like it is full of secrets."

"Hey, what are you gonna do, it runs in my family," said Eli.

"What does—the filthy hair or the secrets?"

A smirk passed across Pang's face, causing Eli's jaw to clench and his fists to tighten.

"Hey if you want to punch me go right ahead. Just remember what happened to your loud mouth friend when he raised a hand to me," said Pang.

"That's it smartass, I've had enough of your—."

"Calm down Brassie."

Eli whipped his head around to find Vance and Conall staring at him. The look of grief was bold on Vance's face, while aggravation masked Conall's.

"Quarrels," started Conall. The mask of aggravation and hostility seemed to instantly dissipate. "Do you mind helping me set up for our guests?"

"Copy!" said Pang leaping to his feet. He followed Conall to the kitchen, and returned with more cups, plates, and a platter of fruits and cheeses.

"You are definitely a spitting image of your father."

Eli looked next to him, and found Vance sitting on the same couch.

"I'm sorry?"

"You look just like your father," said Vance.

"Oh, thank you. So I assume that means that you know him."

"Yes, greatly—your mother Mya as well," said Vance.

"Please tell me, is my father okay? He is alive right? Well of course he is alive, he is great—amazing really. Is he okay?"

"I am afraid I have not had contact with your father since the Necrosis mission. My efforts were primarily geared towards our cities defenses—in hindsight, I should have tried harder."

Eli felt his stomach flee. He knew he should not doubt his father's talents and abilities, but he could not help but worry about Marius being alone in a land controlled by their enemy.

Chairs scraping across the floor trailed after Pang and Conall's activities, followed by the opening of a door. Jude and Sia casually strolled inside, closing the door behind them. Eli noticed Sia's eyes venture his way for a brief second before quickly relocating. His gaze soon fell on Jude.

Ha! Leave it to Jude to pretend like I'm not here.

A knock sounded behind them.

Everyone's eyes met.

"Ensconce," whispered Vance.

Conall crossed the room, and after taking a quick look over his shoulder, opened the door slowly.

"Lieutenant, they are here," said a voice.

"Copy that. Send them in."

Eli was beginning to believe that he was in a never-ending nightmare, where his attacker never ceased his pursuit. Their black hoods and matching combat gear seemed to cast a veil of darkness across the room, making Eli cringe in response. The door slowly and silently closed behind them.

"Everyone to the roundtable," announced Conall.

After a brief pause, the room began to move as one. Chairs slid out then in, and empty cups were soon boiling with steam, before they were handed to their owners. The four Occult Operatives sat in between Vance and Conall, across from Eli and the others. The uncomfortable tension hung high in the air, collaborating with the silence that never seemed to withdraw from the cabin.

"For those of you who do not know, these four make up our Occult Operatives squad. Their main and never-ending objective is the exposure and removal of any and all acts of Kismet treason," said Conall. He nodded towards the four Operatives. Soon the black cloths that were tied around their mouths were removed, and a few seconds later, normality became them. "This is Priya, she is the Commander of this squad and one of our top Combat Specialists. She is known for being adept at anticipating enemy strategies and attacks, as well as turning the tide of battle."

"Salutations fellow Agents," said Priya. Her voice was exotic but strong. Her long black hair was straighter than fresh parchment and shined with a shimmer of magic and mystery. She appeared to be a year or two older than Conall and her slate-black eyes gave no signs of what she was thinking, or who she was.

"The Operative next to her is Tristan. He is a highly-skilled Weapons Master, who has served under both Anya and Priya for many years. He is highly skilled with close combat and projectiles," said Conall.

A smirk and a nod was all that came from Tristan. He looked to be a year or two younger than Priya. His militant short hair, chiseled chin and dark blue eyes made Eli feel more comfortable in his presence. Tristan's hand lightly grasped his chin, exposing his perfectly trimmed nails.

"The gentleman next to Tristan is Jarkko. He is a very advanced Magi, who has extraordinary talents in telekinetics, concealment and ability advancement. I can personally attest to his skills, since he in fact saved my derrière on one of our many missions together," said Conall chuckling.

"It is a pleasure to meet all of you—a pleasure indeed," said Jarkko as he rested his eyes on Sia. The sight infuriated Eli. Jarkko's long blonde hair fell lightly to his shoulders, covering one of his eyes with its blonde strands. His voice was foreign and deep, but to Eli's disgust, was also pleasant to listen to. He seemed to be the same age as Tristan.

You better keep your eyes to yourself. I don't care if you're an Occult Operative, you have never met someone like me before.

"And the man on the very end there is Kai. He is a highly-skilled Weapons Master, and one of the Academy's youngest prodigies. He was admitted to the Academy at the age of eighteen, against all guidelines and advice—if I might add. At the age of nineteen he achieved the rank of Special Agent, and by the age of twenty, he was the youngest of the Occult Operatives. Kai is highly skilled at long-range assault, crowd control and blades. He is know amongst the other Operatives, for playing dead in battle," said Conall with a short laugh.

"Kai is thrilled to meet you all," said Kai with a laugh before turning his gaze to Jude. "Especially *you* fellow prodigy." His bright hazel eyes, straight short black hair and long face were just as familiar as the scars. Memories of Eli's interrogation came and went throughout his vision. "Rumor spreads throughout the land that you will be the light amidst the pending darkness."

Jude's eyes widened. He looked around at the others appearing in disbelief of Kai's words.

"Wait, how can he have been admitted into the Academy at eighteen—it's forbidden," said Eli crossing his arms. Everyone's eyes met Eli's, making him wish he could retract his statement.

"Simple, Kai is a man that knows what he wants—and will do anything to get it. But you know that already—don't you Eli," said Kai with a smile and a glare.

Consider yourself added to my list of people I can't stand—behind Pang and Jarkko.

"The Occult Operatives have been following up on some possible leads. I will let Priya take over from here," said Conall nodding his head towards the Commander.

Priya ran a single finger down the edge of her perfect strands of hair. "Like Lieutenant Titus has stated, we have been following many leads starting with the first Necrosis that attacked our city. Considering the fact that the Necrosis was released amongst our streets without raising suspicion from any of our guards or Agents, proves that they had some connections from the inside. We ran across a couple of stray wanderers within our borders, however, they always managed to take their own life before we could fully interrogate them. Jarkko was able to set a few traps amidst the city streets, and was quick to inform us when he sensed a lead. Our suspect was detected in the Western Hold, and we had reason to believe that his informant held a house in that hold. We quickly apprehended the informant only to find out it was a dead end. Apologies again Mr. Brassie."

Eli gritted his teeth to fight back the words that begged for release. The way Priya recounted the incident after they had broke into his house, attacked him and Marius, apprehended them and then nearly gave Eli a heart attack with Kai's interrogation techniques, was almost insulting. It was as if none of that mattered to Priya—to any of them.

"It was not until the day of the Necrosis mission that we detected a foreign presence at the western gates. I dispatched Tristan there at once. The marks of Fox's hand-to-hand bloodline ability were prevalent on all of the bodies that surrounded the western gates. After rendezvousing with Tristan, our squad immediately returned to the castle, only to find it completely empty. Professor Ivor and a large group of Agents were supposed to be on guard inside the castle. Neither were present. Nothing was adding up. We realized that Council Hall was the last room in the castle that had not been investigated. Upon entering we found nothing short of destruction. Shattered pillars, scattered debris and a destroyed ceiling were just a small fraction of what we discovered there. However, what caught our eye more than anything was the lone lifeless body, which sat across the shattered Council roundtable. We quickly identified it as our former Lord. This was found with his body," said Priya throwing a shinny object on the table.

Jude was the first to grab it. He examined it for a few seconds before holding it up to everyone else "It's a locket."

"Very correct, but open it," said Priya.

Jude opened the locket and recoiled when a small piece of parchment fell from its inner chamber. Eli was growing impatient, and felt like Jude was taking too long examining everything. After unfolding the parchment, Jude's eyes widened. He passed the parchment on to Sia, who continued to pass it around the table. Eli was quick to snatch it from Pang—for more reasons than one. He unfolded the mysterious parchment and examined it:

You are in danger.

Leave Kismet at once, and never return.

ΑΩ

"What is the symbol they used to sign it with?" asked Jude.

"It is the symbol of The Order," said Vance. Eli was shocked at his response, since Eli still held the parchment in his hands.

"So whomever sent the note, knew about The Order and the Guardians—as well as the threat on Bishop's life," said Sia. Eli's eyes drifted to her and stayed fixated, hoping that he could get even a glance from her. After a couple of minutes, he surrendered.

"The real question is, how did this person know ahead of time that there was a threat on Bishop's life, and live to warn him with this note? Sounds shady to me," said Pang with a shrug. Eli got caught in a reverie of him bashing Pang's face into the table, and had to continuously shake off the image.

"Well whomever the person was, they knew about Lord Egon and Fox's treachery, which means they either know them, or collaborate with them on some level. That narrows down our options," said Priya.

"Of all the questions that surrounded these events, we do have the answer to one of them," started Vance. He slowly stood from his seat and clasped his hands in front of him. "The Order is in trouble, which means the three brothers are in danger. The threat rises from this alliance born of deception. Fox and Lord Egon must be apprehended and eliminated before any more harm can come to The Order."

"There is one last thing that we have discovered," said Priya. Her gaze went to Conall, and after receiving a nod, continued. "We have discovered that Ivor has appointed himself ruler and Lord of Kismet."

Eli had to shake his head a few times to confirm that he had heard correctly. After noticing the frequent displays of shock around his side of the table, he decided that he had heard correctly. Since no one would ask the question that was bearing down on Eli's shoulders, he decided to take the initiative to ask for himself.

"How can he do that? My dad always told me that a member of The Council had to be voted for by the people of Kismet."

"We have suspected that Lord Egon has something to do with it," started Conall. He took a sip of his cup for the first time since the meeting had begun, and placed it back in front of him. "We believe that Ivor has been collaborating with Fox and Lord Egon for some time now. Lord Egon probably promised him the throne, as to keep some level of control over Kismet."

"Oh my Aegis," said Vance. It was the first sign of shock that Eli had noticed from the Professor all night. Eli thought about all of the times that Vance had stood alongside Professor Ivor at the Trials, and kicked himself for not seeing it sooner.

It was clear as day. No one could be that crazy and be an honorable man. I should have known there was some kind of treachery behind his insanity.

"We must act, I refuse to stand by and allow my land to fall into the hands of snakes and traitors," said Jude.

"There is a lot more to this than we are being led on to believe. This treachery may run deeper into Kismet than we all know. However one thing is known, we are not capable of going head-to-head with Lord Egon, Fox and Ivor—not to mention the Necroborns, and any other traitors of Kismet that choose to follow them. We will need allies, which is why after speaking with both Priya and Vance, have decided to send you four to Geminate," said Conall.

Eli's adrenaline made its presence known after Conall's words. Eli did not understand why Conall would think it was a good idea to send him and the others to Geminate, when Kismet was in danger—as well as Marius.

"Professor Ivor has been head of our foreign relations. I believe we need to know if our allies really did refuse to give us aid, or if that was just another lie force-fed by Ivor himself," said Vance.

"However, the four of you have not been properly trained in order to successfully adhere to your mission. This is why we have decided that each of you will be assigned an Occult Operative, to help train and hone your abilities," said Conall.

Yes!

"How long will this take?" asked Jude.

"Proper training usually ranges anywhere from one to two years, however, you will only have months," said Conall.

"Months?" asked Eli. He knew that Conall had to be joking. That was a ridiculous amount of time for anyone to go off and train for, while their home was in shackles.

"Yes..." said Conall glaring towards Eli. The glare made Eli afraid to move and stopped any further questions or comments that were pending. "None of you are strong enough to stand in defiance of what we suspect we are up against. After your training, the Occult Ops will stay behind in Kismet and collaborate with the General to try and help take back the city. We will evacuate any survivors to our nearest black sites until the city is back under our control. You four will be responsible for making direct contact with our allies in Geminate, and seeking aid to our cause. I will discuss further details after you return from your training. Lord Egon could move his forces to Geminate and Praxis next, so time is not on our side. Priya, will you be so kind as to inform our Agents as to who they will be training under?"

Priya stood firm and proper from her seat. Her hands clasped behind her back, and her stare bombarded Eli's body with anxiety.

"Agent Bray…"

"Commander!" said Jude rising from his seat.

"After speaking with Conall, I believe that you will benefit tremendously if you were to train with me," said Priya.

"Copy that Commander! Looking forward to it," said Jude taking his seat.

"Agent Wyatt…" said Priya.

"Commander!"

"You will be training under Jarkko," said Priya looking towards her comrade. A quick wink sprung at Sia from Jarkko. Eli thought about objecting to the decision, but came to the conclusion that it would not alter anything, and would probably end with him looking foolish.

"Agent Brassie…"

"Yes mam—commander," said Eli.

Stupid! Stupid! How can I mess up my introduction? I look like a novice in comparison to the others.

"You were definitely a difficult one to place, but after speaking with your Lieutenant, we both have decided that you would benefit the most by training under Kai," said Priya.

Eli felt his heart stop. His eyes grew wider until he could barely feel them. He gasped for air after a few seconds, realizing that he had been holding his breath.

"I'm sorry, I think I was daydreaming. Who am I training under?"

"Kai the sly," said Kai with a smirk.

"I'm sorry but can't I be paired up with someone else, like Tristan?"

The entire room went silent. Eli immediately took it as a sign that he had made a fool of himself.

"Brassie! Backroom now!" said Conall rising from his seat. He exited down the main hallway of the cabin and out of sight. Eli followed the Lieutenant, until they were both in the backroom that Sia had been in earlier. Once Eli had entered the room, Conall closed it shut behind him.

So let me guess, this is the part where you tell me you're sorry for punching me right?

"I do not know what your definition of the word 'orders' is. However, just in case you were not aware, Priya was giving you orders—orders that you will obey without question. Do I make myself clear?"

Who does this guy think he is?

"Clear? You're not my father, you're like two years older than—."

Eli felt his face hit the floor. His teeth and ears both began to ring in unison. For a short moment he was unaware of what had happened.

"I have had enough of your disrespect. I give you more chances than the General would ever consider, but you still continue to try my patience. I am your Lieutenant—your superior. It does not matter how old I am. If I were a toddler equipped with nothing but my bottle and a blanket, you would still follow my orders without question. If being a part of Kismet's armed forces is not something you are capable of or desire, then quit now, head home, and go on with your life. If you choose to remain here, under my command—do you hear me? My command! Then you will follow all orders any superiors give to you without question. Regardless of what you choose, know this, you will learn your place."

Eli felt his brain quickly make up the decision to quit and go home. At least he would get to be with his dad—wherever he was. He knew that his dad would be very disappointed in his decision, but he hoped that Marius would find some way to understand and accept his decision. He rose to his feet and stared deep into Conall's eyes. Eli felt his nose flaring up and his jaw clenching. His fist twitched at his side with the urge to desecrate Conall's smug expression.

"Yes sir Lieutenant. I apologize for all of my outbursts," said Eli.

Conall said nothing. He simply stared at Eli for a few seconds before opening the door and exiting. Eli took Conall's lack of response, as an acceptance of his apology, and decided to follow him back to the main room of the cabin. Tension and wild gazes greeted Eli when he entered the room. Everyone appeared to be finding anything other than him to look at—except for Kai, who had the biggest smile plastered across his face.

Gosh I freaking hate that guy. Him and Pang are running neck and neck on my list.

"I apologize for keeping all of you waiting," started Conall as he took his seat. "Brassie and I were just working out a few details. Isn't that right Brassie?"

I swear you think this is over. You intrude into my relationship with Sia, and then punch me not once but twice. Then you speak to me like I'm your child. You're a fool if you think this is over.

"Yes sir Lieutenant," said Eli.

"Outstanding. So the only issue is the matter of your remaining Agent—Agent Quarrels?" said Priya.

"Don't worry about me. I am good," said Pang crossing his arms.

"Quarrels this is not up for discussion, everyone will receive training. Is that clear?" said Conall.

Yea Pang, is that clear?

"What I meant was, no one in this room is equipped to train me. None of you have any knowledge of blood magic or how it works. I am an anomaly amidst your people. Only the one who taught me my blood magic can further train me—no offense," said Pang looking around the table.

"Very well, and how do you plan on getting in contact with your mentor?" asked Conall.

"I have a good lead—."

"A lead?" asked Conall. He appeared to be both annoyed and tired.

"Yes Lieutenant, my teacher never stays in one spot for too long, but I am almost certain that I know where his current residence is," said Pang.

"Since you are a—how you say—'anomaly,' I will just have to go on your word. I trust I will not regret it—because if I regret it, so will you," said Conall. His expression read *no mercy*.

"Do we know when we will be leaving?" asked Sia.

"Tomorrow morning—so four hours. Each of your Operatives have picked out their own preferred location for your training," said Conall in a matter-of-fact tone.

Eli noticed a look of worry on Sia's face. He tried to pinpoint its origin, but failed.

Maybe she is just afraid to be away from Kismet that long. Four months is a long time.

"Lieutenant I would like to get as much sleep as possible then. I am both physically and mentally exhausted, and want to be at my best for our departure tomorrow," said Jude.

Listen to you. You really know how to show off don't you? Why don't you climb into bed with him so you can be the next Lieutenant?

"Agreed and granted," said Conall slouching in his chair. It was the first time Eli had seen Conall abandon his perfect posture. "I believe we all can use some rest. Unless anyone has anything else to add, I believe this meeting is over."

"Lieutenant?"

"Yes Wyatt?"

"May I speak with you after our meeting?" asked Sia.

Eli's eyes immediately went to Sia.

Say what? Why does she want to speak with him?

"Very well," said Conall standing up from his seat. "Get some sleep everyone, we will reconvene in the morning."

Eli watched closely and distastefully as Sia and Conall retreated to the back room.

A NIGHT AMIDST
THE MARSH

Each second that passed felt like a personal insult. Rocking back-and-forth in his chair at the roundtable, Eli began contemplating abandoning his plan of intercepting Sia's departure from Conall's bedchamber.

She's been in there for like five whole minutes!

After their dismissal, everyone dispersed to either retire for the night or collaborate in the night's cool air. Sia and Conall immediately relocated to Conall's bedchamber in the back of the cabin, extinguishing Eli's hope to speak with Sia. He hated the thought of their last interaction and how angry Sia was with him. He was determined to explain his side of the story, no matter how long it took—at least at first.

Voices sounded down the hallway followed by a door creaking open. The old floorboards beneath the cabin winced beneath the footsteps of their assailant. Sia entered the room casually with a smile that quickly dissipated as she laid eyes on him. Her eyes quickly relocated to the cabin's front door behind him, and after speeding up her pace, was gone. Eli sprang to his feet and crossed the room in a few long strides. Opening the door, he recoiled at the cold air that pillaged him and followed.

A blanket of omniscient stars pulsed above him. The night sky abandoned its usual foggy demeanor and eerily adapted a clear and clean persona. Trees swayed back-and-forth brushing their branches together briefly like conjoining bodies. Giant moths and noisy flies came-and-went at their own accord—brushing passed Eli's face and igniting his annoyance.

The smell of swamp and sour garbage was ever prevalent. Looking around, he quickly located Sia sitting in the middle of the marsh's lake atop a small patch of land. He approached her slowly, like a predator stalking its prey. Every breath, every step and every movement felt like it was haunted with the fear that she would sense his presence and retreat. Trudging through the warm and slimy water that completely surrounded her small island on all sides, he thought about the best way to start the conversation.

Dad always said girls like to hear someone tell them they're beautiful. Maybe it's best to start with a compliment. Or maybe I should start with an apology...

Both Eli's legs shook violently as he came upon the dry land in which she sat. Taking in his surroundings, he became aware of the rise and fall of the water's border from all sides. He pictured drowning if he fell asleep atop the small patch of land in which he stood on. Movement at the corner of his eye drew his attention.

Sia rose slowly with her back turned. The cool air blew her brown curls delicately across her back. Her navy long-sleeve tunic and black leather combat pants gave the impression that she had lost weight recently. She turned around as if sensing his presence. Her eyes failed to live up to the purple brilliance they were notorious for. Her lips were dry to the point of cracking and the bags under her eyes were prominent.

"You look beau—." She slapped him hard. His nose began to run, causing him to sniff consecutively, and his face felt colder in response to the pain amidst the night air. The pain superseded the first time she had slapped him. It left him feeling worthless, shameful and hurt.

Her expression never changed and her body never moved, except for the deep rise and fall of her breathing.

Taking the hint that she was still angry and unwilling to reconcile, Eli turned for the cabin—all without saying a word.

"So now you are just going to leave," she said behind him.

He turned around and studied her.

"Typical," she said with a disgusted curl of her lip.

"You slapped me so—so I didn't think you wanted to talk." He could hear the shame in his voice and felt alien to his own body. Placing his hands in his pockets, he waited for her to make the next move.

"You are disgusting! You took credit for Vance saving me after my Trials battle. You didn't get Vance—Jude did," she said.

"Well I didn't actually take credit I—."

"You said you ran to get Vance and begged him to save me." She crossed her arms and squinted her eyes.

"Well maybe I got a little carried away, but I did tell him to save you once he got there."

"You told Mik we were *together*," she said with a shiver. Eli couldn't be sure, but she almost sounded disgusted by the thought.

"Well we were seeing each other so—."

"You went behind Jude's back after dropping Mik and I off at Ms. Lowell's and told Anya that Jude knew about the Trials beforehand and should be discharged from the squad due to his dishonor."

Eli froze. No one knew about that, not even Marius. Hearing the secret leave Sia's lips gave him pause. "Who told you that?"

"You did! You confessed it you lying scumbag!"

"I just wanted to be on the squad and I didn't know how long my position would last. I was desperate! I wasn't thinking."

"What else is new? You're never thinking—at least about anyone other than yourself!" she said. Tears ran fell from her eyes like hail while her hunched shoulders began to shake.

The sight was devastating. Seeing Sia so pained by his dishonesty was hard for Eli to witness. Fighting back the pending tears, he quickly hugged her.

"Get your hands off of me!" she screamed while pushing him away. Her tone was violent and startling. The bags under her eyes were gone and her vulnerable gaze was replaced with the threatening glow of her Magi glare. "You ruined everything! Everything! I can't even look at you!" Shaking her head she turned around, returning her gaze to the water that surrounded her.

"I'm sorry. I am so sorry. Really I am." He took a spot next to her, examining the disappointment on her face—the refusal to look his direction. "I really didn't mean to hurt you."

Silence.

"Sia, I never want to hurt you."

"Well that's what you did," she said in a whisper. "You emotionally ravaged me."

"I see that—and I'm sorry."

She took a seat on the wet soil beneath them. "I know you are."

Eli saw a glimpse of light amidst the darkness that had shrouded their conversation. He took a seat at her side. With her change in demeanor, Eli saw a hope for forgiveness and refused to let anything hinder the opportunity. "You are right. What I did was absolutely wrong. I wasn't thinking of anyone other than myself. Can you forgive me?"

"You just don't get it," she said shaking her head.

"What don't I get?"

Her eyes finally met his. The gaze brought a reassurance and calmness that he thirsted for. Her willingness to acknowledge his presence next to her made him feel soothed. "You have a really good friend in Jude. You are oblivious to how good of a friend he is to you. I haven't even known you two that long, but I see how good he is to you. He thinks of you before thinking of himself and you—you shame him. You lie to him, deceive him and just..." Her eyes quickly looked away. "I just can't believe someone can be so evil to such a nice person."

Evil?

The word shook him to his core. No one had ever used such a word to describe him before. It was new. It was degrading.

"I'm not—an evil—person. I just made a mistake."

"You did more than make a mistake Eli. You consistently help initiate the demise of those around you. Those who care for you. You just have no idea how your actions affect other people," she said with a deep sigh.

Her words confused him. She made it seem as if things he said or done had some horrible effect on her or Jude. He was already sorry for lying to everyone but Sia would not let it go.

"What do you want from me? I have already apologized."

"Like I said—you don't get it." She flipped her hair to the side and flipped her gaze towards the shining stars above. "I want to get married someday. I want some nice, handsome and *honest* gentleman to come along and sweep me off my feet. He would be an honorable man, Special Agent or Operative perhaps. He will take me on a few romantic outings. Ask me to dance even if no one else is dancing. Order for me at eateries." A small smile teased the corners of her lips. Her eyes came alive and the anger she was once holding seemed to vanish. "I would eventually grow to know every little detail about him: what makes him laugh, cry, happy, sad. I will know his dreams and aspirations the way my lungs know to breathe. I will grow to love him, every inch of him—and him me. Then one special day, one romantic, special and unforgettable day, he will take me to some magical place. Getting down on one knee he will ask me to marry him. Flowers will rain down on our wedding like a never-ending cycle. Nature itself will stop to acknowledge our unity. We will eventually have a little boy and little girl." She sighed again. "It will be perfect."

The water's movement was the only sound to touch Eli's ears. He thought about Sia's dream. Her dream of finding someone special, getting married and having kids. All of that was far from the dream he had for himself. But he cared about her, and couldn't picture her sharing such intimate feelings and dreams with someone else.

"You really have it figured out don't you."

She slapped him. His face hit the mud with a *thud* as she quickly rose to her feet. "Don't condescend to me Eli Brassie!"

"I'm not conde—whatever word you just said. I'm serious!" He quickly leaped to his feet in fear that she would soon runaway. "I care for you and don't want you to share those feelings with anyone other than me."

Sia giggled until a small smile quieted her outburst. The sight made him smile, and happy about the direction things were headed.

"You really don't get it. I want to be with an honorable, loving and *honest* guy. That isn't you. You're a liar, an opportunist and ignorant. You have no idea how your actions hurt and dishonor people," said Sia.

Eli felt as if she had slapped him for the third time tonight. "Is that really what you think of me?"

The sharpest part of her gaze pierced his vision with the darkest Magi glare he had ever seen on her face. "Yes and you will not hurt me anymore. I will not let you hurt me or Mik."

"What? I would never hurt Mik! How dare you accuse me of something like that!"

Sia crossed her arms and squinted her eyes. "You have continuously used, deceived and dishonored your best friend who you have known for all of your life. He is basically your brother. If you can be evil to someone you have known all your life, then I cannot imagine what you are capable of doing to someone you barely know."

"I said I was sorry okay! Shut up about it!"

The next slap was a lot harder than the past ones but hurt less for some reason. "Don't you *ever* talk to me like that. I'm a lady. A man, a *real* man, never raises his voice to a lady. I don't know why I'm surprised."

"You call *me* evil, but you're the one putting your hands on me. You are what Jude would call a hypocrite," said Eli with a smirk.

She slapped him, and when his gaze immediately returned to hers, the back of her hand came back with a vengeance. "You're a pig. Why do you think you can treat people like that? Do you think because you're a guy it's endearing? Do you think because you're a guy you can get away with it? What if I did it—then what? Would it be okay like it is for you? Or would I be a bitch?"

"You're *so* lucky you're a girl."

"No *you're* lucky I'm a girl—because girls think before they act. Right now I want to pull a Pang Quarrels and tear you limb from limb like the scum you are," she said shaking.

"Go ahead, knock yourself out."

"You will *not* take away our happiness and honor. Mik and I have been through a lot and have been alone in this world. I won't let anyone or anything hurt us anymore. I may not be able to stop you from destroying Jude's life, but I can stop you from destroying mine and my little brother's. For your information, Jude is a good person and has a kindness that is rare to find in a person. If you hurt him to the point of no return, mark my words, you will never forgive yourself. Now excuse me." With her departing words Sia spun on the balls of her feet and left.

The sound of feet trudging through water sounded from every angle, but all Eli could see was his feet sinking into the clay soil beneath him. Water droplets fell at his feet causing him to curse nature for adding rain to an already horrible night. Looking up, Eli came face-to-face with a clear and dry night sky.

His hand froze at his face and soon abandoned its intent to wipe away the tears that fell from his eyes.

RESTLESS

Eli found himself both groggy and anxious after a completely sleepless night. His dreams were haunted with the painful images of his father and mother, lost to him forever. The transitions between dreams were no better. They consisted of painful dreams of Sia crying. The closer he got to her, the harder she cried, until nothing was left but the beginning of another night terror of his lost parents.

Considering the fact that he had not had any sleep, Eli was the last to enter the main room of the cabin. Everyone, including the Occult Operatives, were packed and standing by ready to leave. Jude, Sia and Pang, all sat alongside Conall at the roundtable, having light conversation. Eli took one step towards them before coming to a halt. The sight seemed forbidden, as if his presence was not warranted. He dropped the bag that hung from his shoulder and rummaged through it. In his bag he found his family picture, clothes, family mementos and—his mother's journal.

How did this get in here? I left this at home.

Eli retrieved the journal and examined it. He opened the slate black journal and discovered his mother's poems and short stories that she had given to him. It was definitely the journal that he used to cling tight to during sleepless nights as a child. It was his most prized possession, and the last thing his mother had given him.

"Sorry to interrupt, but do you have a second—to talk?"

Eli looked up and found stern green eyes staring back. Jude was dressed in black combat pants and a black belted tunic similar to Eli's brown one.

"Sure," said Eli. He was still wrapping his head around how his mother's journal had made its way into his bag, but decided that this apology that Jude was about to give him, would be imperative to their friendship moving forward. Eli followed Jude out of the cabin and a few yards away, to a patch of land decorated with moist lush trees, brush and heavy fog. The morning birds chirped a less than joyful song than normal, causing Eli to wonder if they were losing their touch.

"So you wanted to talk?" asked Eli. He knew an apology was coming, but felt that it wouldn't be in good taste if he led on that he knew it was coming.

"Eli—you and I have been friends our entire lives," started Jude. His hand kept grabbing the back of his neck, and for the first time since he had known Jude, Eli thought that his friend looked unsure of himself.

"Yeah, we have."

"All of my life I have always looked at you as a second brother and a part of my family. However, recently I have noticed a change—in both of us."

"A change?" asked Eli wondering where the conversation was going.

"Yes—a change. I have always noticed little lies and odd behavior from you, but I always ignored it because you were my best friend. There have been many times where I have felt downright betrayed by you, but I convinced myself that I was the problem. I told myself that because I was holding on to an old memory of us as kids—of who you used to be. Then after the whole incident with the antiom and me hearing all of the different occasions that you have lied and deceived me—it did not sit right with me."

You've got to be kidding me.

Eli felt his rage awakening and his lips snarl. His darker side was laughing at what his brain was concocting to say. During all of this, Eli realized that his ears had been mute to whatever Jude's silent lips had been saying.

"I just wanted to come directly to you and let you know that your recent behavior, ever since you met Zane, has been toxic for me," said Jude.

"Toxic for you?"

"Yes I—," began Jude.

"Wait a minute," said Eli tossing a rock that he had been playing with since the conversation had started. "You hauled me out here in the middle of this disgusting smelling swamp to tell me that I have been a bad friend to you. Is that right?"

"No. I asked you out here just to tell you that I am tired of putting others before myself. I see that your recent random behavior is having a negative influence on me and who I am— and I refuse to allow it to affect me anymore."

"Ha! You sound so idiotic right now. I have been having a negative influence on you, causing you to what—get angry? Or is my negative influence making you cry to your abusive mother every night." As soon as the words left Eli's mouth, he felt his face go into shock. He didn't know where the words came from. They felt angry, hurtful—and right.

"I almost made an attempt on your life," said Jude.

Eli's stomach dispersed a tingling sensation that was too powerful to control. He erupted into laughter.

"You? The bashful, sensitive, overly-religious book addict are standing here telling me that my 'negative influence' on you, caused you to try and kill me. Is that right?"

"Yes. I do not know why the antiom did not force me to confess it. I thought about it all night and came up with nothing," said Jude.

"That's because it's a lie. Even if what you were saying is true, and I'm just playing make-believe, the antiom would have made you tell all of us." Eli stopped and looked at a tree that stood behind Jude. Its branches and leaves fell like vines resembling a curtain. "It gets funnier the more I think about it—you killing me. Ha!"

"It's true. The night after we were both discharged, before the battle with the Necrosis, I found you in a nearby cave sleeping. I had been having night terrors about all of your crap that has pissed me off over the years and I—I wanted retribution," said Jude.

"Okay okay, well then what stopped you big bad killer?"

Eli knew that he had Jude when he saw the blank expression on his face. The entire conversation was a joke, and Eli was happy that he finally caught Jude in the middle of his crazy lie.

"I don't know what stopped me. A voice told me to go through with it—to take your life. Something cleared my head, and I realized that taking your life was not who I was. I could never take someone else's life outside of an honorable battle and in cold blood."

"Of course not, because you're weak and helpless Jude Bray. I know that your brother is badass, but it looks like skills clearly don't run in your family," said Eli. Jude's eyes glared and he gritted his teeth. For some reason Eli found the sight comical, and had to fight to hold back his pending laughter.

"It's irrelevant if you believe me or not. I came to you, face-to-face, to tell you that I had horrible thoughts about taking your life. I know I was wrong and I apologize. I feel like we have grown into separate people and should go our separate ways. We are on the same squad, and I will have your back as much as any other comrade. We make an awesome team. I noticed this during the Necrosis mission—we are just deadly together. I just hope that after time, when we both mature, that we can be friends again. I just wanted to tell you to your face so—."

"Man shut up! Go to hell Jude! You're a joke! Do you know that? Why do you think that Zane thought you were such a freak? You spend countless hours in a freaking library talking to your lifeless books, and you spend every hour praying to some invisible gods that never respond to you. I always thought that it was crazy that you bought into the same crap about the gods and heavens and all that trash like the rest of Kismet, but I kept quiet because you were my friend. If you're saying you don't want to be my friend then go ahead—get out of here. You sit there on your high podium as if I need you—as if I need your friendship. It's quite funny if you ask me. You know what—it's fine. We are good and you don't owe me any apology," said Eli.

"You don't have to understand why I believe in the three brothers, why I pray to them or why everyday I hope that heaven is where I will spend all of eternity. I could tell you about the numerous occasions I have seen angels with my own eyes. I could tell you about how when my mother came down with the disease that took away her bloodline abilities, the healers said her death was absolute; but after months of prayer she was cured without the aid of anyone. I could tell you how when I am lost and need guidance, and I ask Pith for help, he always finds a way to aid me in this journey we call life," said Jude wiping his eyes. "You can ignore all of that though. So what, you don't believe in the three brothers, Anim or heaven—that's fine. But I do. What is wrong with that? What is wrong with the fact that I believe in something that has proven its existence to me? What is wrong with hanging on to something that helps me to cope with the fact that my one and only dad, who I loved very much, is dead? What is wrong with me believing in something that brings me *real* happiness when the people of this world are constantly lying, manipulating and killing each other and hurting others because they're hurting? I believe in the three brothers because I choose to. What I believe in does not affect you at all. It doesn't have even the slightest influence over your life. So why do you choose to insult and ridicule me over it? Why do you choose to attack me for believing in something that makes me happy and helps me get through this never-ending mission we call life? Why take that away from me?"

"You only believe in your imaginary gods because you're weak, and the weak need to know that there is someone stronger to watch over them. It brings you comfort in knowing that as long as you gravel at the feet of the strong, you will be rewarded in your made-up 'afterlife'—it's sad."

Eli expected some witty and pompous comeback from Jude, but all he saw was shimmering eyes and a clenched jaw. His comrade's nostrils appeared larger and his lips appeared to tighten. He waited for the insult that he knew was coming, and began to create a list of better ones to respond with. Jude's lips parted, and Eli braced himself.

"You know after all this time, after all of the anger and arguments with my mom, I think I finally get it. Sometimes people forget that there is more than one way to show someone how much you care," said Jude.

"Trust me, I don't care."

OUT OF TIME

The fear after being shaken from his sleep was enough to make Eli vomit from the anxiety. The cold sweat that caked his brow and the dryness that cracked his throat were quickly ignored, when his eyes set on the culprit that shook him from his slumber.

"There's been a change of plans," said Conall over the loud chirp of the neighboring crickets. His signature silver mail armor and bright-red long-sleeve tunic shined with an impeccable sheen and clarity.

"Wha—What's going on? Why are you in my room?" Eli locked eyes with Conall and knew instantly that something was wrong.

Conall's cold stern gaze enveloped him with worry and despair. The Lieutenant's tongue remained still, refusing to shed light on the meaning of his words. Rising from the one knee he knelt on, Conall slowly turned around and headed for Eli's bedroom door. "Clothe yourself and be downstairs immediately," said the Lieutenant before exiting.

Upon entering the living room of the cabin, tired eyes and shadowed faces quickly found him. Jude, Sia and Pang sat facing the Occult Operatives on the familiar roundtable. Everyone appeared to be just as tired as Eli was, except for Kai, who sat reading passionately to Agent Slate. Word had it that Kai had the tendency to rename Agent Slate whenever the centipede celebrated his day of birth. The large black insect stood tall on its belly and remained still on the roundtable's dark surface.

"Please take a seat Agent Brassie," said Conall. The Lieutenant stood mere inches from Eli, catching him by surprise.

Eli reluctantly took a seat next to Pang and made every effort to not even think about sneaking a glance at his comrades.

"There has been a change of plans," said Conall. He took a seat between Priya and the empty seat that separated him from Eli. After taking a deep breath and clasping his hands, Conall turned his attention towards Eli and his comrades. "I know you four were supposed to be departing for training tomorrow, but that will no longer be the plan."

"Lieutenant if I may ask, where is Professor Vance?" asked Jude.

The four Occult Operatives seemed to shutter collaboratively. Eli quickly turned his gaze their direction only to find blank expressions returning his gaze.

Oh yeah where is the Professor. He was here before I went to bed...

"Professor Vance is..." started Conall before looking off into the distance.

"They ingested the antiom, and as far as we know, are not Rogues. No more secrets. If we are to train them, go into combat with them and rely on them, we need to trust them," said Priya. Her soft face but hard eyes looked conflicting.

Conall's gaze locked with Priya's before returning to Eli and his comrades. "Vance has been targeted for elimination."

A mixture of a cry and gasp escaped from Sia's seat. Her fingers clasped her forehead and her eyes appeared to shimmer in the low light that swung across the cabin. Her shoulders sat hunched over for the first time since Eli had known her.

"Get it together Agent Wyatt!" snapped Priya.

Eli quickly turned to the Commander and saw hostility and disgust on her face. It was the first time Priya relinquished her calm and beautiful demeanor. She looked vengeful and unstable.

"There's no place for prissy whining princesses at this table," continued Priya.

Sia quickly wiped her eyes and returned her posture to the perfection that Eli had come to associate with his comrade. "Yes Commander. Excuse my interruption."

"I will do nothing of the sort. Now pay attention!" said Priya. "Is there a problem Agent Brassie?"

Eli realized he had been staring at the Commander. For how long he could not be sure. His leg was also shaking up and down under the table while his fingertips turned from pink to red in response to the grip on one of his knees. The table shook after something heavy smashed into it.

"I *said* do we have a problem Agent Brassie!" said Priya raising her voice.

"No Commander."

After what seemed like minutes, Priya returned her gaze to Lieutenant Conall—relinquishing the threat that once came from her glare.

"We believe that Lord Egon has somehow discovered the connection between Bishop and Vance," said Conall.

"How?" asked Sia.

"We don't know," said Conall locking eyes with Priya. "What we do know is that a briefing was held a few hours ago by Lord Egon. Professor Vance and two others were targeted for elimination—effective immediately."

"Well who are the others?" asked Eli growing impatient with Conall's vague responses.

"Agent Jed Bray and Ex-Occult Operative Marius Brassie," said Conall. For the first time since their meeting had started, Conall kept his gaze directly on Eli.

"Jude...your brother," said Sia in an apologetic tone.

"Who cares about his brother, he's already dead! My dad is in danger!" Eli's chest began to hurt from the erratic beating of his heart.

"Whether you like it or not Agent Brassie, your dad and Agent Bray's brother are not important right now. Professor Vance is. He is the only one that has a connection to the Guardians. He is the only one that can help us eliminate Lord Egon, Fox, and the Necroborns that we now know have claimed the Land of Kismet," said Conall.

"Necroborns have claimed *our* home—a home that is not theirs," said Jude. His voice was barely louder than a whisper.

"Vance has gone into hiding," interrupted Priya. "He is far too valuable to be out in the open. We believe Operative Brassie has also gone into hiding. Things in Kismet have become far worse. Kai has more detailed information. Kai—."

All of the attention in the room turned to Kai who was still reading to Agent Slate. The Operative would have probably continued to go on oblivious to the attention around him, if it wasn't for Slate's hiss once it sensed the gazes around him.

He doesn't even know what we're talking about and he is supposed to be some great Operative.

"Kismet has fallen under the tyranny of a cold roach," started Kai. Agent Slate slithered into the opening of Kai's armor until he was absent from view. "Professor Ivor has been crowned King of Kismet."

"King? Kismet doesn't have kings!" said Eli.

Kai's cold glare shot towards Eli. A loud hissing enveloped the room and soon a large black object slithered out from Kai's armor and sprang across the table. Instantly Slate was rearing up in front of Eli. The insect appeared ready to strike like the deadliest of snakes. The creature was terrifying. Images of Eli's first encounter with Agent Slate swam through his mind until he found himself scrubbing the feeling of Slate's many legs from his arms and neck.

"Brassie!"

Eli's eyes opened to Conall's voice and realized all eyes were on him. Eli looked down in front of him and noticed Agent Slate was gone. He looked towards Kai and caught a glimpse of a long black object disappearing behind the safety of the Operative's black armor.

"Don't interrupt Kai again," said Kai. "Professor Ivor has been crowned King. This extinguishes the concept of a 'Council' or anything of the sort. His word is law. With this power he has confiscated all food, armor, weapons and water sources from the Kismet people. He is using these necessities to break them. Battles are being held daily. Citizens are being forced to engage in death matches where only the victor is awarded a miniscule portion of food and water. He is calling it 'The Trials of Hunger, Thirst and Deprivation—a clear mockery of our people's trials. Crime in the streets has increased drastically. The Kismet people have turned on one another in order to survive. The lifeless bodies of men, woman and children lay scatted on nearly every other street. At this rate, Kismet will exclusively be home to Necroborns in a matter of weeks."

"This is why we must act now," interrupted Conall. "I have been in contact with General Briars and we have decided that the evacuation of as many of our people as possible is a must."

"But where will they go Lieutenant?" asked Sia. The worry heavy in her voice. "Kismet is our home."

"The original plan was for our people to take refuge amongst the Geminates. Word was to be sent ahead of time to the Priestess to see if she would aid us, but time isn't on our side. Our only hope is to evacuate as many of our people to Geminate as soon as possible and hope the Geminates will have us," said Conall.

So basically just uproot our entire race of people and hope that some strangers will let us eat up their food, drink up their water and steal all of their warmth. Great plan Lieutenant.

"Sunrise is in two hours," said Priya pushing a strand of hair out of her face with the curl of a finger. "Be ready to leave in a half an hour."

The group sat estranged around the campfire beneath the full moon that shined with a silver brilliance. The fire's flames continued to crackle in an infinite cycle amidst the silence that cloaked the night.

The journey back to Kismet's borders did not go as expected. There were no enemies, no resistance—just nothing. The sight was comforting to Jude and his comrades, however to Lieutenant Titus and the Occult Ops, it was a sign that something sinister was in the works. The group crossed the river and arrived in the plains at the border of Kismet in a little over two hours. Tristan instantly divvyed up duties to Jude and his comrades. Jude was in charge of building a small but covert perimeter while Eli was in charge of gathering firewood. Under Lieutenant Titus' command, no one was permitted to use their abilities for their duties. Conall believed that every drop of blood energy needed to be reserved for the infiltration into the city's gates. After the border was complete, a fire was lit and makeshift beds were made. Everyone sat around the campfire waiting for the one that would lead them into the malevolent hazard they all once called home. The silence was brutal.

"So Agent Slate told Kai this hilarious joke today," said Kai breaking the silence. His bravery was rewarded with annoyed glances and tired eyes. "Just trying to brighten the mood around here. You all look deader than a Necrosis. Boom!" Kai laughed loudly to himself while the others seemed to ignore his antics. Agent Slate slithered out from underneath Kai's armor and took a position atop one of Kai's folded legs. "Did you hear that Slate? Kai told them they look deader than a Necrosis. Can Kai get a boom buddy?" Agent Slate hissed immediately, as if in response to his owner. Jude appreciated Kai's effort to raise everyone's spirits in such a dark time. While he understood everyone's wish to be left to their thoughts, he believed it took more courage for Kai to hang himself out there for the ridicule that Jude was sure was coming.

"So what is this joke you speak of?" asked Jude.

Everyone, including Kai, jerked their heads up at the question.

"Oh you're gonna die when you hear this one!" said Kai rubbing his hands together. Agent Slate raised its antenna high in the air, releasing a series of hisses for a few seconds before silence returned. Kai erupted into laughter.

Jude looked around at the others, who seemed to be ignoring Kai's antics—except for Eli, who appeared just as confused as Jude.

"Someone is here," said Priya. Here eyes were closed and her voice was slow.

"What are your orders?" asked Jarkko. His Magi glare instantly activated while miniscule grains of rock lightly levitated from the ground around him.

"Jarkko—defense. Tristan and Kai—frontline assault," said Priya.

◆ ◆ ◆

Eli watched frantically as the Occult Operatives appeared to go into formation without moving a muscle. A branch snapped close-by.

"Agent Slate shall feast on your flesh!" bellowed Kai running in the direction of the noise with two newly-summoned swords in his hands.

"Cease and desist!" yelled Priya.

Kai's lunge came to an immediate halt. The swords stayed summoned but his movement was eerily still.

"It's her," continued Priya.

From the shadows crept a stranger with light armor draping across its frail body. No weapons were visible and the night's shadows continued to mask the stranger's identity.

"Commander you have to give me some credit. Even I know it is impossible to sneak up on an Occult Operative, let alone four of them," said the stranger. Stepping out of the shadows, Eli felt an unexplained relief.

"General, it warms my heart to see your face," said Jarkko with a wink.

"It warms your heart to see any woman's face," said Anya taking a seat in between Conall and Priya.

"You know me so well but still refuse to give me your hand in marriage. You're cruel, merciless and cunning. I love it!" said Jarkko.

"Enough Jarkko!" said Priya.

Eli could tell that any form of comical or entertaining behavior would be forbidden this night. They were here devising a plan that would aid them in infiltrating the city and rescuing their people. Nothing about the danger they would soon face was funny. His dad was in there after all.

Anya looked significantly different than the last time Eli had laid eyes upon the General. Her body was thinner causing her armor to sag slightly along her neck and shoulders. Her posture was somewhat haggard while dark circles controlled her eyes. Her gaze swept across Eli, Sia, Pang and then landed on Jude. "I knew I was right about you four. The next time I see Ivor, I will remember to rub it in his face before taking his head."

"General! The four of them have been administered the antiom and have been fully briefed on everything we discussed at our last rendezvous," said Conall.

"Well done Lieutenant," said Anya smiling at the young Lieutenant. It was the first time Eli had ever seen her smile. She reestablished her sight on the group collectively, raised her chin high in the air and squinted her eyes. "I have been informed that all of you have been fully briefed on Kismet's current predicament. Since we have been desperately gathering pieces of intel, I believe it is up to me to issue you a full report with nothing but all of the factual information. During the Necrosis mission, Lord Egon and a covert squad infiltrated our city's gates. The person who aided him in his mission was none other than our Tactical Emissary—Special Operative Fox. With Fox, Lord Egon succeeded in eliminating..." Anya stopped. Her gaze fell to the floor and Eli thought he saw a shimmer in her eyes come and go. "Lord Bishop was eliminated. With our Lord eliminated, a wave of Necroborns swept through the city imprisoning those that surrendered, and neutralizing those who resisted." Anya nodded her head towards Priya.

"General! The last report I received from Kai, said that the Legacy of the Kings has been reinstated and Ivor has ascended to the throne. Is this correct, and if so, how?" asked Priya.

"Commander, I am afraid that is correct. Lord Egon has reinstated the Legacy of the Kings. He has put Ivor on the throne, to keep his power over Kismet in his absence. I realize now that Lord Egon has no plans of remaining in Kismet. As soon as Ivor ascended to the throne, Lord Egon took a small squad of Necroborns with him back to The Immortal Lands," said Anya. She nodded to Conall.

"General! How many Necroborns inhabit our city?"

The campfire crackled, resisting the silence that came with Anya's frozen gaze. Eli looked at everyone's face, and knew the same anxiety that he was enduring must have its grasp on the rest of the group as well.

"An estimated count of eight hundred."

Eli felt the venison, which he had eaten prior to their journey, threaten to make an appearance. He grabbed his stomach.

"So eliminating all of them is impossible. Your idea is for a stealth mission," said Jude. It was the first thing he had said since Anya had joined them.

"That is correct Agent Bray," said Anya with a smirk. She gave a quick nod to Lieutenant Titus, and soon white folders found their way into everyone's hands.

Eli didn't even attempt to glance down at the folder in his hand. He knew what they contained, and more importantly, knew the proper protocol when it came to briefings.

Once all the folders had been passed out, the General continued. "The Necroborns have laid claim to all of our homes. Our people have been either cast out on the streets, or have been chained and made pets to the Necroborns."

"I'm sorry General, pets?" asked Eli.

"Yes. Yes I am afraid so," she replied.

"General what about the children?" asked Sia. The worry was prevalent on her face as well as her eyes. Eli knew without a doubt that Mik was heavy on her mind.

"They receive no special treatment. They are thrown out on the streets, or made slaves as well," said Anya.

Eli could tell by the anger and pain on Sia's face, that words were pending at the gate. Closing her eyes and extinguishing her Magi Glare, Sia collected herself.

"Listen closely. Our time is up. We must act now. The Trials of hunger, Thirst and Deprivation will be held once again tomorrow. More of our people will be either slaughtered or starve. In a situation such as this, infiltration by night is usually a given. However, The Trials of Hunger, Thirst and Deprivation are only held when the sun is at its highest—and I don't think that's by coincidence." She nodded at Tristan.

"General Briars, why is attacking during The Trials a necessity? Why not just stick to the shadows and use the element of surprise to our advantage?" asked Tristan. His large, perfect bright-white teeth cast a reflection of the campfire's erratic flames.

"Because non-Necroborns are not permitted out on the streets without their 'masters.' The ones, who have not been made slaves, run with the shadows in hopes of not being captured. Their bravery is only rewarded with empty stomachs and cobblestone beds. If we are to rescue as many of our people as possible, it must be during The Trials. Everyone is ordered to be there by Necroborn law," said Anya.

"General if I may," started Priya, and waited for permission from Anya before continuing. "It may seem like The Trials is an advantage because it puts all of our people in one spot. However, we must remember that the place will be crawling with Necroborns, not to mention any other foul beasts that have sworn their allegiance to Lord Egon and Ivor."

"Commander, we cannot forget about Fox either," said Sia in a low voice.

Priya glared at Sia. "I haven't."

"Fox will be tough to take down. He's too fast," said Eli.

"You mean the scrawny, narcissistic refugee with the daddy issues?" said Kai with a raised eyebrow.

Eli laughed.

I hate you a little less after that comment.

"General! Commander! If I may..." started Tristan. After receiving nods from both Anya and Priya, he continued. "Special Operative Fox is a CQC otherwise known as 'close combat heir.' This means that his ability is only effective in close proximity to his enemy. Every living thing has three weak points on their body. One causes paralysis, one causes a blockage of blood energy, and one causes the heart to rupture resulting in immediate death. Fox's bloodline ability allows for his brain to pinpoint those three spots. From there, Fox can pick and choose which to attack."

Death?

Eli thought back to his encounter with Fox. The danger he was in caused nausea to sweep over him. Fox clearly had the advantage. He could have killed Eli with ease, after Eli fell under the paralysis of Fox's attack.

"Because he is a close combat Operative, he is vulnerable at long range," continued Tristan. "He makes up for this with his increased speed, acrobatics and precision. All three of these skills get him close enough to his enemy for his ability to give him the advantage—usually all before the enemy can counter-attack in time."

"You and Jarkko can eliminate him with ease if necessary," said Priya.

Jarkko sighed. "Surrounded by sweaty guys once again. Great."

"Sweating is a sign of hard work. Thank you," replied Tristan.

"Power pieces don't attack until their pawns have. It's the perfect ambush," said Jude looking off into the distance. "If the stealth strategy fails, and we engage the Necroborns in direct combat, we have to expect Fox to attack during the commotion."

"Failing is not an option Agent Bray," snapped Anya.

"Apologies General. Before engaging an enemy, I like to strategize for *every* possibility."

Priya and Anya locked eyes before breaking their bond.

"There will only be one back-up plan; and only *I* will be the one to decide when it goes into effect," said Anya. When the silence returned, a confidence came across the General's face. "Now lets get started with the briefing."

The air filled with the sound of parchment, as everyone opened their briefing folders collaboratively. Eli's eyes laid upon the familiar barbaric enemy he remembered engaging at the Kismet border.

"Enemy number one is the over-powering brutes known as Necroborns," said the Commander skipping their page. "I am sure everyone here can write a book on the Necroborns at this point so moving on."

"Yes—finally! I'm coming for you Necroborns, and this time, I'm bringing retribution with me," said Pang. The red-orange in his eyes diffused and circled each other in an infinite cycle.

Anya cleared her throat; and when all eyes fell to her, began. "Enemy number two, Ivorius Kristoph, is The Council's ex-Foreign Communications Advisor and Kismet's new king. His bloodline is—Weapons Master. Age—fifty-seven. His affiliates include Lord Egon of The Immortal Lands, the Amorphous and most recently, Special Operative Fox. Ivorius Kristoph is a Kismet native. At the age of eighteen he was deemed a master of projectile assault. By the age of twenty-five he orchestrated the creation of the Supremacy ability; and to this day is the only living person capable of using it." The skin was smoother and the face was slightly different, but Eli instantly recognized the chaos behind his mentor's eyes. There was an air to him, and his infamous perfect posture was ever present.

"General, what is the Supremacy ability?" asked Sia. Her heavy eyes and silent yawns signaled her losing battle to stay awake.

"The Supremacy ability is a legendary Weapons Master skill created to bring down other Weapons Masters quickly and effectively. It allows the user to take complete control of any weapon in the area and utilize it, even their enemies. With this ability he was able to initiate the complete suicide of an entire army single-handedly."

"General, how can we win against something like that?" asked Eli after finding his voice. Supremacy seemed like an unstoppable ability that was useless to fight against.

"*You* can't," interrupted Priya. Her folded arms told Eli she was taking a firm stance on the issue. "Our mission is the complete rescue of as many of the Kismet people as possible. We are not here for a battle. If the new king chooses to make an appearance, you can leave him to Jarkko and I." The

Commander eyed the Magi with a precision that made Ivor's death seem absolute.

So a reunion with my ol' psychotic mentor. Looks like it's time for me to show you exactly what I can do.

"Enemy number three is the close combat Special Operative known as Fox. His bloodline is—CQCH. Age—twenty-six. His place of origin is debatable. Fox is a refugee who relocated to the land of Kismet supposedly after his village was annihilated at the hands of Lord Egon—or so he says. With the blessing of Lord Bishop, Fox became both a member of The Council and our land's Tactical Emissary. His strengths are speed, agility and hand-to-hand combat, not to mention his inherited bloodline ability. While his inherited ability is only effective at close-range, it can render an Agent paralyzed, incapable of using blood energy to fuel abilities, and even instant death. Fox's weakness is without a doubt his over-confidence," said Tristan with a quick shake of his head. "He wears absolutely no armor or magical protection. This leaves him completely vulnerable to magic and brute force. Due to his bloodline ability, Fox is known for the silent kill so express caution when engaging this Operative." Fox's plain black shirt and black combat pants made him look defenseless in his briefing photo, however his eyes and hint of a smile screamed danger.

"Here," said Conall handing a concealed item to Jude, Pang, Sia and then Eli.

Eli looked down to find a small diamond-shaped object in his hand. The diamond had an obsidian texture as well as color. The metallic silver, which outlined its edges, added to the appearance of its sharpness. It dangled freely in Eli's hand from the thin rough chain from which it hung from.

"What is this?" asked Eli.

"An S-3," said Jude quickly.

Eli's eyes stole a glance in the green-eyed boy's direction to catch him staring sternly back at him. "I've never heard of it."

Snickering dispersed among the Occult Operatives, as their failed attempts to silence their amusement caught Eli's attention. Sia appeared annoyed while words seem to beg to leave her lips but remained still.

"S-3 stands for *squad surveillance system* Agent Brassie," said Conall. His tone was neutral, cold and unyielding.

"So... what does an S-E do?"

"S-3—and it is a communication device that allows comrades of the same squad to communicate over great distances," said Jude crossing his arms. "Each set of S-3 devices are enchanted to only work with devices they are programmed with. The S-3 is an invaluable tool."

Eli felt himself rolling his eyes. Jude was such a show-off and it was beginning to get on Eli's nerves. Eli placed the chain around his neck and tucked the S-3 inside his combat tunic. The contrast of the cold device against his warm skin made him jump. Looking around he noticed everyone else adorning their chains as well.

Right as Sia's silent lips began to move he heard it. *"Can you hear me?"* Sia's voice sounded clearly in his head with a clarity and volume that felt like she was right next to him. *"The S-3 will only transmit what you want to be transmitted and only to who you want to hear it. Just think of who you are talking to and speak regularly. Even with a whisper, if you're transmitting to them, they will hear you."*

He sat frozen in a trance while his eyes bore into her. She was helping him, why he could not be sure. *"Thank you,"* he whispered while thinking of her, and only her.

Nodding her head once gave the confirmation that she heard him. The S-3 seemed like a gift. It was a door to talk to her even when they weren't on speaking terms. It was a second option when his first option failed miserably.

Anya rose to her feet, which caused Priya and the rest of the Occult Operatives to join her. Eli soon joined, after Jude and Sia leaped to their feet.

The General eyed everyone individually before resting her eyes on Conall. Eli could not help but notice that the General's eyes froze on the Lieutenant for a noticeably longer time than the others. "This is a rescue mission. Our element is stealth. Your mission is the complete evacuation of all civilians. The use of lethal force *is* authorized."

Lethal force huh? I like the sound of that.

Everyone in the large squad eyed one another with a determination that showed that every last one of them would do anything to reclaim Kismet and protect its people.

"Mission accepted," replied Priya. Her long brunette hair concealed the presence of one of her eyes.

"Mission accepted," replied Conall. His notoriously, perfectly groomed hair sat frozen atop his stern gaze.

Don't worry dad I'm coming...and you too Fox

THE GEMS OF
KISMET

"We're in," said Priya. The S-3 transmitted her voice clearly even though she was nowhere to be seen. Hearing the Commander's voice in his head gave Eli the chills and moist palms. "Wait for Lieutenant Titus to give the signal."

The return to Kismet and back to the city, which Eli once called home, was a nightmare to say the least. The white-stone walls were replaced entirely with cold, black sheet metal. The lush green trees were now reduced to a burnt and brittle state, while the once tall green grass that surrounded the city was burned beyond recognition. Only the blackened trees and bare soil occupied the space around the once comforting home.

The Commander and Jude had slipped in through the Eastern Hold's main gates, after assuming their smallest of forms. On this mission they both would be the Recon. Their job was to infiltrate the city's walls and blend in with the crowd; and to only attack if the enemy was alerted of the presence of any other squad members. If this happened, the Commander and Jude were to covertly neutralize the alerted forces before they had enough time to call for reinforcements, or close-in on the detected comrade's location. Jarkko and Sia remained hidden outside of the Eastern Hold's gates. According to the General, a large number of Necroborns inhabited the Eastern Hold. Since the Necroborns were incapable of using magic, it would be difficult for them to resist the combined magical assault of the two Magi. Since Jarkko and Sia grew up in the Eastern Hold, their position also gave them the advantage since they were familiar with the layout. Tristan and Pang remained stationed outside of the main gates. Their objective was to intercept any reinforcements or stragglers that may arise during the mission. Also, they would serve as the squad's defense while the civilians evacuated. Under the General's orders, they were to not enter the city under any circumstances. Pang made a few comments of dissatisfaction, but obeyed orders in the end. The General and the Lieutenant alerted the squad that the duo had an additional mission, and would reconvene with the rest of the squad once their side mission was complete. This left Kai and Eli stationed outside of the Western Hold. Eli's legs began to hurt from squatting behind a large boulder. He wished he had beat Kai to their post so he could have nabbed the large blackened tree that Kai was using for cover.

"Kai counts six Necroborns at the gate," whispered Kai. A bulge slithered around the chest area of Kai's armor, alerting Eli to Agent Slate's restlessness.

"Why do you always refer to yourself in the third person?"

"No other enemy targets detected," said Kai.

Eli took a look around at their surroundings. With the aid of the cloudbank on the western side, it seemed possible to quickly close in on the six Necroborns and eliminate them before they had a chance to attack. "I'm skilled with a bow. You take the three on the right and I'll take the three on the left. Sound good?"

Kai's head turned around slowly with the look of disbelief plastered across his face. "You *do* know what the word 'stealth' means don't you?"

"Yes! It means doing something without being detected!"

"Shh! And you're doing a bang up job right now aren't you genius." Kai closed his eyes slowly and shook his head. "Why do I always get stuck with the imbeciles..."

"Imbecile?" said Eli rising to his feet. "Who do you think you—."

"Silence!" snapped Kai. "If you want to whine and complain about me insulting you, at least use the S-3 so we don't hand this mission over to our enemies."

"Jarkko! Wyatt! Do you think you can put the enemies at the western gates to sleep from your current location if we needed," said Kai's voice over the S-3. Eli guessed that Kai intended everyone to hear the conversation since he was able to hear Kai's voice even though his silent lips showed no words.

"Kai," started Jarkko's voice. *"Your plan is possible, however it would cost a great deal of blood energy due to the distance. We could—."*

"Request denied," interrupted Priya amidst the conversation. *"Jarkko and Wyatt may have to camouflage civilians later on in the mission if things turn ugly. Wasting blood energy to make your job easier is counter-productive to the mission's objective Kai. You know better..."*

The silence over the S-3 was not only awkward but also haunting. Everyone appeared afraid to respond to the Commander's denial of Kai's request.

"Copy that," said Kai.

"Yeah Kai! Stop being lazy," said Eli exclusively to Kai.

No response or movement came from Kai, and just when Eli was beginning to think he was using his device incorrectly, Kai turned around with a blank stare. "Sorry did you say something?"

Just when Eli's lips parted, Agent Slate slithered around from underneath Kai's armor poised for an attack. Eli's eyes tilted up to Kai's and then returned to Agent Slate. Only when the black centipede returned to the confines beneath Kai's armor, did Eli return his gaze to Kai.

"Kai didn't think so," said Kai with a smirk.

The two of them abandoned their squabble and returned to surveying the area. Three of the Necroborns stood as still as stone at the gates while the other three walked in a connected pattern surveying the area. The six of them were fully clothed in the heaviest armor Eli had ever seen. Dark green gauntlets, war boots, cuirass and helmets over-protected every inch of their bodies. Three carried mighty war axes while the other three carried war blades the size of an average man. Their grunts released visible breath amongst the air in front of them as they circled.

Marius and Eli talking in their kitchen flashed across his eyes.

The low light cast shadows across Marius' face, but Eli could see the pain in his eyes. The pain was always there— every second, of every minute, of every hour of every day. It was a pain that Eli refused to acknowledge in his father; why, he could not be sure.

"Then who is going to watch the Western Gates?"

"Who cares? They can watch themselves as far as I'm concerned," said Eli.

"Son you can't just disobey orders it's dishonorable."

The enemy stopped its march, silencing the vibrations around them.

"It's funny," started Eli, breaking free from his thoughts. "Now that I'm the intruder, guarding the western gates doesn't seem as worthless as I originally thought."

Kai slowly turned his head and paused.

"When the Necrosis threat was in full effect, I was originally supposed to be among the offense that would defend our land. The Council discharged me and assigned me to defending the western gates."

"You were spotted numerous times at the Kismet border. So this means," said Kai as his words came to an immediate halt. His eyes turned from confusion to rage, before returning to the neutral expression from which they came.

"I disobeyed orders and went on the mission anyways. I was young so..."

Seconds came and went like the wind, but Kai did not move—or even seem to breathe from where Eli was standing.

"Why are you looking at me like that?"

Kai remained motionless. "You refused the unanimous ruling of The Council?"

"It's not as bad as it sounds."

Kai was upon Eli instantly. His harsh hazel eyes bearing down on him. "The enemy entered through the western gates when Lord Bishop was assassinated and the city was taken."

"I know. I guess I'm pretty lucky that I decided to ignore my discharge, or I probably wouldn't be standing here."

Kai was instantly back at the tree from which he was originally hiding behind. His lips were moving but Eli failed to hear anything. The Necroborns returned to their march around the outskirts of the western gates, causing Kai and Eli to go back into hiding.

"*That explains how the enemy entered the western gates so...*" said a voice over the S-3 before silencing itself. The voice sounded like Tristan's, and was edged with suspicion.

"How accurate are you with the arrow barrage ability?" asked Kai turning to Eli.

What's Tristan talking about?

"Hey! How accurate are you with the arrow barrage ability?" asked Kai again.

Eli thought back to the many times he had used the ability. He even remembered when Dominic Adams had done his Dagger Barrage ability and arrows manifested instead of daggers. It was a novice mistake that showed that many of the participants in the Trials were not experienced enough to utilize their abilities completely.

"I'm pretty good. I can hit people with it."

Kai stared. His unyielding gaze began to annoy Eli. "That means you're horrible," said Kai sighing. He rubbed his chin and shifted his eyes. "Do you know the Execution Style ability?"

"The what?"

Kai closed his eyes and shook his head. "This is ludicrous that they put someone as inexperienced as you on such a high-ranking mission with so many lives at stake."

Eli felt the rage building up inside of him. It was the same rage he felt during his sparring match with Will Keating in Professor Ivor's lecture at the Academy. Kai was flaunting his superiority and experience over Eli. It was both daunting and infuriating. "I'm deadly with a bow—both a regular bow and a summoned one."

"Hmm we'll see," replied Kai.

Eli continued to stand watch behind his boulder while Kai remained covered behind his tree. The cloudbank began to dissipate as the sun reached its highest. Rays poured down from the blue blanket that enveloped them. The air smelled of burning metal while the sound of shaking steel filled the air with each step the Necroborns took. A distant crowd cheering sounded from far away. Marius was in the steel prison ahead of him. Where in the city Eli could not be sure. His only hope was his dad was safe, and Eli would be able to hug him tight and tell him that he loved him. Every possible thing that could go wrong began to cycle through Eli's mind. The more he shook off the unsettling images, the more aggressive they got. The wind blew violently by, sweeping away the silence in its wake. As Eli took a deep breath in an attempt to calm his nerves, he heard it.

"All Agents go..."

TREASON

The light sound of a projectile, followed by a soft crash, immediately caught their attention. If it wasn't for the enhanced hearing of Jude's raven form, he might not have heard it. Two Necroborns stood frozen atop a crumbled street intersecting two rows of homes. One brought its axe above his head while the other readied its dual blades.

"Did you hear that?" snarled one of the Necroborns patrolling the block.

Jude changed back and leaped down, landing atop the closest Necroborn's shoulders, and breaking his neck with a quick jerk of his legs.

"Come on! Could be trouble," growled the other Necroborn. After a few steps he slowly turned around and locked eyes with Jude. His eyes rolled back in his head before his body hit the ground. A lone vial detached from the Necroborn's neck, rolling through the crimson puddle that surrounded it.

After filling up two vials with Necroborn blood, Jude covered himself in the Necroborn's armor and nearly toppled over. The armor was overwhelmingly heavy and smelled of dead bodies and sour garbage.

Now to hide the bodies...

"It came from over here!" said a distant voice. The sound of sprinting feet grew closer by the second.

Jude felt himself panic, as he began to toggle between hiding the bodies and risk being discovered, or fleeing and risking the exposure of the mission.

Dozens of Necroborns filled the street, circling the two lifeless bodies. Each soldier adorned in heavy dark chainmail armor. Jude took slow powerful steps towards the circle, studying more of the enemy's mannerisms the closer he got.

A large soldier, taller than the others, parted the circle and approached Jude. "You! Mogre! Report!" he growled.

Jude hammered his fist over his chest and bowed his head. "Suzerain! Mogre Razul," growled Jude. His heartbeat raced underneath his Necroborn skin.

The Suzerain of the Necroborns peered back at Jude. "These mogres," said the Suzerain pointing to the lifeless bodies. "Who's responsible?"

Jude stared back, feeling uneasy in the body of a Necroborn. His arms, legs and head felt too heavy for his body. His clenched jaw felt uncomfortable.

"Mogre Razul!" yelled the Suzerain.

"Suzerain! A group of five Praxians killed these men and then ran for the main gates. We can still catch them if we act now!"

"You heard him! To the main gates!" The group of Necroborns assembled behind the Suzerain before coming to a halt. "You! Mogre Razul! You will be coming with us to identify the enemy. Fall in line!"

Jude felt the threat of a pending heart attack. Four of the Necroborns circled him and ushered him in line. He was surrounded by the enemy, and as far as he knew, jeopardized the mission.

The Suzerain turned his icy glare slowly until it set on Jude. "Bind his hands!"

♦ ♦ ♦

Eli kept his breathing low, his dagger ready and his mind prepared for the kill.

"*Are you going to kill them or what?*" said Kai through the S-3. Eli almost fell into the trap of responding, but closed his lips quickly. "*Unless you have two extra arms in there, Kai suggests you choose a better weapon.*"

If I'm doing it so wrong, why don't you do it!

The two Necroborns stood motionless in the alley separating two homes. Their backs were turned while their weapons were ready.

Eli summoned a second dagger and brought both up. He sliced the first soldier's neck and then turned for the other. He struggled against the Necroborn's overwhelming strength as the soldier grabbed both of Eli's wrists, holding off his attack.

"You picked the wrong day to rebel slave!" growled the Necroborn through his grunts. He grabbed Eli by the neck with one quick gesture and held him off of his feet.

Eli grabbed the soldier's beastly hand in an attempt to stop his throat from being crushed.

"I need backup! There's a—," started the Necroborn before a large black object slithered quickly over the soldier's shoulder. Agent Slate dove headfirst into the Necroborn's flapping jaws, causing the Necrobrn to release his hold.

Eli coughed hysterically as a rush of cold air spilled down his throat. He looked up quickly, preparing to counter a pending attack.

The large black centipede emerged from the soldier's eye socket, causing the eye to bust, before destroying the other eye in the same manner, as it retreated back into the soldier's head. The Necroborn fell to his knees shaking until Agent Slate emerged from his mouth. The soldier's lifeless body fell to the floor. Blood fell rapidly from the empty eye sockets and mangled mouth. The insect slithered through the puddle of life from which it created. A lone boot stepped into Eli's view, before Slate slithered up its pant leg, disappearing from view.

"You do know that if it wasn't for Agent Slate, that Necroborn would have rang the alarm for backup and exposed our mission; all before killing you and putting your comrades in danger?"

Eli looked up into Kai's bright hazel eyes. They were both alluring and intimidating. "I didn't realize how strong and responsive they were. It's an easy mistake."

"Only the weak make excuses for their errors. A *real* Agent would have been able to takedown two unsuspecting enemies with ease. You even fought these creatures before, there's no excuse for your failure," said Kai glaring.

"Look I don't need you to—."

"Shut up," said Kai closing in slowly, giving Eli pause. "You have already showed Kai that you aren't experienced enough to be on this mission, or really any mission for the matter. The fact that Kai got paired with you is an insult. Our people are slaves. They are in danger. Your dad is in danger. Don't you get it? Kai feels sorry for your dad. His life is in the hands of such a weak and useless Agent. Either do us all a favor and leave now, or grow some balls and get it together. Kai is tired of your weakness."

Eli realized he had been standing there silent for a while now. Kai turned around quickly, propping himself up against an adjacent wall, before looking quickly around the corner and disappearing from sight. Images of Marius smiling flooded Eli's mind. Marius had always been there for him, never failing him in any way. Eli felt a tear fall down the side of his face.

You have always been there for me dad, even when I wasn't the most appreciative son. It's time for me to grow up and return the favor. I will find you. I will save you, and I will show you that I'm not useless. I'm not an unappreciative dishonorable son. I'm the son of ex-Occult Operative Marius Brassie, the number three-ranked Occult Operative in all of Kismet history. With mom gone, you're all I have left in this world. Losing you is not an option.

"Hey Agent useless," said Kai over the S-3. "*Did you run home crying or did you finally realize you're a man?*"

"*Agent Brassie to Kai,*" replied Eli.

"*Go for Kai.*"

"*Let's show them exactly what we can do.*"

"*If you ruin Kai's perfect record, Kai will feed you to Agent Slate for dinner.*" replied Kai.

◆◆◆

Eli scouted the area around him. The Western Hold was a ghost of the brilliance it once was. The large white-stone homes, which he had grown up with, were replaced with rows and rows of metal sheds. Cracked cobblestone streets, littered with garbage, divided the homes. The streets looked bare and cold. The Kismet statues that once basked in the sun-pierced cloudbank, now lay littered in a crumbled sorrow along the city's once thriving streets.

"Unsettling isn't it?" said Kai. He slowly joined Eli next to the once great Lin Kitz statue. "If this mission results in failure, this is all our people, city and legacy will be—a regretful melancholy memory."

"It'll never happen. The people have us."

"*Kai! Brassie! Movement in the Western Hold. Nine Necroborns and a civilian. What is your position,*" said Priya.

"North of Lin Kitz." Eli was shocked at how quick and precise he responded. There was something about communicating over the S-3 that made him feel more confident.

"The Trials are approaching. Eliminate the enemy forces and retrieve the civilian," said Priya. Her voice was firm and absolute. *"Quarrels! "*

"Commander!" Pang sounded as close to Eli as Kai was.

"Prepare a path for the evacuation!"

"On it!" replied Pang.

Eli followed behind Kai quickly through the sheds and haunting homes. The cold that surrounded them never lifted; no matter how many sheds they passed. The cold was ominous.

"Take out the front four as quickly as possible," said Kai. Eli looked over to respond and noticed Kai was gone. "Up here." Eli looked up to find Kai standing atop one of the high metal homes. His wrist flung back over his head, before a large object left its grasp, hurling down at the unsuspecting Necroborns.

A Necroborn hollered. "Get this low-life insect off of me!"

Eli attacked. His blade decapitated two enemies, before coming back for their hearts. The horde of Necroborns spun around collectively with their swords drawn.

"It's the enemy! He's here!" yelled a Necroborn.

Eli's hand flew up. "Arrow barrage!" All of the Necroborns rolled out of the way, except for two, who fell abruptly to Eli's attack.

"I'll call for backup," said one of the Necroborns in a slightly different tone than the others.

Eli blocked the first attack with both swords. Two Necroborns circled him and attacked from behind. His arrow barrage missed as they evaded quickly.

"Back up has arrived," said a voice close-by.

The Coliseum wasn't the Coliseum. The three statues of the three brothers were reduced to rubble, and their respective banners were now the result of a blazing end. Masses of Necroborns and civilians trudged up the Coliseum stairs in waves. Chains hung tight around the necks of every civilian, as their Masters tugged harshly at their bindings.

"Move it maggot!" yelled a Necroborn as he yanked the chain around the neck of a small child who cried hysterically. Her long blonde hair clung to her moist skin.

"Please—water!" cried the child. Her plea as heartbreaking as the chains that ensnared her.

The Necroborn chuckled before rearing his shoulders back and hawking a heavy helping of phlegm down at her. "Water will never touch your lips again maggot. Well unless your weak fragile carcass can win the games!" His bellowish laughter vibrated the shackles that ensnared her.

Jude fell in with the masses. His Necorborn form had faded after escaping his captives during an ambush by Kai's team. The lost time caused him to use the remainder of the Necroborn blood in his vial. He grabbed another vial from his utility belt and stared at it.

I wish there had been more time to extract more. Their strength and aggression would be a huge asset in the future.

Guards, twice the size of a normal Necroborn, stood guard at the Coliseum gates—their large war axes nearly towering over them. "Make sure to get a spot in the front row," snarled one of the guards as Jude walked passed. "There will be plenty of blood today."

"Delicious," said a Necroborn next to Jude sliding her tongue slowly over her wretched teeth.

Entering the Coliseum arch brought Jude directly onto the arena sands. All of the original Coliseum chambers and statues of Trials Champions were now a distant memory. The center of the arena sands was replaced with deep pits filled with vertical spikes that pierced the surface. Rotted flesh and stray bones lay scattered between the spikes. Steam rose vibrantly from a large acid pool in one of the corners of the arena.

Taking a step forward, something hard and cold collided with the side of Jude's face. He looked up to see rusty chains hanging down from the Coliseum ceiling atop the sands. A lone skeleton hanging from its neck by one of the chains, rocked slowly in response to the crowds that scurried around it.

"Agent Bray for Commander Priya!"

A few worrisome seconds passed before a voice responded. *"Go for the Commander."*

"Entering the Coliseum. The General was correct. Every Necroborn and civilian in the city are here. At least they appear to be; and to top it off, the Coliseum battle arena has been converted into a meadow of death traps."

"Copy that, sounds like fun. Can I get a twenty on everyone?" replied the Commander.

Silence trailed after Priya's words before the voices began.

"This is Jarkko. Agent Wyatt and I have just cleared out the Eastern Hold. Approaching Coliseum."

"Tristan reporting in. Agent Quarrels and myself are standing by at the main gates—awaiting civilian evac."

"Kai and Agent Slate here. Agent Brassie, Agent Slate and Kai have just liberated half of the civilians in the Western Hold. Their captives have been neutralized and disposed of. You can expect civilians coming your way in t-minus forty-five seconds Tristan. There's a looker in a potato sack with short hair. You can thank Kai later."

"Ohh is she a brunette?" asked Jarkko quickly.

"Her hair is as dark as the things Kai wanted to do to her," replied Kai.

"Enough!" yelled Priya. Her tone carried both finality and disgust. *"Tristan and Quarrels intercept those civilians and evacuate them to the rendezvous point. Hurry back. My plans are to evacuate at least half of the Coliseum civilians during the Trials, and the other half after."*

"Copy," said everyone in union.

Jude followed slowly behind the child as she ascended the old spectator seats behind her master. The Necroborn continued to pull violently at the chain around her neck, even when she was close on his heels. The sight was infuriating.

Dark cold metal now covered the spectator seats. The red cushions, pillows and banners were no more. Jude turned around and took a seat in the front row, closest to the stairs.

Tall steel gates now replaced the three wooden doors that once announced the contenders of each bloodline. The stragglers found their seats, and soon the commotion came to a halt. Jude's hand clawed at his knee. He began to grind his teeth and his hands couldn't stay dry no matter how many times he rubbed them across his armor. Then he saw him. The entitlement. The authority. The power. King Kristoph parted the sea of Necroborns and took a stance at the familiar balcony that over-looked the Coliseum's sands.

"Agent Bray to all." His lips quivered and his jaw chattered. *"King Ivorius Kristoph has been spotted in the Coliseum."*

THE TRIALS OF
HUNGER, THIRST &
DEPRIVATION

Jude's massive hands tensed at each clap he took. Taking a seat amongst the applauding Necroborns, worry began to creep in.

The vial is wearing off.

He retrieved a vial from his belt and studied the dismal amount of blood that rocked in the vial's chamber. It would only be enough for a half an hour—forty-five minutes if he was lucky. His eyes glanced around at the Necroborns that stood around him still clapping, and after making sure no one was watching, injected his calf with the remainder of the Necroborn blood.

"On your feet you lazy dog!" yelled a voice next to Jude.

Jude looked up to find what looked like a male Necroborn, glaring and growling down at him. His beast-like teeth failed in containing the saliva that fell from his mouth. His cover was blown. The Necroborn must have seen the vial.

Breaking his neck would probably be the quickest. There's no way to prevent others from noticing. Only one option left.

"The King is almost upon us. Show some respect," growled the Necroborn. He returned to his applause while Jude placed the vial, which he was secretly holding, back into his utility belt.

"*Bray! What's your twenty?*" asked Priya.

Scanning the faces of the Necroborns around him, Jude opened his thoughts. "*Coliseum north side—first row.*"

"I am looking at the north side and I see only Necroborns," said Jarkko.

Standing up, Jude clenched his deadly teeth, balled up his mighty fists and felt the savage power of the Necroborn swell up inside of him. He roared. The roar vibrated the ground and silenced the cheering and applause that once came from the crowd around him. Seconds felt like minutes while the quiet refused to budge. Roars soon followed from all around him as the Necroborns went into a cheering frenzy.

"Reckless Bray! But clever," said Priya over the S-3.

"Kai will never look at those innocent green eyes the same way ever again," said Kai softly. *"Can anyone else tell Kai how Bray is a Necroborn brute right now. Kai hasn't even seen you do that yet Priya."*

"Quiet! Keep your eyes open for the last enemy," spat Priya.

A significantly larger Necroborn assumed a position next to the King along the balcony. Confusion came and went from the King's face, as he appeared to be looking for somebody. His eyes soon fell to the bare side next to him, before returning to the Necroborn beside him. The King nodded. The Necroborn's hand darted up, silencing the applause around them.

Oh my Aegis. You're so sententious, that you cannot even silence your own crowd. Hilarious!

"My dearest friends," began the King with the most sinister of smiles. "Today marks the tenth Trials of Hunger, Thirst and Deprivation. Today is a continuation of our celebration of the liberation of this city, this land and the fall of our enemy."

The Coliseum shook with the applause, roars and agreement of the King's audience. Jude knew refusing to applaud would be foolhardy and do nothing short of singling him out amongst the crowd. He clapped. Each clap was heavy and painful. He had to fight with his brain against its apprehension. When the Necroborn next to the King silenced the crowd, Jude wanted to thank him.

"Bring forth the renegades!" announced the King with enhanced bass in his voice.

The sound of crying metal filled the air. The crowd's attention fell to the dark iron rod fence that began to rise. A dark shadow stood dead-center behind the fence's cold metal. A lone woman wobbled out from underneath its teeth. Her body appeared so frail, that the vegetable sack she wore, clung to her body with desperation. Her long frizzled white hair blew slightly across the wrinkles of her gaunt face. Her eyes appeared vacant while her feet seemed to move independently towards the center of the arena.

"*Wait I know her,*" started Eli. The flicker of surprise in his voice made Jude examine the woman in an attempt to identify her.

It can't be...

"*That's Fay—the healer!*" said Eli.

The crying metal returned, causing Jude to shift his attention to the opening door next to the first. Another dark shadow limped out from its depths, holding its side. The stranger's short crumpled black hair sat glued to the side of her face. Her face was smooth but her eyes were puffy. She wore a vegetable sack similar to that of Fay. Her feet stopped and her head tilted up, gazing up into Fay's eyes.

"Ladies and gentleborns! I give you your prey for our first battle!" announced Ivor. His grin shined as loud as the crowd around him.

Jude looked down at the two combatants. They were no Agents. They looked dirty, starved and vulnerable. The stench of death seemed to follow them while their spirits lay shattered in the sands around them. A Necroborn garbed in heavy metal armor strolled out onto the sands from the shadows of the Coliseum gate.

"What is your name maggot?" demanded the Necroborn as he yanked the brunette's head back with a fist full of her short black hair.

Tears and dry sobs seeped from her mouth. "Daliah. My name—my name is Daliah," said the older woman. The Necroborn released his hold, causing her to come crashing down on her hands and knees atop the harsh sands beneath her.

"Which is it do you feebly fight for maggot? Food? Water? Clothes? A bath!" said the Necroborn as he began to chuckle.

"Foo—Food. For my two kids. Please!" pleaded Daliah. Her eyes gazed up into her captive's cold eyes, while her hands remained interlaced begging. A large hand covered her face before pushing her back down to the sands.

The Necroborn turned his attention to Fay. The woman's feet were turned in, while her legs shook with a violence that threatened to buckle. The Necroborn shoved her flat on her back. The Coliseum rang with laughter from the crowd.

"What do they call you maggot?"

"Fay," choked the woman. Her tongue lashed out as she attempted to spit out the black sand that assaulted her mouth.

"What is it you want maggot?" asked the Necroborn.

"Water—for my brother. He has a fever and," started Fay before a hand came crashing down across her face. Her body tumbled across the sands, as if a colossal beast had hit her.

"Your reason is insignificant. You will die nonetheless. It will either be here on these very sands, or you will die on the cold streets while wallowing in the filth you call a home," laughed the Necroborn. He disappeared behind the Coliseum gate.

"One fights for food, while the other fights for water!" said Ivor atop his balcony with his arms outstretched and palms open. "But who will win? Who will gain what they seek only to live to suffer another day?"

Jude stirred in his seat. Rage was ejecting him while pain was keeping him stationary. This was not the Coliseum he remembered. This was nothing like the honorable battles he had grown to know.

"You may kill each other when ready!" announced the King.

Exhausted screams pelted the arena, while the metal chains from above rocked back-and-forth amidst the chaos. Daliah and Fay tackled each other. Their energy was so low and sluggish, that their battle seemed ludicrous to Jude. Their light slaps across each other's faces were embarrassing to watch. The Kismet people had a history of being some of the world's most skilled and deadliest of warriors. Their battles were legendary. But this feeble squabble that carried on in front of him, was not only embarrassing, but also insulting to Kismet's history.

Fay kicked Daliah off of her and came down with her hands firmly around her opponent's neck. Daliah's sand covered legs kicked vigorously while her head whipped back and forth in an attempt to break free.

"I'm sorry Daliah, but my brother needs this," said Fay while tightening her grasp on Daliah's neck. The old woman's struggle stopped for a few seconds, before she bashed her face into Fay's.

Cheering, snarls and stomping rose around the Coliseum. Jude waited to hear Priya's command to interrupt the battle and save the two women. The S-3 was silent.

Daliah grabbed Fay by her ankle and reeled her in. She grabbed one of the thick chains that fell from the Coliseum's ceiling and tied it quickly around the old woman's neck. Choking and rustling chains surrounded the combatants.

"I won't let you take food out of the mouths of my children you harlot! I will see you and your brother die first!"

yelled Daliah. She continued to wrap more of the chain around Fay's neck until the old woman's arms dropped.

Fay's toes dangled slightly above the arena sands, while her head and arms remained motionless. Daliah fell to her knees in tears. Her hands cupped her face and her shoulders rose and fell against the sobs that came from between her fingers. She rose to her feet and turned towards King Kristoph, who now sat in what used to be Bishop's throne. The heads of the large Bishop statues behind the throne were severed, and on their shoulders sat the vile heads of a Necroborn.

Daliah tumbled across the sand with Fay in hot pursuit. A painful-looking circle shined from around her neck from where the chain once ensnared her. Fay's energy level had increased dramatically as she closed in quickly on Daliah's still-tumbling body. Daliah sprang to her feet and wrapped her hands around Fay's neck.

"Why won't you die!" yelled Daliah. The two women began to choke one another while trying to break free from the other's grip.

"Get—off me! You crazy," started Fay before bring her foot up and kicking Daliah in the stomach. The old woman flew back into the rising steam behind her.

Boiling murky green liquid shot up when Daliah's body entered. Heart-wrenching screams wailed from the acid pool. Daliah's arms and hands flung around frantic, while Fay fell to her knees, wide eyes.

"Oh my Aegis! Give me your hand," said Fay extending her hand to Daliah.

The splashing continued until a lone, white flesh hand darted up from beneath the acid's depths. Its skeletal fingers extended towards Fay causing her to leap back in fear. Fay screamed frantically at her victim that cried for help in front of her.

"I'm sorry! I just can't! I can't!" cried Fay.

The sound of splashing began to subside. When the acid pool's steaming surface found its tranquility, a skeletal head pierced its surface—drifting and bobbing. Fay screamed, throwing herself back.

"We have ourselves a victor!" announced Ivor.

Jude looked back towards the balcony and noticed the King had abandoned his throne in exchange for a spot at his balcony.

"What's your name again? Kay? Jay?"

"Fay—my King."

"*Blood energy at full capacity. Wyatt and Jarkko standing by,*" said Sia's voice. The familiar voice broke Jude out of the trance he was unknowingly trapped in.

"*When the second battle begins, move to phase two of the plan,*" said Priya. "*I want no more than half of the civilians evacuated. The others will have to wait until after.*"

Fay limped back towards the risen gate she had previously entered through. Her neck turned slightly, as she looked over her shoulder towards the acid pool, which now lay calm and absent of any inhabitants.

"Now for your prey for the last battle today!" announced King Kristoph.

One of the gates shot down hitting the sands heavily, before rising and unveiling its inhabitant. A large man with short blonde hair, similar to Eli's, trudged across the arena sands. His arms sat folded as if resisting the cold around him. He wore tattered shorts and a bare chest. The last gate opened. A figure limped out onto the arena sands, shielding her eyes with her hand from the sunlight that began to pour down from the opening in the Coliseum ceiling. Her walk was familiar and her long hair was too, but Jude couldn't see passed the abnormally skinny legs and arms that sat barely covered underneath the rags she wore. Then the shadow from the door's archway retreated, and her head tilted up. Then he knew.

PANDEMONIUM

Eli was growing more nauseous from the smell by the second. He began to wonder if Kai's idea of infiltrating the Coliseum through the underground pipes was his way of getting Eli back for their earlier squabbles. The two of them had found a vent that was ground level to the arena sands. Kai called it "front row seats" but Eli called it torture. Due to the narrowness of the pipes, Eli and Kai had to remain in a squat position while peering through the vents. Eli had to admit that their position put them as close to the fight as possible. The first battle was not as action-packed as he thought it would be, but the ending was a shocker.

"These ventilation doors remove easily from the inside," started Kai. Even though they were so close their shoulders touched, Kai refused to voice anything without using the S-3 device. "When Priya gives the signal, unhinge the bottom latch and the door should open."

"Where is Lieutenant Titus and General Briars? I haven't heard from them since we started."

Kai stared. His eyes moved from side-to-side studying Eli, before he returned his attention back towards the vent door in front of him—and beyond that the sands of the arena. "They have their own mission like Kai told you before. Focus on the task at hand."

The ground above them rumbled, signaling the opening of the arena doors once again. Eli set eyes on a tall blonde-haired man, stomping the sands beneath him. He wore no shirt or shoes, only tattered shorts. Most of his teeth had fallen out and his skin was stained with dirt and grime. He made his way to the center of the Coliseum with his back towards Eli and Kai. Before Eli could comment, more rumbling began. A woman dragged herself across the sands until she was toe-to-toe with her opponent. The sun's rays masked her face. The Necroborn from earlier returned, joining the two combatants at the center.

"Speak your name maggot!"

"Madoc you pig!" said the blonde man. He instantly recoiled, when the back of the Necroborn's hand slapped his face to the side.

"Speak to your superior like that again, and it will be the pit for you!" snapped the Necroborn.

"Forgiveness—my master," hissed Madoc between his gritted teeth.

The Necroborn reared his shoulders back and spit at Madoc's feet before turning his attention to the young woman. "Your name! Speak!"

The sun's rays began to dissolve and the woman's face began to uncover. Eli found himself pushing his face more and more into the ventilation bars, in an attempt to speed up the stranger's unveiling. Then he quickly pulled away, tumbling back onto the wall behind him, and splashing the brown water full of waste up his nose. The smell and taste was staggering. He coughed and gagged repeatedly.

"What is wrong with you!" snapped Kai. He had finally broken his pattern and had abandoned the S-3.

Eli tried to respond but continued to cough up more waste from the water around him. "That woman!"

"My name is Aileen. Aileen Bray," said a light dry voice from between the vent bars.

Eli sprang back towards the vent, gripping the bars firmly with his fingers. "That's Jude's mom."

"*Commander are you going to give the signal or what?*" said Jude. His voice sounded desperate and annoyed.

"I will give the signal when I see fit Bray. Remember that!" snapped Priya.

"That's my mother out there!"

"That means nothing to me. Your mother is just like any other civilian and will not receive any special treatment. If you expect me to risk the failure of this mission over one life, your sadly mistaken," said Priya.

Eli looked to Kai, who appeared unfazed. "Does she mean that?"

"Is that a serious question?" replied Kai.

"But that's his mother."

"And?" said Kai.

"You may kill each other when ready!" announced Ivor.

Aileen screamed, as Madoc barreled towards her in a shoulder charge.

"Why doesn't she use her abilities? Isn't she a Combat Specialist like Jude?"

"You know nothing do you?" said Kai shaking his head. "Look at their fragile bodies, sagging skin and blood-shot eyes. They probably haven't had any food or water in days, which is why they enter this suicide."

"But what does that have to do with their abilities?"

Kai sighed while slowly closing his eyes and then opening them. "Abilities are fueled by blood energy. When you don't eat or you're dehydrated, your body begins to consume your blood energy in an attempt to sate the hunger or thirst. When your blood energy drops to a low level, your body begins to eat your body fat and muscle next. They *can't* use their abilities."

The charge was a direct hit. Aileen's body went flailing through the air like a tree branch. She face-planted into the arena sands before returning to her hands and knees.

"Commander I am begging you to spare her! She and my brother are all I have! " yelled Jude.

"*You better calm yourself Bray or so help me Pith,*" snapped Priya.

Aileen returned to her feet just as Madoc towered over her. She went into a slapping frenzy with both hands. The attacks were weak and harmless. Madoc endured her hopeless attacks. His hand shot around her neck, picking her up off the sand. Her feet kicked and her hands clawed at his hand.

"*You have five seconds to give the order or I will give it for you!*" said Jude.

Madoc carried Aileen over to the pit of spikes that sat in the middle of the arena. Her feet dangled freely above the sharp spikes that begged for a taste of her flesh.

"Kai we have to do something!"

"If you value your life you will stay put," said Kai. Agent Slate had slithered out from underneath Kai's armor and sat perched on his shoulder facing Eli ready to attack.

"*Stand down Bray. That's an order!*" barked Priya.

"Please..." cracked Aileen's voice as her eyes looked down at the pit of spikes beneath her.

"My little girl is hungry; and she gets whatever her little heart desires. Even if that means I have to take your life," said Madoc reaffirming his grip. "Forgive me."

A body flipped through the air, blocking out the sun, before landing atop Madoc's shoulders.

"I'm going to kill you!" growled Jude. He locked his legs around Madoc's neck, and after a back bend, hammered Madoc's head into the arena's unforgiving terrain.

Aileen fell into the pit, but quickly grabbed the crater's round surface in an attempt not fall completely in. "Somebody help me!"

"Dammit Bray!" snapped Priya's voice. *"Jarkko! Wyatt! Initiate phase two!"*

"Copy!" said the Magi in unison.

"All other Agents go!"

◆◆◆

Necroborns spilled down from the spectator area in hordes. Jude flipped over Madoc's head, slamming the back of his heels into the man's back.

"This is forbidden! Who are you?" demanded Madoc.

Jude front flipped above the battle and came down in his arachnid form. Madoc turned to flee, but Jude's front legs caught him instantly, spinning him in yards of thick web. Returning to his human form he loomed over Madoc. "My name is Agent Bray, and you hurt my mother. Now you're going to die." He brought both of his mighty troll fists up in the air before smashing Madoc's head beneath their might.

"Help me! Somebody!" The voice sounded like Aileen. Jude searched around frantically until he found her, dangling by a few fingers in the pit.

"Mom!" Racing over to her, he dove with his hand extended. "Grab my hand!"

"I can't! I can't! I'll fall!"

"Jude behind you!" yelled Eli over the S-3.

Jude turned around to find a line of Necroborns closing in on him. A figure and a small snake leaped in front of Jude. Dual swords shined bright in the stranger's hands while the snake reared back ready to strike.

"Come get some!" yelled Kai. He sprinted towards the group of Necroborns with Agent Slate close on his heels.

Turning back towards Aileen, Jude saw the fear in her eyes. "I won't let anything happen to you Mom. I promise. Now please, grab my hand."

Aileen stared at Jude for the longest few seconds of his life. She nodded her head, and with a quick jerk, threw her hand up at his. He caught it and crushed his grip on her hand. He didn't know if he was hurting her, but he did know that he would hold on as tight as he could and never let go. Buried feelings of how much she meant to him and how much he loved her swam through his body making his eyes water as he pulled her up.

"Jude! Jude!" screamed Aileen as she threw her arms around him. She kissed his face harshly before hugging him even harder. "Jude I thought I lost you. I hated myself. I love you Jude. I love you!"

He could not say anything, only hug her back. He was filled with so much emotion that his mouth refused to move.

"Ha!" laughed Kai as he spun across the battlefield with his dual blades.

"There is a small squad of us here to rescue everyone. Stay with me. I'll protect you I promise."

"I'll never leave your side again," said Aileen.

Jude took her hand and ran for the entrance. "Commander where is the evac?"

Silence.

Eli ran by with his bow firing arrows at the hordes of Necroborns that continued to close in. Jude attempted to call out to his comrade, but Eli was surrounded by enemies on all sides.

"If you're mad at me now isn't the time. I have a civilian that needs extraction immediately."

Silence.

He opened his thoughts to the entire squad. *"This is Agent Bray. I need evac for a civilian now!"*

"Why leave so soon?" hissed a chilling voice.

"That voice..." said Aileen in an almost whisper. The two of them turned around causing Aileen to instantly scream. Then Jude saw him.

A man with the palest skin, the greenest eyes and the most sinister whisper. His face weaved back-and-forth like a snake ready to strike while his fingertips tickled the sword that stood between his legs.

"It—it can't be!" cried Aileen. Her hand slowly rose to cover her mouth.

"Can't? But it is? Aly my dear," said Lord Egon with a smirk.

Lord Egon. The one enemy left out of the briefing. The one target they were not prepared for. No Agents or Operatives stood at his side. All of the Necroborns were still engaged in battle with Kai, Eli and another Agent that Jude could not make out.

"Agent Bray to everyone! Lord Egon is on the south side of the Coliseum arena. I need assistance now!"

Lord Egon's head tilted to the side as if trying to understand. "You look so familiar."

"Please! Anyone! Respond!"

"Ah! I see. Are your comrades not responding?" smirked the Lord.

"Jude we should run," whispered Aileen.

"And where will you go," said two voices behind them.

Jude turned around to find two Lord Egon's towering over them. He instantly put himself in between the clones and Aileen. *I don't know how to battle and protect her at the same time. I need help.*

Lord Egon cleared his throat. Jude turned around and found Aileen with her arms pinned behind her back by the Lord. Jude looked down to the hand he was holding and found himself holding hands with a clone. He freed his hand.

"Please don't hurt her! What do you want?"

"Hmm interesting question. A question that needs more time than what exists," said Egon licking his teeth. "For starters I want her."

"You can't have her!"

Shadows covered the Lord's eyes. A snarl controlled his lips. One of his hands jerked back Aileen's hair exposing her throat. "You dare tell me what I can and cannot have. Do you hear that Aly? I sense defiance. I sense superiority."

"Please my lord! Spare him. You can kill me. But please, spare him," begged Aileen.

"What? No! No! You're not killing anybody!" The smokescreen erupted giving Jude enough time to take on his anaconda form. He darted towards Egon, wrapping himself quickly and tightly around the Lord until his tongue tasted his scent. The smoke cleared and Aileen was nowhere to be found.

"Jude!" screamed Aileen far off in the distance.

A heavy blow to the head returned Jude to his normal form as he hit the ground. The air around him spun and he felt his stomach turning. He looked up to find Aileen flung over the Lord's shoulder, disappearing in the distance.

"Mom!" He forced himself to his feet and ran after her. Clones of Lord Egon darted out from the Lord's back, attacking Jude on contact. Jude ducked under their attacks. Leaving clouds of smoke in his wake. "Mom!"

"Jude!" screamed Aileen. Her hand stretched out towards him, pleading and yearning for him to grab hold of it.

His raven form took him up and over the battle—and over the clones that continued to manifest. A circle of fire opened up a few feet in front of the Lord. Its inside was darker than the shadows but swimming with questions. Jude flapped as hard and fast as he could. Arrows pelted him from all sides. Necroborns sat perched in the surrounded seats with their bows. Jude ignored their attacks and kept towards the Lord. He was close. He was going to make it. Sharp pain found his wing and soon sand became his bed. The arrow hurt worse when he returned to his normal form.

The Lord stopped cold. Turning his head around, he smiled. "May the three brothers watch over you." The Lord stepped through the circle of fire and out of view. His sinister laugh filled the Coliseum, ringing in all directions.

Aileen slowly began to disappear through the portal of flames with each step Egon took. Jude ran as fast as he could extending his hand. He would catch her. He would catch her and save her from wherever that portal was taking her. Her body slipped in, leaving her pleading hand resisting to follow.

"Mom I'll save you! Hold on!" He dove for her hand and came down hugging his body tightly. He didn't feel the warmth of her body. He didn't feel the rise and fall of her chest. He didn't feel her soft hair beneath his chin. But most importantly, he didn't feel her love enveloping him in its entirety. He refused to look up, for he knew she was gone. He didn't know whether or not she was alive. What he did know was that he was alone. Utterly and absolutely alone.

Eli ran along Sia's side defending her from the arrows that pelted her from all angles. Her blood energy was running low and she needed time to build it back up.

"Tell me what you need."

"I need you to stop talking and just watch my flank," said Sia. She kept her eyes closed and her hands clasped, but her feet were non-stop.

"*Brassie have you evacuated those civilians yet?*" asked Priya over the S-3.

"*Negative Commander. Sia is still building up her blood energy.*"

"*Who?*" replied the Commander.

"*Wyatt is still building up her blood energy.*"

"*Well hurry up I have major activity headed your way,*" said Priya.

"Hey how much longer do—"

"I swear to Rune if you rush me I will trip you," snapped Sia.

A massive number of civilians ran frantically in front of them. There had to be at least a couple hundred of them. Eli and Sia were to escort them to the main gates to Tristan and Pang; however with their cover blown, more and more Necroborns were spilling out onto the streets attempting to apprehend them.

A young girl somewhere screamed. Eli looked ahead of the crowd to see a small squad of Necroborns running towards them. The civilians staggered back looking in all directions, not knowing where to run.

"Everyone stay with Agent Wyatt!" yelled Eli. He ran through the crowd and met the Necroborns head on.

One Necroborn tossed his mighty axe that continued to slice the air as it whizzed through the air.

"Threat replication!" Two axes fired back, missing every enemy as they rolled to the side and back up to their feet, continuing their pursuit. Summoning his bow, Eli aimed for one Necroborn, and then switched to another just as he let go of the arrow. The first Necroborn he was aiming at dodged for no reason, but his actual target was caught-off-guard and paid with his life. Summoning his shield and sword he leaped into battle bashing the attacks of two Necroborns away with his shield, and engaging the other two with his blade.

"Agent Brassie I'm ready," said Sia's voice.

One of the Necroborns grabbed him and tossed him across the shattered gravel. Coming to his feet he immediately went into a readying stance. "Cataclysm!" The force knocked the Necroborns back but they immediately came to their feet. They were a lot tougher than Eli remembered, and a lot more agile as well. He turned for the group but another Necroborn appeared from one of the surrounding rooftops and blocked his view. His blade hit home, slicing Eli across his side. He looked to Sia for help, and caught a glimpse of her aura enveloping the civilians, taking everyone with her.

"Sia where are you going? You forgot me!"

"The mission comes first. If I have enough blood energy I will come back for you. If not, may fate be your ally," her voice replied.

He felt rage unleash its onslaught. He knew she was doing this out of spite. But was she really willing to put his life in danger because of a few petty white lies? He rolled to the side barely dodging the stomps and blades of the five Necroborns that still pursued him.

"Kai some help please!"

"Kai is busy, and so is Agent Slate," replied Kai. *"Kai will end you—you filthy Necroborn. Ha!"*

The Necroborns engaged, swinging their mighty axes and blades. Eli summoned his dual blades and tried his best to defend against the attacks. A cut to the knee brought him to the floor and a blow to the chin sent him flying.

"We have him! Kill him while he's down!" snarled a Necroborn.

Eli looked up and through the haze and saw his enemies. He couldn't move and pain shot all over. Running feet sounded and soon a cold wind passed his neck.

Jude flipped atop one of the rooftops and came barreling down, hurling vials in all directions. All but one Necroborn fell instantly. Jude went head-to-head dancing underneath the Necroborn's attacks and unleashing punches and kicks to its blind spots when the opportunity presented itself. The Necroborn grabbed Jude by the neck and held him up off his feet.

No!

"You've lost!" snarled the Necroborn.

"No. You've lost!" Jude broke the Necroborn's hold and crawled around the Necroborn's waist, shoulders and then head. The Necroborn fell to his knees, and Jude took his place.

"Need a hand?" asked Jude extending his hand down to Eli. Eli took his hand quickly, grateful to see his comrade.

"Thanks."

"Eli to the," started Jude before his head jerked up to the house next to him. "Down!" Jude shoved Eli to the floor and took cover himself.

Dark purple smoke rose around them, causing Eli to cough violently. He covered his mouth waiting for the smoke screen to attack.

"There! On the roof!" yelled Jude.

Eli caught a lone archer, retreating from rooftop-to-rooftop. Eli concentrated and threw out his hand. "Blunt force!" The assailant continued to flee unharmed. Eli felt nauseous and dizzy. "Something is wrong."

Jude closed his eyes and opened them with alarm. "My blood energy isn't responding."

Eli heard the sound of an arrow leaving its bow.

An archer fired.

Diving to the ground, Eli was late to realize that he wasn't the arrow's target.

Jude turned towards the attack—his eyes wide with shock.

"No!" screamed a voice. A tangle of hair collided with Jude, sending him tumbling to the ground.

"Jude!" Eli ran to his comrade slipping on the puddle of blood that surrounded him.

Jude shot up quickly, cradling a woman in his arms. "Wha-why?"

The woman's mouth released blood as she coughed hoarsely. She smiled. "I have dreamt of the pending darkness. Please, save us Mr. Prodigy. Deliver us from the evil that stirs beneath." Her lip quivered and her breathing slowed. With eyes as still as stone, she released her last breath.

"No, no!" cried Jude cradling her in his arms. "Why would you do this? Why throw your life away for me—a complete stranger?"

Thud. Thud. Thud. The ground rumbled beneath them, causing fractures of the already desecrated cobblestones to come undone. Eli tried to summon a shield and blade and instantly vomited. *Thud. Thud.*

Eli turned around towards the direction of the noise and went into shock. "Impossible! We killed you."

"Your end is now maggot," snarled General Rorik.

♦♦♦

Jude knocked Eli out of the way, but failed to leave enough time to counter himself. Rorik's mighty axe was a direct hit, opening up a crater of cold pain, and sending Jude crashing into an adjacent shed. His body told him to forfeit any chances of moving.

"Curse you! You filthy Necroborn."

Rorik grabbed Jude by his neck and pinned him to the shed behind him. "No! Curse you! You disgusting maggot!" He hawked his shoulders back and spewed a pile of spit that completely covered Jude's face.

The air filled with the sound of Eli's battle cry. He barreled into Rorik's back, causing the General to loosen his hold on Jude. Rorik turned to Eli and brought his hands up over the now frozen comrade. Jude front flipped onto Rorik's shoulders before the General attacked. His snarling was prevalent, as he spun Jude around. He was too heavy for Jude to throw with his legs, and too strong for Jude to break his neck; so instead Jude hung on for as long as he could, in hopes for a miracle that he knew would never come. Eli hollered as he barreled towards Rorik, coming to an immediate halt when he slammed into Rorik's unflinching body. The General tossed Jude over his shoulder and uppercut Eli. The two boys tumbled in a tangled mess until they came to a stop, breathing heavily.

"Without our abilities, we can't win."

The General trudged towards them, spinning his war axe up to his tongue, and licking the flesh from his glistening axe. The clouds began to roll in and the wind began to speed up. Something rose from the cobblestones between Jude and Rorik. Rising through the street like a spirit through a wall, the stranger demanded attention. A black robe covered him and the matching hood concealed him.

"You! What are *you* doing here? Back to your house!" said General Rorik.

The stranger pulled something from his robe and held it out to the General. "Leave now, or face the power of the cards fate has dealt you."

"I'll destroy you!" yelled Rorik. He brought his axe high above his head.

"Perfect. The counter card," said the stranger holding a square object toward the General.

"What are you doing? Run!"

The General attacked and the card magnified, until it was taller than both the General and the stranger. The General's attack struck the card, and the sound of metal through grass consumed the air. Mere seconds passed and the card vanished, leaving the stranger and Rorik standing motionless. Jude rose to his feet and soon Eli followed. Coming in for a closer look Jude froze. A huge gash cut across Rorik's waist. His torso fell to the floor and his legs soon followed.

"How did you? How is that possible?"

"How in the heck did you do that!" yelled Eli.

The stranger turned slowly, exposing a lone black eye—as black as the path of Pith that once led to the Academy steps. "Come with me or perish." The stranger's lips never moved, but his words were as loud as if they had.

Jude looked down towards Rorik's body, and saw the intestines begin to reassemble and the blood retreating back into his torso. Turning his attention back towards the stranger, he noticed the hooded figure never moved. "Who are you?"

"I am your foe. I am your ally. I am your weapon. I am your undoing. I am fate."

A BRUSH
WITH FATE

Thread was woven in every direction, like a web for the prey of the most cunning of spiders. Ducking and maneuvering around the thread that crisscrossed from wall-to-wall, floor to ceiling and corner-to-corner became tiring and unnerving. Old books sat in uneven stacks all around them while scrolls ran freely over their tops. There was something incredibly familiar about the layout of the house. Jude felt like he had seen it time and time again, however, the décor around him made it impossible for him to remember. The walls were completely covered with wall art of men and women, oceans and trees and beasts of every kind. Under their frame was their own set of tally marks in no particular pattern.

"Help! Help!" yelled Eli. Jude turned around and noticed his friend was trapped in the labyrinth of thread that spread out all around them. "I could really use some help." After helping Eli down from his suspended trap, Jude continued to study the photos of the people, creatures and nature around them. One photo was of a man; a strong man with large arms, a chiseled jaw and stern eyes. A duplicate of the figure stood in the background with a bow ready to fire. In the left corner of the photo a card was painted depicting a shattering heart.

"How much time has to pass before you surrender to the question that now haunts your mind?" asked the stranger.

"Who are these people?"

"Forget those people! I've seen you before," said Eli. His words immediately caught Jude's attention. "I just can't remember where."

The stranger took a seat at a dingy old wooden table, which held a small candle that flickered slowly in an infinite dance. Only one other chair occupied the table, which was directly across from the stranger. His hood fell, exposing his tangled white hair. Around his neck fell a medallion, which he quickly tucked away in his robe. He was a young man, appearing to be no older than seventeen. His blacked-out eyes were unsettling, but the innocence of his face was comforting— trapping Jude between intrigue and alarm.

"Who is first?" asked the stranger. His lips never moved while his voice was hollow and enigmatic. The sight was unsettling, and caused more questions to rise the longer Jude stared at the stranger.

I am starting to think coming here was not one of my brightest of ideas.

"You had no choice," said the boy.

Jude froze.

"What do you mean 'you had no choice?" asked Eli.

"Are you reading my thoughts?"

"I don't need to," said the stranger extending a hand towards the empty seat in front of him. "Sit."

"Why should I?"

"So I can read your fortune of course," he replied.

"You've got to be kidding me," said Eli nearly laughing. "Jude come on, we have to get back to the others. Sia and Jarkko have started extracting civilians, and may need our help just in case Fox shows up."

"It's surprising that you are so calm in the presence of what used to be your living room," said the stranger shifting his attention towards Eli.

Eli looked at Jude for a few seconds and then returned his attention to the stranger. He looked over his shoulder and then returned his gaze to the young boy in front of him. "Wait *my* living room?"

The boy smirked. Taking a black rectangular object from his robe, he placed it lightly on the table in front of him. It appeared to be a deck of cards, and just when Jude thought about taking a closer look, a shimmer ran from the top card down to the bottom of the deck.

"Now I know you're crazy. This isn't my house. My house is clean and looks a lot better than this garbage," said Eli.

"Isn't that the chip in the staircase from when you first learned how to summon your first blade?" asked the boy pointing to a staircase the sat in the shadows behind him. Jude ignored the bookcases, the thread and everything else. His eyes traced every inch and examined every detail.

Oh my Aegis! This is his house.

"No. No that is just some crack in a staircase," said Eli.

"I see," said the boy shuffling his cards. "Well I will give you two options. You can leave and go about your mission, absent of any interference by *I*. Or you can swallow your pride, tame your fear, put aside your honor and take the path fate has chosen for you."

Jude weighed his options while studying the boy. The table appeared normal, and the stranger appeared to be carrying no weapons. However judging by what Jude saw earlier with the card and General Rorik, it was a strong possibility that the stranger was a Magi and used magic. But why was the boy so eager to read their fortune? What did he gain from it? And what would he lose if Jude refused. One thing Jude was sure about was that the young boy had saved him and Eli. If he meant any immediate harm, he would have let General Rorik finish them off.

Jude rested his hand on the back of the empty chair in front of him. "You clearly benefit somehow from the telling of our fortune, so you stand to gain more from this than us."

The boy never flinched.

"I will agree to let you read *my* fortune, but not Eli's; and only on one condition."

"Aiso," said the boy.

"Huh?" asked Eli.

"I am known as Aiso," said the boy.

"Wow your mom has a sick sense of humor," said Eli.

"What mom?"

"Eli," started Jude as he took the empty seat. "Return to the mission, ensure that every last one of our people is freed."

"You're not in charge. You don't tell me what to do—got it?"

"Do you forget that we are on a mission? A mission to save our city. Have you even stopped to think about the fact that we haven't heard one sound over the S-3 in almost an hour? The silence is proof enough. Our squad needs us."

"Then why don't you go," snapped Eli. "This guy has been lurking around my house since before the Necroborns invaded us. He is either the head of all this or he knows who is. I demand answers." Eli glared at Aiso, who still sat still and unaffected.

"I am the Recon on this mission. My objective is not to be on the front lines or to be our main offensive force. That's your job. We need you out there. If you refuse…"

Eli turned his glare to Jude as if ready to strike.

"If you refuse then our dad is as good as dead."

The innocence swarmed in Eli's eyes. The edge was gone and emotion seemed to consume him. Jude hated to speak such a horrible thought, but it was the truth. It may be too late to save his mom—a thought that brought intense agony—but they may be able to still save Marius, if he was still alive.

Marius may know where Lord Egon took my mother, or how to save her. I never thought I would miss his suffocating bear hugs.

"Alright," said Eli flipping the drooping hair from in front of his eyes. "But give me your belt with your vials."

Jude felt his head jerk back. "Excuse me?"

"If you want me to leave then give me your vials," replied Eli.

"Why are you asking for my vials? We are on a mission and I will need all the weapons I have at my disposal."

"I know that which is why I want them. If I have your vials, you are more likely to keep your word and come back," said Eli.

"Why wouldn't I return to the mission; and when have I ever not kept my word?" Jude felt his eyes glare but couldn't fight the pending fury.

Eli shot out his hand. "The belt. Give it to me now!"

Jude was just as confused as he was enraged. Eli didn't trust him; and now he was asking for Jude's main source of weaponry. Jude's first instinct was to say no, not because of the obvious reason of him needing his vials, but just to spite Eli for his ridiculous request. However, they were outmanned, and their squad needed Eli. He was the main offense, and with the absence of both of them, their mission would surely fail.

The clasp was difficult to unhinge; almost as if it was fighting Jude's request to unbuckle. Handing his utility belt to Eli, Jude wondered if this would be a decision he would come to regret. "If you lose even one vial or make me regret this in any way, I swear to you I will make it my life's mission to—."

"Yeah yeah," replied Eli quickly. He headed for the door, rustling through the thread that still assaulted him from all angles. "Your threats are as empty as your pockets so don't waste your bad breath Bray."

When the door hammered close, Jude returned to the stranger before him. Aiso continued to shuffle his cards. His shuffling was of another world. It was too fast, too awkward and made Jude dizzy from following the movements. The deck slammed hard on the table.

"Go on. Say what's on your mind," hissed Aiso.

Jude looked into Aiso's grim eyes. If Aiso was in fact fate, then he knew what had been gnawing at the back of Jude's conscience ever since Aiso explained the rules of their meeting.

"We have already alerted the city of our presence. We are a squad of ten in a city full of hundreds and hundreds of enemies."

"Go on..." replied Aiso with a lingering smile.

"We've already lost." The words were hard to speak and even harder to accept. However, Jude felt like the blow was not as staggering as he expected. He knew their mission was a failure for a few hours now—knew it but ignored the knowledge.

"Yes, you've lost."

"Then you're an ally. You intervened in our battle with General Rorik to help us."

Aiso's head slowly tilted back until his mischievous eyes peered down his nose. "Fate is no one's ally."

Jude examined the situation. He never took his eyes off of Aiso, but still took into account everything around him. After the stranger's rescue, Jude was brought to Aiso's home, which was originally Eli's, and informed of what would come to pass. Aiso was an ally unless there was something he wanted; in which case he only saved Jude and Eli to get something in return, which would make him an enemy. Jude chose to play the game. "Then you are an enemy."

"It is shocking that you are more concerned about who and what I am, instead of the deaths of your comrades," said Aiso retrieving his deck and beginning to shuffle once again.

"Tell me how to save them."

"You can't." Aiso continued to shuffle; never taking his eyes off of the cards that ran through his hands.

"Then help me save them."

The shuffling stopped. A ringing came and went throughout the room with no apparent origin. Aiso's eyes locked with Jude's, giving Jude an itch to reach for his vials.

Where are my vials?

Eli's stiff back and hard words came and went. Returning his gaze back to Aiso, Jude was not surprised to see that the Necroborn had not moved.

"What makes you think that *I*, fate, would help you?"

"If you already knew our mission was a failure, which I believe you did, you could have just let all of us die. You're a Necroborn and we are technically your enemy. Intervening in our battle with Rorik and killing him was treason on your part. A crime worthy of death. You put a lot on the line saving us and hiding us here in your home, a home that used to belong to my comrade. No one goes through all that trouble unless they want something. So the question is, what do you want?"

"Let fate tell your fate," replied Aiso.

"What do you gain by telling my fate?"

Aiso paused; and for a second Jude thought he would refuse to answer. "I see your father in those eyes of yours."

Jude's first instinct was to recoil when the emotion invaded him. However, he made sure to quickly cease the impending reaction. He could not afford to let Aiso know that he got to him. Family was always the staple card to play when interrogating someone or threatening them. Most likely Aiso had never even heard of his father.

But then again, he is...fate.

"Well that's disappointing because I hated my father."

Aiso smirked. "When a soul allows me to tell their fortune, both parties get something in the process. The soul gets to know what trials and tribulations are to come, and I get my prize."

"And what prize is that?"

"Their Cipher," he replied with a hard stare.

"What's a Cipher?"

The boy slid his deck across the table, closer to Jude. "It would be best not to meddle with fate. I'm sure your father would agree."

Jude couldn't tell anymore if the constant parading of Aiso knowing Jude's father was a bluff or a fact. Necroborns had always been Kismet's enemy when Jude's father was alive. There was no way the two of them could have known each other on a personal level. Then something else gnawed at the back of Jude's mind. Out of everyone in this city, including Jude's comrades, why did Aiso want to tell Jude's fortune so badly?

My Cipher *that he gets from telling my fortune must be different than the others. There must be a reason, which means I have something to bargain with.*

"Here's the deal," started Jude getting up from the table. "Severe the bonds of every prisoner in this city and help us escape—all of us."

"And what is my prize for such a feat?"

"I will let you tell my fortune. I can tell your desire for the prize you get from telling it is unbearable. Help us and it's yours."

Aiso returned Jude's stare for a while longer before responding. "Very well, but I have my own condition."

Oh dear Aegis what now!

"What's your condition?"

Aiso inched the deck closer to Jude. "Pick a card and keep it with you. When the time comes for your fortune I will have my answer to a question that has been eating away at me for decades." Aiso spread the cards out in an arc, keeping them facedown.

Jude scanned the cards in front of him. Their backs were as black as Aiso's eyes. They had no decoration, no design and no hint of what lay underneath their surface. Anxiety pulled at the right side of his eye. He looked over at a card close to the end of the arc of cards. His instinct told him to pick that card. He stood in a trance for a few seconds and then grabbed the card on the opposite side and tucked it in his combat armor.

"Now what?"

ENTER, MY KING

Eli ran and ran, his feet failing to meet the quota he gave them. The once familiar Kismet streets brought anger and pain as he sped passed them. The cold and damp metal sheds, which were now Kismet's homes, were devastating to acknowledge.

Upon exiting Aiso's house, Eli nearly broke his hand after punching the ground beneath him with rage. He knew Aiso was right. Eli had recognized the layout and hidden décor of his once comforting home the minute he entered the house. The Necroborns had taken over his home and his childhood memories; and since they succeeded in taking his home, Eli began to lose hope for finding his dad. Eli knew Marius would never let anyone take their home. It was the last connection they had to his mother—a woman who meant so much to both of them. The Necroborns had won.

I don't even care about my home anymore. I just want my dad back. At least I have my memories of my mom. No one can take that away from me. But my dad, I'm not strong enough to lose him yet.

Eli tripped over a crack in the street as a lump swelled up in his throat. A scream to the right broke his train of thought and soon sobs followed. Eli turned towards an alley that separated two metal huts. Shadows moved hastily in its mystery. Eli threw his back against the wall of one of the huts and peered around the corner. A large group of Necroborns herded a small group of prisoners, who walked chained together by their ankles. The prisoners came to an immediate halt when the one in front turned around.

"Walk you filth!" snarled one of the Necroborns.

"No," replied the halted prisoner. His red hair concealed his young skin. Dirt and grime had made a home across his neck and face, while his blackened hands shivered underneath his shackles.

"Eli to Kai," thought Eli over the S-3.

Silence.

Really? Still not working! I guess I'm on my own.

One of the Necroborns picked up the red-head by the collar of the sack he was wearing. The young boy's feet left the ground immediately, followed by the retreating hair that once covered his face. Then Eli recognized him. A roar from the assaulting Necroborn blew back Brayden's red hair in a continuous gust while his eyes remained open and set on his enemy.

Eli counted six Necroborns just as his Epee blade cycled through his mind. He locked eyes with Brayden, whose eyes appeared startled before joining his lips in a smile. Eli abandoned the idea of the Epee blade, and summoned his longbow. With his back still against one of the neighboring homes, he took a deep breath and focused on the demolished statue in front of him on the opposite side of the street. He flipped around the corner and fired before instantly retreating behind the house from which he hid. Ignoring a snarl and a heavy object hitting the ground, Eli climbed the shed and took to its roof.

"The enemy! He's here! Find him!" yelled one of the Necroborns.

Eli loomed over the side of the roof and saw five Necroborns, and one lifeless body—an arrow rising from his heart. He summoned two arrows this time and fired. Two enemies, who attempted to race to the streets he once inhabited, fell cold.

"On the roof!" yelled an enemy before firing his bow immediately.

The arrow buried itself into Eli's shoulder, causing him to relinquish his bow, and tumble down the roof and onto the cold cobblestones beneath him. His mouth tasted of warm metal while his face remained buried in the stone he continued to lay on.

"Look it's Mr. Eli," said a small voice close-by.

"Get up Mr. Eli!" cried another voice.

"Kill him!" snarled a Necroborn. "I will wrangle the slaves!"

One set of footsteps sounded. Another set of footsteps sounded. Eli leaped to his feet and back-sliced the Necroborn in front of him with his Epee blade. A head hit the floor just as Eli's arrow barrage formed in front of him and projected behind him. A grunt sounded, followed by a *thud*. A quick stab to the heart of the headless Necroborn was instinctual. Eli turned around and was met with panic rather than victory.

Brayden remained imprisoned in the large arm that locked around his neck. A pending blade shined in front of him in the hand of the Necroborn.

"Drop your weapon, or this maggot dies," grunted the Necroborn. His large nostrils inflated and deflated savagely.

"You really know nothing of our people do you?"

"Drop it!" fired back the Necroborn.

Eli dropped his weapon, which resulted in it dissolving in its familiar purple essence.

The Necroborn's eyes grew wide. "Weapons Master!" The enemy's arm retreated and was replaced by the pending blade that launched towards Brayden's neck. A small object flew across the air pelting the Necroborn. The blade fell just as the rock that assaulted Eli's enemy fell.

"Get him Mr. Eli!" cried one of the prisoners.

Eli darted towards his enemy. The Necroborn shook his head before noticing Eli and attacking. Massive claws whizzed passed Eli. Arrows skewered his enemy's feet then neck.

"Blunt Force!"

The Necroborn evaded the attack and quickly returned to his feet. Eli did not move. He did not try and escape. For he knew his enemy was unfamiliar with his ability. Just as the Necroborn raised his claws, his stray head hit the floor as Eli's spinning axe dissolved.

After ensuring the Necroborn would not rise, Eli turned his attention to the nine children that stood hunched before him. They looked weak, skinny and dirty. The chains that bound them all together looked too heavy for them to bear. Eli searched the bodies of his fallen enemies, but no key was found. His axe was able to cut the chains that bound them together, but did nothing for the shackles around their wrists and ankles that still clung to their skin. Eli went to the last prisoner—a young girl. Her blonde hair was curly and long. Her gaunt face shivered while her eyes cowered in fear.

"I'm not going to hurt you. I promise."

"Can you fix them," said the little girl with a sniffle.

"Fix what?"

She held up her fingers and released a heavy tear. Her fingers were deformed, broken in different directions. Some fingers went right while others went left. Her thumb on her right hand was bent so far back, Eli wondered how long it would take for it to fall of—if that was even possible.

He wanted to vomit. "What's your name?"

"Emma," she said turning her gaze to the floor beneath her.

Eli placed a curled finger under her chin and raised her gaze to his. "It's nice to meet you Emma. My name is Eli. I'm from the Western Hold of the city, and would like to be your friend. Is that okay?"

Emma quickly looked to the others behind him and then returned to his never flinching gaze. She nodded her head with a ghost of a smile.

"No one will ever hurt you again. I promise," said Eli hugging her gently before rising to his feet. He looked at the others. "That goes for all of you." Eli looked around frantically but found no resolution for his painful question. "Where are the rest of your peers?"

The nine children locked eyes. Some sniffed while others cried. Brayden stepped to the front and gazed up into Eli's eyes. While Brayden appeared to be slightly older than his peers, the red-head still had a baby face.

"They didn't make it Mr. Eli. They starved. The Necroborns threw them away," said Brayden. His shivering jaw and glazed eyes was all the proof Eli needed to realize the young boy was trying not to cry.

"I'm getting all of you out of here. Stay quiet, follow me and keep your eyes open."

The group nodded and soon clung to his side. A scratching noise rang throughout Eli's head followed by a familiar voice that went in-and-out. It sounded like Anya, but Eli could not be sure. All he could gather from the distressful voice was something about the Market District.

"Eli to anyone," said Eli.

"Your communicator won't work," started Brayden. "I overhead one of the Necroborns say that something is blocking it."

I guess that explains it.

Eli stared at Brayden for a short moment before finding his voice. "Have any of you seen my dad—Mr. Brassie?"

All of their heads shook in unison. It was the answer he already knew, as well as the answer he feared. A cry rang out from somewhere in the distance. Eli looked around and determined it came from the Market District and sounded like a woman.

"Something is happening in the Market District. I need to get you all out, but I also need to find my comrades. They can help us. Stay together and whatever you do, don't leave my side unless I tell you to."

The children nodded.

This is it. No more snooping around. We make our final stand right now. Even if I have to do it alone.

◆◆◆

"How could you? How could you!" screamed Sia amidst her struggle to break free. She remained ensnared in the grasp of the Necroborn that held her—alongside Jarkko and Conall.

Eli's heart began to beat rapidly at the sight before him. King Kristoph was surrounded by dozens of Necroborns who aided him in capturing Eli's comrades.

"What's going on?" whispered one of the children.

"Shh!"

"Be quiet Logan or they'll hear us," said Brayden.

"But I wanna see! It's not fair!" snapped Logan.

"No I want to see," said Sy.

"No me!" cried a third.

Eli turned around in a panic. "All of you shut up now!"

Pouts and watered eyes stared back at him. The guilt came instantly.

"Look I'm sorry for yelling at you, but you've got to be quiet. Okay?"

They all nodded.

"What makes you think it was me?" laughed King Ivor. His head tilted down to meet his hand, which attempted to silence his amusement.

"Bishop was your Lord," started Sia. "You swore an oath of loyalty to him. Now you prance around in your—." Her face whipped to the side in response to the back of the King's hand. It was then Eli realized that the King was upon her.

"I am King Ivorious Kristoph III. I have no Lord; and I *don't* swear loyalty to anyone! You all swear loyalty to me!" snapped the King.

"Stay here," whispered Eli over his shoulder. He took one step and was instantly grabbed by the wrist. He looked down to find Brayden staring up into his eyes.

"You'll come back, right Mr. Eli?"

"Yeah, I promise." The hand retreated and that was when he set eyes on the utility belt with vials that still clung to his waist. He continued towards the King. So much rage filled his body. How dare the King lay his hands on Sia. Eli would kill him. He would torture him.

Walking through the crowds of Necroborns, Eli noticed the glances that spread out around him. Necroborns threw wide eyes his way and staggered in place as if unaware of what to do.

"My King! The enemy!" yelled a larger Necroborn closer to the King.

Ivor turned around slowly and locked eyes with Eli—who continued to approach the King. "Ahh look who it is."

When Eli finally made it to the King's position he stopped.

"Everyone! This is Eli Brassie, my old apprentice. If I recall, he was an insufferable little cretin. No respect. No skill. No hope to be anything other than a failure and a regret."

Eli clenched his fist and punched the King, who tumbled across the streets and smack into the Three Brothers statue.

"Don't you ever lay a hand on her again."

An object hit Eli's feet and released a cloud of white smoke. The sounds of coughing and a struggle filled the air. When the smoke passed, Eli was looking into the eyes of Commander Priya. The Necroborns who were holding Sia and the others were now nothing more than lifeless bodies. Everyone was here, except for Pang, Tristan and Jude.

Eli ran to Sia's side. "Are you okay?"

"You're an idiot," snapped Sia.

"I agree with that one," replied Jarkko.

Conall approached Sia with his notoriously emotionless stare. Sia stared back, never leaving his eyes.

"Are you okay Agent Wyatt?" asked Conall.

Sia's lips slightly parted while her chest rose and fell rapidly.

Eli was confused as to the sight before him. Sia appeared winded all of a sudden. Also, he didn't know why Conall was asking if she was okay. The Lieutenant never seemed to care about the safety of Eli and his comrades before. An image of the Kismet border flashed before Eli's eyes.

Conall pulled Sia in close as the shields appeared. Necrosis flew in all directions as the two of them began to spin. When the attack stopped, their locked gaze didn't. Sia and Conall remained bound by their gaze, never flinching and never retreating.

"Yeah," started Sia before coughing. "I mean yes, I am fine. Thank you Lieutenant."

"Sinners! Traitors! Malefactors! Seize them! Seize the betrayers!" yelled the King.

Eli turned towards the ocean of Necroborns that began to close in on them.

"Jarkko!"

"Commander!"

"Send word to Tristan and Quarrels to come to the Market District immediately," ordered Priya.

"The S-3 isn't working. Trust I've tried."

Priya closed her eyes and shook her head briefly in response to Eli.

"On it!" said Jarkko.

"Lieutenant, let's de-throne this King," said Anya.

"De-throne him? General you're too kind. I plan on slaughtering him," replied Conall.

Everyone turned towards the ocean of enemies closing in. Necroborns piled in from surrounding streets and rooftops.

"Annihilate them!" yelled the King.

"All agents go!" yelled Priya.

LAST STAND

"Total immobility!" yelled Jarkko extending his hands. The Necroborns closest to them froze immediately.

"Jarkko my man, thank you," said Kai rushing in with his dual blades drawn and Agent Slate tall on his shoulder.

Eli followed after Kai with his bow in hand. Kai's swords were quick and lethal. The Occult Operative moved too fast for Eli to follow. However, a few times some hidden enemy archers targeted Kai, and met their end by Eli's bow. Eventually Eli abandoned his bow as more enemies closed in around them.

There are way too many. I don't see how we can win.

Eli became surrounded on all sides. Casting arrow barrages in all directions, the Necroborns fell.

"Everyone take cover!" yelled Jarkko.

Eli was confused by the Magi's words, so he continued to engage the incoming Necroborns. A few minutes later he was pulled to the side by the collar of his tunic.

"Woah!"

"When Jarkko says take cover, Kai suggests you take cover," said Kai pulling Eli behind a nearby hut.

Eli scanned the area for Jarkko and soon found him with Sia. He was saying something to Eli's comrade as she nodded her head in agreement. Enemies continued to charge towards them.

"They're not going to have enough time," said Kai abandoning his position and heading towards the two Magi. "Come on Brassie!"

Eli trailed after Kai, hot on his heels. Kai leaped in front of Jarkko and Sia just in time to eliminate a small group of Necroborns that had surrounded them.

"I thought I said take cover!" yelled Jarkko.

"You obviously need help—and Kai means that in more ways than one," replied Kai.

Eli set eyes on a small purple sphere that shimmered between the two Magi. Sia and Jarkko both had their hands on the sphere and appeared to be feeding it power.

"Brassie, Slate and Kai will buy you some time," said Kai running off into the crowd.

Eli went to join Kai but was stopped frozen. His body wouldn't move. His eyes found Jarkko who was glaring at him.

"That's my comrade out there. You protect him with your life or you will be my next target," said Jarkko before releasing the paralysis.

Eli stared at Jarkko for a few seconds before nodding and joining Kai in battle.

"Got ya!" laughed Kai as he dove his dagger into the chest of one Necroborn and then another.

Eli leaped to Kai's side and positioned himself back-to-back with Kai.

"Dual blades!" yelled both of them in unison.

"Stop copying Kai!" said Kai.

"You stop copying *me!*"

Necroborns fell from all around them, as Kai and Eli combined their attacks. Eli remained sword-locked with another Necroborn. The two of them grunted as both tried to overpower the other. Eli felt himself losing against the Necroborn's overwhelming strength. Eli's arm tickled as something heavy slithered across its surface. Slate coiled around Eli's arm before pouncing at the Necroborn. The Necroborn released his attack, giving Eli enough time to throw a quick jab to the heart.

"Ever try an aerial arrow barrage?" asked Kai throwing a sword at a Necroborn who fell instantly.

"No. I mean, how would I even get high enough to do that?"

Kai smirked. Grabbing Eli by the collar of his tunic, Kai flung Eli over the wave of enemies. The weightlessness was terrifying until Eli realized he had been thrown before by Pang. He went to speak the words but his brain itched and jam closed his lips.

"Aerial barrage!" Eli's body vibrated at the sound of his words. War axes, blades, arrows and daggers all shot down diagonally towards the enemies below. An unlimited supply of weapons continued to materialize in front of Eli before burying themselves into the cowering enemies below.

"Stop the attack!' yelled Kai.

"Why?"

"Now!" demanded Kai.

Eli focused on ceasing the attack. The second the attack stopped, he plummeted down to the avalanche of dead Necroborns beneath him—their bodies pelted with the projectiles he assaulted them with. Rolling to his feet, he came up with his sword and shield in hand—stepping back-to-back with Kai.

"Kai knows that's fun and all, but you don't want to foolishly deplete all of your blood energy," said Kai.

Eli bashed an incoming Necroborn to the floor and then engaged. He had completely forgotten about his blood energy level. It was something that always seemed to escape his mind.

"Trust Kai. All it takes is nearly depleting your blood energy one time, and you will never do it again."

But I have done that before.

"Eli! Kai! Take cover!" shouted Jarkko from behind them.

Eli followed Kai to a nearby home. Seconds later an enormous sphere, taller and wider than any of the surrounding homes, barreled into the horde of Necroborns. The sphere was gargantuan, burning with amethysts flames that whipped back and forth along the sphere's round surface. Enemies the sphere touched were instantly sucked into its transparent center.

"Sia now!" yelled Jarkko.

The sphere's explosion was staggering and deafening. The force of the explosion was so overwhelming that it tossed Eli yards behind the house he clung to. His face scraped across many rough surfaces until his body came to a halt.

"Hurry up Brassie!" yelled Kai somewhere.

Eli shook off the dizziness and quickly followed after Kai. A smoldering pathway, absent of enemies, spread out in front of them. The victory was short lived. Hundreds of Necroborns continued to pile in from the surrounding streets. Eli followed Kai back to Jarkko, who was holding Sia up by her waist.

"What happened?" asked Kai.

"Her blood energy is low."

"Why would you use such a high level ability with a novice? She clearly wasn't strong enough," said Kai.

"Shut up Kai. You have no idea what Sia is capable of."

"Whoa! Look out for this one Jarkko. This kid has got some fangs!" said Kai.

"I only went through with it because she wanted to. I told her the risks and she accepted them. For the most part she did a great job, but at what cost," said Jarkko.

"Watch over her. We got this."

"We do?" asked Kai.

"Yeah, we do. Now come on!"

Eli engaged the incoming Necroborns. Kai was quick to reach his side.

"Kai thinks it's so cute how you stick up for your little girlfriend," said Kai.

Eli bashed two Necroborns to the floor with his shield before dissolving it and dispatching them with his bow.

"It's sad that you're losing her to the Lieutenant. But then again, he has that effect on women," said Kai.

Eli stopped and stared at Kai, who threw Agent Slate at an incoming Necroborn before stabbing one behind him.

"What did you say?"

"Kai! Brassie! Pull back we have the civilians. To the main gates!" yelled Jarkko.

Kai headed for Jarkko, and after eliminating two Necroborns, Eli went to follow. A tremor vibrated the ground beneath his feet causing him to stop.

"Gonzaga take-down!" snarled a voice from behind.

◆◆◆

Eli grabbed Sia and headed for the retreating crowd—including their comrades.

"Let me go Eli!" yelled Sia. She continued to pelt the incoming Necroborns and General Rorik with an endless barrage of explosive orbs.

"Come on! The others are retreating. We won! Don't worry about him."

She stopped attacking and turned for the crowd. He quickly caught up to her and studied her face, as they ran behind the rest of their comrades who were trailing after the civilians.

"That Rorik knows where my brother is Eli. He knows," she said. Her blood energy level showed no sign of recovering judging by her slow pace.

Eli found himself slowing down so she could catch up, but he couldn't help the burst of energy and will to leave the city he held. "We'll find him. I promise."

"Brassie!" yelled Kai.

Eli quickly ran to catch up with the Operative. Before he could respond, Kai was quick to continue.

"Where is Bray?"

"I don't know. I haven't seen him in a while."

Sia screamed. Turning around, Eli caught her behind a field of black transparent energy; her fist banging against its magical surface.

"Sia!" He ran to her, shoulder-charging the barrier. The barrier warmed and then retaliated, sending Eli spiraling backwards. He returned to his feet and began pelting the barrier with projectiles before diving to avoid his redirected attack. He ran to the barrier and put his hands where her hands were. "We're going to get you out of here okay? I promise."

She shook her head after drying a stray tear. The ground continued to rumble as General Rorik and his army of Necroborns continued to close the distance between them and Sia.

"Eli my B.L. is low. Please get me out of here," she cried.

"Kai! Help!"

Slate was the first to show, slithering up to Eli's foot with his head tilted up at Eli. Kai joined a second or so later.

"She's trapped. Help me get her out."

Kai walked up to the barrier and rested his hand on its surface. Sia turned her back to them and examined the incoming enemies who now surrounded her.

"This is beyond Kai's abilities. We need Jarkko," said Kai turning around and running back towards the civilians—Slate hot on his heels.

Eli turned back around to Sia and locked eyes with her.

"Please find my brother and take care of him. No matter how angry you are with me, please don't let him suffer," she said.

He felt as if she slapped him. "Sia I—."

Rorik grabbed the back of her hair and took her from him.

"No!" he screamed banging his fists against the barrier. Each blow to the barrier retaliated on him, and soon blood fell from his face and arms.

The Necroborns surrounded her while Rorik held her by her hair.

Raising her shivering face to his eyes, Rorik licked the side of her face—his twin black tongue ravaging the surface of her soft skin. "Tasty!"

Tears fell from Sia's eyes as her hands clung to the hair from which she hung imprisoned from. A figure leaped behind Rorik, smashing into him, and sending him flying into the barrier. The collision scared Eli, causing him to retreat. Looking through the barrier, he nearly cried at the sight. Was his eyes playing tricks on him?

Marius grabbed Sia and put her behind him so they were back-to-back. "Don't leave my side!"

Rorik returned to his feet and slowly approached Marius and Sia. "Ahh the silent assailant. It has been too long."

"You've lost General. No one has to die so let us go," said Marius summoning a blade.

"Destroy them!" commanded Rorik.

A shadow crept over the sun, shrouding everything in darkness for a few seconds before the earthquake. Eli rolled across the floor until he collided into what felt like legs.

Kai loomed over him. "Having fun are we?"

Eli jumped to his feet and set eyes on Jarkko.

"What's going on?" asked Jarkko.

"My dad and Sia are trapped behind this barrier and I can't get through. Can you help?"

The three of them ran to the barrier and froze at the colossal troll that swung its mighty mallet at the scurrying Necroborns. A figured leaped down from the troll's shoulders with the silhouette of two blades outstretched in its hands. Marius went into a swinging frenzy, eliminating vast numbers of Necroborns with ease while a circle of spinning daggers circled him—launching at any enemy that got too close. Chaos broke out everywhere.

"This will most likely drain most of my blood energy. I will be deliciously defensive," said Jarkko in a matter-of-fact tone.

Kai stepped forward with a stern gaze. "No one will touch you." Both of them nodded. Jarkko clasped his hands together and closed his eyes.

I guess I'm on my own if Kai will be defending Jarkko.

Eli looked to Marius, who was dancing around Sia in an endless fury of sword strikes. Necroborns continued to fall at Marius' hand while Sia clung to his side. The troll continued its rampage, taking out any who were unlucky enough to cross its path.

Jarkko bellowed. The sound of shattering glass erupted everywhere causing the battling enemies to stop and turn towards the commotion.

Eli ran into battle. "Dad!" He began with a blunt force attack, concentrating on only Necroborns so no comrades would be harmed. Immediately after launching the axes, he followed up with two arrow barrages to clear out the Necroborns that had begun to close in on him. A massive figure leaped fell from the sky, throwing Eli off balance and plummeting to the floor.

"My name is General Rorik Gonzaga of The Immortal Lands. Your end is now maggot!" Rorik lunged.

Eli rolled to the side to avoid the General's mighty axe. Summoning a sword and shield, Eli took on the General. The General swung his axe making Eli hold up his shield to defend the attack. The impact was massive, causing Eli's shield to instantly dissolve upon contact—and sending tremendous pain down his arm. He fell to his knees in pain and a shadow shrouded him. Rorik raised his axe above his head. A foot stepped on Eli's limp shoulder and soon a new contender entered the battle.

Jude faced the General as he wrapped his legs around Rorik's neck, before pushing away, causing the General to stagger a few feet back. Jude wasted no time. He sprinted at the General, ducking under Rorik's axe and unleashing a series of punches to the General's abdomen and back. Rorik swung in all directions as Jude danced around Rorik's blind spots, his hand-to-hand combat pummeling Rorik from all sides.

Eli ran passed the squabble and to his dad and Sia. Marius was in a fast-paced sword fight with a stranger, who was countering every one of Marius' attacks with one of his own.

"You have the audacity to raise your sword to your King!" yelled Ivor.

Marius summoned daggers behind the King that attacked. Ivor immediately spun around and sliced the daggers with his sword before they could make contact. When the King turned back to Marius, Marius punched him. The Kind tumbled across the lifeless Necroborns and came to a stop. Marius ran to the King's body and raised his sword.

"Kill him," said the King in a calm tone.

A figure leaped down from one of the neighboring rooftops, coming down with a sharp punch that Marius was barely able to evade. Eli's eyes widened.

Eli turned back towards Jude, who was still engaging Rorik. "Jude help!"

Jude's head darted up. He sidestepped Rorik's attack and then sweep-kicked the General, sending him tumbling to the ground.

"It's Fox!"

Eli ran towards the battle and soon Jude was at his side. The two of them ran side-by-side using their crisscross method to confuse and eliminate enemies in their path.

"Eli!" yelled Jude.

Eli turned around to find Jude in a headlock by an enemy. Eli summoned an axe behind the enemy and attacked. The enemy released Jude in a howl; allowing his comrade to rip the axe from the enemy's back and eliminate him.

A Necroborn knocked Eli to the ground. The creature soon tumbled as Jude tackled him to the ground. Eli got up to the sight of Marius going toe-to-toe with King Ivor and Fox simultaneously. The troll intervened. Fox gave a few quick punches to the troll's legs and soon the behemoth fell, crushing the Necroborns it fell on. Marius, Ivor and Fox all rolled out of the way and back into combat. The troll shrunk and soon Jude's professor took its place. Lynn laid motionless, her eyes looking around frantically.

Fox's paralysis!

"Jude my dad is in trouble!"

Jude swept the legs of the Necroborn causing it to tumble to the ground. "Marius is here?"

"Help me!"

Jude stuck out his hand. "Vials!"

Eli looked down at his waist and realized he was still wearing Jude's utility belt. No wonder his comrade was using nothing but hand-to-hand combat instead of his transformations.

"Eli now!"

Eli unbuckled the belt and tossed it at Jude, who immediately buckled it around his waist and snatched a vial. The raven appeared and amplified instantaneously before Eli climbed on Jude's back and held on tight. Eli stood atop Jude's back and surveyed the area for Sia. He only saw hundreds of Necroborns pelting them with arrows; as well as Marius, Fox and Ivor who were still engaged in battle.

Jude swerved and evaded the arrows that attacked them, however, Eli could tell the raven was having difficulty. There were hundreds of Necroborns below with bows, and all of them were focusing their attention on the two of them.

Eli summoned his bow and counterattacked. His accuracy was precise, exploding the heads of every enemy he targeted. They were almost to Marius—just a few more feet. Then he saw it. A Necroborn loaded an arrow in its bow with a bomb attached. Eli panicked. He raised his bow and continued to shoot at the Necroborn while Jude continued to dodge the other arrows. Eli couldn't hit him. He kept firing but the Necroborn aimed and fired.

"Jude!" Eli looked down at the raven he rode atop, scrambling for the right words. "Look out!"

Eli's face scorched and his eyes closed as he felt his body fall from the sky. His heart beat violently in his ears and the pain that came was nearly outmatched by the nausea that rivaled it. The impact with the street was so painful, that he felt his teeth jolt in his mouth. He raised his head and saw Jude, still as stone atop their fallen enemies.

"Jude," said Eli extending his hand. He turned his head towards his dad and caught glimpse of Marius overpowering Ivor after kicking Fox away. Ivor and Marius' sword lock gave way as the King fell to the floor. Marius raised his sword to strike and instantly Fox was in front of him.

Fox raised his hands. "Playtime is over!" Fox's palm attacked Marius' chest directly.

"No!"

Marius dropped his sword while his body wobbled back and forth. He fell to his knees and instantly locked eyes with Eli amidst the crowd of enemies.

"Eli! Eli! Eli!" echoed Marius' voice in Eli's head.

Eli's hands grabbed his ears and closed his eyes in reaction to the loudness of his father's voice. Eli didn't understand. The S-3s were useless. How was he hearing his father?

"Eli! Eli! Eli! Run son!"

Eli opened his eyes and locked eyes with Marius just in time to catch him take a knee to the face.

"No!" Eli ran for his dad. Tears fell as fast as his stride. He barreled through the incoming Necroborns, ignoring their petty danger.

Enemies fell in all directions when they came in contact with him. Fox loomed over Marius' body and soon the King joined him. Eli leaped over a body and continued his sprint. He hit a wall and instantly fell backwards. The barrier was back.

"No!" he yelled over and over again as he punched the barrier with his bleeding fists.

The barrier continued to assault him with every punch he took but he didn't care. Fox turned around slowly and locked eyes with him for the first time. A smile slowly spread across Fox's face as he raised his hand to give a delicate wave.

"No!" Eli continued to pummel the barrier.

"Eli?" said a voice next to him.

The voice sounded like Sia, but Eli didn't care. He summoned a blade and continued to strike the barrier continuously, ignoring the blood that began to fall from his tunic and face. The King clasped his hands behind his back and started towards a nearby home. Fox soon followed, dragging Marius by the pant leg of his combat pants as if he was a satchel of garbage. The sight infuriated Eli beyond belief. Then Marius' eyes moved.

RISE

"But he's alive!" Eli glared at Anya, Conall and Priya in hopes that they would see that he would not take no for an answer.

The fire cracked underneath the moon's watchful gaze. The night air was buzzing with the light conversation of the Kismet people. After leaving the city against his will, thanks to Kai, Eli followed his comrades to the familiar shack that Eli was beginning to call home. The ponds and surrounding grassland were covered with the Kismet people. The shack was nothing short of packed, and the description of silence no longer applied to the marshlands.

During their mission, Conall and Anya had liberated most of the food from the city, and stashed it in one spot outside of the city gates. After replenishing his blood energy, Jarkko was able to teleport the food to the marshes, where he was now distributing it the masses of people—along with Kai, Sia and Tristan. Eli asked for a private meeting with Conall, Anya and Priya in hopes of persuading them to help support a covert mission to enter the city to rescue Marius.

"You're such a little daddy's boy," smirked Priya.

"That was uncalled for Commander," replied Pang.

"I beg your pardon Quarrels," started Priya with an icy glare. "Did you say something?"

Is he defending me?

"Commander, all I'm saying is insulting him is probably not the best way to respond right now. I mean that is his dad, what do you expect?"

"I agree," said Jude bandaging his shoulder. "Our mission was to save all of our people. Even if one person is left in that prison of a city, we failed."

"No one cares what you agree with Bray. All of you are barely Agents! You know nothing," snapped Priya.

Anya rose to her feet and walked over to Eli. He looked up into her eyes with disappointment and pain. How many times did he put his life on the line for these people? How many times did he sacrifice being with his dad over some stupid mission that had no way of benefiting him.

"I want to be the first to tell you that I appreciate everything you've done for us. All of us. But the answer is no," said Anya closing her eyes. After the rare softness she was displaying, he was surprised to hear her decline his request. "We were all lucky to make it out of that city alive. We cannot risk the loss of any of our Agents." Anya shot a glare towards Priya. "No matter how young they are. Even if you made it out alive, how can we be sure you won't be followed back here? You would put all of our people in danger." She strolled back to her seat between Conall and Priya and returned to her seat. "Your request is declined."

"You've got to be kidding me! I hate you people! Do you hear me! I hate you!"

Priya was quick to jump to her feet. She looked like she was ready for more action and Eli was ready to give it to her.

"Sit down Agent Brassie," said Jude with a shake of his head.

Everyone's gaze, including Eli's, turned to Jude.

"What did you say?"

"I said sit down!" yelled Jude. "You're making Pang, Sia and I look bad."

I know my dad isn't your dad. But at least he was nice to you Jude. He never had anything bad to say about, only good things, and you're turning your back on him. Coward!

Eli sat in his seat and folded his arms. If no one would help him, he would rescue his dad on his own—no matter what the cost. Eli remained silent for the rest of the meeting. Anya took the opportunity to inform them that Jarkko would need Sia's help to transport the Kismet people. Due to the distance, the two Magi would only be able to bring no more than twenty at a time, which meant the process would be both time-consuming and strenuous. After Sia returned from aiding their people, Anya gave the order for everyone; especially Sia and Jarkko, to get some sleep immediately. The two Magi would need all of their strength for tomorrow's objective; and the others would need to regain their strength just in case a counterattack was necessary if the group was discovered.

"Both Lieutenant Titus and myself have been in contact with Geminate for a while now. They are expecting our arrival and have made the necessary preparations," said Anya rising from her seat. She retreated to a secluded rock where she propped herself up and closed her eyes.

"You're all dismissed," said Conall.

Everyone rose and began to depart. As soon as Sia rose from her seat, the Lieutenant's hand went up. "Wait!"

Eli turned around hopefully. He thought perhaps maybe the Lieutenant changed his mind.

"I have a surprise for you Agent Wyatt," said Conall with the first complete smile that Eli had ever seen from the Lieutenant. He turned his attention to a tree behind him. "You can come out now."

Sia collapsed to the floor crying hysterically. Her shoulders rose and fell abruptly and her emotion was so heavy, that Eli felt his emotions awakening as well.

"Don't cry," said Mik attempting to run to his sister. His run turned into a limp that made Eli's brows curl.

"Run to him," whispered Sia to no clear person. "Run to him you stupid girl! Run!" She kicked up from the ground and scooped Mik up in her arms. She went into a kissing frenzy while swinging him around. "Mik I thought I lost you. I thought you were gone. I love you Mik. I love you little brother." She set him down and cupped his face with her hand. "How is this possible?"

Mik looked up at Conall, who nodded with a small smile.

"It was dad," said Mik.

Eli's legs buckled slightly but he quickly recovered.

Mr. Wyatt...

Sia looked up at Conall. "What does he mean it was dad?"

"Wyatt had him locked in one of the city's underground prisons, guarded by his band of mercenaries," said Conall rustling his own hair. "The General and I were able to infiltrate the prison, eliminate the hostiles and rescue hundreds of civilians—including your brother."

Sia wrapped her arms around Conall. "Thank you! Thank you so much for saving my little brother Conall." She released him instantly and looked at him with wide eyes. "Apologies. What I meant to say was Lieutenant, thank you for saving Mik. Your kindness is greatly appreciated."

The Lieutenant stared down at her. Eli was sure the Lieutenant would punish Sia for touching him and addressing him by anything other than 'Lieutenant.'

"The General's orders still stand. Get some rest and we will begin first thing in the morning," said Conall. He walked to the shack, where Jarkko, Tristan and Kai stood atop its rooftop staring.

Eli looked back towards Mik and Sia and wondered why he wasn't showing happiness for Mik's safe return. He turned for the lone island that marked his heart with the scar of Sia's departure from his life.

Trudging through the water and up the moist soil, he stared at the lone tree that slouched close the soil's surface. The leaves were caked with water droplets and moss began to grow around its trunk. Eli thought about how happy Sia was to see

Mik, and vice-versa. While Eli was happy that the brother and sister were reunited once more, he also hated them for it as well. How could they parade their reunion in front of him knowing that Marius was behind enemy lines, helpless to defend himself. He felt nauseous and angry. Taking a deep breath he realized if he was going to save Marius, now would be the time; and if he failed in his mission, at least he would die at his father's side in the one place that was his childhood home.

◆◆◆

Jude knew Pang would follow him, even without consent. Pang's nonchalant antics of examining nature and striking up small conversation with Sia and Mik made Jude smile on the inside. Trudging through the murky ponds, Jude finally spotted the silhouette of a lone figure kneeling on a small island. Jude made no attempt to mask his footsteps or hide his presence. None of it was necessary, and above all, it was counterproductive to his cause.

"Got a second?"

"You're dead to me," said Eli turning his back to Jude. He crossed his arms and remained silent, as if hopeful that Jude would take the hint and leave.

So now I'm dead to you. That's fine I can be that, but not tonight.

"The others are finally resting. Now would be the time to leave if we are to get back before dawn."

Eli turned around glaring. "I don't know why you would think I would go anywhere with you. Coward!"

"Is now a bad time?" said Pang. He looked from Jude to Eli and then back to Jude. Eventually he took a stance at Jude's side, picked up a boulder three times his size and started lifting it in an infinite cycle.

"Eli we plan on helping you save our dad."

Eli's face scrunched up. "Our dad?' He's my dad not yours, and why would you want to help me. I make you look bad remember?"

Jude looked to Pang for assistance, but he continued to lift the boulder over-and-over. Jude returned his attention to Eli, knowing this was a battle he was alone in. "You weren't being smart back there. I had to say what I said. You're display was telling the three of them that no matter what they said, you would disobey their orders. They would have imprisoned you if not killed you if they thought you were going to jeopardize the mission. Me intervening told them that we all disagreed with your decision, which hopefully sent the message that they didn't need to worry about you. I could tell by the Commander's wondering eyes, that she figured you would only go through with it if you had help—i.e. us. And no matter what you say, Marius is my dad too."

Eli remained silent. The silence would have continued if it weren't for the sound of a landslide that jolted them when Pang dropped the boulder.

"So are we leaving or what?" asked Pang appearing annoyed.

Eli stared at Pang, suspicion heavy in his eyes. "Why do you want to help me? I hate you so bad it isn't even funny and I'm sure you feel the same. Why would you help me?"

"Well if you're going to get all crazy about it then never mind," said Pang turning for the shack.

"Pang..."

"Okay okay," said Pang turning back around. "I just happen to agree that family is number one. Plus I haven't sated my bloodlust for Necroborn blood yet."

"Just to let you know I'm not leaving that city without my dad," said Eli.

"Good, because neither am I." Jude refused to flinch underneath Eli's gaze. He needed his comrade to realize how serious he was about the mission.

"Okay then," said Eli dropping his folded arms. "Let's go."

"Not without me," said a voice from behind a dying a tree.

Everyone's face turned towards the direction of the voice. Jude recognized it but needed confirmation before he smiled. Sia finally stepped out from behind the tree but was not alone. Mik clung to her hand as the brother and sister joined the group.

"It's nice to see you again Eli," said Mik with a small pout.

Eli took a beat before responding. "You too—Mik."

"We have to leave now if we plan on making it back in time," said Sia.

"Are you sure you want to do this? If we get caught it will be more than honor we would lose. We would be pegged a traitor for life and would be executed. I don't know if you want to take that kind of risk. You just got your brother back. We would understand if you wanted to sit this one out."

Sia looked down into Mik's eyes and he returned her gaze. She bent down slowly and kissed him on the forehead and gave him a hug. "Mik, this is something I need to do. Please under—."

"Bring Mr. Marius back okay. He is the reason I'm still here. He snuck me food and water when I was in that place. I never got a chance to thank him," said Mik.

"Sia you're blood energy is expected to be at full capacity tomorrow. You are vital in tomorrow's plan. If you come back tired or depleted of blood energy, they will know."

"My mind is made-up," she said releasing her hand from Mik's. "But I won't be able to teleport us. Jarkko hasn't taught me how to do that yet, and I doubt I could do it on my own."

"Fine. Let's go," said Eli. He turned for the city without so much as a glance to see if anyone was following.

Sia gave Mik a kiss on the head before departing, while Pang gave a wink to the boy. Jude patted Mik on the shoulder and turned to leave but was stopped by a lone hand. He looked down to find Mik grabbing his wrist. His big round eyes shimmered back at him.

"Please take care of my sister Mr. Prodigy. She's all I have. Please take care of Eli too, he's my big brother," said Mik.

The boy's words were heartfelt and heartbreaking. Jude had to fight off the pending tears.

Dropping down to his knees, Jude stared into Mik's glossy eyes. "You are a brave young man. I cannot imagine what you must have gone through in that city. Just know that Sia loves you so much, and I'm sure Eli does too. I will do everything I can to bring them both back to you safely."

Mik's small arms flung around Jude's neck. Jude hugged the boy back but quickly separated himself, knowing time was not on their side. After leaving Mik, Jude quickly rejoined the others. After a little under an hour the city rose up ahead of them. The cloudbank moved in concealing the moon as if in response to their arrival. The sky rumbled while musk ran through the air. Something wet fell on Jude. Looking up he noticed a small drizzle beginning to pour.

"Oh no."

"What?" asked Pang quickly.

"My mom always said rain was a bad omen, if it starts abruptly."

Mom...I miss you. Please be okay. Where ever you are.

"Sounds like liar talk to me," said Eli.

"Hey!" said Jude growing angry. "Watch your mouth. That's my mother."

Eli returned his attention to the city. Jude felt a cold hand grab his. He looked over to find Sia holding his hand.

"My mom used to tell me the same thing before she left," said Sia.

He squeezed her hand once before releasing it. Stepping to the front he turned around and looked at his comrades.

"This is a stealth mission. No one can see us or know we are here. My guess is we won't leave the city alive if we are spotted. Eli will lead us to the last spot he saw Marius. Keep your eyes and ears open."

"Copy," said Pang and Sia in unison. They both clung to the shadows of the nearby trees as they advanced on the city. Eli quickly followed.

Watching his comrades head into battle, unknowing if this would be their last, was unsettling. The sprinkle turned to rain, and soon he felt the puddles rising in his combat boots.

Dear Aegis, Pith and Rune, please protect us. Watch over us and help us deliver Marius safely from this prison that was once our home. I know I have sinned and have disappointed you in many ways, but I still love you and need you. Help us I beg you.

Thunder sounded with each step he took; and soon the four of them were one with the shadows.

◆◆◆

Eli led his comrades through the Western Hold's gates, clenching to the shadows that seemed to move independently against the houses. Sia's cloaking ability was the only reason they were able to make it passed the gates undetected. Eli wondered how they would have made it passed the gates if Sia had never elected to join them. The Western Hold was quiet and deceiving. The dead bodies had been removed and bloodstains were gone. There was no evidence of the havoc and death that was just present earlier in the day.

The four of them ran along Market Road and tucked behind an old shop resembling a house. It was the only building in the area that wasn't a shack.

"Oh my Aegis," whispered Sia. Her eyes were wide with shock.

"Shh," whispered Jude quickly.

"This is Ms. Lowell's shop—her home," said Sia.

The words hit heavy. Sia was right, this was Ms. Lowell's house that they clung to. A stream of memories descended upon Eli, making him relive them. A lone shack in the Market District shined with a small soft light in the window. Eli recognized it immediately.

"That's the house I saw Ivor and Fox bring my dad to."

"It *would* be the only house with the lights on," said Pang crossing his arms. "At least we already know someone's home."

The sound of a march crept up on them. Sia cast her cloak on the four of them, and instantly placed a lone finger over her lips. A squadron of Necroborns marched obediently behind the one Necroborn that Eli felt like he could never escape.

"Enough!" barked General Rorik. He spun around facing his motionless soldiers. "Who is your leader?"

A Necroborn stepped out firmly, separating himself from the others. "I am sir. Loak Rizear of The Immortal Lands—Shadow Region."

Rorik stared at Loak never flinching. Finally he raised a clenched fist to his chest. "Loak today you are the Commander of this attack. We have gathered the remainder of our men at the entrance to this wretched city. Six hundred men are now under your command. We have reason to believe the enemy and our slaves are still in the area. Spread out! Retrieve the slaves and kill the enemy—except for their General, Briars. Bring her to me."

After a quick salute the squadron departed, heading in the direction of the Main Gates. Rorik stayed behind, never moving from his position. Raising his grotesque nose in the air, he sniffed loudly a few times before surveying the area around him. Then he was gone, heading in the direction of the castle.

Sia waited a beat before deactivating the cloak. Eli realized that he had been holding his breath for what seemed like the entire time.

"They plan on a counterattack, and judging by the number of men they have, they might find the black site before dawn," said Jude.

"We need to go back and warn the others," said Sia.

"No! Not without my dad. Man you *would* be the one to want to leave now that you have your brother."

"How dare you! That has nothing to—," started Sia before Jude quieted them both.

"Leaving Marius is not an option, however, allowing the possible genocide of our people is also not an option," said Jude.

I'm so tired of hearing Jude donate his unwanted advice. Rescuing my dad is the only thing that matters. The only reason I allowed you to come with me is because you said it was just as important to you. Big mistake on my part.

"I'll go," said Pang rising from his squat.

"What? Go where?" asked Jude quickly.

"I'll go back to the black site and alert the General."

"No," said Jude, scratching his forehead. "If we are to go through with this, you need to be at the main gates before the enemy leaves. You will need to cause some kind of covert distraction that doesn't signal that we are here."

"I'll control some of them, turn them on their allies," said Pang with a smirk.

Eli liked this plan. "Sounds like a great plan to me."

"No, it won't work," said Jude with a deep breath. He stared off into the distance and then returned his gaze to Pang. "How long can you keep your Blood Domination active?"

"For a group that size maybe five, ten minutes," said Pang.

"What about on one person?" asked Jude quickly.

"One person? Ha! Hours," said Pang with a smirk.

"Without putting yourself in danger, how many hours exactly?" asked Jude.

"Two. Three if I'm closer to who I am controlling. The further away I am, the more difficult it is to maintain that ability," said Pang.

"Jude hurry up. Who knows what they're doing to my dad in there!"

Jude took a vial from his utility belt and opened it. "Eli cut my arm."

"What? Why do—."

"Shut up and do it!" snapped Jude.

Eli summoned a dagger, confused as to Jude's request. However, he didn't care. All that mattered was getting to that house.

"Slice the top of my forearm just enough to make it bleed," said Jude holding out his arm.

Eli did as he was told and instantly looked up at Jude when the crimson trail began to fall. No tears came from Jude's eyes but Eli was sure some were on the way.

Jude tilted his arm over the vial and dropped a few drops of his blood into the vial. Next he retrieved a small leather pouch from his utility belt and sprinkled some black powder in the vial as well. After closing the vial he shook it and then handed it to Pang. "Okay here's the plan. You are going to need to use your Blood Domination ability on Loak, the Commander of the soldiers. Inject yourself with this vial, all of it. It will transform you into a Necroborn. You will look, smell, walk and speak like a Necroborn. After securing some Necroborn armor from somewhere, you will need to fall in line with the other Necroborns. Since you say you need to be in close proximity, try and get as close to the Commander as possible."

"So what do I do to him after controlling him?" asked Pang.

"You know where the black site is, he doesn't," said Jude with a confident smile. "Lead him somewhere far away from the black site. That will give Eli, Sia and myself enough time to rescue Marius. If everything goes according to plan, it should only take us a couple of hours. At some point you are going to want to find a way to make the Commander put up camp for the night. Just make him lay down or anything you can think of to get the rest of the army to join him in retiring for the night. When everyone is sleep you slip out so that when the Commander wakes up, there is no evidence of your presence."

No one said a word. The wind began to blow the harsh rain across the shattered cobblestone streets. Small rivers began to form under their feet while their boots began to squish with every movement.

"Okay," said Pang.

"Pang, are you sure you want to do this. If they catch you I—are you sure you want to do this?" asked Sia.

Pang looked to Eli. "I hate your face."

Eli felt so caught-off-guard that he couldn't respond right away.

"I will hate your face even more if you fail to rescue your father. Don't let him down," said Pang before running off into the shadows. His body went invisible after a few steps, which confused Eli.

Eli looked to Sia and saw that her magi glare was more piercing than usual, and wondered if she had used her cloak on Pang. The cloak soon took its effect on the three of them and then they headed for the house. Crouching underneath the glowing window they all appeared to notice the same thing.

You can't see through the window.

"It's an illusion," whispered Sia.

"How do they work?" asked Jude.

"Magic is placed on an object or person to make others see what you want them to see," she replied.

"Can you get rid of it?"

Sia looked to Eli with annoyed eyes. "No, Vance never taught us how to create or dispel illusions, only how to identify them."

Eli looked to Jude and could tell he was deep in thought.

Jude's eyes looked everywhere frantically and his breathing was slow. He closed his eyes for a short while before opening them. "Okay, Sia we are going to need you to stay out here and be on surveillance. We don't know who is in there or who is planning to return. I need you to use your cloak on Eli and I, to allow us to slip in undetected. Then find a spot to hide where you have full view of the house. If you see anyone coming send us a sign."

"I'll create a small earthquake as the signal. It won't be anything too big so it doesn't raise suspicion—just a shake," she said with a wink.

"There's a chimney on top of the house," said Jude.

"What? No there isn't."

Jude gave Eli a side eye. "Yes there is, and that is our entrance."

"Whatever you say but I'm telling you there's no chimney."

Sia cast her cloak on Eli and Jude. The boys climbed slowly and quietly up the side of the house until they reached the rooftop. To Eli's disgust there was a chimney. He waited to receive the 'I told you so' grin from Jude, but hadn't received it yet.

"You're the offense I'm the Recon. I will shrink down to my arachnid form as small as I can. If there are enemies in there, they need to believe you came alone. Engage them as if you are alone. I will strike from their blind spots while they are focused on you."

"So basically you want me to do all of the work."

"Don't forget," said Jude with a glare. "You're the Weapons Master, offense is what you were born to be."

Eli ignored Jude's words and jumped down.

◆◆◆

Jude injected himself and gave-in to the transformation. After the size reduction, the chimney looked like a castle. His size made him feel vulnerable, which brought uneasiness that made him nauseous. It took him a while to crawl over the mouth of the chimney, but as soon as he made it, he jumped down.

His eight legs hammered down on the wooden floor beneath him. The house had a dingy odor to it reflecting its true shack nature. The wooden floor spread in every direction of the large room, absent of furniture, decorations or life. Jude trailed after Eli's large steps as he surveyed the room. Chains were tied to the floorboards in the corners of the room, as well as hung from the ceiling. Jude watched Eli enter what appeared to be another large room. After waiting a beat, Jude trailed after him. A loud wail so loud, that it filled Jude with the instinct to flee, filled the room. Returning to his normal form, Jude darted after Eli and froze.

Eli dragged his feet like a young child, slowly towards a figure bound to a lone chair—which stood dead center of the empty room. "Dad? Dad?" A dagger begged not to fall from the hand that Eli precariously held it from. The dagger picked at Eli's leg with every step he took—first softly then deeper with each strike.

"Dad!" screamed Eli collapsing to the floor.

Jude quickly raced to Eli's side to help his comrade up—his brother.

"Don't touch me Jude! Don't touch me!" screamed Eli.

Jude quickly released his hands from Eli's shoulders. Turning his gaze to the bound figure, Jude finally felt his own tears surfacing.

Marius sat bound to a plain wooden chair in the center of the room. His arms were bound behind his back to the chair. His armor was torn and soaked with blood. The lacerations across his face were so deep, that the white meat beneath the surface threatened to fall. His nose was broken and both his eyes were swollen shut to the point where they looked deformed. Dried blood clung to his upper and bottom lip. Just when Jude thought he saw the last of the evidence of the torture, burn marks of the third degree pillaged his neck.

Tears began to fall from Jude's eyes in endless streams.

"Daddy! Daddy!" screamed Eli over-and-over again from the floor. His cries were agonizing.

Jude knew Eli wasn't strong enough to ask the question that needed to be asked; so he took it upon himself to check. He walked closer to Marius and reached out his two fingers to check for a pulse and stopped. An overwhelming hiccup of tears controlled him. Jude threw himself back; crushed by the sight of the man he looked at as a father. He collapsed to the floor in a pool of tears that threatened to drown him.

Eli leaped to his feet and threw himself at Marius in a tight embrace. "Dad I love you. I love you dad so much. Please don't leave me. I can't lose you dad I can't. I'm not strong enough. I'm not strong enough dad." Tears muffled the rest of Eli's words. His shoulders rose and fell violently and his knees turned inwards, ready to buckle. "I'm sorry dad. I'm so sorry. I tried to save you I did. I let you down. I *always* let you down. Always!"

Jude wiped his tears and silenced the hiccups of tears that showed no signs of leaving. Returning to his feet, he walked over to Marius and checked for a pulse once more.

Nothing.

Eli looked up at Jude with the heaviest of tears and hope in his eyes. Jude shook his head.

"Dad! Why dad why? Why would you leave me? I need you dad. I'll give you anything you want, anything! Just please come back to me dad."

"Give me a blade Eli."

Eli looked up into Jude's eyes for a few seconds and then summoned a sword. He slowly gave it Jude and then returned to hugging his dad.

Jude severed the chains that bound Marius to the chair. "Come on Eli, it's time for dad to go home."

Jude helped Eli carry Marius from his prison. Marius' armor squished with blood. While helping to hold Marius with one arm, Jude used the other to grab the front door.

"Looks like he had a good time," said a voice behind them.

Jude and Eli turned around to find Fox smiling at them—arms crossed.

"I will kill you!" screamed Eli releasing his dad and tackling Fox to the floor. He pummeled Fox's face in a violent rage as each of his punches scored a direct hit.

Jude set Marius down and went to Eli's aid. Both boys were hurled back towards the door from which they had attempted to flee. Shaking off the dizziness, Jude rested his eyes on a hooded figure, dressed in an all white body suit and matching cape. Her hand remained extended, and Jude concluded instantly that she was the Magi responsible.

A soft applause approached from the shadows. A shine glistened in the darkness. King Ivorious descended upon them.

"The Prodigy of Pith graces me with his presence once again," said the King before turning his attention to Eli. "And you brought the dog."

"You die now!" yelled Eli rising to his feet and charging. Ivor quickly went into a fighting stance.

Jude leaped to his feet in an attempt to stop Eli. Fox and the cloaked figure responded with a ready stance. Then nothing.

"Ah! The chance card. Today, fate is your ally."

The entire room seemed to freeze, and soon a familiar figure rose from the floor beneath them.

Aiso's black eyes released a sparkle. "Fate will see you soon." Aiso remained hovering above the floor. Fox, Ivor and the cloaked Magi remained frozen.

"Now's our chance!" yelled Eli running towards Fox before being hurled back by what appeared to be an invisible wall.

"The deal was for fate to help you escape—not to kill," said Aiso retaining his position. "Last chance, take your dead and leave and tonight will be nothing more than a forgotten dream."

Jude nodded to Aiso and then returned to Marius. "Eli help me."

Eli glared at Aiso. "How can fate protect the evil and kill the innocent?"

Aiso recoiled for the first time at Eli's words. "Fate is not good. Fate is not evil. Fate is fate."

Eli shook his head before turning his back to Aiso. Grabbing Marius' other arm, the two boys opened the door and exited.

Just as he turned around to close the door, Jude took one last look at Aiso. "Thank you Aiso."

Aiso's body turned to shadows before dissolving.

"No, thank you Mr. Bray. I look forward to our meeting," said a loud echo.

Jude closed the door.

"Sia?" called Eli in a whisper.

Sia emerged from a corner alley appearing unfazed. She raced to the boys with wide eyes. "Oh my Aegis! Oh my Aegis! Marius! Marius! Is he okay? What happened?"

"What do you mean what happened? Where were you!" yelled Eli. "Jude and I were ambushed by like three people!"

Sia recoiled and then looked at Jude. "How? I swear I kept watch and I didn't hear or see anything."

"And people like to tell me that I have insufficient skills," said Eli.

Sia's face turned red. Jude could see the pending rage, and knew she was involved in an inner struggled to remain clam.

"He didn't make it Sia. Please, help us take him home."

Sia looked at Jude and released a tear. She gave one nod before the three of them vanished into the invisibility and escaped into the night.

FINAL WORDS

The brutal rain finally began to subside, and took with it the screaming wind. Eli couldn't care less about the will of the weather. The sky could rain with molten lava and the oxygen could vanish for all he cared. The tall wet grass, which rustled with every step he took, began to take its toll on Eli's patience. Finding dry brush and branches was even more difficult with all the humidity. When he returned to their campsite, he was surprised to see Pang staring back at him.

"How did you get back so quick?"

"The Necroborns have a much faster pace than you and I. They cover double the distance than was originally planned. Luckily they also get tired faster with all that muscle they parade around. It allowed me to leave their camp quicker," said Pang never flinching.

"Well that's good."

"So, is that him?" asked Pang with a nod towards Marius' body.

Eli turned his back to Pang and retreated to Marius' body. He returned to putting dry brush and twigs at the base of the altar he had built for him. The sound of crunching grass grew louder with each second, and soon Pang was upon him. He picked up a few branches and began to place them at the base of Marius' grave.

"Look I got this. I don't need your help."

"That's a relief," said Pang rising and leaving quickly.

Eli was surprised at Pang's attempt to show support, but Eli needed to be alone with his dad. Jude and Sia both had left temporarily but promised they would return as soon as possible.

Eli didn't expect Pang to be back. Solitude was his friend right now and that's how he wanted it to stay. He needed time. Time to grieve and time to understand. The loss of his mother was the saddest moment of his life. He cried for too many months to count. At least after his mother's death, Eli had Marius for comfort—and Jude. Now he had another horrendous moment to add to his memory.

"We're back," said a soft voice.

Eli turned around to find Sia and Mik standing before him. Mik's eyes shined in the moonlight. His little feet barreled towards Eli before Mik threw his arms around Eli's neck.

"I'm sorry Eli for the loss," said Mik.

Sia approached them both. "It's 'I'm sorry for *your* loss' little brother."

Eli said nothing to Mik's words. He unhinged himself from their embrace and rustled Mik's hair.

"I apologize for my tardiness," said Jude walking slowly towards the group. "I guess I'm just not as fast as I used to be," said Jude. His eyes shimmered as well, but his nose was also red and his hair messy.

"Well, let's get this started before we're all deemed traitors and have to kill everybody," said Pang joining the group.

◆◆◆

Jude looked down into the four sets of eyes that stared back at him. They were inquisitive and intimidating. *Eli should have been the first one up here* thought Jude. His comrade declined speaking during the ceremony, saying his presence should be enough to show his love and support for Marius' passing. The pain in Jude's heart was overwhelming. The loss of his real father was a crippling experience at such an early age. The loss of his mother was traumatizing passed the point of no return. Lastly, Marius' death would prove to be as painful as the loss of yet another parent. Marius had always been there for Jude like a second father. His kindness, unconditional love and stability were three things that Jude could not picture himself growing up without. Pang cleared his throat and passed Jude a bored stare. Jude wasn't in the mood for Pang's rude behavior today—definitely not today.

"It's not traditional for anyone to speak at a funeral ceremony for one of our own. Even though our people believe that the gods find it dishonorable to take the attention away from those who have passed, I believe that when someone has touched your life in such a special way, tradition can be ignored." Jude looked down at Marius' still body and closed eyes. Soon he felt his emotions creeping up on him. "Marius has been in my life for as long as I can remember. Whether it be ups or downs Marius has always had a special way of making you smile and making you feel safe. When I lost my dad, I was beyond crushed and thought I would have to go through this cruel life without a father. Well, I was wrong. Marius was right there by my side showing me love, support and a way out of the darkness. My mother used to always tell me that naturally kind people are a rare find, a treasure beneath the ocean. Marius wasn't just a treasure, he was *the* treasure. One thing that I remember him always telling me was, 'you may not be my son, but you're *my* son.' At the time it sounded so simple—a general and simple arrangement of words within a sentence that brought a smile to my face. However, now that I replay those words in my head over-and-over again, I realize how much those words mean to me."

Eli shuffled on the rock he sat on, which broke Jude out of his concentration. Eli looked annoyed but hurt at the same time. His crossed arms gave the message of impatience and his scrunched lips gave the impression of disagreement.

"Marius may not have been my father, but he was my dad," continued Jude. "And neither heaven nor hell can separate family." Jude turned his attention towards Marius. "Marius, I love you so much. You have helped me get through so many dark times and have been a part of so many good times. I know heaven is the only place where your soul belongs and where it will go. May the angels and gods appreciate the love and good spirit that is Marius Brassie, the way I have for my entire love. Go with the gods dad. I love you."

With his last words, Jude stepped down from the small hill that overlooked Marius's body. He sat cross-legged on the grass at the base of the branches and twigs that Marius laid on. No feet sounded close-by. No one took control of the hill that Jude once stood on. No one had any final words for Marius—not even his son.

"Marius was always really nice to me," said a small voice.

Mik stoop atop the small hill with his hands buried deep in his pockets—his shoulders nearly touching his ears. "My dad was mean to me—a lot. He used to always say, 'Mik you're such an idiot' or 'Mik how did I end up with such a worthless poor excuse for a son like you.' He also used to hit me—a lot. Each time he hit me hurt worse than the last. He would have hit me more if it wasn't for my big sister." Mik's smile brought a tear down his face that matched his sister's. "Marius was different. Marius loved to teach me stuff and loved having me around. He told me I should never be ashamed of who I am because we are born to be who we are supposed to be. He told me I should be proud to be an Erudite—and I am. Marius was my dad too." Mik started shivering as more tears fell down his face with no signs of stopping. "And I miss him so much." Mik buried his face in his hands while his shoulders rose and fell with each tear he shed.

Sia quickly rose from her seat and joined her brother atop the hill. She cradled him in her arms, allowing him to hug her tight. She kissed him on the top of his head a few times before wrapping her arm around his shoulders and turning her gaze towards Marius.

"Marius had a way of making you feel special, even if it's your first time meeting him. I remember my first time meeting him was *the* most comfortable introduction I had ever experienced," said Sia cracking a small smile. "His smile is a blessing in and of itself. His kindness, like Jude said, is a treasure. It's rare to meet someone who is so full of love and compassion. With so much evil in this world, it is so easy to fall victim to the bitter, selfish, wrathful and deceitful side that is evil. I have seen that evil. I have *lived* with that evil. I thought I would never trust anyone ever again. Marius changed that. His kindness showed me that there are still good people in this world." Her gaze briefly washed over Jude before returning to Marius. "He also showed me how we are supposed to be there for one another, even those who we don't know yet. Mik and I are perfect examples of that. Marius was a gift to this world, an angel from the heavens reincarnated for the rest of us to witness his love. The world has turned darker with the absence of his light. Thank you Marius, for everything. You will be missed."

Minutes went by like seconds after Sia and Mik took their seats in a humble embrace. Jude did not expect Pang to have anything to say since he didn't know Marius and since he was Pang. Jude did however hope that Eli would find the will to say something to his dad before it was too late.

"I was able to secure this from the inner forest at the border of our city," said Jude turning around. He held up the cherry blossom branch he had been holding close since his return. "It wasn't easy to get, but it was worth it." He placed the branch, with its two pink petals, in Marius' hands and stepped back giving Sia a nod.

The inferno roared as soon as it left Sia's hands, engulfing Marius' body in dancing flames. His face was still, along with his body, amidst the chaos that danced around him. Jude knew that this would be the last time he would see Marius—and he hated it.

Jude's tears continued to fall while the hole in his heart continued to grow. Soon Marius' body caught flame, and the essence that is Marius Brassie took to the night sky—leaving its shell, shackles and worries behind.

FAREWELL

Eli began to grow more impatient under the bright sun, which continued to shine. He always thought that the day after a storm was supposed to be filled with clouds and overcast weather. For some reason the positivity of the sun's rays brought more anger than comfort. Anya had tasked Eli, Jude and Pang with being the lookout during the teleportation of all their people. She expected a counter-attack from the Necroborns at any time. Eli laughed at her ignorance. If only she knew the army she would have had to stand against, if Eli and his comrades had not decided to disobey her orders. It was clear that Pang's solo task of leading the Necroborns astray during the failed rescue of Marius, was a complete success. No enemies had been spotted for hours, and more than half of the Kismet people had already set foot in Geminate. The thought was unnerving. Relocating to a strange new land only to beg the people there to spare some crumbs and shelter.

I'd rather take my chances alone. Maybe go visit the Eternal Springs.

"Part two is underway. Time to report in," said a voice behind him.

Eli turned around to find Tristan standing before him, a stern look upon his face.

"Fine. Whatever."

The journey back to the shack was quick. After entering, Eli realized that everyone left was waiting for him and Tristan. After taking a seat at the familiar roundtable, Eli looked around at the faces that were still left. The Occult Operatives, Eli's comrades, Anya and Conall were all in attendance. Everyone appeared exhausted except for Jude, Pang and Eli. Sia had definitely seen better days. Not only was her blood energy low, but her emotions were clearly getting the best of her. Priya informed Sia that where the teams were going next, had no room for kids—specifically Mik. Sia rebelled against the order to leave him behind in Geminate, but her rebellion was short lived. Lieutenant Titus persuaded Anya to allow Mik to stay with her to the very end; why Eli could not be sure.

"Let's make this quick since the enemy is surely advancing against us," said Priya.

"Now that all of our people are safely across the Geminate border and out of the reach of our enemy, we need to prepare our counterattack," said Anya.

"Now you're flirting with me General," said Pang.

Anya slowly closed and then opened her eyes while taking a deep breath. "Lieutenant Titus will head to Geminate to make sure the transition is smooth and error-free. "Tristan and I will continue to surveillance the Land of Kismet in order to figure out our enemy's next move, as well as dwindle down their forces."

The conversation was boring. Eli wished that the General would get to the point already. She seemed to enjoy listening to herself speak—something her and Jude had in common.

"You four will proceed with your training as originally planned," said Anya locking eyes with each of Eli's comrades separately. "Bray will be under with Priya, Wyatt with Jarkko, Brassie with Kai and Quarrels with his mentor. Will that still be possible Quarrels?"

"That is correct," said Pang folding his arms.

"The four of you shall reconvene with Lieutenant Titus immediately after your return," said Anya looking towards the Occult Ops. "You have thirty days to train them. No more."

"Thirty days? Are you testing Kai or something," said Kai with a scowl. "You do remember that Kai has the 'lost cause' to train right?"

Lost cause? Is that the way you and your idiot comrades call me behind my back? Whatever.

"Considering you are supposed to be the prodigy of your generation, I figured Mr. Brassie would be a breeze for you," said Anya with a wink.

Kai sighed. "Kai will see what he can do General. But Kai makes *no* promises. The fool didn't even know you could use aerial abilities." Kai laughed hysterically, followed by the Occult Operatives who joined him in laughter.

Eli was not in the mood to even acknowledge the Occult Ops and their humor. He couldn't picture his dad behaving like them when he was an Occult Operative. Then it hit him. Marius' smiling face flashed before him. The image was pain incarnate.

"Good luck to the four of you with your training. May fate be your ally," said Anya.

The group was dismissed and the table cleared. Sia bid a tearful farewell to Mik. Lieutenant Titus said something about him taking care of everything. Eli wished he could have heard more but Sia and Conall had closed the door before he could hear the rest. Eli and his comrades soon bid farewell, each departing down their own path. Eli with Kai, Jude with Priya, Sia with Jarkko and Pang to his mentor. Eli would have welcomed the departure if it weren't for him having to train under Kai. Exiting the shack he took a look at the setting sun, and wondered if it would look the same when he returned.

RELENTLESS

Jude's vision was filled with haze and blurs, until nothing was left but the mundane presence of his normal vision. An explosion deafened his ears before the impact sent his body flailing through the air. A tree intercepted him briefly, and then his vision was filled with nothing but grass and stray leaves. His entire body felt useless and destroyed. His spine felt like rocks tumbled down its long surface, and his head felt like half of it was on break.

"Agent Bray, it is most imperative that you develop your Optical Tactics. We cannot progress any further until you do so," said Priya.

Jude and Priya had traveled for four long and excruciating days across the marshlands and a small desert, until they came upon a secluded and serene forest that stood underneath a tall and rocky mountain. It had been two months since they had arrived, and after a few weeks, Jude began to enjoy the location. It reminded him of Kismet, even though it was lacking the familiar cloudbank, cherry blossom trees, and countless species of animals. Their training was always held on a large round green lawn, which sat underneath a large mountain that cast a shadow across half of the greenery. Jude's first lesson was endurance training followed by acrobatics in his normal form. He had felt like he had done something wrong when he saw Priya's face after the first month, but was soon comforted when she told him that she had never seen someone of his age master acrobatics already. His confidence boost was short lived when he started his eleventh lesson of visual surveillance. Priya had been working with Jude in an attempt to help advance his Optical Tactics; however after the first week, Jude began to slowly lose portions of his confidence.

"I apologize Commander. I have analyzed every angle of the ability, but I still do not know why I cannot keep it active for longer than a few minutes," said Jude releasing a long sigh.

"It's because you are only twenty young years. A Combat Specialist's Optical Tactics ability, typically does not even become attainable or develop until they are around twenty-two," said Priya.

Jude felt his brow curl above his deep breathing.

"However, according to both General Briars and Lieutenant Titus, you are an Agent that is blessed with a genius mind and prized abilities. So your age will not be a factor of your development. Do we understand each other?" said Priya with a stern gaze. Her perfectly long black hair blew softly through the light breeze that swept across the lush lawn.

"Understood Commander."

Jude closed his eyes and focused his breathing. His mind buzzed with the familiar sensation of the visual ability, but he could not figure out why it only lasted a few minutes.

"Optical Tactics!" said Jude. The white tint covered his vision, and soon his brain felt the urge to instantly calculate and analyze every detail around him.

His breathing quickened when he began to focus it on the task at hand. There were multiple hidden land mines and other traps around him, and he was positive that he could not withstand the recoil of trying to evade another explosion. His body began to shutter, and soon he realized that he had been holding his breath. Right as he was exhaling, he realized that his Optical ability was still active. He inhaled and exhaled slowly, counting the long minutes that passed. Priya appeared to be growing impatient, but he tried to ignore her mixture of glares and abnormally loud sighs.

I got it!

He injected himself with a vial and front flipped above the training field. The bow appeared instantly in his hand, allowing him to fire a handful of arrows at the six landmines and four tripwires that lay hidden around the trees and grass. Explosions ignited all around him, causing soil and grass to rain from the sky. As Jude came down on his knee, the bow dissolved just as he noticed a blank stare from Priya.

"I apologize Commander, was the use of other bloodlines prohibited?"

Priya just stared at him motionless for a short moment before she responded. "No. That will be—fine. How was that possible? I have heard the rumors, but seeing it with my own eyes is just—impossible. Nonetheless you missed one."

Jude's brows nearly fused together. He looked around and only saw the traps, which he had already disabled, trees, grass and a small flock of birds far off in the distance. Just as the birds left the branches they were sitting on, he saw it. A small tripwire tied to a tree that was hidden by a series of long branches that concealed its position. The throwing dagger appeared momentarily in his hand before he tossed it. He missed.

Wow, I really need to train harder with these other bloodlines. I can practically feel the Commander shaking her head behind me.

He summoned a bow and deactivated the trip wire.

"Excellent, and that only took you—twelve minutes," said Priya.

"My apologies Commander I—."

"I want ten laps around the mountain before we turn in for the day," she said quickly.

Jude set off immediately, fighting through the aches and pains that nagged him. The first four laps were a breeze, however once lap number six was underway, Jude began to really feel the pain. As he pushed on he heard a rumbling sound next to him. He stopped and looked behind him. A few stray rocks tumbled down the side of the mountain that he was running around. The blackness of the mountain was perplexing while its presence was haunting. Everything around Jude was caked with lush greenery except for the mountain, which darkened everything that touched it with a slate-black hue of ancient desecration. Its soil, boulders, ridges and peaks all embodied the same absence of color. A large shadow escaped into the mountain bringing a cold chill and anxiety, which replaced the aches Jude was once feeling. He continued to run, but always kept an eye on the mountain. The lush green lawn spread out in front of him. He tossed himself face first into the grass, taking in all its comfort and softness—even though it made his face itch.

"If you ever take that long again I will double your quota," said Priya standing over him. Her shadow blocked out the setting sun, which made him rub his arms for warmth.

"Copy that."

"Now we are going to practice retaining the contents of the vials you inject yourself with. By learning to allow your brain to understand, memorize, and harness the substance, you will learn to be able to transform into forms without constantly using a vial."

Whoa! That would give me room to carry a lot more vials if I do not have to carry any transformation vials.

After a nod from Priya, Jude injected himself with a vial and instantly identified its origin. He closed his eyes and began to meditate. The meditation felt natural and calming, and instantly allowed his body to pinpoint the intruding substance in his bloodstream. The substance felt cold and mobile, and traveled slowly. After slowing his breathing, Jude realized he could control the speed at which the substance traveled throughout his body; and soon discovered he could control where it went and how long it stayed there. He allowed the nature of the substance to take over, and felt the wolf form take control. It was the first time had transformed into a mountain wolf since they were not native to Kismet. Their strong legs, sharp claws, and keen eyesight, made Jude feel powerful and agile.

"Now most likely you will not be able to get it on the first try, but that is what training is for. So return to your normal form," said Priya staring at him.

Jude returned to his human form and then paused.

"Now go ahead and try and," started Priya before she stopped cold at the sight of his wolf form.

The second transformation came natural with his quick meditation.

"You got it— on the first try!" yelled Priya.

He returned to his normal form and felt himself smile briefly before he quickly extinguished it.

"What's next?" asked Jude. He felt himself even more motivated than ever to prove himself, as well as learn as much as he could while he trained under Priya.

◆ ◆ ◆

"Apologies Commander."

"No it is I who owe you an apology. They told me you were tremendously talented, but I doubted you. You're tougher than you look Bray, and that works in your favor. Come, walk with me."

Jude expected the walk back to camp to feel awkward and unbearable, but he was surprised at how comfortable he felt when Priya asked him about his first time in the Trials of Magic, Might and Lineage.

"There are many things that I would do different now."

"Such as?" asked Priya.

"I feel like I did not have an eye on every enemy like I should have. Luckily for me, all of my opponents were skilled and had their hands full, or else I could have lost."

Priya tilted her head from side-to-side slowly before responding. "My first Trials I used up all of my vials in the first ten minutes and had to use hand-to-hand combat the rest of the round. It was a disaster."

"What is my job? I am embarrassed to say that I would not know what to do in combat with a squad, unless the General or Lieutenant was with me."

"Maybe you'll understand your job more, if you understand the roles of your comrades first—I mean, you are a Combat Specialist, so it is part of your job," said Priya.

The warm view of camp made Jude's shoulders drop with relaxation. Priya took a seat on a patch of tall moist grass, and Jude soon joined her.

"Okay, so lets start with Sia Wyatt—your Magi. Her strengths are her magic abilities. Magi magic is usually very strong, once perfected, and typically can nearly fatally wound an opponent if it is a high level ability. However, her weakness for her stronger abilities is time. Magi have to concentrate a lot harder than other bloodlines, because they direct their magic from start to finish. If they launch an attack, and don't keep their concentration on it until it finds its target, the mixture of thoughts in the Magi's mind could end up redirecting it to a comrade. So as you can probably already tell, this leaves Magi vulnerable to many different types of attacks. Now some Magi have mastered their defensive abilities and should be able to keep a magic barrier around them at all times, as long as they have enough blood energy. Remember, with any bloodline, if your blood energy completely depletes, the result can be catastrophic."

"Is it possible for a Magi to put barriers around other comrades?" asked Jude.

"Yes, but it takes great skill, and I have seen Magi overexert themselves trying to shield a comrade, and paid with their lives."

I really didn't know how difficult it was to be a Magi. I always thought it was easy, like thinking of what you want and having it magically happen.

"So, lets move on to Eli Brassie—your Weapons Master," started Priya with a long sigh. Jude could not tell if the sigh was due to her dislike of the bloodline, or her dislike of Eli. "Weapons Masters tend to be an independent type when they are not managed correctly. You see, they are your main offense. They can summon any weapon they have ever held at will, and become deadly with it almost instantly. This is useful because they have a weapon for almost every type of enemy. However, I have to warn you that it is a common characteristic for them to be a little hot-headed, overly-independent and a tad bit reckless at time."

Wow, you have an Eli too?

"I have seen many Weapons Masters run off into battle in an attempt to just kill everything in sight, and have never returned. The worst ones are the ones that take everything that happens in combat personally. Let's take Kai for example. On one of our missions, we were tasked with the retrieval of a piece of intelligence that our enemy was in possession of. We were quickly able to retrieve the intelligence, causing our enemy to flee. Our mission was just to retrieve the intelligence, and not the enemy, so our mission was complete. However, before the enemy left, he bashed Kai in the face before fleeing. As we retreated for home base, Kai ran after the enemy. Our squad ended up having to chase after him, and when we found him, we discovered that the enemy Kai had been chasing had led him into an ambush. Another Weapons Master I know, used to always run off into battle as soon as we arrive. He was impossible to manage, and had been held hostage three or four times because of it," said Priya cracking her knuckles.

"How do you deal with that? How do you make them listen?"

"You can't. That's the problem. I am the Commander of my squad, and even *I* have a hard time keeping our squad focused on the objective and not necessarily the battle. After a few missions, our squad realized why *I* was the Commander, and learned to follow my orders."

Jude thought about Eli, and how he always seemed to want to do things his way and on his terms, and soon Jude felt stressed as if he was already in battle.

"What happens if your Weapons Master refuses to listen? Then what?"

"Well you have to remember that combat is complete chaos. Sometimes giving orders can be just as dangerous as not following them. You have to learn to trust that each person on your squad knows their own strengths and weaknesses, and also knows their role on the team; as well as how to effectively utilize it to raise your mission's success rate. However, when a comrade's defiance of orders starts affecting missions, and private discussions do not help to remedy the situation, you can always meet with the General and request a replacement."

That seems like such a complicated situation—both on and off the battlefield.

"So back to the Weapons Masters. They are your main offensive weapon and able to deal damage to enemies quickly. Their ability for quick offense is probably their most valued strength. They are their own main weakness."

"I am sorry Commander, but I do not follow," said Jude confused.

"A lot of the time Weapons Masters get so caught up in battle, that they are constantly summoning and extinguishing weapons at an alarming rate. Since they are a squad's primary offense, their minds are usually always focused on the battle and not their blood energy. Since they are constantly summoning weapons, their blood energy is constantly dropping and replenishing in a cycle based off of the frequency of the weapons they summon. Many Weapons Masters nearly completely drain their blood energy when in battle. That is the primary reason why Magi started carrying healing substances on their belts," said Priya.

"Okay, well what about my bloodline?"

"As a Combat Specialist, your job is always different from mission to mission. Your bloodline is born of diversity. You can use hand-to-hand combat when in close combat situations, or you can use your transformations to either help take down the most dangerous target in battle, or reduce your enemy numbers as to give your team the advantage. However..."

Jude waited for Priya to continue, but soon felt uncomfortable under her watchful eye.

"Commander?"

"*You* are sort of an anomaly. I say this because *you* have somehow learned how to do the impossible and take on abilities from other bloodlines. You basically could assume any of the roles on the squad you desired—that is if you trained your mind to use the different abilities effectively. You don't want to go to throw a dagger and miss an enemy like you did with your first Optical Tactics training. I mean, have you even given thought to your strategy as an Agent? If you plan to be stealth then what kind of stealth? If you plan to be a part of the offense then what kind of offense? If you plan to be defensive then how will you use that to eliminate your enemy? So my question to you is, who will you be?"

"Neither of those are who I am or who I will be."

"You're an Agent now, so you have no choice. You must choose," snapped Priya.

"Yes, I do Commander. I have always been one to believe in studying my opponent, preparing strategies before entering battle, knowing all strengths and weaknesses of my own abilities as well as my opponents. My Agent motto will be being one step ahead of my enemy at all times."

"You'll die trying," she said with a smirk. "No matter how smart you think you are, no one can be a step ahead of everything or everyone."

"I can and I will. Our people have viewed the role of Recon different than I see it. I plan on evolving that role to fit who I will be on the battlefield; and not even you can stop me Commander."

"Then let us both hope you are never Squad Leader because your team will suffer," said Priya shaking her head. "Another anomaly is your Agent that utilizes Blood Magic. This is definitely a first in Kismet history. Normally a squad has a second Weapons Master. I am curious as to how he will play into your missions, and what his primary role will be," said Priya clasping her hands behind her head.

Jude already had been brainstorming various uses for Pang's abilities ever since Pang won his round of the Trials of Magic, Might and Lineage. However, he did not feel that it was appropriate to share all of Pang's abilities or any of Jude's ideas, especially if he did not even know if Pang would follow any orders from anybody.

"Luckily for you," started Priya. Her words brought Jude back to their discussion, and out of his realm of *what if*. "Lieutenant Titus will be the leader of your squad. Having a Lieutenant or General as your team leader almost never happens, but it a definite blessing. When you have one of them as your leader, you won't have to worry about making any of the hard decisions, or be held responsible if your mission fails. Also, you won't have to deal with the rift raft of clashing personalities on the battlefield—that can get kind of crazy."

"Well anyone can be the Squad Leader in the Lieutenant's absence. It is not always the Combat Specialist right? So it won't necessarily be me if he has to take a leave from our squad— right?" asked Jude. He found himself feeling like Priya was setting him up for something that he could not handle. His anxiety level rose, and he felt like Priya was taking way too long to answer him.

"I am only telling you this because after training with you, I believe you will be great and I want you to be prepared. Lieutenant Titus plans to make you Squad Leader if he feels that you are qualified."

"What? Me!"

"Yes, is that a problem?"

"But why me? Why not Pang or Sia? They are just as qualified," said Jude hastily.

"Two reasons—the first is your reputation as the 'Prodigy of Pith,' or whatever they call you."

"But that is just a stupid title they gave me for doing well in the Trials. I am pretty sure that prodigies are a dime a dozen in Kismet."

"No, that's the thing—they aren't. Our people do not use the word 'prodigy' lightly. From what I hear from General Briars and Lieutenant Titus, you displayed a level of control of not only your own bloodline, but the others as well. That has never been done. It was thought to be impossible for any bloodline to use abilities outside of their own. Your display of this talent, gives our people hope."

"Hope? Hope for what?" asked Jude confused. He could not believe what he was hearing. It was as if his success with the experiment he had been working on since he was young, was now being used as a punishment to remind him of how much he made himself stand out.

"I don't know. You would have to ask them. Perhaps it could be a hope for evolution—the beginning of each bloodline coming together as one powerful mixture of the three. Or it could just be a sense of pride that their land is home to such a prize," said Priya.

"A prize? With all do respect Commander, I am no prize."

"Well, you probably will not like the second reason the Lieutenant is looking to train you to be Squad Leader. News of your battle in the Trials has reached both Praxis and Geminate.

The people there see you as an inspiration. Why? I do not know."

All of this was too much to take in. Jude felt as if everyone was building his match up to be something that it wasn't. Inspiration seemed like the wrong word to describe him. Over-analyzer and over-thinker seemed like probable candidates that he agreed with. The excitement of his training was instantly gone, and the pressure to live up to this false identity replaced it.

"Look Commander, I am flattered by the kind words. Anyone else would be lucky and ecstatic to hear such words and be given such an amazing opportunity. However, I am not an inspiration—or some sign of evolution. I am just a young man that over-prepares, thinks ahead and tries my best. There are countless Agents and Operatives that are stronger, more intelligent and more deserving of such an opportunity. I have always wanted to become an Operative, so nothing will stop me from working hard and trying my best. If the Lieutenant really wants me to be Squad Leader, then I will do my best to live up to his expectations. However, I hope that he gives Sia and Pang a shot because they are highly-skilled and just as capable."

"Hmm not arrogant or power hungry. You will make a fine Squad Leader—that is, if you survive my training and your first missions," said Priya with a smirk.

This is pointless. No matter what I say, people don't realize that calling me some prodigy and placing some futuristic hopes of evolution is not the best way of congratulating someone. I am just so confused as to how one successful experiment can deem me some kind of mastermind in a world that seems almost desperate to be rid of what they come to be so proud of.

TARRAGON MOUNTAIN

He was surrounded. Thousands of Agents circled him on all sides while Sia, Pang and Eli lay bound and helpless at his feet. Jude reached for his belt and realized it was gone. Transformations were not an option and time was running out. A few Agents attacked with bows while the others ran in with various blunt weapons in their hands. Jude back flipped and then launched himself above the threat of the arrows. He came down on the shoulders of an attacking Agent, using the height to deliver an instant death to the heads of the surrounding Agents. Jude rolled across the floor after another Agent tackled him. Enemies attacked from all sides slicing, punching, kicking and firing arrows.

There are too many. I can't win.

"What are you doing?" yelled Priya from somewhere in the distance. "I have spent the last week teaching you every fatal pressure point of the human body and still you struggle against your foe. Eliminate them! Bring your enemy to his knees!"

Two Agents went on the offense. One blade opened Jude's side, while the other was a direct hit to his leg, bringing him to his knees. The Agents kept coming from all sides relentlessly.

"On your feet you weakling!" yelled Priya.

An arrow pierced the air and hit Jude with a direct hit, pinning him to the floor beneath him. His vision faltered and his stomach swayed.

"I'm done here. You're not the Agent I thought you were," said Priya. Her voice sounded further away. "At least you can have the honor to die in combat. Goodbye Bray."

Warm liquid fell down the side of Jude's face. He couldn't tell whether it was blood or tears since both had been present since the battle had begun. He tore the arrow out of his shoulder and rose to his feet. The Agents clanked their swords against their shields. They were taunting him.

"I am the Prodigy of Pith, and I *will not* be defeated."

An Agent raised his sword exposing his chest. A quick punch to the lung pressure point caused the Agent to lose his breath. Jude ended him with a vertical kick to his temples before leaping over three attacking Agents behind him. The three Agents lost balance and continued to stumble forward, giving Jude enough time to stun the three of them with a quick attack to their kidneys.

The Agents kept coming and so did Jude. He could see the weak points of every enemy without his Optical Tactics activated. Piles of bodies began to form at his feet. The more enemies that fell, the quicker Jude adapted to finding ways around their defenses. He was more than some prodigy, he was an awakened Combat Specialist with death on his mind.

◆◆◆

Following Priya, Jude learned that the rest of his training would take place inside the mysterious mountain that commanded his attention ever since they had arrived. Tarragon Mountain was vast, opening up into one large chamber, absent of any tunnels, pillars or obstructions. The sight seemed forced and unnatural, causing him to believe that something had been there—or worse, was still there. Shadows cloaked every corner of the large open chamber all the way up the ceiling, which seemed to have no apparent end. Turning to Priya, Jude realized that his once accompanied adventure had been reduced to a solo mission, with the Commander nowhere to be found. The ground shook, the mountain echoed and the soil continued to leap violently.

"If you think I will intervene when she overwhelms you Agent Bray, you're fatally wrong," said Priya from above. She retained her position stories high atop the mountain shelf behind him.

The roar was immobilizing, causing all breathing to falter, adrenaline to run, and deemed any hopes of escape futile. The beast was massive, towering in all directions with a presence that demanded attention from even the mightiest of gods. The dragon's black scales sat erect with razor-sharp precision, promising excruciating pain and absolute annihilation. Jude went to bend his knees as to anticipate an attack, but was stopped cold by the beast's instant glare. The metallic silver that made up its eyes was both alluring and terrifying due to the absence of a pupil.

"Commander this is impossible. You can't expect me to win against her."

The dragon attacked, its bite striking with both rage and instability. Jude dove to evade the attack, and when he returned to his feet, took off running in no particular direction. An earthquake took control of the mountain as the dragon stampeded after him, unleashing a deafening roar that caused Jude to cover his ears and abandon his plan to go on the offensive. The three makeshift comrades at the dragon's feet rocked back and forth in response to the tyrant before them.

"If even one of your comrades die, this is over," said Priya. Jude could see at the corner of his eye that her firmly folded arms seemed to tighten with anger. "I will no longer train you."

How can I win against something this powerful when I am forbidden to use any blood vials?

KAI, MYSELF, & KAI

The sun's scorching rays showed no mercy or any signs of compassion. The hard cracked terrain caused Eli's feet to hurt and his back to ache. Looking into Kai's hazel eyes, Eli knew that the Operative was not kidding around.

"Come on, just one peck—for Kai," said Kai with a grin.

"Are you kidding me?"

"Please," pleaded Kai.

"Man I'm not going to kiss your black centipede. Kiss it yourself!"

It had been two and a half months since Eli and Kai had arrived—to what Eli called—the middle of nowhere. It had taken them two days to arrive to the dry flat plain. There was absolutely nothing around except for a watering hole and the blatantly scorching heat. Upon arrival, Kai ordered Eli to set up the entire camp, including Kai's tent and Slate's bed. Eli found it extremely irritating and pointless to be training under Kai. The first month of training was filled with nothing but endurance training. Eli feltlike he could run for days while carrying a tree, as well as pass out from the angry heat that poked at his back. The second month was more to Eli's liking. Kai went over some various styles of blade combat that Eli found fascinating. The training sparked the motivation he once had. However, now it was the hottest day since they had arrived, and Kai refused to offer anymore training until Eli made up with Slate after "scaring him" when they first met.

197

"Are you seriously not going to train me if I don't kiss that monster?"

"Monster? Okay now Kai is insulted. You want to train so badly? Fine! Run around until Kai says stop," said Kai.

"You're joking."

Kai stared back motionless, while Agent Slate curled around his wrist shortly before stopping as well.

"How long do I have to do this?"

"Until Kai says stop. But don't worry, we will work on your hearing as well."

Since he was given no clear direction, Eli decided to just run around the watering hole a few times to give himself some kind of guidance. As he closed in on the watering hole, something grabbed his wrist. He turned around to find Kai standing behind him.

"What? How did you get here so—."

"Stay away from that watering hole. You can pick any other area on this large plain, but the watering hole is off limits."

"You're really going to punish me for not kissing that monster huh?"

"Now you get no water for the rest of the day," said Kai.

"What? You can't do that!"

"Keep it up and your bed is next."

Eli bit his lip as to prevent himself from saying what he really wanted to say. He ran passed their camp and towards the endless sight of nothing, which spread out all around them.

Just another example of how I always get stuck with the worse mentor while everyone else gets someone awesome. I swear life isn't fair.

His foot stepped into an unseen hole, causing him to recoil. Something black caught his eye. He looked down to see Slate slithering passed him.

"How in the heck is that thing..."

"If Agent Slate gets back from that next crater before you, consider your food his," yelled Kai.

Okay now I hate you more than Pang.

Eli quickened his pace but found it difficult to keep up with Slate. The black ravage bug moved faster than any bug or animal that Eli had ever seen. As he trailed after Slate around the crater and back towards Kai, he felt his vision blur, his dry throat tighten and his legs begin to give out.

"Ka—Kai! I think I need some—need some," started Eli before his mind began to drift.

It's so—so hot.

"Looks like your rations are slowly slipping away," said Kai.

There was no way Eli could catch Agent Slate. The bug was significantly faster than him and he didn't care. The only thing he could think of was water. When Slate made it passed Kai, Eli felt himself falter. His face hit the terrain hard, causing dry dust to fill his nose, while making his dry mouth and throat seer with pain.

"Why does Kai always get the weak ones?" said Kai.

"Wa—Water!"

"Kai wasn't kidding when he said you lost your water privileges. Suck it up or get off my plain!"

Eli saw Kai's feet exit from view. His hand instinctually reached out and grabbed the Operative's leg.

"Please—water..."

Kai's cold gaze was all the answer that Eli needed to get the message. Kai wasn't backing down even though he could see how desperate Eli was for water. The sun appeared to be hotter than Eli remembered, and soon he felt his eyes independently close. His body felt disconnected from his mind and his hands felt like they were withering away. His breathing slowed and soon her amethyst eyes filled the darkness that now shrouded his vision.

◆◆◆

The cold was both alarming and refreshing. Eli sprang up from the floor and found himself looking through a haze and into a pair of stern hazel eyes.

"There's your water peasant," said Kai shaking his head.

"You could've killed me! What's your problem?"

"Kai never 'could've' kills anyone. If Kai wants you dead, it's inevitable. Don't forget that," said Kai offering a hand down to Eli. Eli was enraged and dreaded touching that hand more than anything. However, he was so weak and cold that he gave in and allowed Kai to help him up.

Eli's eyes widened and his mouth dropped when he noticed the darkness around him. The bright scorching sky was now replaced with a dark veil full of stars and shadows.

"The sun set already? I was unconscious that long and you didn't care?"

"Well, it wasn't that Kai didn't care, it was because Kai had something better to do," said Kai.

Eli went for Kai with his dagger in hand. The dagger was ripped from his hand just as his legs were kicked from underneath him and his arms pinned behind his back. A pinch released a cold sensation around his neck, where his dagger now stood.

"You raise a weapon to Kai? Huh! Do you? You sour piece of garbage!"

Eli felt his shoulder click causing pain to stream down his arm. The pain was unbearable, causing him to forget about the dagger that kept pricking his neck. After a moment of silence, Eli felt the grip on his arms soften and the dagger retreat.

"Go grab the linen from the tents before Kai gets cold," said Kai without looking at Eli.

Eli rose to his feet and ignored the shaking of his legs and lips. He entered Kai's tent and retrieved a few blankets before returning. He handed Kai the blankets and found himself instantly getting them back.

"Put those on, so you won't get sick," said Kai.

Eli found himself extremely confused. After the second cold breeze that blew passed him, he wrapped himself up in the soft warmth of the blanket's embrace.

"Now Kai was trying to teach you one of Kai's signature moves— before you got all crazy that is."

"What move was that?" asked Eli.

"The masquerade of death."

"Huh?"

"Kai was teaching you how to play dead. It can very useful in certain situations," said Kai.

"Play dead? I was nearly really dead!"

"Kai knows. You cannot really know how to pretend to be dead if you don't have some idea of how it feels to be at least dying. So Kai hopes that you remembered how it feels, or we will have to starve and dehydrate you again; and after seeing that last display of craziness from you after you woke up, Kai won't be looking forward to it."

"Please, how can someone forget how it feels to nearly be murdered," said Eli. He felt his patience recede and his anger rising.

"Good," said Kai offering Eli a cup and a piece of bread. After you finish that, Kai will want a front row seat to your demise!"

The bread and cup of water were gone within seconds, causing Eli to release moans of satisfaction. He forgot how good cold water tasted and how delicious bread was.

"You're repulsive when you eat—you know that right?"

When Eli didn't respond, Kai shrugged and continued.

"So go ahead and lay down and try your best to reenact how it felt when you *thought* you were dying."

◆ ◆ ◆

"Look, I don't know what I'm doing wrong. Can you please—help me," said Eli reluctantly. The second the words left his lips, he knew Kai was eating them up.

"Very well, Kai will help, on one condition."

Eli threw his hands up in anger. He knew that he could not have a mentor that just wanted to teach him because it was the right thing to do.

Everyone always wants something from you. Why did I expect this guy to be any different?

"What's the condition?"

"You finally have to kiss and make up with Agent Slate," said Kai with a smirk.

"Again with the centipede? Gosh your," started Eli before he quickly silenced himself. The last time he had disrespected Kai, he paid a costly price. "Difficult."

"Well it's nice to see that the idiot can learn," said Kai laughing. Eli tried his hardest to ignore the comment, in fear of a regrettable response. "That is Kai's condition. Kiss Agent Slate on the head, tell him you're sorry, and Kai will teach you how to properly summon weapons and defenses. If you're so good at pretending that even Kai thinks you're truly sorry, Kai may even teach you some advanced abilities."

Eli felt his hand go to his head as he thought about his possible options. He could refuse and end up angering Kai so much that he refused to train anymore—or even go to the extent of recommending his permanent discharge. Or Eli could just go through with it, and force himself to come face-to-face with the monster that made his skin crawl and his spine slither.

I have already been discharged once. I was lucky to get another chance. I'd be a fool to risk being discharged again, as well as forfeiting an opportunity to learn how to properly use my abilities and a few advanced ones.

"Alright, I'll do it."

Kai quickly grabbed Slate and literally shoved the monstrously large bug in Eli's face. The large feelers dragged across his face, causing him to shutter.

"Which part is the head?"

"Don't listen to him Agent Slate, your sheer perfection," said Kai holding up the end of the bug with the long feelers.

Eli's lips slightly grazed the bug. "I'm sorry Slate."

"No no," said Kai with an annoyed look on his face. "You made him feel self-conscious, shameful and small. Get on your knees and beg for his forgiveness."

"On my knees?"

"Yes," said Kai with a glare. His entire demeanor changed, and soon Eli felt like he looked into the eyes of an enemy—a dangerous enemy.

Eli found himself looking away from Kai's gaze, only to return a few seconds later.

"Well?" said Kai.

"That wasn't the deal. You said a kiss on the head and an apology. That's what I did."

"Well Kai is changing it! What of it!" screamed Kai. He raised his voice so much, that Slate recoiled from the loud noise and began to slither back up Kai's arm. Eli had never known what it meant to be scared stiff, but now he knew. Both of his hands stayed frozen at his waist. His breathing refused to increase or decrease, in fear of punishment.

Man even I don't know what is more important to me right now. I want to say no just because he is trying to humiliate me—and for what? But he is the only one that can help me since my dad isn't here.

Marius passed in front of Eli's vision. Fox's hand came up, smashing into Marius' chest.

"Fox, I'm going to kill you for taking my dad from me. I promise."

"What? What was that?" asked Kai

Eli got on his knees and looked up at Kai. The black bug returned to view, causing Eli to excommunicate his fear. He curled a finger under Slate's head, and felt the hundreds of legs drag across the surface of his finger. His finger shook. Eli's lips felt like he was kissing a wet fish, and his nose was filled with the scent of wet soil and garbage.

"I'm sorry Agent Slate, really."

"Oh my goodness," said Kai with wide eyes.

Eli felt his arms drop and his hope right along with it. He had done the best that he could, but clearly it was not enough.

"That was so—touching. Do you hear that Agent Slate, you guys are friends again," said Kai.

This guy is what Sia would call "certified crazy."

Sia's purple eyes danced in his vision, giving him pause. His throat tightened and his chin grew heavy. He rebelled against the sensation, but soon was over-powered by the warm tear that fell down his face.

I miss you Sia.

"Oh my goodness, Slate look, he's crying. He does care," said Kai.

Eli ignored Kai's antics. His mind was narrowly focused on how Sia's training was going and if she missed him.

I miss you so much. You are the only family I have out here in all of this chaos now that my dad is gone.

A hand blocked his vision. He looked up to see Kai extending a hand down to him. Eli accepted it and was hoisted to his feet. He caught a glimpse of the end of Agent Slate's long scaly body, returning to its hidden spot in Kai's battle tunic.

"Alright stand over there," said Kai designating a spot a few feet in front of him. Eli returned Kai's gaze after relocating. "Since you're a Weapons Master, Ivor must have been your mentor. During his lectures, how were you taught to summon weapons?"

"I wasn't. He really didn't teach us how to do anything properly. He just taught us how to do specific moves, which now that I think about it, they were all weak and basic. It's like he didn't want to teach us anything."

"Okay, so how did you make it through the Trials, and how do you summon weapons now?" asked Kai. He appeared to be studying Eli closely.

"I mean, my dad was an Occult Operative when he was younger so he is pretty skilled with weapons. He taught me how to summon a bow and blade. The rest kind of just came to me."

"Oh—my—Aegis," said Kai with a face-palm. "So you are basically telling me that you have gotten this far on dumb luck. Wait, that would mean you are also telling me that even though your dad was an Occult Operative, and probably has thousands of legendary weapons at his disposal, you not once asked him to teach you how to properly use your abilities, or go down to his weapons room and assimilate all of his legendary weapons to memory?"

"No. I mean yes. I mean—what's the question again?"

Kai shook his head slowly in disappointment. Eli had not thought about it until Kai had brought it up. His dad was one of the strongest Weapons Masters in the city, as well as an Ex-Occult Operative, and he not once asked his dad for help.

I literally could probably be the most powerful and youngest of Weapons Masters in Kismet if I would have asked my dad for help. I bet he had abilities that I couldn't even dream of. I could have been the prodigy instead of Jude and probably even Kai.

Eli shook his head. He felt extremely disappointed in himself, and was too embarrassed to lift his head.

"Wait, why are *you* shaking *your* head?" asked Kai.

"Because I'm so embarrassed."

"Kai doesn't blame you. Kai is embarrassed for you."

Eli found himself laughing hysterically along with Kai. His stomach began to hurt from his laughter, causing tears to form in the corners of his eyes. He thought it was one of the craziest moments of his life.

"Alright no sweat. Kai is here to save the day."

KILL OR
BE KILLED

Eli was moving so quickly, that he wondered how long it would take for the sword he wielded to come flying out of his hand. The Agent he went up against was beyond skilled. This wasn't a mindless Necrosis, a brute Necroborn or a student from the Academy; this was a master swordsman who left no openings and increased his ferocity with each swing he took.

"You're thinking about what to do instead of just doing it," said Kai from the sideline.

The Agent tipped Eli off balanced and countered. Eli felt the cold metal open up his chest and release the pain that spread.

"Attack him with all you've got! Don't even think about the blade in your hand," said Kai.

Eli didn't understand how someone who could attack with a blade and not think about the blade at the same time. Angering Kai was one thing that was scarier than the pain that came from a wrong move, so he obliged. The speed of his blade increased. The sound of metal hitting metal filled the air around him. Eli and the Agent were moving so fast that Eli began to grow dizzy, but continued to focus on his opponent. Eli's sword began to feel like it was alive and thinking for itself, and then it happened. Eli severed the Agent's wrist, which held his blade. Eli flipped around slicing his opponent's neck. The Agent grabbed his neck and returned to Eli with wide eyes. Then the Agent fell. Eli was ready to breathe a sigh of relief.

""Kill him!" yelled the voices around him.

Eli turned around to find himself surrounded by hundreds of Agents. Each Agent wielded a different color blade, which was held high above their heads. They all attacked.

"Uh Kai, some help!"

"Kill them you fool! Kill them! Attack them with everything you have," said Kai.

Eli held on to Kai's advice of not thinking but doing. He continued to go toe-to-toe with each swordsman, eliminating them a lot quicker than the first Agent. Soon he became overwhelmed by all of the enemies. There were way too many. He couldn't even count them all let alone defend against them all.

"If you even think about using an ability, so help me Rune I will maul you," said Kai.

An Agent went for Eli's legs, which caused him to sidestep right into the incoming pommel of an attacking Agent. Eli rolled across the hundreds of boots that stood around him.

"He's down! End him!" said one of the Agents.

Eli looked on in fear. He didn't understand why, but he saw no way out. The Agents closed in from every side brandishing their weapons.

"On your feet Brassie! You're a Weapons Master! Weapons Masters don't cower we make our enemies cower! Kill them! Do you hear me? Kill or be killed you fool!"

Eli rolled to avoid the striking metal around him and brought his blade to the forefront. Kai was right. Why was Eli scared? He was a Weapons Master—he was born to be on the offense.

"Yes! Kai loves the look in your eyes! Look Agent Slate," said Kai.

Eli threw himself back into battle. He did not fear the pain that came from the occasional attacks that hit him directly or the cramps his hands received from the force he bashed his enemies with. Heads began to tumble in all directions, spraying

Eli's face with blood and gore. The blood was exciting. The blood was his reward for his victory. More, he needed more.

"Yes! Kill them! Kill them all!" yelled Kai.

Eli grabbed the pommel of his blade with both hands before spinning continuously in an endless spin. Enemies bellowed and fell at his feet. When he stopped, he was face-to-face with his last enemy, who kept his position far away.

Eli took a step. The Agent took two steps. Eli waited. He thought why rush, his enemy would fall by his hand soon. He wanted to enjoy this moment. His pulse was a drum and his adrenaline was oozing from his pores. The power he felt was seductive and he loved it. His enemy drew closer until he was at arms length.

"You know what to do Brassie," said Kai laughing. "Your opponent made one fatal mistake. What is it?"

"He's in range—and *no one* should ever tread into the grasp of a Weapons Master."

NEW SQUAD

Conall reinforced his clasped hands and forced his back to reassume its perfect posture at the roundtable. Emotions had no place in war and the seed of worry began to plant itself in the soil that was his training. The return to the shack should have been comforting but it wasn't. The old grandfather clock behind him had acquired a beat between clicks, signaling its demise. For the first time in ages there was no screaming wind and no assaulting rain. The sky was clear upon arrival and the marsh was decorated with the unnatural chirping of birds close-by. If the General were here, she would tell him to ease his worry and take the clear skies, singing birds and calm nature as a good sign. However, the cold truth was upon him. The four new recruits would be arriving at any minute. If their training resulted in failure, then Conall would have to decide the next move; a move he was drawing a blank on.

The transition to Geminate went as smooth as possible. Even if the unwelcoming welcome was heavy in the air upon arrival, the Priestess had eased his mind before his departure. One thing was blinking in the back of his mind. Lord Egon's assimilation of Kismet would only be a small portion of his objective. If Conall was right, the Lord would continue to invade every surrounding land until he secured his grasp on the entire eastern region.

Two knocks. One knock. Two knocks.

Conall slowly rose from his seat and then darted to the window. A hooded figure stood at the door—expected but still suspicious. Conall surveyed the trees and surrounding area. There were no signs of others. The arrows hovered around his shoulders as he opened the door.

"Good morning Lieutenant," said Vance. His haggard face and chapped lips were proof that his journey from Praxis had not been easy.

"Please, come in."

Vance took a seat at the table while Conall poured them both a cup of hot tea. Sitting across from the Magi, Conall hoped that his faith in the positive signs outside would ensure some good news from Vance.

The professor slowly drew his tea to his lips, waited a second, and then sipped. After returning the cup to the table, he repeated the motion a few more times.

"Excuse my impatience but well?"

Vance returned his cup to the table, wiped his lips and then met Conall's gaze. "Well the good news is Lord Egon's reach has not extended to Praxis. They remain unaffected by his imminent invasion. However, the King has no interest in aiding our people or allying his people with ours. We will receive no aid from the Praxians."

Damn!

"So then we have no other option."

"That is correct," said Vance with a small smile. He looked around the shack and then returned to Conall. "Where are they now?"

"They have not returned yet and I have received no news in regards to their training. Don't tell the General but I'm worried."

"Do not feel ashamed of your human emotions. We are who we are and we are made how we are made," said Vance with a tilt of his head.

Before Conall could respond, a light knock brushed the door.

"Ensconce," whispered Vance.

Conall opened the door and was both anxious and relieved by the sight.

Sia stood before him in a purple robe. Her hood was drawn but her permanent Magi glare was prominent. "Hello Lieutenant. May I come in?"

"Yes, please."

Sia nodded her head before entering slowly. She took her time approaching the roundtable. When she got to Vance's seat she appeared to be preparing to sit down, before taking her hand off of the seat and relocating to the one across from it.

"I am glad to see that you are well Professor," said Sia.

What?

Vance's body appeared again. Conall took a seat in between the two Magi, astounded by what he just saw.

"I see your training went well. However, I must say that I am surprised you were able to see through my spell," said Vance.

"Apologies," said Sia resting her hands on the table. "I meant no disrespect."

"No no you misunderstand," began Vance. "I'm not upset about it I'm just—."

"Relieved," said Conall. He was embarrassed by his outburst but could not hold his tongue any longer.

Sia cracked a smile. "The others aren't here yet?"

"No, but they should be here at," started Vance before falling silent to the firm knock at the door.

Conall looked to Sia who was staring at Vance.

"No need for your Ensconce spell professor. I believe I know whom that reckless knock belongs to," she said.

Vance nodded to Conall, who instantly answered the door. The stranger was familiar but not quite identifiable. His blue eyes stared back firmly while his wet blonde hair stuck to his forehead.

"Is something wrong Lieutenant? Am I late?" asked the stranger.

That voice.

"Brassie?"

"Yes Lieutenant. Your orders were to meet back here right?" said Eli.

"That is correct. Please, come in."

Eli entered and walked to the roundtable. He took long heavy steps and nodded once to Vance and then to Sia before taking a seat between the two of them. Conall was surprised that Eli did not take a seat next to Wyatt. He clearly had some kind of attraction towards the Magi, but wasn't wearing it on his sleeve anymore.

Conall began to close the door and then it stopped. A hand was propping it open. Opening the door, Conall came face-to-face with a pair of unforgettable green eyes.

"Good morning Lieutenant. I apologize for my tardiness. The desert proved to be quite a challenge," said Jude. His stare was so unnerving that Conall found himself looking away.

"Bray, please come in."

Jude entered quickly, taking long light steps that were so light, that he appeared to be gliding across the room. Arriving at the table almost instantly, Jude greeted everyone at the table before taking a seat. There was something different about him. Conall sensed something different about all three of them. Both Bray and Brassie filled in their armor a little more and Sia walked with power in her steps. But there was something else different about Bray. The longer Conall thought about it, the more it escaped him. He closed the door and joined the others.

"Since the three of you are here, I assume that means your training went well."

"Yes," said Eli.

"Correct," said Sia.

"Flawlessly," said Jude.

The house shook beneath a heavy sound. Everyone's eyes went to the door.

Was that a knock?

The door flew off its hinges and slid into the kitchen. Conall prepared himself, along with Jude and Eli. A significantly muscular stranger patrolled through the door. His chest was bare and did little to hide the long scar that intersected his chest. His arms were massive and his abdominals looked as if they could withstand an assault from any blade.

"What? I knocked," said the stranger entering the shack.

"Quarrels?"

Pang stormed to the table and hammered down in the seat next to Jude. Everyone's cups of tea spilled over when he took a seat next to Jude.

Conall ignored the fact that a behemoth had just entered their safe haven. He propped the door up, in an attempt to close it, and returned to his seat in between Jude and Vance.

"How's it going Quarrels?"

"It's going," said Pang.

A smirk was present on Jude's face while a blank expression was present on everyone else's. Conall took Pang's abnormally larger body as a sign that his training went well. He had no time to interrogate the four of them. He would just have to take their word that they were thoroughly equipped for what lay ahead.

"Before I forget, here." Conall tossed four small pouches towards the center of the table. Each of his subordinates took a pouch before everyone grinned at its contents—except for Jude, who appeared unaffected by his prize. "Five hundred gold. Consider that payment for your mission at the city borders."

"Enough to buy a nice-sized cottage and then some. Not bad," said Pang approvingly.

"*Very* generous of you Lieutenant," said Sia.

"The four of you earned it. But pushing on to more important matters, we're out of time so let's cut right to the point," said Conall retrieving a roll of white combat tape from his pocket. He began to wrap his hands before continuing. "Vance has just returned from Praxis. He ventured there to see if the King would offer any aid to our people. He will not. The good news is, Lord Egon's reach has not reached Geminate or Praxis. The bad news is, it won't be long before he tries. Your permanent residence moving forward will be Geminate for the time being. Everything has already been taken care of. From this day forward you are no longer Agents-in-training and you are no longer Agents. Your ranks are as follows: Wyatt, Special Agent. Brassie, Special Agent. Quarrels, Special Agent. Bray, a customized rank was in order so—Tactical Agent. The four of you will make-up the Kismet Task Force. You will no longer receive orders from the General. You will receive orders from me and me only."

Nods spread out around Conall. Their silence showed discipline but their demeanors showed readiness.

"While you're in Geminate, you will tell no one, and I repeat no one, about any missions or your true identities. Questions?"

"With the four of us constantly leaving Geminate for missions, it is inevitable that our absence from the rest of the Kismet people will draw attention," said Jude.

"That's correct. You will need an alias. Any ideas?"

"B.B.Q.W.," replied Jude instantly.

"Come again Jude?" asked Sia.

"If we are going to have an alias, it has to be something believable just in case we are questioned. Anything too fancy and we will draw suspicion. B.B.Q.W. is our last names. Our alias can be some kind of Kismet organization. Since our real last names are a part of the name, it is more believable," said Jude.

Conall was at a loss for words. Jude's plan was perfect. The use of real information to help conceal their true identities was genius.

Such speed.

"Agreed. B.B.Q.W. Bray, Brassie, Quarrels and Wyatt. Your cover will be that the four of you are our resources team. You four are responsible for gathering food, water and funds for our people. This won't be the case because that will be my job and the General's."

"Yes Brassie."

"Excuse me Lieutenant I am confused. The Geminates won't be providing any food or water for our people?" asked Eli.

"Correct and we can't expect them too. We have a little over four hundred Kismet citizens staying there. It's already kind enough for them to allow that many people to stay in their city. We can't expect them to offer anymore aid."

"Agreed," said the four of them in unison.

"I'm sure by now you will have already guessed that Fox and Lord Egon must be eliminated."

A shutter came from Eli. Conall looked across the table only to find Eli void of any emotions, but with hands shaking slowly around his cup.

I know Brassie. I get it. You want revenge for what those two have taken from you. I hope fate blesses you with the opportunity that I never had when I was in your boots.

"Before that can be done, Vance needs your help with a different matter."

The K.T.F. turned their heads to Vance. Curiosity was buzzing in their eyes. Vance rose from his seat and looked at everyone individually before beginning.

"First let me say that I know I speak for the entire Kismet people when I say we are most grateful to the four of you for all you have done and will accomplish. We need you. We all need you. There is great hardship ahead. I can feel it. For your first mission, you will need to rendezvous with Special Operative Jamieson Edric," said Vance. He set a stack of white folders on the table in front of him.

Conall passed each of the K.T.F. a folder before opening his. A young man with dark hair and hazel eyes stared back at him. The report was extensive, reporting everything from his physical characteristics to his fighting style. Whoever collected the report had done a thorough job. Conall wondered if Kai or Priya was responsible for the information.

"Special Operative Jamieson Edric is one of the many gems of Geminate. He is considered to be one of the top stealth operatives in the world. Edric has been dispatched on a top-secret mission. He has been tasked with the neutralization of a dangerous Operative that has been responsible for the deaths of hundreds of the Geminate people. The only problem is, it's a trap. The Operative has been informed of Jamieson's mission and will be waiting with a handful of mercenaries at his disposal. Your mission is to find Jamieson and bring him back to Geminate—alive! Your mission is *not* to eliminate the Operative or the mercenaries. Lethal force is authorized if and only if it is absolutely necessary. You must not fail," said Vance.

"Also, you cannot relay to Jamieson that his mission is a trap or your true identities," said Conall cutting in. "If he refuses to abandon his mission—."

"And he will," interrupted Vance.

"Then you will have to temporarily incapacitate him. Unfortunately I will not be able to join you on your mission," said Conall turning to Sia. "Your father has been spotted in the Relinquished Isles. We believe he has plans of allying Lord Egon's forces with the Amorphous that reside there. We cannot allow it to happen, so the Occult Operatives, the General and myself will have to stop him by any means necessary." Conall looked for any signs of resistance from Sia but saw nothing. Her Magi glare continued to glow while her face remained frozen. He couldn't tell whether she was angry, indifferent or relieved. She had shared with him the nightmare of living with Mr. Wyatt as a father. Part of him was sort of relieved that he could bring the life of such a miserable soul to an end however, Conall knew finding enjoyment in the death of another was completely and utterly wrong.

"Everyone has forgotten one thing. Us four have not been to Geminate before, so how will we bring in the Operative if he is incapacitated?" said Eli.

"You don't need to worry about that Agent Brassie," said Sia brushing a strand of hair away from her face. "Both Jarkko and myself were responsible for the transportation of the entire Kismet people to Geminate's borders. Even though I have never done it alone, I am sure I will be equipped to open a portal to Geminate once again."

"This will mean the entire mission will rest on your shoulders Agent Wyatt," said Jude looking to Sia. "If you fail, we all fail. Can we count on you that when the time comes, you will deliver?"

"I will not fail," said Sia.

"Who will be Squad Leader in your absence Lieutenant?" asked Jude.

Conall could sense more than curiosity behind Jude's words. He didn't need to guess; he knew that Jude knew who the Squad Leader would be on this mission. "Bray will be the Squad Leader in my absence. You *all* will be under his command on this mission."

"Copy that," said Pang and Sia in unison.

"Copy," whispered Eli.

Conall could already hear the rebellion in Eli's voice. He hoped that Brassie's training gave him some kind of discipline. This would be the first mission for all of them, not to mention Jude's first mission as Squad Leader. Conall began to wonder if Anya's little favorite would live up to her expectations.

Jude looked to each of his comrades separately. He nodded once, which brought the rest of the Kismet Task Force to their feet. With a quick side-eye to Conall, Jude smirked. "Mission accepted..."

THE COLD ZONE

"It's mirror magic," replied Sia with a sigh. The excess air released after her words alerted Jude to a pending catch to entering the cold zone.

Thanks to Sia's portal, Jude and his squad were able to turn a journey that would normally take days, into a journey that took less than an hour. Portaling was beyond explaining with mere words to Jude. Amethyst flames hissed and whipped back and forth along the edges of the giant oval when Sia summoned the portal. The blackness inside the circle was infinite and unyielding in its mission to conceal its path. Upon entering the portal, Jude fought against the heaviness that descended upon him. His muscles refused to move against the high velocity at which Jude was now traveling at through the portal. Warm wind whipped at his face and neck while his arms and legs remained imprisoned in the invisible force that was the portal. Seconds later a white light opened up in front of his eyes, and soon he felt the gravel and dead grass crunch beneath his combat boots. The designated cold zone rose up ahead of them in the form of a cold and desolate cave. The cave was larger than some of the surrounding mountains, but absent of neighbors of its kind. A cold wind whizzed passed Jude and his comrades from behind, while the echoes of the cave assaulted them head-on. The entrance was blocked by an invisible shield, which only showed Jude and his comrades in its surface.

"One way in and no way out unless you have been trained in the art of mirror magic. I have not," said Sia over the S-3. They all stood side-by-side, but Sia still used her S-3.

It was Jude's first rule. He would not leave it up to chance that even one of his comrades misinterpreted or failed to hear any orders or intelligence. Jude wanted the squad's communication to be flawless. He felt like the more aware everyone was of what was going on with their comrades in battle, the stronger the squad would be. Also, if any enemies were tracking them, they wouldn't be able to ease drop on any of the squad's conversations.

"Bray for Lieutenant Titus."

After a few idle seconds, Conall's voice boomed through the S-3 from whatever location his current mission had taken him. *"Go for Titus."*

"Kismet Task Force reporting in. We will be entering the cold zone shortly, in which the entrance is encased in mirror magic. We have no knowledge of its properties, so we will need assistance with our escape."

"I hear you loud and clear Squad Leader," replied Conall breathing heavily. After a short moment, he steadied his breathing. *"Proceed into the cold zone. I will consult with Vance and formulate an escape plan for your squad. Titus out."*

Jude looked over his shoulder at his comrades. Except for Sia, they were all dressed in the same black armor and combat pants with black velcro straps along their arms and legs. Dark red accents colored various portions of the armor. Sia was dressed in an all black body suit that clung tightly to her athletic figure. Black velcro swarmed around her arms and legs as well.

"Lethal force is not authorized unless I give the order." Jude didn't even wait for confirmations from his comrades. He was the Squad Leader and his word was law. They would follow his orders no matter what the circumstances—or they would die by his hand.

"Entering the cold zone."

Jamieson recalled his ipseity before checking on his fallen victim. The mercenary's breathing slowly came to an end, confirming that his life had followed. A small rockslide close-by caught his attention amongst the fallen foes that now lay at his feet. He summoned his ipseity to the ledge leading to the tunnels that spread out above the mountain's chambers. The dark but identical twin appeared on the ledge and offered a hand down to him. Jamieson accepted the help, and after reaching the upper tunnels, recalled his ipseity once again.

The tunnels were still darker than shadows. His armor scratched across the jagged rocks beneath him and on the walls around him. Large obstructions of boulders blocked his path every few feet, causing him to either sneak under or find a new tunnel to follow. The tunnels were a labyrinth, barely big enough for Jamieson to fit through. Voices sounded beneath him. A small beam of light shot through a tiny crevice on the wall next to him. He halted and peered through.

The mercenaries were doing battle with two Agents dressed in all black armor. Their faces were slightly covered by the black cloth that sat tied snuggly around their mouths. One was a swordsman with impeccable speed. Mercenaries fell continuously at his feet as he continued to engage them. Enemies that leaped out of the shadows to ambush him met a quick demise at the end of his blade. It was as if the swordsman knew where all of the enemies were before they even targeted him. The second Agent was a barbarian—plowing into groups of mercenaries and sending them flying; before tearing them limb from limb. Then Jamieson spotted it. A set of footprints ran along the mountain's dusty surface signaling a presence. There were three Agents. Very odd.

Outsiders. But what do they want?

The barbaric Agent tossed a mercenary at the swordsman, who retaliated with a wall of what looked like arrows. The mercenary now hung dangling from one of the surrounding walls.

A young woman appeared as if out of nowhere. Her brown curls pulled neatly into a tight ponytail. Her head slowly turned around exposing eyes unlike any Jamieson had ever seen. Her eyes were sharply purple.

The three Agents stood motionless and silently. The absence of words was eerie and suspect. A body appeared in front of the female Agent, his eyes glowing with a white glow that was looking directly at Jamieson. The other three whipped their heads Jamieson's direction, along with the fourth Agent.

They've found me!

Jamieson quickened his crawl through the tunnels. Whoever these Agents were, they were highly skilled. He needed to find the target fast, eliminate him and retreat before they reached him. Jamieson thought about his partner Lo, and wondered if the Agents had gotten to her already.

TRACKING

Eli trailed closely behind Jude and the others. He continued to look around cautiously even though he knew that Jude would spot any assault before the rest of them did. His newly-acquired visual ability was proving to be extremely useful in battle. The four of them had encountered a large group of mercenaries on their way through the catacombs. Jude relayed invaluable information on the enemy's movements, numbers and positions over the S-3. Apparently they had missed one because Jude quickly scanned and discovered another person hiding in a hidden chamber above them. Jude immediately targeted them for elimination. The four of them now continued down a long passageway opposite the direction of the target. Jude explained that he could detect a hidden passage that would get them through the catacombs quicker.

The path began to open up into a dark circular chamber.

"Wait!" screamed Jude's voice over the S-3.

His abrupt outburst alarmed Eli, but Eli quickly regained his composure.

"Someone is here," continued Jude. *"Sia..."*

"On it," replied Sia quickly.

Jude, Pang and Sia disappeared before Eli's very eyes. He knew that he too would appear that way with the aid of Sia's invisibility spell. The four of them watched attentively as a lone red-headed Agent did battle with a gargantuan behemoth.

"We will not engage," said Jude over the S-3. *"We must assume that everyone other than the Operative we are looking for is an enemy."*

The Agent was agile, ducking beneath her offender's attacks before retaliating with her own. However, the behemoth was strong; and once his powerful fist connected, the Agent was hurled across the rocky surface. The Agent rose to her feet as the behemoth closed in on her location. She ran for the door behind her. A large object fell from the ceiling and landed in front of her, blocking her path. The second giant grabbed her by her throat and lifted her off her feet.

Eli was waiting for Jude to give the order but heard nothing. The woman was clearly done for. The squad needed to help her.

"Well are we going to help her?"

"Brassie! You will stand down. That's an order!" snapped Jude.

An order? An order!

Eli fought back the acidic words that began to pillage the back of his teeth. His training with Kai taught him to build a barricade for certain words that rose up quickly when he was agitated.

The giant slammed the Agent to the floor and held her down. Then one-by-one, the behemoths took turns bashing her body into the rocky terrain with their massive mallets. The ground jumped beneath Eli's. Blood splattered the floor and walls around the chaos. Then the commotion stopped. The giant's turned towards the door the Agent had tried to retreat to, and exited.

Jude surveyed the area and then nodded. The four of them descended upon the once battlefield towards the fallen Agent. Heavy burgundy armor covered her from her shoulders to her toes. Her body was broken in so many different ways that her arms and legs were crushed beyond repair. Her pale face, which probably once glowed with a beauty that gave others pause, was now bashed into a bloody mess of skin and bones.

"She was beautiful," said Sia pulling the black cloth down from her own mouth—exposing her face. "Rune be with you stranger."

"I want the Operative found. Split up and find him. Radio in when you find him and we will all meet back here," demanded Jude.

"Copy," said the rest of them.

♦ ♦ ♦

Jude activated his Optical Tactics multiple times before confirming that no one else was in the chamber. Judging by the brushed away footprints, carcasses and fresh acid that still lay caked atop one of the pedestals, someone was just here.

Let's just hope that it was the Operative.

Jude crossed the bridge cautiously before arriving at the door across from it. He opened the door gently and entered. A battle raged on ahead of him. Mercenaries fell in all directions as two assailants danced around their enemies. Then the chaos ended. One of the assailants stood with his back to Jude, staring down at his fallen victims. The other assailant was nowhere to be found. Jude activated his Optical Tactics and scanned the chamber. The single assailant in front of him was the only other person present.

Jude took a vial from his utility belt and shoved it up his sleeve. "Show me your face!"

The assailant stiffened, bringing his head up but refusing to turn around. "So, you've finally found me."

"I won't ask you again."

The assailant raised both of his hands and turned around slowly. The image of the Operative in the white folder flashed before Jude's eyes. Messy black hair cascaded down across his hazel eyes. His arms were large, far surpassing Pang's with rock-hard precision. His jaw sat pronounced atop his strong chin. His entire body screamed brute force. Jude knew if it came down to one of them overpowering the other, Jamieson would win hands down.

"Operative Jamieson Edric. Please come with me, we have to get you out of here."

"Then what," replied Jamieson.

Jude was caught-off-guard by the Operative's resistance. Surely Lieutenant Titus or Vance had let Edric know of their rescue mission right?

"Then we bring you to Geminate. Once you are safe you are free to go."

"Really," replied Jamieson. The suspicion was heavy in his voice. "And why would four Agents, who I've never met, put themselves in danger to ensure my safety? What's in it for you?"

Four? He must have been the person I detected earlier. He knows I'm not alone. But how to rectify this?

Jude opened up the connection with his S-3 so his comrades could listen in on their conversation.

"My name is Jude Bray. I am head of the Kismet resources team. We are tasked with gathering food and supplies for our people when our land is in distress. Our people have taken up refuge in your homeland of Geminate. I was asked to make sure you return safely."

Jamieson stared back harshly. His trust would not come easy and he would not be easily fooled. The longer Jude stared into the Operative's eyes, the more he was beginning to spot a plan behind them.

"Very well. It's a pleasure to meet you," said Jamieson lowering one of his hands to shake Jude's. It was then that Jude saw the stranger leap from the shadows and rise up behind Jamieson—blade in hand.

"Get down!"

A flicker of shock washed across Jamieson's face; and just as the stranger raised his blade to attack, another silhouette appeared behind him. The stranger fell at their feet. Blood continued to fall from his severed neck. Jude looked up to find a copy of Jamieson standing at the Operative's side. The copy was identical in every detail, including posture. The only difference was a shadow that remained glued to the copy as it moved closer. Then it was gone.

How...

A heavy pressure descended on Jude. There was something familiar about Jamieson. He had a face that Jude had never seen before. His voice was foreign and unfamiliar to Jude's ears. However, there was something there—a connection. Something was present in the room that turned every second with this stranger into a second with a colleague.

Who is Jamieson Edric and why was his rescue so important?

◆ ◆ ◆

Jamieson matched each of his captive's steps equally. Even though he was sure this Jude Bray was watching him, Jamieson didn't want to give him any reason to watch him even closer. The two of them continued over the bridge and passed the pedestal room, venturing closer to the entrance to the mountain. Even though Jude's story of why he and his colleagues were here appeared legitimate, Jamieson was still suspicious of the dark-haired boy. His green eyes looked like they were caked with secrets. However, there was something familiar about the young man that Jamieson could not shake-off. He was positive he had never seen the young man before, but at the same time he felt as if he shared some kind of connection with this Jude Bray.

Could be some kind of magic at work to coerce me into going willingly. The General didn't mention anything about reinforcements for this mission when he assigned it to me. I did hear word of a large group of Kismet civilians relocating to Geminate temporarily so I guess his story checks out. But still, I don't know.

As Jamieson entered the next chamber, he heard footsteps from all around him as Jude Bray joined him in the center of the room. He knew it had to be Jude Bray's colleagues. The chamber was large and square, stretching out in all directions. Shadows cloaked the corners, making them invisible to the eye. The ceiling was too high to see its surface and the dozens of dead mercenaries that lay scattered at Jamieson's feet were proof that Bray's colleagues had to be close.

The swordsman from earlier stepped out of the shadows in front of him. He had long blonde hair and an athletic build. His dark armor carried the same straps and craftsmanship as Jude Bray's. His eyes were the color of the sea, and carried tremendous pain in its waves. He had no weapons in his hands, on his back or at his waist. Jamieson found this unnerving because he knew he saw the swordsman use a blade and arrows earlier. Something was—off. A second pair of feet approached from the left. A silhouette too dark to distinguish approached slowly. Then he saw them. Piercing purple eyes opened up in the shadow that approached him. The purple was sharp and powerful. He dared not look directly into them. A young woman in a fitting combat body suit stepped out of the shadows. Her long brown hair was neatly secured in a knot that fell down her back. She was beautiful, mesmerizing and terrifying all at the same time. A third set of footsteps approached from the right. The barbarian in all his madness cleared the shadows and approached. His armor matched the swordsman's; but instead of empty hands like the blonde, the barbarian held a severed arm.

"Mr. Edric this young woman on our left is Sia Wyatt," said Jude pointing to the woman with purple eyes. She returned a small smile before extinguishing it. "The young man in front of you goes by the name of Eli Brassie." The blonde boy gave no reaction to his introduction. He maintained his position as if waiting for something—maybe for an attack. "Lastly on your right we have Pang Quarrels." The barbarian was terrifying. There was something dark about him. His pores sweated evil while his smiling eyes continued to threaten. There was more to this Pang Quarrels than his appearance.

Jamieson looked at each of his captives individually, making sure to lock eyes with each of them. "Pleasure to meet all of you."

"That's a good point Sia," said Jude looking around.

What's a good point? She didn't even say anything.

Something was going on behind their expressionless faces and Jamieson didn't like it. If everything Jude Bray had told him was the truth, why were they keeping things from him? Jamieson looked around at their ears, mouths and hands to see how they could be communicating.

There has to be some kind of hand signs or facial gestures they are using to communicate. Doesn't matter either way. They are hiding something, which means I have cause for suspicion. First chance I get I'll make a run for it but I'll still need to find Lo in order to get out of here.

Everyone, including Jude Bray, stared back harshly at Jamieson. He couldn't tell if they were waiting for him to say something or if he had accidentally thought out loud.

"Are you okay?" asked Jude.

"Yeah why shouldn't I be?"

"Sia was just telling me that we still have the issue of the mirror magic blocking our exit. I asked you if you knew of an alternate route," replied Jude. His eyes studied Jamieson, making him nervous to answer Jude's question. Jude's stare made Jamieson afraid to lie and afraid to move. It was obvious; Jamieson would need their help to find Lo before he could make a run for it.

"We need to find my partner Lo. We split up a few hours ago so she could find the Umron Crystal."

"What's an Umron Crystal?" asked Sia Wyatt.

"It's what powers the mirror magic at the entrance to this mountain. Only with the Umron Crystal can we get out of here."

"You said your partner Lo left to retrieve the crystal," started Eli. He took a few more steps towards Jamieson until they were nearly toe-to-toe. "What's her stats and what does she look like?"

"She's about your height maybe a little shorter. She has long red hair and," but before Jamieson could finish, he caught the locked eyes of Jude Bray and his colleagues. Judging by their expressions they had already spotted Lo—or worse killed her.

"Your partner was killed," said Jude dryly.

"Killed? No not Lo!"

The chamber remained silent.

"How can you be sure? When did you see her? Where did you see her?

"We stumbled upon her in combat with two other hostiles. She made a run for it but was ambushed," said Jude.

"They beat the living flesh off her bones," said the barbarian Pang Quarrels. His tongue ran savagely across his lips.

"Pang that's enough!" ordered Jude. The finality in his voice was surprising.

"I refuse to leave without knowing for sure if she's dead. If she is, her body must be brought back to our homeland. I will find her." Jamieson took a few steps and was immediately stopped by a firm hand.

"You will stay here," demanded Jude. His eyes were fiercely sharp and unyielding with every word he spoke. "The three of you start with Lo's body in the eastern chamber where we first encountered her. Let's hope she already had the crystal before her death."

Nods and no words was all that came from Jude's colleagues. In a flash they were gone, leaving Jamieson alone with the cold and mysterious Jude Bray. Jude's eyes met with Jamieson's as if in response to his words. The sight was unnerving and filled Jamieson with overwhelming anxiety.

You better keep more than an eye on me, because the minute you even think about turning your back—I'm gone.

DIVIDE & CONQUER

Jude continued to meditate while keeping his ears alert to any movements from the Operative, who never stopped pacing in front of him. Jude could sense the suspicion from the Operative. A person who was grateful for their rescue would be much more receptive to the squad's help. Jude knew he needed to keep an eye on the Operative not only because of the potential threat of an attack from the enemy, but also an attack from Jamieson himself. Jude's meditation was also giving him the perfect disguise for communicating with the others without drawing too much attention. Sia, Pang and Eli had returned to the chamber where they first encountered Lo, only to discover her body was missing. The three of them spread out to find her and would report back in when they've found something.

"What are you're doing?" asked Jamieson.

Jude opened his eyes and found the Operative in a sitting position staring back at him. The way he was sitting was weird and looked awkward and uncomfortable. "Meditating."

"And what is that?" asked Jamieson with a curl of his brow.

"You've never heard of meditating before?"

Silence.

"It's the act of focusing your mind on one thing at a time, usually your breathing. It helps some people relax."

Jamieson shuffled in place. "Why do *you* do it?"

The question was so direct it blindsided Jude. "Well I first started doing it because our people believe its one of the vital practices that lets the three brothers in. After meditating for a while, I realized how calming it is. It also helps me think."

Jamieson mimicked Jude's position by crossing his legs and placing a hand on both knees. "So you're people are still loyal to the three brothers?"

"Yes. Most of us still are. What about your people?"

The question made Jamieson recoil as if he had just been assaulted. "You must know nothing of the Geminate people."

Jamieson's words were not entirely true. Jude knew he had never physically set foot in Geminate before, but he had read a lot on their culture and beliefs. He was sure Jamieson would be shocked at what he knew about the Geminates, even if it wasn't that much. However, Jude was given orders to not disclose too much vital information, so ignorance would have to be his friend."

"I'm afraid I don't. I apologize if I disrespected your people in any way."

Minutes passed like seconds amidst the silence around them. Jude came to the conclusion that any disrespect, even disrespect born of ignorance, was something Geminates took seriously; since Jamieson hadn't said a word for what felt like hours.

"Our people were born loyal to the three brothers. Pith is our champion, and in turn he is the brother we follow closely. Of course we respect all three of the brothers equally," said Jamieson.

"Brassie look out!" yelled Pang's voice in Jude's head.

"Pang. Eli. What's going on?"

The chamber rocked and soon tiny rockslides came to life around Jude and Jamieson. The abrupt quake was all the report Jude needed.

"Wonder what that was," said Jamieson.

"Jude for Sia."

"Go for me," said Sia.

"Eli and Pang may be in trouble. Find them."

"Permission to obtain this crystal first," she replied.

This crystal?

"Wait you have eyes on it?"

"Yes it's right in front of me. I just need to figure out how this trap works," she said.

"Describe it to me."

"The crystal is in a small gold box. If I take steps away from the box it opens. If I am close to the box, it remains sealed shut. There are statues surrounding me with jewels for eyes. Something tells me those jewels aren't just for decoration so I'm afraid to touch anything."

Jude began thinking about the mechanism Sia described, while Jamieson stared back attentively at him.

"Remove the eyes from the statues and tell me what happens."

Jude waited a few minutes for Sia's response. Jamieson continued to stare and appeared fidgety.

He either wants to attack me or run. Either one is unwise since we are here to help him.

"I removed the eyes from the statues. Now the statues have retreated to the walls and the box is open. I can grab it now," said Sia with heightened breathing.

"Don't move!"

"Standing by," replied Sia. Her voice was comfort to his ears since he thought he might have been too late.

"Where are the jewels at, you know, the eyes from the statues?"

"In my pocket," she replied.

"Find a place on the other side of the room to put them. Doesn't matter where, just make sure they are as far from you as possible." He waited.

"Copy, jewels are under a stone on the other side of the room," said Sia.

"Now put a shield around yourself and grab the crystal."

"Do you mind showing me how to meditate?" asked Jamieson. His voice brought Jude back to the chamber he was in.

"Sure. First keep your legs crossed and put one hand on both knees like me. Then inhale through your nose and—." An explosion threw the two of them on their backs. Jude leaped to his feet and caught a glimpse of Jamieson barreling through a dark opening. "Jamieson wait!" Jude sprinted for the Operative. Rocks and pillars began to fall from the ceiling nearly crushing Jude. Jude found himself quickly closing-in on the Operative who immediately caught sight of his pursuer. *"Jude to Sia. What happened?"*

Heavy breathing answered first. *"The jewels! The jewels you had me get rid of exploded! The entire room is coming down! But I have the crystal."*

"Perfect! Get back to the entrance," started Jude as he opened his mind up to Pang and Eli so they could hear their conversation. *"All Agents rendezvous at the entrance. I am in pursuit of the Operative who is making a run for it."*

"Copy that," said Sia.

Nothing came from Eli or Pang. Jude hoped for the best and focused all of his attention at turning the next corner sharply after activating his Optical Tactics. The second he turned it, Jamieson attacked and Jude countered with a sweep of Jamieson's legs. The Operative fell to the floor but Jude immediately found himself dodging the incoming daggers that Jamieson threw after hitting the ground. Jude shattered a vial and embraced the smokescreen that fell on them. Coughing filled the room while Jude sprinted for Jamieson. The Jamieson copy returned and launched for Jude, who flipped over the clone's head and came down with a heavy palm to Jamieson's chin. The copy fell to the floor, followed by Jamieson. The smokescreen cleared, bringing Jude face-to-face with two identical Operatives. Then the shaded clone was gone. Jude took a vial from his belt and hammered it into Jamieson's neck. He didn't know where the added roughness came from when he injected him. The serum would act as a muscle relaxant, preventing Jamieson from moving if he came to before the squad reached Geminate.

"Bray for Lieutenant Titus."

After a few minutes the Lieutenant's voice boomed in Jude's head. *"Go for Titus."*

"Mission complete."

FAR FROM HOME

Conall waited anxiously underneath the familiar but foreign white trees. The white flowered vines that fell from every branch of the surrounding trees were aggravating but comforting. The vines did help conceal his presence even though he had to slap them away with each step he took. The Geminate Forest was just how he remembered it. The seclusion, the exotic birds singing, and of course the snow-white grass, all jogged his memory of his first mission within Geminate's borders. Everything from the rocks, to the dirt, to the animals themselves was as white as snow. The contrast was painful to the eyes at first, but after a few hours, Conall's eyes began to adjust.

Tactical Agent Bray had reported completion of his squad's mission a little over an hour ago. Surely with his Magi's portaling they would be here by now. Worry danced around him in an endless taunt, just before a rustling drew his attention.

Conall looked up at the arrows he summoned amidst the surrounding trees. Thousands of arrows remained motionless, concealed behind the branches and leaves, ready to fire at his command. A duo of amethyst orbs pierced the white blanket that was the Geminate Forest. Wyatt's eyes enchanted him. Her eyes were home when he looked into their center. Each occasion that he was able to be closer to her was short-lived; for he was her Lieutenant, and commingling intimately with subordinates was dishonorable and frowned upon. But he wanted her, wanted her with every inch of his being.

The air filled with the sound of leaves crunching and soon Sia's arms were around his neck. His brain told him to push her away. Half of his heart told him to listen to his brain, while the other half told him to give-in and embrace her. He wrapped his arms around her. The smell of cold leather filled his nose as her armor rustled beneath his embrace. Her arms finally retreated, and soon he found himself lost in the Magi Glare that never ceased.

"I heard the pain in your voice over the S-3 during our mission," she said with worry on her face. She quickly looked away, blinked a few times and then returned his stare. "I did not know what to think."

Is she telling me what I think she's telling me? Or is she telling me what I'm hoping she will tell me? It's irrelevant. Article nine, section one of the 'Lieutenant Code of Conduct' tells me that this is wrong.

"Bray's report said the mission was a success."

Her change of demeanor told him that he succeeded in diffusing the situation. Her emotions had clearly gotten the best of her. Special Agent Wyatt was smart, honorable, disciplined and knew the rules. If it wasn't for her emotions, she would have never hugged Conall the way she had.

I believe this is the second time she's hugged me like she would never see me again.

"That is correct Lieutenant. The Operative gave chase, but Bray was able to apprehend him. The others are just taking a quick break, to regain their blood energy, and should be here any second," she said.

He could not look away from her stare even though he was willing himself to. "And why did you decide to not take a break? Aren't you exhausted as well? Surely portaling must have taken its toll."

I'm playing with fire. Why did I ask that question? I know what her answer will be; and even though I want to hear it, I shouldn't want to hear it.

"You are correct Lieutenant," she said regaining her composure and acquiring a stern demeanor. "I am foolish for not joining the others. The portal consumed most of my blood energy, and I should always be prepared for an ambush. My apologies."

That's not what you wanted to say. It can't be. You wanted to see me didn't you? I can see it in your eyes the same way I see it every time you look at me. I know you feel the same way—know it but refuse to act on it. Nice work Wyatt, I'm glad I can count on you.

"Calm yourself. Your first mission was a success, it is only natural that you would be excited to report-in after such a triumph."

"Thank you Lieutenant," she replied slowly.

The rustling of leaves caused Wyatt to relocate a few steps back. Conall turned towards the commotion to find Bray approaching him with Quarrels hot on his heels. Conall began to worry when he saw no sign of the Operative, until Brassie stepped through the white brush with Operative Jamieson Edric.

Funny. They make Brassie carry him. Looks like we have identified the pack mule of the group.

"The Operative should be waking up soon so I would prefer if we get him to his destination beforehand as to avoid any complications," said Jude.

"Agreed. Follow me and stay close."

◆ ◆ ◆

Eli could smell the dirty and sweaty musk with every step he took. The Operative definitely had the 'I just got out of combat' smell. The smell was one thing Eli could overlook, even hold his breath if he had to, but his main complaint was the weight. The Operative had to weigh twice Eli's weight, and he assumed it all came from the Jamieson's massive arms.

Now I know why Kai made me lift all of those boulders during my training. He claimed it was for weapon handling but now I know it's so I can carry heavy piles of salty garbage like this guy. I still don't get why I was elected to carry him over Pang and his freakishly large scarred up arms.

Eli didn't know what triggered it, but suddenly all he could think about was his dad—chained to that chair, helpless to fend off the attacks that left him scarred and deformed—the endless river of dried blood that fell from his body.

He must have been in so much pain.

"Stay close to me," said Conall brushing branches and debris out of their path.

"I'm tired of these freaking leaves!" yelled Pang with some added bass. "Can't we just cut them all down!"

"Never willingly harm any type of nature when in the domain of the cursed lady," said Conall.

"Who is the cursed lady?" asked Jude.

Conall went silent, making Eli wonder if the Lieutenant heard Jude's question or if he heard it and refused to answer.

"I do believe you've lost your touch Lieutenant," said a voice from in front of them.

Eli froze, along with the others, at the tall man that stepped out of the white trees and bushes. He was dressed in some of the most impressive armor Eli had ever seen. Black and white armor perfectly outlined his broad shoulders, massive chest and flexed arms. His arms remained glued to his sides with every step he took while his nose and chin remained high in the air.

"General Mather, I didn't expect to be meeting you here. I thought you would send one of your other men—perhaps Garrett," said Conall.

"Well that is why you're a Lieutenant and I'm a General," said the man chuckling. "I don't assume things, I *know* things," said Mather.

The air reeks with the arrogance of this guy. Conall please shut this guy down.

"I see," said Conall.

"There are nine Agents approaching from the east and west," said Jude over the S-3. "None have their weapons drawn and their arms are at their sides, however, I'm assuming they have some sort of Magi with them on account of I was not able to spot them earlier."

"None of you say a word," replied Conall.

"Hello, hello hello. Lieutenant?" said Mather.

"Apologies General, we have had a long journey and I'm a bit tired. Did you say something?" said Conall.

General Mather wrapped his arm around Conall's shoulders and walked with him towards the nine Agents that appeared before them. "Eh old news. Let us visit more important matters shall we."

"Follow us slowly and carefully, but not too close," said Conall's voice in Eli's head. "I don't want him to think you're trying to listen. By the way, no magic Wyatt. No matter how harmless, General Mather will immediately take it as a threat."

"Copy," said the four of them in unison over the S-3.

"Loyalty my dear Lieutenant. Loyalty!" said Mather. "Loyalty is what separates the honorable from the dishonorable. Man from the animals. Strong from the weak."

When the lake opened up in front of Eli, he thought he was looking at the edge of the world. Two large green mountains sat on either side of an enormous dark lake. The surface was violent. Cold waves crashed into one another for no apparent reason. Nothing appeared to be disturbing the lake, so Eli was perplexed as to why the lake was in such an uproar. The unidentified Agents circled behind General Mather and Conall. One separated from the crowd and approached Eli.

"Here," said the Agent holding out a small black velvet pouch. "Try not to lose them so I won't have to kill you."

Eli's hand took the bag without his command, while he scowled at the Agent's words. "Try not to threaten me again, so I won't have to kill *you!*"

"Brassie!" screamed Conall's voice in Eli's head. Eli had to claw his ears in order to withstand the volume of the Lieutenant's voice.

General Mather's head whipped around. "Well well well, it looks like you have a spitfire in your group Lieutenant. Tell me, does the little monkey do tricks?"

Eli felt his blood boiling and this time it wasn't his blood energy.

"Brassie! You will not say a word! Do you hear me? Stand down," said Conall.

General Mather lowered his head until it was level with Eli's gaze. "Do you little guy? Do you do tricks? Do you spin on that big, dirty, oblong head of yours? Huh? Do ya?" General Mather rose from Eli's sight. "Or are you a baby dragon with a tough roar but no flames?"

"I could really go for a Blood Execution right about now," said Eli over the S-3. His comment returned some mental muffling that resembled laughter.

"Well at least the dumb animal knows when to keep its big mouth closed," said General Mather returning to Conall.

Just before he reached the Lieutenant, he turned a lone eye back towards Eli. "Don't worry, you will learn your place."

Eli returned his attention to the soft black pouch in his hands. He loosened the tassel and looked inside. He reached in and took out what appeared to be a small black diamond no bigger than a pebble. The diamond was elegant and sharp. No matter which way Eli held the diamond, a tiny shine sparkled from its core. Eli handed the pouch to Pang, who took out a diamond and then passed it to Jude, who eventually passed it to Sia.

"Don't lose it," boomed Conall's voice over the S-3. *"This gem is your key to enter Geminate. Without it, your fate will be reduced to that of the Praxians from the story—at least that's what the legends say."*

Eli hugged his diamond tight just as the sound of a tidal wave came to his ears. His eyes widened and his mouth dropped as the large ravenous lake parted, unveiling a path unlike any he had ever seen.

UNDER THE
WATCHFUL EYE

Jude continued behind General Mather's squadron of men, as they all descended the clear glass staircase. Looking up, Jude nearly panicked as the ocean's dark waves splashed closed over their heads. The entrance was replaced with the dark surface of the lake's waves. With each step they took, their path grew darker while the steps appeared endless. Sia screamed. Looking her direction, he found her fixated on the transparent glass walls around them. A massive yellow eye shot open. It's size larger than any creature Jude had ever encountered.

"Don't worry little girl he can't hurt you," said Mather.

"Little girl?" said Sia over the S-3.

"These staircase walls are enchanted with the magic of Pith. Nothing can stand against them. Not even magic," said General Mather turning his head back towards Sia's direction as he led on.

The eye was gone. In its wake it left a blanket of bubbles. Jude felt nauseous being underneath the water's surface. He felt like each step he took brought him one step closer to the walls caving in—bringing with them a cold onslaught of the lake's power. The fish and creatures that swam on either side of them were captivating. Fish of every color and size swam over and under them as if the staircase Jude walked on was completely and utterly invisible. Jude looked down at his feet at the transparent glass that displayed the dark, bottomless depths of oblivion below.

I think I'm going to be sick.

Minutes turned to hours and hours to miles of anticipation. Then Jude remembered that Pang was still carrying the Operative. Focusing on the S-3, he found himself whispering even though he knew no one but his squad and Conall could hear him. *"Doesn't anyone find it suspicious that General Mather has not said a word about the unconscious Operative that Pang is carrying over his shoulder?"*

Silence.

"Good observation," said Sia.

"Isn't there some saying about arrogance blinding you?" replied Eli. *"Maybe that's why."*

"Right Brassie," said Pang with a hint of sarcasm in his voice. *"General Mather was able to see every last one of us perfectly but happened not to see the giant arm wrapped around my neck or the tall body that it goes with."*

Conall laughed slightly at the conversation. It was abnormal for the Lieutenant to display any kind of positive emotion around them so Jude began to become suspicious of the Lieutenant's chipper behavior.

"He saw the Operative," interrupted Conall. *"He either thinks he's dead, which I highly doubt, or he is pretending like he isn't interested in the topic."*

"Regardless, any normal person would have acknowledged it so we know something is up." As soon as Jude finished his sentence, he felt a picking at the back of his head. The sensation was like a fragile knock and was something Jude had never experienced.

"You're right Jude," said Sia sharply. *"There is a Magi in their group, and whoever they are, they are trying to enter our thoughts."*

Conall cursed while continuing to follow the General.

"His words are a decoy to divert our attention away from the Magi's attack. What would you like us to do Lieutenant?"

"We can't use magic. He will see it as an attack," said Conall. *"Bray, what do you recommend?"*

Hmm how to defend against an enemy without using magic, weapons or any sort of attacks.

Jude activated his Optical Tactics just as a school of pink fish swam above them. The white hue descended upon his vision. His mind quickly counted everything around him without him even trying. The fish, the steps and the Agents all read like numbers to him. Focusing on the hands of the General's soldier ahead of him, he quickly spotted a miniscule burn on the corner of one of the Agent's nails. The Agent was slender with barely any muscle mass whatsoever.

He must be strong with magic if he is one of the General's personal bodyguards without any athleticism. I mean even Sia looks more built than him.

"Bray?" asked Conall's voice.

Jude strolled towards the Agent, who instantly turned around when Jude was upon him. The Agent's curly black hair shook slightly above his brown eyes.

"Hi my name is Jude."

The Agent blinked violently before tripping over his own feet and regaining his composure.

"Hello, hi!" replied the Agent quickly. "Raslo is my name."

"Nice to meet you Raslo. I am sorry to bother you, but I am a little uneasy in regards to all of this." Jude's gaze swept from one side to the other of the lake.

"Keep it up Jude, I can feel his reach weakening," said Sia's voice.

"Brilliant Bray," said Conall's voice.

"I hear you it can be intimidating. I'm comfortable with it now. When I was younger I used to travel these steps a lot," said

Raslo. Each word he spoke was quick. Jude felt like each sentence was thrown at him.

"Yes! Very intimidating," Jude quickly answered. "How much longer do we have to go? Are your legs as tired as mine are? What was that large yellow eye we saw earlier?"

Raslo stared. "Not too long. I'm fine and what used to be a Geminate secret."

"Well what is it?"

Jude deactivated his Optical Tactics, but not before catching the silence of the General's ramble. The General's lone eye looked their direction while he continued to take each step with powerful steps.

Raslo's eyes attained small red cracks before closing. He shook his head back-and-forth before returning to Jude's gaze. "It wasn't an eye it was just a cluster of fish that travel together. Many people mistaken them for other things but that's all it was—a school of fish.

"Sia what's happening to him?"

"What do you mean?" asked Sia over the S-3.

"He had red cracks spread along his eyes before closing them."

"IIe has a heavy spell active. But that's strange because I sense his energy and it's not going anywhere," said Sia.

Jude stared deeply into Raslo's eyes as he went on about the different kinds of fish that existed in The Great Lake. Raslo's brow began to sweat while he began to stutter at the beginning of each new sentence.

"He forgot to deactivate his spell. His blood energy is low."

"You ask too many damn questions that's why he forgot," fired Pang with some heavy breathing in his voice.

"Raslo switch with Dane," ordered Mather.

Raslo quickly relocated to the first spot behind General Mather, and was replaced with a different Agent, who refused to even give Jude a glance. Jude retreated to his squad behind Conall and turned his attention towards the massive yellow eye that returned once again. The eye was enormous blinking once, twice and then dissolving into the water's cold depths.

"General Mather definitely did not like what you did," said Eli.

"We may have made a mistake by countering," replied Sia.

"No," replied Conall's voice quickly. *"We could not afford to have his Magi read our thoughts and discover what has transpired. We did what needed to be done, and it could not have been done better. Good work Bray."*

Jude didn't know why, but he felt a surge of confidence after Conall's praise. He tried to extinguish it but couldn't help it. He had been through training and had already proved his skills. However, Jude valued Conall's opinion greatly, and he could not help but admire the Lieutenant's status as a Lieutenant at such a young age.

"Finally," said Mather.

Jude turned his attention ahead of him, only to come to an immediate halt—causing Sia to run-in to him from behind. Two large statues towered over them all. The detail of the statues was extensive. The first statue, depicting a male in light but sturdy armor, was as white as milk and looked as smooth as the walls of the Coliseum. The statue held a dark orb in his raised, open right palm and a sword in his left. The other statue was a copy of the first; except for the second statue had a sword in his right hand and a light-colored orb in its left. It also had a dark shade across its surface from head-to-toe. In between the two statues was a pair of tall glass double doors. Through the glass was a blinding light, which concealed whatever was on the other side. The statues were familiar. Jude looked down at the armband that was tied firmly around his bicep. The same statues stared back at him.

"*From this point on you will always be under surveillance,*" said Conall with a flicker of worry in his voice. "*From now on, you are the Kismet Task Force in combat and the B.B.Q.W. outside of combat—especially here in Geminate.*"

"*Copy,*" said the squad simultaneously.

GEMINATE

The thousands of fish swam aimlessly above, below and on the sides of Geminate's great walls. Clear glass walls surrounded the city on all sides, giving Eli and his comrades a clear view into the aquatic world around them. All of the marine life was unsettling. A very large city, larger than Kismet, sat in the middle of an aquatic world of various creatures Eli had never seen.

Hundreds of rows of identical homes sat intersected by the single large clear path Eli stood on. The path turned to stairs at the beginning of the first row of houses, ascending with each new row of homes. Each row was higher than the last—their identical rooftops growing taller and taller the further up you ventured. The houses all shared a theme of twisted white and black patterns and symbols. To Eli, the architecture surpassed Kismet's and was a lot more advanced. At the top of the cascading staircase was what looked like a large temple, much larger than the homes beneath it. Standing large and strong behind the temple was a statue similar to the duo Eli passed on the way into the city; only this time there was only one statue with a line that ran down its center, separating the light side from the dark. The sword was absent. Two open palms hovered above the temple's rooftop—a black orb in its right hand and a white orb in its left. While the black orb was inactive, the white orb resembled the sun, shining with bright rays that gave light to the entire city.

The streets were a buzz with life. The citizens of Geminate thrived differently than the Kismet people. The Geminates walked faster, spoke faster and multi-tasked activities that didn't require them to. In addition to their quick and effective behavior, the Geminates also had a glow to them that had no clear source. They were enchanting to stare at and mesmerizing whenever Eli locked eyes with them. On the other hand, Eli was finding it difficult to focus solely on the natives in front of him, due to the enormous aquatic life that continued to swim around him from every angle.

"I really don't like this place or those—things," said Eli.

"I don't either," replied Jude quickly. "I feel like the floor beneath us is about to shatter; dropping us into a feeding frenzy of savage proportions."

Eli looked down at the transparent streets beneath him as a black shadow swam underneath him. His stomach sank. "I'm going to throw up."

"You do and I'll kill you," said Conall.

"Well I trust that you know your way around Lieutenant," said General Mather. "After you're done getting your—um who are these delightful people again?"

"General, this is our city's resources team. They are in charge of gathering food, water and supplies for our people," said Conall.

"Hmm, a lot of help they will be. Luckily for you and your people, our Priestess has agreed to supply you with all of those necessities—lucky you," said General Mather with a scowl. "Well after you're done getting your useless 'resources team' situated, come see me Lieutenant. We have business that needs to be settled." Without waiting for Conall to respond, General Mather and his men disappeared into the crowd of civilians. After a few seconds, Eli saw the back of Mather's armor, ascending the stairs that led him through the homes and towards the temple.

No one moved and Eli was growing restless. He expected someone, specifically Conall, to say or do something.

"So are we sleeping with the fishes or what?"

"I will show you to your houses shortly, but first I want you all to meet someone," said Conall.

"Lieutenant, what about our good friend Mr. Sweat and Musk?" asked Pang.

"He comes," fired Conall.

◆ ◆ ◆

Eli's leg began to shake in his chair, causing the legs of the chair to creek. If it weren't for the pleasant smell of herbs and berries in the air, he would have lost it and went on a rampage. The house was quiet, except for the light commotion upstairs. The owner of the house, a woman by the name of Kyla, was upstairs preparing a bed for the Operative. Jude and Conall were helping Pang bring the Operative upstairs to a loft that overlooked the living room, which Eli and Sia inhabited. Eli's legs were killing him from both the long journey and carrying the Operative out of the previous cold zone; so he decided to take a seat. Sia on the other hand, stood dead center of the living room examining the many miniature statues on various end tables around the room. The statues resembled the large one behind the temple. Weapon racks hung from the walls on one side of the room, while soft and dainty furniture occupied the other side. The weapon racks reminded Eli of his dad's old Weapons Room.

Marius sat on the fountain of the three brothers under the night sky's cool embrace. Eli took a seat alongside Marius. "When a comrade falls in battle, if there is even the slightest chance that they could be saved, you take it."

Sia's voice caught his attention and brought him back to the present.

"I'm sorry did you say something?"

"Never mind, I see you're being as clueless as ever," said Sia.

Eli felt himself roll his eyes, a gesture he was not accustomed to.

Dad I tried to save you—I really did. The Council was right, I didn't have the skills to be in combat back then. But I'm stronger now dad I am. But now it's too late. You're already gone. You left me. No! No! I left you—and spit on you on my way out.

Conall, Pang and Jude returned to the room and took a seat. Kyla soon came down the stairs, brushing her brow with the back of her hand. She was a tall woman with a small frame and flat stomach. Her long brown hair swayed freely at her back. Her voice was light and sweet, similar to the healer Fey's. A small star sat etched in the center of her forehead, something Eli noticed was present on all of the Geminate's brows.

"I left some hot tea and lavender next to his bed for when he wakes up," said Kyla.

"Thank you Kyla," said Conall rising to his feet. He gave a quick nod to the rest of them, and soon Eli rose to his feet along with the others. "This is Kyla Aaia. Kyla this is Jude Bray, Sia Wyatt, Pang Quarrels and Eli Brassie. They make-up our resources team."

"It's a pleasure to meet all of you," said Kyla with a smile.

"We appreciate you inviting us into your home Ms. Aaia," said Jude.

"My pleasure! Oh and it's Mrs. Aaia. My husband should be home soon and I'm sure if he ever found out that I was going by Ms. Aaia, he would surely think I was leaving him," said Kyla with an upbeat laugh.

Her laugh was uplifting and made Eli feel more comfortable in Kyla's home. They all took their seats. Eli found himself looking to Jude for instruction, a habit he had recently acquired which disgusted him. Jude sat calmly examining the woman, so Eli took it as a sign that they all could interact somewhat normally.

"So I take it you're all from Kismet as well," said Kyla rubbing her stomach in a circular motion.

"Yes," replied Sia softly. She stared closely at Kyla's revolving hand. "We are."

"I hear your land is plagued by a vampire," said Kyla with worry heavy in her voice.

Eli and his comrades looked at each other immediately. Everyone looked startled, except for Pang, who appeared to be fighting back laughter.

"How do you survive?" continued Kyla.

"We don't go out at night," said Pang with a smirk that was loaded with laughter.

"You know," started Conall locking eyes with Eli. "Kyla's husband, Eio, is a good friend of Marius."

Eli saw everyone's gaze set on him. Why should he care if some stranger's husband knew his dad? Marius was legendary, and Eli was sure many people were friends with him. He refused to talk about his dad with these people—including his comrades.

"I love your weapon cases."

"Do you? I'm sure my husband would be thrilled to hear that," said Kyla with a smile.

"Yeah, my dad and I had a Weapons Room back home and he had some similar weapons cases. He was sort of a collector."

"Ahh that's great. You know news of Kismet's invasion reached our city a little while ago. I trust it your dad made it out okay," said Kyla.

"No—I'm afraid he didn't make it."

"I'm so sorry to hear that Eli," said Kyla with a frown.

Silence.

"So when can we expect Eio to be home?" asked Conall.

"You know my husband should be here by now, and I don't know where my son Alistair is either. Maybe he," started Kyla before stopping at the sound of the front door opening.

A tall man with short, messy brown hair entered the house and closed the door behind him. He was drowned in heavy black metal armor from head-to-toe He had two long blades in a belt around his waist, in which he unbuckled and threw on the floor. Sweat shined on his forehead while his noticeably dirty hands went to wipe it.

"Eio! You're home," said Kyla running to greet him. She kissed him quickly on the lips before he picked her up and swung her around.

"How are my two favorite people in the world?" asked Eio before kissing Kyla on the lips and then kissing her on her flat stomach. His light-brown eyes quickly found Eli and the others. "Conall, you finally made it."

Conall rose from his seat and greeted Eio with a quick but firm handshake. "How are you doing my friend? I would like for you to meet our resources team." Conall extended an open arm and hand to Eli and his comrades. "This is Jude Bray, Sia Wyatt, Pang Quarrels and Eli Brassie."

Eio recoiled. "Brassie eh?"

Eli met Eio's gaze. "Yes sir. I understand you knew my father."

"I better since he was my best friend," said Eio extending a hand to Eli.

Eli shook Eio's hand and instantly recoiled at the man's tight grip.

"Come on, I know a Brassie can do better than that," said Eio tilting his head with a frown. "You know what they say about a man with a weak handshake..."

"They're not a man," said Kyla and Eio in unison.

It's a handshake for heaven's sake.

"Now I'm sure you can do better than that so let's try again," said Eio extending his hand.

Eli exhaled quietly and grabbed Eio's hand with all his strength and shook it.

"Ouch! Ouch! You're tearing my arm off," said Eio with a laugh. "Now that's a handshake." Eio looked to Conall before continuing. "This one is going to be a leader some day. Mark my words!" Returning his gaze to Eli he frowned. "Perhaps you can give my son Alistair some pointers on being a man. Pith knows I've done all I can do."

"Eio!" yelled Kyla.

"What?" replied Eio.

"You know Alistair is doing his best. Why don't you lighten up," said Kyla. She gave Eio a light slap on the shoulder.

Eio took a seat and patted his leg with a smile. Kyla sat in his lap and wrapped her arms around his neck. "Okay, okay, but only because I love you so much." He looked down to her stomach. "Both of you."

"Oh my goodness congratulations!" said Sia.

For what?

"Thank you! Thank you!" said Kyla appearing bashful. "I'm around ten months now! The baby will be here any day! I really hope it's a girl. But if it's a boy, I will love him just the same."

"We need another man in this family, that way when I'm dead and gone we have a man to carry on my name!" said Eio.

"Hunny you already have Alistair for that," said Kyla.

"I said a man Kyla. A man!"

Eli was confused as to how Sia could even tell that Kyla was pregnant. It's true that Eli had never known a pregnant woman—at least to his knowledge. Kyla looked so normal and had a flatter stomach than his. With no telltale signs that she was pregnant, Eli was sure that Sia either used magic to tell that Kyla was pregnant, or just knew because it was a woman thing.

The door creaked open slowly.

"Ah speaking of my son," said Eio.

Eli turned towards the door and set eyes on a young man with short dark brown hair like Eio's, except Alistair's was groomed. He had the same light-brown eyes as Eio, but where Eio had a muscular build, Alistair had an athletic build. Alistair was fully dressed in a dark light armor, similar to his dads, but far less bulky.

"Afternoon Ali!" said Kyla.

"Kyla don't call him that. Ali is a girl's name," said Eio with a shake of his head. "So how did training go?"

Alistair closed the door behind him and set a large weapons bag on the floor. "It went."

"Answer your father Alistair," said Kyla with a light rise in her tone.

"I did answer him," said Alistair dryly.

"No you didn't. You snarked at me the way a woman snarks at a man when she's mad about doing the dishes," said Eio.

"It went well. Baul said I'm advanced for my age so he's thinking about moving me up," said Alistair.

Eio's fist came down hard on the end table next to him. "Well by the name of Pith that's great! I knew you had it in you. You're an Aaia! A natural. In a few months you will be one of the youngest Agents under the Priestess' command."

"But dad I don't want to be an Agent. I don't like combat," said Alistair.

"Nonsense! All boys become Agents and all boys like combat," said Eio.

"Maybe most boys do but I don't," said Alistair with a drop of his shoulders.

Eli noticed a dark shade begin to fall down Eio's body. It was as if Eio's shadow wasn't attached to him, but moved around at his command and had just fused with Eio himself; giving him a darker hue.

"Please dad can I just be a—."

"That's enough!" yelled Eio pushing the end table next to him over. He quickly rose to his feet. His demeanor had changed along with his posture, which to Eli, looked like Eio was ready to do battle. "You're a boy! All boys like combat. All boys become Agents. Boys who claim they don't like combat are not boys; and if you're not a boy, then you mines well be a girl!"

Alistair's head dropped. "But dad..."

"End of discussion!" snapped Eio.

In a quick second, Alistair snatched his weapons bag and disappeared down the hallway, which ran alongside the staircase and up to the loft.

Sitting back down in his seat, Eio began to rub his head. He appeared to have a headache. The shade was gone, nowhere to be found. Kyla finished returning the end table to its rightful place.

"I don't know what I'm gonna do with that boy," said Eio.

"He'll be fine Eio. Stop worrying," said Kyla.

"I don't know hun, I have already taken him to see Alize and she can't do nothin' for him," said Eio.

"Are you sure that's what she said? I have known Alize my entire life, and I have never known her to give-up on someone," said Kyla.

"Alize is Geminates go-to ipseity Practitioner," said Conall to Eli and the others.

"Yes and my good friend," said Kyla. "I strongly recommend each of you go see her at least once while you're here. I'm sure she will give you a complimentary session."

What the Pith is an ipseity Practitioner?

"We surely will," said Jude.

You mean you surely will.

"Eio is in charge of the city's security. However, he is also a very resourceful guy so if any of you need anything and I'm not here, Eio is your go-to guy," said Conall.

"That is right," said Eio with a more positive demeanor. "Any friends of Conall's are friends of mine. Come over any time!"

"Thank you Mr. Aaia," said Sia.

"Well I need to show them where they will be staying," said Conall rising from his seat. Jude soon followed, which made Eli and the rest of them rise.

"Just a second Conall. Is you-know-who upstairs yet?" asked Eio.

"Yes. He is still unconscious. When he wakes up just tell him that you found him in The Great Forest. He will most likely go looking for answers, however, we all should be gathering supplies for our people. So hopefully we won't have to run-in to him," said Conall.

"Very well. Perhaps having a top rank Operative in my house will help with that son of mine," said Eio with a sigh.

Conall shook Eio's hand. After everyone said their goodbyes, Eli followed Conall and the others out of the Aaia household and back to the streets of Geminate.

THE LOCALS

Eli had no idea why he was so angry. Looking at his closet with all of the new clothes provided for him made him feel a tad bit spoiled. He closed the armoire and looked around his bedroom. Painted black walls with various artwork surrounded him. A large bed, big enough to fit four full-sized adults in it, lay comfortable in front of him. He exited his bedroom and looked out from the loft over his very own living room, kitchen and furniture. He was eighteen going on nineteen and already had his own house.

Why am I so mad?

Walking down the stairs, he took it all in. He had his own house and could come and go as he pleased. The freedom felt amazing. He walked to the front door and turned around to get a better view of the entire house. The luxury reminded him of Sia's old luxurious emerald green and white house. The black and white décor gave the room an artful look of sophistication and luxury.

Jude's house is bigger.

After leaving the Aaia household, Conall showed each of them to their new homes as well as rewarded them with another small bundle of five hundred gold. The Kismet people were sharing homes in the first row of homes on the bottom level of Geminate closest to the main entrance. As many people as comfortably possible inhabited the homes. Luckily, the Geminate's architecture was large and realistically one house could fit eight to ten people comfortably. Right now, twelve to thirteen people occupied each house. Conall had instructed for

Eli and his comrades to have their own house for alias purposes. He didn't want to risk anyone asking too many questions or to even have knowledge of when Eli and his comrades came-and-went from the city. Jude's house was first, which was located on the very last row of homes at the very top of the stairs—closest to the temple. Eli noticed that the very last row of homes broke the status quo of identical homes and were significantly larger than the rest of the homes in Geminate. Everything about the homes was more upscale and larger than the rest. Walking inside, Eli was in shock at the size of the house. Jude's house contained multiple rooms and bathrooms. He had a large kitchen and a mini kitchen, as well as a built-in spirits closet. To top it off, his living room was filled with hundreds of gifts from the Geminate people to the Prodigy of Pith. After leaving Jude to get settled in, Conall took Eli and the others to Eli's house, which was at the very bottom of the stairs on the first row. Eli was annoyed by the relocation at first, but figured having multiple bedrooms, kitchens and bathrooms would make up for it. The excitement was short-lived. When he walked into the house it was nice and luxurious. He was embarrassed to say that it was even more luxurious than the home he and Marius had. He thought maybe a tour of the house would extinguish the rising anger he felt inside, but after taking a last look at his house, he realized he was even angrier than he was when he first arrived.

Typical life of Jude Bray. Everything comes easy for you doesn't it? You're too good to have a normal sized house like the rest of us. You have to have a castle with extra rooms and bathrooms that you probably won't even use. And with all of those gifts, he's basically royalty. Whatever.

A knock sounded at the front door behind him.

Opening the door, he found himself gazing into a pair of eyes he thought he would never see outside of a mission. A tight-fitting burgundy dress clung to her curves ending slightly above her knees. Her S-3 now hung from a golden chain around her neck, along with a few other pendants that Eli wondered if they were just decoys. Her hair sat whimsically contained over one bare shoulder.

"Good evening Special Agent Brassie," said Sia.

"Hello."

"May I come in?"

Eli opened the door wider and instructed her to come in. A clicking followed her every step. Eli looked down at a pair of black shoes she wore with a raised heel. He closed the door and followed her to the sitting area of the living room. She quickly took a seat at one of the two black armchairs that faced his un-lit fireplace and crossed her legs—causing her dress to slightly rise at its end.

"Jude and Pang sent me to get you. You should get dressed. We are going out to what the Geminates call a tavern tonight. I forgot the name of it," she said.

Eli looked away from her and stared at the loft that sat perched overhead. Going out sounded like a bad idea. They had just returned from an intense mission *and* had traveled to a foreign land—all in the course of a day.

"I really don't feel like going out tonight. I think I will sit this one out."

She sighed and rolled her eyes. "Oh don't be difficult. Go in there, get dressed and don't take too long."

Eli felt himself stagger. Who was this forceful aggressive person, and why did she think she had the authority to tell him where to go?

Perhaps being alone with all these thoughts of my dad isn't the best thing.

"Fine make yourself at home."

His legs cramped at each step on the return back to the armoire. All of the clothes smelled even fresher than when he looked at them a few minutes ago. He grabbed a pair of dark, smooth pants and a fire-red collared shirt. The red shirt took no thought and was fueled by instinct. He turned around and tripped over his knapsack that sat next to his bed.

You're alright Lieutenant. You're alright...

He picked up the knapsack and sat on the bed. He instantly found his mother's journal of poems. The familiar smell of flowers and berries, the smooth surface under his fingertips and the memories the journal brought, all were comforting. He opened the journal to the first page and began to read.

"You're of course rude as always," said Sia.

Eli looked over at the beautiful woman in the doorway of his bedroom. "Sorry I got sidetracked. I'm ready we can go now."

"Not like that we can't," said Sia crossing the room and standing over him. "Here stand up."

Eli did as he was told.

Sia quickly unbuttoned the top two buttons of his collared shirt. "Never button up a formal shirt all the way to the top. Always leave two buttons open, no more no less. Two buttons are just enough to remain formal and appropriate for the occasion, but just enough skin to give woman something to look at."

"Sure. Whatever. Can we go now?"

Sia curled her brow and glared at him. "If you don't want my help Brassie, just say so. Oh and yes, we can go now." The clicks that followed her every step were harder and more powerful when she left the room. Eli placed the journal in the top drawer of the table next to his bed and followed.

The night air was surprisingly warm, making Eli wonder how a city buried thousands of leagues under a bottomless lake, could stay so warm. Eli followed quickly after Sia. Looking back over his shoulder at his new house, he wondered if he would ever be at home after all that had transpired the past few months.

♦♦♦

Jude studied Pang while they waited for Sia and Eli outside of Mother Nature's Tavern. Something was different about Pang, ever since the four of them had returned from training. His demeanor had always been a little strange yet aggressive, but now Jude sensed something different. Pang felt off. Studying his gestures and activity, Jude read him as someone who is unstable.

"Go ahead. Ask away," said Pang. He was dressed in dark dress pants and a smoke gray collared shirt. His arms appeared to be even more muscular due to the fact that Pang had his long sleeves rolled up to his elbows.

"You seem different and I just wanted to let you know that if you need someone to talk to, I will keep whatever you tell me between the two of us."

Pang's mouth opened and then closed at the sound of the nearby footsteps. The two of them turned around to find Sia strutting quickly ahead of Eli up to them.

"Sorry we're late. I'm sure you already know why we're late so I won't bore you with the obvious," said Sia.

Jude looked to Eli, who appeared unaffected by the comment, and then returned to Sia. "No apology needed. Tonight I believe we should get to know this city and its people if we will be living here for however long."

"I agree," said Sia with a nod and a smile.

"Sometimes it's not the first thing you notice that is the most important, a lot of the time it's what follows. But, I also want us to have a good time." Jude stopped and relocated his focus to his S-3 that was in his armband under his shirt. "We had a tough mission and I believe aside from the minor things, the mission could not have gone better. We deserve to have a fun night."

"I am so ready for a good time," said Pang.

The comment was out of the ordinary for Pang, but Jude took it as a sign of good things to come tonight.

The Tavern was located next to the entrance to Geminate. The streets were more bare than when they had arrived to the great city, but the sea creatures below and beneath them continued to swim by at random times, giving Jude a few scares. From the outside, the tavern looked more like one of the many identical homes around them, except for its name in calligraphy letters above its door. Jude opened the door and entered.

The tavern air was loud and filled with the scent of a fresh meadow and the ocean. To the left was a man and woman behind a long counter serving drinks and food. On the right were rows and rows of small roundtables and chairs. Everything in the room matched the twisted black and white theme that occupied most of Geminate's homes. Jude looked down in hopes of seeing an actual floor, and instead came face-to-face with a giant red eye that opened and closed, before the creature swam off into the darkness.

"There's a table over there," said Sia pointing to the back of the tavern.

Jude followed Sia and the others to a secluded table in the corner. It was the perfect spot to get a good view of the entire tavern. A young woman in all white stood taking orders at a nearby table. After Jude and his comrades piled in to their seats, she snuck a glance over her shoulder and then was upon them. But something was off about her. Her body had a dark shade to her now. Jude looked back over at the table and noticed the same woman taking orders at that table. Then he remembered the Operative and his copy.

This must be the legendary ipseity I read about in that Geminate History book. She can be in two places at once.

"I don't have all day!" yelled the woman. "What will you be having?"

"We haven't even received menus," said Eli.

Jude noticed another glance from the original woman and then she was upon them as well. What Jude took as the ipseity was gone, and now a smiling young woman with long blonde hair and pearly white teeth stood before them.

"Hello! Apologies I have had a long day," said the woman.

"No apology needed," said Jude studying her. He took a menu when she handed it to him.

"My name is Tae if you need anything. I will be back in a few minutes to let you guys look over the menu," said Tae. She gave a big smile before departing to the next table.

"What a nut job," said Eli.

"She obviously has some past demons. We shouldn't judge her for being a little on edge," said Sia.

"I thought she was nice," said Pang. Everyone looked at Pang in shock. "What?"

"Well I'll be the first to say that I found our visit to the Aaia house to be highly uncomfortable," said Sia with raised brows. "I don't think I will be returning there again."

"Really? Why?" asked Eli scrunching his face. "I found it to be okay."

"Because he's ignorant." Jude shook his head in annoyance of Eli's oblivious perspective. It was clear as day that Eio Aaia had a narrow view of the world, a view that he was forcing on his son who was crying for help.

"Who do you think you are to call someone ignorant just because they're different?" said Eli.

"This coming from the guy who pre-judged and verbally attacked me because *I* was different," interrupted Pang. He shook his head slowly but continuously while mumbling under his breath.

Jude wouldn't let this one go. He had a point and wanted Eli to get it. "Alright Eli moving forward you will be our Scout.

From now on I will need you to gather intel on all of our targets and report back to me."

Eli's shoulders fell while the disappointment on his face couldn't be more obvious. "But I don't want to be a Scout I hate it."

"But in Kismet *all* Weapons Masters are the Scouts, and are responsible for gathering intel for the squad. You already know that Kai is the Scout for the Occult Ops. So what's the problem?"

Eli slammed his menu down and folded his arms. "But that's not fair Jude. You know that means I will have to do a lot of reading and research and I hate both those things. I don't want to be a Scout! Just because all Weapons Masters like being Scouts doesn't mean I do."

"But you *are* a Weapons Master." Jude had to fight back the urge to smile.

"Yeah I am, but I'm different. I like to be the offense not the Scout," said Eli sulking.

"Well if you're not the Scout then you're not a Weapons Master; and if you're not a Weapons Master then you have no spot on this team and we will replace you."

"That's not fair," whispered Eli.

"Calm down Brassie," laughed Pang closing his menu. "He's not making you a Scout, he's just making a point."

Eli appeared lost, but by the look on his face a few seconds later, appeared to eventually get it. "That's not funny."

"I just think you should know how it feels to be a prisoner of social norms, especially when you have no say in the matter. My mom tried to force me to be a prophet instead of Agent, just because I was a follower of the gods. I tried to explain to her that I was different and loved combat just as much as I loved the gods. She didn't want to hear any of it. She told me *all* followers of the gods want to be prophets and that's what I would be as long as I lived under her roof. I refused; and endured the punishments that continued to rain down on me with every rebellion. Eventually she surrendered to the fact that it's my life and she can't tell me what I like based on what others like."

Eli looked back at Jude with wide eyes. It was a secret Jude never shared with his comrade when they were growing up. It was something so personal and so painful to have to deal with on a daily basis, which Jude kept it locked deep inside. Jude hoped that Eli would learn from the lesson Jude was trying to teach him.

"Oh my Aegis," said Sia in a whisper.

"What?"

"Jamieson Edric, the Operative, he's here," said Sia nodding towards the door.

The second Jude spotted Jamieson the Operative spotted him back.

Dirty bloody sheets!

Jude had to think quickly. The Operative was awake and surely would approach them for answers. When they first met, the Operative appeared to have an idea of their true identities, so Jude concluded that he must have spotted them in combat. If they refused to answer his questions, it would only draw more suspicion.

What to do...

"What do we do? He's on his way over here now," said Sia over the S-3.

"Just do what the Lieutenant told us," said Eli's voice. *His gaze was fixated elsewhere while his lips gnawed on one another.*

"No, when I first encountered him he appeared to know that we are Agents. He must have seen us in battle. So just let me do all of the talking. After I set everything up, proceed normally as to avoid any suspicion."

"I could just kill him and then we could stop worrying about it," said Pang's voice. When no one responded, he continued. *"I'm serious it won't be any trouble I promise."*

A shadow descended upon the table. Jude looked up expecting to lock eyes with Jamieson and instead locked eyes with Tae.

"Hi! I'm back. Have you had enough time to look over the menu?" said Tae.

Jude looked around the table. "I apologize but I think we need a few more minutes."

"You got it!" said Tae with a wink before leaving.

"I was just two seconds short of a heart attack," said Sia.

"Regain your composure. You can't look nervous if he comes over here. In this situation, nervous screams your hiding something. Remember, you've done nothing wrong."

Sia took a deep breath and regained her composure.

"Are we having fun yet?" asked Pang.

"Looking for fun are we," said a familiar voice. Jamieson looked down at the table with his inquisitive hazel eyes. His armor was replaced with black dress pants and a black dress shirt. His black hair was neatly contained while his massive biceps continued to steal the attention away from everything else in the room.

"Well look who's up," said Eli.

Jamieson stared at Eli for a second too long before grabbing a nearby seat with one hand and planting it down next to Jude's comrade. "Woke up at a friend's house. Usually when that happens, it's a sign of a good time."

The table laughed lightly.

"Only this time," continued Jamieson turning his gaze to Jude. "I know it wasn't due to a good time."

"I apologize. The plan was to just bring you back safely but, well you know."

Jamieson stared at Jude. Jude wasn't intimidated by the Operative's stare. He was confident in his ability to keep enemies guessing at what he was thinking. Jude's mind was his own personal machine surrounded by a labyrinth of defenses against prying eyes.

"Well our last meeting was a little on the unorthodox side, so let me take the time to introduce myself. My name is Jamieson Edric," said Jamieson turning to Eli. "And you are?"

"Good to meet you I'm Eli. Eli Brassie." Eli shook Jamieson's hand.

"It's very nice to meet you Mr. Jamieson," said Sia. She held her hand out and was surprised when Jamieson grabbed her hand and kissed her wrist from across the table. "Oh!"

"I must ask for your forgiveness. I forgot you all are not from Geminate. It is custom for a man when he meets a beautiful woman to kiss her wrist," said Jamieson releasing her hand and rubbing the back of his neck. His gaze bore softly into Sia's eyes. "I'm sorry for my inappropriate behavior."

Sia stuttered before her words were understandable. "No *I'm* sorry. If this is the custom in Geminate, I'd be ignorant not to follow it. It's a pleasure to meet you." Her gaze tilted down to Jamieson's lips and then arms, and eventually Jude realized what was taking place.

"Pang Quarrels," said Pang extending his hand. After shaking hands with Jamieson, his brow curled. "That's a strong grip you got. How much do you lift? I lift about two fifty."

"Three seventy-five," said Jamieson without hesitation.

Eli whistled. "Sorry to be the first to tell you Pang, but you're no longer the strongest person in the group."

"Don't tempt me Brassie. You know just how strong I am," said Pang.

"*Pang!*" yelled Jude over the S-3.

"*Calm down I'm good,*" replied Pang.

"I've been lifting since I was nine. I know some secrets to muscle gain that are native to Geminate that you may be interested in," said Jamieson.

Annoying laughter and loud commotion interrupted their conversation. Jude joined Jamieson as he looked towards a group of men at a large table in the center of the room. They all had various weapons on their belts and all were dressed in black armor from head-to-toe. One tall man with a shaved head and broad shoulders caught Jude's attention. Jude looked over to Jamieson and noticed a slight glare.

"Who are they?"

"Garrett Bramwell and his—clan," said Jamieson. He seemed to spit the words out in disgust. "Since you're new to this land I feel like I owe it to you to warn you. Don't get involved with those guys. They are the top soldiers of the Priestess' Guard and they know it. While I would rather you not be swayed by my opinion of them and to judge for yourself, I will warn you not to get on Garrett's bad side. You'll never get off of it."

"He doesn't look so tough," said Pang.

Jamieson turned around with a smirk. "He may be an arrogant piece of garbage, but he has the means to back it up."

A thin young man around Jude's age with short straight brown hair entered the tavern. In his arms he carried various heavy weapons that appeared to be getting the best of him. The young man staggered towards Garrett and his group.

"What about him? Who is he?"

Jamieson's glare turned to sorrow. His brow curled while he released a sigh. "Hunter Jaxon. Probably one of the nicest people you will ever meet. He just turned eighteen but has been training to join The Guard his entire life. He's sort of Garrett's personal dunce."

Jude watched Garrett's leg dart out just in time to catch Hunter's ankle. The young man face-planted onto the glass floor beneath him, giving rise to laughter all around him. Garrett beat on the table with one of his massive fists while he laughed hysterically along with the other soldiers of The Guard.

"That's awful," said Sia.

"Well if he doesn't like the way they're treating him, he should stop being weak and stand-up for himself," said Eli. His comment immediately caught Jamieson's attention, who turned his scowl Eli's direction.

Jude envisioned taking Eli's face and beating the table with it. "He's not weak. People are just evil!"

"I don't agree," said Eli. "There are two kinds of people in this world, the people who go out and make things happen and the people who sit back and hope things will happen. Only the strong make things happen."

"Yes, well there are also two other kinds of people in the world, the ones who tell the truth and the ones who can't stop lying," said Sia.

Jude returned his attention to Jamieson and realized the situation was getting out of hand however; he couldn't help how he felt. He recognized that his emotions were taking over and quickly extinguished them. His fast heartbeat soon subsided, and he found himself watching Hunter return to his feet after picking up all of the weapons he had dropped. He placed them on the table in front of Garrett and turned for the door. Garrett's hand quickly pushed Hunter's back forward. Hunter hit the floor. The laughter returned.

"Excuse me. I'll be right back." Jude rose to his feet and walked over to Hunter. The young man looked a little shaken up and his eyes shiny when he looked up at Jude. He looked up in Jude's eyes with shame and pain all over his face.

"I'm Jude. Use a hand?" Jude extended a hand down to Hunter and hoped he would take it.

Hunter took Jude's hand and leaped to his feet. "Thank you but I really should be going," said Hunter quickly turning for the door. He was halted when Jude grabbed his wrist.

"Wait!"

Hunter turned around slowly.

"There are good people out there. Do yourself a favor and surround yourself with them. My house is on the last row in front of the temple, third over on the left if you need a friend."

Hunter didn't answer. He quickly headed for the door and exited. Jude instantly felt a presence behind him and turned around. Garrett and two other soldiers stood before him.

"What do you think you're doing?" said Garrett.

I'm holding back bringing your miserable life to an early end.

Garrett's half-finished drink caught Jude's eye. "Nothing that concerns a bully." Jude turned for the table and was immediately stopped by a firm hand that grabbed his shoulder. "Get your hands off me you piece of garbage."

Jude turned around just in time to catch the ipseitys of Garrett and the two soldiers appear. Jude was now facing six soldiers instead of three. He looked over at the table and noticed the soldiers at Garrett's table had summoned their ipseitys as well.

"It's sad that you're so weak that you have to intimidate others to make yourself look so great. By the way I'm not scared of you if that's what you're wondering—of any of you."

"Whoa what's going on here?" asked Jamieson taking a position next to Jude. Eli, Pang and Sia soon joined him.

"Jamieson," said Garrett with a flicker of surprise. "Didn't know you sunk as low as hanging out with these Kismetians."

Kismetians? Is that what they call our people? What an ugly name.

"Ha! We shouldn't be surprised right guys," said one of the soldiers nudging Garrett. All of them burst into laughter and only stopped when they noticed no one else was laughing.

A soldier screamed, drawing everyone's attention. Garrett's over-filled drink rocked back-and-forth in response to the commotion. Pang held one of Garrett's men by the neck—his feet dangling above the ground.

"I could take your head off so easily and the blood would flow like a tidal wave beneath my fingertips," said Pang.

The sound of metal filled the air as Garrett and his men drew their weapons.

"That's enough!" yelled Jamieson jumping in the middle.

Pang released the soldier but Garrett and his men kept their weapons drawn.

"Why don't we all just take it easy. Jude, why don't you and the others return to our table," said Jamieson.

If Jude wasn't the leader of a squad, and didn't have more important matters to worry about, he would have gladly met Garrett and his lackeys in combat. Instead, he ordered his comrades to retreat over the S-3. The four of them returned to the table, never taking an eye off of Garrett and his men. Jude returned to his seat with a smile, anticipating the show that Garrett would soon show. After some light conversation, Jamieson returned to the table and the loud voices of the surrounding guests returned.

"Garrett says you're on his list," said Jamieson to Jude with a shake of his head.

"I hope he'll still have the stomach for it later."

"Can I just say you all have just become my favorite people," said a voice.

Jude turned around to find Tae standing before him with a small notebook and pen in her hand.

"Come again?" said Eli.

"Garrett and his men really bring unwarranted hostility to this tavern. They order drinks and never pay for them. They assault guests and break things; and we can't say anything because they are a part of the Priestess' Guard. It's about time that someone stands up to him," said Tae.

"It was the right thing to do. He was picking on someone for no reason."

"I know," said Tae with a frown. "Poor poor Hunter. Little does he know, thanks to Garrett, he will never be in The Guard. But they continue to string him along with the false hope that someday he will be."

"Why haven't you told him and stopped this?"

"Look I don't want any trouble. I have to deal with Garrett and his men every day and it will just be a lot easier if I stay out of it," said Tae.

"Don't lie to me! You're a coward that's why. Let's just be honest here!"

Tae recoiled as if she had been slapped. The hurt was prevalent on her face.

"Jude!" yelled Sia. Her face looked shocked.

"Hold on, I'll be right back," said Tae. She soon returned with five glasses that she placed on the table. "These are my treat for your bravery. Let me know if you need anything else." Then she was gone.

Jude watched Garrett laugh uncontrollably while his eyes stayed fixated on a young woman who was on her way to the restroom. When she disappeared around the corner, he downed his drink and followed her. "Cheers!"

GUILTY PLEASURE

Eli found himself actually listening to every word Jamieson said. He didn't know why, but Jamieson had a magnetic element to him that made Eli want to socialize more with the Operative. Jamieson continued to tell Eli and his comrades about the mission he was on when they had encountered him. Jude quickly penetrated Eli's thoughts over the S-3 telling everyone that it was a trap and that no sane Agent or Operative would disclose the contents of their mission to any unauthorized individuals—especially strangers they just met. Regardless, Eli found himself drawn into Jamieson's story of taking down a dangerous Agent who was responsible for multiple attacks on Geminate.

Jamieson's attention turned away from the table and towards the door. Eli followed his gaze and noticed a tall man—a little taller than Jamieson—with large arms and dark brown hair, standing by the door. His blue eyes were bright enough to pierce the dimly lit lights in the tavern, as they scanned the room.

"If you all will excuse me," said Jamieson rising from his seat. He went to the long counter as if he was going to order a drink, before relocating to the door and meeting the tall man.

"How is everything?" Tae looked down at Eli and his comrades. Her eyes snuck low glances at Jude, who jerked his head away.

Whoa! I've never seen this side of little Jude before.

"No we're fine, thank you," said Sia finally.

Tae smiled before quickly retreating to the safety of another, probably more friendly, table.

"I'm down to kill him if that's what you're thinking," said Pang. His gaze set on Jude, who looked up immediately at Pang's words.

Jude stared at Pang.

Is he actually thinking about it?

"No! No that's not what he's thinking Pang," said Sia. "Jude is a Squad Leader with a lot of responsibilities and things riding on the safety of our people. He wouldn't dare poison his mind with such thoughts over some dishonorable reject. It's not worth it. He's smarter than that."

Eli felt like the last sentence of Sia's big speech was more of a question by the way her voice trailed off. He took a sip of his drink and was pleased by the cinnamon taste.

Jude looked to Pang. "If my orders are for a target to be neutralized, I will give them." He then turned to Sia and glared, causing her to forfeit her perfect posture and slouch slightly in her seat. "As for you, that will be the last of your condescending motherly speeches. Do I make myself clear?"

Eli choked on his drink, causing a nearby table to turn around briefly. His throat felt scratchy after he finally got his drink down, causing him to continue to cough.

"Clear Squad Leader," said Sia slowly.

Eli coughed one last time feeling like it would be the last.

"And you," said Jude jerking his attention to Eli. "Stop coughing! The Operative is on his way back with a new individual and I can't think with your annoying gasps for air."

Eli got an instant adrenaline rush. He felt like he had just been attacked. "Copy that Squad Leader."

Jamieson plopped down in his seat next to Eli, who welcomed the Operative's return. Jude was clearly on some sort of power trip and the mood of the night had changed for the worse.

"I would like for you all to meet Special Operative Talon Tatum—A.K.A. The Four-armed Beast," said Jamieson with a small laugh as his shoulder crashed into Eli's.

Talon glared at Jamieson before closing his eyes and shaking his head. His dark gray combat pants and black belted combat tunic told Eli that no matter what the circumstances, he was prepared for battle. Talon single-handedly picked up a chair and set it at the front of the table so his back was facing the rest of the tavern. Eli could not help but notice how large his arms were and how broad his shoulders were. His arms looked like they were the same size as Jamieson's but his shoulders were slightly broader.

Holy Aegis! Who are these guys? Muscle head one and two?

"Evening. Jamieson tells me you're from Kismet," said Talon looking around the table starting with Jude.

"Yes, we are Kismet's resources team. It's a pleasure to meet you," said Jude extending his hand. Talon cracked a small smile and shook Jude's hand.

"That's Jude," started Jamieson while pointing to Jude. "Next to him is Pang, then Sia and this is Eli."

Eli shook Talon's hand and fought back the urge to tense at the crushing of his hand.

I really need to step my game up.

"So, what was the first thing you noticed about Geminate upon arrival?" asked Talon.

"The freakishly big fish that come at you from every direction non-stop!"

Talon sat back in his chair, folded his arms and smirked. "Scary huh? Being so close to ancient animals that have the power to kill you with ease."

"I'm liking this guy already," said Pang.

The room went completely black. Someone close-by screamed.

"*Attack on my command*," said Jude over the S-3.

"Uh oh, looks like the party is about to begin," said Talon.

"What do you mean?" asked Sia.

"One word. Josline," said Talon with a grin.

A bright spotlight hit the front of the tavern landing on a small stage that Eli didn't see when they arrived. A lone figure, with her back turned, stood motionless center stage. The music came slowly but strong. The music was unlike any Eli had ever heard. It was patient, seductive and calming. The woman turned around and was instantly bombarded with whistling and male shouts of approval. Eli's lips dried as he took in Josline's beauty. She was tall and slender with a small waist, voluminous backside and a chest worthy of a second look. Her long black hair cascaded down on both of her bare shoulders, while the skin-tight navy blue dress she wore sparkled in the spotlight. Her red lips parted, releasing her seductive will upon all who stared:

"You say you want a classy woman, but is it true? Now would a classy woman do the—things I do?"

Josline stepped off the stage with both hands on her swaying hips while she made eye contact with every person in the front row, men and women alike.

"Now you're a man and I'm a woman so let's—skip the games. I know how to make you grunt and holler, can she—do the same? Your toes will curl and spine will tingle—is that okay? Can you bind my hands and legs until I—cry your name?"

Sia gasped drawing no one's attention but Eli's. "Oh my Aegis what is she doing?"

Talon and Jamieson whistled loudly while Pang and Jude tried their best to contain the huge grins on their faces.

"She looks my age! That is just shameful and degrading!" snapped Sia folding her arms.

Josline made her way from table-to-table until she found a bashful looking young man. She sat on his lap facing him and raised her lips towards the ceiling continuing to sing:

"I'm your baby hot and ready can you—make me coo? Your classy woman won't hear my cries unless you—want her to. Now I'm a six foot walkin' up-all-nighter can you—make it through?"

Another woman appeared behind the young man identical to Josline.

What the Pith?

The first Josline whipped her head back-and-forth while still sitting on the young man's lap, who looked like he was going to faint. The second Josline placed her hands over the young man's eyes and put her lips close to his ear. Her singing was light, but still loud enough for the rest of the tavern to hear:

"Now you're a man and I'm a woman so let's—skip the games. I know how to make you grunt and holler, can she—do the same? Your toes will curl and spine will tingle—is that okay? Can you bind my hands and feet until I—cry your name? Come get me going."

Eli's table rocked back-and-forth. He looked up and saw Sia stepping around Jude and Pang.

"I refuse to sit here and watch that filthy, temptress drazel spread em' for all you desperate juveniles," said Sia. She stormed towards the restroom. Josline had made he way to the other side of the room, and just as Sia walked by her, Josline turned around and blew Sia a kiss. Sia opened the restroom door and slammed it closed behind her.

Josline's green eyes shot to Eli.

Uh oh...

Josline's hips swayed, hair bounced and lips parted as she hummed the melody of the song. When she got to their table she cleared it with one swoosh of the back of her smooth hand. One knee came up on the table and then the second. Eli had to fight to keep his eyes from falling down to the top of her chest, which was void of any coverage.

"Go Brassie!" yelled Pang.

Eli looked over to Pang and Jude and saw them laughing hysterically. Talon and Jamieson elbowed each other while laughing at the show. Josline seemed unaffected by the responses. She made Eli forget who he was with her green stare. Her body made his leg jump under the table repeatedly, while his hands clawed at his knees. Her soft red lips opened and he knew he was in trouble:

"You know my name so call me when you're—ready babe. Just in case you forgot it let me—C.Y.A. "It's J—O—S—L—I—N—E there's no, other way. I'm always gagged so none will know you—came by today."

Josline swung her legs over the table and plopped down in Eli's lap. Her smell was light. Her smell was sweet. Her smell was addicting. She lightly placed one hand on both of his shoulders and blew in his ear. The hairs on the back of his neck felt like they were ready to detach and flee at any minute. He fought the urge but gave-in to the desire to close his eyes and fall victim to her spell. Her red fingertips glided down from her neck to the top of her strapless dress and then it happened. Josline ripped the top of her dress down exposing herself. Eli felt his mouth drop, as he looked around frantically for his mom and dad to come scold him. When his eyes returned to Josline, she had covered herself.

"I'm done come find me."

Her weight lifted from his lap and he knew the bliss was over. The spell had been broken. Eli opened his eyes just in time to catch the sashaying of Josline from their table all the way passed Sia and back to the stage. Eli's eyes remained glued to Josline's curves. She turned around and winked.

That wink was for me! I just know it was. She doesn't care about any other guy in here. She wants me to know that.

"Come find me," said Josline. She elongated the three words until the spotlight went dark. When the lights to the tavern sprang on, she was gone.

Eli looked around frantically for the whereabouts of the woman who had just held him captive to his guiltiest of desires. She was gone.

"Are you done dishonoring yourself?" Sia glared at him.

"Ah calm down. Just a little fun. That's all it was," said Jamieson.

"A little fun? Thanks to Josline, I'm good for the rest of the week," said Talon.

Jamieson wrapped Talon in a headlock as they both laughed and argued over who would go out with Josline first.

"Men are disgusting," said Sia with a snarl. She returned her gaze to Eli. "I expected more from *you* Agent Brassie. But you're just as gross. I'm going home." She returned her gaze to Talon and Jamieson. "It was nice meeting you both." With her parting words she stormed around the tables, knocking into any who dared to get in her way, and slammed the tavern door closed behind her.

"*After all her training, she let her emotions get the best of her,*" said Jude over the S-3. Afterwards his eyes got big as if he unintentionally communicated that.

I really hope Sia didn't hear him say that. She looked crazier than a Necrosis on fire when she left.

"Ouch! Some history there?" asked Jamieson.

Eli sighed. "Yeah I'm afraid so.

"Hey hey don't worry. She will get over it. They always do," said Talon with a wink.

The guilt was slow but painful when it finally reared its head. Eli didn't mean to make Sia angry. There was just something about Josline that made him lose control of his body. But what he didn't understand was why Sia even cared. She told him to his face that she didn't want to be with him anymore and that he wasn't the right man for her. Those painful words haunted him clear up until Marius' death, which now controlled his emotions. He felt himself sigh.

Dad.

A KNOCK AT
THE DOOR

Eli knew sleep was unrealistic. The tears that continued to run as he tried forcing himself to sleep, was the only sign he needed that he would never get over losing Marius. He was all alone. Marius, Mya and now Sia were all gone from his life. He had no one. Or did he? Leaping up from his bed, Eli ran to his armoire, grabbed a sweater and pants and left his bedroom. He was having trouble getting his arm through one of the sweater's sleeves when he finally made it to his front door. He stopped.

I really don't want to go to him for anything.

He secured the last sleeve, grabbed his mother's journal, opened the door and exited. The night air was surprisingly warm considering the fact that they were so far underneath The Great Lake's depths. The Lake's darkness did little to show the creatures that made the large bubbles come and go on the other side of the glass barrier. Eli did his best not to think about it. He turned for the ascending steps and climbed. The streets were noticeably bare, something Eli had noticed since they had arrived earlier that day.

The city is so backwards. At least in Kismet, there would be at least a handful of friendly neighbors walking about.

The climb was a lot steeper than Eli remembered. The large house began to rise up on his left the further he climbed. He quickly extinguished the anger boiling at the sight of the luxurious house. He knew why he was here and anger had no place right now. Walking up to the door, he noticed a botanical garden on the side of the house accompanied by a small pond. Clearly it was one of the numerous amenities that he did not have at his own place. He closed his eyes, took a deep breath and knocked. His heart began to beat faster with each passing second like a drum that got louder and louder. After a few seconds he heard footsteps from the other side of the door that came to an immediate halt. For a moment, Eli thought the door would never open. Just when he was ready to give up and return to the confines of his bedroom, the door opened.

The green eyes that stared back at him were not the same green eyes he had grown up with. They belonged to someone else entirely.

"Hi."

"Good evening," said Jude with a blank stare. His hair was wet, which gave Eli the impression that his Squad Leader had just showered. "What can I do for you?"

Eli started to feel the pain that had kept him from his sleep begin to dissipate. He took a step into the doorway and was instantly blocked. Jude stared back at him with a stern gaze.

"You're not going to let me come in?"

"What is it that you need Eli?" asked Jude. He appeared annoyed and tired at the same time.

"I came over to talk." Eli stared back at Jude confused. There wasn't tension in the air but something entirely different. Distance.

"What happened? Did you blow your cover?"

"No."

Jude's brow curled. "Are the other Agents in trouble?"

"No."

"I'm confused," said Jude shrugging his shoulders. "Then why are you here?"

It was all or nothing.

"I miss my dad Jude. I really do! It's so hard to—."

"Wait! Wait! Wait," said Jude holding up his hand. "You came over here to talk about Marius?'

"Yeah." Eli was even more confused by the annoyance on Jude's face. Even though Marius wasn't Jude's dad, Eli knew Jude had to be feeling at least a fraction of the pain that he was feeling. "I thought maybe since you were somewhat close to him too that—."

"Let me stop you right there," said Jude lowering his voice with crossed arms. "I don't have time to sit around with you and cry about your fallen father. I'm not your mother, I'm not your brother and I'm not your friend. I am your Squad Leader. Unless you have something relating to the mission, your comrades or our enemy targets, we have nothing to talk about."

Eli felt his head recoil. He blinked a few times and realized it wasn't a dream. This was happening. "Where's all of this anger coming from?"

Jude shook his head with a light laugh. "No one is angry Eli. You just need to remember that I'm your Squad Leader and not your buddy. I'm not here to solve your personal issues. Now goodnight."

"But Jude I have no one else to—."

The door slammed closed. The living room lights soon retreated. The walk back down the steps and back home was like razor blades of ice cutting the bottoms of his feet with each step he took. He really was alone. He felt it now.

Returning home, Eli sat on his doorstep and opened his mother's journal. He flipped half way through the journal to the first blank page and retrieved the pencil from the holster in the inside cover. He made a cover page titled: *Eli's Journal* before turning to the next page. Breathing in the aquatic air, Eli put the pencil to the blank page and began:

Location: Geminate

Time of day: Late

Dear Mom & Dad,

Hi. A lot has happened since I've last seen you both. Dad, the invasion of Kismet was a success. Our city is lost and our people are without a home. It still hurts so much to even remember the city because all I can think about was that battle between you and Fox and how he took you from me. How he took my only family from me. I miss you so much dad and I'm so lost without you. The Necroborns took our home dad. So now I don't even have our home to remember you by. All of our memories of you, mom and I…lost. Mom, amidst the chaos I have been lucky enough not to lose your journal. It is the only thing I have left to remember you by now that I don't have a home to go back to. Your poems are both pain and comfort. They bring me closer to you but not close enough. Will the pain of your absence ever go away? I have started a section of my own in the blank pages of your journal. Writing is not my strong point. I'm finding that making bad decisions is more of my specialty, so I hope it's okay that this entry is not a poem. I'm finding it hard to breathe with every word I write so let me tell you what has happened since Lord Egon and Fox laid siege to Kismet.

The Lieutenant and General have relocated the remainder of our people to Geminate. The city is far to the east, as I'm sure you already know, and located beneath an amazing lake. Jude and I underwent training from the Occult Operatives. When we returned, we were put on a squad called the 'Kismet Task Force' with a girl by the name of Sia Wyatt and a weird guy by the name of Pang Quarrels. Everyone's demeanor changed after training. They all seem like slightly different people. Mom just to bring you up to speed, Sia and I once had something, but because of my stupidity, she no longer wants anything to do with me. Sorry dad. After all that fuss and turmoil, it didn't even last. One thing I know you and mom will be disappointed to hear is that Jude and I are no longer friends. We went through a spat and I don't think we will come back from this one. He now looks at me as just another comrade, and I'm sure if we weren't on the same squad, he most likely wouldn't have anything to do with me, which is fine. Moving on, our squad's objective is to eliminate Lord Egon and Fox, and stop the spread of their tyranny. To be honest, I look forward to the next time I see Fox. I was naïve and young before and did not have the skills I needed to take him down. Now post-training, I feel like an unstoppable force of power and destruction. The next time Fox and I meet, it will end with his body lying at my feet. I'm sorry mom I know you have always been against revenge but you have to understand, this guy killed dad. Don't worry dad, I will avenge you. Anyways, I have my own house and have been spending a lot of time by myself. It has given me a lot of time to think about you guys and how much I miss you. I feel alone in the world and it's becoming more difficult as the days come and go.

Well, the longer this entry gets the more I feel like I'm complaining and the further I feel from you both. Maybe next time I'll write you guys a poem as funny as that sounds. I'm laughing now thinking about me of all people writing a poem filled with emotions and clever words and all that. Maybe it will bring me closer to you mom. Maybe I will eventually be able to see the world the way you once did. If I don't, at least I can be closer to you and dad through this journal. Well I have to end this. I need to get some training done in the next few days since I am the only Weapons Master on the squad. As the main offense, I need to make sure my body is always at its best. I remember you mentioning that some time ago dad, even though I can't remember when. Well it was nice talking to you again. Talk to you soon.

Your son,

Eli.

◆◆◆

Aileen leaped and pleaded as she tried desperately to free herself from the pool of flames that held her captive. The scorching white flames showed no mercy as they sizzled away her skin and hair. Her eyes were too hot to create tears but the anguish on her face was enough to show the torment she was ensnared in. She continued to jump until the inevitable truth of death dawned on her. "Save me," she said before Lord Egon's hand grappled around her neck, crushing her throat and forcefully submerging her head into the dancing flames below.

Jude flung his head up from the sweaty cloth that was his pillow. He looked around at the large vacant bedroom adorned with black walls with assorted paintings, silver ceilings and more armoires of clothes than Jude would ever need. If the walls could talk, what stories would they tell? What secrets were they hiding? The cool air from the open balcony window next to his bed was comforting. His breathing took a while to stabilize. He felt conflicted, not knowing whether or not he should pray to the gods for aid. The past few months, he felt more unsure than ever about what to do anymore. Retrieving his ceramic box from the nearby end table caused his hands to shake. The second the ceramic box touched his chest, the shaking stopped. He was content. He was safe.

"A dream! All a dream," he said aloud.

He opened the box and smiled at the small family portrait inside. This one was different than the one in his old living room. This one had Marius and Eli in it instead of Jude's dad Mathias. Another photo leaned against his S-3 wristband at the bottom of the box. Jude took it out and found a smaller version of the large family portrait that once hung in his living room. Seven small glass cylinders rolled around clashing into one another. Out of the seven, one stood out the most. He took out the vial he won from Lynn and rolled it around in his finger. He still had no idea what it did, but he promised himself he would find out soon. A light single knock rose from downstairs causing Jude's knee to jump. He returned the photos and vial to his box and placed it back on his end table. Climbing out of bed he hurried out of his bedroom and down the stairs and stopped. It was well passed midnight. Who would be at his door? After the embarrassing and awkward encounter with Eli a few hours ago, Jude felt like he had already had his full share of visitors for the rest of the week.

A muffled voice called through the door.

Jude crept across the first sitting room and the first living room before arriving at the door. He activated his Optical Tactics and surveyed the porch through the door. A single person stood at his doorstep. Judging by the proportions, he assumed it was a woman. No one else appeared to be present.

Her backup could be concealed by magic.

He opened the door to a smiling face, which showed no attempt at concealing her phosphorous white teeth. Her reddish-brown hair was short but long enough to leave a small swivel atop her forehead. Her body was full but her skin was smooth. Her fingers remained interlaced together in front of her plain black slacks while her dark eyes stared back with dozens of questions. A long silver jacket covered her shoulders and stopped at her ankles.

"Can I help you?"

Her eyes smiled with a squint. "I believe you have it backwards. The real question is can I help you Mr. Bray."

I should be unnerved by the fact that she knows my name, however, it's a given she would know at least something about me if she was able to find my house. Her timing is what's unnerving.

Jude felt the urge to activate his Optical Tactics once again to foresee the pending attack, however, he was aware that the ability filled his eyes with a white mask that could cause his unwanted guest to attack. "I'm sorry but you must have the wrong house. I don't need any help but thank you." He began closing the door.

"You're father couldn't sleep his first night in Geminate as well Jude," she said.

The door stopped along with Jude's heart.

"Allow me to introduce myself. My name is Alize. I am the Medical Specialist of Geminate," she said.

"Alize?" The name was familiar. Eio had mentioned that he had taken Alistair to see Alize. But why was she here and how did she know his father?

She nodded her head.

"And why are you here and how do you know my name?"

"How could I not know the prodigy from Kismet—the chosen one said to return peace to the world," said Alize.

There it is again that stupid title. But how can Alize know about the Trials and my victory? And what is this about a chosen one and returning peace to the world?

"I think you're mistaken about me being some sort of chosen one, but I would like to know how you know my father."

She smiled sharply with a glint in her eye. "I will gladly tell you how I know your father but first I would like to have a session with you first."

"A session?"

"Yes, I always volunteer to sit and meet any newcomers that visit Geminate. I always offer one free sit-down session," said Alize.

The danger swam around every word she said. The art of temptation was mixed with the allure of forbidden knowledge and accompanied with a charitable gesture. He could see through it all. It would be the perfect trap for the unsuspecting.

"Let me get my jacket."

BEHIND THESE
GREEN EYES

Jude refused to show any emotion or release any hints of what he was thinking through his eyes. Alize appeared unfazed by his stern gaze. She sat down slowly in the wooden chair across from the black sofa he sat on. She looked on either side of her before nodding her head to no one in particular and reaching underneath her chair. Her hand returned with a small white journal. She retrieved what looked like a pencil from her silver jacket. She crossed one leg and returned his gaze. Her dark eyes were soft and open.

"So, I always begin with some simple questions. Nothing too personal," said Alize with a smile.

"Okay."

"What's your favorite color?" she asked exposing some teeth.

He analyzed her question. His first instinct was to lie. Alize was a stranger to him—a stranger that could be a potential enemy. However, he was tired of looking at everyone as a potential enemy. He needed a break from being Squad Leader. He had only adorned the title a few days ago and he was already feeling the stress that it came with. He needed one day, one day to completely let go and let his defenses down. If he was walking into a trap, he would deal with the consequences head-on with less stress and anxiety than he would have had keeping up his walls.

"Baby blue."

293

Her head tilted. "Now you paused on that question. May I ask why?"

"Because I was going to lie to you and say black."

His statement instantly caught her attention.

"And why were you going to lie about something so miniscule?" asked Alize with a vacant stare.

"Because I don't know you and I'm a private person when it comes to my personal business. However, I decided that I will be open to this session to see if it can benefit me in some way."

"I see. Well I appreciate your honesty. Usually people lie the first half of their session. So baby blue," said Alize writing in the white journal. "Where are you from?"

"Kismet. It's just southeast of here."

"Beautiful land known for your beautiful cherry blossom trees, lush forests and legendary white-stone city," said Alize with a smirk. "Do you have a girlfriend?"

The question caught him off-guard. He changed his position on the couch. "No."

"Still looking for the right one...or just broken up or..." she trailed off.

"Had a few when I was younger but they never worked out."

"And why's that?"

Jude thought for a few seconds. "All three of them said I was too nice and in turn boring."

"All three said the same thing?" she asked with astonishment.

"In so many words," he said. He didn't care what she thought.

"Do you plan on trying to meet someone anytime soon?"

"No."

"Too soon?" she asked. The question almost felt rhetorical.

"No I don't want a girlfriend or a wife," he said.

"Why not?"

"Because I hate people."

Alize recoiled, and for the first time appeared caught-off-guard. She uncrossed and then re-crossed her legs before returning his gaze. "Why do you hate people?"

He felt like he had gone too far. What he was telling her was something that he had never even had a chance to discuss with his mom, Jed or even Eli. She was in too deep but he didn't care.

"Because people are evil, even if most are too ignorant to realize it."

Alize's eyes got slightly wider. She appeared to be even more interested in what he had to say than she was when they first sat down. "Please go on."

"When you meet someone you're pulled in by the charade of their niceness, beauty or whatever. But in reality, there is a monster underneath the surface of what you look at. Majority of people are selfish and they only look out for themselves. Even when you feel like you've met someone that is a good person you're fooling yourself. It's only a matter of time before they find some way to hurt you, betray you or destroy you. Just think about it, if people weren't evil we wouldn't need Agents, Operatives or battles."

"I would like to go back to what you said about most people being selfish," said Alize leaning closer. "Can you explain that to me."

"Take myself for example. My mother brought me up to always think about how my actions will affect other people first and how they will affect me second. In a sense, she brought me up to be selfless which is how Aegis, Pith and Rune want us to be. But most people don't care. If it came down to them killing you to ensure their own success they would. If it came down to them stealing from you just to get ahead they would. If they are having a bad day and just feel like being a completely horrible person to everyone because they feel horrible, they would—and feel good doing it. There have been times when people have put their hands on me, lied to me and disrespected me for no reason. I constantly put myself into the shoes of others and I have never given anyone a reason to disrespect me in any way—but they do it anyways. People as a whole are born to only care for themselves and bring pain and suffering to any who get in their way. Only those raised to be selfless are the exception and that portion of the human race is nearly extinct."

"Okay so I met a young woman the other day that seems like a nice woman," said Alize writing in her journal. She finished what she was writing before continuing. "How do I know if she is one of the many selfish people in the world, or if she's the small portion of 'selfless' people?"

"You can't. But chances are she isn't selfless. She's most likely a snake like the rest of the world."

"But she hasn't done anything that has shown me that she's a snake," she said.

"Just give it time. She will eventually do something that will hurt you beyond belief and you will ask yourself why she did it. A lie, betrayal, an attack, the possibilities are endless. You will realize you did nothing to warrant such behavior. You won't be able to come up with a reason because there is no reason. She just did it because she wanted to."

"So you are against freewill?" she asked quickly.

"I don't believe in freewill."

"Oh," she said surprisingly. "And why not?"

"Freewill is supposed to be our inherent human right to carry out our will in whatever way we see fit but then people are born certain ways that they can't change. We are destined to be the people we are. To me, that's fate and fate contradicts freewill in my eyes."

She inhaled and exhaled. "So you said you believe in the gods, how do they fit into the grand scheme of things?"

He paused.

"Tough question?" she asked quickly.

"No. It's just I know how I am going to answer this question now, and it's *way* different than how I would have answered it a few years ago."

"Well sometimes our opinions of something or someone can grow and evolve right along with us. How does Jude Bray feel Aegis, Pith and Rune fit into what we have talked about now?"

"They're a disappointment." When he saw she wasn't going to respond he continued. "As loyal followers of the gods we are supposed to praise them and have faith in them that they are always there for us, love us and all that crap. I have had faith in the gods my entire life. I was brought up reading the sacred text of the gods. I have never witnessed the gods being there for me in any way. I was brought up to believe that when evil happens around you or when someone is carrying out evil that it's Anim's work."

"The devil," she interrupted.

"Yes. I was brought up not to call him that because that name sparks fear in people and when you fear him you give him power."

"I see," she said with an incline of her head. "Please continue."

"I spent my entire life praying, meditating, following and loving the three brothers unconditionally. Some bad things have happened in my life, truly bad things that have corrupted me. Where were the gods when this happened? Where were they when Anim ran rampant through this world infecting those around me with his evil? We are supposed to have faith in the gods that they will protect us but they never showed. Never! Instead I was at the mercy of Anim himself while the gods I bow to, pray to, follow and live my life by their approval, ignored my cries for help. I've wasted my entire life praying to gods who sit by and let the few good people in this world suffer at the hands of all the evil people in this world. If the gods loved us as much as they claim they do, why would they standby and watch us suffer? They say they will never put more on us than we can bare, but maybe I don't want to constantly bare pain. Maybe I want the gods that I have faith in to come down and rescue me from the evil of this world or at least punish those who hurt and corrupt me."

Alize's gaze never left his. "So you believe that people should be punished?"

"I believe that if someone hurts someone else for no reason just because they feel like it—yes the gods should punish them. If you're not going to save the good from the evil at least punish the evil for harming the good."

Alize stared back for what felt like minutes. The more her gaze bore into his eyes, the more uncomfortable he felt. He felt vulnerable and hated it.

"Jude I think we have accomplished a lot for our first session. Before we go I would like to try something that I try with all my guests," she said getting up from her seat. "Is that okay?"

"Sure."

Alize retreated to a cabinet behind her and returned with a small bottle. She sat in her seat, uncorked the bottle and smelled it. After smiling she replaced the cork. "This is a substance known as Syphon. Are you familiar with our people's path to enlightenment and our acquisition of our ipseity ability?"

"Not a lot, only what I read briefly in a history book."

"Our people believe that every person is comprised of both a light and dark side. That person needs both sides to remain balanced and in turn in control. If a person was to only do what would be considered good and relinquish the bad, they would become unbalanced and self-destruct—and the same vice-versa with the dark. Balance is what keeps all living things at peace, in control and pure in the eyes of the gods," she said.

"I don't mean any disrespect but what peace are you talking about? The entire world falls into darkness with each passing day. With each passing day, people become more and more corrupt, kill each other and come one step closer to complete and utter annihilation."

"Bare with me," she said with a smile. "Now the Geminate people are the only race that have walked the path of enlightenment and in turn obtained the ability of ipseity. However, there is another way for outsiders to see the world through the eyes of a Geminate—at least somewhat," she said with a wink.

"And this Syphon is the key to that?"

She nodded.

"Why do I need to see the world through the eyes of a Geminate. What's so special about that?"

"Only through Geminate eyes can one see all of oneself—both the light and the dark. Only then will you see the world through unbiased eyes. Even if you are reluctant to benefit from what I'm offering, at least you will get a chance to understand the people of the city you live in," she said with a smile. "Nothing wrong with understanding another culture is there?"

Jude looked down at the Syphon and then back up at Alize. He would be a fool to drink some concoction he had never heard of. He could be drinking poison or something similar to Antiom. He could end up disclosing all the squad's secrets and their mission and put everyone in danger. He thought about all the times he made decisions that benefited others before benefiting himself. He thought about all the times he thought about how his actions would affect others before worrying about himself. He had done that his entire life and was punished by evil every step of the way. No one appreciated his kindness and no one appreciated him. Majority of the world was evil, selfish and hurt others; how come he couldn't? Even if it was a one-time thing, it was his turn to only think of himself. It was his turn to be selfish. He had seen what happens in life when you are a good person and only thought of others and it got you nowhere but hurt and angry. But who was he? He knew who he was and he would never think like this. His mother would say to pray to the gods for forgiveness when such evil thoughts crossed his mind but he didn't want to. He used to hold on to his adolescent innocence even when the adolescent years were over. The innocence was his most prized possession.

"Innocence lost..."

"I'm sorry Jude," said Alize confused. "What did you say?"

He snatched the Syphon, uncorked it and downed it to the last drop—licking his lips with a vengeance.

◆ ◆ ◆

The being was terrifying. The mere air around him was significantly colder than the rest of the room. Its darker shade made the copy look sinister and deceptive. This thing was evil and Jude wanted nothing to do with it. He waited for the order to neutralize it—permanently.

"Jude. Jude are you okay?" asked Alize.

Jude met her gaze. "Yes I'm fine."

"I can tell that this is unsettling for you. Do me a favor and look at him and tell me what you see," she said.

"Okay." Jude swallowed hard before turning to his left at the ipseity copy that sat next to him. "He is without a doubt completely identical to me. The eyes, nose, height and weight—everything. The only difference I see is the dark shadow that appears to be sewn into his being."

"Jude this is your ipseity, your other side. He is your passion, your desire, your confidence and your strength. He is everything within you that aids you in survival. You must embrace him. He has been within you this entire time whether you knew it or not. He is what keeps you balanced and in control of who you are," said Alize pointing to Jude with the tip of her pencil.

Jude looked at his ipseity and saw every impulse decision he had ever made or wanted to make. He saw the strength he utilized in battle but also the things he was ashamed of. This thing was pure evil and he couldn't look at it any longer.

"No Jude don't look away. You need to—."

"I don't want to. He's evil. He's the sinful and corrupt thoughts I suppress when they arise. He's the embodiment of corruption and what I was brought up to resist. I have nothing to say to him. He's not welcome here."

"Jude he has always been inside of you. He is exactly one half of who you are," said Alize.

Jude looked the opposite direction towards a painting depicting the two silhouettes that were inscribed on his armband. He needed to look at something that didn't make him come face-to-face with the evil that sat next to him. Unfortunately, every painting in Alize's house had something to do with ipseitys.

"Okay Jude I understand. Let's try something else," she said.

Jude met her gaze.

"We are going to try an exercise called shuttling," said Alize pulling her chair closer to Jude and the ipseity. "Why don't you look at your ipseity and tell him what bothers you about him. What he has done that you don't like. Can we do that?"

Jude sighed. "Okay." He looked at the intruder next to him. The nefarious aura swam around him. "I don't know where to start."

301

"How about 'because of you I' and then tell him what you have done because of him that you don't like," she said softly.

He took another deep breath and jumped when he noticed his ipseity taking the same deep breath in unison.

"Because of you I hate people so much that I cringe." While the statement was unnerving it was also liberating. The ipseity recoiled as if he had been slapped but remained silent and motionless. Jude looked to Alize for approval and instruction.

"Go on," she said with a small smile.

"Because of you the mere thought of getting close to someone makes me uncomfortable." He again looked to Alize who returned a nod. A weight had been lifted and took with it the walls and chains that had bound him to being overly-calm and collected. The liberation was exhilarating and relaxing. Looking to the ipseity he saw rage in its eyes but also pain. Jude thirsted for more. "Because of you I'm afraid to stick up for myself! Because of you I pray *every* night that the gods don't send me to hell!"

The ipseity's lip curled into a snarl and just as its mouth opened, Alize's hand came up towards the ipseity. The copy's mouth closed and he returned Jude's gaze.

"Because of you I want to hurt *so* many people! Because of you dad left us and is *never* coming back!" Jude found himself gasping for air. He had been talking so fast he had forgot to breathe. He looked up into the darkness of the ipseity's eyes and saw the pain. "Because of you I've lost my innocence—forever."

The ipseity looked angry. The ipseity looked vengeful. While the being looked ready to pounce and show no mercy to his victim, Jude was scared to lift his finger. His courage was gone. His power was gone; and in its place was fear and worry.

"Now Jude it's your darker half's turn," said Alize

Jude jerked his attention to Alize. "What do you mean it's his turn?"

"Jude you need to understand that he is a part of you. Just like there are things you don't like about him, I'm sure there are things he doesn't like about you," she said in a matter-of-fact tone.

Jude looked back towards the ipseity, who returned a gaze full of rage, pain and vengeance. The sinister smile spread.

◆◆◆

It was a standoff. Neither the weakling nor Jude moved or said anything. It wasn't as if the weakling had a choice to say anything in the matter. Alize specifically instructed him not say a word while Jude said his piece. Jude slouched in his seat and broke his index finger. The crack was loud and painful, nearly too loud. Jude felt himself smile. The pain would soon swarm within the alter ego's body bringing him to the realization that he was not in control of the matter—a fact Jude knew terrified his weaker more vulnerable alter ego. The pain was comforting to him but as he looked into the eyes of this inferior being, he saw the pain in his green eyes. The weaker Jude saw his finger bend all the back to his wrist. He went to scream but the pain choked him while the nausea swam within him. Yes the mind-numbing pain. Jude felt it. It was powerful. The alter ego began to panic and looked to the female as if she would save him from the torment. Jude reveled in his weaker half's torment.

"Because of *you* my opinion *never* matters! Because of *you* people walk all over me!" Jude stood up loving the superiority he felt from standing above his weaker self. "Because of *you* I'm a slave to the tyrants you call gods! You weak fool!" The weakling began to choke as Jude grabbed him by his throat and held him off the couch. Yes, Jude could see the vulnerability in his eyes as the cries for help turned to dry gasps. "Do you hear me? You're weak! You're weak! Because of *you* people view *me* as weak! Because of *you* Lord Egon took mom away and she's never coming back. That was because of *you!* Because *you* were too weak to stand against him!" He tightened his grasp as far as he could without risking unconsciousness or death. However, seeing his inferior self squirm in his gasp and cry through his eyes for help and mercy, filled his body with warm, sweet liquid bliss. "Because of *you* the evil go unpunished! Because of *you*..." he stopped to think about what was next. He knew it was true but he refused to say it. It would mean they were connected by something.

"Go on," said the female.

"Because of *you* I'm afraid," he said. He immediately looked up into the closing eyes of his weaker half. Jude could feel his own eyes growing heavy and he knew unconsciousness would soon follow. He tossed the alter ego to the couch and returned his gaze. The mere sight of this weak piece of garbage made him sick. Who did he think he was chaining Jude up in his own mind and refusing to adhere to his will or acknowledge him as an equal? This Jude deserved punishment just like those who had wronged him. He would pay.

CONCERNING MATHIAS BRAY

"Why didn't you stop him? He was choking me!"

Alize left and returned with two glasses of water. She gave one to Jude and the other to the ipseity.

Jude instantly knocked over the ipseity's glass of water before he could grab it. "Don't give him any! That demon tried to kill me! Have you lost your mind!" He noticed movement in Alize's eyes and followed her gaze to the spot next to him. The being was gone. A cold spot pulsed in his chest causing him to panic. "Get him out! Get him out!" Jude began to punch on his chest over-and-over again in an attempt to drive the being from his body.

Alize leaped up from her seat and came down on him. "Jude that's enough! You will only hurt yourself—and when I say yourself I mean both of you. He is you! You are him! Understand that and accept that," she said restraining him.

Jude began to wish he never accepted Alize's invitation for the session. She had opened up a door that he wished never had been opened. Worst of all was that it was too late to go back. He was aware of his darker side and his darker side was aware of him. If killing Jude didn't also kill his darker side, Jude was sure the ipseity wouldn't have hesitated. He felt lost the more he thought about everything that had transpired since he sat on the couch.

"You said you knew my father. Please share."

She sighed. "I will but first I believe we should talk about what just—."

"I said now!" Jude looked at Alize angrily and noticed her eyes rested on his feet. He looked down and realized the table that he had been sitting in front of him was tipped over, and the two cups that had been there, now lay shattered on the floor at his feet. "I'm so sorry. I don't know what's happening to me. I have to go." He turned for the door but was instantly grabbed by the wrist.

"Your father Mathias came here years ago but it really feels like months," said Alize softening her grip.

Jude returned to his seat and studied her.

"When he arrived he was suffering from amnesia. The only thing he remembered was that he had been held prisoner in a dark place in The Immortal Lands. He didn't remember how he escaped or who had imprisoned him. Of course the General's first instinct was to lock him away. Anyone venturing to Geminate from The Immortal Lands was a threat. However, I saw pain in his eyes and no signs of deception so I ordered for his release," she said.

"Wait they released him because you said so?"

"The Priestess honored my request for his release because she trusts me. The General called for his execution," said Alize.

"But why would the Priestess release someone who could pose a threat?"

"No one knows why the Priestess does what she does. Perhaps she saw good in Mathias the same way I did. That would explain why she placed him in The Palace of Champions. No one is allowed to stay in that house," she said.

"Where is this palace?"

Alize glared. "Your residence."

The cold feeling of being caught doing something wrong descended upon Jude. He couldn't have heard her correctly. His house was enormous and had more rooms than he needed, not to mention the ones he hadn't discovered yet, but he couldn't believe what he was hearing.

"Your father's first night here was a painful one. The neighbors claim they heard cries from his bedroom throughout the night so the city guard was called. Luckily I was in the area and arrived first. I offered to take him in for a session where he too would attempt the shuttling exercise."

"Well what happened?" Jude became more anxious and curious the more he heard.

"The Syphon didn't work. His amnesia controlled him. I had never seen amnesia strong enough to immobilize one's alter ego. The only thing that appeared was a haze before it dissolved. I came to the conclusion that his amnesia was no normal amnesia but something not of this world," said Alize with wide eyes.

"What do you mean not of this world? I'm not understanding you!"

"I can't explain since I never discovered the source of his amnesia. Mathias eventually started a new life here in Geminate. At first the locals were resistant to accept an outsider. Geminate has been in hiding ever since the Praxian war. How he discovered our city beneath The Great Lake is still a mystery. But he was open and dedicated to learning our culture. He began attending our sermons at the Cathedral the first of every week like the others. He soon started his own shop where he sold various elixirs and substances that could aid Agents in battle. Then *that* day came," said Alize coming to an immediate halt. Her eyes fell to her feet and soon lifted as it shook back-and-forth as if refusing to believe whatever she was thinking.

"What day?"

"Mathias had been training with Baul along with some Agents-in-training. Baul was teaching Mathias the art of Geminate combat. Of course Mathias was always at a disadvantage. What Agent could go toe-to-toe with a fully trained Geminate and his ipseity? But then it happened. A perfect ipseity formed at Mathias' back blocking the attack from his opponent's ipseity. Everyone in the city was there since it was the final exam—even the Priestess and General. Mathias' ipseity took on his opponent's alter ego with ease and soon his opponent fell. It was unheard of. An outsider acquiring the ipseity ability without walking the path to enlightenment. The city was in an uproar of confusion. Everyone wanted to know who this man was and where he had come from. The Priestess ordered for an audience with him immediately in seclusion. No one knows what happened in their meeting except for the fact that he was awarded The Palace of Champions as his permanent residence even when he was away. It was out of this world. Many saw him as a prodigy and a prophet. Others saw him as a blasphemous symbol of the desecration of our way of life. No matter what their view, they all wanted him on Geminate's side. They believed he would be the chosen one to bring peace to the world and bring Geminate out of hiding," she said.

Jude was shocked when he saw a tear fall from Alize's eye. There was emotion behind her words. She had feelings for his dad, he could tell. "What happened next?"

"I woke up one day and he was gone. His bed was made and all his things were packed. The only thing that was left was his Combat Band of Recognition the Priestess had given him for his accomplishments. Everyone figured his amnesia had finally lifted and he had returned to his previous life—wherever that may be."

"Combat band of Recognition? Like a ring?"

"No," she said with a shake of her head. "It was an armband given to him by the Priestess of a warrior and his ipseity. It was the only one of its kind. It was made to honor him for not only adapting the Geminate customs, but also making the impossible possible with the acquisition of his ipseity," said Alize. She appeared sad, and for the first time, vulnerable.

Jude's mind instantly wondered back to his black ceramic box in his bedroom with his armband in it. He was sure it was the same one Alize was referring to. It had belonged to his father.

But if dad left it here, how did it make it back to Kismet along with his journal?

"Did you love my father?"

Alize's head jerked up with wide moist eyes. The answer was all over her face. She wiped her eyes, sat back in her chair and crossed her legs. "He was a good man. I am ashamed to say that I had feelings for a man that I knew was married. His wedding ring remained glued to his finger. Even though he claimed he had no recollection of who his wife was, he felt some attachment to her through the ring. He never took it off. So I refused to look at that hand." She quickly wiped her eyes. "Pith oh my I don't know what has gotten into me or why I am sharing such secrets with you. You—a complete stranger. It's just..."

Jude met her unflinching gaze. "It's just what?"

"It's just you look just like him and I need to know. Is he okay? Please tell me he's okay and he's happy. I won't interfere if he is happy I swear it. All I need to know is that he's happy. Please!"

Jude looked down at the hand that grasped his. Alize's words were heartfelt and desperate. Jude became overwhelmed over all that had happened tonight.

"I'm ashamed to say I don't know. He never came home."

Disappointment, agony and sorrow all crawled across Alize's face. She never looked away but her bottom lip and hands continued to shake. "I apologize but this session is over. Thank you so much for coming by."

"I'm sorry but—."

A shadow descended across Alize. "I said get out!" The house shook and the sound of shattering glass erupted around them.

Jude instinctually hit the floor. After he was sure an earthquake had not occurred, he looked up to find all the windows in the house were broken. Glass now lay scattered at various points around the room. Alize was nowhere to be found.

The night's warm air was aggravating when he exited Alize's house. The night-stalkers that were the aquatic beings circled the city from all sides. It appeared that not even they could succumb to the night's call for rest. Walking back up the city's stairs he kept his head low along with his breathing. He still felt vulnerable and afraid. However, his fear did not stem from the threat of an external attack but an internal one. His alter ego was with him. He could feel it. The thought began to grow in Jude's head that this would not be the last he saw or heard of the evil being that was his alter ego.

A PAST LIFE

Jude closed the door behind him and came face-to-face with a march of civilians heading down the city steps. Each of them individually dressed with formal robes and various dark clothing, socializing as they made their way towards the large cathedral Jude had watched them enter and exit the past few weeks. Identical small black books hung in their hands.

"Are you going to join us this week?" asked a voice.

Jude turned around to find Jamieson detaching himself from a small crowd. His hazel eyes stood out against the black collared shirt and dark pants he decorated himself in. A small orb hung from a silver chain around his neck, while the silver Geminate star etched in his forehead pulsed.

"Operative Edric, hi. Where is everyone going?"

"Can we please cut the formality? I'm Jamieson. You're Jude. Let's keep it that way," said Jamieson with a sharp smile. "First day of the week. Time to receive Pith's blessing."

Confused, Jude just nodded his head with a small smile.

"Your people don't worship and pray to the gods?" asked Jamieson.

"We do. Just not as a group—or on a certain day of the week."

"Oh what's that Jude? You're dying to accompany me? Well why didn't you say so come on!" yelled Jamieson pushing Jude towards the crowd.

Jude's veins rushed with anxiety as he struggled to unhinge himself from Jamieson's grasp. "Wait! Wait! I didn't say I wanted to go. I really have some tasks that need completion so I'm afraid I can't—."

"You don't have to beg! You're more than welcome to come along," said Jamieson with a huge grin.

Jude knew what was going on and found himself shaking his head and laughing at Jamieson's stubbornness. His visit to Alize would apparently have to wait, but what made Jude the most uncomfortable was what lay ahead. It had been a while since Jude and the gods had been on good terms since the invasion of Kismet and the loss of his mother. The cathedral was comprised of thick but sturdy dark stones and pointy towers. Multiple stain glass windows of various illustrations decorated the building. Two large wooden dungeon doors opened up as if in response to the civilians that made their way towards its entrance. Jude looked around at the small black books in everyone's hands and was surprised when he noticed that Jamieson was the only one that did not carry one.

"Where's your book?"

"Huh?" asked Jamieson with a comical curl of his brow.

"Everyone else is carrying a black book except for you."

"That's not true you don't have one either!" said Jamieson with a grin.

"What? Are you kidding me? I'm not even from here and this is my first time!"

"Alright alright," said Jamieson raising his hands. "The book in their hands is The Book of Worship."

"Okay so why don't you have one?" Jude continued to follow Jamieson through the double doors and almost paused when he set eyes on the large inner chamber within. Long connected benches stretched out across the silver marble floor leading up to a cascading staircase. Stain glass windows lined the walls on either side of them. Jamieson took a seat on a bench towards the middle of the cathedral. Jude joined him.

"Because people use that book to judge people and that's not what the gods have taught us," said Jamieson with a clench of his jaw.

"What do you mean?"

"Pith, Aegis, Rune! Pith, Aegis, Run!" yelled a voice from the front of the cathedral. A tall man with short brown hair and a dark dress robe held his hands in the air with a large warm smile on his face.

"Good morning how are you?" said a voice next to Jude. He turned to his left and locked eyes with an older Geminate woman smiling back.

Jude was confused. He was positive he didn't know the woman and definitely had not seen her before. Instead of listening to his Agent side, he returned her smile. "Good morning! How are you?"

"Well my illness is acting up. They say my time may be upon me but I'm blessed. I'm sure Pith will find a way to heal me," said the woman.

Jude nodded and inched himself closer to Jamieson, who looked down at him in response to the touch.

"You alright?" asked Jamieson with a grin.

"Sure! Doing great."

Jamieson laughed before rising to his feet. Soon Jude felt a hand on his shoulder hoisting him up. "Time for the best part."

A blast of music assaulted Jude from all sides. Shouts of approval and applause soon accompanied the song, as Geminates rose to their feet clapping along to the beat. Jude looked down and noticed his hands were clapping.

Not even Pith can save you from me weakling.

The rest of the worship inside the cathedral consisted of a lecture from the tall man in the dress robe that led the worship. The man spoke from a small black book similar to the one Jude had seen in the hands of the other Geminates. Jude didn't know why, but he felt embarrassed when he was the only one that wasn't following along in the book—except for Jamieson. Jamieson appeared to still be listening to the lecture despite the fact that he didn't have a book like the others; however, he not once showed any regret for not having one.

Random conversation and signs of affection were what greeted them when Jude followed Jamieson out of the cathedral.

"What did you mean by 'people use that book to judge people?'"

"I'd rather not talk about it," said Jamieson walking up Jude's doorstep. "Well thanks for accompanying me today. I hope you enjoyed yourself at least a little." Jamieson turned his back and headed down the steps.

Jude fumbled with his words and couldn't get them out quick enough. "Wait you're leaving?"

Jamieson turned around with curled brows. "Um yes. Didn't you say you had something you need to tend to?"

"Well what are you going to do?"

"Me? Me me me. Hmm, well I'm going to head to the tavern. I need a drink to balance myself out. It's definitely in bad taste considering I just left the cathedral but my ipseity and I need it—balance reasons." Jamieson continued down the stairs.

Jude looked towards the direction of Alize's house and then looked at the back of Jamieson's head disappearing from view. "Hey!" Jude sprinted down the stairs and caught up with Jamieson with ease.

Jamieson turned around with squinted eyes.

"Use some company?"

"Only if you're coming to drink and not to watch me drink," said Jamieson continuing towards Mother Nature's Tavern.

Jude wasn't big on consuming what his mother called "the devil's nectar;" but if having a few drinks was what he needed to decipher the Special Operative known as Jamieson Edric, a few drinks is what he would have.

Mother Nature's Tavern was empty to say the least upon entering. One gentleman behind the counter and Tae, the young woman who served Jude last time he was at the tavern, were the only other people there. Jude started towards the back tables and stopped when he saw Jamieson heading towards the stools at the counter.

"You don't want a table?"

"For two people who are only having a drink? No," said Jamieson sitting down. "What are you having?"

Jude took a seat on one of the stools next to Jamieson. "Whatever you're having?"

"Says the man who doesn't normally drink," said Jamieson with a grin. "Doesn't mean I'll go easy on you."

"How ya' doin J," said the man behind the counter. He scrubbed a cold stone cup aggressively.

"That's not true I drink occasionally. I'll have an Anti-gravitatis."

The man behind the bar and Jamieson both shared a look of confusion.

"A what?" asked Jamieson.

"Oh I've heard of those," said the man with a flicker of disgust. He leaned in closer to Jamieson in an attempt to whisper. "I heard it's one of those underprivileged drinks that they only make in the east."

Jude glared at the insult.

Jamieson laughed. "Shut up Lyle!"

Lyle cracked a grin before continuing to polish the cup he was holding.

"We'll have a Broken Neck," said Jamieson with a squint.

"Comin' up," said Lyle. He soon returned with two tall black ceramic cups that boiled at the top. He set one down in front of Jamieson and the other in front of Jude. "I'll be in the back. Just yell if you need me to take out any garbage." Lyle's eyes went right to Jude and hovered for a few seconds before he departed.

"Kind of rude."

"No. *Very* rude," said Jamieson sipping his drink while staring at Jude.

Jude picked up his cup and was surprised by the arctic temperature. He smelled the cup and gagged.

"I rest my case," said Jamieson taking a larger sip of his drink.

"On what?"

"On the fact that you don't drink. Even a school of fish know not to smell before they drink. Just so you know, it tastes better than it smells," said Jamieson.

"That doesn't even make sense."

Jamieson set his cup down. "What doesn't?"

Jude decided not to argue. He took a sip and immediately put the cup down. The drink was refreshing but strong with the devil's nectar. He would have to approach this drink with caution.

"So what do you have planned for the rest of the day?"

"Go home, lift and train. Fill an order then lift some more," said Jamieson staring down at his cup.

"An order?"

"Yes sir. I own my own weaponry. I have a large order for the General that is due in a few days." Jamieson met Jude's gaze as the last word left his lips.

The General.

There was something about the Geminate General that Jude didn't trust. He had no reason not to trust the General except for the warranted dislike he had for the man. There was a voice in his head that told Jude that he would need to keep an eye on the General.

"Well that was quite a spectacle during worship today," said Jamieson with a small smile.

Jude felt his forehead slam against the counter. The pain hurt but was quick. The embarrassment soon followed but quickly left as well when he realized he shouldn't be embarrassed about anything. "That was something I wouldn't expect out of me. Not anymore."

"Why is that?" Jamieson turned his seat completely around so he was staring directly at Jude. The shift of attention made Jude uncomfortable, but he did his best to ignore the anxiety. "We are all blessed by the gods and able to connect with them."

"Yes I guess. I'm just complicated."

"Hey Lyle! Make it two Black Eyes this time!" yelled Jamieson. Lyle soon returned with two black cups and set them down on the counter.

Jude looked down and noticed that his first cup sat empty in his hand. He didn't know when or how he had finished the drink, especially how strong it was, but he figured it was dearly needed.

"Try me," said Jamieson handing Jude his new drink.

Jude returned the Operative's gaze in hesitation.

"Don't worry I will let you know if you're boring the living Pith out of me," said Jamieson.

"You seem to be a very spiritual person. You appear to follow and worship the gods like we're supposed to. I used to be like that—like you. I prayed before every meal and before bedtime. I prayed for loved ones and in tough times as well as thanked the gods for every blessing they have given me. That was who I was—who I was born *and* raised to be."

Jamieson took a sip of his drink before releasing a chuckle. "What's complicated about that? Sounds pretty straight-forward to me."

"I'm mad at the gods. I feel like they are letting some of us down and I don't want to worship them anymore."

Tension exploded in the tavern. When silence strolled in behind it, Jude looked Jamieson's direction; who stared back at him with wide eyes.

"You know that's Anim talking. You should pray to the gods for aid," said Jamieson.

"If this was a year or two ago I would agree with you. But I disagree. It's not Anim talking it's me."

"The gods do many things that we don't understand, especially Aegis—since he is known to punish, but they do it for our benefit," said Jamieson retreating to the safety of his beverage.

"Well we obviously are on two different sides of the argument. So to sum it up I am not the same person I was a few years ago. I have been at odds with the gods for months now and the fact that I even entered the cathedral, let alone had that outburst, is not who I am now. The gods know I am angry with them so they have left me alone. No blessings, love or guidance come from them anymore and it's bittersweet." Jude snatched his cup and downed half of it. The Black Eye tasted like a mixture of blackberries and vinegar. The taste was awkward but satisfying. The effect it had on him soon became apparent, which made Jude realize that he had enough for the night.

Jude looked over to Jamieson, who appeared to be lost in thought. He stared harshly at his cup while his eyes appeared to be begging to blink. He soon broke out of his thoughts and took a sip of his drink before wiping his mouth with the back of his hand.

"Well I hope everything works out for you. I know the decisions the gods make can be confusing at times," said Jamieson with a smile that came and went in the same second.

Jude realized he had brought awkwardness to the night and quickly regretted it. He decided a change of subject was best. "So where is your weaponry?"

UNDESIRABLES

Eli picked the closest café and ushered Brayden and his friends in. Brayden had explained that the food rations for the Kismet people were running low so the two meals a day promised had turned into one small meal a day. The hunger was prominent on the gaunt faces of Brayden and his peers. Their clothes had a hard time staying on their bodies and the bags under their eyes were proof of the pain the Kismet people were enduring. The café was packed to say the least. Dozens of wooden roundtables covered the transparent glass floor inside. The tables reminded Eli of Inzanity, minus the tree trunk theme. Upon entering, the sounds of conversations, eating utensils and the gnawing of food ceased. Every face in the café stared back at them including the few young children that ate next to their parents. Something small and delicate tugged at the bottom of Eli's foul smelling tunic. He looked down to find one of Brayden's peers staring up at him with big sad eyes.

"I don't like it here. Can we go?" Logan whispered. His sparring buddy, Sy, nodded in agreement.

The commotion soon returned and the Geminates returned to their conversations. A large table in the middle of the café caught Eli's eye.

"It'll be okay. Look there's a table right there."

Eli headed for the empty table. Brayden and his peers waited a few seconds before following. Each of them clung together like bees in a hive. Eli pulled out all of the seats for Brayden and his friends and was relieved when there were exactly enough seats. Brayden went to sit down and a body leaped into his seat. A young man around Eli's age glared back with arms crossed. Brayden went to sit in the seat next to him and a shaded clone of the young man appeared in that seat. Eli figured it had to be his ipseity.

"Excuse me we were going to sit here."

Suddenly men and women of all ages piled in to the seats releasing their ipseitys to fill the seats that no one occupied. Glares darted back at Eli from all of their faces.

"We're not that hungry. It's okay Eli let's go," whispered Brayden.

Eli felt his rage boiling. He hadn't received such rude behavior at Mother Nature's Tavern when he went out with the squad. The Geminates were clearly going out of their way to make Eli and the Erudites feel unwelcomed.

There has to be something I'm missing. Maybe there's some custom I forgot to adhere to before entering. There's still a lot I need to learn about this city.

A nicer table with cushioned seats seemed to glow in the back. Eli sprinted to it and sat down before signaling for Brayden and the others. Smiles swarmed their faces before Brayden and his peers piled into the seats next to Eli.

Eli passed menus to everyone else before opening one himself. The menu was extensive and had two whole pages devoted exclusively to soup. Eli felt his stomach rumbling. Training had taken a lot out of him but he didn't realize how hungry he was until he thought of how good a bowl of warm chicken and potato apple cider soup sounded. "Get whatever you want. It's all on me." Brayden's peers all high-fived each other before diving their noses into the menus. Eli felt himself smile for the first time in a while. He did feel guilty however for not once thinking of Brayden and the others since the invasion of Kismet. He knew they weren't his responsibility, but he still felt like he should have visited them at least once when he got settled in.

An older woman with a uniform took a spot in front of their table. Eli passed a grin to Brayden and his friends, who returned the same grin. The woman however looked irritated, but Eli decided not to read too much into it.

"Excuse me," started the woman as she put one hand on her hip. "Can I help you?"

"Yes good morning! Can we start with whatever fruit beverage you guys have today. I think we may need a few more minutes before we order." Eli had been looking at his menu and didn't look up until he realized that a response didn't follow his words.

The woman looked back at him with a glare. "Why don't you and your little pieces of garbage remove yourselves from my café before there's any trouble."

Brayden started coughing.

Eli locked eyes with the boy before returning the woman's gaze. "Excuse me?"

"You heard me," said the woman before releasing her ipseity. Her ipseity's eyes were completely black and looked possessed by some sort of monster. "I can put up with having to make nice with you Kismetians swarming our city. On the other hand, I refuse to have to breathe the same air as these pieces of unholy Erudite garbage!"

"Hey!" Eli rose to his feet ready to teach this woman a lesson. The entire café rose from their seats but they didn't scare Eli. His trainer was an Occult Operative and Eli knew he could take every last one of these filthy Geminates if he needed to. The destructive force he now wielded thanks to Kai's training was staggering and pulsed in his veins. The only thing holding him back was Brayden and his friends. Their safety would be in jeopardy not to mention Eli risking exposing the identity of the squad. Combat was not an option in this situation. "I apologize for any inconvenience. We didn't mean to start any trouble." Eli exited from behind the table and nodded for the Erudites to follow him. When Eli and the others got to the café door, Eli looked back at the café and noticed that no one had returned to their seat or removed their glare. Eli could read every bit of the message their eyes were sending. They thirsted for blood; and would kill Brayden and his friends the second Eli turned his back.

◆◆◆

Eli's house was a freak show. Brayden and his friends ran rampant upstairs and downstairs while he occupied the kitchen. After leaving the hostility that was the Geminate café, Eli and the others went to the shops so Brayden and his peers could pick out their favorite foods to bring back to Eli's house. He used the gold he received from the Lieutenant for their Necrosis mission. The Erudites were amazed at Eli's residence and took advantage of the fact that they were the only ones there. Eli immediately headed to the kitchen and began cooking. Even though the day was early, it had been years since Eli cooked a lot of the different foods that some of the kids had picked out. Eli knew he would need as much time as possible. When all of the food was finished, Eli realized he had missed one. Sy, Logan's Partner in crime, had asked for caramelized honey bananas and Eli had no clue how to make it.

He took a look at the kitchen table and counter. The entire kitchen was completely covered with more food than any of them could finish. He would have to skip the bananas.

Eli washed his hands and splashed some water on his face wondering why he had taken on such a task.

A Special Agent cooking in the kitchen. Kai would never stop making fun of me.

A knock sounded at the door. Eli curled his brow before drying his hands and heading to the door. He opened the door to what felt like a ghost. The brown eyes, innocent face and small stature had all changed. Mik had changed.

"Hi Eli," said Mik with a small wave.

323

Eli tried to move but just stared. He missed Mik so much and now he was standing right here before him. "Hi."

"Who's at the door?" yelled one of the Erudites.

"One of my friends. One of my really good friends." Eli turned back to Mik expecting no one to be there. Mik's changed brown eyes stared back at him. "We were just about to sit down for dinner Mik. Would you like to join us?"

Mik smiled causing the tension to melt. "That sounds great." Mik strolled in and took a seat in the dining room.

Eli closed the door in disbelief at who was in his house. "Alright everyone grab a plate from the kitchen and help me bring them into the dining room."

Brayden and his friends poured into the kitchen and after a few short minutes, everyone was ready to eat. Eli took a seat next to Mik. Brayden soon took a seat on the other side of Eli alongside Sy and Logan—who were arm wrestling vigorously.

"Everyone I would like you to meet Mik. He's—." Eli didn't know why the words stopped. Why was Mik being in his house so awkward? "Mik is a really good friend of mine. He's like my brother."

"Hi Mik!" said Brayden and the others in unison.

"Hi everyone," said Mik.

"I was able to cook everything except for the caramelized honey bananas. I apologize Sy."

"That's okay!" said Sy shrugging with a smile. "Everything looks great!"

The dinner was refreshing. Everyone socialized as a whole, and everyone, including Mik, appeared to be having a great time. Brayden and the others were ecstatic when they realized that Mik was also an Erudite. Brayden and his eight peers introduced themselves to Mik, which was a relief to Eli, because he got a reintroduction to everyone's names. Brayden and the others discussed the hardships of the Kismet people and how they all like to retreat to the Geminate Forest to train. Since none of them were able to complete their training with Marius before the invasion, they all felt like they were at a standstill with training.

After dinner, Brayden and the others helped Eli wash the dishes and put up the remaining food, which was a lot. Eli decided to allow the Erudites to package up as much food as they liked and take it home for them and their families. Everyone appeared to be highly thankful and loaded as much food into bags as possible. Eli insisted on walking them home, however Brayden assured Eli that he would make sure everyone got home safely since most of them lived in the same area. Eli forgot how much Brayden had grown. He was seventeen now and the others were sixteen. After everyone had left, Eli closed the door behind them and turned around to a pair of serious brown eyes staring back at him.

"Eli we need to talk," said Mik.

Eli felt caught-off-guard. Mik's words sounded serious and Eli felt like he was in trouble somehow.

"We do?"

"Yes. Do you have a second?" asked Mik never leaving his gaze.

"Sure." Eli instructed Mik over to the sitting area in front of the lit fireplace. It was the one place in the house closest to Eli. It was where he went when the solitude and sorrow got to him. "Would you like some tea or—."

"This won't take long," said Mik taking a seat at one of the cushion black seats. "Please sit."

"Um okay." Eli took the other seat and met Mik's gaze. "What did you want to talk about?"

Mik sighed. "Eli I know with the invasion and all that you and my sister and Jude have had a lot on your plates. But it has been weeks and you have not once came by to visit me."

Eli felt terrible. "I know Mik I'm—."

Mik held up his hand. "Please let me finish."

"Okay."

"You were there for me during a really difficult time in my life, you know, with my dad and all that. You were there for both my sister and myself and I really appreciate it. You are like an older brother to me and I worry about you like I worry about my sister. You guys are the only family I have left—and Jude is slowly joining that too. I just hoped you felt the same about me, but it is clear to me now that you don't feel as close to me as I feel to you—."

"Mik please stop." No tears came or even threatened to make an appearance, which surprised Eli. The absence of sorrow but the presence of guilt felt awkward. "You are absolutely right Mik. I should have come by to make sure that you were okay. You have to understand that I *do* feel closer to you. I *do*. It's just with everything that has happened with Kismet things have been crazy. Your sister and I aren't seeing eye-to-eye anymore either."

"Why not?" asked Mik. He appeared to be very concerned, and the longer he looked at Eli awaiting a response, the harder it was for Eli to respond.

"It's a long story. All you need to know is that she probably doesn't want to see me anymore unless it's during a mission."

"So you're taking it out on me," snapped Mik.

"What?"

"You're mad at my sister and you were only being nice to me because you liked my sister. Now that you and my sister aren't talking, you have no reason to talk to me anymore," hissed Mik.

"Stop it Mik! It's not true. I care about you Mik. I know I haven't shown it lately but I honestly *have* been thinking about you. Things will be different now I promise."

"You promised me you would teach me some new moves months ago. You promised me that you would teach me to dual wield. You make a lot of promises that you don't keep," snapped Mik.

Eli recoiled. His words were harsh. After some thought, Eli realized that he had made Mik promises he had not lived up to. The guilt returned.

"Your promises mean nothing," said Mik with stern eyes.

"No. They *do* mean something. What can I do to show you that things will be different?"

Mik stared back for a few seconds. "*Show me* that things will be different. Since I can't take your word for it, I need you to *show* me." Mik got up from his seat, which made Eli join him.

Eli readied himself to give Mik a hug and nearly fell over when Mik extended a hand. Eli stared back at the young man before shaking his hand.

"I have to get home, but hopefully I will see you soon," said Mik heading for the door.

Eli rushed to follow him to the door. "You want me to walk you home?"

"No I can handle it. But thank you," said Mik opening the door and exiting out into the cold. "Good evening."

When the door closed Eli stood with his mouth open.

"Okay who in the heck was that? That could not have been Mik. He has grown up so much!" Eli walked back over to the fireplace and added some firewood to the dying fire. Looking down into the smothered retreating flames, Eli breathed a sigh of relief when the flames rekindled and the fire began to return to its once voluminous splendor. A knock broke him out of his thoughts.

Eli turned around at the sound of the door. Crossing the room he opened the door. A pair of stern green eyes stared back at him. Jude's nose winced. Eli figured he had to be smelling the day-old clothes that still draped Eli's back.

"We have a twenty on Fox," said Jude.

Eli tore his shirt off and snatched one of his K.T.F. black combat tunics from under his bed. When he returned to the door, Jude was already retreating up the Geminate stairs. Eli closed and locked his door before following Jude to what Eli hoped would be the mission briefing that would bring him Fox's head.

DEPLOYED

Eli hated to see Vance so haggard. The Magi mentor stood a broken shell of the magical perfection he once embodied. The cabin, which once served as their black site, had become a cold zone. Necroborn scouts had discovered its location so Vance had to set fire to the cabin before they could return with reinforcements to uncover any secrets. Instead, the six of them sat around a large campfire in the middle of an all too familiar desert. The ghosts of Kai's cruel and unusual training danced around Eli's vision as he sat on the desert's surface.

Lieutenant Titus handed out black folders this time. When everyone had a folder, Eli looked to Jude who looked to Conall. After Conall and Vance opened their folder, Jude opened his, and the rest of them followed. A heavily built Agent stared back at Eli. His body was covered in heavy metal armor while his menacing light brown eyes squinted at Eli. His hair was tightly pulled back into a long tangled ponytail that ran down his back with various ornaments throughout its braid.

Conall cleared his throat. "Our sources have tracked Fox to a small village just southeast of Geminate. He was first spotted there a week ago and seems to come and go at various times throughout the day—but always returns. He was most recently spotted there yesterday. We believe he is either trying to coerce the natives there to join Lord Egon's forces, or the village has already pledged their allegiance. Target number one is an Emissary, age—unknown. His strengths include weaponry and magic so be warned. From my field report I have gathered that he fancies blades in close combat and magic at long-range. However, I have witnessed him use magic and his blade at close range as well to take out a small army with ease. His weakness isn't some large weakness that will be easy to take him down. He is highly skilled with both close combat and long range but he seems to lack strategy. He fights only in the now. He will most likely be adorned in the heaviest armor he can find, so finding a weak spot for a quick kill is not an option. Chances are a small army of highly-skilled Agents will surround him. As far as I know, the Agents are unable to use magic, but are exceptional with all kinds of weaponry so approach with caution. From here on out your enemies will not be the novices you've faced in the past. They will be highly-trained Agents, Operatives, whatever. You cannot afford to underestimate anyone."

"Sia your senses must be keen for any magical traps moving forward," said Vance rising from the desert floor. "Chances are you will be the only one able to detect them. You must be vigilant."

"Understood," said Sia.

"Your mission," started Conall as he rose to his feet. "Is to enter the cold zone immediately. The portal's magic will most likely attract some attention. If you arrive and the Emissary and his men attack you, they must all be neutralized. If they enlist your help, then they are being held captive and will need assistance. But you must be wary of any traps so the decision will of course fall to Bray. Regardless, target one must be neutralized. He is too dangerous to keep alive. Fox on the other hand needs to be taken alive. We need to find out what Lord Egon is up to and Fox is Egon's right-hand man."

Sorry Lieutenant, but I won't make any promises. Fox killed my dad, and my hands thirst for his blood.

Conall met Jude's gaze. "I don't care how you do it, but Fox must be taken alive. If you're attacked upon entering the cold zone, everyone has to die. Do *all* of you hear me? Moving forward *everyone* is an enemy down to the last child. I don't care if it's the cutest little girl in the cutest dress. If the civilians get in your way, then the civilians become targets. And all targets, but Fox, *will* be neutralized."

"If you succeed, we will be one step closer to ending the madness," said Vance with sorrow in his eyes.

"Any questions?" asked Conall.

The question was rhetorical for everyone but Jude. As Squad Leader, if Jude had a question, he would ask the Lieutenant. If Eli or the others had questions, they would ask Jude. The rules were garbage to Eli but he knew it wasn't his place to decide not to follow them.

Jude rose to his feet. "Mission accepted."

Part Two
Retribution

◆◆◆

A PORTAL OF BLAZING AMETHYST FLAMES OPENED
ATOP THE ROLLING HILLS LIKE AN EYE AWAKENING
FROM A PROLONGED SLUMBER. THE NIGHT'S VIOLENT
WIND HOWLED ACROSS THE SWAYING GRASS LEAVING
AN ECHO IN ITS WAKE.

A DARK SILHOUETTE WITH GLOWING EYES EXITED THE
DANCING FLAMES, OPPRESSING THE GRASS BENEATH
HIS FEET. THE SLEEK BLACK ARMOR BOUND WITH
CRIMSON RED STRAPS, ALONG WITH THE BLACK
CLOTH THAT COVERED HIS MOUTH, HELPED CONCEAL
HIS IDENTITY AMIDST THE NIGHT'S EMBRACE. THREE
SIMILARLY DRESSED FIGURES SOON APPEARED AT HIS
SIDE, MOTIONLESS AND LIFELESS AMIDST THE
TURMOIL.

FEAR IS WHAT BECAME OF THE NIGHT...

B.B.Q.W

THE KISMET
TASK FORCE

Eli forced his way through the portal, taking an immediate position at Jude's side, followed by Sia and Pang. The wind assaulted Eli from all angles as he set eyes on the unarmed villagers that stared at them from afar. The outline of a medium village rose up behind them as they slowly began to approach the squad with caution. Eli looked to Jude, who remained motionless atop the rolling hills. His eyes were consumed with a white hue as they twitched in all directions like a predator stalking its prey. The realization that no blood would be shed on this night was disappointing. The thought was dark and briefly dumbfounded Eli.

"One step ahead of every move you'll make," said Jude aloud. His eyes squinted and grin widened. *"Mission update,"* said Jude over the S-3.

"Eli, reporting in."

"Pang, reporting in."

"Sia, reporting in."

The wind's attack, along with the villagers' footsteps, came to a halt, as if in response to the tension in the air. The seconds that passed awaiting Jude's command were brutal; and just when Eli thought he would lose all self-control, Jude's voice forfeited the S-3 and filled the night air.

"Kill them all!"

◆◆◆

Jude's Optical Tactics instantly detected the villagers' concealed armor and weapons, along with the village's hidden traps, just seconds after exiting the portal. It was at this moment that Jude not only realized that these villagers were actually disguised Agents, but patted himself on the back for creating one of the Kismet Task Force's first cardinal rules: Jude is always the first to set foot in any and all cold zones. The plan of attack became as vivid as the mission at hand. Jude promptly gave the mission update to the rest of the squad then bolted towards the incoming enemies. The Emissary rose up, as if from the ashes, towards the back of his armed forces. His hands equipped with both magic and metal.

"Kill the Emissary!" As soon as the words left Jude's mouth, an Agent leaped in front of him with dual blades drawn. He began to attack Jude with an endless dance of exceptional strikes. Jude ducked, dodged and side-stepped around every attack finding it remarkably simple to continue to read his enemy's movements. The Lieutenant was right; this enemy was highly skilled and would not fall easily.

Eli intercepted the dance, summoning his own set of dual purple blades. Bombarding the enemy with lightning-fast attacks of skill and destruction, the two of them became entangled in a dance of metal and skill.

"You're in range," said Eli.

"I need back-up!" yelled the swordsman as he began to grunt underneath the power of Eli's attacks. "Help me!"

Jude catapulted over the melee, launching a vial down at the incoming reinforcements. The poison was instant. The poison was deadly. The sound of metal soon ceased, and Jude knew that the swordsmen had met their brutal end. Jude's Optical Tactics activated, and soon the enemy's strategy became visible. He opened his mind to the S-3 so the entire squad could see what he saw, hear what he heard and understand what he understood. "Subterranean traps detected forty degrees out in the northern and eastern quadrants."

"Copy," said the squad in unison.

◆◆◆

Eli single-handedly went blade-to-blade with two soldiers while eradicating a small group of incoming henchmen with his Cataclysm ability. The tremor that followed the attack pushed the engaging swordsmen off-balanced, allowing Eli to severe the head of one, and stab the heart of the other. The battle proved easy with the aid of not only Eli's mastered abilities, but also Jude's Optical Tactics. The ability broadcasted everything Jude saw and heard to the rest of the squad, allowing Eli to intercept any ambushes that came his way.

While Jude continued to disarm the hidden traps, Pang barreled down in the midst of the chaos, drawing the attention of nearby enemies. Clapping his hands together he palmed the ground creating an insignia of enormous proportion. Just when his work was done he was surrounded. The enemies rose motionless from the ground as Sia's telekinesis lifted them briefly, before slamming them down into the insignia that Pang had just created. A crimson shade descended upon the battle as Pang brought a horde of twenty or more enemies front-and-center to their first and last Blood Execution.

"Eli! On my heels!" yelled Jude over the S-3.

Then Eli saw it, a shimmer following Jude as he continued to ambush enemies and disarm traps. Eli ran after Jude, following semi-close to his comrade. Jude jumped into battle quickly aiding Pang by eliminating three enemies with a jab to their chins, sides and backs before continuing to run. Then Eli saw the trap that he was there to intercept. The cloak dissolved, and in its place was a soldier with twin daggers running hastily after Jude. Then Eli saw Jude's next move through his eyes. Jude fell to the floor, giving the enemy the opportunity to end him. Bringing his dagger up behind Jude as he returned to his feet, Eli summoned a blade and severed the soldier's head. The ambush was ambushed. A flicker of images passed his sight before Eli saw a sparkle closing in behind him.

"Jude, what are my options?" asked Eli over the S-3.

"You attack one, the others will ambush you. You have one chance, make an explosion," replied Jude's voice.

Turning around, Eli palmed the floor. "Landmine!" The explosion revealed the invisible soldiers, sending them tumbling. Then Eli saw from a different angle, four soldiers closing in on him from various angles—with the aid of Jude's Optical Tactics. He waited for the first to attack, and with a simple back-swing, beheaded the enemy. The other three soldiers trembled before him with wide eyes. For every step Eli took towards them, they took two steps back.

"He's—he's unstoppable," said one of the soldiers dropping his shield and sword. "I've never seen anyone with that kind of destructive power. He see's everything."

Eli summoned three spinning axes above his shoulders and closed in on his enemies. When he got closer, the other two soldiers dropped their weapons and fell to their knees.

"He's Anim," said the second soldier clasping his hands together in prayer. "Aegis be with me. I am your humble servant in this life and the next." Two of the spinning axes buried themselves into the foreheads of two of the soldiers, leaving the third to cower in fear before Eli.

The soldier's hands shook and his jaw jumbled as a lone tear from his eye fell. "Wha—What are you?" stammered the soldier.

Eli leaned in close until their noses nearly touched. He smiled just as the remaining axe stopped spinning.

"I'm Anim—the fallen one."

Jude sprinted towards the onslaught, flipping over the incoming enemies and intercepting their attack on the weakened Pang. Hand-to-hand combat versus the countless blades that assaulted him from all angles would have overwhelmed some, however, Jude reveled in the turmoil. An open palm to the first quadrant of the chin of the first enemy knocked him out cold. Back-flipping over Pang, Jude landed on the shoulders of an incoming enemy before breaking his neck.

Pang was lifted in mid-air, drawing Jude's attention. The Emissary pulled him in from far off in the distance. Just when Jude was ready to abandon his brawl and intercept the Emissary's attack, a portal appeared around Pang and soon Sia took his place.

"Rune's Rein!" yelled Sia. The sky rumbled as Sia bombarded the Emissary with the bolts of lighting that continued to follow his every dodge.

"You witch!" shouted the Emissary as a bolt staggered his defense.

Enemies continued to fall at Jude's hand. As their numbers dwindled, Jude realized his body would not be able to continue the neutralization of such a large number of enemies.

"I found the leader!" yelled an Agent that drew his bow at Jude.

Jude activated his Optical Tactics and counted sixteen Agents that surrounded him.

"Who sent you? Who are you? What do you want?" demanded the Agent. Jude said nothing, but kept his Optical Tactics activated. The enemies attacked.

Eli rolled into battle and to Jude's side, unleashing a three hundred and sixty degree attack of arrows that buried themselves into the throat of their foes. Jude broke out of his normal form and ascended the night air filling it with the battle cry of his gargoyle form.

"Monster!" yelled a soldier pointing from below.

"Run!" yelled another soldier as the mass began to retreat to the Emissary.

"Yes I'm bleeding!" yelled Pang before his sinister laugh filled the air with nefarious intent. It was one of Jude's other rules. If one of them was injured, they needed to let the squad know over the S-3 so the injured party could be defended if necessary. Pang on the other hand, had abandoned the S-3 and decided to taunt his enemies with the news of his injury.

Pang cut off the fleeing enemies throwing both his hands up. "Blood Domination!" Allies soon turned on one another, attacking their brothers with the same rage they once had for the squad.

Jude landed, returning to his normal form while Sia and Eli went toe-to-toe with the Emissary. Inferno comets rained from the sky and redirected to Eli before Sia pushed Eli aside and redirected the attack back at the Emissary; who evaded. When he returned to his feet, Eli's blade came down with a vengeance.

"Sia..."

Sia's eyes darted to Jude who continued to sprint towards their location. A portal soon took Sia's place before Jude found himself entangled in Eli and the Emissary's brawl. Eli had an advantage over the Emissary whenever they engaged in close combat. Just when Eli found the opportunity to end the Emissary, the enemy would bombard Eli with flaming projectiles or apprehend him with his own telekinesis.

Jude flipped in between the Emissary and Eli, landing a kick on the Emissary that tossed him across the rolling hills. Jude tossed Eli an empty vial before engaging the Emissary with his hand-to-hand. Jude attacked as hard and fast as he could. The more he smothered the Emissary, the harder it would be for him to use his magic. An arrow hammered into the Emissary pinning him to the ground. Jude took the opportunity to end him but was thrown by the Emissary's telekinesis. Returning to his feet, Jude caught the now full vial from Eli. He reached into his combat belt and added the necessary ingredients to the vial before injecting himself and returning to the battle.

Jude and Eli went on a tag-team assault. The Emissary had his own strategy for defending against the double team until the vial took effect. Two Eli's now engaged the Emissary. Whichever weapon Eli summoned, Jude summoned the same. The display was a gimmick merely meant to disguise which of them was the Combat Specialist and which was the Weapons Master. Eli would need to be the one to end the Emissary since he held the advantage. All Jude needed was to give him the proper opening. The Emissary pushed Eli off his feet giving Jude the opportunity to land a blow with his blade; which he soon followed up with a smoke cloud.

Eli summoned dual blades and quickly entered the cloud of smoke with the Emissary. "You're in range," said Eli's voice from the turmoil of the smoke cloud. "And *no one* should ever tread into the grasp of a Weapons Master!" The smoke cleared just as Eli's speed went out of control until his movements became a blur. His blade bisected the Emissary's chest causing the enemy to drop his blade. Eli went into a rampage slicing in all directions as his battle cry eclipsed the battle; then it was over. The Emissary had been reduced to five dismembered body parts in a meat pile at Eli's feet.

Jude looked to Eli and then turned for the village, wondering if Eli's training had taught him what needed to be done next.

"*Target one neutralized*," said Eli.

Jude came to a halt at the village's gate accompanied by Eli. Sia and Pang soon joined them via a portal at Jude's side. The village was eerily quiet considering the destruction that had just occurred. Through his Optical Tactics Jude saw no sign of any hidden enemies.

Fox your time is up. The Kismet Task Force has you on their radar.

Sia's invisibility overtook them all, and after Jude reconfirmed that no enemies were hidden behind the gate, the squad infiltrated the village completely and utterly undetected.

FAILURE OR FATE

Eli kept his gaze low and his thoughts secret. Since the mission was over, he didn't believe he was breaking Jude's rule of leaving the S-3 connection open. Disappointment and rage were his friends right now and he refused to rid himself of their presence. After infiltrating the village, both Jude and Sia scanned the grounds for Fox's presence. With his Optical Tactics Jude looked for people while Sia surveyed for any magic at hand. The village was completely deserted. Open doors, scattered belongings and toppled over tables and chairs were the norm upon arrival. The presence of lit candles and warm plates were evidence of life prior to their arrival. The evidence was as clear as it could be. Fox had gotten away.

Sia and Pang hovered over the campfire of the new black site while Jude stood close-by the camp mumbling to himself. A shadow clung to the side of his face with no clear culprit. Eli on the other hand found himself sitting far away from the others. Even though Sia and Pang appeared to not be in deep conversation, he still didn't feel a part of whatever discussion they were having. He knew Sia would probably not be in the mood to socialize with him, and Pang was never a fan of his to begin with. Jude had made his position clear when Eli had shown up at his doorstep a few nights back. Jude had sent word to Lieutenant Titus to rendezvous with them for a mission report. Eli didn't know why, but he was anxious about what the Lieutenant would say when he saw that Fox was nowhere to be found.

Around an hour had passed before the portal opened. The Lieutenant exited the portal first followed by Vance. The Lieutenant stood adorned in heavy metal-plate armor with red detail of the Kismet city on his chest. A shield and sword had already been previously summoned and now sat glowing in the palms of his raised hands. Vance's eyes darted in all directions beneath the cover of his black hooded robe—a color Eli had never seen the Magi wear before.

"Squad leader," said Conall taking a spot at Jude's side. Vance was quick to follow. "So, where is he? Is Sia concealing his body? Were you followed?"

Eli joined Sia and Pang next to the campfire. His comrades appeared to not even feel his presence. All attention was on Jude, who was unflinching to the Lieutenant's long list of questions.

"We failed to acquire him Lieutenant," said Jude in a sturdy but dry tone.

Vance stepped away from the Lieutenant and joined Eli and his comrades, leaving Jude and Conall to their conversation.

Conall's brow curled and uncurled, his eyes squinted and relaxed and his jaw clenched and unclenched. "What do you mean you failed to acquire him?" Conall walked away from Jude and paced temporarily before returning to Jude. "What do you mean you failed to acquire him! Where is he! Where is Fox—*Squad Leader*?"

Jude never left Conall's gaze despite the yelling and intensity of the conversation. His composure never faltered, however, his eyes looked like a storm was brewing in their depths. "Target one was easily eliminated, along with his comrades, however—."

"I don't want to hear 'however' Squad Leader!" snapped Conall. "However means something went wrong, and *nothing* is allowed to go wrong do you hear me?" Conall stormed over to Pang, looking him dead in the eye. "Where is he Quarrels? Where is Fox!"

Pang snuck a glance to Jude and then to Eli. Eli was just as perplexed as his comrades at the Lieutenant's newfound anger.

"Or should I be asking *you* Brassie," said Conall in an accusing tone. "Let me guess. Your team infiltrated the city and you did some idiotic amateur garbage to expose your presence and drive *the* most imperative target away. Huh! Is that what happened? Answer me Brassie! I want Fox you imbecile! Give me Fox!"

Eli's first reaction was to fire back at the Lieutenant but he didn't. Instead, Eli looked away, refusing to acknowledge the anger in front of him.

"You *will* direct any and *all* questions in regards to the mission to me Lieutenant," said Jude. He never left his original position, and stared at the Lieutenant with a stern expressionless gaze.

Conall's head whipped back to Jude and then back to Eli. Glaring at Eli for a few seconds, Conall returned to Jude in a destructive display of rage and disgust. Eli saw movement from Sia; however, Pang was quick to grab her wrist. He shook his head slightly at Sia, who nodded and forfeited whatever action she had plan to take.

"I knew I shouldn't have sent you four," said Conall shaking his head at Jude. "Three of you are beyond weak and one of you is wasting away on this so called *squad*." Conall stormed over to Vance, who had taken a position away from the camp at the recent area of their once blazing portal. "We should have sent the Occult Ops."

"You know we didn't have that option," said Vance with an incline of his head. "We utilized what we had. We just have to accept the fact that the gods didn't feel like it was Fox's time to depart this life. We *cannot* fault ourselves."

"Even if the gods didn't desire us to capture Fox, the Occult Operatives would have successfully captured him anyways. The Occult Operatives are perfection. They never fail," said Conall.

A portal opened up behind Vance. The Magi waved briefly before disappearing inside the portal's depths. The Lieutenant soon joined him, but before he disappeared completely, turned his gaze back towards Jude. "You four may have damned us all. Return to Geminate. I will be in touch." With his departing words the Lieutenant was gone, along with the portal.

Jude approached Eli and the others slowly after the Lieutenant's departure. Without giving any signs as to what he was thinking, he cocked his head towards Sia. "The Great Lake."

◆◆◆

Jude poured his squad some black honey tea before pouring himself some and returning to the sitting area. The tea was a Geminate favorite among the civilians; and also one of the many gifts he had received since coming to Geminate. While the prodigy title was an annoyance, it definitely had its advantages. Jude had not acquired a taste for the tea yet, however, it was the only tea he had in his house and thirsted for something warm to calm his nerves.

"Do you mind lighting a fire Sia?"

"Sure," said Sia squinting towards the fireplace. The dry dusty wood exploded into sparks and flames, giving the sitting room a much-welcomed warmth.

"I was two seconds away from relieving the Lieutenant of his head," said Pang.

"Seriously!" said Eli quickly. He returned a confused expression to Pang who awaited his response. "Mister I'm more honorable than everyone else was all in our faces with his 'where's Fox' insanity. Not very honorable if you ask me."

"No kidding," laughed Pang.

"Be quiet Eli," interrupted Sia. "Conall is just under a lot of stress. I mean he has a lot on his plate. You don't even know half of what he does for our people here in Geminate. Oh and he *is* honorable—*a lot* more honorable than you could ever hope to be."

Jude fell speechless. Eli and Pang had apparently hit a soft spot in the Magi, a soft spot that Jude was sure she would never reveal.

"Excuse me your highness," started Eli with a hostile cock of his head. "Are you defending him? Are you defending the Lieutenant?"

All eyes swept to Sia. Even Pang appeared to be desperately awaiting her response.

"All I am saying is that none of us know anything about what the Lieutenant does for our people," said Sia regaining her composure. "I mean, it's not like he has the General's help anymore—wherever she is."

"No no! Don't try and downplay it now sweetheart," said Eli with a grin.

"Sweetheart?" said Sia with a glow of her eyes. I'm *not* your sweetheart little boy and I'm not downplaying it," fired back Sia. "I'm just—."

"It does sound like your downplaying it," laughed Pang with a fold of his arms. "What is he your lover now?"

Uh oh!

"No, is Eli *your* lover?" shouted Sia shaking her head. "Since when do you agree with Eli anyways? Last time I checked you hated him because he was a 'sloppy, seven year-old amateur that got lucky," said Sia with a glare. It was the first time Jude had seen Sia lose her composure and stoop to Eli's level.

She probably feels double-teamed.

"Don't get all irate with me!" yelled Pang slamming his fist into the table next to him and shattering it into pieces. "No one has to die tonight."

Sia turned her gaze and body back to Jude and crossed her legs in her seat. "Only men, who are dishonorable garbage, talk to a woman like that—and trust me, if I have to come out of this seat, I won't be the one dying tonight little boy."

"I don't care if you're a man, woman or piece of fabric. You get irate I get irate. Period. End of discussion. The end," snarled Pang while cracking his knuckles. "Just say the word—sweetheart."

With a clenched jaw and parted lips, Sia twisted her gaze to Pang and Eli. "Next person who calls me sweetheart..." The sound of a drawer opening in the nearby kitchen gave warning before the duo of large kitchen knives entered the room and hovered in the faces of Pang and Eli.

Eli got up from his seat and slowly walked over to Pang, Sia's knife following his every move. "Sloppy, seven year-old amateur huh?" Eli slowly looked towards Sia but kept his position in front of Pang. "Oh and I almost forgot—sweetheart!" Instantly the conversation went left. Eli, Sia and Pang began shouting undecipherable insults back-and-forth at one another. At one point Pang lifted the sofa chair he was sitting on and threatened to beat Eli over the head with it. Sia's magic apprehended the chair as she threatened to pommel Pang with it.

"That's enough!" Jude's voice became lost in the chaos.

No one appeared to have heard his command. Suddenly Eli became ensnared in Pang's Blood Domination and began punching himself repeatedly in the face while Sia lifted and slammed Pang onto the living room floor continuously.

"I said shut up!"

Wide eyes stared back at him when the turmoil ended. Jude's comrades returned to their seats, refusing to look at one another. Sia combed her hair with her fingertips and adjusted her combat body suit; while Pang began to lick the blood out of the wound on his hand that Sia had just given him.

"Remarkable." No one responded, just stared. "The three of you have undergone *the most* rigorous and high-level training anyone could ever hope for. It's amazing how different, how

347

mature and effective, you three are in combat and mission briefings. You are almost different people. But even after all of the training you three have received, you are all still the same. People never change. That much is clear."

"Squad Leader I apologize for my," started Sia before falling silent to Jude's glare.

If I were our enemy, I could use your ridiculous behavior against you.

♦♦♦

Eli laughed along with the others, beneath the dim hanging lights of Mother Nature's Tavern. Pang repeatedly hammered the table with his mighty fist threatening to bend its will beneath his power. The drinks kept coming, courtesy of Jude's popularity as the Prodigy of Pith, and everyone's guard appeared to be down and long gone. Sia was the only one not partaking in a drink that had any real substance. She finally agreed to stay at the tavern, and not request a change of venue, when she found out that Josline would not be performing tonight. The disgust Sia had for the girl was far from discreet. Eli on the other hand, found himself yearning to see Josline at least one last time.

"Jude what was your favorite part?" asked Sia with a grin.

Jude looked up at the light above their table, appearing to be deep in thought. Suddenly a smile leaped to his face. "Ah! Mine would have to be shortly after I gave the command to kill the Emissary and that highly-skilled swordsman leaped in front of me in a feeble attempt to 'catch me off guard," laughed Jude uncontrollably. "His face when Eli sprang up in front of me was priceless!"

The entire table laughed so loud, that Eli could see the stares from the surrounding guests that came and went at their laughter. Eli was surprised that Jude's favorite part of their last mission included him in it. Even though Eli was sure that it had nothing to do with Eli in particular, and more to do with that moment, he still found himself feeling a little closer to the group once again.

"Poor thing didn't realize he was going up against a Weapons Master and the longer he sparred with his enemy, the stronger his enemy got," continued Jude.

"Wait! Wait I think I remember his words," interrupted Pang in laughter. "Help! Oh help! I'm weak and defenseless and need backup!" Both hands went to Pang's face as he tried to calm his laughter.

"That's not exactly what he said," said Sia shaking her head with a smile.

"Mines well have!" laughed Pang.

"Another round?" asked a whisper amongst the laughter. It was Tae. She balanced a small square tray with empty glasses on one of her hands.

"Jude! Jude! Jude!" chanted Pang while beating on the table. He quickly punched Eli with wide eyes in an attempt to get Eli to join him in persuading Jude to get more free drinks. Eli obliged.

"Jude! Jude! Jude! Jude!" chanted and cheered Eli and Pang as they beat on the table, rocking it and its contents back-and-forth.

"Will you both stop! We're in public and your acting a fool," whispered Sia.

The chanting continued. Jude eyed Sia before returning his gaze to Tae. "Only if she has a *real* drink." Jude's eyes swept to Sia and then returned to Tae, who looked at Sia awaiting her response.

"Peer pressure is a bully technique Mr. Bray—one I refuse to partake in," said Sia crossing her arms and retreating her gaze to the wall behind her.

"Well, guess everyone is paying for their own drinks," said Jude.

"Boo!" said Eli and Pang in unison. "Sia! Sia! Sia! Sia!" Their chant raged on, until the table behind them joined in out of nowhere.

Sia turned around with wide eyes and looked at the dozen of people cheering her name. The embarrassment was clear on her face. "Okay! Okay! I'll have a drink."

"Yeah!" screamed the tavern as their hammering fists appeared to rock both the ground and the walls.

"I'll bring you something mild," said Tae with a small smile.

"Pith bless you!" whispered Sia.

"How are you doing sir?" asked Tae to Jude. Eli realized that Tae had been going out of her way to be nice to Jude since they had arrived. At first he thought it was because of Jude's prodigy status. Now he wondered if it was her attempt to reconcile their last disagreement about Hunter and the hostile treatment he received from Garrett.

"Fine. If I needed something I would have let you know," said Jude.

"Very good sir," said Tae retreating to the front of the tavern.

"You know, you could be a little nicer to her," said Sia.

"I know. But I don't want to," said Jude finishing the last of his drink and then sliding it over to Eli, who had been making a fort out of the empty cups all night.

"Jude it's not her fault that Garrett treats Hunter so badly. What do you expect her to do? Not everyone is as strong as you," said Sia.

"I have an announcement to make," said Jude quickly. The entire table came to a pause, as everyone's eyes swept to Jude, who looked at Sia with a sharp stare.

Sia noticed Tae on her way with a small tray. She allowed the woman to leave their drinks and regarded her with gratitude, before confirming no one else approached their table. "Ensconce."

"Regardless of what the Lieutenant says," continued Jude. "I think the three of you did an excellent job during our mission. The fact that the entire village was empty and Fox was nowhere to be found, was something none of us could have prevented. We did as we were told and that's all a Squad Leader could ask for. My only issue was that little unwarranted squabble back at my house."

"Unwarranted?" snapped Pang. "Were you paying attention? Sia was coming for me. I was in fear for my life and the life of my kids!"

Eli choked into laughter.

"Oh shut up Pang," said Sia shaking her head with a smile. "I can't even deal with you right now." Pang grinned at her words.

Eli felt a large weight leave his heart. While the dagger of agony called Marius was still buried deep within its depths, the weight of solitude and isolation was fading away. Everyone was getting along and he was included in the fun. It had been weeks and weeks since the squad had engaged in any social activity with him outside of a mission. His pride told him that he shouldn't care if he was included or not. If they didn't want to hang out with him, then he didn't want to hang out with them. But deep down inside he knew that he did care, and tonight was comfort for his wounds.

"Which brings up my next point of what happens if I ever do get injured in combat," said Jude with worry. "There are a few things we need to go over, and a few combat techniques that I will be implementing. Tomorrow night we will have a training session so I can fully explain. Keep your day open."

"Well the night calls," said Pang stretching. "Off to my midnight lifting. Jude you're coming right?"

Eli's brow curled in confusion as he looked to Jude, whose shoulders dropped at his sigh.

"I promised didn't I?" asked Jude.

"Yes! Yes you did Bray," grinned Pang.

"Alright let's go," said Jude finishing his drink. "Pang and I are off to do some duo heavy lifting that he tricked me into agreeing to."

Eli could sense it in the air. Everyone was leaving. "You guys want some company?"

Jude looked to Pang.

"I'll have to say next time Brassie. I got this lifting exercise from Jamieson and he says it only works with two people," said Pang with a yawn before shaking his head. "I swear I will make it my life's mission to have arms bigger than that guy."

"Alright," said Eli trying to neutralize any hint of disappointment or sorrow in his voice. He turned to Sia and noticed that she was packing up as well. "Where are you off to?"

"Well I really should be getting home to Mik," she said with a smile. "It's really late and I promised him I would help him with his combat project and be there when it's time for him to go to bed. I'm probably already late."

"I could help—with his combat project." Eli heard the desperation in his own voice and cursed himself for failing to conceal it.

"That's nice of you," said Sia giving Eli an urge to smile. "But, right after his project I will be making sure he goes right to bed; and if we have company, I'm sure it will be hard for him to go to sleep."

"Oh. Okay."

Pang and Jude rose from the table adjusting the Geminate clothes they wore. Sia soon joined them and right as the three of them began to depart, they all turned back towards Eli.

"What do you have planned for tonight?" asked Jude.

"Me?" Eli's mind reached in all directions for any ideas. Cups, people, garbage and lights all failed to aid him in his attempt to come up with a plausible story. "I'll probably just turn in for the night. My blood energy is still recovering and I'm a little tired."

Eli's comrades all nodded before Pang saluted and they departed. On their way to the exit, Jamieson entered the tavern and engaged in light conversation with Eli's comrades before they departed. Eli returned his attention to the table he sat at. Memories mere minutes old of Eli and his comrades laughing and enjoying each other's company manifested ghosts in the empty seats around him. Then they were gone and Marius took their place. His warm smile teasing Eli with love and support. The dagger in his heart began to turn clockwise and then counter-clockwise, feeling his heart with agony. The tears in his eyes began to form, and just when one was about to take a plunge down his cheek, a voice interrupted his thoughts.

Eli looked up and found Jamieson staring down at him. Quickly blinking to exterminate any pending tears, Eli forced a smile upon his face.

Worry descended upon Jamieson's face as his hands grasped Eli's shoulders. "Pith oh my are you okay?"

Eli became confused by the antics. He curled and uncurled his brow before coming to the conclusion that Jamieson wasn't joking. "Uh yeah."

"You're responsive and you're looking right at me so you don't appear to be blind," said Jamieson appearing slightly relieved but still concerned. "But who knows, it could be deep-seeded."

"What are you talking about?"

Jamieson's eyes widened. "You looked directly into one of the great wonders of the world and lived!"

Eli was growing more confused by the second. "Looked into the what?"

Jamieson took a deep breath as if he was about to deliver some bad news. "Josline's perfect breasts. They say, one look at her divine chest can drive a man to the point of madness!"

It took Eli a while, but once he got it, his laughter nearly suffocated him. He laughed and laughed, feeling his legs continue to hit the underside of the table.

Jamieson's pearly white smile turned into laughter while his chest rose and fell abruptly. "How's it going buddy?"

Eli tamed his breathing and silenced his laughter. "Good how are you?"

Jamieson took a seat across from Eli and waived over Tae, who appeared almost instantly.

"What will you be having handsome?" asked Tae with a wink.

"A piece of whatever you got," replied Jamieson with his own wink.

Umm...

Tae giggled underneath Jamieson's attention before regaining her composure. "Will it be the Busted Rib or Neck Breaker this time?"

"Just water tonight thank you," replied Jamieson.

"How boring!" said Tae.

"Have we met? I'm probably *the most* boring person in existence," said Jamieson.

"One water coming up," said Tae turning away.

"Wait!" shouted Jamieson reaching for Tae, who turned around immediately. "Eli might want something."

Eli was shocked that Jamieson remembered his name considering they had only officially met once. Eli looked from Tae to Jamieson and then back to Tae. "Oh no I'm good. Thank you though."

Tae smiled before she took her leave. Eli looked down at his full glass between his hands. He didn't even have a chance to taste it before his comrades decided to leave. Pang and Sia's half-full glasses shook beneath Jamieson's shaking leg as he surveyed the tavern before returning his attention back to Eli.

"You know, I just saw your friends when I came in," said Jamieson.

"Yeah, we all came for a short night out but we still have a lot of work to do so they retired early."

"Oh yeah I forgot the Kismet resources team. Does your team have a name?" asked Jamieson.

If it wasn't for the pre-planned answers and aliases, Eli realized he would have stumbled and most likely failed to answer Jamieson's question. "B.B.Q.W."

Jamieson looked off into the distance nodding his head. His finger rose in the air as if he was counting something. "So Brassie, Bray, Quarrels and what was Sia's last name again?"

Eli felt anxious. Jamieson decoded the squad's alias with ease. Since it was their alias, the group's identity was in no real danger. The purpose of the alias was to flash it around to any who questioned their identity. However, Eli couldn't help but feel a little unnerved that Jamieson had read through it so fast. "Wyatt."

"That's right! That's right!" said Jamieson nodding. "So Brassie, Bray, Quarrels and Wyatt. Very cool."

"Actually it's Bray, Brassie, Quarrels and Wyatt. Jude's name is first since he is the—." Eli stopped himself immediately. He was mere seconds away from exposing Jude as the Squad Leader, which he knew would result in more questions. "Since he's been with the resources team the longest. He's kind of a veteran."

"Oh nice nice," said Jamieson noticing Tae approaching their table. He took his water from her with a flirtatious smile before returning his gaze to Eli. "I invited Jude back to my shop the other night after we went to the Cathedral. He seems like a really nice guy."

"The Cathedral?"

"Yes for worship," replied Jamieson in a baffled tone.

"What's that?"

"I swear you Kismetians," said Jamieson shaking his head. "Worship is when you go to a blessed location and praise the gods."

Eli laughed. "I can't believe you Geminates call us Kismetians. The name sounds so ugly."

"Well what do you call your people?" asked Jamieson appearing confused.

Eli thought about it and was surprised when he came up empty handed. He shrugged his shoulders. Instead, he decided to change the subject. "So you believe in the whole gods thing too?"

"Gods thing?" replied Jamieson. His face turned sharp as if he had just been insulted. "Oh I get it. You're one of *those* people. Let's change the subject so we don't argue."

Fine by me. Crisis averted.

"How come you're still here?" asked Jamieson with a concerned look on his face.

"What do you mean?"

Jamieson sipped his water. "I mean why didn't you leave with your friends?"

Because they didn't want me to come with them.

"I don't know."

Seconds came and went before a minute had passed. Eli kept his gaze at the still full cup in his hands that was probably beyond room temperature now.

"Wanna talk about it?" asked Jamieson.

"About what?" Eli knew exactly what Jamieson was inquiring about. No matter how many times he tried to persuade himself otherwise in his head, the truth that the solitude he had been experiencing the past few weeks was eating him alive.

"You don't have to talk about it if you don't want to," said Jamieson interrupting Eli's thoughts. "I just thought I'd offer since you look like something is bothering you.

I do wanna talk about it! I shouldn't want to but I do!

"I've angered two if not all three of my teammates in the past." That one sentence chipped off a particle of the anxiety Eli was holding. It felt good. Jamieson said nothing but continued to stare. "While it seems as though we've put it behind us, part of me feels like we are only getting along because we have to—because of our duties."

Jamieson nodded while biting the inside of his cheek. "So basically everything appears to be fine when you and your 'friends' are doing things that pertains to the B.B.Q.W, but any other time you find yourself alone."

Eli's mouth dropped as if on its own.

"What?" asked Jamieson quickly.

Eli shook his head trying to find his voice. "Uh nothing."

"Well whatever your past is with your 'friends' is really none of my business. The three of them have been nothing but kind to me. What I will say is that you shouldn't let yourself sit here and waste away. Trust me. The longer you sit here, the more time you give your hurts of the past to catch up to you. You don't want that because it never ends good."

Eli was annoyed by Jamieson's advice. He knew what the Operative was saying was true, however, he hated advice that offered no real solution. "Then what do you suggest when you are subjected to isolation on almost a daily basis?"

"The way my life is, I'm *far* from being in a position to give any advice," said Jamieson with a small chuckle. "Eli sometimes you have to walk alone." His words were simple. His words were heavy. The message they sent failed to extinguish his agony, but succeeded in calming its rage.

"I'm meeting with Talon, the General and his men in a couple of days," said Jamieson rising from his seat. "We have some big important combat meeting so I will need all the rest I can get for the next couple of days to put up with the General." Jamieson raised two fingers to his brow. "Good evening sir."

Eli returned the gesture. He watched Jamieson walk around the emptying tables before disappearing from view.

Sometimes you have to walk alone.

NO MORE PAIN

"Now you can take your socks off now, or I can knock them off once you see our secret weapon," teased Marius. He stepped through the door with a dressy black long-sleeve sweater with silver stitching. The sleeves naturally cuffed at the wrists and had tiny silver swords sewn into the exposed cuffs.

Eli drowned his tongue in the Neck Breaker. The drink made the contents of his stomach threaten to show itself while his body began to lightly shake. Lyle, the gentleman that served the drinks behind the counter, stared down at Eli while his eyes ran down the menu. The stools at the counter were far less comfortable than the table he once sat at, but with every sip he took, the stools became a little more comfortable.

"What's the Hemorrhaging Coma taste like?"

"Like death sprinkled with insanity," replied Lyle.

"Alright I'll take..." His brain paused. "I'll take..." Eli became annoyed and mentally gave his brain a kick under the table. "I'll take that one and the Bleeding Brain."

Silence.

Eli looked up to make sure Lyle had heard him. The Geminate stared back at Eli with a vacant expression.

"What?"

"Maybe I should bring you some water first," said Lyle.

Eli summoned a blade in front of him on the counter and smirked back at Lyle. "Maybe I should show you who the boss is in this..." He hiccuped. "In this relationship."

Lyle's expression never changed. He didn't reply right away, just stared. "Your threats are as useless as that poor excuse of a sword you summoned Weapons Master. Save them for your next inevitable drunken squabble." Lyle turned towards the back door. "I'll be back with your drinks."

"Yeah. Yeah that's what I thought you stupid!" Eli looked down at the blade in front of him and noticed that it had the handle of a sword but the point of a dagger.

Oh man I messed up.

He quickly dissolved the blade before anyone saw it. Looking around the tavern made him dizzy, but gave him confirmation that he and Lyle were the only ones there.

That's right Tae went home like two hours ago. What time is it?

Lyle returned with two cups. One cup danced with flames at its mouth while the other bubbled like a cauldron. Eli felt his mouth water when Lyle set them down in front of him.

"Thanks handsome."

Lyle recoiled. "I'll be in the back if you need anything." He quickly retreated to the back as if a fight had broken out.

"What? It's not like I called you...it's not like I called you ugly!"

Marius' ghost that had been sitting next to Eli since he had relocated was fading—and with it the pain.

"Almost gone! Almost gone," he said to himself as he stared at the cups in front of him. The memories of Marius stepped atop a sharp high cliff looking over a raging sea. The two drinks were all he needed to push them over the edge and banish the pain from the depths of his mind.

Sia played with each of Eli's fingers individually, while they both lay amidst the amethyst meadow. "So if everything is okay, and life goes on—then what?" asked Sia. "What do you mean?" asked Eli. "You know," she started as she raised her head from his shoulder. "With us. Where do we go from here?"

Eli blew out the flames atop the cup and downed half of the drink and then the other half. His chest burned briefly before he felt the tightness under his chin and the vomit rising quickly. He felt his eyes widen. He continuously gulped the second cup until the vomit was forced back down into his stomach. The room began to spin. His eyelids felt like stones but the pain was subsiding. He closed his eyes.

"Why hello," said a voice next to him.

Eli opened his eyes and saw rows and rows of beverages. His head bobbled back-and-forth as it swiveled to the stool next to him. A beautiful woman sat next to him in a tight-fitting white dress that ended far above her knees. Her dress was barely containing her chest with each breath she took.

Eli felt tickled and began to laugh. "Hello beautiful."

"Stop!" she said with a slap on his shoulder. Her smile was both bashful and seductive. "You are just being nice. I'm Josline." She turned her stool his direction bringing her warmth his direction. She folded her buttermilk legs and blinked twice.

"I'm not! I'm serious you're beautiful—and I'm Eli." He put his hand on her leg wanting to feel the smoothness of her skin. Her legs were smoother than they looked and warm to the touch. His eyes glanced at her knees, up her legs and found them at her lips, which were under siege by the bite of her teeth. Then there was two of her. He blinked and then there were five sitting in front of him as the tavern behind her increased the spinning. He felt like he was going puke.

"Are you okay?" she asked.

He closed his eyes and smiled. "Yeah I'm great." When he opened his eyes he saw her smile.

"I know what you need," she said rising from her stool and grabbing his hand that still rested on her leg.

Before she tugged him off his seat, he finally regained control of his stomach. "Where are we going?"

"To make you feel good," she said with a wink.

I must be dreaming.

Eli let Josline pull him towards the exit of Mother Nature's Tavern before they came. The amethyst orbs were large when they opened up in front of him. Guilt was their power and the past was their strength.

"Wait!"

"Yes," said Josline turning around. Her fingertips danced at her leg.

"Maybe another, another, another," he stammered before closing his eyes and taking a deep breath. "Maybe another time."

Her bottom lip poked out. "Ah okay then." She released his hand and approached him slowly. She pushed her chest against his. Her smell was light but intoxicating. "Next time I'll expect double the fun." Turning on the balls of her feet, Josline was off. Just when Eli began to smile he fell to the floor and vomited in an endless stream. The more he tried to close his mouth, the harder the shutter that released more. The smell was heinous. His nostrils flared as they took in the odor from the never-ending waterfall.

"By the name of Pith!" yelled a familiar voice.

Eli thought it sounded like Lyle, but he was too sick to try and figure it out. Two feet stepped into his line of sight away from the foul-smelling pond that he had just spewed. Eli looked up and saw Lyle and his darkly shaded ipseity standing over him.

"Now here's what's going to happen," said Lyle with his arms crossed. "You are going to clean every inch of that up."

The ipseity began to punch its fist into its open palm. Its aura was dark and terrifying. It bent down until it was eye level with Eli. "Then I'm going to kick your ass!"

AN UNKNOWN
MISSION

Jude stared down at the piece of parchment. Its folded nature concealed its contents. The unsettling feeling it brought forced Jude out of bed and over to the washroom. He quickly cleaned up and got dressed before re-entering his bedroom and hovering over the end table that held the ceramic box and mysterious parchment.

After lifting with Pang, Jude felt like he was going to keel over and die. The exercises were clearly not designed for someone with Jude's body type, but for that of a god. After making it through a brutal torture, Jude returned to Alize's house. He needed to speak with his other side again and hoped she would help him. The trip was in vain. Alize explained that because he wasn't a Geminate, the shuttling he did was a one-time occurrence and that drinking the serum again would produce nothing but an upset stomach. She advised him to open up the lines of communication with his other side and learn to accept all of himself instead of only the side he had grown up to accept. Returning home for the night, he climbed into bed and opened up the ceramic box that never left his bedside. Three small statues depicting the gods rolled around inside next to his vials and family photos. The statues were purchased from a shop around the corner from Jamieson's weaponry. He didn't know why. For a second, the statues compelled him to pray or at least communicate to the gods, but he quickly closed the door to those thoughts. After waking from a dreamless night, he turned over in bed to his end table just in time to catch a piece of parchment explode onto the table.

Activating his Optical Tactics unlocked the mystery. *B.B.Q.W.* shined clearly through the parchment's surface without even opening it. Jude snatched the letter and focused on the S-3. Signs of confirmation from Pang and Sia responded to his command to rendezvous at Sia's for an emergency meeting. For some reason Eli didn't respond.

He must not have his S-3 on.

The streets were filled with civilians. It was probably the busiest day in Geminate that Jude had seen. The sight of Pang's house was overshadowed by the grunts from the silhouette that stood in front of the house. Jude opened the small gate and entered the front yard to find Pang lifting a massive boulder like one would lift a piece of firewood. His bare chest glistened with caked sweat and dirt. Suddenly his hands slipped and the boulder fell on top of his bare feet. A thunderous shout released before Pang barreled his fist into the boulder, shattering it into tiny pieces of gravel and dirt. His face was savage. His hands sat clawed.

"Pang!"

Pang's eyes found him with ease. The beast was gone but the terror never left. "Morning Squad Leader."

"Ready to go?"

"Oh yeah," said Pang walking over to a precariously thrown tunic and putting it on.

Eli's house sat only a few doors down, so the two of them walked casually down the block.

"Have you heard from Eli?"

"Brassie? No. I was almost surprised when he didn't confirm your command," said Pang wiping his face and neck.

"I hope he just forgot to put on his S-3—in which case he's in trouble."

Eli's house rose up quietly and untainted. The curtains in the windows were closed and the look of abandonment was present. Jude ascended the few steps up to Eli's door and knocked once, twice and then a third time. No answer. Jude met eyes with Pang and then descended the steps, scouting the neighborhood. The S-3 always remained open so Sia's voice soon boomed through it.

"Why isn't he answering?" asked Sia with worry.

"Activating Optical Tactics." Jude tried to scan the house, however, the only thing he saw was a plain house.

"Sia my Optical Tactics can't pierce the walls."

"Apologies Jude, I enchanted our homes on my way home last night, to ward against prying eyes and ears," said Sia in a matter-of-fact tone. *"Try it now."*

Jude reactivated his visual ability and instantly saw a thermal view of the house. One body was visible on the top floor, lying facedown on the floor. The second Jude saw it, the rest of them soon followed.

"Brassie!" yelled Pang barreling through the front door and knocking it off its hinges. Jude followed Pang upstairs until they both were looking down at Eli's lifeless body. A foul odor hung in the air.

Jude checked for a pulse.

"He's alive." Jude threw Eli over his shoulder, something he would never be able to do prior to training. Splashing water on Eli's face just once resulted in his arms and legs flailing around. His eyes opened and rested on Pang.

"What are you doing in my house Quarrels?" asked Eli.

"Taking advantage of you," said Pang crossing his arms. "I didn't enjoy myself so it was a one-time thing."

Eli coughed violently before laughing. "Whatever man."

"Eli what happened? Did someone do this to you? Where are they?"

Eli stared at the washroom wall in front of him before turning to Jude. "I didn't feel good when I got home last night. I was a little nauseous and had a bad headache. I must have overslept."

Jude studied Eli with every word he delivered. His words were stammered, his eyes kept drifting to the same spot and one of his ears kept twitching—a habit Eli never had.

He's lying.

Jude made sure to keep the thought far away from the

S-3 so the others wouldn't hear it, especially Eli.

Eli's head suddenly jerked up as if hearing a voice. He shook his head before rolling his eyes. "Yeah whatever Sia. Why don't you go work on that ugly drawing you call a dress."

"Alright wash up and get dressed. Pang and I will be downstairs." Jude exited the washroom after receiving a nod from Eli. Pang helped himself to every piece of meat in Eli's refrigerator while Jude paced the dining room. Every seat was staggered as if they all had been in use.

Ten guests and then Eli makes eleven?

"Brassie needs to go grocery shopping," said Pang entering the dining room while gnawing on a piece of meat.

"You're shameless," said Eli entering the room shortly after.

"You have some people over?"

"No," replied Eli. His eyes scanned the dining room table and set on one of the chairs before returning to Jude, who bore his gaze deep into Eli's eyes.

He's lying again.

"Alright well let's get to Wyatt's."

B.B.Q.W.

Forgive the change of communication. I am afraid rendezvousing with you anywhere but Geminate will no longer be possible. I will now be communicating with your Squad Leader via writing, and with the aid of "V," be teleporting it to you at the safest moments.

A few days ago the General and the four responsible for your training were sent on a covert mission to The Immortal Lands in a desperate effort to eliminate the ruler. Their mission was not successful. Fox was waiting for them; and with the Lord's help, proved to be a worthy adversary. So it is with a heavy heart that I must inform you that Tristan and General Briars are no longer with us—casualties of war.

Their failure is not without consequence. The ruler of The Immortal Lands is now aware of the rebellion and pending attack and has made haste in invading other lands and villages. Kai was able to retrieve some intel indicating that the Relinquished Isles is next, followed by Praxis and then Geminate. So as you can tell, our time is running out and our numbers are dwindling. In two days I will be rendezvousing with you at the residence of your Squad Leader at midnight. Keep your eyes and ears open and be smart, safe and brave.

Until we meet again,

"L.T."

As the last sentence was read, the parchment grew warm, before igniting into an explosion of black flames. It was gone. Eli realized he had been holding his breath, and after willing himself to breathe again, looked up at the vacant eyes that stared back at him.

"Oh my Aegis," said Sia softly.

"Wow," said Pang with a curled brow.

I don't believe it. The General—dead? And Tristan too?

Jude rose from his seat. "This means from now on there *cannot* be anymore mistakes. We all have to be perfect during every mission. You will train twice as hard so we can be sure that everyone is *always* at their best."

"Copy," said Eli along with Pang and Sia.

◆ ◆ ◆

Eli walked with his comrades down the steps behind the Priestess' temple, and through the hundreds of shops that ran in all directions. Each step felt like hell. Eli still felt so sick from the night before that his empty stomach still threatened to show itself. Jude wanted to show them the weaponry of the Special Op. Jamieson Edric. A dark building rose up ahead of Eli when they reached the last shop. The sound of a hammer on metal banged through the door.

Entering behind Jude, Eli felt like he was in a dream when he entered the shop. Every weapon you could possibly imagine hovered around him. The lights were beyond dim, which did wonders for Eli's current condition.

Footsteps grew closer drawing everyone's attention. Jamieson stepped through a doorway from the back; his bare chest shining with sweat and littered with specks of dirt. Eli felt awkward looking, but he couldn't help but notice how chiseled Jamieson's torso was. His abdominals and chest looked like they could bend an incoming blade. His enormous arms shined as well but were not a surprise. Eli hated to admit it, but he was jealous. Even after all of his intense training with Kai, his body wasn't close to looking like Jamieson's. Where Jamieson had a six-pack Eli had a four-pack; not to mention that Jamieson's arms looked like they were at least three times the size of Eli's.

"Oh—my—Aegis," said Sia.

Eli joined the stare of Jude and Pang as they turned their attention to the Magi. Sia stood fanning herself with her hand.

Eli focused on the S-3. *"Calm down Sia. I mean, how many times have you seen me with my shirt off?"*

"You have the body of a boy. *That* right there is the body of a man," said Sia.

"Ouch!" said Pang looking over to Eli.

She knows that isn't true. I even had muscles before training. After training my arms had doubled in size and my chest and abdominal muscles drew attention even when I wasn't flexing. She's such a witch.

"Witch..."

A hovering blade fell from the ceiling in front of Eli and stabbed the floor, standing in place. Jamieson had been approaching them and recoiled at the sight. He now wore a shirt that was doing little to hide his muscles.

"Sorry about that," said Jamieson extending a hand to Jude. "Don't know why that fell. The holders are enchanted. That's never happened before."

Jude shook Jamieson's hand. "No apology needed. I just wanted to bring everyone by your shop so they knew where it was. You remember Sia, Pang and Eli."

Jamieson nodded his head to everyone. "Well take a look around. I have some great offensive and defensive weaponry.

The squad took a look around while Jamieson disappeared to the back. When he returned, Jude had already regrouped with the rest of the squad.

"We're heading out," said Jude.

"Already? You just got here," said Jamieson with a frown.

"Rough day," replied Jude shaking Jamieson's hand.

"Well you guys are welcome to come back anytime. Remember, last row, large dark building," said Jamieson.

Everyone offered gratitude before turning for the door. When Eli turned to follow, a hand grabbed his shoulder. He turned around to find Jamieson staring back at him.

"Brassie you know you can't leave here without shaking the shop owner's hand," said Jamieson.

Eli laughed before extending his hand. Jamieson took a while to grab it, but when he did, Eli felt a smooth piece of glass between their hands.

"See you guys later," said Jamieson turning for the backroom and disappearing.

Eli looked down at his hand and found a very small bottle with a small piece of parchment tied to its neck. He untied the parchment and opened it:

Sometimes you have to walk alone…

But sometimes walking alone doesn't mean being alone.

Drink up and feel better.

—Jamieson

"Eli are you coming?" called Jude from outside the shop.

Eli tucked the note and the bottle inside his tunic and exited the shop, guilt of his previous night heavy on his heart.

FATHER & SON

The return to the Aaia house was far from comforting. It was for this very reason that Jude forced the rest of the squad to accompany him. However, Conall had pressed to them that Eio Aaia was someone they could trust in his absence. The Lieutenant even went so far as to express to Jude in secret that if Jude really needed answers, Eio was the person to go to. The four of them sat patiently in the living room while Kyla Aaia warmed up some herbal tea in the kitchen. Eli was the only one of the squad that appeared excited to return to the Aaia house. Jude figured it was because Eio Aaia and Marius used to be best friends; at least according to Eio.

Kyla entered the room with a small tray with five cups on small plates. She still showed no signs of pregnancy, which was always a mystery to Jude. She passed everyone a steaming cup, before taking one herself, and joining them on the couch. "My husband should be back soon. He and Alistair went shopping for a new blade for Alistair. So exciting!"

Jude smiled but did not feel like responding.

"Did you ever meet my dad?" asked Eli eagerly. He pushed himself to the edge of his seat, giddy with anticipation.

"I did a few times. Very nice man. He taught me to play chess, even though I am ashamed to say I have forgotten how to play," said Kyla blushing.

The front door slammed open drawing everyone's attention. Alistair stormed in, followed by his father Eio.

"Dad I am begging you. Please!" said Alistair.

"As long as you live under my roof, there will be no more of this writing!" yelled Eio holding up a worn journal.

"Eio, Alistair what's going on?" asked Kyla rising from her seat.

"Mom I—."

"Shut up Alistair!" yelled Eio. He waited for Alistair to close his mouth before returning his attention to his wife. "I found our son writing some piece of fictional garbage in this journal after I specifically told him that writing was out of the question."

Jude looked to Kyla in hopes that she would put an end to this madness. Jude felt like he would have laughed at how crazy the entire situation was, if it wasn't bringing so much pain and suffering to poor Alistair.

"Mom, I love writing. I don't like combat," pleaded Alistair.

"Quiet!" yelled Eio throwing the journal across the room. "All boys love combat. How many times do I have to tell you that?"

Alistair stared back at his father, and for a second, Jude thought Alistair might attack Eio. "None father. I'm sorry—for everything." With his apology, Alistair disappeared to his room, leaving his scattered journal behind.

Kyla greeted Eio with a hug before retreating to the kitchen to finish preparing dinner.

Eio took a seat in front of Sia. "I apologize for my son. Sometimes I feel like I'm raising a girl. He's so soft. If it wasn't for his little girlfriend he's been with forever, I would assume he *was* a girl; especially with all that nonsense about him not liking combat."

"Are you sure pushing combat on him is the best thing though? He seems to really enjoy writing. Maybe combat just isn't for him." Jude hoped his suggestion would not send Eio into the rage he had come to associate with the man.

"Oh no Alistair likes combat trust me. He just doesn't know it yet. But he'll eventually come around," said Eio.

Pang cleared his throat. Soon a small crash came from the back of the house, drawing the squad's attention.

"Don't mind that. It's just Alistair letting off some steam," said Eio. "Now you wanted to ask me about something?"

Jude forced his personal feelings about Eio aside and focused on why they were here. "Yes sir. The Operative we brought to you when we arrived to Geminate—Jamieson Edric—what do you know of him? Is he someone we can trust?"

"Who Edric?" asked Eio. When Jude nodded, he continued. "Of course highly-skilled Operative and a very respectable young man. His parents were killed shortly before he became an Agent so he's had to raise himself. Very smart boy with a talent for smithing some of Geminate's finest weapons."

"Dinner is ready," interrupted Kyla.

"Now Kyla, you know better than to interrupt a man when he's talking," said Eio.

"But of course. Forgive me honey," said Kyla kissing Eio on the cheek while drying her hands with a towel. "You finish your conversation and I will go get Alistair." Kyla disappeared to the back, causing Eio to lean forward to watch her backside as she disappeared.

"Gotta love that women," said Eio whistling. "Now as I was saying I can't think of anyone more trustworthy than Edric. He's—."

A scream boomed from the hallway.

"Kyla!" shouted Eio running to the back.

Jude looked around the room at the wide eyes. Something was wrong. Jude's thoughts instantly went to Fox. Perhaps he had shadowed them and infiltrated Geminate's walls.

"Be on your guard!"

"Copy that!" said the squad in unison as they rose from their seats.

Jude walked slowly down the hallway, keeping his Optical Tactics activated. Family portraits and paintings decorated the wall as he ventured down it. Every portrait was of Eio, Kyla and Alistair. Everyone smiled in the portraits, except for Alistair, who had the same flat line expression in every photo. Walking into the open door, Jude prepared for the enemy that lay ahead.

Eio embraced Kyla tightly as she fought and struggled to break free from his arms. Her sobs were loud and her tears ran wild down her face. Then Jude saw him. Alistair's body rocked back-and-forth, ensnared by the rope around his neck that hung from a hook in the ceiling. A chair lay on its side beneath his feet. It was horrifying. The young man that once walked, talked, lived and breathed just a few minutes ago, now hung from his neck in his bedroom—eyes too wide open to be natural.

Jude looked down to an unfamiliar sensation. His hands were shaking. It was baffling. After all of the enemies he had eliminated in combat, this brought his nerves to their limits.

"Not my baby! No, no, no Pith no!" cried Kyla falling to the ground along with a shocked Eio. "Why Pith? Why!"

Jude took a few steps closer to the body. Unloosening the noose around Alistair's neck, he laid the boy's body down on the floor. A note ruffled in his hand. Jude retrieved the letter and turned to Eio and Kyla, holding it out for their retrieval.

"What does it say?" demanded Eio. "Who did this to him?"

Even Jude could tell without his Optical Tactics that no intruder had been here. Alistair had done this to himself. The level of denial displayed by Eio was almost shocking. Eli and the others soon slowly entered the room. Sia's hand instantly covered her mouth before she buried her face into Pang's shoulder. Jude opened the letter to some scribbled handwriting and read it aloud:

Dear Mom & Dad,

I'm sorry I didn't turn out to be the son that you guys always wanted. I have tried my entire life to make you both happy and to make you the proudest parents in the world. I'm sorry to tell you once again that I don't like combat. I know you think all boys are all alike but we're not—I'm not. I don't yearn to wield a blade, train hard and become an Agent. I dream of expanding my knowledge and writing stories of legendary heroes and epic battles. Dad I know you're probably very angry right now and I'm sorry. I'm sorry I'm not a son you can be proud of. I have tried to be someone I'm not, the someone you want me to be. Unfortunately I can't. I am who I am. Even though you have brought me up to believe that taking my own life will seal my fate in Anim's realm of darkness, I believe that fate will be less painful than living a life as the disappointment you wish was never born. I just hope that Pith and the other gods are forgiving of my choice. I love you both so much with all of my heart and please never forget that.

Your son now & forever,

Alistair Aaia

"Shut up! Not another word," yelled Eio.

"Mr. Aaia I'm so—."

"Quiet! We were fine until you four started coming around," shouted Eio. "You did this to Alistair! Out! I want the four of you out of here!"

Emotion told Jude to rebel against Eio's words. It told him to tell Eio that he did this to his son and that Jude and the others had nothing to do with it. The squad had only come over twice. Those two visits could not amount for years of bottled despair and pain. Jude folded the note and placed it next to Alistair's hand. He nodded to the squad, before following them out of the bedroom. Exiting the Aaia house did not extinguish the silence or tension. On the contrary, it haunted them with a silent grief that would follow them for days to come.

ENLIGHTENMENT

Jude paced back-and-forth across his bedroom floor. The three small statues of the gods stood on the end table staring back at him. He looked back towards the full-length mirror and made his decision. Walking up to the mirror he peered at the mirror image of his stern green eyes.

"Show yourself."

The room was silent and everything went unchanged, except for Jude's patience. He knew the being was there, and refusing to show himself.

"Jude, show yourself."

The alter ego now inhabited the mirror. The darkness in his eyes was staggering but familiar. His pain and rage were clear across his face.

"What do you want?" asked Jude's alter ego.

"For you to listen."

The being in the mirror said nothing. But his eyes were filled with secrets.

"First, I want to apologize to you for repressing you my— *our* entire life. While I do apologize, you have no choice but to find in whatever darkness of a heart you have to forgive me. You know how our mother raised us. Always think of others before yourself. Always do good and honorable things. Love people and forsake any evil or sinful thoughts. I was raised to forsake you and that's all I knew. So you see, while you have every reason to be angry with me, you have every reason not to be angry with me."

"Why am I here," echoed the alter ego's hollow and nefarious voice.

"It's time for you to become me and I to become you."

The mirror being looked slightly caught-off-guard as if not expecting the answer. Still he said nothing.

"I'm strong and you know this. I can read people like a book made for babies. I can tell when people are lying and when they're telling the truth. Today I looked into Eli's eyes and saw his light side and dark side, something I've never been able to do with anyone. Everyone seems to be whole, utilizing their light decisions and their dark—especially the Geminates. My mind is quick to not only create a strategy for me and my team, but also to brainstorm the best options and strategies for my enemy and which one they are most likely to take. Due to my training I am fast and nimble. However, I also know that you're strong. You have confidence. You have power. You are cunning. You are determined. Also, just like me you're goal oriented. The only problem is, without me you wouldn't last a month."

The mirror shook, as if an earthquake was erupting.

"And why wouldn't I last a month!" snapped the alter ego.

"Because without me, your rage would just act on impulse getting you and your comrades killed. Thinking ahead and efficiently is my quality, something that would help to keep you alive. While you may have power, the majority of the best Combat Specialist traits lay with me. Adapting to combat as it unfolds, knowing the best ways to aid my comrades and ensure they come out on top and being one step ahead of the battle is all me. The aggression in other forms, ability to deceive an enemy and brute force are all you. While mine are both powerful and can keep me and my comrades alive, yours are just powerful."

"What do you suggest?" asked the mirror image.

"You and I as one. Like everyone else is. The way we should be. As one there would be no secrets from one another. There would be no lies. My opinion would not hold more weight than yours, because we would be one and not think of us as two separate beings, but remember us as one person. The way we are supposed to be—balanced. You and I would be unstoppable."

The room was silent. With each passing second, Jude began to wonder if his darker halve would refuse.

"Unlock the part of your mind you have locked me away in, and let us be one," said the alter ego. Then he was gone. Jude breathed in deeply, and submitted to himself.

THE RETURN TO TAARAGON MOUNTAIN

The letter could not have been any clearer or any more startling. Kai had been discovered during his mission to obtain intel on the next move for Lord Egon and Fox after the invasions. His abductors now held him captive somewhere inside a place called Taaragon Mountain. The letter was sketchy and left many questions. The handwriting was messy while the letters themselves looked terrified. Eli flew on the back of Jude along with the others. The Squad Leader's gargoyle form had become even larger and more powerful than the last time Eli had seen it. Sia appeared delighted at the change of transportation since portaling always took a substantial amount of her blood energy. Kai was in trouble and needed to be rescued immediately; and the Kismet Task Force would be the squad to rescue him.

The night air was cold and violent when the rough, rocky mountain pierced the sky before them. The trees beneath Jude's wings looked lush and soft, reminding Eli of Kismet. Landing on a wide, oval patch of greenery, the squad dismounted. Jude quickly reverted form and activated his Optical Tactics. The ability was eerie but was growing on Eli. The squad moved quickly towards the whistling mouth of the mountain.

"The Lieutenant was right," said Sia strutting in front of the squad. With one open palm she attacked the air in front of her, bringing a wall of cascading, cerulean glass tumbling down before them. "The arcane arts are at work here." She returned behind Jude and let him take the lead once again.

The cavernous mountain was beyond dark once they entered. Eli found himself on edge, waiting for the enemy to leap out of some kind of hidden cavern and ambush them. As the squad's main source for offense, he needed to be ready. Spears of rock shot down from the ceiling above them while lose earth lay scattered at their feet as they turned every corner. The passage soon opened up to a fork.

"Activating Optical Tactics," said Jude over the S-3.

Eli quickly followed Jude down the left tunnel, leaving Pang to bring up the rear. A hoarse scream echoed throughout the mountain sending shards of rock detaching and falling all around them. The scream sounded familiar. Eli focused on it once it returned.

"That's Kai. I'm sure of it."

"He's trapped in an illusion—a strong illusion," replied Sia. *Her thoughts were jittery to the point of alarm. "I can feel it."*

"They're torturing him for information," replied Jude. His thoughts were just as erratic as always when the squad communicated via S-3. His mind always thought of too many things at once for Eli to follow. It was like listening to a crowded room of people debating at the top of their lungs.

"Torture huh?" replied Pang with a giddiness in his voice. "I love the sound of that word.

◆◆◆

The path opened up into a rocky, circular chamber. Boulders and small rocks decorated the dry terrain while the shadows cloaked the corners. Three hooded figures stood with their arms outstretched in front of a lone body that lay sprawled out on the floor beneath them.

"This one is harder to break than the last one," said one of them.

"He's from that *cursed* Kismet. Hurry up before those Kismet Task Force swines find us!" said another.

Pang coughed. The male spell casters turned around, unveiling Kai's motionless body beneath them.

"Hello gentlemen! My name is Pang, and I will be your executioner for today," said Pang cracking his knuckles.

"The Kismet Task Force! Get them!" yelled a spell caster.

"Battle formation Tau!" yelled Jude, before somersaulting in front of the squad.

Pang leaped to Jude's side, shaking the mountain when his feet met the ground. Sia cloaked herself in invisibility before walking behind Jude and Pang, tapping them both on the shoulder with two fingers once, before disappearing. Jude raced to the spell casters with Pang hot on his heels. Two of the spell casters stepped to the front, lifting chunks of earth with their magic, before hurling them at Jude. Jude didn't flinch nor did he slow down, causing the spell casters to smirk. The large boulders hit Jude directly, exploded into clouds of smoke and rubble as Sia's arcane armor took effect. Jude contorted and took flight into his raven form, exposing Pang running in for a direct attack.

"Boom!" shouted Pang barreling his fist into the face of one enemy sending him crashing into the wall behind him. Quickly snatching the collar of the second offensive spell caster, Pang hurled him Eli's direction.

Eli readied his bow. Once he had a clear shot at the incoming body, he buried an arrow in the spell caster's face, shooting the enemy's body back the direction from which it came. "Down for the count."

Pang walked slowly towards the recovering spell caster he had attacked earlier. Waves of magic, rock and projectiles shot at Pang from the spell caster's hands as he screamed for aid.

"Why—won't—you—die!" shouted the spell caster while continuing to attack. When Pang finally got to him the attacks stopped. "Please! Please don't kill me."

"Oh I'm not going to kill," said Pang crouching down to the spell caster's line of sight. He pointed one finger up, causing the enemy to look up just in time to catch the razor-sharp fangs of the incoming gargoyle.

The last spell caster threw Kai's body over his shoulder quickly and headed for the back of the cave. Eli didn't even think about taking a step to go after him. In battle formation Tau, Sia took Jude's normal role as Recon; and would have an eye on the fleeing Magi. The portal around Eli opened quickly, and as soon as Eli stepped through it, he found himself on the other side of the room facing the fleeing spell caster that ran his direction.

The enemy skid to a halt, dropping Kai's body. His eyes were wide and his palms were poised for the attack. Eli felt a tap on the back of his shoulder and then he was off, closing the distance between him and the enemy. A mist of spectral soldiers appeared around the spell caster just as Sia secured Kai's body under the cover of her invisibility.

"Operative secured," said Sia over the S-3.

The soldiers charged. With his blade, Eli eliminated five of his attackers before turning towards the line of incoming attackers behind him. "Landmine!"

The landmine activated, unleashing a massive explosion that sent a tremor throughout the mountain. Spectral body parts rained all around Eli while he closed in on the last enemy. The arrows Eli summoned behind the spell caster deflected upon contact, telling Eli that his enemy had armor of his own. That didn't matter to Eli. Every Magi's number one weakness behind the lack of blood energy was close combat—and close combat was Eli's specialty.

The spell caster snarled, forfeiting his stance and charging Eli.

You know it's over don't you...

With a clean back-slice of his blade, Eli beheaded the spell caster, bringing the mission to an end.

"Target neutralized. Mission complete!"

THE ESCAPE

Jude led the squad back towards the passage from which they had entered. Pang carried an unconscious Kai over his shoulder, while Eli watched his flank. A rumbling began echoing throughout the mountain the second Eli reported the last target's elimination. They needed to get out of the mountain as soon as possible. The way back was a lot quicker than the way in. The passages shook upon entering them, causing chunks of rock to fall over their heads. Sia's magic kept the debris from becoming an obstacle. The mouth of the mountain opened up to a dawning light filling Jude with comfort, which a voice in his head quickly struck down.

Jude ran to the center of the familiar green lawn he had trained with Priya on. It's soft surface was no longer a sense of comfort but annoyance. He took a few more steps before he heard it. The familiar sound of power, legends and the ancients roared around them.

"Brace for impact!"

The dragon stomped its massive weight down on the grass's surface, throwing the squad off their feet. The metallic silver eyes surveyed each squad member one-by-one. The sharp black scales appeared even sharper than Jude remembered. A closer look at the dragon's neck revealed a large healing bite mark from Jude's last battle with the creature. No scales covered the wound. The dragon's eyes went from Eli to Jude and then stopped. Opening its jaws at Jude, the dragon roared.

"Prepare yourselves! This is a foe unlike any you've ever seen!"

◆◆◆

Eli allowed Pang to toss him above the dragon's attack, landing him atop its shoulders, before the frenzy of his epee blade wore away at the dragon's only defense against his attack. Bursts of flames shot in all directions, lighting the surrounding trees in destructive fury.

Leaving the mundane chains of earth beneath her, Sia took flight, bringing herself eye-to-eye with the beast. Eli found himself airborne, leaving the sharpness of the dragon's shoulders, as Sia's telekinesis forced the dragon's attacking flames to submit to her will. The flames came together, drawing in the ring of fire that once trapped the squad. With a cold swoop, the raven swept under Eli, flying him to the safety outside of the flaming prison.

"I'm going in!" yelled Pang sprinting towards the beast.

Sia contained the flames while simultaneously levitating Pang from the ground beneath them.

"Boom!" yelled Pang slamming his fist directly into the dragon's snout.

Using its wings, the dragon recovered before hitting the floor. It quickly attacked with a breath of flames at which Sia quickly slid in front and countered; redirecting the flames and charring the dragon's flapping wings. The beast took to the sky, engulfing the area around it in flames and ashes.

"Oh no you don't," said Sia flying after the dragon. Her magic quickly grasped a hold of the creature before hammering it down onto the ground beneath her—never leaving the safety of the sky. Just when Eli was ready to attack, Sia lifted the dragon's massive body once again and this time continuously pummeled the floor with the enemy. When she was done the dragon went still, but its chest continued to rise and fall.

"Let us end this mission!" Eli ran for the incapacitated dragon. Blades summoned all around it slicing and attacking as if being held by invisible master swordsmen. He soon joined the attacking blades, using his dual blades to unleash every bit of anger and darkness he had felt over the past few days. Scales and skin fell at his feet. The countless blades never stopped attacking and neither did Eli. With each swipe he found himself closer to the attack that would end his enemy's life. The attack proved strenuous when Eli felt his blood energy drop and his attacks grow lighter. Jude ran by in his peripheral vision, tossing a vial at Eli that stuck into his back. Immediately Eli felt his blood energy return with a vengeance. His attacks grew more powerful and more deadly. The independent attacking blades began striking with such speed that their movements became untraceable, while Eli found himself spinning and dancing in an endless dance of stabs and strikes.

"Not gonna happen!" yelled Jude tackling Eli to the floor. Shortly, the dragon's massive tail whizzed passed them.

"Time to get dangerous," said Pang sliding in front of Eli and Jude. Intercepting the dragon's attack, Pang knocked one wing away and then the other before locking both hands around the dragon's neck. The dragon kicked and roared in an attempt to break free. "Blood Deprivation!"

Finally releasing itself, the dragon knocked Pang off his feet and returned to the sky. Endless trails of blood continued to fall from the dragon with each flap it took. Its eyes, nose and wings continued to ooze blood from areas that showed no wounds. With a staggering roar that made Eli freeze in place, the dragon unleashed another challenge into the night air.

"This is it!" yelled Jude running for the beast. "Battle formation Alpha!"

With Jude's command Eli and Sia leaped to one another's side. Sia ran to the right, unleashing her chains of paralysis around the beast and freezing it in place. Eli summoned his bow and ran to the left, firing an endless quiver of arrows that buried themselves into the soft flesh of the dragon's belly—never missing their mark. Pang and Jude ran side-by-side, Jude covering ground faster than Pang before his hyena form took control. Pang quickly caught up to Jude's side, feeding his blood magic into Jude's side. The hyena continued to grow until its head was to the dragon's neck. The hyena leaped and attacked— its sharp fangs ripping into the dragon's neck and forcing it to land. Then the feeding frenzy began. Snarls and bites from the hyena sent dark flesh in all directions before Jude reverted form.

The body of their fallen foe twitched but remained on its back. A weak roar followed by another came-and-went. A twinkle rippled through the air like a sparkle from the night sky. In the wake of the twinkle came four strangers adorned in all white combat armor as white as snow. The black straps around their arms and legs were similar to the red straps of the Kismet Task Force. White masks concealed their identities, except for one, who only utilized a hood that cloaked his face in shadows. Whoever they were, readied hands and feet gave the warning that they were ready to engage.

"K.T.F. Operatives," said the Agent with the hood. The Agent sounded female, however, Eli didn't know if it was only due to the magic that floated around the stranger. "Recover the target. Kill any who get in your way!"

With a flash Eli was surrounded by two of the Agents, entangled in a dance of blades as he tried desperately to fend of the precision of their attacks. It took only a few seconds for Eli to quickly realize that his opponents were also Weapons Masters. The lethality and precision of their attacks were too perfect for a normal Agent or even an Operative. His blood energy was draining and he could feel the power and force leaving his attacks with each swing he took. Dissolving his blades, he made a decision that if he would die, he would make an impression. Ducking beneath both his assailants, he palmed the floor. "Land mine!" The explosion was tremendous, knocking back his assailants but leaving him unscathed.

The female Agent wasted no time abandoning her battle with Sia and rushing for Eli. He could feel his heart fluttering and his hands shaking. His body was strained and it would only be a matter of time before he lost consciousness. The Agent leaped above Eli's head ignoring him, but soon came crashing back down underneath the ravenous jaws of Jude's arachnid form.

The two Weapons Masters quickly returned to the battle. With blades drawn they landed direct blows on the arachnid, drawing rivers of black blood. Screeches and staggering came from Jude as he tumbled off of the Agent.

"Jude she's a Magi!" Eli jumped to his feet but found himself dragging every part of his body towards the inevitable massacre ahead of him.

The Magi clasped both sides of her head with her hands before racing to Jude in a flash. Her magic was effective, making her movements untraceable. A blue aura covered her hands as she struck Jude repeatedly drawing his screams and reverting his form. Jude turned to run for Eli but the Magi's magic turned the surrounding trees against Jude, using their branches to ensnare his arms and legs.

"Pang help!" cried Sia over the S-3.

Turning to his other comrades, Eli found Pang and Sia locked in a battle with a Combat Specialist. A blue aura surrounded the Combat Specialist in whichever animal form he manifested into. Sia's magic and Pang's Blood Magic continued to be intercepted by the aura, sometimes turning Sia's and Pang's attacks against them. Turning back to Jude, Eli wished he had not been so careless as to expend so much blood energy. He forced himself into a run for the battle in front of him. He was the only one that could save his Squad Leader; and even with no blood energy, he would find a way.

Jude flipped around the battlefield in an attempt to evade the attacks from all three of his assailants. The victory of his strategy was short-lived once the Magi returned to her feet and intercepted Jude's acrobatics and throwing him to the ground. The other Weapons Masters smothered him with attacks as he tried to return to his feet. It was a blood bath as the Magi trapped Jude's feet in place while the other Weapons Masters went into a slicing frenzy.

"Injuries at critical level—beast awakening!" shouted Jude over the S-3.

Jude's gargoyle form released him from the prison but his form quickly reverted back. Limping to his feet, Jude turned around and saw the three incoming assailants and then returned to Eli with wide eyes—the black scarf that concealed his identity rested caked with blood.

His blood energy is low too. He's not gonna make it...

"Jude!" Eli ran for his comrade fighting through the pain and dizziness. He reached his hand out towards Jude in hopes of snatching him from the danger that pursued him. Jude's hand extended to Eli, driving Eli to quicken his pace and get to his comrade faster. Then the Weapons Master blade loomed up behind Jude as he unknowingly continued to run for Eli.

Oh no! It's over...

Jude's Optical Tactics activated, turning his eyes a bright white, before he reached for his combat utility belt and retrieved a vial. This was it. This was when Jude would inject himself and some ingenious plan would come to fruition. The thought was calming until Jude flicked his wrist burying the vial into Eli's shoulder just as the purple blade broke through Jude's chest. Blood propelled from Jude's mouth and then his body hit the ground.

"No!" Eli's scream drew the attention of Jude's assailants. The vial quickly induced the familiar effects of the Faliche Plant through Eli's veins, but also gave his blood energy a quick boost. It may not have been a lot, but it was enough for Eli to will himself into battle with his attackers. The Weapons Masters were easy prey to his increased speed. Placing a landmine beneath the feet of one, and impaling the other with projectiles from behind before they could react, was child's play. The Magi proved more of a challenge, as her magic increased her speed so she moved almost at the same speed as Eli. With a slight advantage over the Magi, Eli was always able to dodge her elemental and palm attacks, but was not able to land a fatal blow. Even though he pelted her from all angles with every type of arrow, blade and projectile, her magic dissolved the attacks. Considering a Weapons Master was supposed to be a Magi's weakness, she was proving to be a formidable opponent.

In his peripheral vision, Eli caught an uprooting tree coming for him. He dodged but wasn't quick enough. The force of the trunk cracked his back, sending him tumbling into what felt like a body. He turned over to find himself lying on top of an unconscious Sia. "Get up Sia!" He shook her as hard as he could but she refused to wake. One of the Weapons Masters blocked his view of the battle. His laugh filled the air as he took off his mask revealing his identity. Will Keating loomed up over Eli with the most arrogant of smiles. Memories of Eli and Will's last battle in Professor Ivor's class flashed in front of his eyes.

Will summoned a blade and put it to Eli's neck; and then summoned another blade and put it to Sia's unconscious neck. "I won. You lost. The end!" Will's blades attacked, burying themselves into Pang, as he charged Will to the ground.

Eli threw Sia over his shoulder before Pang's painful grunt caught his attention. Will summoned pits of spikes, which Pang eventually stepped into, lacerating his leg, and bringing him to his knees.

Will's dual blades crisscrossed around Pang's neck, shining in the moonlight with a burning brilliance. "Praxian filth! Your parents also resisted me when I came for them in the night—*especially* your wretched mother."

Eli dropped Sia next to Jude's lifeless body and went for Will. The Combat Specialist quickly loomed up over Will as the largest amongst serpents, bringing Eli's revenge to a halt.

"Eliminate them," commanded the Magi.

The other Weapons Master soon appeared alongside Will. Extending his hand to the moon, a bow fell from the sky surrounded by silver rays. Its presence was blinding, causing Eli and Pang to look away. As the Weapons Master pulled an invisible arrow back, the moon's shine began to darken. The arrow fired, carrying an aura of the moon with it. A serpent's tail intercepted the attack, reflecting it back on the Weapons Master. Eli turned around and locked eyes with a second dragon.

The massive beast unleashed its blazing fury among the enemy as they tried desperately to flee. A scar bisected the dragon's chest, causing a flashback of Jude's death to replay in Eli's head.

"Jude..."

The dragon pounced on its prey, tossing Will and the Weapons Master to the side, and meeting the serpent Combat Specialist in a battle that was over quicker than it started.

"Eli here," said a soft voice from beneath him.

Sia looked up at Eli with fluttering eyes. In her hand was a small vial. Eli took the vial and helped her to her feet. Jude's tail came back swiftly, knocking Eli to the ground, before coiling around Pang. Jude snatched up Sia with his cringing claws and took to the sky.

"Jude what are you doing!"

"Shoot him Eli!" screamed Sia as Jude took her and Pang higher into the night air. Pang struggled in the dragon's grip before being tossed to the floor by Jude's mighty tail. The other Magi pelted Jude with elemental attacks and attempted to imprison him with the surrounding forest, but Jude was too powerful. The Weapons Masters fired countless arrows and unleashed a rain of projectiles, which showered over Jude's path.

"The beast before death..." Eli held up the vial and willed it into a projectile. Instantly the vial acquired the tail of an arrow with the needle of the vial at the head. Eli summoned a bow and aimed. "Luckily for you, I'm the best archer Kismet has ever seen." The dragon was too quick to hit directly, so Eli followed his movements until he saw where Jude would fly next. He fired.

Sia plummeted from the dragon's grip but quickly levitated before she hit the ground. The dragon dissolved into itself until Jude cascaded down from the night sky. Sia's magic gripped Jude before he hit the ground while Eli grabbed Kai's body from behind a shattered boulder. The enemy ran for Sia, as she hovered above the forest holding Pang and Jude's lifeless bodies in her telekinetic grip. All of their attacks Sia countered back at them while still in flight and still holding her comrades. Eli ran with Kai's body as fast as he could, knowing that Sia would not be able to hold out for too much longer.

Sia's eyes went to Eli just as the Magi jumped to Sia's position. A portal opened up behind Sia just as a second portal opened up in front of Eli. Holding his breath, Eli rolled into the portal, alongside Kai.

NEW ENEMY

Jude awoke to the eyes of Lieutenant Titus and Vance. It took him a few seconds, but he eventually recognized his room around him. He shook off the headache and rose in bed. His body screamed at him as it shuttered with shattering pain.

"You were right Professor. This one is a fighter," said Conall. With his less than joyful words, the Lieutenant exited the room, leaving Vance and Jude to the light commotion downstairs.

"Glad to see you're awake," said Vance taking a seat at Jude's bedside. His face looked less haggard than the last time Jude saw the Magi, and he actually looked like he gained some weight as well.

"Where's the squad? Is everyone okay?" Jude couldn't get his words out quick enough. The last thing he remembered was Eli's fearful eyes as the icy-cold metal sliced into Jude's insides. The mere memory of the incident was jarring and seemed to awaken his howling agony.

Vance sighed. "Mostly everyone is fine. Pang took a bad fall and is still unconscious..."

Jude threw back the covers and reprimanded his body when it had the nerve to retaliate with massive pain. Vance followed quickly after Jude, pelting him with words Jude was too busy to decipher. He needed to see Pang and figure out what happened to him.

Eli and Sia sat in the armchairs in front of the fireplace looking down at Pang, whose body lay on the adjacent sofa.

When their eyes found Jude, they both shuttered. Eli even rose from his seat in alarm for a second before returning to his seat.

They look so unnerved...

Kai exited to the kitchen in the background, only giving a nod when the two of them locked eyes. He was clearly not going to show any signs of appreciation for his rescue. Jude walked over to Pang's body and studied him. His chest rose and fell slowly but faintly. Bruises and cuts decorated his arms and face. His right leg and foot looked horrific with holes and gashes as if he fell into a pile of knives. His KTF black scarf was pulled down around his neck and it too looked like it had withstood the worst of battles.

Jude's tail came back swiftly, knocking Eli to the ground, before coiling around Pang. Jude snatched up Sia with his cringing claws and took flight.

"Jude what are you doing!"

The memory seemed to rush back like a tidal wave, and with it the truth about what happened to Pang Quarrels.

"I came down here thinking I was going to find some evidence of which of those Agents did this to you but I was wrong. *I* did this to you. *Me*, your own Squad Leader."

Sia was quick to step to his side. "Jude you couldn't help it. You weren't—you."

Jude kicked himself for not anticipating the ambush. Recovering Kai's body was too easy.

Those Agents weren't just any Agents. They had to be Special Agents or even Operatives. The foundation of their attacks was nothing short of perfection.

"A.R.S.—Anti-Resistance Squad. That's who attacked you at Tarragon Mountain," said Conall emerging from the kitchen. He took the last remaining seat, leaving Jude and Vance to stand. "Judging by Wyatt's report and your injuries, they're good."

It was light, but Jude could since a hint of insult being thrown his squad's direction. "With all do respect Lieutenant, our squad had just infiltrated the dragon's nest you call Tarragon Mountain—undetected I might add—eliminated three high-level spell casters, recovered Kai's body, eliminated a full-grown dragon on our way out *and* survived the onslaught of a high-level squad. All of this while still being able to return with Kai's less than helpful body." Jude turned his attention to the Lieutenant and met him on this battlefield of egos and disrespect. "Don't test me."

"We're being hunted," said Sia resting a hand on Jude's shoulder. "Who are they? What do they want?"

Conall extinguished his glare and rested his eyes on Sia. "We believe they are Lord Egon's personal security service. Every land and village the Lord has invaded, the A.R.S. has been right at his side. If I had to guess I would say that he deploys them to take out high-level enemies to ensure his invasion is swift and easy."

"They knew our squad name—not alias—but squad name," said Eli rising from his seat and joining Jude and Sia by Pang's body. "How is that possible?"

Conall's confidence seemed to shatter at Eli's question. For once, Jude's comrade was on to something. Jude could see in Conall's eyes that his brain was manifesting an artificial story. He was thinking of a way to lie.

"If you lie right now *we* will be your next enemy."

Conall sprang to his feet. "How dare you Bray! I am your Lieutenant. Respect me! I order you to respect me!"

"Conall..." said Sia approaching the Lieutenant. "You can tell us. We are *all* on the same side." Conall locked eyes with Sia and his rage instantly dissolved. He collapsed into his chair and threw his face into the palms of his hands.

"They know because I told them," said Conall.

"I'll kill you!" yelled Eli coming down on Conall and lifting him out of his seat by the Lieutenant's collar.

"Get your hands off of me Brassie! I had to do it!" yelled Conall.

"Why?"

Conall plopped back down in his seat and began shaking his leg. For the first time he looked extremely nervous and unsettled. "I met the Lord." The uproar started. "If you want to know the truth, shut up and listen!" When Jude and his comrades settled, the Lieutenant continued. "I trailed after the Lord after a recent invasion. I offered a peaceful conversation and he accepted. It was my feeble attempt at trying to reason with him. He of course laughed in my face and paraded around the fact that he could have me killed at any second and my followers would meet the same fate. So I threatened him. I told him that the Kismet Task Force has risen, and if he didn't cease his invasion and withdraw his forces from Kismet, the K.T.F. would be on his doorstep."

The tension came and settled on the walls, ceiling and everywhere else it could cling to. Jude couldn't believe what he was hearing. It was so shocking, that he didn't even have a response for the Lieutenant's confession. Instead, Jude knelt to his knees in front of Pang, hoping to notice some signs of his condition improving.

"Now I may not be the smartest person in the room," said Eli returning to his seat. "But even *I* wouldn't have done something *that* stupid."

"No you would have just strutted into The Immortal Lands by yourself, challenged the Lord to a battle and lost miserably within the first few seconds," said Conall.

"Say what you want—*Lieutenant*—you know that what you did put all of our lives in danger and has now put a powerful enemy in the way of our goal. Your decision was foolish," said Eli.

Conall laughed. "Says the pig calling the garbage stank."

Jude ignored the childish bickering behind him. All he could think of was the fact that he was the one that hurt Pang.

If it wasn't for those damn A.R.S. Agents this would have never happened.

"No matter what anyone's opinion is," interrupted Conall. "To get to Lord Egon, you will have to go through the Anti-Resistance Squad."

Pang's eyes fluttered and soon opened slowly. He stirred before sitting up.

Jude rose to his feet and faced Conall and the others. "It won't matter, because next time we'll be ready."

THE FOURTH
BLOODLINE PT. 2

Eli walked the Geminate Forest observing the techniques of Mik and the other Erudites. Brayden's skill with a bow had improved tremendously, and after some pointers from Eli, became a deadly long range foe. Mik was slightly behind the others to Eli's distaste, despite his training in Geminate. Eli felt partially responsible since he had made countless promises to Mik in the past to train him. Eli found himself spending more time helping Mik than any of the others. Luckily, no one seemed to notice.

Thanks to the substance Eli received from Jamieson earlier, his sickness was in the past. The concoction nearly worked instantly to Eli's surprise. He was feeling so much better that he rounded up all of the Erudites, as well as Mik, and decided to pick up where his dad had left off with their training. Eli knew nothing about being a professor or tutor, but he hoped he could help just the same. He made the official decision that he really liked Jamieson. The Operative was funny, sympathetic and non-judgmental. Even after hearing the negative things Eli had to say about his comrades, Jamieson didn't automatically decide to bad-mouth them or reprimand Eli for his feelings. He was a humble person that came across very trustworthy. Eli decided that he would find some way to thank Jamieson and hoped they would eventually become great friends. Being friends with Jamieson is something Eli highly desired the longer he thought about it.

If Jamieson turns out to be as trustworthy as I think he is, maybe I can tell him about the squad if he agrees to keep it a secret.

Eli walked over to a brunette boy by the name of Sy and a blonde one by the name of Logan, who were sparring lightly. Sy wielded dual swords, while Logan wielded a shield and sword. The brunette was forgetting to block since he didn't have a shield. Eli wondered if the boy knew that you could still block with a weapon despite not having a shield. The blonde was barely utilizing his shield since he only used it defensively to block. He never tried any bashing or rushing techniques. Eli took each boy aside and amended their techniques, and after joining each other in battle, engaged in such a heated and highly-skilled match, that they drew the attention of the surrounding Erudites who stopped and cheered them on.

Someone cleared their throat. To his right Eli saw Brayden standing strong and tall. "Yes Brayden?"

The red-head nodded away from the others, causing Eli to follow Brayden when he departed. He lost sight of Brayden shortly but soon found him sitting on top of a large boulder that overlooked the training camp. Eli joined him.

"What has become of us," started Brayden staring down at his comrades. "We are, normal."

Eli stared down at the Erudites and watched Sy charge Logan with his blade. The blonde countered, causing them both to come tangled in a stalemate of blades. "No, you're better than normal. You're Agents." Three Erudites fired volleys while Logan and Sy deflected the arrows with their blades.

"All my life I heard the word 'Erudite' from my parents and others but never really understood what it meant until I was ten. My father brainwashed me into believing that being an Erudite was shameful and it was a curse for my past sins," said Brayden spitting. "I despised my mother the most."

Eli finally turned to Brayden in curiosity. "Why your mother if your father was the cause of your pain?"

"Because my father used to beat me every night after dinner. He was in denial of my Erudite bloodline and thought that if he beat me hard enough, my abilities would awaken from being dormant. Mothers are supposed to love their children, and in my opinion, even more than fathers since they carried us in their bodies. All my mother did was watch—one beating after the other. You see the only thing worse than being the cause of such a brutal act, is being present to witness it and do nothing. She was just as guilty."

First Sia and now Brayden. All my life I thought our people were so peaceful and loving. Blind as a boy and ambushed as a man to the truth that has always been in front of me.

"We owe it all to you," continued Brayden.

Eli looked up unbeknownst to what Brayden was commending him for.

Brayden stood from his seat, staring down at Eli not as the young red-haired boy Eli had first met, but as a young man with strength and presence. "You have given us all purpose and have shown us a kindness that is rare for us. Thank you for not turning your back on us the way so many of our people have our entire lives. I promise we won't let you down."

Eli rose and stared at Brayden, wanting to give him the same hug he had given Brayden since they had met. Eli's chin rose high, looking down his nose at Brayden, before extending his hand. Brayden's grip was firm and strong, laced with the rough coarse skin of an Agent.

◆ ◆ ◆

After training, Eli relocated the group back to his house after nabbing some groceries from the Geminate markets. He made everyone a quick meal before the group departed. Eli hoped it was as productive of a day to them as it was to him. Entering the kitchen, Eli quickly located the black bag he had hidden from the Erudites in the top cupboard. He took it to the sitting area and sat in front of the fireplace. He placed the bag on the table next to his family journal and ignored the *clank* the bag made. He lit the fireplace, removed his combat boots and took a seat in the armchair closest to the fireplace. He grabbed the bag from the table and untied the knot. A calm and sense of piece washed over him at the mere sight of the bottle. It was as if the bottle was telling him that everything was going to be okay. Stress, pain and anguish would be a thing of the past. He held the bottle up to his line-of-sight:

HEMORRHAGING COMA

WARNING:

Large servings and excessive use is not recommended. Please consume with caution. Recommended serving: 1 oz.

"One ounce! They got me twisted." Eli unscrewed the top drank a fourth of the bottle and ignored his heart when it began to race and thump. As if all at once, the ghost of Marius disappeared from the seat across from him and the duo ghosts of him and Sia kissing on the stairs disappeared as well. Hugging the bottle against his chest, his heart seemed to calm itself and neutralize the thumping. "I'm okay now. I'm okay. I'm going to be okay." It wasn't long before Marius appeared. He was late, but Eli wouldn't point it out in fear of causing his dad's retreat.

"You know you've come this close to emptying your blood energy on the past two missions," said Marius holding up his almost-touching fingers. "How many times will you do this before it kills you?"

Eli winced in response to the bite from the spirits but enjoyed the rebellion in the liquid's presence. "I had everything under control."

Marius took a seat in the armchair across from him and sighed. "You know, killing yourself won't bring me back and it won't make her want to be with you."

His father's words stung like a new burn. Deciding to take advantage of their time together, he ignored Marius' words. "Are you going to grade me on my mission or not?"

The empty armchair no longer creaked beneath its inhabitant's presence. Apparently his words stung Marius with a poison more painful than Marius' burn. Eli stared into the swaying flames of the fireplace and then reached for the journal. He opened up to a blank page, took a gulp of the bottle and began:

I Feel the Curses...

Curses are memories that walk these halls.

Bound to my grief, I hurt.

I hurt because I'm not in control.

In control of what is and hurting from what's no more.

Then, when the skies are dark and the moon is full, I hurt myself

to see if I still feel—feel no more.

SOME HISTORY

Jamieson's eyes washed over the familiar knick-knacks, photos and other familiar mementos that he had come to know over the years. Calling it a house would be an insult considering its large size and vast halls. It was more of a palace to Jamieson than a house. However, his people were notorious for constructing homes that were far larger on the inside than the outside. The three floors felt like a city in and of itself. Looking down at the black hardwood floors of the living room beneath his feet and then to the smoke-gray walls littered with maps and art, Jamieson welcomed the familiar feeling that always consumed him whenever he visited Talon's home. Jamieson thought of his parents, and wondered if they were still alive, how it would feel to have a family home to go back to.

"I know! I know," yelled Talon running down the stairs in his black combat pants, drying his bare chest with a towel. "Shut your mouth alright. Just shut it!"

Jamieson laughed. "But I didn't even say anything."

Talon dried his hair and then tossed his towel in a random direction. "Yeah yeah but don't forget I know you J, and you're probably thinking I'm never on time and how can a Captain not be punctual. Regardless, before you desecrate my perfect image, help me find a shirt."

Jamieson shook his head and hid his grin before looking around the large living room. Assorted weapons, quilts, candles and books lay on various end tables around the room. The black couches surrounded a long, rectangular silver table underneath a grand chandelier—adorned with translucent and black jewels. The chandelier was a gift from the Priestess from a few years back after Talon single-handedly infiltrated an enemy fortress to recover one of their top Operatives. The chandelier could have been classified as pure perfection if it wasn't for the dark gray cotton shirt hanging from one of the jewels. Jamieson pointed to the chandelier.

"Crap!" yelled Talon. He released his shirtless ipseity, who instantly walked over to the couch and climbed on top of it. The ipseity unhooked the chandelier, while Talon joined him underneath it. After lowering the chandelier to Talon's line-of-sight, the ipseity waited for Talon to retrieve his shirt, before returning the chandelier to the hook it once hung from. "Alright you ready?"

"Are *you* ready?" Jamieson couldn't help but throw a dig Talon's way.

"Don't do it J. Don't do it. I don't want to have to kill you tonight," said Talon with crossed arms. His arms were getting larger and close to catching up with Jamieson's.

I have to increase the training ten-fold. Can't lose my reputation.

Jamieson rose from his seat and walked passed Talon without responding or looking at him. Venturing into Talon's war room, everything looked exactly how it was last month when Jamieson was here. Gray cobblestones made up the walls and floor while a large square table stood dead center in the middle of the room. The table was completely covered with a massive map that showed Geminate, the fallen Kismet and the other lands and various regions. Pre-lit candles on standing pedestals stood in all four corners of the room.

"So I really could use your advice on the General's next mission," said Talon shouldering passed Jamieson through the war room doorway and taking a position at the map in the center of the room. Jamieson joined him. "Most of the General's men will be attacking from the east side since it's the only penetrable part of the city due to the surrounding mountain. Since I won't be going, I need to make sure the General and his men are fully prepped for the entire Operation."

Jamieson looked down at Stronghold City. It was located on the coast but surrounded by an impenetrable mountain on both the coast side and two other sides. Only one side was penetrable, and that was the main entrance. The architecture was smart. Whoever built the city and picked its location centuries ago, was a genius.

"Well," said Talon. He stared down at Jamieson with annoyed eyes.

"It's suicide." Jamieson retreated from the map, and in turn ventured over to one of the cobblestone walls. A sketch Jamieson drew of some new combat armor he had been working on a few years ago still hung on its rocky surface. Jamieson's quick eye had already located a weak spot in the armor about a year ago, so a newer more effective version had already been produced.

"Nothing is suicide for me I'm the best," said Talon laughing. "So I need to come up with the best strategy for the General."

Jamieson turned around and stared at Talon. The Captain's arrogant grin was something Jamieson thought was an endearing quality, however, he knew to everyone else it was probably the most annoying frustrating look in existence. Probably annoying enough to make someone want to kill the Captain. "Well if you're the best then why are you asking for my help?"

"Because many consider you the best assassin in all of Geminate. Stealth, silent kills and survival are your thing," said Talon grinning.

"Is that sarcasm I hear?"

Talon chuckled. "Don't take it personally. We know you're the best, at least assassin wise, but I'm the best all around."

Jamieson sighed. "Alright what is it?"

Talon slouched against the table and tightened his crossed arms. "What do you mean?"

"Don't play dumb with me. You never *ever* parade that arrogant, narcissistic, annoying over-confidence to me, only to everyone else. You only go into 'I'm the best' mode with me when there is something on your mind that is bothering you. So spill it."

Talon's eyes widened. He covered his mouth with his hand and started laughing. It was a defense mechanism that Jamieson had come to spot over the years. It meant Talon was either feeling nervous, caught-off-guard or both.

Jamieson responded with raised open palms. "So..."

"You've gotten kind of crazy over the years J," said Talon turning his back to Jamieson and focusing on the map in front of him. "I think you've been spending too much time smithing in that intense heat in your weaponry. Don't worry though, not everyone can take the heat. I on the other hand, can handle anything. Perks of being the best."

Jamieson turned for the doorway leading out of the Weapons Room. Right as he exited, he turned around and couldn't resist throwing one last dig before leaving. "Is one of the other perks of being 'the best' being responsible for the deaths of fifty Agents during an imperative mission due to your over-confidence. The best huh? What a joke." Jamieson exited the Weapons Room and entered the living room. He grabbed his daggers from the living room table and returned them to the hidden holsters in the sleeves of his tunic. He grabbed his blade, which stood in the corner against the wall, and sheathed it in the holster on his back. Making his way to the door, he was quickly stopped by a hand that grabbed his arm. He turned and faced Talon staring back at him with squinted eyes and a snarled top lip.

"You may be a Special Operative," started Talon letting go of Jamieson's arm. "You may be an alright assassin. But I am your Captain and you will not *ever* speak to me like that. Do I make myself clear soldier?"

The perks of being best friends with someone with a higher rank...

Talon recognized the magnitude of the situation. He had never pulled rank on Jamieson before. Jamieson had struck a nerve. He knew he was hitting below the belt with his comment. However, throwing digs at an overly-confident person when he was being provoked was a golden opportunity he couldn't pass up.

"You got it Captain. Forgive me."

Talon stared back harshly. His jaw remained clenched and his fists remained balled-up. Jamieson wondered if the night would turn into one of the many nights of them mauling one another in hours of body slams, fist fighting and black eyes. That didn't bother Jamieson. It had been a few weeks since their last brawl when they were arguing over whose biceps were bigger. Jamieson walked away with swollen knuckles and a slight black eye while Talon walked away with a bleeding ear, bruised rib and a busted lip. Needless to say, Jamieson was sure Talon knew which one of them won that argument. They were guys and enjoyed a good brawl every once in a while. The only problem was they were both very competitive and Talon always took the squabble too far. The second it felt like an injury was about to happen Jamieson would back off; however Talon was a different story.

"Have you changed your mind yet?" asked Talon softly. His hands were calm and his eyes and voice were soft.

Jamieson could play coy, however, him and Talon both knew what Talon was asking. They had the same conversation nearly every few weeks for three years now. It was a sore subject and one Jamieson tried to stay far away from in fear of the consequences. "No."

"Alright," said Talon in a disappointed tone. His dark brown eyes were like a black hole pulling you in the longer you looked at them.

Jamieson turned his back and headed for the door. "There's an underground sewer pipe on the side of the coast big enough to fit two men at a time. That is your best bet if you want to infiltrate the city undetected and have the upper-hand."

"You *are* the best," said Talon following Jamieson to the door. His words brought back the not-so-distant argument they recently had, making Jamieson shake his head.

Jamieson opened the door and looked back towards an expressionless Talon. "So I'll see you tomorrow at the war meeting."

"Should be a riot," said Talon opening his arms up as if for an embrace. When Jamieson remained still, Talon opened his arms wider. "Come on bring it in!"

Jamieson knew the hug was most likely a trap. It was true that they hugged when greeting each other and departing since they had known one another for going on eight years now. However, whenever an argument had just occurred, seventy percent of the time Talon's hugs resulted in Jamieson being body slammed before another brawl began.

Jamieson came in for a hug. Pulling away, he was surprised he was coming away unscathed. Then it happened. Talon's hands grabbed his waist. "What are you doing?" Talon's grip tightened until the warmth of his hands passed through Jamieson's combat tunic. Jamieson used both hands to shove Talon away. "Get your hands off me man!"

Talon recoiled and then came back quickly. "Why? It was just a hug."

"That's a lie and you know it! That was more than a hug. You crossed the line!"

Talon's face tightened. "I could tell everyone you know. I could tell everyone that you and I are together. As a Captain, I'm sure they would believe me—even those temple dwellers you praise the gods with."

Jamieson's dagger pricked Talon's neck, as he held it to the Captain's throat. One of the perks of being one of the top assassins was the skill to instantly put your enemy in harms way. "You do and I will gut you and then drag you up and down the city steps. All eight hundred and fifty of them." Talon said nothing and appeared afraid to breathe let alone move. Jamieson took the silence as confirmation that his point had been heard loud and clear. In one quick movement, he sheathed his dagger, exited the house and slammed the door closed behind him—all without Talon moving a muscle.

Jamieson closed his eyes and prayed to Pith for forgiveness; and hoped that Talon's inappropriate behavior would not result in Jamieson's demise.

GOOD & BAD

The Erudites' training was coming along a lot better than Eli had hoped. He knew his advice and guidance was valuable to the young soldiers, but the credit for their inspiring progress had to go to their motivation and unity. He never planned for any of them to ever have to utilize what they learned in real combat, however, he was still happy to provide an activity that kept their spirits high in a land of people who despised them based on their bloodline.

Brayden's skill and accuracy with both a bow and blade had increased ten-fold, along with his endurance, leaving nothing more for Eli to teach him. Eli now looked to Brayden to help him teach the others. Sy and Logan, along with the other Erudites, still needed a little work with their close-combat skills, but that would be remedied today when Eli stepped into combat with each of them individually. The training for their long-rang combat would begin next week, and Eli was happy he had Brayden to help him assist the group since there were quite a few of them.

Sipping his canteen, Eli made sure to guzzle it so he gave the impression that he was drinking water. One thing he didn't want was for the Erudites to start drinking spirits as well. Mik was nowhere to be found. After the first hour of training, Eli pulled Brayden aside and asked him if knew where Mik might have gone. The two boys had become close friends and nearly went everywhere together. Both of their Geminate mentors taught on different sides of the same training field, so Mik and Brayden were nearly always together.

Downing the last drop of his spirits, Eli found a large rock behind a tree and dug a hole. He buried the bottle inside, covered it with dirt, and then threw some grass on top. Returning to the sparring Erudites, he halted at the surrounding stares from the students around him.

"Is something wrong?"

The wall of students parted at Brayden's entrance between them. The young red-head stared at Eli with stern eyes and a stiff lip. "We've all been training for a while now; learning how to defend ourselves and overcome our enemies. While all of that is great, we still need to know."

The forest swayed around the younglings, making Eli clench his jaw in hopes of remaining on his feet. "Know what?"

Brayden looked back at the others. After receiving a nod from Sy, he returned with squinting eyes. "What it's like to be in combat."

The question, born of innocence and curiosity, is a question Eli never had a chance to inquire about prior to joining the academy. It was a question that would bring the Erudite's training to an abrupt end, or it would be the question that would fuel their drive to perfection. "Well I could tell you that it's amazing. I could tell you that it's the best feeling in the world and that no other feeling in this life can compare. I could tell you that wielding the power to destroy any who cross my path is exhilarating and that I never want it to end. While all those things are true, I would also have to tell you that combat is horrible. Combat is a nightmare; a nightmare you continue to relive and continue to find relief for when you awake from it." Confused young eyes surrounded him.

Not the answer you were expecting I guess.

"But how can something be both good and bad?" asked Brayden shaking his head. To Eli, it was a fair question, a question he himself would have asked long ago.

"Imagine going into combat with hundreds of skilled opponents who all have one objective and one objective only—to take your life. Then mix that with fighting side-by-side with a handful of allies who you have grown close to over the years, even when you have more bad times than good with them. Then imagine the fear of those same comrades entering the beast of combat with you and never leaving. Look around at the friends at your side." The Erudites looked to their lefts and rights, staring into the eyes of their peers. "Imagine doing anything to protect them, including taking an innocent life or mutilating a guilty one. Knowing that what you are doing is murder no matter what the cause. Then imagine the eyes you now look into cold, still and vacant of any life. Then imagine the pain that comes with the realization that you will never see them again. But then imagine those very comrades alive, healthy and smiling. Imagine them standing at your side while your enemies now lay still at your feet. Imagine the joy and relief. When it comes to life there's no such thing as good and bad. There's only choice."

"Hi Eli," said a voice behind him. Eli jerked around and set eyes on a haggard and vulnerable-looking boy. "I'm sorry I'm late I got—held up," said Mik dropping his head with his hands in front of him.

Eli walked closer to Mik to get a better look at him. His left cheek was swollen and he had a shiner on his left eye that could only be created by someone with massive force. Eli's stomach was already burning but began to boil at the sight. He clenched his jaw and began to grind his teeth, a habit he never had before. "Mik what happened? Who did this to you?" When Mik didn't answer, Eli grabbed the boy's chin and gently lifted it up so they locked eyes. "It's me. Please tell me."

A tear fell from Mik's swollen eye, shattering the tough persona he had adapted over the last few months. "A boy in my training workshop. He likes to mess with me sometimes but it's okay—I can handle it." His face dropped from Eli's stare and his shoulders began to tremble. "Don't worry I know men are not supposed to cry. I will be fine. I'm a man..."

Eli felt his eyes water while looking at Mik. The young man's spirit and self-esteem were crushed into pieces too tiny to find.

Who would do this to someone like Mik? He is such a happy kid. He's nice to everyone and very polite. He's such a loving person. I don't understand why someone would pick on him like this. His eye is darker than Jude's combat armor in the Trials of Magic, Might and Lineage.

Eli wrapped his arms around Mik and pulled him into a tight embrace. Immediately Mik started crying hysterically.

"He just wouldn't stop Eli," cried Mik hugging Eli tighter. "He kicked my feet from underneath me and kept kicking me in the head over-and-over calling me a filthy Erudite. I couldn't defend myself because I was dizzy and my eyes were blurry. I tried to remember your training Eli I really did. I'm sorry."

Eli stared at Brayden and the others, whose faces softened at the conversation. They all dropped their weapons and began to close-in on Eli and Mik, but made sure to keep their distance. Eli held Mik at arm's length and waited for the boy to look at him. "Don't let anyone ever tell you that men don't cry. That's a lie. If men didn't cry they wouldn't be human. Tears come from sorrow and pain, which are feelings. Feelings and being human are interlaced and unable to be separated." He pulled Mik in for an even tighter hug, wanting this moment to end so the revenge could begin. "I love you Mik. I love you and I'm so sorry this happened to you. That boy will *never ever* lay a finger on you again do you hear me?"

Mik stared back unflinching. His trembling began to subside, but the tears continued to flow.

"Now you know how you can get him back?"

Mik shook his head.

"You can become *the most* powerful Agent this world has ever seen."

Mik wiped his eyes and formed a small smile. "Okay. I mean yes you're right."

"Are you okay Mik?" asked Sy. He and Logan both wrapped an arm around Mik, and escorted him to the others.

"Yeah I'm okay," said Mik wiping his eyes. "I just had a bad day."

Brayden quickly found a spot at Eli's side. "It was that bully in his training lectures wasn't it?"

Eli slowly looked down at Brayden, interested by the boy's familiarity with the situation. "You know him?"

"I know who he is if that's what you're asking," said Brayden combing his red hair with his fingertips. "I always see him picking on Mik and another boy, but it was always just words. If I would have known it had gotten physical I would have been there for him." Brayden's face looked grim and ashamed. "Mik is just like the rest of us—different; and when you mess with one of us, you mess with all of us."

Eli felt his head swimming and the bliss descending across his nerves. "What's this bully's name and where can I find him?"

THE MESSENGER

Eli waited behind a lone tree next to one of the large steaming basin that sat on the outskirts of the training head quarters. The training grounds were located just on the other side of the Priestess' temple, down a sharp stone hill. Outside of the main HQ was a grassy sparring field, as well as a few large basins that lay spread out at various points along the grounds. According to Brayden, Mik's bully was a sixteen year-old young man by the name of Seit who was notorious for spending every evening soaking in the large steaming basins after a day of training. Eli decided he would wait until the young man showed up so he could have a talk with him.

Eli sat at the base of the trunk with his legs parted and began to sip on his last bottle of spirits. He looked up at the nearly-setting sun that came and went around the Geminate city.

Well, going on three hours now. He better show up.

As if like clockwork, a splash sounded close-by. Eli tucked his head around the tree to find a tall pale boy with dark hair removing his shirt and stepping into one of the basins. His arms were significantly larger than Mik's but perfect tools for asserting one's dominance over smaller foes. Seit released a loud sigh of comfort before dunking his head and then resurfacing.

Like a fly in my web.

Eli finished his drink, looked around for witnesses and then sprang to his feet. He casually walked over to the basin undetected. When he was standing over Seit, the young boy finally whipped his head around in alarm.

"Who are you?" shouted Seit with hostility heavy in his voice.

Eli gripped Seit's throat with one hand tight enough to prevent any screams or cries for help. Then as forcefully as he could, Eli dunked the boy's head beneath the water's hot surface. The basin sprang into a panic of violent waters, flailing limbs and choking whispers. After a little under a minute, Eli pulled Seit back up, but kept his grip tight around his neck. Seit's head wobbled back and forth with a daze.

"There's a handsome, intelligent and wonderful young man by the name of Mik Wyatt that trains with you here at the HQ. Word on the street is that you and your unstable adolescent hormones like to bully him and put your hands on him." Eli shoved Seit's head beneath the water's surface before he could reply. The violent struggle and splashing water returned while Eli looked around for any incoming witnesses. After the struggle began to weaken, Eli pulled Seit back out and then hurled him to the rough terrain beneath them. Immediately Seit began to choke and cough up water. His body heaved as if he was about to vomit before he looked up into Eli's eyes.

"I...I don't know what you're talking about," coughed Seit staring up with wide eyes.

Eli raced to Seit, snatched him up by the arm, kicked the back of his knees and trapped him in a headlock. "Listen here you little *shit*. You're going to stay far away from Mik Wyatt do you hear me? Whenever you see him coming you run. You got it? If you're paired up with him by your mentor during training, you tell your mentor you refuse to fight him because he is better than you. I don't care if he threatens to kick you out of training; because if I hear that you have come within even a yard of Mik Wyatt, I will *traumatize* you! You won't ever be able to walk, breathe or even think without remembering the pain and trauma I will subject you to." Eli face-planted Seit into the ground.

Seit turned over sobbing and coughing. Eli expected him to make a run for it, but all Seit did was stare back up at Eli with terror in his eyes.

"One other thing." Eli punched Seit in his left eye, causing his head to hit the ground with a *thud*. "Consider you and Mik even." Eli turned away and began towards Jude's house. His mind went back to Mik's black eye and the tears and pain in his face. His anger instantly resurfaced. He turned back around and came across Seit grabbing the wall of the basin in an attempt to return to his feet. Eli grabbed one of Seit's fingers and broke it, releasing a howl of agony across the terrain. "Now you're even."

THE PRIESTESS

Jude followed Garrett and his soldiers down the long, winding staircase beneath the Priestess' temple. Various artifacts lined the walls, along with portraits of the same woman every few feet. Her pose was always her standing in a lavender dress with delicate open palms and a bright white light behind her. The background's depicted different time periods, time periods centuries apart.

"I went over to Jamieson's shop earlier today. It was really busy," said Eli over the S-3.

"Many people around the city say that his craftsmanship is unparalleled."

"His work is impressive. He gave Mik a few weapons and refused to take any payment for them. He offered to train Mik in his trade as well. He's a really nice guy," said Sia.

"Yeah he is! I really like him. I can see myself hanging out with him a lot," said Eli.

"You will have to pry him from my blood-soaked fingers Brassie. Jamieson is a god among fitness! I never thought my arms could get any bigger, but thanks to him, they have doubled in size!" said Pang.

"He seems trustworthy too. Maybe I can talk to the Lieutenant and see what he knows about Jamieson. I think he can be a valuable inside contact to Geminate, if our missions take us elsewhere."

A tall double-door rose up in front of them at the turn of the next corner. Garrett came to a halt and fanned out his men on either side of the door.

"Alright Kismet scum get in there," said Garrett with a scowl. When Jude took a step forward, he was immediately stopped by Garrett's hand. "Just remember to be yourselves, that way I'll have the pleasure of coming in there and taking you down!"

Jude locked eyes with Garrett, refusing to flinch. They both continued their stare. Garrett's grin showed no signs of retreat, while Jude searched his dark green eyes for the source of his piggish behavior. All he saw was weakness.

Jude finally grinned. "If you knew what I was, you'd run and hide." His words were sharp. His words cut deep. His words were not his own. As soon as the words left his lips, Garrett's grin retreated and his eyes turned to large orbs of worry and fear. The solider took a step back and then glared at Jude before nodding his head towards the door.

The circular chamber was massive, lined with large, silver oval mirrors that hovered side-by-side all around the room. The room's architecture was similar to that of the Kismet Coliseum. White-stone floors and walls shined blindingly bright all around the squad. Reflections of Jude and his comrades came and went from mirror-to-mirror, as they ventured up the three long steps towards the center of the room, occupied by a figure in a bright lavender robe. The squad fanned out, so the four of them stood side-by-side.

"The Prodigy himself, blesses this hallowed ground with his presence," boomed the Priestess' voice as she turned to face the squad, unleashing a bright light that appeared to sit frozen behind her. A larger oval mirror, larger than the others, hovered high above her head.

"*Do what I do,*" said Jude over the S-3 before kneeling to one knee. He heard the rustling behind him and was glad the squad had reacted with haste.

"Much respect given from strangers of our customs," said the Priestess taking a few steps forward looking from one face to the next. The bright white light seemed to follow every step she took. "Or perhaps one born from following orders." Her gaze sat on Jude, which brought alarm.

"Priestess, it's our pleasure to meet you. From what we've been told, you wanted to see us?" With his words a hidden chamber opened in his chest, and a connection was made. The Priestess was a question mark, someone he had never met. However, he could not deny the connection they now shared; a mutual connection showing proof of its presence across her soft face. It was similar to the connection he felt upon meeting Jamieson—but not as strong.

"Yes, but not for what you have been told," she said turning her back and returning to the spot she once stood at. Now all the mirrors showed the reflections of the squad and not one showed a reflection of the Priestess—even the mirrors right next to her. "Has Bishop's assassin been identified yet?"

The question was a surprise attack, one Jude hadn't anticipated. A meeting with the Priestess didn't seem like one he would need to strategize for or even worry about. He now realized that was foolish, because ambushing the unexpected was a move born of perfection. It wouldn't happen again.

"*We can trust her*," said Eli over the S-3. Alarm from the rest of the squad immediately followed his words.

"*How can you be sure?*"

"*My dad told me that Bishop and the ruler of Geminate were closer than close*," replied Eli. His thoughts accompanied his words, showing the squad a montage of past memories of Bishop and Marius speaking fondly of the Priestess and their trust for her. The montage had a tendency to shake every now and then, making Jude wonder if it was difficult for Eli to relive the memories of his fallen father.

"Yes Priestess." The second Jude began to speak, his reflection appeared in the larger mirror above the Priestess. The other mirrors, now only represented the reflections of the rest of the squad. "You already know that Lord Egon of The Immortal Lands and his Necroborns were responsible. However, a man by the name of Fox was Egon's inside contact, and helped him infiltrate our city. Fox was our Tactical Emissary."

"The Emissary is familiar to me. He has ventured to our city numerous times," she said with a slight edge in her voice.

"What was the nature of his visits, if I may ask?"

"Our city has been requesting aid from Kismet for some time. Fox was the liaison between us. His treachery was abundant considering he claimed Bishop refused to send us aid due to your land's lack of men," she said with a sinister smile and incline of her head. "Bishop and I go *way* back you see. As Guardians of the gods, we have existed for lifetimes—at least he used to."

"Forgive us Priestess, but how can we be sure you are who you claim to be?"

From beneath her robe came a locket, coated in silver and carved into a heart. Shining bright with a glow across its smooth surface, sat the inscription:

$$A\,\Omega$$

A gasp released from Sia, drawing the attention from the Priestess, and switching the reflection in the large mirror above the Priestess from Jude to Sia.

"I know you've seen a similar artifact before, however, it is yet to be known whether or not you know exactly what it is," said the Priestess with a grin.

"You are correct."

"This locket that hangs from my neck is my Guardian Medallion. I'm sure after Bishop's death, his was discovered on his body, a silver loop cross with a sapphire in the middle," she said.

Jude focused on the S-3. *"She appears trustworthy. Speak at your own risk."*

"Apologies Priestess," interrupted Sia. "But the medallion we found was a round gold locket, not a cross. It was found with a note."

The bright light behind the Priestess turned from bright white to black smoke and shadows. "No, that's not possible."

"Priestess," started Eli stepping forward. "What do you mean? Why isn't that possible?"

"Because that would mean Cur is still alive," she said glaring at the mirrors around her. "What did the note say?"

"It was a warning. Whoever wrote it said Bishop was in danger and that he needed to leave Kismet at once."

"It was signed with the same symbol on your medallion and the medallion we found," added Sia.

The Priestess held her medallion up so its surface was visible. "This symbol is the mark of The Order—the Guardians whose job is to serve and protect the gods. If someone knew that Bishop would be assassinated, and knows the mark of The Guardians..." Her voice trailed off as she appeared to retreat to her thoughts. "If what you say is true about the medallion you found, then Cur is still alive. Find him!"

"But who is Cur?" asked Sia quickly. "And how do we find him?"

"Cur is of one of the sacred families responsible for guarding the sacred knowledge and connection of the gods. His family was responsible for safeguarding the resting places of the gods. The sacred family was said to have the power to infiltrate the barrier around the god's resting places, in order to hide the power of the gods from our enemies. Many years ago The Immortal Lands invaded Cur's village. My sources say that none escaped the Lord's will—except one." The Priestess' eyes darted to Eli. "Fox."

THE BLOODLINE REVELATIONS

Screeching doors opened up on the other side of the chamber, drawing everyone's attention. General Mather, accompanied by three men, strolled into the chamber with his head held high and his hands firmly at his sides.

"Ah Priestess! Forgive my interruption," said General Mather with a quick bow. He and his men took a spot next to Jude and the squad. It was then Jude realized that one of the men was Jamieson's friend, Special Operative Talon Tatum. The General took out a napkin and handed it to one of his men. "Hand this back to me and tell me you are handing it to me."

The soldier took the napkin from the General, held on to it for a few seconds, and then handed it back over the General's soldier. "I'm handing you your napkin back."

The Priestess squirmed in place.

"How's it going Talon?" said Eli eagerly.

The General turned around slowly, as if he just noticed the squad's presence. "Spitfire is that you?" The General's men turned to face the squad as soon as he acknowledged their presence. Mather turned his attention back towards Talon, who quickly turned his attention to the General. "Captain do you know this monkey? He must know you well since he addresses you so informally. Too bad scum aren't capable of comprehending the concepts of rank and respect."

"That's enough General," interrupted the Priestess. She took a few steps forward before stopping. "These are my guests. Please refrain from insulting them."

"Oh but of course Priestess," said Mather with heightened energy. He looked to the squad with a large grin that was far less than genuine. Turning his attention back to the Priestess, Talon discreetly shook his head as if warning them. "I just wanted to let you know that we are moving forward with Operation Stronghold City."

"Thank you General. I know the operation will be a success," replied the Priestess.

General Mather returned his attention to the squad. "Again I apologize if any of you were offended. You know what? I have the perfect idea!" A smile from the General, accompanied by the grin he sent to the Priestess, told Jude that the General was up to something. "Priestess would it be okay if I borrow these four. The war meeting for the Operation will be starting at my return, and I would love to get the opinions of the..." The General looked to Talon and then to Eli. "What do you call yourselves again?"

"B.B.Q.W.," said Eli with added bass to his voice. "We are the resources team for Kismet."

"B.B.Q.W. is it? A pretty serious name for just a resources team if I do say so myself," said the General with a chuckle that his men soon joined in on. "Sounds more like the name for a squad."

The S-3 was filled with shock and worry. Jude instantly gave the command for the squad to calm themselves and not give any signs of nervousness.

"I guess," said Pang nonchalantly. "If we were five-year-olds." He began to laugh which made the rest of the squad join him. His tactic was great. His comment not only deflected the General's suspicion, but also calmed the nerves of the squad.

The General glared. "Really? How so?"

"It's only our last names," replied Pang crossing his arms. "Only kids make a secret squad name with their identity in it." More laughing followed him. Soon, the General's men joined the squad in laughter, including Talon.

Mather turned to his men with the iciest of stares. The room was silent. "Well I would love it if the resources team could join our war meeting so I could pick their brains."

"I apologize Priestess, but we have a lot to do today. Perhaps another time?"

"*Thank you!*" said Eli over the S-3. "*I'm not being forced to deal with this guy longer than I have to.*"

"*It's a trap,*" replied Sia. "*There is a magic user in his group. Whoever it is, they have been targeting us since they entered the room. If I had to guess, they can read minds. At least they would if I weren't around.*"

"Keep it up Sia. We should be out of here soon."

"This is a difficult mission Priestess," said the General in a sad tone. "I believe we need to utilize *every* resource at our disposal if we are to be victorious."

"This is true," said the Priestess turning to Jude. "Consider it a favor that I would be forever in your debt for."

"*Don't fall for it Jude,*" said Pang over the S-3. "*Don't fall for those pretty eyes. She is baiting you. This General clearly has something up his sleeve. He probably wants to try and reveal our identity.*"

"*Your absolutely right. But since the Priestess just asked us as a favor, it would not only be disrespectful to decline, but suicide considering our people inhabit their city.*"

"The answer is no," snapped Eli. He turned his attention to the General and glared. "Monkey!"

"There you have it!" yelled the General. "That's all the evidence we need. They're spies! Kill them!" The General's men attacked.

Sia twirled in front of the squad, shattering the large mirrors that surrounded the room, and projecting the razor-sharp shards at the enemy. A soldier threw himself in front of the General, absorbing every glass shard, before falling lifeless at the General's feet. Battle cries from Talon and Pang filled the room as the two behemoths charged one another after Pang's Blood Magic took a hold of the General in a struggling Blood Execution. Then the General was on his feet. Talon and Pang ran backwards until both men were at their respective sides. The fallen soldier returned to his feet while the bloody shards that had impaled him left his body and restored the mirrors that once hung around them.

"This is a difficult mission Priestess," said the General in a sad tone. "I believe we need to utilize *every* resource at our disposal if we are to be victorious."

This conversation just happened. Yet, it is happening again.

Jude looked to the Priestess and discovered her already peering stare just before her voice boomed in his head.

Find Cur young prodigy. He holds the answers you seek and the answers to stop the Lord of the Immortal Lands.

An image of a faceless man pierced Jude's mind giving him both direction and clarity. He met her gaze and nodded.

◆◆◆

"This is true," said the Priestess turning to Jude. "Consider it a favor that I would be forever in your debt."

"Don't fall for it Jude," said Pang over the S-3. *"Don't fall for those pretty eyes. She is baiting you. This General clearly has something up his sleeve. He probably wants to try and reveal our identity."*

"Your absolutely right. But since the Priestess just asked us as a favor, it would not only be disrespectful to decline, but suicide considering our people inhabit their city," said Jude.

It couldn't be heavier in the air and Eli could feel it. The squad was being forced into a corner with no correct way out. The thought was infuriating. Eli hated being forced to do something he didn't want to do; and being forced to fight under Jude's command was already aggravating enough. Eli would not be forced into another ridiculous situation. He felt his lips part, and then they halted when his eyes fell to the Priestess and the mirrors that now sat absent of reflections.

"One's actions are immortal and live on through the ages even after death," said the Priestess' voice in his head. Her lips

never moved, but her words were as clear as the mirrors around them. *"While people believe that the actions they get away with have no consequences, I must assure you they do. On the contrary, the actions that don't have immediate consequences are the ones that house the most severe. Everyone must be rewarded for their good deeds and punished for their bad ones. One can only hope that in the end when death is ready to claim them, that their good deeds outnumber their bad; or victory shall fall to evil and Anim shall claim their soul."*

The Priestess relocated her attention. The mirrors returned to broadcasting the reflections of the squad as well as the General and his men.

"For you Priestess, we would be glad to," said Jude.

"Excellent! Loyalty my dear friends. It's all about loyalty," said the General.

"And the power of choice," echoed the Priestess.

"THEY WILL COME FOR ME..."

Jamieson was beyond enraged by the presence of the B.B.Q.W at the war meeting. He knew it was a scare tactic by the General to show the B.B.Q.W. that he was in charge and everyone had to do what he commanded. The meeting comprised of the Kismet team and the General's personal guard on one side of the table, and the General, Talon and Jamieson on the other side of the table. Sitting next to Talon was awkward to say the least. Their last interaction was far from pleasant, but Jamieson knew they would get over it. They were best friends and they had been through worse. What was odd was the absence of Ket, the Lieutenant of the Geminate Guard. Jamieson hadn't seen him since the General came back from their mission and wondered if he was ordered to stay behind for some reason. The first half of the meeting was spent talking about an infiltration strategy and bombarding the B.B.Q.W. with various combat questions. The questions would have been out of place if it weren't for the memories Jamieson had of his rescue by the team. They were a resources team after all. Combat was clearly just an added secondary skill to help them get supplies to their people. If the General had any questions about combat, he should be directing them to him or Talon.

"Mr. Bray," started the General as he flipped through his papers. "Which part of the city do you think would be most accessible for a successful infiltration?"

"Infiltrations aren't exactly our strong points," started Jude with a small smile and risen shoulders. He appeared slightly embarrassed with each word he spoke. "As the resources team, our job is to just run in and deliver resources and supplies, or retrieve them, and leave. So we primarily use the main entrance ninety percent of the time."

The General appeared to not be amused at all. His lip curled into disgust while his fingers drummed the table beneath his hand. "If your 'team' is not even knowledgeable about infiltration strategies, then what's the use for you?"

Here we go. Let the your weak and I'm strong speech begin.

"Excuse me General," interrupted Talon. When the General gave permission to speak, he continued. "I have already discussed the infiltration with Special Operative Edric. I believe your Operation will be a complete success."

Jamieson froze beneath the General's stare. Their dynamic had always been a difficult and confusing one. Jamieson decided years ago to just assume the General hated him and would never like him. It took a lot of stress out of deciphering the intent of his comments.

The General's hard stare soon turned into a smile. "Very well! You know what Captain, why don't you come along with me on this mission as my Lieutenant. I'm sure the men will feel more comfortable with you there."

What? Lieutenant?

"But Ket is the Lieutenant," said Talon. He looked as confused as Jamieson was.

"Oh I'm sorry didn't you hear? Ket has unfortunately fallen," said the General acquiring the look of sorrow on his face.

Jamieson jumped to his feet. "What? Fallen? When? How? And why are we just hearing about this?"

The General rose to the challenge, rising to his feet as if preparing for battle. "You are just hearing about this because I wanted you to just hear about it." He turned his attention to Talon and continued. "Ket was a brave Lieutenant, and if it wasn't for him, I wouldn't have made it back to the city alive. It's a tragedy, but one we must learn to move on from. So what do you say Captain? Do you accept the rank of my Lieutenant?"

"Excuse me General! I believe the Captain and I may have brought the map that shows all of the secret entrances of the city."

"Oh excellent," said the General rubbing his hands together. "May I see it?"

Jamieson rose from his seat. "You sure can! Talon you want to help me carry the board it goes on?"

Talon's eyes showed that he knew what was going on. He stared at Jamieson for longer than Jamieson would have hoped. The General was a smart man, and the longer Talon stared, the greater the chance the General would pick up on the lie. "Sure. I think we left it in the Armory Repair cabin."

Jamieson didn't understand why Talon didn't get it, or for the most part, why he refused to get it. The longer they argued, the more emotional he became. He soon wondered if this discussion would end in a violent brawl or violent tears.

"I'm done with this conversation Edric," said Talon crossing his arms. Jamieson knew that Talon was referring to him by his last name as a means to draw distance between them.

"Just please don't go on this mission. That's all I'm asking." His request didn't feel unreasonable.

Talon turned for the door unresponsive. "The General is waiting."

"You walk away from me and I will bash your teeth in!" Threatening physical harm was all Jamieson could think of. Talon was stubborn and refused to change his mind at times, even when he knew it was for the best. Jamieson had no intention of attacking Talon, but he knew that the Captain was competitive, and couldn't walk away from a challenge.

Talon turned around cracking his knuckles. "Go ahead—try! And see where it gets you." When Jamieson said nothing, Talon decided to make the first move and walk to Jamieson with his hands ready to strike.

"Just don't go."

"Why? Tell me why you don't want me to go," said Talon dropping his hands.

"Because no one ever comes back from missions with the General—ever!" The General's record of being the only one to return from his missions was no secret. Jamieson had many friends that went on missions with the General, highly-skilled and well-trained friends, who never returned and were reported as a casualty. Jamieson couldn't have that happen to Talon.

"You don't trust him," said Talon with wide eyes. "You don't trust your own General. Treachery!" Talon paced back-and-forth around the room with his arms behind his back as if deep in thought. He soon stopped in mid-stride, locking a stern gaze with Jamieson. "So you think if I go on this mission with the General, I won't come back. Is that it?"

Jamieson held his chin up high. "Yes."

Talon nodded his head. "But why do you even care?"

Jamieson staggered. "How can you ask that? You're my best friend and have been for years. Is it only natural that I wouldn't want to lose my best friend? You're basically the only family I have left."

Talon's unflinching stare was hard to look at. The Captain forced his arms down to his side, held his chin up high and marched straight to Jamieson—eyes looking down at him. "That's it? That's your only reason?"

Not this again. Please, this is serious.

"Yes, I don't think I could handle it if you didn't come back." Jamieson hoped Talon would understand. He hoped that Talon would be made to see that his life was important.

The Captain studied him with a faint shake of his head, almost too faint to notice. "Not good enough." Talon turned his back to Jamieson and headed for the door, his decision absolute.

Jamieson had enough. He wouldn't allow Talon to walk out of this room. His best friend's life was in jeopardy, and he wouldn't let him be just another casualty of the General. Chasing after him, Jamieson grabbed the back of the Captain's arm and hurled him at the adjacent wall.

After smacking his head into the stone-wall, the Captain charged Jamieson, wrapping his hands around Jamieson's neck and pinning him to the wall behind him. "You know by Guard Law I have the right to kill you. Putting your hands on a high-ranking official is punishable by death."

Jamieson knew there was nothing he could do. Talon was stubborn and would not change his mind just to spite Jamieson. Every funeral Jamieson had been to for his fallen friends, under the General's command, flashed before his eyes. The last funeral would be for Talon, and that would be the last straw. "Just don't go. Please."

"Give me the *real* reason. Don't give me any of that family or best friend crap! Tell me the *real* reason dammit," demanded Talon. The finality in his voice was unnerving. For a second, Jamieson thought Talon was capable of breaking his neck, and leaving his lifeless body along the cold stone beneath them.

"I...can't."

Talon tightened his grip on Jamieson's neck and shook him. "Don't give me that! Why! Why can't you tell me?"

The deep-rooted pain, which Jamieson had carried around his entire life, began to uproot itself. It was years of repression, shame and fear. The memories of seclusion and self-loathing and the lies all emerged with a vengeance, bringing tears down his face. Talon's grip slightly loosened at the sight of the tears. It was the first time Jamieson had shed a tear.

"Please don't make me say it. They will come for me..."

The room spun before Jamieson's head came crashing down onto the cobblestone floor. He blinked his eyes a few times to shake off the pain, before noticing that Talon now stood on top of him with his grip now even tighter around his neck.

"The gods aren't going to hurt you J! They know who you are. They created you for Pith's sake," shouted Talon. Jamieson said nothing, just returned the Captain's stare. How could Talon ask him to do such a thing? He knew how painful the discussion was, but he still kept pressing him. "Give me a good reason not to go J, or I leave."

"You're torturing me right now. The gods wait for me to answer wrong so they can punish me and condemn me; while you wait for me to answer wrong so you can punish me as well." The weight lifted from Jamieson's torso, along with the grip around his neck, allowing Jamieson to return to his feet.

The Captain clearly had enough. He dusted his armor off and adjusted his medals. The look he gave Jamieson after returning to his feet, made Jamieson feel ashamed and miniscule. "I know now that they will always come before me— and they should. It's the way we have been raised to worship anyways. I don't blame you."

The Captain's departing back was a drum of anxiety against Jamieson's ears. His eyes opened and closed abruptly, trying to shake-off the realization that he would not see Talon ever again. His soul felt torn and his heart felt shattered. There was no right answer in this situation, but Jamieson knew that he couldn't bear to lose his best friend and his family. "I love you."

The footsteps stopped. The sound of swinging medals filled the air when the Captain turned around. His look of shock showed he never thought the words would ever leave Jamieson's lips. "What did you say?"

One tear fell then the other. "I love you Talon."

The warmth of the overwhelming embrace from Talon felt comforting and wrong at the same time. With each passing second, his soul erupted into turmoil trying to decide which one he felt more, comfort or shame.

Talon released Jamieson and held him at arm's length. "So has the time come? Will you be with me?"

Jamieson didn't understand why the Captain was asking so much. He had already expressed his feelings for Talon, something he vowed never to do aloud. "Talon I just can't. You want something I can't give you. But Josline—Josline can give you what you want."

"I don't love her! I love *you* dammit!" The happiness in the Captain's face fell into rage and then vacancy. His head nodded in understanding and released his hold on Jamieson. For a few seconds, Jamieson missed the touch, but willed himself to despise it. Talon turned for the door and ignored the constant call of his name from Jamieson. When he got to the door, he opened it and looked back with a soft face.

Aegis hear my thanks! He's staying.

"I'll see you when I get back J," he said calmly.

"What? You're still going? Why? I gave you what you wanted! I told you how I felt. I gave you your reason to stay!"

"What you said means nothing, if all it will become is a memory once we leave this room," he said. He brought two fingers up to his brow and saluted. "I'll see you when I get back. Do work on your abdominals while I'm gone. You're gettin' a little flabby." The door closed and the battle was over. But no one would claim victory on this day. For when pain and imminent death were present, victory no longer mattered or was considered.

DISCOVERY

Jude hurried desperately, along with Pang and Sia, in an attempt to catch up with Eli. During the war meeting, the General had asked Eli to go see what was taking Jamieson and Captain Tatum so long. After a few minutes, Eli emerged into view with anger and instability. He stormed out of the war meeting, leaving Jude to apologize to the General for their departure. Weaving between buildings towards their homes, Jude and the others were filled with curiosity and concern since Eli was refusing to answer their calls over the S-3. When the last row of homes rose up first in front of the temple, Eli stopped at the large statue of Pith for a breather, giving the rest of the squad time to catch-up.

"Eli what in the Pith is going on?"

"Yes, that was very rude and left a very bad impression for us with the General," said Sia.

"I rather enjoyed the exercise," said Pang with a smile. "Jamieson said I need to keep my heart rate up more."

"Yuck! Don't even say that name around me again," spat Eli.

"What? Why? What happened when you went to go get them?" asked Sia.

"Did they attack you? Did they uncover your identity?"

"Please as if they had the time. They were too busy kissing and being all over each other!" spat Eli.

"Come again?"

"Jamieson and Talon are—together!" said Eli in disgust. Every time he spoke Jamieson's name, he had to spit a ball of saliva to the side.

"Quit lying Brassie!" laughed Pang. "Jamieson is like the most masculine guy in the world—Talon too!"

Eli shook his head back-and-forth uncontrollably. "No! No! No! No! I'm telling the truth. I went back there to tell them the General was tired of waiting and I heard them arguing behind the door so I listened. Apparently Jamieson doesn't want Talon to go on that mission with the General because he's in love with him or something. He thinks the General will make Talon not come back somehow."

"Interesting. If he thinks that, then that means he doesn't trust the General either."

"True," said Sia in agreement. "Maybe we can talk to him, and see why his trust is shaken since no one seems to trust that tyrant."

Eli clapped his hands together once. "Hello! Are you guys even listening to me? Jamieson is a—freak!"

"Freak? Why, just because he has feelings for Talon? Big deal!"

"Yes," said Sia appearing confused. "Why does it matter?"

"For two 'smart' people, I can't believe I have to spell it out to you. Jamieson, a guy, has intimate feelings for Talon, another guy! What—the—Pith!"

"No! No," shouted Pang with his hands over his face while shaking his head erratically. "You're telling me Jamieson Edric is a dainty.

"What's that?" asked Eli.

"A sick and twisted ankle grabber!" shouted Pang at the top of his lungs.

"Pang!" yelled Sia.

Eli erupted into laughter, high-fiving Pang in between laughs.

Jude was embarrassed by the conversation. "That was uncalled for Pang. I really don't think his love life is any of your business!"

"The two of you were just talking about how much you liked him like an hour ago," said Sia flipping her hair and crossing her arms.

"I never said that," said Eli and Pang simultaneously.

"I can't believe you two. It's not like he's changed. He's still the same person you liked. You just learned about another side of him. What's the big deal?"

"It doesn't matter. I won't be hanging out with him again, that's for sure. Who knows, he could try and kiss me or something," said Eli with a snarl.

Pang laughed and high-fived Eli. "I'm with you on that one Brassie. I can't believe I was taking training tips from that guy. He was probably getting some sick kicks out of watching me do them."

"I hope you didn't bend over in front of him," said Eli laughing.

"Pang you never trained with him," said Sia glaring. "He gave you tips and you did them on your own time."

"So. Whose to say he wasn't imagining me stretching and bending over and stuff," growled Pang. His body shook off a shutter as if a chill had descended upon him.

"Well Mik and I like him and will continue to be his friend because we don't have a problem with him," said Sia turning her attention away from the conversation.

"Are you insane? I don't want Mik anywhere near him. He could try something with him!" yelled Eli.

"Oh Eli that's foul! You're way out of line!" snapped Sia going toe-to-toe with him.

"I don't want him anywhere near Mik!" yelled Eli.

"Well he's *my* brother not yours and I say who he hangs out with," snapped Sia.

"Yo!" yelled a voice from behind them. The squad turned around to find Jamieson running to catch-up. When he got to the squad he took a spot in between Pang and Sia. After spitting once, Pang relocated to the other side of Eli, unleashing a wave of tension onto the group. "Everything okay?"

"Yes, everything is fine. We just had to leave the meeting early."

"Yeah I was feeling sick," said Eli.

"Eli stop!" demanded Sia.

"Yes, a dainty will do that to you," said Pang.

Silence. The tension became unbearable as all eyes covertly snuck to Jamieson. Jude felt ashamed of his squad. After all of their training, Eli and Pang had been very good at holding their tongues with General Briars, Lieutenant Titus and even General Mather. But they refused to hold their tongue on this, and it made Jude hate their immaturity.

"Hey J, General needs to see us again," said Talon joining the group; his presence bringing more tension and awkwardness to the situation.

"What did you call me?" demanded Jamieson. The veins in his neck began to come alive while his clenched jaw and flexed arms showed exactly where this conversation was going.

Jude quickly stepped in between Jamieson and Pang. "He didn't say anything. Don't worry about it."

"I called you a dainty," said Pang. His words were met with Captain Tatum's hand around his neck as he asserted himself between the group and to Pang.

"Who do you think you are little man," snapped Talon.

In one quick jab, Pang's fist came crashing into Talon's face. The punch was fueled to the max, however, it barely moved

Talon's face to the side when it came in contact with him. It only took a beat before Talon and Pang to become entangled in a violent squabble of punches and headlocks. Pang held his own, but Talon was the walking embodiment of power, and returned every punch from Pang with three of his own. Soon the two of them tripped over one another and began tumbling down the city stairs, punching and kicking on the way down.

"Oh my Aegis!" yelled Sia running after them. She pulled her arm away when Jude tried to prevent her from running after them.

"Beat him down Pang!" yelled Eli.

Jamieson grabbed Eli's chin and jerked his face back his direction. "Shut your mouth! That's my Captain!"

"I bet he is an ankle grabber!" snapped Eli with a glare.

"Eli shut up!"

Then it was over. One quick direct punch from Jamieson and Eli was down for the count. Laying flat on his back, his eyes closed and barely moved. "What now Brassie? Look at ya! You were talking all that big talk a second ago!" Jamieson went to continue his assault on a still unconscious Eli, however, Jude quickly leaped in front of him begging him to stop.

Sia soon returned to the top of the stairs with Talon, who looked like he was ready to go on a killing rampage. Pang was nowhere to be seen. Without saying a word to anyone, Talon grabbed Jamieson by the shoulder and ushered him back to the Temple. Jude guessed they were heading back to the General, but hoped they would not alert him of the squabble. The people of Kismet had already overstayed their welcome, and Jude began to wonder how long the Priestess and General would be sympathetic to their situation.

"Eli! What happened to him?" shouted Sia hysterically.

Eli still laid flat on his back. His head now moved slowly side-to-side but his eyes were still closed.

"Him and Jamieson got into it. Where's Pang?"

Sia gave an exhausted expression, alerting Jude to what was potentially a fight of gargantuan proportions. "I think his ego is bruised a little. I'm just happy he didn't use his Blood Magic because then I don't know what would have happened."

"None of this should have happened. If the Lieutenant were here, he would chew me out for losing control of my squad. This is my fault. I should have ordered them both home the second Jamieson got here." Jude threw Eli over his shoulder and grunted under the weight. Eli had definitely built up some muscle post-training, and the weight was staggering.

"You can't blame yourself for the actions of other adults," said Sia trailing behind Jude as he made his way to Eli's house.

Jude dropped Eli off at his house and made sure his comrade made it into his bed. He asked Sia to stay for a little while until Eli woke up, to make sure he was okay and ensured he remembered to meet at Jude's at midnight for the rendezvous with the Lieutenant. Jude would meet up with Pang to make sure he was okay and his mind was clear since retribution and revenge were at the top of his list of hobbies. Sia was apprehensive at first, asking if Jude could stay while she checked on Pang. Jude didn't want to put her in that situation, but he knew how Pang was when he was at his worst and didn't want to put Sia in harm's way if Pang had not calmed down yet.

The streets of Geminate were filled with conversation. Many civilians now stared at Jude as he made his way to Pang's house. He hoped that it was due to a few stragglers seeing the fight and not because Jamieson and Talon had alerted The Guard, Priestess or General. Walking up Pang's doorstep, Jude could already tell that it would not be an easy task to calm Pang down. The front door had been punched off its hinges and now lay in a wreck in the doorway. *I know deep down inside that if you resist me, I will have to hurt you. Don't forget we are one.*

ONE LEG

Eli was halfway through his bottle of spirits before his headache began to subside. It was going on thirty minutes since he had been awake, however, he made sure to stay in his bedroom since he spotted Sia downstairs from his open door. He already knew what kind of conversation was heading his way, and the stress and drama that was standing by waiting to pounce was something he couldn't deal with without a drink or two. He already began devising a revenge plan for Jamieson. He thought of Jamieson as a coward for punching him when he wasn't expecting it. After a quarter of the bottle was left, the air in his room began to smell lovely. He put the top on the bottle and then walked over to his armoire of clothes. He wrapped the bottle in a sweater and put it towards the back of the armoire; and then placed some shoes on top of it for good measure. After splashing some water on his face from the washroom, he took his time descending the stairs.

"Finally!" said Sia getting up from her seat at the dining room table. Eli's house looked like someone had picked up a bit and he wondered if Sia was bored enough to clean his house. "It's been like an hour maybe more!"

"No one said you had to stay," said Eli walking to the kitchen. He had his mind set on the cold steak he had in there from when he had the Erudites over for dinner. He hoped it was still okay to eat.

"Don't you walk away from me like that," said Sia following him. "I stayed to make sure you were okay ingrate!"

"I don't even know what that word means, and frankly, I don't even care. You can go now." A hand spun him around until he was locked in a stare with her purple glaring eyes. Her nose inhaled and exhaled.

"By the name of Rune, are you drunk?" she asked in disgust. Her judgmental tone told Eli that arguing with her was pointless.

"No! I had a sip."

"Stand on one leg," she demanded.

"No! Who do you think you are?"

"Stand—on—one—leg," she demanded through her teeth.

One thing dad always taught me is to do whatever women say and call it a day. It will make my life a whole lot easier.

He put one hand on his head and then the other, and then before he knew it, he was laying on his side on the kitchen floor with eating utensils pouring down upon him. A falling heavy drawer ended the parade. Sia helped him to his feet and fixed his shirt.

"Oh my goodness Eli, what have you done to yourself?" she asked with less anger.

"What do you mean? You're acting like I died. All I had was a sip. That's all."

"You don't get this destroyed by a sip of the devil's nectar," she said with crossed arms.

"Oh you just want a kiss, come here!" He leaned in waiting for her to submit to the kiss he knew she wanted, but was rewarded with a slap across the face that nearly knocked him off his feet.

"You're disgusting! Stay away from me," she said barreling out of the kitchen.

Eli quickly jumped to his feet and found himself angrier than ever. "Don't you walk away from me you witch!" He quickly caught up with her before she got to the front door and quickly blocked her path.

"You're an alcoholic! You were drunk that day Jude and Pang found you. You were drunk when you were over my house when we read that letter from the Lieutenant, and you're drunk now. The devil's nectar has its fangs in you deep and I don't know who you are anymore," she said with glazed eyes.

"You must be drunk too then, I see that shimmer in your eyes." He felt like he won that argument, and felt himself smile while he crossed his arms.

"These are tears you drunken idiot!" she yelled.

Eli felt bad for her because she was so convinced that he had a drinking problem when he didn't. It was an honest mistake for someone as close-minded as her. He opened his arms up to her. "Come on give me a kiss and I promise you will feel better. Then I will give you a kiss back and you will feel even better." He licked his top lip feeling his mouth water. "Then I can carry you upstairs and *really* make you feel better."

She slapped him and then pushed her way to the front door. It was then he realized what was going on in front of him. He loved Sia with all his heart. His love for her was one of the things he so desperately wanted to forget since he couldn't have her.

"Wait! I love you." The room stopped spinning as soon as the words left his mouth. It was as if the world was waiting for her response.

Sia opened the door and looked back over her shoulder. "You're drunk! I don't want you around my brother anymore. You're toxic. And just to let you know, I'm telling Jude too." After her threat she was gone, with the door slammed tightly behind her. Eli tried to go after her, but tripped on his combat boots, which sat by the door, and fell. The impact of the floor on his chest broke the wall that secured his stomach. Warm, foul-smelling vomit spilled from his mouth and flooded the floor next to him making his stomach feel better. His eyes fluttered open and closed, until Marius was pouring him hot cider at their kitchen table, and then Eli knew he was daydreaming.

Forcing himself to his feet, he stepped over the vomit and used the furniture around him to guide himself to the guest room down the hall. After a quick shower that resulted in the hot steam making him vomit all over the shower, Eli felt the nausea subside.

The kitchen lights shined too bright for Eli's liking. He opened his secret cupboard and went into a panic at the empty bottles lying aimlessly on their sides. He threw one bottle after the other over his shoulder ignoring the sound of shattering glass behind him. He found one bottle with a drop of spirits in it and quickly consumed it before tossing that bottle as well.

Oh man I feel a massive headache coming on and why is it so freaking hot in here!

Grabbing the closest dish to him, Eli tossed it at the kitchen wall. Exiting the kitchen, he felt himself ready to cry. A half-emptied bottle of his favorite spirits lay underneath a stack of firewood next to the fireplace. Snatching it quickly, Eli fell into the armchair closest to the fireplace and hugged the bottle. After lighting the fireplace, he took a sip. His headache immediately retreated with a smile. With each sip, he thought about the way Sia looked at him like he was a stranger. Suddenly, she appeared in the armchair across from him with her legs and arms crossed.

"Now before you say anything your highness, let me just have a little sip." He took a gulp and smiled at the burning sensation that trickled down the back of his throat. "Okay so you see I'm not an alcoholic. I just like to have a little beverage here and there."

Sia's face tightened while she shook her head.

"I don't know what you're talking about okay? I just don't have time for this."

She uncrossed her legs, rose from her seat and walked over to the fireplace.

"Look, my dad isn't coming back okay? Why do you keep asking me where he is?"

The look on her face when she turned around looked angry, which made him submit to the pressure.

"Alright I'll tell you what I do if you'll stop yelling at me!"

Sia returned to her seat and re-crossed her arms and legs.

He sighed. "Every night when the sea monsters are few and the rest of the city has gone to bed, I talk battle strategy with my dead father. He grades me on my missions and gives me advice on future ones."

Sia fought back a smile.

"Look I know he's gone but he still visits me—well, at least his memory does."

Sia rose from her seat, adjusted her clothes, and retreated into the flames of the fireplace; evaporating into the fire's embrace.

Mother Nature's Tavern sat dark and empty behind Eli, while he sat in solitude hugging his knees amidst the cold breeze. By the looks of the shimmer in the water surrounding the city, dawn was a few hours away.

Eli arrived to the tavern in hopes of having a sip or two of his favorite drink. He failed to realize that the tavern was not open throughout the night. Instead of returning to an empty home, he decided to remain on the steps leading up to Mother Nature's Tavern. Surprisingly, the proximity to the tavern put his anxiety of being without spirits, somewhat in check.

"Nothing more charming than a man loyal to who he is," said a sharp voice.

Eli cursed. He was caught-off-guard and the extra few seconds that it would take to decide where to direct the attack could mean the difference between life and death. Rising to his feet, he prepped his hands and located his enemy. The General stared back with a sinister smile. Eli quickly looked around for other soldiers and in turn an ambush.

"Calm down, calm down mister—Brassie is it?" said the General.

"What do you want? I haven't done anything wrong."

The General looked up at the tavern behind Eli and broadened his smile. "Waiting for yet another performance from Ms. Josline I see." Eli's unflinching gaze made the General return his attention towards the tavern's door. "Or perhaps just looking to drink from the fountain of fun."

Josline? Fountain of fun? How do you know about my after-hour activities?

"Hello, hello is anyone in there?" asked the General looking at Eli from different angles.

Telling Jude would pin blame on me considering our current relationship.

"I'm just having some thinking time."

The General studied Eli. His face appeared to be in a war with itself, as if trying to force itself to do something it wasn't accustomed to. A soft smile soon followed. "Look, I know how you must feel. Being on some—resources team—headed by a man that isn't fit to be captain."

The conversation was far more than an attention-grabber. It was a seed of curiosity that began to grow out of control the longer Eli thought about the General's words. "What are you saying?"

The General rested a hand on Eli's shoulder; causing Eli's extinct to attack to awaken. "I'm saying sometimes life rewards the wrong people. I'm saying, sometimes we need a friend to help us through life's unfairness when others have turned their backs on us."

"So what's changed? What is it that you hope to gain from deceiving me? Last I checked, I was a spitfire—a monkey. Now you're offering me a friendship, born out of the goodness of your condescending dark hole, which you call a mouth. Forgive my skepticism. Forgive me for being tempted to punch you right in the throat."

The General recoiled but recovered with a light chuckle. "Spitfire as always. I don't take *my* subordinates for granted and I believe in rewarding those who deserve it." He turned his back to Eli, and started towards the direction of the temple. "When you're tired of suffocating under that low-life's boot of command, come find me. I will make sure you are rewarded with what you deserve."

SEARCH AND CAPTURE

Eli arrived to Jude's residence ten minutes before midnight, making sure he wouldn't be late. He walked into Jude's lavish sitting room only to find the entire squad already there. When all of their eyes instantly flung his direction after closing the door, his eyes went to Sia. She shook her head slowly before flinging it towards the fireplace. Eli could tell that she was still mad at him, but he didn't care about that. He was desperate to know whether or not Jude was informed of an inaccurate drinking problem.

"Eli you're here," said Jude. He appeared surprised.

"Yeah. Midnight here right?"

"Midnight here, that's correct," he said turning the chair next to him around so the opening faced Eli. "How are you feeling?"

Eli looked to Sia, who still refused to look at him. Pang wasn't looking his direction either, which made Eli wonder if Jude was waiting to see if he was going to lie or not. "I'm not at my best, but I will be fine."

Jude paused for a beat before extending his hand to the chair next to him. Eli took his seat, but kept his eyes low. No one seemed to be up for conversation, which was a relief. If Sia had told Jude, Eli was sure that his drinking would be the topic of the night.

Unless he's waiting to have a one-on-one conversation with after the meeting with the Lieutenant.

The Lieutenant slipped through the front door without even knocking. Eli guessed Conall assumed the door would be open. When the squad went to stand to salute him he declined their greeting. His demeanor was melancholy to say the least. Eli wondered if the Lieutenant was taking the General's death hard, or if he was just tired from his journey.

"I have to make this quick because I'm also meeting up with Vance in Praxis in the morning," said Conall.

"How is Vance?" asked Sia quickly. She leaned forward in her seat as if desperate to know.

"He's—fine," said Conall dropping his gaze. "He's not fine. The constant traveling and lack of sleep is taking a toll on his health. I don't know what to do because I need his help and—never mind. On to your mission." He grabbed a lone cup from the table next to him, smelled it and then took a sip. No one stopped him or said anything. "Fox has a contact. Special Operative Palorious III. He lives in a small village on the other side of Kismet, opposite of the marshlands."

"Kendall Village?" asked Pang.

"Yes you know it?" asked Conall.

"Very well," replied Pang.

"Good. Then infiltration should be a breeze for the squad. If you're coming in the main entrance, his house is the first on the right," said Conall building a diagram with his hands. "His alias is P.K. He is blindly confident that no one knows that he is Fox's right-hand man so capturing him shouldn't be too difficult. You just need to make sure no one sees you. By the way, your cover is somewhat blown."

Everyone but Pang and Conall stirred.

"How can it have been blown Lieutenant? We have been *extremely* careful," said Jude.

"Fox must have got a glimpse of the squad on your last mission," said Conall sitting back in his seat and crossing his legs. "While he doesn't know who you are exactly, he knows you're the next generation Kismet Task Force. The squad name and uniforms have been synonymous for decades."

"That piece of garbage!"

"I'm not telling you this to scare you," interrupted Conall. "I'm telling you this because you need to know that people will be looking for you—hunting you. You must always be aware of your surroundings and leave none alive who spot you. *None!*"

"So what happens after we secure the target?" asked Pang finally joining the discussion. "We get to kill em' right?" Eli noticed a slight black eye and wondered if his comrade had received it from Talon earlier.

Conall took his combat boots off and placed them next to the fire. The water droplets began to run and soon dry. "You will need to—persuade him to give up Fox's position. Apparently, Fox was severely injured in his battle with the General and Tristan and is now on bed rest at some unknown location. He will of course have the best healers that Lord Egon can supply at his side so time is of the essence. You need to find his location before he is fully healed. His injuries will give you an advantage if you can catch him early enough."

Jude offered the Lieutenant his cup. "Copy that. Infiltrate the village, apprehend the target and find out Fox's location. Then what?"

"Then I may be sending you to Praxis. That is where Vance and I will be. We will need the King's help for the invasion on The Immortal Lands. We cannot risk going on in with just one squad anymore," said the Lieutenant.

"Praxis," interrupted Pang. "Praxis Praxis?" When the Lieutenant nodded, Pang's brow curled.

Conall put his combat boots back on and rose to his feet. "You will need to leave first thing in the morning. The Operative usually meets with Fox in the early afternoon. You will need to have him by then. I would also start thinking of a good spot to *persuade* him at. Good luck on your mission. Perhaps the gods will smile upon us this time." The Lieutenant started for the door, and after opening it, looked back towards Sia. "Wyatt, I need to speak with you."

All eyes swept to Sia as she rose to her feet. The request was odd and Eli didn't like it. Why did they need privacy to talk? Sia was part of a squad. Whatever he had to say to her he could say in front of her comrades.

"Of course," she said walking to him and then exiting. He closed the door behind them, leaving Eli and the rest of his comrades in silence.

Eli stood up, refusing to allow them to meet in private.

"Eli sit down," said Jude. He stared sternly at Eli until he retook his seat. "We leave at seven in the morning here. Get some sleep and be at your best. I don't want *any* hiccups tomorrow. I'll pass the word along to Sia."

Eli was ready to turn in for the night but not to sleep. He tried to leave Jude's house as fast as he could, but Jude refused to let him walk home alone. Eli guessed that Jude didn't want him to go look for Sia and the Lieutenant. Eli wondered what they could be talking about anyways. If Eli had to guess, she was telling the Lieutenant about his drinking and wanted to be reassigned to another squad. She was such a snob that Eli wouldn't put it passed her. Turning the last corner, a tall man took powerful strides towards them. Eli continued to walk alongside Jude since there was ample room for the man to pass. Suddenly, the man decided to walk right through Eli and Jude, pushing them out of the way as he passed.

"Are you serious?" Eli turned around towards the man but he kept walking.

"Really!" shouted Jude at the top of his lungs. "All the space in the world and you had to barrel through us like that."

"Tell it to your mother Kismet scum," shouted the man without breaking stride.

"Seven in the morning at my house. Goodnight," said Jude walking towards the direction the man was walking.

"Hey where are you going? Your house is the other way."

Jude quickly strolled towards the direction of the man, his hands buried deep in his combat tunic. "You heard him disrespect me. Now I have to kill him."

He's being dramatic. I don't have time for this.

Eli unlocked his door and entered. He took off his shoes and headed for bed. He noticed his hands were jittery and he was sweating tremendously despite how cold it was in the house. His head drummed and he found himself rubbing it over and over again without relief. Throwing his legs over the side of his bed, he buried his face into his palms and began to sob underneath the increasing nausea and pain. He blinked his eyes over-and-over again until he realized it was all in vein.

What the heck is wrong with me?

SAVED IN VEIN

Mother Nature's Tavern sat silent in the presence of Josline's beauty and melody. She stood elegantly on the stage in her painted on red dress—sparkles shining like the stars in the night sky. Her light, seductive voice spread out across the tavern, entrancing all who listened. Eli found a spot in the front row, due to his early arrival. By the time Josline hit the stage, Eli was comfortable and full of a new spirit by the name of Double Tap.

Josline's enchanting melody was hard to follow for some reason. In fact, every sound and movement in the tavern was hard to follow. From what Eli gathered, the song had something to do with a painful journey with no clear end. As the spotlight dimmed at the last of her words, the crowd quickly rose to their feet, unleashing thunderous applause. When the light returned, she was gone once again; leaving Eli thinking of the next time he would see her again. A young woman soon appeared in Josline's place, her beauty paling in comparison to Josline's. While her song was less touching, it was catchy, and didn't take long for Eli to tap his foot while finishing his drink.

"Why do you come here so often?" asked a voice next to him.

Eli noticed Josline standing over him, her delicate hands grasping the chair in front of her. Eli grabbed his second cup. He never ordered a drink alone; it always needed an ally. He took a sip before returning her stare. "To see you." He smiled when she smiled, before nodding to the chair she grasped.

Josline sat slowly, adjusting her dress in various spots. Eli noticed eyes from all around the tavern staring at him.

Garrett sat in the back corner eyeing him with his goons mimicking his every move.

This time Jude isn't here to keep me from taking your head!

"So," started Josline as she crossed one bare leg over the other. "You come here just to see me?" Her wink sprung a smile.

"I come here to feel better and you and this drink I'm holding do just that." He picked his cup up for another sip and instead smelled the alluring sent of Josline's delicate hand over the top of his cup.

"You don't need that to feel better," she whispered in his ear.

"Then what do you suggest?"

The room was dark but spacious. Luxurious jewelry and clothing lay scattered along her vanity countertop. Lit candles danced in the shadows at various points in the room, courtesy of Josline. Entering the bedroom from the washroom, Josline strolled out in her transparent night clothes—the light pink failing to hide anything beneath its surface. The pink was familiar. The pink was memorable. That night entering through the double doors of that nightmare would haunt his mind forever. How foolish of him to not savor those moments with *her*.

Josline laid her body along the silk surface of the large pillow-top bed. She covered herself with one cover before his time was up. Eli kicked off his boots and unbuckled his combat tunic. His bare chest welcomed the coolness of her room. Her lips exhaled at the sight, noticing his hand as it traced his abdominals. He tugged off his combat pants and stood idle in trousers, not embarrassed but afraid. He slipped under the covers and immediately fell into the warmth of her embrace. The kissing was passionate. Her hands were claws down his back. Placing both hands on his bare chest she climbed on top of him, never missing a kiss. After taking off her night clothes he stopped kissing her.

"What's wrong?" she asked.

The spirits' effect was failing. He became more self-conscious as time passed. Looking up into her eyes he saw his reflection, dancing in their center. "I've never done this before."

She sat back but stayed on top of him. Brushing her long hair out of her face she studied him. "Are you sure?"

"Yeah. I was saving it for someone." His words felt foolish and childish. He hoped she wouldn't be turned away by his immaturity.

"Oh I love it," she said licking his chest. "Well today, you handsome devil, is your lucky day."

Warmth was first, followed by awkward movements, intensified breathing and savage desire. Then all that was left was his eyelids closing to the blissful blanket of indescribable pleasure.

OPERATION: KENDALL VILLAGE

The plan was simple. Sia would infiltrate the city and locate the target. With her Halcyon Trance, she would put the target to sleep and teleport him to the black site. Eli and the rest of the squad remained cloaked by her invisibility at various points throughout the city, just in case reinforcements happened to show up for absolutely no reason other than bad luck. The S-3 was never silent, since the mission had begun. The breathing and rustling of his comrades began to wear on Eli's nerves. Kendall Village was a quiet medium-sized village. The villagers that walked along its dirt roads seemed friendly. They seemed like they would be welcoming to the squad if the situation was different. Children fought with wooden swords while mothers shopped close-by. Out of every place Eli had been, this village held the largest tavern Eli had ever seen. Rising up in front of him at over three stories tall, the air salivated with the smell of spirits and other delectable smells.

"Who are you?" said a male voice over the S-3. The sound of a struggle and commotion quickly followed before Sia's heavy breathing filled Eli's ears.

"Target is immune to magic," said Sia while breathing rapidly. *"He's headed for the watchtower!"*

"Spread out and find him quickly!" shouted Jude's voice. He didn't appear angry but excited. *"A round of drinks to whoever apprehends him first."*

Eli thought he must have been hearing things. Free drinks for doing his job seemed too good to be true.

"Ten gold coins says Jude gets him first," laughed Pang.

Eli set eyes on the watchtower and felt the invisibility dissolve. Villagers screamed all around him as they set eyes on his K.T.F. uniform. The scarf covering his nose and mouth would help conceal his identity. The villagers would not be on his radar. The only thing he could think of was capturing the target *and* that round of drinks.

◆ ◆ ◆

"Boo!" said Pang's voice before the abrupt crashing filled the S-3. *"Apparently he's immune to Blood Magic as well. That little dainty! I should have just grabbed him and let him break his own arm trying to escape. Looks like the insect is heading for the tavern."*

The screams and panic from the villagers continued to erupt from different locations throughout the village. Eli forced his way through the crowds of gawking and cowering villagers trying to make his way to the tavern.

He would be at the tavern. I was just there. If I would have stayed there, I would have been right next to him. Typical.

Then he saw the tavern, rising up behind rows of homes. Going around them would take too long. He gritted his teeth and barreled through the door of the first home.

"Who are you?" screamed the woman inside. She grabbed the hand of a young boy and pulled him close. "What do you want?"

Eli ignored her and continued through the back door. Leaping over the second home's fence, he broke down that door as well, but this time came face-to-face with an older gentlemen armed with a rusty blade.

"Now you stay right there!" the man demanded. "Now what do you—." His neck split open as Eli sped by him with his own blade.

Exiting the last door, Eli emerged into the village streets at the center of the panic. Men and women cried and ran in all directions amidst the chaos.

"It's the Kismet Task Force! The Lord was right! They're going to kill us all!" shouted one woman.

"Grab the children!" shouted a passing guard. His armor and weapons appeared rusty and unusable.

Eli ran through the crowd, drawing everyone's attention immediately. He threw himself on to the wall next to the tavern and flung himself to the second floor.

"Help! Someone help! They killed my honey bunny! Help someone please!" shouted a woman behind him.

Entering the tavern from the second floor, he discovered the building appeared abandoned, perhaps due to Eli and his comrades. Chairs and tables were flipped over and perfectly good spirits now lay in puddles on the floor.

What a waste! What a stupid stupid waste!"

Eli ran to the center of the tavern and noticed that a square staircase rose from the middle of the tavern. Eli looked down to the first floor and saw nothing. Then a crash came from the third floor.

"Ugh! Someone help! He's here! He's here! Send the guards! He's going to kill me!" shouted a man's voice.

Eli ran up the stairs, through a storage room filled to the max with various produce. Opening the back door, he stumbled across Jude dueling with another man.

"You'll have to kill me!" shouted the man bringing his blade down on Jude.

Jude's Optical Tactics activated, the white sheen covering his eyes like a blanket. "One step ahead of every move you'll make." With calculated precision, Jude countered every movement of the man as if foreseeing it minutes before. Jude disarmed the man with ease.

Tumbling out from underneath Jude and returning to his feet, the man quickly regained his footing and went on the offensive.

"Three blocks and two strikes is all I need," said Jude side-stepping the stranger's attack. He landed a direct hit to the back of the man's knee and secured him in a chokehold—all in what seemed like a single move.

"Operation complete," rang Jude's voice. "Jude for Pang."

"Go for Pang," replied Pang with giddiness heavy in his voice.

Eli stared at Jude; curious as to what would come next when the mission seemed complete.

"Kill them all!" ordered Jude.

AN AGENT'S CODE

Memorable knick-knacks and organized clutter smelled like wet books. Wooden floors with creaky floorboards were the only signs of what life within the taken home used to be. A man and woman lay lifeless in the corner of the home, slain by the end of Eli's blade. Special Operative Palorious III sat with his hands and legs bound to the chair he sat in. Jude thought the bruises and burn marks looked painful enough to break even the mightiest of men—but not this one.

"I really don't like hurting you Palorious. I want to help you. Will you allow me to help you?" Jude stood from his chair across from the Operative, and began circling the prisoner's chair.

"But I don't know where Fox is I swear!" cried Palorious.

"Maybe if we—," started Eli before Jude sprinted to his location.

"Not a word." Jude waited until Eli nodded before returning to his seat—dragging it closer to the Operative. "Palorious you see, I know you know where Fox hides. Nothing you can say will convince me otherwise. But like I said I want to help you. When I was rummaging through your home before you ran, I noticed you live with your mother. A lovely woman—."

"You stay away from my mother!" yelled Palorious. He struggled against his shackles, but his binding was tight.

"Shh shh! I won't do anything I don't have to. You see, I have a mother too that I love *very* much. Can I tell you about her?" After the Operative nodded, Jude continued. "My mother is all I have. My dad left us at an early age and she is all I have left and I would do anything to protect her. I would go to the darkest, wettest trench of hell to protect her. Anim, the devil himself, could not keep her from me. I can tell that you feel the same about your mother. Am I right?"

"Yes! I would do anything for her," he cried desperately.

"You see, you and I are the same. Now I will do everything in my power to make sure you return to her safely if you just reveal Fox's location. He will never know it came from you. If you refuse to help me, then my boss will make me hurt you, and I don't want to do that. So please help me help you."

The Operative stared back at Jude through tired eyes. His mangled face began to shake along with his sharp chin. A single tear dropped from his eye. Jude lifted his face and wiped the tear away, forcing the Operative to look him in the eye.

"I can't," cried the Operative in hiccups. "He's the most dangerous Rogue to ever walk this Earth. He will kill me."

"I'm so sorry Palorious. I'm trying to help you, but you won't let me." Jude rose sternly, staring down his nose at his prey. "Pang!"

"No please! I don't know anything I swear!" cried Palorious.

Jude retreated to Pang and Eli. Sia soon entered the home after setting a barrier around the house to make it invisible and harm anyone who got too close.

"Shatter his kneecap."

"Don't you think that's a little extreme," said Eli quickly.

Eli would be the next one in that chair if he questioned Jude one more time. Jude turned his gaze to Eli and took in the resistance he clearly displayed. "I'm sorry did I ask you?"

Eli said nothing, which made Jude hope he had remembered his place.

Pang walked over to the Operative cracking his knuckles. "I'm going to enjoy this." He brought his fist back and attacked.

The howls of agony echoed throughout the house. The Operative flailed and squirmed in his seat while continuing to scream at the top of his lungs. The tears were thick and endless. It took some time before Jude decided the Operative was as calm as he would ever be. The cries and groans still came, but the Operative clearly had tired himself out.

Jude took his seat, crossed his legs and waited for the Operative to notice him. "I'm sorry I had to do that. The young blonde gentleman over my shoulder is our healer. He can heal your knee and take away all the pain—once you reveal Fox's location."

"Alright alright!" yelled the Operative. His chest rose and fell violently, while his twisted leg continued to fidget in place. Jude jerked the Operative's head up so his eyes remained locked with Jude's. "Underneath the rug in my bedroom is a trap door. Follow the trap door and it leads down to a small passage. Follow the passage and you will find a door. Through the door is where we were holding Fox."

"He could be lying," said Pang taking a spot next to Jude. "How do we know he's telling the truth? Maybe I should dislocate his arms to be sure."

"He is. I can tell," said Jude leaving his seat and signaling for Pang to follow him. When the four of them were a significant distance away, he looked at the staring Operative and gave him a thumbs up with a smile. The Operative breathed a sigh of relief and dropped his head.

"So if he's telling the truth should we move out?" asked Eli.

"No because Fox won't be there."

"But I thought you said he was telling the truth," said Sia.

"He was." Jude walked back over to his seat and sat down. He put a hand on the Operative's shoulder and smiled. "Thank you so much for telling me the truth. For doing that, I can help you now." Jude looked over his shoulder to Pang. His comrade soon came with a plate of bread and a cup of cold water. He placed it down on the floor next to Jude, who picked up the bread and placed it at the Operative's mouth. The Operative turned into a savage beast as he gnawed and attacked the bread with hunger and desperation. When he was done, Jude put the water cup to his lips until he finished it.

"Oh thank Anim for your kindness!" shouted the Operative. Someone behind Jude shuffled at his words.

"So you pray and worship Anim. I do too. There aren't a lot of us around. It's refreshing to find a fellow believer."

"I agree," the stranger said slowly.

"So you see how I was able to help you when you helped me?"

"Yes! Yes! So you're going to let me go right?" he asked.

Jude got up from his seat and began circling the Operative, trying his best to keep him off-balanced. "You see I can't let you go because even though you were telling the truth about where you 'were' keeping Fox, we both know that's not where he is now." Silence. "You see, you making us chase you around the village created quite the show. If I had to guess, news got back to Fox and whoever is in charge of his care. If I had to guess, he was moved to some sort of back-up location for when things don't go according to plan. Tell me where *that* location is and I will let you go."

The Operative opened his mouth.

"Before you answer, just remember that I'll be forced to hurt you if you lie to me; and trust me, I will know if you are lying," said Jude activating his Optical Tactics.

Seconds passed followed by minutes. Then finally the Operative looked up from his lap. "You're right, but I don't know where that location is because it was never supposed to come to that. They told me the second location wouldn't be needed. I'm telling the truth."

"Just great well what now?" said Sia.

Jude shook his head back-and-forth in disappointment before leaving his seat.

"Where are you going?" cried the Operative. "I'm telling the truth! Say something dammit say something! Say something!"

"Standby and don't talk to him."

◆ ◆ ◆

Eli paced the outside lawn trying to focus on anything that would keep his mind occupied. According to Sia, as long as he kept within a few yards of the house, he would not be spotted. It was going on three hours since Jude left. The rest of the squad was getting tired and Pang had already cleaned out the refrigerator of the house they occupied. Food wasn't what was putting Eli's nerves on edge and his cold sweat returning. He thought about how refreshing a drink would be right about now. He deemed it only natural that he would have a thirst for some spirits considering how intense the current situation was. Jude was completely out of control with his persuasion techniques, and Eli didn't know how much longer he could witness the cruelty.

Entering the house, Eli found Sia and Pang chatting quietly on the couch next to the slain bodies. The Operative's head was tilted down until Eli walked through the door.

"You—healer!" said the Operative. He continued to call Eli until Eli looked at him. "He said you would heal my knee if I told him the truth. Well I did, so can you heal it please. The pain is excruciating."

Eli didn't know why Jude said Eli was a healer. The statement was more than far from the truth. Not speaking to the

Operative under any circumstances was Jude's orders, so Eli retreated to the couch with Pang and Sia.

"No! Where are you going? Come back! He promised!" yelled the Operative while shaking in his seat.

"I'm so tired right now," said Sia slouching in her seat.

"I'd rather be tired than hungry," replied Pang.

The front door opened. In stepped a stranger with a black bag over his head. Jude walked closely behind him. Kicking the door closed behind him, Jude pushed the stranger to the seat in front of the Operative. After the stranger was seated, Jude looked back towards the squad. The three of them joined Jude next to their two guests and awaited orders.

"Pang, restrain the Operative and don't let him break his bonds," said Jude over the S-3.

Pang walked behind the Operative and stood idle. *"Copy that."*

"Sia make sure your barrier is still cloaking sound and keep an eye out," said Jude walking in between the stranger and the Operative. *"Eli, you are to restrain the stranger. You don't say a word to anyone—not to me, not to them, not to anyone."*

Eli didn't like the sound of what was going on. Judging by Sia's face, she was a little on edge as well. Eli took a spot behind the stranger, growing more curious as time passed. The hooded stranger smelled like a heavy musk of flowers and outdoors.

"Who is that?" asked the Operative struggling in his seat until Pang restrained him.

"I'm done trying to help you Palorious. Do you hear me? I'm sick and tired of your *crap*! Now I tried to help you, but you still lied to me—after me giving you food and water and us connecting on a personal level," said Jude walking over to Eli's captive. He yanked the hood from the stranger's head and exposed an elderly woman with curly white hair and creased skin.

"Mom! Mom! What are you doing? That's my mother!" yelled the Operative as he fought beneath Pang's grip.

The woman began to cry, and as soon as Jude ripped the scarf from her mouth, she began to scream. "Palorious what's going on? Who are these people? Why are they doing this?"

"Mom shh it's going to be okay," said the Operative sobbing. "What do you want from us?"

Jude turned his head slowly to the Operative feeling annoyed. He walked over to him and backhanded him across the face. "Don't insult my intelligence! You already know what I want!" Jude grabbed something from his combat belt and approached the woman.

"What's that? What are you doing to her? Answer me!" yelled the Operative.

Jude held a vial in the air. "My answer." He ripped open the woman's shirt and plunged the vial into her chest.

"Stop it! Stop it!" shouted the Operative.

The woman began to shake violently as her chair rose and fell off the ground. Jude took out a second vial and walked behind Eli and the woman until he was staring at the Operative. "I've injected your mother with a viral poison of my own making. As we speak, it's attacking her nervous system. As seconds turn into minutes, her body will begin to attack itself. In my hand I hold the cure."

"I am going to kill you!" yelled the Operative. "Do you hear me? I'm going to rip out your throat you piece of garbage!" He tried to bite Pang's hand, but Pang grabbed his hair and pulled his head back.

"Now tell me where the second location is and I will end her suffering," said Jude.

"I don't know I swear," he replied quickly.

"Please! Please Pal Pal tell him whatever he wants to know," screamed the woman. "Please son, it's spreading. It's spreading everywhere and it hurts. Please tell them!"

The Operative's chair rose and fell continuously as he tried desperately to escape. "Mom! Mom I'm so sorry I'll save you I promise."

'Tell me Palorious," said Jude.

"I'm telling you the truth I don't know," he replied.

Eli lifted his hands to a wet feeling along his fingertips. Fresh blood glistened on his fingertips from the trails that fell from her eyes. He felt like he was going to be sick.

"The blood from her eyes tells me she only has about four minutes left," announced Jude. "Looks like we will be burying two more bodies tonight."

"Okay I'll tell you. But first help her," cried Palorious.

"Tell me where Fox is *first*," demanded Jude as he rested his hands on the Operative's chair and stared at him nose-to-nose.

"The Silent City! Now save her!" yelled Palorious.

Jude turned quickly and plunged the vial into the side of the woman's neck. After a beat, her shaking stopped and her breathing stabilized. Jude retreated to the couch on the other side of the house, and the rest of them soon followed. Jude retreated back to the woman and released her from her bonds and watched her come crashing down on her son in a tight embrace and tears. The two of them hugged each other, not moving from their spot.

Jude returned to the rest of the squad and wiped his brow. "Good work."

Silence.

"Sia will portal us back to Geminate for food and an hour of sleep. Then we go after Fox," said Jude.

Sia recoiled. "But the Lieutenant said for us to rendezvous with him first once we retrieved Fox's location."

"Well your little boyfriend isn't here now is he Wyatt? I'm the Squad Leader and I say we go after Fox. Is that a problem?" snapped Jude.

"No Squad Leader," replied Sia.

The four of them headed for the door, but stopped when Jude guarded the door.

"Pang un-tie the Operative. The lady comes with us," said Jude.

"What? No!" shouted the Operative. "We had a deal! I told you where Fox is!"

"Yes you did," replied Jude quickly. "This is just a little insurance. Your mother comes with us. If Fox is where you say, I will have Sia bring her back to your village. If he's not, then you'll have an extra bedroom in your house."

"No! That wasn't the deal!" shouted Palorious.

The second Pang un-tied the Operative, he went to attack, causing Sia to encase him in paralysis. Pang flung the woman over his shoulder as she cried and bid farewell to her son. The five of them exited the house, and after a few steps, stopped behind Jude.

"You know what to do Pang," said Jude.

"Copy that," replied Pang. He began walking to a patch of secluded trees and bushes.

"We're going to kill her?" asked Sia.

"Of course," said Jude in a matter-of-fact tone. "We can't cart her around all day can we? If we leave her somewhere she will starve to death and we can't let her go because we don't know if she will tell anyone or is working for Fox. At least she will go quickly if we kill her now—unless the two of you have a better suggestion. I'm all ears."

Silence.

Who is this guy? This isn't Jude. Jude would never do something so cold and heartless.

Eli racked his brain for a better alternative, anything that would end in the woman living. Everything resulted in the woman either going free or starving to death. Watching Pang carry the woman into the bushes and behind the trees, Eli flinched when her hand rose calling out to him to save her.

"It's not her fault," continued Jude picking his nails. "She just knew the wrong people."

"Blood magic!" echoed the night air.

A blood-red blanket branched out from behind the trees, coating the entire sky and moon in a red hue. The nocturnal creatures stirred and screeched.

"Blood execution!" growled Pang. The sinister laugh of Trials winner, Pang Quarrels, made its debut. Then the sky was clear. The sound of a disturbed lake soon followed, before Pang appeared between the bushes. He walked calmly and quietly as if he had just risen from an afternoon nap.

"Water burial," said Pang.

"Good work," said Jude turning to Sia.

The portal opened quickly. It's violet flames hissing and whipping back and forth along its black vortex. Eli followed his comrades inside, erasing from his mind the blood moon night of pain and death.

UNITY

The squad entered Jude's home swiftly and silently. The warmth across Jude's face gave the warning that the fireplace was lit and someone was home. The squad immediately went into battle formation with Eli stepping in front, dual blades drawn, and Pang at his side, ready to turn the tide of battle. The only person who didn't appear alarmed was Sia, who took her time stepping between Eli and Pang, and ventured to the kitchen—the sounds of plates and cupboards soon following.

Jude passed his comrades and made his way up the stairs and to his bedroom. "You guys can help Sia prepare the food, we will need to be fully charged before we leave."

The bedroom door sat cracked three-fourths closed, the same way Jude had left it, even though the doorknob was now stuck in the turned position. Entering the bedroom, he found Lieutenant Titus sitting on his bed, staring at a photo. Jude's ceramic box sat open on the end table.

"Bray!" said Conall springing from the bed and setting the photo down. "I didn't think you would be back so soon."

Jude decided not to respond, only stare.

"You're probably wondering why I'm here?" asked Conall approaching him.

"You're here because Sia secretly went behind my back and contacted you, telling you that I was planning on ignoring your orders to rendezvous in Praxis before pursuing the target."

Conall remained unaffected. He walked around Jude to the bedroom door, peeked through the crack and then closed it.

"What the heck were you thinking exposing yourselves in the cold zone while pursuing the contact. Did you ever once think that revealing your plans in an open city would hurt your cause?"

Jude walked to the washroom, keeping the door open so their conversation could still continue. "So Sia told you that? She told you that I chose to make a spectacle?"

"She said that you offered to buy whoever caught him some drinks that would impair their judgment and jeopardize future missions," snapped Conall. His words caught Jude's attention, making him turn around and face the Lieutenant.

"She said that?"

"More or less," he whispered.

"Well how I run my squad is none of your business. If you don't like the way I do things then leave—and take your backstabbing, big mouth girlfriend with you. Otherwise, get your musty carcass out of my face."

Appearing dumbstruck and puzzled, Conall stared at Jude before closing his mouth and leaving. Jude let a few seconds pass before following the Lieutenant down the stairs and into the dining room. The rest of the squad sat anxiously waiting, hunger running rampant on their faces. The Lieutenant took a seat next to Sia, something Jude was not surprised about. The five of them began eating the food the squad prepared, and left the talking to the assaulting wind outside—something Jude never understood considering they were underwater.

"The Lieutenant will be joining us on our mission. The extra help will further ensure our success." Sia's eyes darted towards Conall, who didn't look up from his plate.

"That wasn't part of the plan," said Pang. He quickly looked to the Lieutenant, who joined his stare. "No offense Lieutenant. It's just four is the perfect number for a covert massacre."

A knock at the door interrupted their conversation.

"He won't be the only one joining us." Jude put his fork down and left the dinner table full of gawking eyes. He opened the door and welcomed in his guests, and the new additions to this mission's squad.

"Are you serious?" snapped Eli rising from his seat and knocking over his cup.

"This has to be a joke," said Sia pushing her hair out of her face and then resting her cheek on her hand.

Jamieson's black and burgundy combat armor shined in the dining room light. Its detail screamed rarity and protection. He didn't appear to be anymore enthusiastic to see everyone, as they were to see him. Josline on the other hand, smiled gently before strutting over to the dinner table in her skin-tight white dress. She walked over to Pang, who sat by Eli, and winked.

"Um can I help you?" asked Pang.

"Do you mind changing seats so I can sit here?" asked Josline with a smile.

"What makes this seat so—," started Pang before looking at Eli and grinning from ear-to-ear. "But of course madam. Please sit." He got up from his seat, pulled out her chair, and waited for Josline to sit down before pushing the chair back in.

"What a gentleman! I see Kismet is full of em," said Josline looking as comfortable as ever with all of the attention. "Oh my let me catch my breath it's getting hot in here! Gentleman one, two and three," she said pointing from Pang to Eli to Jude.

"Are you sure this is a good idea?" asked Jamieson quietly. His worry was obvious, but his face remained neutral. "I'm with you, but I don't want to cause any trouble."

Jude wrapped his arm around Jamieson and walked him to the predator's table. "I really appreciate you being here." He let Jamieson take the seat between him and Conall, and passed him a plate.

"Bray what's the meaning of this?" asked Conall pushing his plate away and looking from Jamieson to Josline and back to Jude. "I believe introductions are in order."

"Lieutenant, the man to your left is Jamieson Edric, the Special Operative we were instructed to rescue. He is Geminate's top assassin, as well as extremely knowledgeable with all sorts of weapons and armor."

Jamieson extended a hand to Conall, and after some hesitation from the Lieutenant, shook it firmly. "Honor to meet you sir."

"Next to Eli is Special Agent Josline Verisity, a pro of the supernatural arts."

Josline raised a delicate hand and waived it gently side-to-side like a flower blowing in the wind. "It's a pleasure to meet such lovely people." After waiving she blew a soft kiss to the table.

"This is a joke!" snapped Sia springing up from the table and storming into the sitting room.

Jamieson leaned over to Jude and whispered. "Does she have a problem with me too?"

Jude sighed. "No, not at all." He opened the connection to the S-3, knowing that Sia was a just a few feet away. *"You're dishonoring yourself right now. Do you think real Special Agents act the way you are acting now?"*

Sia slowly entered the room adjusting her armor and fixing her hair. Conall watched her every move as she returned to her seat. "Apologies— to all."

"Since the Lieutenant decided to join us, I decided to look at this as a sign for the upcoming mission." Standing to his feet, he backed up so he could see everyone. "I do not believe it is farfetched to say that Fox will be heavily guarded. So it may serve our interest to put Josline and Jamieson under the Lieutenant's command. Both of them have been informed of our *true* identity, and have elected to help. Josline and Jamieson can deal with any reinforcements or distractions, giving us enough time to infiltrate the walls and neutralize Fox—*not* capture him."

"Have you lost your mind?" asked Conall. Everyone's eyes swept from the Lieutenant to Jude, and then back to Conall. "Vance and I have worked so hard to orchestrate and sustain your alias and you just throw it away by disclosing your squad's identity to two people you barely even know?"

"Our numbers continue to fall and we seem to be at the end of this struggle. If we are to succeed, or at least survive, we will need as much help as we can get; and last time I checked, this was still *my* squad."

"For now," hissed Conall.

"What do you think we can expect from the bodyguards?" asked Eli.

"I don't know." Jude returned to his seat after feeling like the conversation was heading in the right direction. "What I do know is that Fox will be tough to take down. If I had to guess, he will have some subordinates for us to deal with that will serve as his distraction for him to use his bloodline ability. All of that will be enough for us to deal with. It would be reckless for us to try and deal with that, as well as any reinforcements."

"Agreed," said Conall rising from his seat. "If it's not Necroborns guarding the cold zone, it will most likely be highly-skilled Operatives." He turned to Jamieson and then Josline. "I have never fought by your side. Can I count on the two of you to deliver on the battlefield?"

"Just give me five seconds to show you exactly what I can do," said Jamieson slamming his fist on the table.

"You'll never want to leave my side after I'm done," said Josline giving Conall a wink. The cup in front of her randomly tipped over, soaking the top of her dress. Her eyes darted to Sia.

"What bad luck," said Eli grabbing a dinner cloth. "Let me get that for you." He began to dry Josline's chest.

"I could make a joke about this water on me, but I'd rather let your mind wonder," she said to Eli. Sia's grin turned to a glare before she rolled her eyes.

Jude grabbed the tablecloth beneath the plates and yanked it as hard as he could, sending dishes and cups flying behind him. The silence came immediately, as well as the wide eyes. "I'm going to say this one time and one time only. A few of you in this room have problems with one another. My advice to you is grow up—now! I don't have time for popularity contests and boring drama. Just remember, when you think about throwing that insult, or glass of water, just think of you and that person being the last ones alive on the battlefield, surrounded by enemies. Suddenly your foolish crap won't seem so important. Do yourselves a favor and don't dishonor yourself in front of me or the Lieutenant."

No one in the room could look at one another. Every person found anything they could to stare at. Conall and Jude were the only outsiders amongst the tension.

"We won't be able to portal into the cold zone without risking being spotted so we will portal to the Rocky Highlands and go by foot."

"Get some sleep," continued Conall. "We leave in three hours."

CONSEQUENCES

The night air finally calmed after the tents were pitched and the campfire was lit. The tents were compliments of Jamieson, and considered a lifesaver to everyone who weren't too prideful to admit it. The tents were compact enough to fit six tents in a small bag, which Jamieson was able to carry over his shoulder. Everyone had their own tent, except for Sia and Conall, an arrangement that was luckily made when Eli decided to wash up in the small lake close-by.

Jude sat with Pang and Eli around the campfire, while the others turned in early for the night. It would take a little under an hour to get to the cold zone, and the night was already going by fast.

Jamieson exited his tent and joined the three of them at the campfire, his eyes staying glued to Jude. "The tents seem to be working out and Josline already completed the perimeter around the camp. I was thinking of turning in early. Since I haven't fought alongside your Lieutenant, I want my mind to be sharp."

"Good idea. Thank you again for the tents. Even if no one has said it, everyone's grateful for them. Really."

"They're not that great," whispered Pang. His words were light but loud enough for Jamieson to hear.

"Mine smells like nude male body," said Eli.

Jamieson returned his attention to Jude and smiled. "Let me know if the squad needs anything else." He held a hand out to Jude, who rose quickly and shook it firmly before giving Jamieson a tight embrace.

"No I believe that will do. Go get some sleep." As soon as Jamieson peeled back the flap of his tent, Jude quickly called to him. "Thanks again for everything." Sitting back down to the warmth of the campfire, Jude counted down in his head to the inevitable objections.

"You know you're making a huge mistake by allowing him on this mission," said Pang.

"Yeah, I don't trust him," added Eli.

"And why don't you trust him?"

"He's not from Kismet and we don't know if he will turn on us," said Eli glaring.

"Neither is Josline, and you don't have a problem with her being on the squad."

Silence.

Jude looked from Pang to Eli, awaiting a response, but only found vacant expressions.

"Well that's different," said Pang finally. "She looks like we can trust her."

"Yeah," agreed Eli.

"She *looks* like we can trust her?" Jude shook his head and returned to his feet, over the conversation. "We all know why the two of you don't want him here. If I remember correctly, before you guys objected to him so much, *both* of you nearly worshipped him and said how much you liked and trusted him. I'm starting to get whiplash from the back-and-forth."

"Jude he's not normal," shouted Eli.

Jude was sure Jamieson heard Eli's words, judging by their volume, so he decided to put the conversation to rest. "Normal? Let me tell you something Mr. Brassie. Normal to you is something or someone that is just like you. People who are normal, are people who act and think like you. And any who don't act and think like you are abnormal, and in turn your enemy. Those are the people whose stories you will never know. You will never know their struggles, their victories, their dreams or what keeps them going. Just remember, you and Zane judged Pang before knowing him. Matter of fact, both of you verbally attacked him constantly because you didn't think he was 'normal.' You have an extensive track record of judging people you don't know. Look, I'm not here to change your opinion on Jamieson. You don't have to like him, but you *will* respect him because I'm the Squad Leader." With his closing speech he looked to Pang. "Period. End of discussion. The end!"

Leaving his comrades behind, Jude threw himself into his tent. When he entered, he set eyes on a puffy bedroll with two pillows with extra blankets, as well as a small light and knapsack. The sight looked comfortable and welcoming. He retrieved the photo of his family from his knapsack and laid with it on the bedroll, staring at his mom's smiling face.

Either Lord Egon holds you captive, or you have passed on to the other side. Either way I will join you shortly, once Fox and the Lord have been slain. After all, this life is only temporary, while my love for you is not.

Jamieson's tent was a war zone to say the least. Clothes lay scattered all around the tent while half-finished piles of food covered his wooden table. Surprisingly, the only clean and tidy area of the tent was his bed, which sat neatly made with impeccable detail.

"So what did you want to see me about?" asked Jamieson taking a seat on the floor. He began removing his combat boots but never took his eyes off of Jude. "Did I not bring enough tents for everyone?"

"No. That's not why I am here. I wanted to see if you were okay. I know Eli and Pang are not the easiest to get along with. To be honest, they can be the most difficult people I have ever met." With every inch of his apology, Jude began to feel even more guilty and embarrassed of his squad's antics.

"No worries I'm a big boy," said Jamieson laughing. "I mean it's what we do as men. We berate and emasculate each other for fun. I mean it's better than the bloody noses and broken jaws Talon and I give each other." He threw his boots to the side with more passion than normal.

"You know I don't have a problem with you and Talon liking one another right?"

Jamieson halted his activities for the first time since Jude had entered his tent, and met Jude's gaze. He smiled. "Well that would be nice to hear, if we were *actually* together." He rose from the floor and began cleaning up the old food and scattered clothing.

"But you have feelings for each other, right?"

"You're asking a lot of questions. Is this a requirement for being a part of your squad?" said Jamieson chuckling.

Jude could tell that Jamieson had no intent of opening up about his personal life so he decided that asking more questions would not be the best thing. If Jamieson wanted to talk about it he would. "I apologize for prying. I didn't mean to." Jude turned for the exit and decided that a good night's sleep would probably be the best thing right now.

"Alright, I may like the guy—a little," said Jamieson chuckling. When Jude turned around and showed no signs of leaving, Jamieson continued. "And he has expressed the same towards me."

Jude walked to Jamieson's bed and took a seat. Jamieson flipped over a fallen chair and took a seat.

"Then how come you aren't together? Are you both too busy with missions?"

"We're not together because..." Jamieson looked towards the tent's flaps and then down at his feet. His breathing escalated and his foot began to tap in place. "We're not together because I won't let us because I know the gods won't like it."

Jude found himself confused and could have sworn he misheard his new comrade. "Why do you think the gods care about who you love?"

Jamieson sprang from his seat and began pacing around the tent, spilling tension everywhere. "I don't know. But my people claim that somewhere in the book of worship, Aegis claims that my feelings for Talon are sinful and an abomination. I know that book like the back of my hand and I can swear to you that it doesn't."

"Then why do they say it does?"

"The Book of Worship speaks vague and in generalizations in regards to everything. To many it's an interpretive text and its meaning is different depending on the reader. Basically, people who read it decide what it says based upon their experience and upbringing. But then when they go to the Cathedral, they are taught what the Cathedral members want them to learn. Then everyone magically interprets the Book of Worship the same, claiming it says something it doesn't. That's why I don't carry the book," said Jamieson.

Jude thought about Jamieson's words and became even more confused by the discussion. The thought that divine beings such as the three brothers, cared about something so small and irrelevant as mortal relationships seemed ludicrous and farfetched. However, judging by Jamieson's story, it seemed like he was more afraid of what his people thought about his relationship with Talon than the gods. "Are you sure it's not your people that are making you afraid of your feelings of Talon instead of the gods?"

Jamieson pulled his chair close to Jude and stared deeply. "The first time Talon and I kissed, was the happiest moment of my life. It felt a little strange considering I had only had relationships with women at the time, but he was my best friend and I loved him dearly. I went home, had some dinner and went to sleep. When I woke up my lips were gushing blood as if someone took a knife and split them both open. The blood continued to run no matter how many salves and pressure I put on it. I finally fell to my knees in tears because the pain was unbearable and I had no parents to turn to for support. I begged the three brothers to make the pain and bleeding go away. Five minutes later the bleeding ceased and never returned."

"Now I'm definitely not the gods' biggest fan right now, but even I don't think you can blame that on the gods. I think it was just a coincidence."

Jamieson smiled. "That's what I thought. The next time I saw Talon we didn't kiss. Instead, he kissed me softly on my right eye wishing me sweet dreams. The next morning I woke up with a black eye that was swollen shut for three days. Can you guess which eye it was?"

"But why? Why would the gods do that to you? You're always praying, always going to worship, always being so nice to people, even strangers like me. It doesn't make sense."

"I don't know," said Jamieson getting up from his chair and returning it to the table. He walked to the tent's flaps and held them slightly open, looking up into the night air. "But I'm scared of the consequences. Enemies of the gods go to hell and I don't want to go there. I love them, and I wish they truly loved me back."

"But you don't even know if your fear is valid. What if your people and their book are wrong?"

Jamieson closed the flap and turned to face Jude. "I believe they are. But look at it this way. Let's say I decide to take a chance and be with Talon. I know his love for me is unconditional and would last for centuries. I would be the happiest person in the world being with him, and never want anything ever again. Then I find out that my people and the book were right and my feelings for him are sinful. So I spend eternity in the burning flames of Anim's realm. But then let's flip the coin shall we? Let's say I refuse my feelings for Talon and always keep him as a friend. I'll be miserable the rest of my life knowing that I can't be with the only person I love. However, when I die I have a better shot at going to heaven because whether my feelings for him are right or wrong it doesn't matter because I was never with him. Now tell me, which is safer?"

Jude weighed the consequences and calculated the cause and effect. Jamieson was right. It was better to completely eliminate the chance of doing something that could possibly bring you pain, rather than taking a chance at fulfilling a desire; only to find out that you will pay dearly for it for the rest of your eternal life. Even though Jamieson's choice of taking the cautious route seemed like a win in the end, the entire situation seemed like a lose-lose situation to Jude. "But isn't life about doing what makes *you* happy and not what makes other people happy?"

"I thought it was. I've grown up going to the cathedral almost daily and always trying to do the right thing. I thought that with all the time and love I give the gods, they could award me this one small shot at happiness by letting me be with the person I love," said Talon examining his biceps before dropping to the floor and doing push-ups. "The black eye told me otherwise."

"But that's not fair."

"Nothing is fair," said Jamieson turning over for sit-ups. "Life, death, people—none of it. The only thing that you can count on are these massive biceps baby." He puckered up and began kissing his arms passionately before flexing. "Well it was nice getting all deep and stuff but I'm tired. Let's kill the girly conversation."

Jude rose from the bed and extended a hand to Jamieson. He nearly fell trying to help Jamieson to his feet. When Jamieson shook his hand Jude pulled the Operative in for a tight embrace. "I'm sorry."

Jamieson pushed Jude away, leaving him shocked by the response. "I'll see you bright and early Squad Leader."

Jude ventured out of the tent and into the cool night air. Tip-toeing back over to his own tent, he snuck a glance up at the night sky. Many stars shined bright, but three seemed to shine brighter than the rest. "Were you wrong mom—about the three brothers? Are they actually my enemy instead of my friend?"

BREAKING POINT

Light! So bright!

I see the light by bringing the dark.

They see the dark but I bring the light.

Then still eyes.

I turn from the dark and come into the light.

For I brought the dark, while the light was so bright.

Eli awoke in a cold sweat but toasty blankets. The tent was warm but his body felt cold. This wasn't the first time the uncomfortable episodes woke him from his slumber. It took him a few occasions to understand what it meant, but he now understood what needed to be done. Pulling off the blankets, he reached into his utility bag and pulled out his last bottle of spirits. Just holding it in his hands seemed to begin the process of ending the night sweats. He unscrewed the top, sat in the corner of the tent, and began his recovery. The night was so quiet that it was unsettling. The constant missions full of death and rage turned silence into torture. He needed to do something to escape the prison of idle nothingness.

After finishing half the bottle, he tucked it away in his bag and exited the tent. The camp was bare and uninhabited, except for the squad's tents and the unlit campfire. Eli grabbed two rocks and sparked a fire and then sat and watched the fire come alive. The swaying flames reminded him of his fireplace at home.

Wow! I actually just thought of my house in Geminate as home.

All that was missing now was a bottle in his hand to compliment that warmth from the flames. With everyone asleep, he decided it should be safe to grab his bottle and drink by the campfire briefly before going back to sleep. No one would be awake to catch him and that made the idea even more enticing. Getting up from the campfire, Eli turned for his tent just in time to catch Sia leaving a tent, dressed in her night clothes.

She's supposed to be sharing a tent with Josline. What is she doing coming out of that tent?

Sia buttoned the top of a see-through night shirt and giggled quietly at a nose that erupted from the tent she had exited from. Conall exited the tent and wrapped his arms around her from behind, passionately kissing her neck as she giggled.

"You son of a..." Eli stampeded to Sia just as she turned around to kiss Conall. Grabbing her wrist he yanked her away from him.

"Brassie what do you think you're doing!" yelled Conall.

Eli clenched his fist as tight as he could and punched Conall, sending him tumbling across the terrain.

"Eli what are you doing! Stop it!" shouted Sia

Eli ran to Conall and climbed on top of his fallen body. The Lieutenant was quick to counter, flipping Eli over and climbing on top of him. The frenzy of punches clouded Eli's vision but the blow to the nose gave birth to a hidden rage that gave him the strength to fight back with a few punches of his own. Soon Conall was off of him and Eli was on his feet. Sia clung to Conall's arm with all her might, trying to pull him away. The anger on Conall's face said she was wasting her time and Eli was glad.

"Jude! Pang! Jamieson! Someone help!" yelled Sia before Conall pushed her to the side and hurled a sprinting right hook too quick for Eli to dodge.

"I'm done with this!" Eli summoned his dual blades and crouched.

Conall summoned two larger blades engulfed in flames and crouched.

"Whoa! Whoa!" yelled Pang walking out of his tent. Jude soon joined him, and then the two of them hurried to Sia's side.

"Eli stand down!" yelled Jude.

"Stay out of this Jude." Eli summoned his war blade and two spinning axes over his shoulders.

"Novice," laughed Conall clapping his hands together. "Dominion!" The ground around them began to shake, causing Eli to dissolve his weapons and hang on to the ground beneath him for stability. Pebbles and dirt rose slowly from the ground, while fissures shot out from Conall's feet, knocking Eli to the ground.

Eli rolled over opening his mouth as wide as it would go. A massive blade taller than any house or tree towered over Eli from the Lieutenant's hands. Bolts of lightning coiled around its blade like a snake, while flames hissed and roared at its edges. "Oh—my—Aegis!"

Conall smirked. "Yeah I know. Mine's bigger!"

"Lieutenant stop. You won okay," said Jude stepping between them.

A tremor radiated as the blade dissolved. Eli grimaced watching Sia throw her arms around Conall, showering him with kisses and affection. It was nauseating to watch and painful to think about. Then he fell into the pitfall of thinking about all of the things Sia and the Lieutenant have most likely done together. A shadow coated Eli in darkness, causing him to search for its source.

Jude stood over Eli drumming his foot. "You, me, over there—now!"

◆ ◆ ◆

Jude paced back-and-forth in front of Eli trying to contain his rage. The magnitude of what just occurred was overwhelming. He knew what he was supposed to do, but his anger kept him sidetracked.

"You're wasting your—," started Eli before Jude backhanded him.

"Shut your wretched mouth!" Jude stared at his comrade, unsurprised by the situation. It was clear as day what needed to be done. Eli assaulted a high-ranking official and threatened his life. Dishonorable discharge would be a generous notion if the Lieutenant didn't want to invoke the code of conduct. If he did, Jude would be responsible for the execution. "So you've left me no choice but to let you go on a dishonorable discharge."

"Dishonorable discharge?" said Eli laughing. "We have no home or armed forces so who cares."

"You *would* say that." Jude turned his back to Eli and started towards the camp, hoping to do damage control with the Lieutenant; and to see how the Lieutenant wanted to handle the situation.

"Don't you turn your back on me Jude Bray!" snapped Eli grabbing Jude's shoulder.

Jude shrugged his shoulder from Eli's grasp. "You picked the wrong one."

487

◆ ◆ ◆

Jamieson sat alongside Josline and Conall at the foldout table towards the back of the camp. The midnight antics had sparked hunger in everyone, except for Jude and Eli, who had been gone for a long time. The thought of the blonde boy made Jamieson shake his head unknowingly. The guy was trouble and disrespectful. Jamieson decided to give Eli a pass after their mishap in the city a few days ago. However, after hearing Eli tell Jude that he wasn't normal, Jamieson was done making excuses for the ignorance of others. Pang was another one on Jamieson's list. The boy with the scars had been glaring at Jamieson across the table, ever since everyone decided to sit down to eat. Jamieson began to wonder if accompanying Jude on this mission was a mistake.

"Just don't be angry with him okay babe," said Sia feeding Conall a strawberry. The couple sat snuggled together, ignoring the presence of everyone else.

Conall sighed. "I'll try not to be. You do know what this means though."

"Yeah I know," replied Sia.

"So," said Josline turning to face Pang. "What are you into?"

"Everything that has to do with dominating my enemy," replied Pang yawning. His eyes were fluttering closed, making Jamieson wonder why he didn't just go to sleep already.

Josline's eyes widened, along with her smile. She began to fan herself with her hand. "Oh really." She repositioned herself in her seat as she took a sip from her water cup. "What did you say your name was again?"

"I didn't," said Pang.

Jamieson looked from the catastrophe to Conall and Sia, who were rubbing noses, and began to feel like a third wheel.

Getting up from the table, he decided to go look for Jude and see what was taking him so long. The campfire was dying when he walked passed it. For some reason he thought of Talon, and how his mission was going. It was a thought he tried to keep at the back of his mind. It was only a matter of time before the General returned alone with some farfetched story of Talon's demise. Circling around the campsite, Jamieson stumbled across an eye-opener. Running back to the camp, he hopped over the unlit campfire and up to the others.

"J what's wrong?" asked Josline turning her smile away from Pang.

"Eli is fighting Jude!"

BROKEN SHELL

Eli attacked with all his might, slicing and bashing with his shield and sword while blades rained from the sky atop their battle. This was a fight he had thirsted for, ever since Jude was named Squad Leader. Now with Jude turning his back on Eli because of his squabble with Conall, Eli had nothing holding him back from putting an end to Jude Bray and his tyranny.

Jude danced around Eli's attacks and side-stepped around the falling blades. It was as if Jude knew every move Eli was going to make before he made it. Eli's comrade knew when to block, when to attack and when to evade as if instinctually. Eli found trying to land a blow exhausting. Finally a raining blade caught Jude's pant leg, trapping him in place.

"Ha! You're mine!" The chest was his target, and he wasted no time plunging his blade quick and hard.

Jude's forearm knocked the blade away, while his free leg came up and disarmed Eli's shield. Then with a quick punch to Eli's already-broken nose and torso, Jude knocked Eli off his feet.

Eli leaped to his feet. "Come on! Why not use your transformations!"

Jude front-flipped forward, propelling himself high above the battle. Eli knew Jude's moves. This would be when he would use his arachnid form. Eli summoned a blade and tossed it right where the arachnid would appear. Jude twisted and stepped on the incoming blade before landing on Eli's shoulders. The ground hammered Eli's head when Jude forced him down. Eli returned to his feet with his dual blades but Jude quickly swept the back of his foot, throwing him off-balanced.

You asked for it.

Jude sprinted to Eli, gaining ground fast.

"Landmine!" The explosion triggered an earthquake, kicking up dust and gravel everywhere. When the dust cleared, a giant crater was all that was left of Jude, causing Eli to feel proud and in awe of his own power. Then his knees caved-in and soon the crater became his home.

Jude stood over Eli inside the crater, arms crossed. Eli was sure Jude's over-confidence was kicking in since his Squad Leader had made one fatal mistake. He was in range and would be punished. Eli summoned his blade. Jude crouched with a flicker of worry. Eli attacked.

"Playtime is over!" yelled Jude. Then the painful memories resurfaced.

Fox's hands rose quick and sharp. "Playtime is over!" Fox's palm attacked Marius' chest, bringing him to his knees. "Eli! Eli! Eli!" rang Marius' voice in Eli's head. "Run son!"

Jude came barreling down with both feet stomping into Eli's stomach once, twice before somersaulting backwards out of the crater.

"Jude stop!" yelled Sia from somewhere close-by.

The spinning allied itself with the pain in his torso and head. The night sky continued to spin while her familiar eyes went from four to two.

"Jamieson can you help me?" asked Sia.

Eli looked up to find Jamieson reaching down to help him up. "Get your filthy hands off of me you dainty! I don't do that kind of stuff." Jamieson's hand retreated and then he was gone. Pang soon took his place, helping Sia return Eli to his feet. The second Jude's face resurfaced, Eli wanted his head. "How could you say such words? You know Fox said that to my dad before killing him! You were there! Why would you do that?"

Jude slowly closed the distance between them, never leaving Eli's stare. When they were toe-to-toe, Jude stopped. "Because I knew those words would hurt you since they hold such painful memories. Don't get mad at me because I bested you at every turn." Then the Squad Leader turned away, retreating to the camp, and never looking back. Eli no longer knew who that person was anymore. While that creature paraded around in the shell of the boy Eli grew up with, he was not Jude. That boy was gone, lost to the ages.

◆◆◆

The morning was difficult to rise to. A pounding headache, dry mouth and twisted insides were the works of none other than the now empty bottle of spirits that Eli clung to like a baby blanket. Regret was waiting for him when he finally rose from his slumber. The sun began to rise, half-lighting Eli's tent with a clear line between light and dark. Eli stepped out of the comfort of his tent to find Jude and Jamieson dressed and packing up camp. They walked back-and-forth in front of Eli, but said nothing or even looked his direction. The tension was everywhere. Conall's tent rumbled announcing the exit of the couple from its shelter. Both their eyes darted to Eli, caution and worry heavy in their eyes.

"Good morning."

Silence.

A rustling to Eli's right caught his attention. Pang joined the group after leaving his tent. His large arms sprang for the sky in a stretch that signaled the roar that soon left his mouth.

"How'd you sleep?" asked Pang. His question was directed towards his tent, which made Eli wonder if his comrade knew that he was awake.

Josline exited Pang's tent with her own delicate stretch. Her night clothes twisted and contorted in a manner that spoke violence. Eli shielded his eyes slightly at the sight of her half-exposed breast. "Too well. I hope I'm able to move today," she said winking.

Pang covered her chest and planted a kiss on her forehead. When she walked to meet the others, he pummeled her with a slap on the rear. "Morning Brassie!"

"Good morning Sia," said Josline heading in the direction of the lake. "I love your sexy get-up. Quite the show-stopper."

"*Disgusting* little harlot," replied Sia. Someone close-by dropped a heavy object.

Josline stopped in her tracks fidgeting her fingers. Conall left Sia's side and relocated to helping Jude, who appeared not to be listening, clean up the rest of the camp. A few seconds passed before Josline turned back around and strolled back over to Sia. "Excuse me? I compliment you and tell you good morning and you insult me?"

"First Eli then Pang? Who's next—Jude?" asked Sia flipping her hair. She looked at Josline up-and-down slowly before gagging. "Looks like I better keep my man close whenever you're around."

Wait! How did she know Josline and I slept together?

"You know it's girls like you that give men the power to call us crazy and a witch. It's not cute," said Josline flipping her own hair. "You're making me angry and I'm losing my balance. Excuse me." She shouldered passed Sia and headed back to Pang's tent.

Eli began to breathe normally at Josline's decision not to let the situation escalate. Sia was clearly out-of-line for attacking Josline for no reason. To Eli, Josline was always nice to everybody, including Sia. The fight seemed ridiculous.

"It's girls like you that make the rest of us *women* have to turn over in bed every second of the night to make sure our man isn't missing," snapped Sia.

Josline halted again.

"Don't feed into it Josline," said Jamieson walking by with a few packed-up tents.

Josline turned around and smiled. "I'm not going to even dignify that with the response that has been brewing at the back of my mind ever since I met you and your split ends." She turned back around and began towards the tent once again. Sia mumbled something under her breath with her tongue out and the most disgusted look on her face.

Josline was halfway through the tent when she froze once again. "What was that?" Spinning on the balls of her feet, Josline quickly closed the distance between her and Sia, as she stormed over there with tremendous power in each step. "Was that the come back and slap me face?"

Sia stepped toe-to-toe with Josline. "You're a dirty hussy. Now get out of my face."

Josline back-handed Sia, causing her face to jerk to the side. The second Sia's face returned to its neutral position, Josline's other hand came back with a vengeance, knocking Sia to the floor. Josline kicked up a dirt cloud at her fallen victim. "Dusty witch!"

"I'll show you a witch!" yelled Sia flinging her hand up. She levitated Josline off of the ground before face-planting her onto the ground beneath her. The entire camp moved at that moment.

Jamieson and Jude grabbed Josline just as her ipseity appeared behind Sia with open palms. Conall and Pang grabbed Sia while Eli apprehended the ipseity, who felt and smelled just like a normal person—just like Josline. Insults were thrown while both girls, and the ipseity, were dragged in opposite directions. Shortly after, the ipseity vanished, leaving Eli alone to watch the madness all around him.

The squad is falling apart.

ASSAULT ON SILENT CITY

The sun's rays shined bright on what would normally be a beautiful day. All of the trees, hills and grass around Jude shined with a sparkle which made the scenery a glittering display of the perfect dream. The others stood one next to the other, behind the smooth round hill that served as their cover before the pending storm.

"Since invisibility favors me, I will survey the area," said Sia removing her cloak and casting it aside.

"This sector is enormous," replied Josline strutting to the front of the group. "How do you expect to survey it in its entirety?"

"I wouldn't expect someone like *you* to understand the inner workings of a proficient squad such as the Kismet Task Force," said Sia. With grace and elegance, her feet left the ground as she took flight, concealing herself in a veil of invisibility.

"Really? Really! Now the witch can fly," snapped Josline.

Jude felt a hand around his arm, before Conall dragged him to the side. Suspicion and worry filled the Lieutenant's eyes. Eli was quick to join them, clearly consumed by, what Sia would call, the devil's nectar.

"I don't like this," said Conall clenching his jaw. His eyes looked up at the others before returning to Jude's.

"If you don't have the stomach for the mission at hand, you can leave. Go ahead, run!"

"You are way out of line Bray!" snapped Conall.

To Jude, this conversation was a waste of energy and time. He had no time for allies with weak knees and upset stomachs. "Look Lieutenant, the General and Tristan are dead. I don't know about you, but I refuse to sit and wait around until my enemy finally brings death to my doorstep."

"This is exactly how the General died," said Conall glaring. "She couldn't be patient, devise a plan and do things the correct way. She would be alive if she would have listened to me!"

Sia appeared in the midst of the conversation, causing Jude to look away from the Lieutenant's fuming face. "Not the best news I'm afraid." She gathered the group, positioning herself in front of Josline as if in an attempt to exclude her from the conversation. "I count at least two hundred well-armed soldiers blocking the entrance to the city. There are at least five to six magic users amongst their party."

"I can control half of them causing a distraction so the Lieutenant's team can take them on while we infiltrate the cold zone," said Pang.

"That sounds like the best idea," said Conall nodding his head.

"No." All of their missions seemed to count on this one. All mistakes would have dire consequences and all victories would have major rewards. Nothing could be left to chance. "Pang will need all of his blood energy. I can't risk him going into battle with Fox weary from helping your team do their job."

The Lieutenant recoiled as if enduring a small quake.

"I don't need a man to do anything for me that I can't already do for myself hun," said Josline shouldering herself into the group. "If you need a distraction, I can give you one."

◆ ◆ ◆

Conall waited patiently alongside the Special Operative, Jamieson Edric, while Josline and her ipseity stood face-to-face charging their power. The murky green aura consumed them both, enveloping them in a chain of swirling magic. The Kismet Task Force waited yards away, awaiting Conall's team to draw out the enemy forces and the attention of the spell casters.

I should have never let Bray talk me into this. We are supposed to learn from the mistakes of our ancestors not repeat them. He's putting our last hope for survival on the line due to his inexperience. What's worse, he's putting Sia in danger, something he shall pay for if anything happens to her.

"Raise the curtain boys," said Josline withdrawing her ipseity. She walked up to the top of the hill before stopping. "When the thunderous applause begins, that's your signal." With those words she was off, running hysterically down the countryside screaming in a panic.

"Don't worry," said Jamieson drawing Conall's attention. "She's invaluable on the battlefield."

"Seeing as how I don't have a choice, I will have to trust that you know what you're talking about."

Josline ran rampant up to the rows and rows of tan tents that blocked the city. Crowds of soldiers equipped with various weapons ran out to meet her in organized squads of archers, swordsmen and cloaked figures. Josline tripped and fell, landing flat on the ground, before jumping to her feet and continuing towards the soldiers.

Not off to a good start are we...

"Help me! Help me! It's going to kill me. Please! Someone help," shouted Josline waving her arms.

The soldiers stared at her and then looked behind her, staggering in place before pointing at the hill that Conall and Jamieson stood on.

"Dragon!" shouted a soldier pointing towards Conall.

The organized masses dispersed in various directions, abandoning the power of their unity. Archers formed two long lines in front of the tents, firing arrows as fast as they could load them. Soldiers readied their swords and axes behind the archers; ready to do battle with the enemy they saw. Screaming covered the hills, sending chills down Conall's spine.

"*That* would be the thunderous applause she was referring to," said Jamieson running over the hill towards the commotion.

Conall looked towards the last location he saw the Kismet Task Force. After deciding to abandon all S-3 devices due to the danger of the enemy tapping into them, Conall began to wonder if eliminating their only line of communication was a horrendous mistake. Summoning his shield and sword, Conall followed after Jamieson.

The archers were swift in response to their incoming danger. With a few quick hand formations, a rune appeared in front of Josline, before evaporating into the ground beneath the entire camp of the enemy. The archers prepared their bows. The bowstrings snapped as they fired, leaving them wide open for Conall's direct melee attack. The swordsmen and hooded figures quickly retaliated, closing-in with their weapons in hand. Jamieson went into a fighting stance with a blade and quiver of daggers—his ipseity appearing at his side with its bow and arrows ready. Running in front of Conall, the ipseity never stopped firing its bow at the incoming enemies. The targets it failed to hit, fell to Jamieson; who appeared behind the mass of enemies, slicing their throats without detection. With countless enemies, ignorant of who they faced, it was an assassin's paradise. Being a master of close combat and silent kills, along with the aid of his ipseitys long bow, Jamieson was more than a worthy adversary.

"Impressive..."

Owners cut war hounds loose from their chains before they stampeded for Conall and Jamieson. Conall and Jamieson's ipseity readied their bows, while Josline twirled in a straight line in front of them, leaving a green smog in her wake. When the hounds reached the smog, the ground caved-in, swallowing the hounds in an endless trench.

"It's a witch!" screamed a soldier, drawing the attention of his allies.

Thunder shook the sky. Josline's ipseity appeared in midair at her side, glaring with the same ferocity as Josline. "Why is it every time a woman outsmarts a man they call her a witch?" said Josline charging her hex. Her ipseity looked up at the sky, encasing it in a murky green aura. "You want a witch, I'll show you a witch!" growled the ipseity.

Enemy tents catapulted from their mounts, revealing pending ambushes and hiding enemies. Soldiers fell to the floor choking, grasping their throats and gasping for air. Josline's hexes continued to wreck havoc across the battlefield even after Conall and Jamieson took the opportunity to attack. Multiple incidents of bad luck continued to pillage the enemy. Random gusts of wind would knock them into attacks, enemies would swing their blades too hard only to kill an ally, and spells of enemy spell casters would charge up only to backfire—taking the lives of fellow allies.

For the first time in his life, Conall enjoyed being in combat. He felt as if no matter what he did, the mission would be a success. For every enemy he engaged in battle, Jamieson's ipseity appeared behind the foe; quickly ending their life before they knew what hit them. All projectiles that made it through Josline's magic were halted with the aid of Conall's total defense perimeter. The spinning shields not only reflected all projectiles, but opened up space in the sea of enemies, long enough for Josline to cast her illusions and hexes; and Jamieson to nail every surrounding enemy with a perfectly thrown dagger. Even though Conall hated to admit it, they were a deadly trio; and if the situation was different, he would want to take more missions at the sides of Jamieson Edric and Josline Verisity.

Their diversion was turning into more of a slaughter, with enemies trying to fend off the attacks of both the manifested dragon and Conall's squad. Ready to end it, Conall came up the middle. Then came the spell casters, dropping their hoods and exposing their hollow eye sockets and beastly fangs.

"Oh my Aegis! The damned walk the earth..."

◆◆◆

Eli thought about the time leading up to this moment. The pain, anger and vows of vengeance all resurfaced alongside his grief for Marius. There would be no mistakes and no way out. He had a sufficient amount of spirits before the mission began, and the tingle in his hands and the numbness in his lips made him feel at ease. Fox would die.

After slipping through the city gates undetected, Jude's Optical Tactics instantly located a subterranean chamber beneath the city's streets. According to Jude, a lone body lay still within the chamber's walls, giving him the confirmation that it had to be Fox. Dozens of traps, both physical and magical, filled the rocky path into the underground lair; however, they were no match for the combined abilities of Jude and Sia. Eli's comrades were quick to not only locate, but also dispatch, every trap and obstacle in their path. Stepping through a narrow doorway, Eli set eyes on a single body hovering above the ground in a ray of bright light.

"Target acquired," said Jude. The volume of his voice was normal as if uncaring of any listeners. He began towards Fox's hovering body, giving Eli the confirmation that the moment had come.

"Wait!" said Sia throwing her arm out to halt the squad. "We're not alone."

All Eli could see was the head he thirsted for hovering in front of him like a prize on a glowing platform. Fox was finally in range and helpless to defend himself. His revenge would come quickly and easily. "I don't have time for this." He took out his blade and started for Fox, smiling wider with every stride. Mere feet from Fox, a shimmer of sparkles rippled in front of him, giving him pause. Out of the shimmer appeared the nightmare from Eli's mission at Tarragon Mountain. The four Agents adorned in all white armor with black accents, stood tall and proud in front of Fox. White masks concealed their identities, except for the hooded agent, whose face was only concealed by her cloak.

"K.T.F. Operatives," announced the hooded Agent.

Her voice was familiar and tickled the back of Eli's memory. He was sure he recognized the voice, but still couldn't place it. Retreating back to the safety of his squad, he still couldn't help focusing on his prize hovering in front of him.

"A second chance at retribution," said Pang cracking his knuckles. "Fate is more than my ally today, it's my lover."

"Stay out of range of the Weapons Masters," said Jude looking from Sia to Pang. "They are both fully realized heirs; clearly traitors from our land."

"Abandon all thoughts of utilizing projectiles," replied Sia shifting her weight. "The spell caster has placed a barrier on all of them—including Fox. I can deactivate them but it will take time. Until then, no Blood Magic Pang; unless you want to be your own executioner."

"Eli I'm leaving it to you when it comes time to kill Fox, should he wake up," said Jude tightening his Geminate wristband. "Close combat is his advantage, but it's also yours. Can we count on you?"

Dad it's time...

"He won't make it out of here alive."

The hood of the cloaked Magi dropped, unleashing one last twist before the battle could commence. Meara glared back at them, her blue eyes filling with the dark purple of her Magi Glare. She walked to the foreground of her squad and smiled. "Annihilate them!"

SQUAD VS SQUAD

Jude already decided that this would not be a long battle. The longer they took, the longer their enemy had to adapt to their new strategy and style of combat. It also would give Fox extra time to awake from his slumber, if death had not already claimed him.

"Assailment formation!" commanded Meara. Her Weapons Masters asserted their way to the front, while the Combat Specialist took on the form of a dark wolf that instantly doubled its size.

"Battle formation Omicron!" Jude took out his vial, and with the aid of his Optical Tactics, saw his comrades grab theirs from their belts. After injection, four Jude's stared back at the A.R.S. The smokescreen came next, surrounding the chamber in a mask of blindness.

"All Agents go!"

◆◆◆

Eli and his comrades sprinted for Meara. Not knowing who was who, the Weapons Masters and wolf engaged the foe closest to them, resulting in Will taking a direct hit from Pang. The formation's only objective was to get them close enough to their enemy to engage without the threat of any magical or projectile attacks. Through Jude's Optical Tactics over the S-3, Eli saw Will and the other Weapons Master summon their blades.

503

Sia tapped Eli on the shoulder before portaling back over to Meara, intercepting her paralysis hold on Pang. The two Magi took flight, engaging in an aerial battle of elementals—Sia with her lightning and telekinesis and Meara with her speed and flames.

Will and the other Weapons Master came swift, assaulting Eli from all angles as Jude and the Combat Specialist went head-to-head as serpent and dragon.

"What's the matter Brassie," laughed Will pelting Eli with daggers while the other Weapons Master went in for a direct assault. "Am I too much for ya?" Pang interrupted the battle, absorbing the attacks from both assailants, and leaving a puddle of blood at his feet.

Will and the Weapons Master laughed. "Amateur!"

Pang's fatal wounds began to heal instantly until his skin looked as soft as a newborn. He turned to the second Weapons Master and smiled. "A new ability." Pang and the Weapons Master engaged in combat with Pang enduring any attacks that would get him close to his victim.

Eli ran for Will in an attempt at retribution. The sword dance went unstable with both Eli and Will matching every strike of their opponent. The battle erupted into both of them pelting each other with every projectile they could as their blades continued to tango. Will's projectiles were deflected by Sia's barrier around Eli while Meara's barrier deflected Eli's. Will's knee finally came up, kneeing Eli in the crotch, and forcing him to his knees. He felt like he was going to vomit, as he dissolved his blades and grabbed his crotch. Shaking off the nausea, he forced himself to his feet.

"Sia I'm ready." As Will summoned his bow, Sia glided by, with Meara hot on her heels, and tapped Eli on the shoulder one last time. Eli took short but powerful steps towards Will; building his blood energy with each step he took.

"Giving up?" laughed Will firing. His arrow was a direct hit, bouncing off Eli's forehead, and allowing him to continue his pursuit. Axes and arrows bombarded Eli as he continued to close the distance between him and Will while simultaneously building his blood energy. Will would still have Meara's barrier protecting him. If Eli's plan was going to work, he would need every drop of blood energy he could use.

"Uh Meara some assistance. Our little annoyance is being—well annoying," shouted Will.

The Combat Specialist ran to Will's side but was tackled by Jude in his arachnid form. When Eli was finally to Will, Meara appeared at Will's side, before Sia's portal surrounded her and teleported her to the other side of the room.

For the first time, rage and fear both filled Will's eyes. He lifted his bow and chucked it at Eli, who barely felt it when it fell to the ground.

"Checkmate." Eli exhaled, looked down at the ground, and unleashed all of his blood energy. A field of landmines lay underneath Will's feet, more landmines than Eli had ever seen.

Will gasped. "Oh—my..."

"Boom!"

The explosion detonated, sending Will to the ceiling and back down. The explosion caused Eli's ears to ring but did no damage. As Will's charred body turned over, Pang's laughter filled the air. "Blood Execution!"

Eli smiled and then walked over to Will and picked him up by his collar. The magic still drummed in Will's clothes under Eli's fingertips, but one of his eyes was swollen shut and he was missing teeth. "I won. You lost. The end!" Eli spit in Will's face. "Oh Pang my dear!"

As if he was death itself, Pang turned away from the Blood Execution in front of him. The Weapons Master's body hung lifeless by its neck. Pang grinned.

Will looked at Pang and then up to Eli. "Wait what are you doing? Kill me! Come on you hate my guts kill me!"

Pang stalked slowly towards Eli and Will, cracking his knuckles along the way. Eli dragged Will by his collar towards Pang, as Will kicked and screamed in Eli's grip.

"You weak piece of garbage kill me! Kill me!" screamed Will.

When Pang was close, Eli tossed Will at Pang's feet. Will squirmed to turn over, before looking up at the sinister grin on Pang's face.

Pang cracked one knuckle and then the other. "You better notify your next of kin!"

Will tried to crawl away but Pang grabbed his ankle and reeled him in before climbing on top of the Weapons Master. Pang ripped one arm off and then the other, causing Will's horrific screams to fill the air. Then one leg detached and then the other. The mangled corpse that was Will Keating stirred faintly in place as his eyes fluttered open and close. Pang gripped Will's head with both hands. "Perfecto!" Then the head gave way.

Sia tumbled from the air, face-planting at Eli's feet. Jude soon joined them just as the Combat Specialist joined Meara next to Fox's body. The body stirred.

◆ ◆ ◆

Jude readied himself as Fox threw his legs over the side of the altar he lay on, and stood up. The Tactical Emissary yawned and stretched, before noticing the spectacle in front of him.

"Just the two of you?" asked Fox joining Meara and the Combat Specialist. "What happened to Will and Qui?"

"Sir, Qui is dead," said the Combat Specialist.

"Shame," said Fox.

"Sir, so is Will," said Meara.

"Good I hated that kid. Talked *way* too much," said Fox shaking his head before noticing Jude and his comrades. "Eli Brassie is that you?"

Eli started for Fox, but Sia quickly grabbed his wrist.

"You *just* missed your dad. I saw him around the corner," The graveyard was buzzing with life," said Fox.

"Give the word Jude. Just give the stupid word!" snarled Eli.

An inferno ignited the altar behind Fox and his minions. A portal of flames served as the entrance for a guest no one thought would make an appearance.

"The point of an Anti-Resistance Squad is to prevent resistance," said Lord Egon. He was familiar. The memory of Aileen asserted its way into Jude's vision. The pain and tears in her eyes was so vivid, as Lord Egon dragged her to the unknown.

"Jude..." trailed Sia's voice.

"I know, we don't have enough blood energy to take on the four of them."

"But we can't run," replied Eli quickly. "We've been waiting for this moment. I've been waiting for this moment.

"And if we fall?" asked Sia. Her voice had traces of fear, a quality she rarely showed.

"If we go down, we take them with us," said Pang.

"We don't play around. We begin with the end."

"Agreed," said the squad in unison.

"Bring me the Combat Specialist," said Lord Egon brandishing his blade. "I would like a word with him."

THE FINAL STRUGGLE

"Battle formation Omega!" shouted Jude.

Sia and Pang retreated to the background, after Sia tapped both Eli and Jude on the shoulder. Eli pushed to Jude's side, his heart was pounding louder and louder with each passing second. He could feel his knees begin to shake—with excitement or fear he could not be sure.

The Combat Specialist assumed his serpent form, amplifying its size, and then speeding towards the squad. Meara took to the sky, showering the serpent in protective spells before readying her own attack. Jude assumed the diversion of his enlarged arachnid form, before Eli jumped on his back. Summoning his bow, Eli drew his arrow and locked his legs around Jude's body. The chamber rocked as the giant arachnid and giant serpent barreled towards one another while Meara readied her attack to fire on Jude. Sia's cloak of invisibility protected Eli from view, and gave him the time he needed to find his opportunity. The serpent sprang for an attack. Just as Meara was ready to fire, Eli's arrow buried itself into her chest—pinning her to the wall behind her.

The serpent screeched in the prison of Jude's web. Eli went to strike, but was scooped up by Jude in his gargoyle form, Fox hot on their trail. The serpent and Meara regrouped alongside Fox and charged after them. When Eli and Jude returned to the squad, Eli knew what needed to be done. He built up his blood energy, and met Fox and his comrades in battle. Fox opened his palm and attacked.

"Landmine!" The explosion was absorbed by Meara's attack. She had taken the bait. The portal appeared around Eli and soon he found that he switched spots with Pang and Sia. A swaying vortex built of blood magic and elemental magic towered into a screeching pillar.

"What is this tomfoolery?" demanded Lord Egon.

Jude appeared behind the Lord, landing on his shoulders, and hammering his head into the ground. He quickly back-flipped above Fox and his comrades, tossing a smokescreen down at them, and retreating to Eli's side. "This—is battle formation Omega."

Sia took flight, taming the top of the swaying vortex while Pang tamed the bottom. "Which means this..." shouted Sia before falling silent to the screeching vortex.

"Is the end!" roared Pang.

Both Pang and Sia thrust their palms forward, unleashing the screeching vortex upon their foes. A body shot out from Lord Egon, snatching up Fox, and returning him to the Lord's side. Meara and the Combat Specialist weren't so lucky. The vortex swallowed them up, spinning them violently in its belly like a tornado. Then the blood magic took effect, as the giant insignia formed at the base of the pillar, imprisoning its victims in a Blood Execution. Their bodies went limp and the vortex dissipated.

Jude's Optical Tactics sent an image of Fox on the move. Eli jerked his head to the Emissary, finding the Special Operative jumping to the wall and running along its surface. Jude's head jerked to Fox, before somersaulting to the wall, and meeting Fox's wall run with his own. Jude intercepted Fox's attack and forced him to the ground.

◆◆◆

Lord Egon's clones covered the entire battle as Jude engaged the Tactical Emissary Fox. The Emissary was quick and nimble but Jude was able to follow his movements. Fox consistently attacked with open palms. With the rest of his comrades busy with the Lord and his clones, Jude knew he was alone in this fight.

Jude swept Fox's legs, causing him to fall backwards, however, Jude didn't take the opportunity to attack while Fox was down. Fox's tensing when he went down signaled an anxiety linked to anticipation, which meant he was expecting an attack. Instead Jude flipped forward above Fox, just missing him, as Fox attacked forward with an open palm. Jude threw Sia a vial, who covered Eli and Pang in a barrier, before releasing the poison within. Dozens of clones melted before disappearing.

Fox swept Jude's feet from underneath him, but Jude used the momentum to flip behind Fox. Attacking one of the several weak points in the spine, Jude brought Fox to his knees. Spinning to face Fox, he attacked the third quadrant in Fox's chin, an attack that would have knocked him out cold if Fox wouldn't have evaded.

"Get off me!" yelled Pang before Sia's scream filled the chamber.

Jude didn't turn around in fear of being caught-off-guard. Instead, he continued to engage Fox while making a decision on what he would do next. Killing Fox would help stop the Lord's invasion however, without his squad, Jude didn't knowhow far he could get without them. The voice in his head told him to kill Fox, but he chose otherwise.

"Eli!" Jude released his thoughts and vision to the squad over the S-3, knowing his comrade knew what it meant. After all, the squad had already decided that Eli had the advantage over Fox and would be the one to kill him. With a quick portal from Sia, Jude swapped positions with Eli.

Clones attacked from all angles as Pang released blood magic attacks everywhere, turning the clones against Lord Egon. The Lord went on the defensive, summoning new clones to combat the afflicted ones. Sia served as Pang's defense, as he remained stationary in between attacks. Jude looked at his armband and realized the time had come. He unclasped the buckle of the two identical soldiers and retrieved the small vial within. He opened his thoughts to the S-3, allowing Pang and Sia to gain distance before the show began.

Pith be with me...

He injected himself.

◆ ◆ ◆

Eli enjoyed every ounce of blood he made Fox spill. The Emissary was quick, but was no match at close range for Eli. Summoning landmines with each step he took, Eli not only kept Fox on the defensive and away from attacking him, but also found enjoyment watching the annoyance in the Emissary's eyes.

The air became rank shortly after their battle began. A lone Necrosis ran freely amongst the clones, delivering instant death with each bite and scratch. Sia and Pang engaged Lord Egon, since he had finally left his position and joined the battle.

Fox jumped to the wall and began running along its surface in an attempt to aid Egon, but Eli summoned his bow and fired. Fox's body tumbled from the wall with a direct hit.

"No it's not fair! Oh Pith why?" yelled Jude drawing Eli's attention. His comrade was holding Lord Egon in his arms atop the altar, while Sia and Pang tried to pull him away.

"The time has come!" announced Fox. He jumped to his feet and started running for Eli.

"Eli don't let him get away!" shouted Jude tearing his attention away from the body he held.

Yes the time has come—for your end...

Eli summoned his shield and sword and prepared for Fox's attack. The Emissary limped but continued to charge Eli. However instead of engaging, Fox ran around Eli in an attempt to flee. Due to his injuries, Fox moved so slow that it was easy for Eli to block his path. He used his shield to bash Fox across the face. The Emissary tumbled to the floor and struggled to get up. Eli went to end it and instantly felt his nausea kick in.

No! Not now!

Eli's body broke into a cold sweat even though his insides were on fire. All he could think about was a drink. He attacked, but Fox knocked his weak attack aside and ran around him. Eli went to follow and instantly collapsed to the ground, shaking before spewing vomit everywhere.

"Are you kidding me!" yelled Jude's voice. "Sia after him!"

Two pairs of feet ran by Eli before he lost consciousness. He failed in his vengeance. The guilt made him hope he would never wake from the descending darkness.

FORK IN THE ROAD

The voices around Eli came-and-went. The headache on the other hand, showed no signs of mercy. He never completely awoke from his slumber, but would hear portions of conversation around him before falling completely back to sleep. Apparently something was wrong with Jude, while Sia and the Lieutenant hadn't been spotted in days. The voices of Pang and Vance were the most common, excluding the voice of a woman who Eli did not recognize.

Light assaulted his vision all around him when he finally awoke. Concerned dark eyes stared back at him underneath a swivel of reddish-brown hair.

"Glad to see you're awake," said the woman with a bright white smile. She put a hand to his head, appearing to look for a temperature. "My name is Alize. How are you feeling?"

His throat was so dry that talking was a task in and of itself.

"Water..."

A cold cup soon found Eli's hand. He guzzled it down before returning it to her in hopes of more. She obliged. "You're back in the safety of your home here in Geminate. You're safe."

"Well look who decided to forfeit the sleeping princess act," said Pang entering the room. He took a position next to Alize at Eli's bedside. Vance entered the room a few seconds later. When Eli locked eyes with Vance, he expected to see hostility, and instead saw relief.

Turning to Alize, he found a calmness under her presence. "What happened to me?"

Alize looked to Pang, Vance and then back to Eli. "Well, you see your body started experiencing episodes from the lack of alcohol. It seems like you've been excessively consuming alcohol and thus building your body's dependence to it.

"She means you have a drinking problem," snapped Pang.

"Pang," said Vance putting a hand on Pang's shoulder. He shook his head, clearly not approving of Pang's harshness.

"But I don't have a drinking problem."

Everyone's eyes in the room met.

"Since your body is so dependent on alcohol, and you didn't consume the amount it needed, your body started feeding on your blood energy in an attempt to fill the void of the alcohol," said Alize rubbing Eli's leg. "Your blood energy level reached a horrible low. It was touch-and-go for a while. You've been unconscious for going on several weeks now. I wasn't sure..."

"She's saying you could have died idiot," snapped Pang.

Eli stared at Pang, uncaring of his harsh words. "He got away didn't he?"

The hostility in Pang's eyes retreated and disappointment took its place. He nodded.

"And Jude?"

Pang shook his head.

"What about Sia? Where is she?"

"She and the Lieutenant have been staying in Praxis for a while now," said Pang yawning. "She contacts me every couple of days to check on your condition—and Jude's."

"We should let him rest," said Vance. He came and kissed Eli on the top of the head before exiting with Alize. Pang walked up to Eli, staggering awkwardly, before giving Eli a light punch on the shoulder. It of course still hurt. Then Eli was alone.

Closing his eyes, Eli willed himself to evade worry and stress. He focused on recovering and soon drifted it off into the safety of his dreams.

◆◆◆

Eli awoke to the familiar smell of light perfume and fresh linen. Sitting up in bed, he smiled at the visitor staring back at him.

"Don't push yourself," said Sia jumping to help him up. She sat at his side before handing him a cup of cold water. "How are you feeling?"

"Better now that you're here."

She waited for him to finish his water before retrieving the cup and setting it on his end table. She appeared uneasy.

"I had to visit you one last time before the move," she said.

"What move?" He felt bad news approaching. It was written in fine print in the core of her eyes.

"Mik and I are moving to Praxis—with Conall," said Sia. She studied him as if searching for a rebellion.

"But what about the squad. You're abandoning us?"

Sia shook her head and smiled, before kissing Eli on the forehead. She rose from the bed and walked over to retrieve her coat from the chair she was sitting on. "There is no squad Eli—not anymore. It's time for us to move on; for how long, only fate knows."

"What do you mean there's no squad?" He threw his legs over the bed and nearly collapsed when he tried to stand. Sia quickly came to his aid, helping him to his feet. That was when he saw it; the largest and most perfect, brilliant-cut diamond he had ever seen—shined effortlessly on her finger.

She took a deep breath. "Jude disbanded the squad after our last mission. So we're all kind of doing our own—."

515

"What is *that* on your finger?" Even though he realized the question was rhetorical, he hoped that she would surprise him with a different answer that would confirm a misunderstanding.

She walked to his bedroom doorway, paused and smiled. "Care to walk a lady to the door?" She waited patiently as Eli walked slowly to meet her.

"Please don't go. I have no one left. My mom is gone. My dad is gone. My best friend is gone; and now..." He grabbed both of her wrists and forced her to stop. The closer they got to that door the closer she was to leaving him forever. "I will do anything you ask. Please don't go."

She shrugged. "Eli I can't. I love him."

Her words staggered him. He nearly collapsed at their power, causing Sia to grab him when he nearly met the floor.

"But what about me? What about all of the things that we've been through? We were supposed to be together, not you and him. You can't just walk away from us."

She sighed. "You just have to accept the fact that sometimes people aren't put in our lives to stay. Sometimes people are put in our lives to help us find ourselves. Then...they're gone"

"Be with me. Forever."

"Eli, you are an alcoholic. You need help. Your actions are destructive and your lifestyle is toxic. I can't be around you—not even as friends," she said.

So now she was insulting him. In his weakened state and after all he said to her, she was insulting him. How could she not care about him anymore after all that has happened? It's so easy for her to just throw him away.

"So you're just going to stand there and watch me self-destruct?"

"You can self-destruct all you want, but you will have no one to blame but yourself." She continued towards the door, walking slowly and elegantly. "You know a long time ago, I once told you that you were unaware of how your actions affect other people. Look at yourself. Your lies and cruelty have lost you your best friend. Your alcoholism has taken away your honor, integrity and has helped destroy the closest thing we have had to a family since we lost our parents. What's funny is the ignorance could have been forgiven if a lesson had been learned—but you haven't. You still don't get it, which makes all of the terrible things that have happened a waste. It was all for nothing." She opened the door and paused. A single amethyst eye looked back at him through her new princess lock. "Mik and I will be in town for six more days. I know how much he means to you, and you to him, so take as much time as you need to say goodbye." Then she was gone.

Eli picked up his KTF boot and tossed it as hard as it could at the living room window. Glass fell in countless shards along the floor. Racing to the kitchen, he pulled open every drawer and opened every cupboard until he found it. The HC bottle shined like a beacon of hope. He drank and drank until his stomach rumbled.

Marius came through the walls and leaned against the counter. "Son don't. Please—stop."

"Shut up dad!" Tears began to stream down his face. For every tear that fell, he took another sip. "You're not even real. You're just the alcohol trying to make me feel better." The spectral ghost dissolved until Eli was alone once again. "This is all your fault. You did this to me. You force me to honor you as Squad Leader even though you don't deserve it. You force me to follow you along like some weak and pathetic puppy while you bask in the glory of honor. You turn your back on our friendship after all these years leaving me weak and destitute." He fought the urge to gag as he finished the rest of the bottle. His body felt right again. "All of that could have been forgotten but you decided to take away the last trace of family I have, along with the love of my life. If those weak and pathetic gods you pray to are actually real, let them be my witness that you, Jude Bray, will pay."

PATH OF THE ROGUE

The room was cold but bright with numerous lights, which confused Eli. General Mather signaled for his guards to leave them, before retreating to a long table on the other side of the room.

"Can I get you a drink?" asked Mather.

"Yeah. Yes—please." Eli didn't know what he hoped to accomplish by being here. Then he realized he was lying to himself. He knew exactly what he hoped to accomplish. The guilt was jarring until the first few sips of the spirits spilled down the back of his throat. Then the calmness came.

General Mather poured himself a glass before taking a seat across from Eli. "I'm glad you finally decided to take me up on my offer. No one should feel alone in these dark times."

"Look, I'm not here for a friend. I have something you want and you can give me something I want."

Mather smiled. "Go on..."

"The B.B.Q.W. *is* the Kismet Task Force, or at least was. Our Squad Leader was Jude Bray. None of us wanted to be a part of the squad. Jude forced us to. He threatened to have us killed if we didn't go along with it. The rest of us decided we don't want to be a part of the Kismet Task Force anymore but fear retaliation. That's where you come in."

"So...you want me to take *care* of Jude Bray. What's in it for me?" asked Mather.

"The glory of bringing a traitor of Geminate to justice. I'm sure the Priestess and the Geminate people would commend you *and* you get the chance to be rid of someone you hated from the start." Eli finished his drink, got up to refill it and then returned to his seat.

General Mather played with the hairs on his chin while smiling. "I like the sound of that. However, it will be difficult to capture the traitor since he doesn't trust me. But you on the other hand, he trusts you."

"Not anymore."

Mather got up from his seat and began pacing. "That could be a problem. What about your other comrades? We could use them to aid us in our mission."

Eli took another sip. "What do you mean?"

"I mean we can stage your other two comrades being imprisoned by some unknown enemy. Then you can run to Bray and tell him that your comrades have been captured. Even if he no longer trusts you, his worry will cloud his judgment. You lead him to the others, and when he's not looking, incapacitate him and leave the rest to me," said Mather.

"But Sia and Pang won't be harmed right?"

"Of course not. I look at them as allies—just like you. I promise you, you will be rewarded," he said.

"Alright, I'll do it." Eli felt the room turning and knew he had too much to drink. He put his cup down on the table in front of him and focused on the General.

"If this is to work, then I will need to know all of Jude's strengths and weaknesses, as well as the other comrades, so the battle is believable," said Mather.

Eli was feeling so much better after all of the turmoil that had transpired. "Sure. Anything you need I'll tell you."

"Perfect! You will no longer be a part of the Kismet Task Force. For this mission you will be our Rogue. But first," said Mather taking a seat in front of Eli. "Tell me about the beast before death."

CODE: 12

Jude's fangs sank deep into Lord Egon's flesh, bringing him to his knees, and eradicating the horrific mask that was the Lord. His dad, just as he remembered him, lay in his arms.

"Jude, my son, I have dreamed about the day when my eyes would lay upon your face, curse-free. Come, let me show you what has transpired since you last saw me—before I became what I am."

Jude sprang from his dreams gasping for air. It was the same dream he had night-after-night since the death of Lord Egon—his father. Jude kicked his legs over the side of the bed, and rested his eyes on the large damaged book on his nightstand—a gift from Lord Egon as life left his body. Jude had read it three or four times now. Each time made him angrier.

After washing up and putting some new slacks and a sweater on, Jude decided to check on Jamieson. It had been a while since he had seen his friend, and Jude could use a friendly face or even one of Jamieson's jokes right about now. Quickly descending the stairs, Jude opened the door, and set eyes on the last person he wanted to see.

"What do *you* want?"

"Jude it's Sia and Pang. General Mather has taken them!" said Eli panting.

Jude knew it was only a matter of time before the General discovered the squad's true identity. He had hoped that Sia would be long gone to Praxis, along with Conall and Pang, before the reveal.

"Where are they?"

◆ ◆ ◆

Eli found it difficult to keep up the charade, as the two of them made their way to the rendezvous point. The General was correct in that worry distracted Jude enough to allow Eli to lead his old comrade undetected. If it weren't for the cuts in the trees, Eli would have gotten lost in the Geminate forest. An open field soon spread out in front of them. Two bodies stood tied to two trees.

"Eli it's Sia and Pang!" yelled Jude.

I don't remember us saying anything about tying them up. Well at least he's thorough.

Eli followed quickly behind Jude and up to Sia. Untying the scarf around her mouth, Jude's hands began to shake. What looked like bruises and burns decorated Sia's face and arms. The same could be said for Pang, except his were more severe.

Artifice...

As Jude went to untie Sia, Eli summoned his blade.

"Jude look out!" screamed Sia.

Jude spun around and caught the incoming pommel of Eli's blade. It was difficult, but Eli soon over-powered Jude and threw him to the ground.

"Eli stop it!" shouted Sia.

Jude jumped to his feet and began to flee. An army of Geminate soldiers surrounded them, bows shining dangerously in their hands. General Mather stepped through the crowd with his arms firmly at his sides. "Take him!"

The battalion attacked, causing Jude to take on his gargoyle form and flee. Arrows followed his path, but were too slow to hit. The hidden Magi immobilized Jude, bringing him crashing to the ground. Jude retrieved a vial and injected himself, before taking flight. The Magi's magic now failed every attempt to apprehend Jude Bray.

"Jude run! Get out of here!" yelled Sia.

"Silence witch!" shouted a soldier.

Eli was sure Jude would get away. He was stories above them all and had a clear path to escape. Instead, Jude returned to the area and scooped down in an attempt to grab Sia and Pang. The soldiers fired, ceasing his attempt. Eli looked to the General and received a nod. Summoning a bow, Eli aimed for Jude. He knew Jude's flight patterns and knew where he would go next. As soon as Jude made a second attempt for Sia and Pang, Eli fired and landed a direct hit.

The gargoyle tumbled from the sky, crashing onto the forest lawn beneath it. His form reverted.

"Quickly the gas! Hurry you fools before the beast arrives!" commanded the General.

A canister of red smoke surrounded Jude causing him to choke. Seeing his comrade crawl for his life should have made Eli feel good, but he felt nothing.

Jude clawed his way up to Sia and untied her and then untied Pang. "Run! Save yourselves." As his body collapsed, Sia scooped him up in her arms. A canister of black smoke erupted around them, rendering Eli's comrades unconscious.

FINE PRINT

The Geminate prison was held in the dungeons beneath the Cathedral. The cold stone staircase led Eli down a spiraling path lit by hanging lanterns and horrific art. Finally getting the best of Jude should have been beyond blissful, but the feeling was late to make an appearance. Eli decided to pay Jude one last visit in order to revel in that feeling of superiority.

A broken lantern decorated the wall a few feet before Eli collided with a soldier. The solider summoned his ipseity and drew his blade to Eli. "State your business!"

Eli held up the badge the General had given him. The solider examined it before returning a glare. "Fine be on your way. But remember the rules, no food or water for the traitors."

Every cell was empty, except for one in the middle. A single dirty male lay haggardly on the floor. His cell smelled of feces and urine. What looked like fresh vomit sat in the corner. A lone green eye turned to Eli, peering around the scattered strands of dirty black hair before retreating.

"You know you brought this on yourself right?"

Silence.

"Everything always comes easy for you in life and you have no respect for those of us who have to work for what we have."

Silence.

"I could have forgiven all of that if you wouldn't have stabbed me in the back by disbanding the squad. Looks like I had the last laugh huh?" Eli began to chuckle but stopped.

A whimper came from behind Eli. He turned around to find a lone female inhabiting the cell.

"Just stop it! Leave him alone," whispered the prisoner.

Eli recognized her instantly. He grabbed the bars and shook them as hard as he could. "Sia! What are you doing in here? Guards!"

Three guards and their ipseitys came barreling around the corner, blades in hand.

"Sir?" asked one of the guards.

"Why is she in here. That wasn't part of the deal. She's not a traitor only he is."

The ipseitys slid into their hosts. The three guards laughed uncontrollably while elbowing each other.

"Right," said one of the guards before following the other still-laughing guards back around the corner.

Eli knelt down in an attempt to get closer to Sia. "I am *so* sorry. This wasn't supposed to happen. Not to you."

Silence.

"You were right. I *was* unaware of how my actions affect those around me—but not anymore. I will fix this! I promise."

General Mather sat slouching at his desk, when Eli entered his chambers. Bookcases lined the circular room while four or five chandeliers fell from the ceiling at various heights. The two guards, who escorted Eli in, took a firm stance at the door—facing the action.

"You wanted to see me?" asked Mather appearing un-amused

"Why is Sia Wyatt your prisoner? That wasn't part of the deal. Only Jude Bray was supposed to be your prisoner."

The General puckered his lips to the left and then to the right, while hitting the side of his face with his pencil repeatedly. "Yeah I don't recall that conversation. Besides, I'm in charge of the city's security. So what I remember is what happened." He smiled and then returned to his writing.

"But we had a deal!"

"Guards, Mr. Brassie and I are done here," said Mather. The guards were quick to apprehend Eli.

"What? You can't do this!"

"Don't worry Mr. Brassie, you will be compensated for your heroic efforts," said the General.

Jamieson stared unflinching up at the photo he held in front of him, as he lay on the living room sofa. The fireplace was beginning to become too warm and the silence in his house was beginning to depress him. Talon stood back-to-back with Jamieson, smiling back. His perfect white teeth and pink lips taunting Jamieson with their absence.

"I'm sorry..."

A hard knock pummeled the front door. Jamieson rolled off of the couch, hitting his face on the table next to him. He swore and then asked Pith for forgiveness. Scurrying to the front door, Jamieson clenched his jaw and knew it couldn't possibly be who he hoped it was.

Well you never know!

Swinging open the front door with an open mind, Jamieson instantly felt himself frown. Burying his face into his hands, he shook his head back-and-forth. "Oh Pith no! No! No! No! I *really* don't feel like knocking you out again right now." But then Jamieson noticed something off about Eli. Something was wrong.

"Can I come in?" asked Eli.

"No, but what's wrong?"

"I...I..." started Eli.

"So you finally betrayed your comrades by revealing their identity to General Mather and now you realize it was a bad idea."

Eli's head shot up. "How did you know?"

"Well it is *my* city and I *am* one of the top assassins. It would be quite sad if I didn't figure it out."

"I made a deal and the General didn't honor his side of the bargain. Now my friends are in trouble. Will you help me?" asked Eli.

Jamieson nearly fell over. "Wait a minute hold the bow and hold the arrow. You want *my* help? Me? The ankle grabber, the dainty, the person who you both verbally and physically attacked and *still* got knocked out cold?"

"I don't have anyone else," said Eli. His gaze fell to the floor. "Sia was right, I'm not aware of how my actions affect other people."

"Ya think?" Jamieson knew he was going to help Eli regardless of what came out of the blonde boy's mouth. He just wanted to mess with him for a little. Earlier that day, Jamieson had gotten wind of two incoming prisoners, who he later found out were from Kismet. Putting two-and-two together, he guessed at what had transpired. The only thing he couldn't figure out was what happened to the Quarrels guy.

"Get in here!"

BATTLE SCARS

Eli followed Jamieson through a secret pathway into the Cathedral. He left his ipseity at the entrance, just in case someone had spotted them and was planning an ambush. Eli didn't like Jamieson's plan but found himself in no position to complain. As much as he hated to admit it, he needed Jamieson. Jamieson was the only one that could help him save his comrades. When the familiar broken lantern appeared before them, Eli knew a guard was nearby.

"Alright Mr. Traitor, you're on," whispered Jamieson.

"Please don't call me that." Eli took a deep breath and continued down the path.

"Well it's true," mumbled Jamieson.

When Eli set eyes on the guard, he was relieved that it wasn't the same one from earlier.

"This is a level four lock-down. State your business," demanded the guard.

"But you don't understand, he's gonna get me!"

The guard drew his blade. "Who is?"

Jamieson loomed up behind the guard before opening the guard's neck with a slice of his dagger. "Me." Jamieson looked around before resting his eyes on Eli. "There should still be three more guards. You lay next to the guard I just killed and I will wait around the corner. When the first guard comes, you attack."

"How can you tell there were four guards? There were only three when I was here."

"Because I'm from here, plus there are four sets of foot prints in the dust beneath your feet," said Jamieson climbing the walls and finding a crevice to slip into. "Learn to see what you're looking at."

Eli laid his body haggardly on the floor in an attempt to reenact death. Two sets of footprints came before rushing to his position. "Call for back-up!" Eli snuck a glance at the guards and summoned a ceiling of arrows that soon pelted the necks of the guards. Their bodies fell hard.

Returning to his feet and dusting off his shoulders, Eli turned around to find two more guards staring back at him with drawn weapons.

"Don't—even—blink!" said one of the guards. A dagger buried itself into the forehead of one guard and then a second came for the remaining guard.

"That was close." Eli waited for Jamieson to climb down from his hiding spot but the Operative didn't. "Are you going to come down?"

"Stop right there!" yelled a guard from behind Eli.

Really? Five guards?

A dagger whizzed past Eli's ear and then the guard fell. It was then that Jamieson climbed down from the ceiling.

"Cardinal rule number one for being an assassin: Just when you know you've killed the last enemy, wait another sixty seconds just in case."

Eli mocked Jamieson silently when the Geminate turned his back.

"Oh no," said Jamieson coming to a halt.

Eli ran to Jamieson's side and looked around at the empty cages. "They're not here."

Jamieson led the way to the end of the path, which went in two separate directions. "The left path will take you to The

Never Ending Stairs. Tread carefully and be wary of any stray guards."

"Wait where are you going?"

"The dungeon, where the General likes to torture and dismember his victims," said Jamieson with a glare.

"Good luck."

Jamieson grinned. "You too."

After their separation, Eli took no chances at being caught-off-guard. He walked on the tips of his toes and kept arrows summoned above his head and a blade in each hand. He wondered what The Never Ending Stairs was and when he would reach them. The stairs he now climbed felt like they were never-ending. But Eli pressed on in hopes of saving Sia and Pang from a mistake he regretted more than anything.

Her screams desecrated the air around him, causing his body to cringe and his heart to shatter. The more strikes she took from the cat o' nine-tails, the more her pale skin was coated with the crimson stain that was her pain.

"Stop! Please stop!" screamed Sia. Her voice was weak and submissive, while her Magi glare continued to come-and-go; as if in response to the pulsing pain that continued to enslave her.

Jude fought against the chains that held him, hoping and pleading with fate that he could somehow free himself from the shackles that held him in the center of her anguish.

"Who wants to see more?" announced the General with a wide grin on his face, and a twinkle of amusement in his eyes. The crowds that surrounded them responded with applause, cheers and continuous signs of enjoyment and thirst.

"Look at me! Look at me!" yelled Jude as he stared at Sia's drooping head and motionless body. The air was filled with the sound of chains blowing in the wind while her wrists and ankles remained outstretched atop the cold stone floor that held them.

"Please—protect Mik Jude. Protect my brother," she said.

"No! No! We are going to make it through this," said Jude rocking back-and-forth amidst his shackles.

"This is the end. I can feel it," said Sia slowly tilting her head up. Her eyes were bloodshot and the rivers that fell from her eyes showed no signs of stopping.

"Again!" screamed the General.

Sia's head jerked in all directions. Her screams were heart-wrenching. With each strike, Jude's face was sprayed with warm fresh blood. The sight was horrifying and continued for an eternity in his eyes. After the next forty lashings her body fell. The crowd went wild.

"No!" screamed Jude. He felt his shoulder come out of socket. The pain was unbearable for the first few seconds before it intensified, due to the shackles that forced his shoulder to remain pinned in the torturous agony it just endured.

"Give her fifty more!" screamed a man somewhere in the crowds. His outburst was rewarded with cheers and signs of agreement.

"Sia look at me!" screamed Jude.

The wind gently blew Sia's hair away from her face, exposing her puffy cheeks, motionless eyes and blood-drenched skin.

"Fifty more!" announced the General.

The nine-tails failed to provoke any form of a response from her hanging body. No screams. No movement. Nothing.

"It's just you and I now," whispered the General. His voice no longer made Jude cringe. It no longer brought life to a once horrific nightmare. Instead it brought a command of submission, in which Jude humbly obeyed.

Jude looked in front of him and saw no movement from Sia. Her body continued to rock back-and-forth within the chains that held her. Her blood-soaked fingers did not twitch in response to the angry wind that blew. He was alone.

I'm sorry. I'm sorry I couldn't save us.

"All I need is one confession from you. *One* confession saying that you meant us harm in any way, and you will have sealed the fate of your people," said the General. The sensation of victory was heavy in his voice.

"I won't do it." The General slapped him. Jude instantly felt his nose break and his face swell. His squinting eyes watched the departure of the General's boots from view.

"Ladies and gentlemen. I give you—the leader of the traitors of Kismet!" announced the General.

Rough and hard objects pelted Jude, pummeling his body and shattering his hopes of survival. Boos and curses poured down from the surrounding audience in waves, growing deadlier as time passed.

"Bring forth—the cauldron!" yelled the General. His command was greeted with cheers and whistling, while the air sounded of heavy wheels across sandy rock. The temperature rose significantly, causing Jude's face to cry with discomfort.

Jude looked up. A large cauldron steaming with boiling water lay before him. Water rose and burst in response to the heat that empowered the cauldron. The heat was so unbearable, that Jude found himself coughing erratically. His chains fell around him. Just when he thought the nightmare was over, his back burned with intensity unlike any he had ever felt—causing him to scream as loud as he could. He jerked his head around to find the cauldron strapped to his back; boiling hot water spilling out of the lid and over its edges, ravaged his flesh. His jaw clicked in response to the screams that continued to fall from his mouth.

"Now walk!" ordered the General.

Jude looked up to find a long stone staircase, cascading down from the sun's rays. No top was visible. Along the staircase, stood ravaging Geminates on both sides. The look of disgust, anger and savagery sat present on their faces. More boiling water continued to topple over the cauldron's brim, scorching his flesh with so much pain, that his stomach turned. He vomited.

"I said walk!" yelled a voice as the cat o' nine-tails struck Jude's ankle, causing him to fall face first into the pile of vomit he had just spewed.

The scorching hot metal of the cauldron buried into Jude's neck, causing his mouth to open to scream, but only to choke on the vomit he lay facedown in. The weight of the cauldron was staggering and the heat was merciless, but as Jude returned to his feet and gripped the straps that held the cauldron over his shoulders, his eyes rested on the fate before him. He started walking.

"You're gonna burn traitor!" yelled a man from the side as Jude passed him on the stairs.

"I hope Anim feasts on your soul!" yelled a woman.

The more steps Jude took, the longer the cascading stairs appeared. He looked up towards the top of the mayhem he was climbing, and saw no end to his pain. Someone spit on him, causing his face to jerk away. His legs felt light and his feet struggled. The stairs bashed the side of his face as he came down on its rough surface.

"You will die on these stairs you Kismet scum!" yelled a man.

Jude forced himself up, only to be pushed back down by the heel of a merciless spectator. Jude looked over his shoulder and locked eyes with a young boy. He couldn't be any older than Mik. His eyes held the same anger and hostility as the others. He spit in Jude's face.

"Stay down weakling!" yelled the boy.

"Walk!" yelled the General from somewhere in the distance.

Jude returned to his feet and continued up the stairs. Sweat poured from his face, neck and chest. Hot searing pain sliced his back and depleted his energy. His eyes returned to the path that lay ahead, and all that greeted him was the endless stairs and the continuous assault from the Geminates, which rose up on either side of him.

◆◆◆

Eli walked out into the hottest day he had ever experienced. The sun's rays were blinding and the air that blew passed his face caused his lips to feel instantly cracked. He wiped his face.

Massive amounts of people circled around an empty stone area in front of him. Shouldering his way through the crowd of screaming and cheering people, Eli finally pushed his way through the last wave of spectators, and into the empty circle. There was nothing, except for a few Geminate guards that stood with empty buckets and thirsty grins. Eli looked back towards the crowd and noticed their attention was diverted towards some old stone stairs that spilled over the edge of the hill. A few footsteps brought Eli face-to-face with the steepest stairs he had ever seen. The stairs cascaded down for what seemed like miles—lined with countless angry Geminate citizens.

What are they screaming at? And why?

Eli stood atop the colossal stairs, staring down at the perplexing sight before him. Then he saw it. A lone figure slowly trudged desperately up the dry countless stairs that lay at Eli's feet. From both sides Geminates hurled garbage and insults as the figure continued to ascend the stairs. A large pot swayed from side-to-side atop his bare back. A veil of steam rose continuously from the pot while water fell from the sides, tumbling down the flesh of the stranger.

"Kismet will burn for your treachery!" yelled a woman.

A shutter ran through Eli just as the sun's rays parted, and the stranger's eyes locked with his.

Jude...

Patches of blisters caked Jude's shoulders and neck. Sweat littered the steps he ascended, and various pieces of garbage clung to his hair. His lips were parted while his chest rose and fell abruptly. Tears demanded attention against the sweat that clung to his face.

"Die you Kismet demon!" yelled a young girl next to Eli. The innocence of her face was only outshined by the brightness of her long blonde hair. However, her words lifted the mask.

A dagger shined in the sun's rays before it came down on Jude's back. Heartfelt screams covered the stairs as Jude collapsed to the floor. Water fell from the sides of the pot, burning Jude's flesh instantly upon impact. Steam and mist hovered in the air around Jude like a veil. Jude clawed up the last few steps until his hand grabbed Eli's foot unknowingly. A swollen-shut eye and a blood-shot eye looked up at Eli with fear, hunger and desperation. Jude's bottom lip quivered as he retracted his hand and forced himself up on one knee and then the other.

The smell of burning flesh filled Eli's senses as Jude trudged passed him. The large pot continued to spill steaming water across the blisters and red skin that covered Jude's back. Marks and scratches resembling lashings covered the back of his legs and his lower back.

"Jude..." said Eli. He could barely hear his own voice.

The circle of citizens spread out, circling Jude as he entered the uninhabited area Eli had ventured into earlier. The General appeared between the crowds, bringing with him several guards that followed as he approached Jude.

"It is with great pleasure," started the General while raising his hands to silence the crowd.

Eli stood frozen unable to move, as Jude's body collapsed to the floor. Steam rose from the flesh that stuck to the pot on his back.

"It is with great pleasure, that I give you—the hero of Geminate! Eli Brassie!" announced the General.

The once angry and hostile crowd showered Eli with cheers, whistling and applause. Eli felt a few hands on his shoulders, and turned around to find a few men congratulating him. Eli returned his gaze to the General in awe. Obfuscation became him.

The General waved Eli over, and he obliged. Taking careful and hesitant steps, Eli glanced at Jude's motionless body before taking his position next to the General.

"This, ladies and gentlemen, is the man we owe our lives to. This man, saw the treachery and dishonor of the Kismet filth, and decided on another path. He decided on a path—of honor," said the General. His words inspired even more cheering and applause from his spectators. A soldier appeared next to the General, carrying with him a glass box that shined effortlessly in the sun's rays.

"Let today mark the fall of the snakes of Kismet, and the rise of a great and honorable Lieutenant. Ladies and gentlemen, I give you—Lieutenant Brassie!" announced the General.

Wait, Lieutenant?

The words were mute and took a while for Eli's brain to process. There was no way the General was making him Lieutenant. The thought sent a smile to his lips, but also made him wander what happened to the last newly-appointed

Lieutenant—Talon Tatum. The box the solider was carrying opened up to the most stunning medal Eli had ever seen. A smooth gold medallion hung from a small royal blue ribbon. Etched in the medallion were two identical soldiers that stood back-to-back in front of the Geminate insignia. The gold nearly blinded Eli the longer he stared at it.

Retrieving the medallion, the General held it up for the crowd to see. The crowd went wild, chanting Eli's name and calling him a hero. The sight made him feel wanted and good. The General quickly pinned the medal on Eli's tunic, and then dismissed him out into the crowd with a flick of his wrist. The medallion felt right. It felt like it had always belonged to him.

"Now for the main event!" announced the General. The words caught Eli's attention, causing him to immediately return his gaze to the General, who commanded his men to remove the still-boiling pot from Jude's back.

Eli found himself nearly gagging when he saw the severity of Jude's swollen eye. The swelling appeared to cover half of his face. His other eye was swollen halfway closed. The eyelid was barely open enough for the frightened and erratic eye to surveillance the chaos around him. The large pot slammed down next to Jude, while the soldiers grabbed the empty buckets around them. Each dressed their hands with thick gloves before dunking their buckets into the boiling pot.

"You may now—begin!" announced the General.

Jude screamed at the boiling water as it pillaged him. Each soldier took their time filling their bucket with the scorching liquid, before hurling it at the piles of blisters that swarmed Jude's bare flesh. New blisters began to form atop the old. Clusters of blisters began to form like massive flesh bubbles.

"What are you doing?" yelled Eli.

"We are punishing the leader of the traitorous dogs!" said the General.

The buckets continued to release their scorching fury of pain and suffering. Massive burns began to form all over Jude's body. The skin on his shoulders began to shed and fall off. His skin turned red while his screams turned into shrieks.

"Mom help me!" screamed Jude in no particular direction.

A small voice told Eli to go to him. The voice told him to save Jude from the torture he was enduring, while another told him he wanted what he saw. The more Eli thought about intervening, the stronger his self-paralysis became. This was what he always imagined; to see Jude get exactly what he deserved.

Jude fell to the floor and began to crawl away. His body scurried a few feet before a soldier grabbed him by his feet and dragged him back to the center. His fingernails clung to the stone beneath him, peeling back before detaching from his bloody fingertips.

"Help! Jed! Big brother! Help me—please!"

"Hold him up! Make him take it!" yelled the General. Two soldiers held Jude up by his arms, stretching his body out as far as it could go. A bucketful of boiling water pummeled Jude's face.

What am I doing? That's Jude! That's my brother!

"Stop it! Leave him alone!" yelled Eli. He ran to Jude but was quickly apprehended by two of the General's men.

The General's head quickly whipped to Eli's position, the giddy smile vanished and in its place was the glare of a predator. His steps were more like lunges and in no time he was at Eli's side. "Say one more word or interfere again, and you're next. Trust me, yours will be worse. Take your treacherous medal and shut your mouth boy!" The General returned to his original position and regained his happy composure. "Let the judgment—continue!"

The scorching assault went on. Jude's screams grew more and more hoarse while his voice began to sound like that of someone three-times his age. Both eyes swelled completely shut.

So many clusters of blisters covered his body and face, that he was barely identifiable to Eli. The sight hurt. Eli fought against the urge to rebel and the fear of the punishment. Tears fell heavily from Jude's swollen eyes. His body began to tremble.

"Help—me," whispered Jude. His voice became faint. "Please. Somebody—anybody—help..." His voice trailed off into a whisper that was kidnapped by the warm wind, which covered his swollen eyes with his garbage and blood-infested hair.

"Now, everyone!" yelled the General.

All of the soldiers filled their buckets together and prepared for a simultaneous assault. Eli knew what was next. He knew how this would end. While Jude hung in the grasp of his captives, his swollen eyes remained locked closed and his body remained limp.

"Kill him!" yelled a man.

Eli turned away from the sight, causing the soldiers holding him to release their grip. Eli trudged towards the door he had entered through. His head remained tilted down and his eyes were too scared to open. The sound of splashing water filled the air. Just as Eli reached the door, his ears were able to catch the last and final scream of Jude Bray.

NEW PATH

Returning home one final time brought up a lot of emotion that Eli thought had died over the years. He hastily packed all of his bags and anything that could be of use to a wanderer on the road. Sia and Pang were gone and the revenge on Jude Bray was more real than ever. Eli decided it was best to take his medal and leave the city of Geminate. He had already written two separate notes; one to Mik and the other to Brayden and the others. He would drop those off discreetly on his way out. All of his things were nearly packed when a rumble sounded at the door.

Throwing his bag over his shoulder and his new hood up above his head, Eli crossed the room and answered the call. Jamieson stood staring back at him with blood soaked skin.

"What's with the bags and travel clothes? Going somewhere?" asked Jamieson.

"Why are you here?"

"I found her. She's alive," said Jamieson with relief heavy in his voice. He began massaging his shoulders.

"Who's alive?"

Jamieson rolled his eyes and shook his head. "Who else?"

Eli's bag dropped harshly to the floor in response to his shock. "Bring me to her."

♦ ♦ ♦

Jamieson washed and shined his daggers while Eli had some alone time at Sia's side. After a few minutes, the blonde boy took out a small book, which he had either drawings or writing in—Jamieson couldn't tell which. Alize came-and-went, checking on Sia's condition every half hour. The young girl had endured over three hundred lashings as well as being subjected to malnutrition and dehydration. The young woman was so traumatized, that her brain turned on itself, telling her lungs not to breathe, her blood not to flow and her heart to race as fast as it could. Using her ipseity's special ability, Alize entered Sia's dreams and calmed her mind. Afterwards she focused on feeding and hydrating the young woman. For the most part her condition was stable.

"Can I get you anything?"

Jamieson turned towards the kitchen and found Alize staring back at him. Bags were heavy under her eyes but she still looked as alert as ever. Her ipseity cleaned the kitchen ferociously behind her, while Alize dried a glass.

"No I'm fine. Thanks."

Alize studied Jamieson with such focus that he knew something was pressing on her mind. "How have you been since our last session?"

Jamieson recalled his sessions with Alize. They mostly talked about his longing for his parents who had passed. The conversation ended up evolving into his dilemma with Talon. While Jamieson knew the Geminate in Alize told her to scold and punish him for his feelings, the specialist in her remained neutral and helpful during their sessions. "I've been—content." He forced a smile before returning the last dagger to the quiver on his back.

"So you've made your choice?" she asked almost desperately.

He nodded. "I chose the will of the gods. Hopefully I will find some kind of peace or happiness in my decision."

Alize's face swam with relief as her shoulders fell slightly. She set the cup she was drying on a nearby table and pulled him in for a quick embrace. "You're making the right decision. If you weren't blessed with loving correctly, the least you can do is live correctly." Her words hit a nerve, but Jamieson ignored it. Instead he thought of what it would be like to see Alize and her ipseity battling each other in a dance. The thought brought him a few seconds of joy.

"Has there been any word about either of the boys?" she asked attentively.

"The big one has been sent to the Immortal Lands prison. We'll never see him again." Jamieson thought about his first time meeting Pang Quarrels. The young man seemed smart, witty and funny in a dry humor sort of way. Further down the line, Jamieson found Pang ignorant, intolerant and lost. However, even after all of the ill feelings that have made several appearances, Jamieson still felt pity for the young man.

Alize grabbed Jamieson's wrist, bringing him back to reality. "What about the one with the green eyes—Jude?"

"The last I saw him, his body was being taken to the Priestess' temple. The punishment mutilated his body leaving it deformed and barely identifiable. You probably wouldn't even recognize him." Alize clawed at her ears shaking her head.

Jamieson unbuckled his quiver and set it down next to a pile of old books that lay in the corner. His lips opened to speak and then closed. "The orders came from the Priestess herself, for his body to be taken to her. Somewhere along the transition, his body never made it to the Priestess."

Alize's eyes widened. "You don't mean..."

"According to the report, his body was nearly to the point of immobility. There is no way he could have left on his own. We believe someone has taken his body." Jamieson shuttered at his own words and knew that Alize had to be feeling the same discomfort. It was one of the many questions that had been running through Jamieson's mind ever since he trailed and then spied on General Mather's men after investigating the dungeon. What happened to Jude Bray? Where was his body now? Who took it and why? The longer he thought about it the more the yawns began to resurface.

"You've done a great deed today young Edric," said Alize clearing the dining room table. "Rest your weary mind. Life's answers only come to those who don't seek them."

Jamieson checked-in on Eli before his departure. The Weapons Master showed no signs of wanting to leave Sia's side, which Jamieson expected. If he was in Eli's spot and that was Talon lying on the bed, Jamieson knew he would never leave Talon's side—not ever. The thought was enlightening but the enlightenment was perplexing.

THE IMMORTAL PRISON

Eli tiptoed over the piles of dead bodies that lay scattered at his feet. Daggers sat wedged in the backs and foreheads of some of the guards, while the others lay lifeless with only a simple gash across their necks. The evidence of Jamieson's presence was everywhere and a relief that the mission was going well. The prison's walls and floors rumbled with the activity of the volcano they swayed in. Sharp pillars of rock decorated the ceilings while jagged rocks jutted from the walls around Eli. Prisoners glared at him from both sides of the path he walked. Some called out to him begging for their release while others spit his direction while slinging insults. A long winding river of molten lava continued to flow and bubble when Eli reached its edge. Hundreds of prisoners hung tied by their wrists to a single wire that draped them collaboratively over the river—their toes barely hovering above the lava's surface.

Eli's blood energy continued to slowly rise, but was still dangerously low after his scuffle with reinforcements who were clearly responding to some distress call from inside the prison. The temperature inside the volcanic prison was beyond dangerous while Eli's exhaustion fell to critical. Finding Pang as soon as possible was at the forefront of his mind, while the overwhelming fear of Pang's wrath raged in the back of his head. He knew now that he had done many horrible and unforgiveable things. Annoyed that it took him this long to realize the severity of his actions, he began to hope that he could find some way to persuade Pang to forgive him; and help him with what lay ahead.

Eli followed the river of molten lava until he came to an empty arch comprised of rock and earth. A weak but malicious laugh blew from its depths. Voices talked over the laugh while it continued to come-and-go. Eli pressed his back against the wall of the arch and tensed at the sweltering heat it attacked him with. Sliding down to the floor against the wall, Eli peered through the archway. A frail young man with dark hair hung from his wrists, bound by a chain that hung from the ceiling. The prisoner was nude, except for a small cloth that barely covered him from the waist down. Burn marks covered his entire body while pieces of loose flesh dangled from various parts of his body. A bench of various tools, both sharp and blunt, sat in front of the prisoner's scarred and swaying body. A large branding iron sat in a cauldron of molten lava next to the bench, boiling ferociously. Two Necroborn guards spoke casually in front of the prisoner as if ignorant of his presence.

"They're all dead! Every last one of them," said one of the Necroborns with his fist to his chest. He was dressed in dark metal-plate armor despite the immense heat.

The second Necroborn reached for the soaking branding iron, and retrieved it from the cauldron. His armor was slightly heavier and was far more luxurious than the other Necroborn. A gold pendant shined from his chest, making Eli conclude that he had to be some sort of Commander. "Impossible! None have ever set foot in The Immortal Prison that wasn't a prisoner. The volcano must be playing tricks on your eyes." He raised the branding iron high above his head and then struck the prisoner in the side. Heart-felt screaming, followed by villainous laughter, spilled from the prisoner.

"My eyes see the truth. The men are dead," said the Necroborn guard never releasing his fist from his chest.

"What levels?" asked the Commander returning the branding iron to the cauldron and dusting off his hands.

"One through four," replied the guard.

The Commander laughed hysterically. "That's it? There are over fifty levels in The Immortal Prison with over two hundred men on each level." He picked up a chain and tied it around the prisoner's neck and began choking him. "Whoever the intruder is, he won't get out of here alive. The Immortal Prison always claims the life of those who enter uninvited." The Commander dropped the chain he was holding. "Secure this prisoner's chains and follow me to seal off the first floor exit. Whoever the intruder is, I hope he loves to climb."

After tightening the prisoner's chains, the guard lead the Commander through another arch on the other side of the room—haste heavy in their footsteps. Eli waited a few seconds before barreling into the room. Instead of summoning a blade and expending blood energy, he grabbed a bloody scythe from the bench and slashed the chain that held the prisoner—catching him before he hit the ground.

Pushing the stray wet hair out of the prisoner's face, Eli stared down at a face full of burns, cuts and hunger. The man's eyes remained closed while his face kissed death. "Don't die! I need your help."

The prisoner choked.

"I'm looking for a prisoner by the name of Pang Quarrels. He was brought here less than two weeks ago—tall, muscular with dark hair. Have you seen him?"

The prisoner's eyes shot open with rage. "You! I'll destroy you!"

"Pang?"

◆ ◆ ◆

Jamieson reached the forty-third floor, on the back of his ipseity, quickly and covertly. The ipseity breathed heavily when they finally reached the prison's surveillance chamber. Jamieson looked at it as a small price to pay. It was better his ipseity be tired rather than him. He had already expended enough energy eliminating hundreds of guards on the first eleven floors. That would be the only spare time he could provide for Eli. The Weapons Master would have to fend for himself if any new threats should arise.

Climbing off the back of his ipseity, Jamieson recalled his doppelganger and climbed up the side of the surveillance room—keeping an eye out for any enemies. Nine Necroborn guards huddled closely in the surveillance room, looking out through a window that peered over the center of the prison. Jamieson summoned the hands and feet of his ipseity on top of his—a trick Talon had taught him—and like an insect, began climbing through the surveillance room archway. He quickly climbed up the walls, and eventually across the ceiling, until he hung upside down from the ceiling above the commotion.

"The Jackal should be here shortly. In the meantime, do anything and everything to prevent the intruder from escaping," said a guard.

Did he just say The Jackal is on his way?

"Do what you want, I'm getting out of here!" replied a guard. His colleagues nodded in agreement.

"You will do no such thing!" replied the first guard.

"Don't be a fool Kiez! The prison hasn't been the same since his grace Egon fell. We've all felt it, and I know you have too. Something is wrong!" said a guard.

The adrenaline began to flow while the truth of General Mather's involvement was clear. The General was working with Lord Egon before the Lord met his death at the hands of Jude

Bray. This collaboration went against everything the Priestess stood for and what the Geminate people fought for. The Priestess needed to be warned; but first, Jamieson and Eli needed to find Pang and escape before the General arrived. Jamieson knew for a fact that neither he nor Eli would want, or survive, a fight with the General.

Kiez drew a blade and an axe from his belt and pointed them at the other guards. "If even one of you attempts to escape before The Jackal gets here, I will hunt you down and take your head!"

The remaining Necroborns revealed their beasty fangs and growled. A few seconds of tension passed through the room before the opposing Necroborns retracted their fangs and bowed to Kiez. Just as they turned to exit, one of the guards turned around and halted. "We all know what's hidden beneath this prison; and I plan on finding it," said the guard.

In a quick flash, Kiez stormed the room slicing, stabbing and decapitating his comrades, until they all lay in a bloody pile beneath his feet. "Woe to those who uncover the secret that lays beneath The Immortal Prison." Kiez returned his weapons to their holsters and peered through the window at the prison before him. His eyes looked down at what looked like a map of the command center. His large hand snatched up the map, rolled it up and tucked it away under his armor.

"For all of our sakes I hope they're wrong," said Kiez pressing a button in front of him. Immediately all of the doors barred closed, imprisoning Jamieson in the room with the Necroborn. "Whoever you are, come out now!"

Perfect he knows I'm here...

"I know you're in here and I know you're human. I can smell your rotting flesh!" said Kiez drawing his blade and axe. He looked around the room until his eyes ventured up and found Jamieson.

Kiez smiled. "You're as good as dead!"

548

"I'm afraid you have it backwards," said the ipseity rising up from behind Kiez, causing him to turn his back to Jamieson.

"A Geminate?" mumbled Kiez. Right as the ipseity's blade came up, Kiez's hands released their weapons. "Wait! I'm on your side!"

Jamieson grabbed a dagger from his quiver and threw it. The dagger planted itself in Kiez's torso, throwing him to the ground. Falling from the ceiling, Jamieson landed easily on his feet. "No—we're not." The ipseity flipped Kiez over before disappearing. Jamieson grabbed Kiez by the collar and forced him up. "What were your men talking about? What lays hidden beneath this prison?"

Kiez coughed up a laugh, while blood fell from the corner of his mouth. "Woe to those who uncover the secret that lays beneath The Immortal Prison."

Jamieson snatched another dagger from his quiver and dug it into Kiez's knee. The Necroborn howled in pain before releasing another laugh. "The next one is headed for your unmentionables. Now talk!"

Kiez forced open his falling eyelids. "What my fallen men speak of are the five seals of Anim, the fallen one." Kiez laughed.

"Are you telling me the five seals lay beneath The Immortal Prison?"

Kiez grinned before wincing in pain. "You humans are so dumb. You all deserve what's coming to you. Don't you see? The seals have shaken, the seals have stirred—the Arch-Demon will soon be here." Kiez's eyes closed.

Jamieson shook Kiez but received no response. After retrieving the map from Kiez's armor he grabbed the S-3 from his boot. Tying it around the chain on his neck, Jamieson opened his mind to Eli.

CONFESSIONS

Eli rolled underneath the branding iron Pang swung at him with ease. While the rage behind the attacks could not have been stronger, Pang's weak body and low energy made his attacks as harmless as a slap across the face.

"Pang it's me Eli. Stop attacking!"

"I looked at you as my comrade—as my brother in combat! Your betrayal will be your undoing!" shouted Pang charging for Eli. Eli ducked under Pang's jab but didn't anticipate Pang grabbing him around the neck with his other hand. Dragging Eli over to the cauldron of molten lava, Pang snatched a second branding iron from the cauldron and hammered it into Eli's neck.

The agony from the iron was immobilizing. As the pain continued to rise, the paralysis from the pain it inflicted rose with it. Finally Eli released himself and then tossed Pang over his shoulder before falling to the ground in agony. The burn continued to bite at his neck while the smell of burning and rotting flesh crawled up Eli's nose. He grabbed his neck with both hands hoping the pain would subside. Pang jumped on top of Eli, choking him with both hands.

Overpowering Pang, Eli rolled over on top of Pang and pinned his hands to his sides. "Now you're going to listen to me dammit!" Eli reconfirmed his grip on Pang's wrists. "Yes I was the Rogue. But I didn't intend for any of this happen I swear." Pang spit in Eli's face. Not wanting to release his grip, Eli wiped his face on Pang's chest. "I was angry at Jude for disbanding the group and blaming me for Fox's escape. I was hurt that the love of my life was marrying another man. Since my father was killed it's hard for me to deal emotionally with crap that happens to me—so I started drinking. I wanted revenge on Jude because I never saw all of the times I have betrayed, mocked and took him for granted. I only saw how I felt and what I *thought* was the reason for how I felt. I went to General Mather asking for help in pinning Jude as a traitor. He said he needed to use you and Sia as bait but that no harm would come to you. He lied to me. He lied to me the same way I have been lying to so many people over the years. He imprisoned you here and nearly killed Sia. And Jude, I witnessed first hand what he did to Jude; and now I don't know where Jude is or if he is dead or alive. But it's only because I helped him. I was wrong and all of you were right. I *am* responsible for Fox getting away. I *am* responsible for our squad not being as strong as it could have been and I *am* responsible for you being here. I'm sorry Pang." Eli looked for any signs of surrender from Pang and saw only rage. "You have every right to hate me and to take my life. All I ask is that you wait until after I get you out of here. So please, help me get you out of here."

Eli climbed off of Pang and stood up. He had apologized and poured his heart out, something he was not used to doing. If Pang still refused to let Eli help him, Eli would never find out what happened to Jude's body.

"*Jamieson for Eli.*"

"*Go for Eli.*"

"*Did you find Pang?*" asked Jamieson over the S-3.

"*Yeah I found him. He's not looking too good.*"

"*We have to get out of here fast. General Mather is on his way and I know he will bring a small army of Geminate soldiers with him. We can't afford to get into a squabble with him, especially if Pang can't help us.*"

Eli watched Pang get up from the floor. His comrade's eyes never left him, but soon softened.

"*I have a score to settle with General Mather. Let him come. He won't lay a finger on Pang.*"

"*Stop being overly-dramatic. Besides, something else may be coming—something dark,*" said Jamieson.

Eli's anger subsided at the fear in Jamieson's voice. He allowed Jamieson's thoughts to pass into his conscience, and soon Eli saw the potential threat of the Arch-Demon.

"*Okay. Pang and I are on the seventh floor, how do we get out of here?*"

"*There's a secret exit half-way up on the twenty-fifth floor. That's our only shot,*" replied Jamieson.

"*Twenty—fifth—floor...are you joking?*"

Jamieson laughed. "*No time, even though that would have been funny if I was. I'll release some of the prisoners and cause a prison break. That should keep all of the guards busy. I'll meet you on the twenty-fifth floor as soon as I can.*"

"*Alright see you soon.*" Eli thought about the hundreds of guards on every floor that the Commander spoke of; not to mention the hundreds of bloodthirsty prisoners desperate for vengeance. "*And Jamieson...*"

"*Yeah,*" replied Jamieson after a few seconds.

"*Be careful.*" A few idle seconds went by, causing Eli to wonder whether or not Jamieson had heard him.

"*You too.*" Then the connection was severed and the closeness gone.

Turning to Pang, Eli was relieved that he was standing before him. "Ready to get out of here?" Pang punched Eli in the face. Eli fell to the floor clutching his nose. He checked for blood and saw none. He looked up at Pang, who had acquired a small smirk.

"Now we can get out of here," said Pang.

CHAOS

Jamieson pulled the lever releasing all of the prisoners on every level above the twenty-fifth floor. From the window of the surveillance chamber, he witnessed hundreds and hundreds of prisoners spill out across the volcanic prison. Guards attempted to contain the outbreak, but were soon overwhelmed. Prisoners looted weapons from guards they killed and used them on both guards and other prisoners. Jamieson opened up his mind to the S-3 in an attempt to contact Eli, but recoiled at something sharp blocking the connection.

"Come on Eli where are you guys?"

A large explosion erupted on the seventeenth floor disturbing the pool of molten lava that bubbled at the center of the prison. The magnitude of the explosion was staggering, which made Jamieson assume it couldn't be natural. He searched for the source, and smiled when he found it.

"There's our little troublemaker."

Eli rushed through falling bodies of guards and prisoners with Pang draped across his shoulder. Pang looked less buff and more fragile since the last time Jamieson had seen him. Even with their past of ill will, the sight of Pang Quarrels in such a weakened state was disturbing. Then Jamieson saw them. A large group of Geminate Agents cut off their escape when Eli and Pang got to the next staircase, which lay next to rows of large kennels. Eli's head turned around to the large group of incoming Agents. They were trapped.

Jamieson searched frantically around the command center for anything to help. His eyes found a small lever labeled: Prison hounds.

"Now this sounds like fun." Pulling the lever, Jamieson watched as the kennel doors next to Eli and Pang released dozens of ravaging prison hounds. Arrows fell from the ceiling killing two hounds that went for Eli and Pang, while the other hounds ambushed the Geminate Agents. Ipseitys were released everywhere by the Agents in an attempt to aid them in eliminating the prison hounds; while Eli and Pang slipped into the staircase.

That was too close.

Jamieson sighed heavily, watching Eli drag Pang's limping body up the staircase and to the eighteenth floor. The floor was empty of guards while prisoners still remained contained in their cells, allowing Eli and Pang to move quickly up to the nineteenth floor and eventually the twentieth floor. Jamieson knew he would need to leave now if he wanted to get to the twenty-fifth floor when Eli and Pang arrived. Looking across the last five rows Eli and Pang would have to cross, Jamieson spotted the hazard, he hoped they could avoid, descending from the twenty-fourth floor.

General Mather stomped down the prison hall towards the twenty-third floor staircase. At least twenty Geminate Special Operatives surrounded him, eyeing every inch of the room they stampeded through. Jamieson's head jerked down towards Eli and Pang who were coming to the twenty-third floor staircase and panicked. He tried to call Eli over the S-3 and nearly smashed his own head into the command center when the same sharp sensation blocked the connection.

"The General must have a Magi in his ranks that's blocking our connection." Jamieson watched Eli set Pang down against a wall, clearly giving him a rest. The two talked for a few seconds before Eli pulled Pang up and continued down the prison halls.

"They'll be massacred..." Having no choice, Jamieson pulled the two levers releasing all of the prisoners on the twenty-third and twenty-fourth floor. Inmates sprung from their cells attacking the General and his Special Operatives, but were easily slain within minutes. Jamieson pulled the lever for the prison hounds on both floors, which bought a little more time than the inmates had. Pressing the button to open the doors of the surveillance room, Jamieson looked from the remaining levers to Eli and Pang and then to the General and his men. "Please Pith, help me." He pulled all of the levers releasing the hounds and prisoners on every floor and then exited the surveillance room; hoping to make it to Eli before any of the other threats did.

◆◆◆

Eli targeted the incoming hounds, summoning landmines around their collars before activating them. A battle between prisoners and hounds raged on around Eli, while he tried desperately to drag Pang up to the twenty-fourth floor. The Immortal Prison had turned into absolute chaos after they had crossed the seventeenth floor. The cells for both the prisoners and hounds opened on their own, as if in defiance of the rebellion that was underway. In addition to the prison's own chaos, Geminate soldiers had stopped their progress numerous times, but were soon overwhelmed by either inmates, hounds or both. They were so close to the twenty-fifth floor that Eli began to feel a sense of relief when he got to the twenty-fourth floor staircase.

"Let me go first." Eli unhinged himself from Pang and propped his comrade up against the wall, so he could use it to guide himself up the staircase.

"Brassie just leave me. We both know you can't hold me and fight at the same time," said Pang breathing hastily. His eyes fluttered semi-closed before opening a few times.

Eli knew Pang needed healing now. It was then that Eli wished he had Sia or even Jude with him. They always knew what to do in rough situations. Eli walked up to Pang and grabbed his chin, making Pang look at him. "Will you shut up and stop complaining. I mean I knew I was stronger than you but come on Pang, even Mik could fare better than you are."

Pang's brow and lip curled. He forced himself to stand on both his legs and shook his head at Eli before laughing to himself. "You always did talk too much."

Eli laughed slightly before treading up the staircase, cautious of any hidden enemies. After they reached the twenty-fourth floor, Eli held his arm out to stop Pang. The two of them stared at the dead bodies that lay scattered across the twenty-fourth floor. A Geminate Operative went head-to-head with a small group of inmates who fell quickly to his blade. When only one prisoner was left, a prison hound emerged from one of the cells from behind the Operative. Pouncing on his back, the hound ripped into his neck with its rigged fangs. After the Operative was dead, the hound looked to the prisoner who remained still. The two stared at one another for a beat before the hound sprinted for the staircase to the twenty-fifth floor—the prisoner following hastily behind him.

"Come on Pang."

The dead bodies were quite the hassle to maneuver around while trying to hold Pang up. The further they walked, the more weight Pang put on him. When they finally got to the staircase, Eli decided they would both ascend it together.

"Do you remember when you hated my guts?"

"It wasn't you I hated, it was your little loud mouth boyfriend," said Pang coughing. "Why do you think I barely went after you in the trials and why I didn't kill you when you were under the control of my Blood Domination?"

Eli shook his head at the confession of Pang and the truth that Eli had looked at Pang all wrong from the very beginning. "Jude was right."

"Huh?" asked Pang ascending the last few steps.

"I judge people before knowing them."

"Ya think?" fired back Pang shaking his head. "Why do you think you're such a little—." Pang collapsed to the floor in convulsions.

"Pang!" Eli fell to the floor alongside Pang just as the sound of metal-to-metal sprang from the corridor in front of him. "Just a little further okay? I promise, I *promise* we're almost there." Eli threw Pang's arm over his shoulder and forced him to his feet. Turning to the twenty-fifth floor, Eli saw large open archway leading out to the night sky, and next to it saw the heated battle of Jamieson and General Mather going at each other with everything they had.

General Mather threw a flask on the floor that shattered into a puddle of ooze. Gooey creatures formed and darted for Jamieson, binding his legs and holding him in place while the General approached him. Grabbing Jamieson by the neck, the General spit in his face. "I know that blonde little shit is here! Tell me where is or die!"

Jamieson stared.

The General shook his head in disappointment. "You would die for them and turn your back on our people? Why? I demand to know why!"

"Jamieson!"

Jamieson and the General turned around immediately, eyeing Eli with shock.

"I tested my hypothesis and the results couldn't be any clearer. Find one enemy, you find them all," said the General smiling.

"Eli the door on the right! Go on, get out of here!" shouted Jamieson. His ipseity formed in front of the General, just as the General began closing the distance between him and Eli. General Mather and the ipseity crossed blades in a lighting-fast match, while Jamieson released himself from the creatures that bound him.

Eli locked eyes with Jamieson, and after receiving a nod, headed for the exit.

ABANDON ALL
HOPE...

Pushing Pang into the night air, Eli's stomach dropped at how high up he was. The volcano roared while geysers of molten lava sprang up into the night sky. The sight felt comforting for a while until Eli began to have a hard time breathing.

"Do you feel that?" asked Pang amidst the sound of rising and falling molten rock. "Something is wrong."

The night sky turned darker, demanding Eli's attention. A dark shade covered the stars and moon. A violent wind began to blow just as thunder shook the sky and released the rainfall. Eli looked at the remaining floors above him and saw prisoners and hounds collaborating on the balconies over their floors—peering at mother nature's call-to-order. More and more geysers of molten lava continued to erupt from the volcanic pool beneath Eli until the earthquake awoke, knocking Eli and Pang to the ground. Looking over the edge, Eli watched as the molten lava began to turn until a whirlpool of hot lava swirled and swayed. Lightning began to light the sky, striking the volcano multiple times, and sending chunks of volcanic rock tumbling into the blazing whirlpool below.

The lava soon turned black and continued to turn. The temperature in the air dropped from boiling to freezing. The sound of a screeching horse came from beneath them, followed by a galloping echo. From the depths of the black whirlpool, emerged a pale horse saddled by a dark cloaked figure, wielding a pulsing blade.

"Black as coal. Red as blood. The stars of heaven shall fall like all who oppose him," echoed the volcano as the horse and rider ascended to the night air. The silhouette of the horse blocked the moon as the dark figure's red eyes pierced the night. He swung his blade twice before stabbing the stars. "Rune no more. Pith no more. Aegis no more." The horse reared back on its hind legs while calling to the night sky. A black hole appeared around them, swallowing them whole and returning the night sky to its once peaceful state.

"Show off," coughed Pang.

The dark shadows began to move. Painful moans crept out from the shadows, along with the echo of gnashing teeth. Dark creatures with tormented eyes, grinding teeth and bodies embodying the silhouette of a person, detached from the shadows and collectively appeared on every floor of the prison. Prisoners screamed and fled with the hounds hot on their heels.

"What are those things?"

Pang coughed, spewing blood on the rocky floor beneath him. "You ignorant fool! They're demons! Don't you read the sacred text?"

"I thought they were just a myth to scare kids into behaving."

Pang's hand grabbed a hold of Eli's jaw, forcing him to look at the demons diving into the bodies of fleeing prisoners and hounds—forcing them to claw their eyes out, before turning to attack others fleeing.

"Time to go!"

The volcano began to collapse, rumbling as the bottom floors began to detach and spill into the inferno below. The volcano wouldn't last long. Eli looked around for the rendezvous point just on the other side of the lava pool. They were going to make it. Eli forced Pang to begin walking. Climbing over rocky ledges and under fallen boulders, Eli took the lead, helping Pang up when he needed him.

A dark shadow rose from the ground, blocking their path. "Heir of Aegis, your body is mine!" In a flash the demon dove into Eli's body, swallowing him into darkness.

He felt his hands glide across his face, his teeth assault his tongue repeatedly and the thirst to destroy himself and all around him take over. Bishop's violet eyes opened and closed amidst the darkness, then the rocky terrain returned. The assaulting demon appeared, turning from black to navy before its combustion.

"Eli answer me!" yelled Pang.

Eli snatched Pang up from the floor and forced him to run. "I'm okay. Keep moving!" The two of them hurried across the ridge, finding an alternate route whenever a demon would block their path. After possession, many prisoners, Operatives and hounds jumped to their doom, with no attempts at salvaging their lives. The untainted ran frantically searching for a way out of the volcano and away from their dark assailants; while others climbed its collapsing walls. Then the rendezvous point rose up ahead of Eli. Mik stood by clutching the reins of the steeds that would deliver them from this nightmare. His tall arm waived back at Eli when he saw them.

"We made it Pang!" The words felt so good to say.

"Making it to me is laying face-down on a nice warm bed with dead silence around me," replied Pang.

Eli smiled and then laughed. He helped Pang across the last bridge while the rumbling continued to grow, until the sound of detachment caused Eli to cease and look up. A large boulder fell quickly above them. Eli pushed Pang out of the way. The boulder crushed the bridge, leaving a large trench between them and the rendezvous point. After they returned to their feet, Eli helped Pang over the remaining portion of the bridge and towards the trench.

"We'll have to jump."

"Do I look like I'm in the mood to jump?" said Pang unhinging himself from Eli's grasp. Boulders began to fall behind them, taking the floor with them. "Fine, fine, fine! On three!"

Eli jumped, alongside Pang, across the trench. The ground became closer-and-closer, along with the light at the end of their mission. Then at the corner of his eye Eli saw him. General Mather soared through the air towards them with his powerful grip leading him. Eli bent down grabbing his legs, which caused him to fall quicker to the floor, evading the General completely.

Pang bellowed.

Eli rolled to his feet and looked back to find the General and Pang freefalling while entangled in a brawl.

"No!"

Demons surrounded Eli. He closed his eyes and thought of Bishop's eyes, and the power they brought him the last time. He opened his eyes with clarity, summoning a bow encased in amethyst, Eli fired. Demons fell in growls and explosions instantaneously. Pang and the General fell a few floors before hitting a still-intact rocky floor. Molten lava rose and fell on all sides of them. Eli ran for the cliff next to him and jumped down to the next floor. Leaping over ledges and climbing down walls, he rushed to get to the same level as Pang. The General jumped to his feet, followed by Pang, who looked like he was ready to defend himself, despite his weakened state.

The General drew two blades. "You won't get away you Kismet scum!" The floor beneath him began to chip away, causing the General and Pang to stagger.

Eli became angered by Pang's stubbornness. "Run Pang! Run!"

Pang turned away from the General and tried to flee. Limping as fast as he could, Pang ignored the pillars that continued to fall around him. The General sprinted for Pang, covering more ground while Pang limped away, clutching his injured leg. Demons lunged after them, falling from overhead and clawing their way up from beneath. Eli's assault began. He ran along the ridge, dispatching demons with every infused arrow he fired. Leaping down to the final floor, Eli ran to Pang.

"I'm coming Pang!" He was almost across the final bridge that would bring him to Pang when another boulder fell, shattering the bridge in front of Eli, and preventing him from venturing further. "No! Come on!" Both his hands grabbed the sides of his head while he desperately searched for a solution.

Pang tripped and eventually fell, sliding slightly before coming to a stop. The General jumped and landed over Pang—blades drawn. Eli summoned a bow and drew an arrow. An ipseity appeared in front of the General, catching his blades as they came down.

Jamieson jumped on the General's back, blood pouring from his face. "Run stupid! Run!"

Pang looked back at Jamieson and then forced himself up to his feet. The General went head-to-head with Jamieson and his ipseity; with Jamieson's ipseity saving him just as the General saw an opportunity to strike. Pang finally found the will to run and looked around frantically for an escape.

Eli eyed a section of the trench that was more manageable. "Pang over here!" Tremors and cracking floors disheveled Pang while he continued to flee but he pressed on, running as fast as he could.

Jamieson screamed.

"You insignificant, filthy specimen!" shouted the General as he jumped down to Pang's level and ran for him.

Eli could see the fear in Pang's eyes as he ran the border of the trench looking for an option other than the inevitable.

"Pang you have to jump!"

"I won't make it," shouted Pang.

"No you won't. I'll make sure of that," shouted the General in hot pursuit.

"Yes you will. Trust me!"

Pang kept his eyes locked with Eli. He nodded and then quickened his pace. Eli slid to a halt just as Pang ran for the edge and jumped. The General attacked; his blade licking the back of Pang's leg. Pang recoiled mid-jump but his eyes remained glued to Eli's.

He's not going to make it...

Pang extended his hand for the cliff but was too far away to make it. His body shook when Eli caught his wrist. The sweat from Pang's hand made it difficult to get a grip but Eli found one anyways. His comrade's body swayed above the rising pool of molten lava.

Pang looked down at the lava swirling beneath him. "Eli."

"Yeah buddy."

Pang turned his gaze from the lava up to Eli. "I don't want to die." A tear formed at the corner of Pang's eye but refused to fall.

"You're not going to! You're going to make it you hear me?" Footsteps scuffled behind Eli. Turning his head behind him, he set eyes on the dozens of Geminate Special Operatives surrounding him with their blades and ipseitys ready to attack. He looked back down at Pang, still dangling from his grip and began to pull him up. A projectile whizzed in front of him and barely missed Pang.

The General stood on the other side flinging attacks, until Jamieson tackled him to the ground, locking eyes with Eli. Eli turned around and found Jamieson's ipseity trying to hold off the incoming Operatives. The Operatives went into formation, dodging attacks and landing blows on the ipseity. Jamieson screamed in front of Eli, even though the General had not landed an attack.

When his ipseity takes damage, so does he...

"Mik! Help!"

A small silhouette ran into view, maintaining its high vantage point. "Yes! Mik for the win!" Arrows began to rain from the sky. Operatives fell as Mik's arrows pierced their throats and chests. The ipseity soon took back control over the tide of battle with the aid of Mik's ambush. Eli looked back down at Pang and began to pull him up with two hands.

Jamieson screamed.

A sharp pain struck Eli's shoulder causing him to release Pang and then grab him again. The General fired arrows one after the other. "Pang I need help, you'll have to climb."

Pang began to climb up Eli's arm as Eli pulled as hard as he could. The General fired another arrow that missed and dug into a boulder above Eli. The boulder fell fast, picking up more speed as it closed in. It would crush Eli.

"Pang hurry!"

The boulder came in closer. Eli rolled to the side dodging the boulder. A tremor erupted shaking his grip on Pang. The stronger the tremor got, the further Pang slipped.

"Eli I'm falling!" screamed Pang.

"No, I got you!" Eli heard an arrow fire and then the pain took over his other shoulder, causing his hands to loosen their grip. "No!"

Pang looked up with wide eyes screaming, as he slowly fell into the molten abyss beneath him. The lava rose when his body entered. His body immediately caught fire as he kicked and screamed in an attempt to escape. The thrashing subsided and his body sank, finally covering the orphaned hand decorated with the ring of Isaac Quarrels.

SECOND CHANCES

Jamieson removed the hot water from the flame and poured it into the patiently waiting teacup. The lemon on the saucer, which the cup stood on, shined bright despite the darkened mood. Alize entered the kitchen with old blood-soaked rags. She grabbed the hot tea from Jamieson's shaking hands and kissed him on the forehead.

"You are a great man," said Alize tilting her head. "I believe Pith himself couldn't be more proud."

Alize stared aggressively, as if trying to unearth some sort of truth. "May I ask you something?"

Jamieson locked eyes with her. "Sure."

"Why do you do so much for those who have done so little for you?" she asked softly.

Brainstorming for the best response, he came up with nothing—but the truth. "It's the right thing to do."

Silence.

Alize's ipseity took over, darkening her appearance in a black aura. "If you think your good deeds will make it okay to give-in to your sinful, lustful feelings then you're wrong. Those feelings are an abomination that will secure your place with Anim if you act on them."

Jamieson laughed. "Someone got up on the wrong side today. Get it, wrong *side*."

Alize's ipseity retreated, restoring the balance. She exited the kitchen and took a turn for Eli's bedroom.

Hmm, guess she didn't get it.

THE BLOODLINE REVELATIONS

The escape from The Immortal Prison was a nightmarish struggle that would traumatize Jamieson for the rest of his life. His ipseity took massive damage, causing Jamieson's body to instantly recall it. After landing a few direct hits on the General, many of the Special Operatives ignored Eli and came to the General's rescue, scooping him up and retreating while others engaged Jamieson. The collapsing volcano aided Jamieson in his escape but that wasn't the hard part. When he finally got to Eli, he realized the hard part wasn't completely over. The young Weapons Master still hung over the cliff looking down at the molten lava that now covered the body of his fallen comrade. No matter how much Jamieson tugged and screamed at Eli, he wouldn't budge. His grief had chained him to the final resting place of Pang Quarrels. It took Sia's younger brother, Mik, to shake Eli from the mental prison he had imprisoned himself in. The horses aided them in their escape, but the failure of their mission set the guilt against them, causing Eli to falter into a darkened state of unconsciousness. Alize came to Eli's house as soon as she received word from Jamieson. Eli had already awoken, but stared motionlessly at the wall in front of him. After a few failed attempts at conversation, Jamieson abandoned his hopes of shaking Eli from his agony.

Jamieson walked into the living room and set eyes on a shattered living room window. A long black boot sat beneath it. Taking a seat in one of the chairs, he thought back to their mission and wondered if there was anything he could have done to make the mission end in success and not death.

"He will come around," said Alize entering the room. "Greif is hard, but rarely fatal."

"Thanks." He returned to his thoughts and staggered when he saw Alize standing in front of him.

"Why did you do it?" she asked.

Jamieson felt his forehead scrunch. "I already answered that but you didn't like my answer, remember? Something something hell, something something abomination, something something Anim. Remember those words?"

Alize sat down in the seat in front of him. "Why did you help *him* specifically? Jude told me in one of our sessions that he was cruel and intolerant towards you and that he didn't deserve a friend like you."

"Jude said that?"

Alize nodded.

"I don't know why. I guess, beneath the cruelty, beneath the lies, beneath the selfishness and ignorance, I see a man. I see a man who sees who he was and knows who he wants to be."

"And who does he want to be?" asked Alize softly.

"Only he knows that. I just see a chance at change when I look into the blue of his eyes; and I am a man who believes in second chances."

A NIGHT WITH THE DAMNED

The cold woke Jude from his painful slumber. The familiar sound of Jed's voice caught his attention, but he kept his eyes closed. His body was mutilated and barely responded to his will—he was dying. Perhaps it was for the best since his captives now loomed over his body sniffing his flesh.

"Get away from him!" snapped Jed.

"I am underworld leader of this clan you peasant! You will refrain from disrespecting me with your wicked tongue," said the stranger.

"Forgive me," replied Jed.

"I shall not. But *you* shall remember our deal."

"I won't as long as *you* don't remember our deal," replied Jed raising his voice. "You get his blood and I get his body."

"Are you sure this will work? I will drag you down to Anim myself if you double-cross me" said the stranger.

"A sip of his blood and you and your entire clan will be able to walk in the sun just like me," replied Jed. "But you can't bite him. If you bite him he will turn into us and his blood will be of no use to you."

"My clan is full and he has no place with us," replied the stranger. "I have to ask, why is his body so important to you?"

"His body still holds the magic of Pith in its blood and bones. I know someone who can make his body my own, and restore the abilities I lost so long ago," said Jed.

"A vampire infused with the magic of the three brothers? Impossible!"

Silence.

"I see. So it's power you seek," continued the leader. "You seek a way to become more powerful than I. You aim to slay me and take over this clan by our ancestor's sacred right of passage."

"Even if that *was* my plan, we both know you need me. So stop stressing about my motives and make sure your clan is fed and ready for the march on Praxis and the return of our dark lord," said Jed.

A hiss filled the air and then nothing.

"Hey you hungry," hissed a voice.

Jude opened his eyes to find a pair of familiar all white eyes staring down at him. A young man with short snow-white hair stared at him with fangs drawn. Jude opened his mouth to speak, but his tongue was too swollen to form words. He nodded.

The vampire handed him a bread roll and a dirty cup of water. He stared anxiously back at Jude waiting for him to eat. Jude took the roll and ate it slowly, wincing at the pain in his jaw and tongue. The water was icy cold and felt good to his tongue and throat.

"Thank—you."

The vampire hissed. "My name is Damien. After I was bitten, my soul was born out of the fourth realm of hell—the realm of chaos. It's a pleasure to meet you." Damien appeared on the other side of Jude and poked his cheekbone with his finger. "Is it true what they say about your blood?"

Jude studied the thirst in Damien's eyes. "Yes, and more."

"More?" hissed Damien.

"Yes. My blood can allow you to live in the sun. But that's not all it can do with *my* help."

"Well what else could there be?" quizzed Damien.

Jude forced a smile. "Bring me to the Hallowed Sanctum in Mt. Perennial and I will make you more powerful than your Underworld Leader."

Damien hissed. "Deceiver! Mutiny!"

"Why do you think they brought me here instead of just killing me or turning me?"

Damien stared.

"Your Underworld Leader plans to drink my blood so he can live in the sun like my brother Jed. He plans to use me to secure his position as Underworld Leader and remain more powerful than all of you. Then he will dispose of me. The only person left to level the playing field. Call me what you wish. My life is over. I feel my clock waiting to stop any minute now—and I fear no death."

Damien revealed his fangs and then was gone. Jude shrugged off the failure. He didn't care about what lay ahead or what would come. The journal of Lord Egon provided much insight into the gods and their deception. Jude kicked himself for blindly following the three brothers considering the massive secret they withheld from him and his family—not to mention the pain and turmoil they had caused his father Mathias. Jude knew that if his body had not been handicapped at the hand of Eli's betrayal, he would get revenge on the gods for their cruelty.

Damien appeared. "We leave now! Make a sound and I will snap your neck."

INNOCENCE LOST

Hallowed Sanctum was now home to grotesque bats and hordes of spiders and their webs. Skeletons and dried bloodstains were the norm in the inner chambers. A heavy presence was definitely here and that reassured Jude that he had followed Lord Egon's journal thoroughly.

"I don't like this place," hissed Damien while whipping his head back-and-forth. His cold hands held Jude like a newborn, while his footsteps made no sound.

Bats descended from the doorway in front of them and closed in on them. With one hiss, Damien turned the bats against one another. Bats screeched and attacked one another until they all lay flat on the dusty ground beneath them.

"This better be worth it. I love bats," hissed Damien.

"You'll get what's rightfully yours."

The door from the journal stood tall and old in front of them. A crack in the wall released a ray of sunlight across the door.

"You get half your prize now and the other half upon completion."

Damien licked his fangs. "Delicious."

Jude held out his wrist and scraped it as hard as he could against the jagged walls. Warm fresh blood fell from his wrist. Damien licked greedily at Jude's mutilated flesh. Jude could feel death upon him. They were running out of time. Jude's body would not last if they did not hurry.

Damien's head jerked up with wide eyes before he inhaled deeply. He propped Jude up against the wall and placed his hand in the ray of sunlight before them. Walking into the ray of sunlight he smiled and hissed.

"Take me *inside* Damien."

Damien jerked his head back at Jude and glared. He picked Jude back up and walked to the door. "What now?"

Jude placed his bleeding wrist on the door and smeared a blood trail across its surface. "Geais Hipt Neur!" The door screeched open at the dark sacred words, releasing a stale cold wind that assaulted them instantly.

A cold stone altar decorated by skulls and extinguished candles sat in the middle of a perfectly round chamber. Three statues stood against the wall on the other side of the chamber. Jude released himself from Damien's grip and limped over to the table. Placing his hand on its cold surface, he could feel the power waiting to be awakened. He turned to the statues. They were similar to the statues of the three brothers back in Kismet; only their faces were twisted into foul demons with fangs.

"Geais, Hipt and Neur awaken!"

The chamber shook and then steadied. The candles in the corners of the room lit, followed by the candles on the stone table.

The eyes of the Rune statue glowed blue. "What do you want insect? Pride has no time for your insignificant soul." The voice was proper but deadly and hollow. It spoke with superiority and arrogance.

The Aegis statue's eyes glowed a piercing red. "Who cares! Wrath hates him! Kill him! Let him rot! Let him die!" The voice was angry and demonic, striking fear with every syllable of the words it spoke.

The last statue of Pith slowly dimmed on before its eye sockets grew black. "It's Envy's turn! Why should he be allowed to walk the earth unchained by the holy prison? I hate him! I want his eyes, his bloodline—his body! Envy is kept last when it comes to his judgment, but why shouldn't I be first to speak?" The last voice was high-pitched and squeaky with venom heavy in its voice.

Jude looked into the eyes of all three statues. "I have something you want."

"Please...you have nothing I want. I possess knowledge and things you couldn't possibly fathom," said Pride. Chains shot out from the Aegis statue, barbed with razors. The chains wrapped around Jude's wrists and ankles, holding him up off the ground. A pool of blood forming beneath him. A second set of chains darted behind him and soon Damien hovered next to him.

"What is this? I am not your enemy! I am merely the courier of this man," hissed Damien.

"But Envy wants you both!" squeaked the Pith statue.

"My father is Mathias Bray." The chamber went silent. "I have seen the truth. I know of the curse bestowed upon my father by those tyrants—a curse bestowed because of his defiance to allow me to suffer. You are the counterparts of the three brothers. My father's journal told me of your forgotten legend so I know what you seek."

"I seek your suffering. I seek your blood and your life!" shouted Wrath.

"You seek acknowledgement of your existence and retribution for your wrongdoing," said Jude smiling when he heard no rebellion.

"And what do you want from us *peasant*?" snarled Pride.

Jude looked at his reflection in a shattered mirror on the wall behind Rune's statue. His eyes were still somewhat swollen shut covering his green eyes. His face was scarred and mutilated beyond recognition. One arm was thicker than the other while half his black hair was burned away exposing his scalp. He didn't recognize himself. "I want your power—all of it. All three of you."

"Pathetic! You are filth and grime. I am a god, superior than you," spat Pride. "Why would I ever give you the reins to my chariot?"

"I should have his reins and his life!" shouted Envy.

The chains around Damien threw him from wall-to-wall, before slamming the Vampire into the ceiling, and then down to the ground. "I don't have time for this!" screamed Wrath.

"I know why the Combat Specialist line has dwindled. My father's journal told me. You have tempted and corrupted the Combat Specialists before me. The power of their bloodline would allow you to possess their bodies without destroying it. They would adapt to your darkness allowing you to walk the Earth with your powers intact. Pith probably knows of your treachery and has halted the continuation of his bloodline. I will never forget that night when you came for me at the Kismet border and tempted me with your power. I will never forget Wrath's rage as I put the dagger up to the neck of my best friend in an attempt to take his life. I will never forget Envy's ill will for the ignorance of my best friend to go on harming others without guilt or hesitation. And I can't forget Pride's mirror showing me the truth that I am a good person and therefore superior to Eli. I want all those back to do what I wish to do. You give me your powers, make the sacred oath of fealty and I will give you what you seek. Otherwise, good luck waiting another millennia in hopes of another Combat Specialist that will allow you to dominate them."

"This is not what I came here for! This, is unforgiveable!" hissed Damien.

"Then *burn* demon!" roared Wrath. The chains holding Damien tossed him out of the chamber, slamming the door closed behind him.

Eli could have stayed staring at his bedroom wall for a few more days if it wasn't for the hunger gnawing at his belly. He blinked many times due to the dryness of his eyes, and moved his jaw side-to-side in hopes of releasing the lock. *Pang is gone, and there's nothing I can do about it*, he thought to himself. He abandoned his bedroom and stalked down the stairs yawning and scratching his side.

Jamieson sat lying in one of the chairs next to the fireplace; his head slanted to the side and eyes closed. His massive biceps were sufficiently acting as the world's largest pillow causing Eli to laugh slightly. A loud knock sounded, causing both Jamieson and Eli to stagger in place.

Jamieson looked around frantically and then rested his eyes on Eli. "Man were you watching me sleep?"

Dumbfounded Eli didn't know how to respond so just stared.

"Just creepy," replied Jamieson.

Eli ignored Jamieson and turned his attention to the door. He opened it to find Josline breathing heavily behind it.

"Thank Pith I thought you would never answer," said Josline. She seemed a little erratic which was out of character for her.

"J what's going on?" asked Jamieson joining the conversation.

"I can feel it," said Josline choking hoarsely. "I can feel the darkness awakening."

Eli became alarmed but confused. "What darkness?"

"Mt. Perennial. Hallowed Sanctum, "she said breathing heavily with wide eyes.

Eli looked from Josline's wide eyes to Jamieson's wide eyes and became frustrated that he was the only one that did not understand what she was trying to say. "Will somebody please tell me what Mt. Perennial means and why I should be alarmed?"

"It's the place where the gods succumbed to sin due to Earth's corruption," interjected Jamieson while looking back-and-forth between Josline and Eli. "Enraged that they could be so easily tempted by sin like the mortals they punished for it, the gods separated themselves from their corrupted sides. Those banished sides became the world's first ipseitys: Geais, Hipt and Neur. The gods imprisoned them in stone far beneath the Earth's surface in an attempt to rid themselves of sin and shame."

Eli thought of the dark rider from The Immortal Prison. "Could that dark rider we saw at The Immortal Prison have anything to do with it?"

"What dark rider?" asked Josline alarmed.

"Maybe," said Jamieson ignoring Josline's question. We won't find out unless we infiltrate Mt. Perennial and see what stirs there.

"We will need Alize's help," said Josline. "For some reason luck favors us when I picture her with us."

The three of them nodded collaboratively.

"Perhaps we have judged you incorrectly," said Pride. A blue spectral of a man manifested in front of the Rune statue until a tall, clean-cut man garbed in luxurious robes stood before Jude. "But if we are to have a deal, you will have to know exactly what you are asking for, what we are asking for and who we are." The black and red spectral forms of Envy and Wrath materialized, leaving Jude face-to-face with the spectral forms of Pride, Envy and Wrath. But Pride was the one who took the lead.

"Pride has been my name since the very beginning. I wouldn't be lying if I said they got it wrong. I'm a god among you mortals and I'm always chin-up tall. Can you blame me? I'm a god whose got it all.

You think I care about these whiney peasants? They have nothing that compares to what I do. But when I'm honest and speak the truth about the facts I'm telling you, they damn and curse me. They call me Pride. I'm not Pride!

I'm the voice that gives you confidence in the heat of battle. I'm the power that lets you always stand up tall.

You sad, sad little peasant. Go ahead—cry and weep! Aegis, Rune and Pith are tyrannical gods among you humans and what are you to them? You're all ants! You're all dust!

Sad, sad little peasant. Go ahead—cry away! There's no one here to save you and your sins are ready to drown you! Don't blame me! Blame your Pride!"

Pride extended his hand to Jude. Jude stared down at it and shook it. A dagger with a jagged hilt manifested in front of Jude that absorbed Pride's presence at the end of the handshake. Envy stepped in between Jude and the dagger and wrapped his arm around Jude, guiding him to the stone table.

"Come on it's Envy's turn!

You tell me that you understand the terms of our contract. You tell me that I can have what I seek.

But what I seek is the skin that coats your bones, and the feeble breath that fills your lungs and while you're at it— the entire world.

I'm the forbidden taboo you shouldn't speak of loudly. But when I am, they minimize and call it jealousy.

While you do this I'll take your wife, and your money and that knife—if I can't have you, I'll take your life!

Come on it's Envy's turn to rule you stupid mortal! Without me you'd always come in dusty last. It's time to take the reins of the one who runs this game; and claim your prize! Claim your fame!

And when you're done, you're never done, so do you realize, it's never fun. Do you get it? You get what you deserve!"

Envy snatched a lock of Jude's hair and rubbed it across his face. He extended his hand, and when Jude shook it, Envy placed the lock of hair in his mouth and swallowed it. Immediately his soul was absorbed into the dagger that hovered above the ground. Wrath crossed the room snatching the dagger. The rage in his eyes roared with power. He signaled for Jude to lay across the table. Jude obliged, feeling his back complain about the cold and roughness of the table. The ceiling sat comprised of metal spikes littered with old skeletons. Wrath's face jerked in front of Jude's eyes.

"Wrath is the blood bath I spill when in agony.

They named me Wrath because they misunderstand what I do. I'm the power that lets you rule. I'm the power that's telling you, that when you're angry—kill the fool!

So you think you're sweet and innocent and love all people? Well good luck my dear and we'll see how long that lasts.

Because when you get a little older, you'll realize life is a wee bit colder and you'll curse them. Yes you will!

So go ahead and bring the death and all the suffering! Kill all who dare to cross your wrathful path! And when there's no one left to kill, and you feel you've had your fill, don't stop there! Kill yourself!

I'm not crazy, I'm just Wrathful!

Wrath placed the dagger in Jude's hand and grinned slowly. "Now, only a person whose soul is stronger than Pride, Envy and Wrath can wield our power. If not, you'll usher in eternal damnation and spend eternity in the darkest realm of hell—torn limb from limb for eternity. Now cut your throat and seal the deal!"

Jude rose, throwing his legs over the side of the altar. He held the dagger up and glared at his mutilated reflection in the dagger's surface. He placed the dagger at his neck just as the chamber shook, drawing his attention to the stone doors.

Eli barreled through the doors bow loaded with a shining arrow and Jamieson and Josline at his sides. Jude walked towards the center of the chamber as the visitors scanned the room. Then Eli's eyes met Jude's.

Jude fell to the floor and began to crawl away. His body scurried a few feet before a soldier grabbed him by his feet and dragged him back to the center. His fingernails clung to the stone beneath him, peeling back before detaching from his bloody fingertips.

"Help! Jed! Big brother! Help me—please!"

"Hold him up! Make him take it!" yelled the General.

"Jude," said Eli appearing shocked alongside Jamieson and Josline.

Jude felt himself shake his head. "No more..."

"What?" said Eli lowering his bow.

"No more!" Jude raised the dagger up to his neck and released the river. Someone screamed off in the distance as Jude felt himself choke before collapsing to the unforgiving surface.

Eli ran to Jude's side. Scooping him up, he raised Jude's head up and locked eyes with him. Jude felt his tongue go crazy in his mouth. He was choking to death, he could feel it.

"Alize!" screamed Eli.

"Get him on that table!" yelled Alize appearing in Jude's sight.

Jude felt himself rise and then felt a hard cold table beneath him. The chamber roared and stirred beneath Jude's body as he choked and gasped for air. His hands grabbed his bleeding throat while his body jerked and convulsed.

"Oh my Aegis Jude, what have you done to yourself?" said Eli.

Something was wrong. Jude could feel his death as his eyes began to flutter.

"Hang on Jude!" shouted Eli somewhere. "Don't you quit on me dammit!"

This wasn't supposed to happen. He should be absorbing Wrath's, Pride's and Envy's power right now. Instead, he felt himself slipping. *They tricked me*, he thought to himself

"Alize do something we're losing him!" shouted a female voice.

Then it was over. A calm swam across his body. A bright white light replaced the entire room. A faceless figure with large wings flew slowly towards him. Jude rose from the stone table and looked down at the lifeless mutilated body before him—his body. He then looked around the room and saw Alize, Eli, Jamieson and Josline frozen in time—crying hysterically. He returned his gaze to his deformed body. That body carried so many painful memories and so many good ones. But the chains were off and he was free.

Jude looked back towards the angel and surrendered himself when it reached out to him. Jude reached out to the angel, and when their fingertips touched, terror consumed the angel as the surroundings rumbled violently. *He's mine!*

Jude fell. He fell through the table, through the Earth's crust and couldn't stop falling. He fell for what felt like eternity before he slammed down onto an icy surface. The icy was so cold that it burned and stuck to his skin, imprisoning him on his back.

Pride appeared over him, a grotesque demon, who looked far more horrific than he portrayed himself to be. When Jude opened his mouth to scream, Pride placed his hand over Jude's mouth and smothered his cries for help. Wrath appeared next, his devilish form manifesting fear in Jude unlike any he had ever seen. Wrath placed his hand on Jude's neck, crushing it. Then came Envy, grinning from ear-to-ear. Envy jumped into Jude's body, followed by Wrath and then Pride. The sensation was jarring, like a wall crushing Jude until it finally entered his body.

Jude ripped his arms off of the icy surface and clawed at his face, digging his fingernails into his flesh and clawing at his eyes. He felt his teeth gnash and his body convulse, while the beings desecrated his inner body and found a place to settle. Jude grunted and growled. He gnashed his teeth and barked like a beast. Then the calm came once again.

"What's happening," cried Envy.

Jude and Jed frolicked in the front yard while Mathias and Aileen snuggled up under the family tree.

Then Jude was older, kneeling next to Aileen at her garden—socializing beneath the night sky.

The coliseum rose up on either side of Jude while Jed, Marius and Aileen cheered from their seats.

Jude and Jamieson clapped their hands and praised beneath the cathedral's sacred roof.

The angel flew down, releasing Jude from his bindings to his flesh. Silent emptiness and then pain.

"Let them rot! Let them die!"

GOODBYES FOR TWO

Eli stared motionlessly at his bedroom wall—an activity he was beginning to wonder if he should add to his list of hobbies. Nightmares no longer came since he had abandoned sleep. Through Jamieson, Eli found out that Lieutenant Titus had returned to Geminate, along with the Praxian royal guard. While the Lieutenant claimed his visit was due to an attempt at creating peace between Geminate and Praxis, Eli knew vengeance was what truly brought the Lieutenant back to the underwater city. Jamieson cautioned Eli to not leave the house, at least until the Lieutenant returned to Praxis. Conall was the last thing Eli was worried about. He had been hastily making funeral arrangements and was ashamed that he would not be able to acquire enough guests to attend. *Jude deserves the entire world at his funeral* Eli thought to himself.

Since the incident at the Never Ending Stairs, the Kismet people were labeled a threat to Geminate security, by General Mather, and banished from Geminate forever. They now occupied the Geminate Forest scrounging the ground for scraps. Eli used up all of his gold and valuables on supplies for his people. He didn't know how long the people would last until anonymous donations of food and water covertly made their way to the Kismet people. Eli suspected the Priestess but could not be sure.

Three strong knocks brought Eli down the stairs and to the front door. He opened it slightly and gently smiled when Jamieson looked back at him. Eli swung open the door and threw his arms around Jamieson before pulling him inside.

"So you'll be happy to know that everything is ready," said Jamieson.

Eli studied Jamieson. "Good morning, how are you doing?"

Jamieson tilted his head and curled his brow. "Fine—and yourself?"

"I'm doing okay. Thanks for being here."

Jamieson walked over to the couch and took a seat. He removed one boot and then the other. "Of course. I may not have known him long, but Jude was a good friend of mine."

Eli took a seat across from Jamieson and stared.

"Um are you okay?" asked Jamieson quickly.

"Yeah why?"

"Because you're kind of freaking me out," replied Jamieson shaking his leg.

"I just wanted to say I'm sorry for all of the horrible names I have called you and all of the times I made you feel uncomfortable and unwelcome."

Jamieson swatted the air in front of him. "No worries."

"I mean it. I was wrong. You are a good person and I'm sorry I didn't see that earlier. Thank you for helping me break into the Geminate Prison and helping me infiltrate The Immortal Prison."

Jamieson reached his hand to Eli, who quickly shook it. A low knock on the door caught their attention.

"Perhaps I should get this just in case it's the Lieutenant coming to kill you," said Jamieson. He retrieved a dagger from inside his boot and held it behind his back before opening the door. His head tilted slightly down before he opened the door completely. Mik stepped through the door.

"Mik!" Eli ran to the young man and hugged him tightly. Mik returned the hug. "I am so glad to see you buddy."

"I really miss Jude. I wanted to say my goodbyes," said Mik frowning. "When are we leaving?"

"His body is being delivered to the requested spot in the Geminate forest as we speak. We should probably get going," said Jamieson.

"Okay. I'll meet you guys at the double doors. I have something to pick up from my house for Jude," said Mik rushing out the door.

"He's a great kid," said Jamieson.

"No he's not."

Jamieson turned to Eli.

"He's a great young man."

Jamieson smiled and nodded his head. "I have something for you." He reached into his armor and retrieved an armband and extended it to Eli.

Eli felt something cold on the armband so he flipped it around. Two identical warriors stood side-by-side wielding orbs and weapons. One was shaded while the other wasn't. A small bloodstain dampened the corner of it. It was Jude's wristband. Instantly the day upon The Never Ending Stairs formed in front of him. Jude's heart-felt screams for help and his painful injuries tore at Eli's heart. A warm tear fell from his eye and landed atop the wristband, slightly calming his heart.

"I'm sorry I thought you'd want it," said Jamieson reaching for the armband.

Eli jerked the armband away and hugged it. "No I do. It's perfect, thank you."

Jamieson patted Eli on the back. "I'll wait for you outside." The door closed lightly behind him.

Eli fiddled with the armband willing himself not to release more tears. He knew he couldn't do anything about the past, but still wished he could.

The least I can do is give you a proper funeral buddy and show you how much you meant to me.

◆◆◆

Jude's body looked far worse than Jamieson remembered. The gashes, burns and pillaged skin were hard to look at. However, even with all of the various injuries, what drew Jamieson's attention the most was Jude's severed neck. It was something that seemed out of place, but something no one else seemed to notice. Jamieson stood next to Mik, who came running to the burial site as if in fear he was missing the ceremony. Eli stood in front of them next to Jude's body. He had been whispering something to Jude since they had arrived, and Jamieson had no intentions on rushing him.

"I don't know what to say when it's my turn to speak," said Mik. He bit his lip and shifted his weight. "I don't want to say the wrong thing."

Jamieson wrapped his arm around the young man and rocked him. "When all else fails, crack a really cheesy joke."

Mik looked up confused.

"Or...something about his accomplishments?"

Mik nodded back with a smile. Jamieson looked ahead of him and found Eli on his feet frozen in place. His eyes were wide as if he was in shock. Jamieson turned around and found Lieutenant Titus and Sia approaching them. They both were dressed in matching black robes. Despite the severity of her injuries, Sia had healed pretty well. She walked independently without any guidance and only a few small scars now showed on her cheekbone. Eli walked down to meet her but stopped when the Lieutenant stepped in the way, glaring down at him.

Jamieson rushed over to the commotion in hopes of preventing any ridiculous behavior at such a difficult time. "We saved you a seat over here."

"What do you mean saved *us* a seat," snapped Conall. He let Sia sit down first before joining her. "We're the only ones here besides you, Mik and the treacherous dog."

Sia grabbed Conall's chin and lightly forced him to look at her. "You promised."

Conall's shoulders fell as he sighed. "I know. I'm sorry." He kissed her lightly on the lips.

"I wouldn't say the only ones," said Jamieson looking to the trees behind them.

Men, women and children poured in from the surrounding trees, their faces heavy with grief. Sia and Conall turned around in shock.

"Mr. Kaas?" said Conall running to an old man in tattered clothes. He wrapped his arms around the old man and hugged him tightly. "How is this possible?"

"How is *what* possible Lieutenant?" asked Kaas confused. "When one of our own pass on to the three brothers, it is custom for the Kismet people to come together."

Sia appeared at Conall's side, taking in the crowd before her. "You are all most welcome."

An arm pulled Jamieson to the side. He found Eli looking as worried as ever.

"Do you mind starting?" asked Eli. He shoved both his hands in his pockets. "I just need some time to gather my thoughts."

Jamieson nodded and then took a place behind Jude's body. He waited for Eli to take his seat next to Mik and for Sia and Conall to end their private conversations with those around them.

"It's funny, I wasn't nervous about getting up here until now," laughed Jamieson aloud.

Silence.

"Right…" Jamieson cleared his throat and re-gathered his thoughts. "I didn't know Jude long. When we first met I classified him as my enemy. Boy the gods know I had that wrong. Jude was smart, kind and *very* understanding. He was someone you could rely on when you're in a dark place and someone who could make you feel strong even when you're the most vulnerable. He was also the first person that didn't judge me when he finally got to know the *real* me." Jamieson felt the back of his throat get itchy, which confused him. "I'm going to miss Jude very much. I hope Pith, Aegis and Rune realize the treasure they now have in their home. But no matter how many seconds, how many days or how many years go by, I will never forget how Jude made me feel. He made me feel unashamed of who I am; and that's something I never thought was possible. Goodbye buddy. I'll miss you." Jamieson put a hand over Jude's heart and kissed the back of it. It was the 'departing palm,' a Geminate custom meant to display that Jude had changed Jamieson's life for the better, and in turn, would be rewarded in the afterlife.

Jamieson took his seat on the other side of Mik. The young man jumped up quickly and took his position next to Jude's body. He spoke of Jude kindly, describing him as the brother he never had. He spoke of Jude's victory in the Trials of Magic, Might and Lineage, and of his title as 'Prodigy of Pith.' After he was done, he knelt to his knees and hugged Jude, telling him goodbye as tears fell from his eyes. After returning to his seat, the Lieutenant rose from his seat and strolled to the front. The Lieutenant, for the most part, spoke of Jude's talents in combat and his accomplishments in missions. He rarely showed any emotion, but saluted Jude when his speech was over. After the Lieutenant took his seat, there were only two people left.

Eli looked at Sia, who returned his stare before looking away. She rose from her seat with a small pouch in her hand. Conall rose with her when she began to cry, but she assured him she was fine, so he returned to his seat. When she got to the front, she looked out at her people just in time to catch the entering Erudites take their seats. A smile nudged at her lips.

Sia took a deep breath and fluttered her eyelids. "You know, there aren't many people in this life that you can hand your soul over to unprotected, and trust that it will remain protected. There aren't many people who make you smile just by being present or truly understand your pain when listening to your sorrows. When I speak of these things, I speak of Jude Bray. Jude was too kind, too loving and too forgiving. Even though those traits were what took him from us, I am glad he had them. His love and kindness helped me through so many dark times in my life. I wouldn't be lying if I said I wouldn't be here today without him. I could choose to remember Jude as one of the gems of Kismet. I could choose to remember him as the best Squad Leader I've ever had. I could choose to remember him as the brother who knew me through-and-through and always had my best interest at heart. But I choose to remember him as my guardian angel, loving me unconditionally and placing my happiness before his." She opened the pouch she held and pulled out a small plant, bare of anything other than a small pink petal. "Where Jude and I come from, back in Kismet, it is custom for the fallen to be buried with the rare and beautiful cherry blossom tree. It's a tradition we both held dear, and it's a tradition that will live on through me as long as I live." She placed the small plant down next to Jude and then kissed him on the forehead. "I love you Jude."

A wave of hoods simultaneously went up around Jamieson. He looked around at all of the attendees and each person had a hood up. Some were tattered and some were like-new. He found himself confused by the gesture and out of place as well since he didn't have a hood of his own.

After Sia returned to her seat, her face filled with tears. Conall pulled her in close, comforting her as she sobbed. Jamieson looked over to Eli, whose eyes did not rest on Sia, but rested on Jude. He stood from his seat and took his spot next to his fallen comrade. He waited for Sia to look up before beginning.

"I'm not someone who is good with words or explaining how I feel. Come to think about it, I'm not good at thinking on my feet either—which is kind of ironic considering my bloodline," said Eli stirring in place. "Wow 'ironic'—a word I would never know how to use if it wasn't for Jude."

Jamieson could sense Eli struggling so he did the one thing he knew how to do. "You wouldn't know how to stand on two feet if it wasn't for Jude either." He started laughing hysterically at how funny the joke was but silenced himself when he saw that no one else was laughing.

A chuckle erupted from the front. Jamieson looked forward and found Eli laughing uncontrollably.

"You know what's so sad about that. It's not the bad timing but how true it is," said Eli continuing to laugh. Soon the entire crowd joined him in laughter.

"Thanks J," said Eli with a wink. "I have had some dark times in my life, as I am sure we all have. Besides coping, in what I now know are destructive ways, I have also coped through writing." Eli took out a piece of parchment from his pocket and unfolded it. He cleared his throat and looked down at Jude. "This is for you Jude."

Jamieson turned around and found Josline taking a seat towards the back. She wore a tight-fitting black dress with her hair thrown whimsically over her shoulder. Jamieson smiled. She smiled back.

Jude, my brother, so kind.

Searching for the answers to the riddle of what drives the beast.

Too kind.

Loyal and loving against all odds.

So kind.

Bitten and ravaged but still loving.

Too kind.

The beast is gone and so are you.

Dark does not sustain when light departs, but joins it.

Be at peace while the world shines a little less bright.

"I don't think this day is big enough," continued Eli. "It isn't big enough because we aren't just losing Jude today, we are losing Pang as well."

Sia gasped. Her eyes widened before she began crying hysterically. She buried her face in Conall's armor. Shortly after Josline erupted into tears, frantically wiping her eyes before the tears fell too far. One of the Erudites, Logan, was quick to run to Josline's side—trying his best to comfort her. Mik also began to cry, but buried his face in his hands so no one could see.

"For those of you who didn't know. Pang Quarrels has also left us. When I first met Pang I was a lost soul. I judged him. I belittled him. I insulted him. I did everything in my power to prove that he was this horrible monster. Little did I know that *I* was the monster. It took a lot of time, but Pang and I grew really close. He was the kick in the pants I needed when I was too stubborn for my own good. He was the big brother that watched out for me on the battlefield, who always defended me in my time of need. He was also the only person who came to see me everyday after my alcoholism drained my blood energy and forced me into a coma." Eli looked up at the bright sky and laughed. "Even though I am sure you enjoyed it sometimes, the pain is over my friend. Go now and rest. You've earned it."

Eli turned around and shuttered at Jude's body. Jamieson began to wonder if he should go up there and comfort Eli, but decided against it. He figured Eli needed to let all of his emotions out.

"I've known Jude longer than anyone here. But at the same time I've *known* him the shortest. Jude and I were always family. We grew up together playing with fake swords in my backyard. We went to the Junior Academy and Academy together. Jude was the hard worker of the two of us. While I was always running around and getting in trouble, Jude was always studying, reading or just bettering himself. He always helped me with my homework and defended me when trouble came my way. My mother passing was one of the darkest moments of my life, and Jude was right there on the front lines comforting my dad and I. It was Jude who helped me see the light after the darkness that was my mother's death. He fought by my side to help try and free my dad—our dad—and was there for me at my father's funeral. I never really knew how lucky I was to have a friend like Jude. He was a friend who forgave me *way* too many times, especially when I didn't deserve it. Even when I hurt him to his core, he was always there to watch out for me. Jude taught me what being a friend really means. Being a friend is accepting someone for who they are, even when you don't agree with them. But most importantly, being a *real* friend is being there for someone even when you aren't friends anymore. That is what Jude did for me. I just wish I wasn't blind to what was in front of me. Jude may be gone, but he has changed my life tremendously. Wow, tremendously. A few months ago I wouldn't even know what that word means. Thanks Jude for your vast and confusing vocabulary. I love you my friend—my brother. I will *never* forget you. I will *never* judge someone before getting to know them. I will *never* take the kindness of others for granted. I will *never* forget how lucky I am to be standing here breathing. I will *never* forget the meaning of true friendship and loving someone unconditionally. But most of all, I will never forget our sword fights in the backyard or the hot cider talks in the kitchen. Goodbye brother. I'll miss you."

Eli leaned down and hugged Jude. After returning to his feet, he knelt back down and kissed Jude on the forehead. Jamieson helped Eli lower Jude's body into the ground, while the Kismet people surrounded them humming an indecipherable tune. Josline forfeited her disgust for dirt and helped Mik fill Jude's grave—with Logan nearly begging to help her. Sia and the Lieutenant planted the small cherry blossom tree atop Jude's grave. Josline found the seed of a small orchid and planted next to Jude's grave, in remembrance of Pang. The sun began to set when both graves were made. But just before the sun completely departed from the darkened sky, two rays touched the graves of Jude Bray and Pang Quarrels.

Nothing was right but everything was as it was. The sunset was home across many cultures. No one could deny the overwhelming feeling of potential acceptance and imminent peace; including Jamieson, who had enough moments of pain and death to last a lifetime.

IN THE SHADOWS,
IT WAITS

Lyle kept the drinks flowing while Eli kept guzzling them down. Mother Nature's Tavern was a buzz with socialites. Friends, family and peers laughed and socialized amidst the live entertainment. However, they would not see Josline perform tonight, since her grief over Pang's passing had her held up in the confines of her home. Eli found being out having drinks with Lyle a lot more healing, especially since the drinks were free.

"So how did the, you know, go?" asked Lyle. He refilled Eli's glass before polishing another.

"It was hard but I got a lot off my chest. I think it will take a lot of time for me to heal completely." He downed his drink in one gulp.

Lyle stared at Eli. "I'm sorry I can't take it. This is *way* too heavy for me to handle. I need a drink." He retrieved a clean glass from underneath the counter and poured himself a drink and guzzled it down.

"Excuse me," said a voice behind Eli.

Mik took a seat next to Eli and stared up at him. "What are you doing here?"

Eli waited while Lyle refilled his glass. "No the question is, what are *you* doing here little mister. This is a place for grown-ups."

"I grew up a long time ago Eli," replied Mik exhaling. "I came to say goodbye. My sister and I leave for Praxis in the morning," said Mik unflinching.

What am I doing? Two hours and I am already taking someone for granted.

"Thank you Mik." Eli reached into his pocket, took out his house key and handed to Mik. "Do me a favor and meet me back at my house. I will clean up and when I get back we can have one final lesson before you go."

Mik smiled and then extended his hand. "Deal!" Eli shook the young man's hand and smiled back.

After Mik left, Eli ordered a glass of water and some bread. Lyle ridiculed him vigorously for it, but Eli didn't care. He loved Mik very much and hated to see him go. He didn't know what he would do without Mik's bright young face shining light on Eli's darkest days. He figured that after some time had passed, he would visit Mik in Praxis—if Sia allowed it.

"One more glass of water Lyle. I have a sparring lesson to teach."

◆◆◆

Mik placed the key in the keyhole and turned it. A heavy musk and a messy living room greeted him when he entered Eli's house. He closed and locked the door behind him before setting the key on the end table next to him. He began tidying the living room and then washing the dishes. It was the least he could do after all Eli had done for him. Eli had always been there for him despite his scary father, and Mik appreciated that. Eli also brought Mik and his friends together—a meeting of Erudites that Mik never thought would be possible. He would miss them terribly, especially his best friend Brayden.

Climbing the stairs, Mik entered Eli's room and set eyes on a small journal on the table next to the bed. He sat on Eli's bed and opened the journal. Various poems decorated the pages.

Mik began to read one but then set eyes on something peculiar. Another larger journal sat on the table next to the bedroom door. The journal was dark and had a note tied to it. Placing the first journal down on the end table, Mik crossed the room to the second journal and reached for it. A creaking noise from downstairs halted his progress. He stopped himself from calling out to Eli. Instead, he peered through the doorway down to the first floor. The house was empty. Tip-toeing down the stairs he looked around at the vacant living room.

"Just a little jumpy I guess." Mik entered the kitchen, poured himself a glass of water and finished it. He washed the glass out and then re-entered the living room, stopping cold at the figure before him.

♦♦♦

Eli attempted to steady his walk back home. The homes around him, along with the pedestrians, continued to multiply the longer he looked at them. After leaving Mother Nature's Tavern, Eli walked a few blocks and instantly started having episodes. After the episodes reached a staggering rate, he stopped by a smaller local tavern and had a few drinks before progressing home. When his house rose up ahead of him, he breathed a sigh of relief before realizing he gave Mik his house key. He retrieved the spare key from the small assortment of rocks in the garden and unlocked the door.

All of the lights were off when he entered.

"Mik?"

"Hi Eli," said Mik's voice softly.

Eli flicked on the light switch next to him and froze at the sight. He blinked once, twice and then a third time, knowing his eyes had to be playing a trick on him.

"Evening Mr. Brassie," said Jude standing behind Mik with his hands on the young man's shoulders.

"Jude?" Eli fell to his knees in disbelief but quickly stopped himself from succumbing to joy after studying Jude. He was dressed in dark armor and a black cape. His face was no longer scarred and his scalp was no longer burned. His eyes were no longer swollen shut, but what was most unnerving, was the red that replaced his once emerald green eyes. Eli rose to his feet.

Jude formed a small smile. "Nice of you to join us." His voice sounded deep, hollow and wallowing.

"Jude, how is this possible?"

"Happy to see us are you?" said Jude tilting his head to one side and then the other.

Even with the swaying room and blurry vision, Eli could tell something was wrong. "Mik are you okay?"

"Eli, did you really betray the squad and nearly kill my sister?" asked Mik with a quivering lip.

Eli nearly burst into tears at the question coming from one of the few people he loved so dearly. Eli looked up at Jude, wondering what all he had told Mik. "Jude what have you told him?"

"The truth, dear friend," said Jude.

"So it's true," said Mik releasing a tear.

"Yes, it's true Mik. But it was an accident. I would never intentionally hurt your sister. I love her."

"I don't know if I believe you anymore," said Mik.

Eli looked up at Jude's smiling face. His crimson eyes looked down at Mik before he whispered something in the young man's ear.

Mik's eyes widened. "Did you also try to kill Jude?"

"Jude stop it right now!"

"Answer me!" shouted Mik.

Eli looked down at Mik and fell to his knees at the question. "No. I mean, yes. Well it was an accident I swear."

"An accident Eli! Really? Is everything an accident? How do you accidentally try to kill someone?" yelled Mik.

Eli opened his mouth to respond but nothing came out.

"Answer me!" yelled Mik.

Eli closed his mouth and looked up at Jude. The smile never left Jude's soft reborn skin.

"Mik I know you're mad, but please, come here."

Mik wiped his tears and took a step forward before Jude jerked him back.

"But we're not done playing," said Jude abandoning his smile and adopting a frown.

"Let him go Jude. This has nothing to do with him."

"Do you ever stop lying? This has *everything* to do with him," said Jude looking from Mik to Eli. "You love this little creature. You care about him and his wellbeing. If we pluck a hair from his tiny head, it triggers you." Jude snatched a patch of hair from Mik's head sending the young man howling in pain.

"Jude leave him alone!"

"Eli," pouted Mik.

"Shh it's going to be okay Mik okay. I promise."

"Ah there there little man. Don't cry. We're sorry," said Jude rubbing Mik's head. He produced a small dagger from behind his back and held it to Mik's throat.

Eli's open palms rose quickly. "Jude stop!" Eli tried to concentrate on summoning a weapon but his concentration was still blurry and his mind still raced. "Okay you obviously came here for something. Why else would you come here in the middle of the night? Just tell me what it is. What do you want and I will give it to you."

Jude smiled. "Whatever we want? Envy likes!" spat Jude in a high-pitched voice.

"Yes Jude, whatever you want. Just please don't hurt Mik and you can have anything."

Jude snarled while gnashing his teeth. "You have *nothing* we want. If anything, we have *everything* you want. You are *nothing! Nothing!*" exclaimed Jude with a proper and confident tone.

"Okay I have nothing. Just please, don't hurt him."

Mik's chest continued to rise-and-fall violently while Jude's face went from hostile to neutral.

"Do you want us to release him to you Mr. Brassie? Is that what you want more than anything right now?" asked Jude in a bland tone.

"Yes Jude. More than anything."

"Okay Eli we'll release him. But only because we love you," said Jude with a small smile.

Eli closed his eyes and released a silent exhale. "Thank you so much Jude. I love you too."

Jude released his hold on Mik.

"Come on Mik. It's going to be okay."

Mik walked slowly to Eli quivering, while tears continued to fall from his eyes.

"Shh shh it's going to be okay." Eli wrapped his arms around Mik when he got to him. He smothered Mik with kisses on his head and the sides of his face. He couldn't remember the last time he felt so happy.

"It hurts Eli," said Mik.

Eli's eyes flung open just as the worry began to take hold. "What do you mean it hurts Mik? What hurts?" Just as he finished his question, Eli's hand found a foreign object jutting from Mik's back. Eli pulled out a small vial. Mik collapsed in Eli's arms shaking.

"Jude what have you done?" Eli rocked Mik in his arms hoping it would help somehow.

"Cold—hearted—kill!" hissed Jude. The power of his laughter shook the house.

Eli began to choke on his tears while he rocked Mik in his arms.

"I'm sorry Eli. I'm not as strong as you," whispered Mik.

"Shh no you're very strong. You're much stronger than I am. You're going to be okay I promise. I promise, just hold on."

Mik blinked slowly. "I can't feel my legs."

"Tell us, does it hurt yet—the pain?" grinned Jude approaching them. "Go ahead, tell us how much it hurts. Let us revel in your pain!"

"Somebody help me! Please! Somebody!"

"Sad, sad little peasant. There's no one here to save you," snarled Jude.

The front door slammed open. Jamieson and Josline ran through door and jumped in front of Eli and Mik.

"Eli what happened to young Mik?" asked Josline.

Eli could say nothing. His pain crippled his voice. All he could do was raise a finger to the monster who had caused all of this.

"You get what you deserve," squeaked Jude. Chains emerged from his back swatting at Josline and Jamieson, while simultaneously tearing the house in two.

"He'll bring the whole house down!" shouted Josline rolling on the floor.

"Jude stop this, are you crazy?" yelled Jamieson.

The chains stopped in mid-air, hovering above the ground.

"I'm not crazy, I'm just Wrath!" barked Jude. The chains darted for Jamieson reeling him in while the other chains swatted away a hex Josline through at Jude. The chains threw Jamieson through the window while the others wrapped around Josline's neck and brought her to him. "In life, evil always wins. You know why? Because the gods don't love us like they claim they do. If they did, they would intervene and save us every time evil deceives or torments us."

"Enough demon!" shouted a voice from behind Eli.

Eli turned around to find the Priestess glowing vibrantly with the whitest of lights. "Release her!"

"A guardian!" hissed Jude in a high-pitched voice. "I want to be a Guardian!" Jude showed his fangs. "Kill her! Kill them all!"

The Guard appeared behind the Priestess, bows drawn.

The chains tossed Josline at the Priestess, sending them both tumbling across the floor. The chains twirled around Jude blocking the arrows that assaulted him before he emitted a blinding light. Everyone looked away and when the light was gone, so was Jude.

A soldier of The Guard ran to Eli. The soldier's lips moved but Eli couldn't hear anything. Instead, Eli lifted Mik up to the soldier. "Please. Help him."

IN NEED

The infirmary was similar to the Medicinal Quarters back in Kismet, except it was much larger and stood independently amongst the other buildings. The white walls and bright lights were familiar, but the large number of healers, which the Geminates called medics, was both comforting and overwhelming. Eli rushed hastily behind one of the practitioners as he rushed Mik into one of the rooms.

"I've got a waning child!" shouted the practitioner. Immediately three more practitioners entered the room, surrounding Mik's bed and administering care.

A female practitioner rolled Mik over on his side and then placed her ear to Mik's back over the area where the vial once stood. She then rolled him back on to his back and listened to his heart. "It's poison."

"Do we know what kind?" asked another practitioner as he placed a washcloth on Mik's forehead.

"I would need a sample to tell," replied the female practitioner.

"I have the vial that held the poison," said Eli holding it out to her.

She snatched the vial from his hand and shook a loose drop into a bowl of water. She then cut her finger and flung a droplet of blood into the bowl. "Optical Analysis activate!" Her eyes turned gray and then returned to their normal brown. "This poison is unlike any I've ever seen. It's strong."

"How strong?" asked her colleague.

"It's a killer," she mumbled.

"We'll need to cleanse his blood stream!" shouted an older man.

"Go get the toxicology kit!" yelled another.

Eli looked around at the chaos and then down at Mik's barely-breathing body. "A killer? No he can't die. You have to save him!"

"Get him out of here!" shouted the woman.

Guards entered the room and drug Eli out of the room, locking the door behind them. Eli ran to the window of the room and watched as every practitioner poked and studied Mik.

"Where's my brother!" shouted a voice down the hallway.

Eli turned to find Sia storming down the hallway with Conall at her side. Worry and rage controlled her face, while her hands remained glued to her sides.

"Excuse me miss," said a guard stepping in front of Sia.

She slapped him hard, causing him to recoil. "Get out of my way!"

When Sia got to the door, the two guards who escorted Eli out, blocked her path.

"Excuse me I need to get in there," said Sia.

"I'm sorry miss but you will have to leave," said one of the guards grabbing Sia's arm.

Conall immediately jumped in the middle shoving the guard back. "Keep your hands off my fiancé!" Conall continued to argue with the guards while Sia looked into the window and began to cringe with rage. She turned to Eli as if seeing him for the first time.

"Eli what happened to Mik?" she asked.

Eli opened his mouth but couldn't find what to say.

"Answer me!" she yelled. The way she said those words reminded Eli of Mik shouting the exact same words at him before everything happened.

"I did it," said Eli. A tear formed in the corner of his eyes when he saw the shock and pain on her face. "I did this to Mik. But I didn't mean to."

Sia's face contorted into a cry as she screamed at the top of her lungs. "I hate you! I hate you!" She started pummeling Eli with violent fists as she grunted. "Why won't you leave us alone!"

Conall broke away from his argument with the guards, removed Sia from hitting Eli, and punched him straight in the jaw. Eli fell to the floor while Conall tried to finish what he started. The guards immediately apprehended him, dragging him down the hallway.

A hand helped Eli up off the ground.

Josline lightly grabbed his chin and looked at it from all angles. "You're okay." She quickly ran to Sia and wrapped her arms around her. "Hunny it's going to be okay."

"No it's not! He did this to my brother!" screamed Sia pointing to Eli.

"Hunny you have to calm down," said Josline rubbing Sia's shoulders.

"I don't *want* to calm down! I want my brother! Do you hear me? I want little Micky!" shouted Sia.

"Okay, okay," said Josline releasing Sia and entering Mik's room. She pulled aside one of the practitioners who shook his head back-and-forth appearing to be giving her a hard time. Shortly after, Josline opened the door and ushered Sia inside.

"Oh my Aegis! Thank you Josline! Thank you!" exclaimed Sia running inside.

Eli tried to follow but was stopped by Josline's hand.

"I'm sorry only the two of us are allowed in. You'll have to wait out here," she said.

"But he's like my brother."

"I'm sorry," said Josline closing the door behind her.

Jamieson walked up behind Eli, with gashes decorating his face and neck.

"It was an accident I swear. I didn't mean for this to happen."

"Hey, hey calm down," said Jamieson rubbing Eli's back. They both looked into the glass window and watched Sia and Josline stand at the foot of Mik's bed while the practitioners worked on him.

"He's gonna make it J," said Eli nodding his head. "Mik is a fighter."

"I know he is," said Jamieson.

One of the practitioners at the head of the bed slouched over Mik and shook his head. He rose and covered Mik's face with a sheet. Sia collapsed to the floor in tears while Josline cradled her in her arms.

"No!" Eli banged as hard as he could on the window. Mik couldn't be gone. They just weren't trying hard enough. "You were supposed to save him! He's not dead! You're supposed to save him!"

The guards came back for Eli, but Jamieson ushered them away and pulled Eli aside holding him. Eli struggled to release himself from Jamieson, but the Operative was stronger than him.

"Let me go J! Let me go! My Mik's not dead do you hear me? He's not dead! He's a fighter!"

"He's gone," whispered Jamieson tightening his hold on Eli.

"No he's not! Don't say that!"

"He's gone," continued Jamieson over-and-over. "He's gone."

MISSING
PUZZLE PIECE

Death clearly has it out for us thought Jamieson after returning to his own home with Eli. The blonde boy hadn't said a word since they left the infirmary but Jamieson didn't worry. Absolute silence seemed to be Eli's way of dealing with grief. Jamieson witnessed it first-hand after Pang's death and Sia's near-death experience. Josline stayed with Sia and Conall at the infirmary and promised to check-in once they left.

Jamieson helped Eli up to his bedroom, removed his shoes and helped him climb into bed. Exiting to the living room, someone knocked at the door just as Jamieson cleared the last step. Josline stared back at him when he answered. He smiled and asked her in. The two of them sat in the living room next to the fireplace staring at each other, but not saying a word. Their relationship stemmed back many years from a destined friendship, to a long and passionate relationship, and back to friends again. They were kindred spirits.

"Okay I'll be the one to ask it," said Josline breaking the silence. "What in Pith's name happened tonight?"

"I don't know. All he would say over-and-over was 'Jude what have you done?' Nothing else."

"But how is Jude still—alive?" asked Josline in disbelief. "We buried him. I was there!"

"I know. So was I, remember?" Jamieson got up from his seat and began to pace. "What is so baffling is did you get a look at his face? It was as if The Never Ending Stairs never happened.

He had no burns, cuts or bruises anywhere. He didn't even have the gash across his neck from when he took his own life."

"His eyes were healed and glowed with the crimson light of darkness! It just doesn't make sense," said Josline shaking her head. "Could it be an impostor?"

Jamieson stopped. "Not an impostor, but maybe an Amorphous."

"The predators?" Josline's hand went to her mouth. "There's only one way to be sure though."

"You go. I don't want to leave him."

"Okay," she said standing from her seat and walking to the door. "I won't be long."

"Be careful."

"Be safe," she replied.

◆◆◆

Eli awoke to a few light taps on his bedroom door. He rose up to find Jamieson peering in.

"You have a visitor," said Jamieson looking behind him and then back at Eli. "Do you feel like entertaining guests looking like that?"

Eli nodded.

Sia stepped through the doorway, absent of Conall— something Eli thought he would never live to see the day. He sat up in bed and brushed the hair out of his face and the tears from his eyes.

Sia pulled up the chair from the side of the armoire and set it at Eli's bedside before sitting down. "Hi."

"Hi."

The crickets chirped loudly outside.

She cleared her throat. "How are you feeling?"

"Horrible. You?"

"Same," she replied. She got up from her seat and walked to the other side of the room and closed the bedroom door. "Why did you lie and tell me that you murdered Mik?"

Eli never left her gaze. "I didn't lie. I'm the reason he's gone."

She folded her arms. "The practitioner told me the cause of death was poison and showed me the vial you gave him. It was one of Jude's."

"I know."

"Eli why are you covering for him?" asked Sia as she returned to her seat appearing agitated. "If Jude killed Mik then why don't you just say it? Be a man for once in your life!"

"Because he didn't! I killed Mik! How many times do I have to drum it across your tiny little ears? I killed your brother!" He realized both eyes were wet with tears so he wiped them. "I'm sorry for yelling."

Sia crossed her legs. "Eli what happened tonight. Tell me the truth."

"Please don't make me relive it. Please." He covered his face with his hands, seeing the image of Mik walking slowly towards him. A hand grabbed his wrist, interrupting his thoughts.

"Eli he was my brother. I need to know," she said softly while releasing her own tears.

Eli gave-in and recalled the entire night, starting with the end of the funeral. He didn't want to leave one detail out, including his drinking at Mother Nature's Tavern. After finishing, he awaited patiently for Sia to come down on him with a barrage of slaps and punches.

"You were trying to save him," she said.

"Yes, but I killed him."

"Why do you think that?" she asked grabbing his wrist. "It was Jude's vial and his poison."

"Don't you see?" Eli threw back the covers and snatched his hand from Sia's grip. He stalked over to the other side of the room before turning back towards her. "I was drunk when I came home. I was too drunk to summon weapons. I was too drunk to attack Jude and I was too drunk to save Mik. I'm an alcoholic Sia. Alcohol prevented me from saving my little brother. If I wasn't drunk, I could have saved him."

Sia rose from her seat and walked to the bedroom door. "You are right when you say you're an alcoholic, but I can't agree or disagree with the rest." She opened and then closed the door behind her.

I'm an alcoholic...

FELLOWSHIP

Jamieson sat eagerly at the roundtable, awaiting a private audience with the Priestess. The remaining attendees were Lieutenant Titus, Sia, Josline, Eli and two members of the Priestess' personal Guard. Mirrors shined all around them as a clear sight that the room they were in was a safe haven for the Priestess and her ability. The seconds that passed were agonizing since they were all meeting in secret without General Mather's awareness—a crime punishable by imprisonment and potential exile. Jamieson stared at Eli. He was sitting in Talon's seat and looked more like Talon the longer Jamieson stared at him.

"Everything alright?" asked Eli across the table.

Jamieson shook himself from his thoughts and longing to see his best friend. "No, but I will be."

The Priestess entered, blinding everyone with the bright light that trailed after her. The two members of her personal Guard stood saluting her, and didn't take their seats until she took hers.

"Make this quick. I have more pressing matters to attend to," said the Priestess.

Jamieson eyed Sia and coughed twice. Her eye quickly caught the glance before looking away.

"How long has the General been in charge of The Immortal Prison?"

The Priestess recoiled with a slight laugh of annoyance. "The Immortal Prison is not in our jurisdiction nor has it *ever* been. Please tell me this meeting is not a waste of my time."

Jamieson eyed Eli, who was quick to eye him back. The Priestess noticed the exchange of glances and her smile soon turned to a frown. "I ventured to The Immortal Prison on a mission to rescue a friend. I know the General runs the facility and is operating under the name The Jackal."

The Priestess gasped. The mirrors shined while her eyes outlined in white and then stopped. "Make this quick. I have more pressing matters to attend to." Everyone around the table, minus Jamieson and the Priestess turned to one another confused by the repeat conversation.

"It didn't work. We came prepared." Jamieson snuck a glance at Sia and smirked.

"How dare you defy the will of the Priestess! If you are planning on betraying Geminate, I will be on the front lines ready to take your life," said the Priestess rising slowly from her seat. Her Guard moved their hands to their weapons but did not draw them.

"We aren't your enemy. We called you here to bring you warning and offer our support."

She looked to her Guard and commanded them to return to their seats with a simple nod. She continued to stand but opened her robe, exposing her Guardian amulet. "Why should I trust you?"

Jamieson looked around at the eyes of his new friends and potential comrades. "I think it's obvious why you should trust me. But maybe *they* should explain why you should trust them. Lieutenant, would you like to go first?"

Lieutenant Titus rose from his seat and bowed. "Your grace. I have served on many missions that benefited both the Kismet people and the Geminate people. I understand that your people once called out to us for aid, and the traitors of our land denied you support and concealed this from the rest of us. I think it's time for us to finally rise to that call." As he took his seat, Sia rose next.

"I am not a native to your land. I do not know your people or you completely, but I *am* an advocate for honor and loyalty. What I do know is that you showed my people kindness when they were plucked from their homes. You gave them a home, safety and a second chance at life. I have heard of your anonymous gifts and continued kindness. This is a debt I aim to repay." Sia sat down and looked to Josline who brushed the air in front of her and pointed to Eli.

Jamieson felt guilty when he began to feel worried about Eli's response. It is without a doubt that he had seen a significant change in Eli's perspective and was impressed by his progress. On the other hand, Eli wasn't the best person with words, and the Priestess was known for only giving everyone one shot with her.

"My name is Eli Brassie," began Eli rising from his seat. He bowed to the Priestess and then to her Guard. "Words are not my strength, and I refuse to lie to you by pretending otherwise. Geminate has become my home and now I know my home is in danger—in danger due to your General, who manipulated and used me to do his bidding. I think it's time for your General to be exposed as the vindictive coward he is." The speech wasn't the most glamorous speech Jamieson had heard, but it was honest. He saw the confusion come-and-go frequently across the Priestess' face. She was clearly baffled about Eli's 'speech.'

Rising from his seat, Jamieson bowed to the Priestess. "We all know why you should trust me. I have lived and breathed Geminate since my first mission as an adolescent. I have proved that my loyalty is stronger than the treachery that surrounds you. I bring you allies while your General surrounds you with enemies. Mostly everyone at this table knows who you *really* are, but still hold the secret close. We *are* Pith's gift to you before the inevitable betrayal. Use us—or stand from your balcony and watch Geminate drown at the hands of the man who swore to protect it."

The Priestess bowed her head to her Guard, closed her eyes and clapped twice. Immediately her Guard dispersed, one covering one exit while the other covered the other. She rose from her seat and opened the top of her robe, exposing her Guardian medallion. "As Priestess of the realm of Geminate *and* as a Guardian of The Order, I accept your allegiance. However, if we are going to bring down General Mather *and* the Geminate Guard, we are going to need some help." Her Guardian medallion flashed.

ABDUCTED

It had been three weeks, four days and twelve hours since the Priestess accepted the aid of Eli and the others. Eli only knew that because it had also been three weeks, four days and twelve hours since he had a drink. The side effects were brutal at first, but with some herbs he received from Alize, he no longer experienced them. The physical urge still came at odd hours in the day, but Eli stayed strong. The Priestess requested that no one contact her while she rallied their unknown allies, in fear that the General would catch wind of the pending rebellion. On the other hand, she helped orchestrate a retrieval of all of the Kismet people, allowing them to live on the other side of her castle. It was then that Eli realized how much extra space the Priestess had at her disposal.

Meanwhile, people were disappearing from all across the realm. Men, women and children continued to be abducted from Praxis, Geminate and the surrounding villages. Most of them were never seen again, while a few of them eventually showed up one-by-one a few days later—their deaths always different from the others and growing more brutal. While everyone's immediate thought was Fox and the remainder of Lord Egon's army, Eli wasn't too sure. He couldn't help but remember the dark rider atop the pale horse who brought down The Immortal Prison. It was the only other culprit Eli could conjure. Refusing to stress over the unknown, Eli sent word via the Erudites, to the rest of the Kismet people to meet him at the border of The Great Lake. After the water parted and his feet stepped onto the soft soil, he smiled at the hundreds of faces that stared back at him.

Brayden emerged from the crowd waving at Eli, followed by the other Erudites. They all surrounded him with eager smiles.

"I believe this is everyone!" said Brayden with a grin. "How did I do?"

Eli laughed and patted Brayden on the shoulder. "More than good."

"Yes!" exclaimed Brayden turning to the others. "Did you hear that Logan? More than good."

"I wish Mik could join us," said Sy. His face turned into a frown that soon swept across the faces of the others.

"While I'm happy that Mik was so close to your hearts, today is not the day for mourning." Brayden and the others nodded and abandoned their looks of grief.

Eli stepped around the young men that surrounded him and approached the crowd before him.

"Who in Rune's name are you?" shouted a man in front. He was familiar but Eli couldn't remember his name. He did know however, that the man had worked in the Market District before Kismet fell.

"My name is Eli Brassie—son of Marius Brassie." Commotion rose as men and women turned to one another. Eli waited for them to settle down before continuing. "Ever since our arrival to Geminate, a few of us have been part of a covert task squad called the Kismet Task Force. Our mission, was to neutralize the two people responsible for taking your home— Lord Egon and Kismet's very own Tactical Emissary, Fox." The crowd went into an uproar at the mention of Fox's name. A few people spit on the ground in front of them while others simply booed his name. "While our squad was able to eliminate the Lord of the Immortal Lands, Fox slipped through our, *my* fingertips. With that failure our squad was disbanded. I tell you all of this now because I believe you deserve to know that I plan on taking Kismet back from the enemy."

"And how do you plan on doing that smart guy?" shouted a man.

"I don't have a plan yet. But whatever plan I come up with, it will start with taking down Fox." Nods and confident faces reassured Eli that the Kismet people still supported him. "I also asked you all here to offer my apologies. I not once came by to check on you—any of you. I consider you *all* my family and not once checked-in to see personally how the transition from Kismet to Geminate was for you all and if you needed anything."

"Don't fret son of Marius," shouted a woman from the middle of the crowd. "The Lieutenant and the Prodigy of Pith took care of us. Food, water and money they covered all of it."

Jude gave them his money and provided them with food and water? When did he find the time to check-in on them?

"Please, whatever you all need, just let me know. The Lieutenant plans on returning to Praxis and I don't know how often he plans to visit. I don't have much, but I can offer what I have."

"The Kismet people may have been wounded once, but we are strong now. We will rise once again; and *you*, Eli Brassie, will help bring back our home," said Brayden. His words were inspiring and uplifting. The crowd began to cheer and clap, while whistling rose from their depths. Just as a smile began to form on Eli's face, a man screamed somewhere close-by.

"Somebody help!" screamed a figure erupting from the Geminate forest. He ran frantically towards the Kismet people until he locked eyes with Eli and redirected towards him. It was then Eli was able to clearly see Eio, approaching quickly with desperation in every step. It had been months since Eli had seen the man, after the suicide of his son Alistair.

Eio collapsed into Eli's arms. "Please Mr. Brassie, help me." Blood ran from his wrists and face.

"Eio, what happened?"

"He took her Mr. Brassie. He took Kyla. He took my pregnant, defenseless wife. You've got to bring her back. Please!" said Eio erupting into tears.

"Who took Kyla?"

Eio cried hysterically, wiping his eyes repeatedly. "Mirrikh!"

♦♦♦

Jamieson arrived to Eio's house as soon as he received Eli's message. The note said that the person responsible for the abductions had been identified and Eio was the person who witnessed an abduction first-hand. Jamieson was the last to arrive behind Eli and Josline. The Erudites stood in the corner of the living room staring back at Jamieson when he entered the Aaia house but he ignored them, taking a seat next to Josline.

"So now that we're all here," said Eli looking from the young men to Jamieson and then to Josline. "Explain again what happened."

Eio inhaled and exhaled deeply. He wiped his mouth and scratched his neck. "The baby is due any day now, so Kyla and I decided to take a trip to our secret spot in the forest before the baby came. The sun shined bright and the light breeze was so comforting. The trees welcomed us. Then we saw him. That devil appeared between the trees, sending squirrels, birds and other animals fleeing at his mere presence. I stepped in front of Kyla, demanding to know his name. He stopped and smiled, uttering his name slowly and deadly. 'Mirrikh' he whispered across the breeze that glided by. Casting me aside, he snatched up Kyla. She screamed and screamed for me to help her but I couldn't. I chased after her as he dragged her away but I was too late. They were gone. Just like that they were gone. He took them both. My Kyla and my unborn child." Josline comforted Eio when he began to sob.

Eli met Jamieson's gaze and then returned to Eio. "Can you describe to me what he looks like? Height? Hair color? Anything?"

Eio wiped his nose and then his eyes. "A little less than six feet tall maybe. Dark-black hair. He wore some sort of antique armor."

"Anything else you remember about him?" asked Eli.

Eio looked through the window behind Jamieson, lost in thought. He scratched his head a few times but continued to stare motionlessly. His body shuttered. "Yes! His eyes. I'll never forget those eyes. They were red."

Eli coughed hoarsely. He repeatedly cleared his throat but the assault against his windpipes continued. "Did you say red?"

Eio nodded his head. "Yes, blood-red."

ENEMY RISING

Allowing distance allowed hope, which to people, was the only thing they had when swallowed up in the darkest moments of their lives. The assault on the scattered leaves continued with each desperate footstep, as the peasant attempted its unknowingly pre-planned escape. It was frightened. It was female. Her name was irrelevant, because tonight she would be who he desired her to be. The forest was dark and vast, and potentially hopeless, to anyone else who had nothing left but hope. A small house marked every half-mile. The repetitiveness was both boring and intriguing. Inhabitants peered out their windows and doors but never got involved, despite the hysterical cries for help the woman threw at their doorsteps.

"Why won't anyone help me?" she shouted at the night sky. "Help me!"

He purposefully stepped on a tree branch and brushed across the tree next to him. Her head flew up, eyeing his location, and then rushing back into the forest labyrinth. He wondered how long he should allow this game to continue. How long did a person hope for salvation from their pain, from their attacker and from their life? It was a question that he once could have answered. Now, it was something he would have to learn all over again; and would enjoy the entertainment of this lesson.

The woman climbed over a small wooden fence, tripping as her last leg cleared it. She ran up to the doorstep, tears streaming continuously down her face. She knocked, and never stopped knocking. The door creaked open, revealing an older, potentially kinder, woman.

"Thank Pith! You have to help me! Please, he's after me," cried his prey panting. She collapsed to the floor, allowing the resident to kneel down and comfort her.

"Shh shh don't cry my dear. Don't cry," said the old woman rocking her back-and-forth.

"What are you doing? We have to go inside! We have to get out of here before he finds us!" cried his victim.

"It's going to be okay my dear. He's already here, and trust me, you're the only one he wants—not me," said the old woman. She smiled when her visitor looked up with fearful eyes. "There there now. All he wants is to kill ya'—nothin' more, nothin' less. Well, unless you've done something to anger him, then it will be worse. You see, it's all a part of his little game."

She struggled in the arms of the old woman, trying to break free from their embrace. "He's not playing any game. He's trying to kill me! Why don't you understand? Why won't you help me?"

The old woman released her from her grasp and rose to her feet, pulling her visitor up with her. "Oh but I do understand my dear. He took you from your home, the one place on Earth you feel safest. He tortured you in a way different from those before you; and then when you were seconds from death's kiss, he let you escape."

"*Let* me escape?" she asked confused.

"Why yes," replied the old woman kissing her brow. "You see in the end, no one ever truly escapes." She unhinged herself and quickly closed the door behind her.

"No don't leave me! Open the door!" she cried clawing at its rough surface. "Open the door!" She collapsed to the floor the same way her predecessors had.

Entering the fence he halted, allowing her to find him.

Her eyes soon found him, faltering at the mere sight of him. "No...No..." She broke into a stride, pushing anything and everything out of her way to escape. She cleared the fence with ease this time, throwing herself into the forest. He followed.

After a mile of running, limping and eventually crawling, she fell. In a split second he was upon her.

She flipped herself over and stared up at him. This time she didn't run, only watched. "Who are you? What have I done to deserve this?"

He leaned down, falling gracefully to her level. He studied her long brown hair and frightened dark eyes. He instantly felt the presence of another, and dropped his gaze to her stomach, before returning to her eyes.

"Please," she quickly said. "I'm pregnant."

"Eli, how can a mother cling to the unborn with such desperation, but abandon her first born with such disdain?" he asked.

Her eyes widened. "My first born? I don't know what you're—."

He quickly put his finger to her lips. "Shh don't lie Eli. If you continue this nasty habit, we might change our minds about letting you live."

"We?" she asked.

Tear her limbs! Mutilate her flesh!

"Who—who are you? And why do you keep calling me by the name of that Kismetian?" she asked.

She's asking for my name! Tell her Envy is who we are! Tell her now or I will curse her to kill her!

"Mirrikh. *We* are Mirrikh." His hand independently rose and caressed her throat. "Now, run!"

She didn't waste any time returning to her feet and departing. For a few seconds, he continued to hear the crunching of leaves, the swaying of shrubbery and the echoing sobs that filled the night air.

"Peasant be gone. Peasant be still."

A NIGHT
IN PRAXIS

Jamieson wasn't used to being the odd man out but decided he would make it look good nonetheless. Hundreds of party guests socialized and mingled under the night sky. Low-hanging soft lights draped around a large rectangular dance floor giving it a small glow. Countless tables lined the dance floor, but remained empty of inhabitants—but not their belongings. It was going on a month since Jamieson had arrived to Praxis. The lone stone city, surrounding snow-capped mountains and freezing night air were things he was having difficulty adjusting to. His stay in the city marked the first step in uniting Geminate and Praxis by allowing the citizens to get to know him. It was an idea hatched by Sia, who agreed that an alliance between the two cities may be the only way to stand against the enemies that continued to take rise all around them. To Jamieson, the people of Praxis were practical, inviting and had a thirst to learn about other cultures—which Jamieson found refreshing. Geminate was the opposite in terms of learning about other cultures. The Geminate culture was the *only* culture in his people's eyes.

"Josline did say you clean up nice, but wow!"

Jamieson turned to find Sia standing before him; dressed in a luxurious fire-red ball gone and drenched in fine diamonds. Her engagement ring was breathtaking and looked too heavy for her one finger to hold.

"That's because I don't clean-up. You haven't noticed the odor when I'm around? Pretty rank."

She smirked slightly and released a soft laugh, almost uncomfortably. "I always remember you smelling beautifully."

"And since when do you and Josline get together for girl talk about me and my dressing arrangements?"

Sia's face darkened while her eyes looked away and then returned to him. "Since I lost my brother."

"I'm sorry." Jamieson had to fight back the urge to joke his way out of the awkwardness but felt like comedy had no place here.

"Any word from him?" she asked slowly.

Jamieson studied her wondering where this conversation was headed. "Which him?"

"*Him*," she replied.

Jamieson thought of he and Talon's last interaction. The desperation and pain associated with the inevitable loss of the one person he could not live without. Now gone. "Nothing, and with the treachery of the General, I doubt I will ever get a chance to see his body. It will just be another tool of leverage the General can use against me. I have already started forgetting about him to prepare myself for the day those feelings are used against me."

She frowned. "But why would you do that? You love him—more than anything or anyone."

"Don't act surprised. I am sure you did the same thing about Eli or else how could you move forward with the King?"

She recoiled, opening and closing her mouth.

"Having a good time I hope," said King Titus joining the conversation. He was dressed in bright yellow gold armor garbed with a red cape and red sheathe.

"Such a good time that I became overwhelmed and went into shock. Can you tell?"

Titus shook his head back-and-forth with a smile. "Not one of your better jokes."

Jamieson let out a laugh agreeing with the King. "Okay okay how about, such a good time I needed to catch my breath?"

The King smiled nodding his head. "Much better."

"So how are we looking? Was it all a waste?"

The King's expression hardened. "My council believes it would be too great a risk to form an alliance with Geminate while it is in its current state."

Jamieson began to laugh. "Oh I get it they are one of *those* friends. The ones that are your friends when everything is going well for you, but when you are going through bad times, they disappear or don't know you anymore."

"I can see how you could view it that way," said the King shrugging. "They are just more concerned about bringing Geminate's enemies to Praxis. But that won't matter."

"What do you mean it won't matter?"

Titus smirked. "Last time I checked I was King and what I say goes."

Jamieson felt like screaming at the top of his lungs. Eli and the rest of Geminate would be ecstatic at the news of the new alliance—at least Eli would, since the news would have to be kept top secret until General Mather could be taken care of. "Thank you King Titus. Truly on behalf of the entire Geminate race, thank you." He extended his hand.

The King shook Jamieson's hand firmly. "To you I am Conall, Lieutenant or whatever you decide on—but not King."

A slow humming melody gave rise, summoning couples to the dance floor.

Sia came alive. "KT this is a new song! Shall we?"

Jamieson looked from Sia to Conall. "KT?"

Conall giggled, looking into Sia's eyes before returning his gaze to Jamieson. "Stands for King Titus." He kissed her on the side of her face making her face tilt and come into the moonlight. A scratch and a little swelling unveiled under Sia's right eye.

"What happen, you get in a fight with a tea cup?" Jamieson was sure that joke was a success.

Sia recoiled under Conall's kiss, grabbing for her eye she appeared alarmed. "No no, it's just we got a cat and he's not listening to me right now."

"Maybe you're just not listening to him," said Conall kissing her neck.

Jamieson looked from Conall to Sia and studied her. She shook her head softly.

Conall pulled Sia towards the dance floor kissing her hand. "Alright QW time to go take a stroll amongst the people. Besides, Jamieson's surprise just got here."

Jamieson broke his lock on Sia and returned to the King. "Surprise?" Someone tapped him on the shoulder. Turning around, Jamieson tripped over his own feet and fell to his knees.

Soon Talon was kneeling down meeting his gaze. Grabbing Jamieson's wrists, Talon helped his friend to his feet.

"Wha...What?"

"Are you really going to ask what I am doing here?" replied Talon shaking his head in a mocking tone.

Jamieson threw his arms around Talon as hard as he could. All of the pain, sorrow and longing went into the embrace. Talon hugged him back. He smelled of pine and ocean. Jamieson soon came to and released his hold on Talon—looking around and hoping there were no spectators.

Talon tilted his headed to the side and frowned. He looked down and then back up at Jamieson. "I missed you."

Jamieson couldn't breathe. He felt like choking. "I need some air."

"You're outside go crazy," replied Talon annoyed. "Why Jamieson?"

Jamieson began to laugh. "Why do I need air?"

"No," he said closing his eyes and shaking his head before opening them. "Why do you do this to yourself?"

That's when Jamieson realized it. The two of them were standing too close. Two normal gentlemen wouldn't stand that close or look at each other that long. He looked around frantically searching for how many people noticed. A hand grabbed his chin and forced his gaze to Talon's.

"No! No you don't look at anyone else. I am right here! Do you hear me? Right here!" snapped Talon.

Jamieson smiled and pinched his nose between his thumb and forefinger. "You don't have to remind me man, I am pretty sure Geminate can smell you from..."

"No! Shut up! No more jokes I'm tired of it," said Talon. He grabbed Talon's wrist and began dragging him away from the tables.

"Where are we going now?"

They came to a halt, right dead-center of the dance floor. Hundreds of couples slow-danced intimately to the beautiful harp-fueled hum of the surrounding melody. Talon grabbed Jamieson's wrists and placed them around his neck. He wrapped his own hands around Jamieson's waist and began to rock. Jamieson felt his eyes widen as he began to detach his hands from around Talon's neck.

"If you move one finger I swear to Pith I will break it," said Talon in a neutral tone without missing a step.

Jamieson locked eyes with Talon before returning his hands to their uncomfortable position. "Why are you doing this to me? You know what this means. You know they will come for me—them and everyone else."

Talon dipped Jamieson unexpectedly causing Jamieson to look around wondering how he was not falling right now. Talon stared down at him studying him, before pulling him back up into their rocking intimate dance. "How long have we known each other Jamieson?"

Jamieson was caught-off-guard by the question and didn't know how to answer. "Um a long time. Too long for me to remember."

Talon spun Jamieson around once before continuing the dance. "And would you say I know you well?"

Jamieson opened his mouth to respond but fell silent at Talon's rough finger across his lips. His finger was warm and alluring.

"Before you answer," interrupted Talon. "Let me tell you how well I know you."

Oh Pith help me...

"You're stubborn but practical. Your empathy blinds you from the neglect of yourself," he said dipping Jamieson a second time and pausing. "You're smart and handsome."

Jamieson looked away, fighting back the urge to smile.

"Hey!" said Talon. When Jamieson returned to his gaze amidst the dip, Talon continued. "You have a *very* nice body. And those arms..." Talon licked his lips before pulling Jamieson up from the dance.

As the two of them rocked back-and-forth now closer than before, Jamieson slowly felt himself submit. "Alright alright we know my arms are awesome. But what else do you think you know about me?"

Talon locked eyes with Jamieson. "I know you're in pain."

Their dance stopped but their embrace continued. There was absolute silence amidst the still-playing music.

"You're in pain because you are afraid to be with the one person you want to be with," continued Talon.

Oh no, not now!

Jamieson felt his eyes watering but willed his eyes not to release it.

Talon pulled Jamieson in close and continued the slow dance. "Look, I know our people's religion is very important to you. It's important to me as well. But J you can't let it define you. Why would Pith and the other brothers create such a wonderful person only to damn him for being who they created him to be? Answer me that."

Jamieson said nothing, only detached from the dance to showcase some footwork and return to Talon's embrace. He realized he was getting the rhythm of the dance.

"While I was away on that suicide mission I thought of you and only you. Is that normal for a couple of guys like us?" continued Talon while breaking away to do some awkward footwork of his own—which made Jamieson laugh. Talon was not a dancer no matter how hard he tried. Returning to Jamieson with his hands snugly around his waist, Talon pulled Jamieson in. "If it isn't normal then I don't care—not anymore. If it *is* normal, then I don't care either."

The melody slowed, causing couples around them to pull each other in for hungering kisses and passionate embraces. A finger gently returned Jamieson's gaze to Talon.

Jamieson smirked. "Since when did you become so in tune with your emotions? I mean, what do you want from me?"

Talon pulled Jamieson in as close as the couples were around them—licking and then biting his bottom lip.

Oh my Aegis what is he doing? Please do it...I mean don't do it! What am I thinking? This is my best friend!

"Here I am, Talon Tatum, newly-appointed Lieutenant of the Geminate forces and prisoner of my love for you. If you want me, here I am. If you don't, then walk away from me right here right now—and tomorrow the amnesia of my love for you, as well as my happiness, will mark the first day of the rest of my life."

Without saying the word, Talon was giving Jamieson an ultimatum. Jamieson didn't understand why Talon would do such a thing. Wasn't it good enough to have them both here alive, safe and healthy. Wasn't it enough to be able to go on through life being close friends, fighting at each other's side and being there for each other? As the questions manifested, Jamieson internally answered them.

Unhinging his hand from Talon's he studied his friend. The rebellious tear fell from Jamieson's eye as his head shook. "I'm sorry. I can't." He turned away and retreated as fast as he could towards the tables. Then the second tear dropped causing Jamieson's legs to weaken and knees to buckle. He fell. A cold stabbing ache pierced his chest forcing more tears. No hands were there to help him up this time. No love to ease the pain. Returning to his feet he turned back towards Talon, who remained frozen on the dance floor staring shocked. He looked frozen in between wanting to help Jamieson and remaining immobilized. The look of sorrow and betrayal sat so heavy on his face—a face Jamieson had never seen, a face that he had caused.

Jamieson shook his head slowly. "I'm sorry I can't," he mouthed.

Talon forced a smile and nodded back. "It's okay, I know." Talon turned for the main gate, his departure an all too familiar sight for Jamieson.

"Wait!"

Talon turned around with wide eyes, along with the hundreds of couples abandoning their hugs and kisses at Jamieson's outburst. Everyone's eyes fell on Jamieson. Talon looked around at all of the spectators shocked.

Jamieson ran to Talon, collapsing into his embrace when they reunited. Pulling away, Jamieson locked eyes with his friend. "I love you."

Talon's eyes widened before his lips came down hard and then soft on Jamieson's. Talon's hands clawed at Jamieson's waist while Jamieson's hands never left Talon's face. The kiss grew more passionate by the second with Talon biting Jamieson's bottom lip followed by a kiss. The hunger was there and the thirst heavy. Just when Jamieson was beginning to feel the tears dry, Talon pulled away.

"I love you too," said Talon wrapping his arms around Jamieson and pulling him in for the tightest and warmest hug Jamieson had ever experienced.

Whistling and applause erupted around them causing Jamieson to look around at the audience of cheering spectators around them. There was no hostility or objection in their eyes. There was no judgment. There was no threat to crucify or condemn. There was only love and the full silver moon that watched over what Jamieson felt like was the best night of his life.

A LEAD

Eli became restless, feeling the opportunity slowly falling through his fingers as time passed. He waited for Sia and Eio to make Kyla comfortable before the onslaught of questions began. Brayden and his team remained perched at the windows and front door, keeping watch for any uninvited guests. It had been four months since Mik's death and the founding of his alliance with the High Priestess of Geminate. It had also been four months since Eli had last seen Jude. After taking a trip back to his empty grave, Jamieson reported his findings, as well as his search for Jude's whereabouts. Eli was both hopeful and fearful of finding his best friend. The disappearances continued to sweep the neighboring lands, with the deaths becoming more violent with each kidnapping. No evidence of the attacker could ever be found; neither on the body nor at the location the body was recovered from—until now. Kyla was found wondering the streets of Praxis by Jamieson during his stay in Praxis. After caring for her wounds, Sia and King Titus transported her immediately back to an anxiously awaiting Eio. Jamieson stayed behind and was vague about his reasoning. Eli was eager to gather as much information from Kyla as possible while it was still fresh in her mind, but found himself heavily impacted by Jamieson's absence.

"Can I get you some tea my love?" asked Eio attentively. He knelt down rubbing Kyla's hands while she sat motionless in her chair, staring at what appeared to be nothing in particular. When she didn't respond, Eio looked up at Sia in worry.

"I think we could all use some," said Sia softly with a smile. Eio returned the gesture and exited to the kitchen, leaving Kyla alone with Eli and the others.

"Do you remember where he imprisoned you at?"

"Eli!" snapped Sia glaring at him.

"Stay out of this Wyatt. I need answers." He returned his attention back to Kyla who was now staring back at him.

"You speak to the future queen of Praxis like that again and I," started King Titus before falling silent to Sia's nod.

It was a lot to take in. Sia was to be Queen and Conall her King at the conclusion of their wedding—a wedding Eli was sure he wasn't invited to.

"Alright I have some for everyone," said Eio returning with a tray full of teacups. He passed everyone a cup, starting with his wife, before taking a seat next to her.

"Do you remember where he held you at?"

The teacup in Kyla's hand began to shake while her bottom lip began to quiver. A tear formed at the corner of her eye, while her gaze never left his. "Eyes as red as blood."

Eli face-palmed. "Okay so he has red eyes. What else?"

Two tears fell simultaneously from Kyla's eyes. "His voice, as cold as ice."

"Stop this charade and tell me!" He found his patience dwindling and didn't have time to play the concerned role right now.

"How dare you speak to my wife like that, especially after all she's been through! Have you lost your mind?" shouted Eio rising from his seat. King Titus quickly got in between Eio and Eli, something that baffled Eli completely.

"I'm sorry. You're right." He looked to Kyla and smiled. "I apologize Kyla." She remained unaffected, never flinching. Eio slowly returned to his seat, resting a hand on his wife's knee and glaring back at Eli.

"Just anything, anything you can remember about your attacker will be helpful."

The cup continued to rattle in her hand until it finally fell to the floor, shattering into tiny pieces. Everyone, except for Eli and Kyla, jumped up at once to help clean up the pieces.

Kyla slowly rose from her seat, her gaze becoming more hostile the further she rose. "Eyes as red as blood. A voice as cold as ice..." She came down on Eli biting and growling at him. He struggled to fend her off, unaware of how strong she was.

"Hun what are you doing?" cried Eio as he joined Sia in securing Kyla. After she was back in her seat, her face went vacant and the hostility departed. She was as calm as ever.

"I think that's enough questions for now," said Sia pulling Kyla up to her feet. "Perhaps a bath would be nice right about now?"

Kyla nodded her head.

"Do you need help?" asked King Titus rising to his feet.

"No I'll be okay," said Sia kissing the King on the cheek as she passed him with Kyla. The two women exited into the guest bedroom down the hall, closing the door behind them.

"No more questions," said Eio crossing his arms. "I don't like your methods and right now I don't like you."

"You can not like me all you want. The point is, she knows who the person is that's responsible for all of the killings. Every one of the attacker's victims has been killed and the evidence lost. We may not *ever* get a chance like this again."

The King sighed. "Brassie is right. The killings have even stretched to Praxis. People are afraid to leave their homes. If she knows anything about who is responsible, we have to find out."

Eli eyed the King, awaiting some sort of pending sarcasm. Titus rose from his seat and began speaking with Brayden, who had been listening covertly to the conversation. Then the sound of something heavy falling against the front door, shook everyone in the room.

Brayden eyed the other Erudites, using two fingers to command their locations. He then looked back at Eli and the others, raising a single finger to his lips. Brayden opened the door and staggered back.

A lone body fell into the house, an arrow rising from his back. Eli ran to the stranger, helping him up to his feet and to the adjacent couch. It was then he realized it was one of his people—Morgan from the Lin Kitz neighborhood.

"They found us..." said Morgan collapsing to the couch.

Sia screamed.

"Sia?" shouted King Titus rushing down the hallway. Eli and Eio quickly followed and stopped at the King's location.

Kyla approached; shaking frantically as she held up a bloody knife freely. "Eyes as red as blood. A voice as cold as ice— and a soul, *darker* than the evil that drives the madness." She held the dagger to her throat, causing commotion to erupt around her. "For Lord Mirrikh!" The dagger glided smoothly across her neck, bringing her and the trail of blood, to her feet.

"Kyla!" screamed Eio rushing to her side. "Go get help!"

Eli fell into thought, reminiscing about that night when the shell of his best friend came to him. Kyla's repeated words finally processed completely. "Eyes as red as blood and a voice as cold as ice..." A tremor shook the house, causing décor and bookcases to tumble to the ground.

"Everyone take cover!"

"Sia!" Titus rushed passed a still-sobbing Eio and into the backroom. Shortly after entering, he screeched in pain. "Oh my Aegis, why?"

Metal-on-metal took the air from the living room. Sprinting across the rocking hallway and fallen debris, Eli made his way to the center of the pandemonium. Brayden and the other Erudites went head-to-head in all out war with a familiar adversary of the past—the Necroborns. Erudites yelled Brayden's name for aid from all directions as the Necroborns easily over-powered them in brute force. The battle was one-sided, with the advantage lying with the enemy. Erudites began to fall one-by-one. Behind Brayden stalked a large creature with bestial teeth and tremendous stature. The ground itself shook beneath each footstep the beast took.

"Peasants of Geminate, your end is now!" roared General Rorik.

Eli ran through the battle, summoning a blade in preparation, but recoiled when it dissolved instantly. He summoned his bow and cursed at its departure.

Brayden met Rorik's gaze and went into shock; standing motionless while his enemy prepared to attack.

"Brayden what are you doing? Defend yourself!"

Eli threw himself on Rorik's back. "Brayden what are you doing? Snap out of it! We need you!"

"Get your paws off of me maggot!" growled Rorik. He snatched Eli off his back and tossed him across the room.

Eli hit something hard and jagged before rag-dolling to the floor. He blinked numerous times, going into shock at both the pain and the failure of his eyes. His eyes found Brayden, who looked down at him—his face coming into focus.

"Eli are you okay?" What happened?" asked Brayden. The worry was prevalent on his face.

"My abilities—they're not working."

"That's our mentor!" yelled a voice far off in the distance.

Rorik roared as Erudites attacked him from all sides. The Necroborn General threw his weight around, barreling into attacking Erudites, and sending them flying in all directions—a true force to be reckoned with.

Brayden helped Eli to his feet just as the Necroborn reinforcements strolled in. Leaning on Brayden, Eli looked around and counted at least a few dozen enemies. They were surrounded; and all Eli could hope was that King Titus would somehow find a way to release them from their fate.

"Victory is mine!" yelled Rorik beating on his chest with his fist. "For my prize, I claim your heads." He charged for Eli.

Eli pushed Brayden out of the way and braced himself.

"No!" yelled Brayden. He appeared back in front of Eli with his bow drawn just as Rorik's axe hit—removing Brayden from sight.

"Brayden!"

White smoke erupted causing Eli to look away.

"Target acquired. Activating Supremacy!"

Supremacy? It can't be...

The sound of metal and commotion was short lived. When the smoke cleared, a lone Agent stood strong and tall above Eli. "Mission complete!" The Agent knelt down until his hazel eyes were level with Eli's.

Eli's brow curled. "You?"

Kai extended an open hand to Eli, softening his face. "Eli, my brother in arms, Kai has come to take you home."

EPILOGUE

Fox swam The Great Lake, bypassing the hundreds of nightmarish creatures that swam next to him. They were animals he had seen many times during his multiple visits to the Geminate land and secret meetings with General Mather. His phobia of them had diminished somewhat, however, his fear of the one great beast, which is said to protect The Great Lake, lived on. Tentacles and barnacles mounted the underwater walls and ceilings when Fox broke the water's surface inside the cavern. Climbing up on the rocky surface, he stuck his finger down his throat and regurgitated the desert herb that allowed him to breathe underwater. While its other properties of heightened awareness and tolerance to underwater pressure were invaluable, it was first and foremost a poison used to incapacitate the lungs. Fox wouldn't make such an amateur mistake by allowing something so deadly to linger in his body; especially when his mission was reaching the peak of its objective.

"The fall of The Immortal Prison and the rise of the pale horse and its rider are signs that my mission is not yet complete. Soon evil shall sweep every land in existence, preying on the sins of mankind." He leaped down into a small river that ran inside the subaqueous cavern. He swam a few yards and emerged into the center of the formation. "Luckily for me my sins aren't too bad. Just some murders, thefts, lies and a few promiscuous activities." He stopped and thought for a second. "Okay okay, *a lot* of promiscuous activities."

He walked the uneven surface, hearing the gurgling of the lake's water on both sides of the walls. Reaching the center of the room, he looked down at the circular trench of water with the emerging pedestal of earth. He jumped in, tensing at the unusually cold temperature. Swimming to the pedestal, he retrieved the urn and climbed out of the trench.

"So happy to be done with this place." Before he made it all the way back to the river, he paused. The urn felt cold and lighter. It no longer drummed with the immense power inside. He felt his stomach drop and his heart spill into his ears. Placing his hand over the lid of the urn, he did what no living being should ever do—he opened it.

A charred and vacant urn whistled back at him. The fear settled in, followed by the rage-induced realization of inevitable failure. The countless missions surrounding the retrieval of the urn and its power glided across Fox's vision. All of the people he killed, pain he endured and mental anguish he suppressed, all for this fragile, *empty* piece of porcelain.

"Pith has chosen his champion. The rise of the Protectors is upon us." He slammed the urn onto the cavern's floor as hard as he could, feeling his anger recede at the sight of the shattering pottery. "And from the bowels of the Earth rose he, for he is only fallen not beaten. With death, the immoral and the pained at his side, the battle of the gods—and our salvation—has begun."

The story continues and ends in

Mission: 3
of

The Bloodline Revelations

ΑΩ

www.ingramcontent.com/pod-product-compliance
Lightning Source LLC
Chambersburg PA
CBHW021330070726
47496CB00016B/9